Jericho

Ann McMan

Nuance

Bedazzled Ink Publishing Company • Fairfield, California

978-1-934452-67-7 paperback
978-1-934452-68-4 ebook

Library of Congress Control Number: 2011937166

Cover Design
by
TreeHouse Studio

Nuance Books
a division of
Bedazzled Ink Publishing Company
Fairfield, California
http://www.bedazzledink.com

For Sheila, who will live forever in my own story.

Acknowledgments

I have many people to thank for this book:

Jessica Hayes, who convinced me I should write it—and who regularly suited up in her dominatrix gear and cracked the whip over my head to be sure I did; Montine, who steadfastly read every fragment of every chapter as I cranked them out, and never complained about getting it piecemeal; my mom (dee dee) who brazenly told me the awful truth about adverbs, and swore she "skipped over" the sex scenes; my dog, Maddie, who allowed me to borrow her identity; Domina, who honored me by reading the entire thing during a long, Vermont winter (I strongly suspect she used it for kindling); Claudia and Carrie at Bedazzled Ink for taking a chance on me; my talented, longsuffering, and esoteric editor C.A. Casey (another ex-librarian), who taught me about dangling participles and women's basketball—with varying degrees of success; the many wonderful people I've gotten to know at The Academy and The Athenaeum; my soul sister, Luke, who always tells me the truth; Michael and Matthew, who graciously permitted me to clone Ward Manor (the best Inn in Virginia); Trently, who always loves me—even when I get how I get; to Joni Mitchell, for writing the amazing song that inspired this story; and, finally, an obsessive-compulsive named "Bagel," who loves Maine, muscle cars, and this book—not necessarily in that order.

I am indebted to you all.

"By faith the walls of Jericho fell down . . ."

— Hebrews 11:30

Chapter 1

Durham, N.C.

The last couple of boxes barely fit into the crowded station wagon. Syd waited until the last few minutes to pack up the essentials of her daily life—the things that would keep her company for the next eighteen months during her sojourn in the tiny mountain town. The things that would keep her sane and remind her that the rest of the world's cranky machinery was chugging along, even if her own had frozen to a complete stop. The movers had already been and gone, and the majority of her personal belongings were now on their way to a climate-controlled storage facility west of Raleigh. She'd figure out what to do with it all once she figured out what to do with what was left of her fractured life.

After closing the tailgate on her car, she walked back inside the shopworn bungalow that had been her home for the last four-and-a-half years. She walked slowly from room to room—five rooms in all. Sturdy, spare, and still resonating with the sounds and smells of the life she had lived there. The familiar shotgun design of the house—one room behind another behind another—again struck her as curious. Why would anyone choose to live in such a straight line? It didn't make sense. Life wasn't like that—people weren't like that. People were bent and contorted by life into all kinds of irregular shapes. Life was anything but linear.

Architecture like this was a distinctly Southern invention—stubborn in its implied insistence that life was a straightforward thing that would always work out, and always proceed according to some master plan. It was no accident that all of the houses on her street opened onto wide front porches that seemed to converge with nature. They were designed like ludicrous parodies of religious parables—imitating a person's plodding and unvarying path through life—culminating in a grand and glorious reward.

Well, sometimes, the rewards weren't so glorious. And today, she was moving, but it wasn't toward anything glorious. It wasn't toward anything; it was just away from here.

Syd walked back through the house, taking a last look inside closets and cabinets. Something caught her eye in the back of a kitchen drawer, and she bent over to see the corner of a white piece of paper wedged between the drawer and its backstop. She tugged at it gently, and was surprised when it turned out to be a badly creased photograph. It was a picture of her with Jeff—taken outside her parents' house in Towson, on the day they had packed up to move to North Carolina together. They looked happy and in love as they posed with their arms wrapped around each other in front of Jeff's impossibly overloaded 4Runner.

Syd shook her head as she gazed down at the tiny image of herself. *Stupid. Stupid. What a waste.* She tucked the photo back into its hiding place and closed the drawer. After turning off the kitchen light, she made her way back through the house. On the threshold of the front door, she paused briefly, then exhaled, pulled the door shut, locked it, and slid her key back through the brass mail slot.

She walked around her car one last time to ensure that it looked fit for travel. The sturdy, '95 Volvo station wagon was mostly reliable, but a daylong drive in September heat wasn't like her usual twenty-minute commute to the Carolina campus. She prayed for the millionth time that she'd reach Jericho without incident.

She climbed into the car, started the engine, and snapped her seatbelt into place. After setting the trip odometer, she popped a disc into the dashboard CD player. Without looking back, she pulled away from the house on Broad Street and drove toward the Interstate as strains from Bonnie Raitt's "Nick of Time" filled the car.

Virginia

Maddie wished for the hundredth time that she'd left Pete back at the house. Her five-year-old golden retriever frantically paced back and forth in the rear of the Cherokee. Any time Maddie made the trek to Charlotte for supplies with Pete in tow, she had to endure his excited behavior whenever the New River snaked into view along the roadside.

"C'mon, Pete. Please settle down. We'll stop for a swim on the way back. I promise. Be a good boy, now."

In the rearview mirror, she saw only the strobe-like flash of the dog's tail as he continued his frenzied pacing, which now was accompanied by a high-pitched whine. She only had a few more miles of this to endure. Once they crossed into North Carolina, he would settle down and sleep the rest of the way.

Maddie brought her eyes back to the road and noticed a blue Volvo wagon ahead—halfway pulled off onto the grassy shoulder. Its flashers were on. A woman stood at the back, leaning into the open cargo area, pulling out boxes and suitcases. As she slowed to pass, Maddie saw the culprit—a blowout on the left front tire. She pulled over and turned on her own flashers, then hopped out of the Cherokee and walked back toward the stranded motorist.

"Stay," she commanded Pete sternly, whose curiosity was rapidly overcoming his excitement at stopping. The woman behind the car had stopped unloading, and now stood a little warily as she watched Maddie approach.

"Having some car trouble?" Maddie asked from a respectful distance.

"You might say that," the woman said, gesturing toward the shredded remnants of her front tire. "Funny. It was fine when I put it on the car sixty-thousand miles ago."

Maddie smiled. "Well, then, I'd say you definitely got your money's worth."

"That's me—a shrewd consumer. I just have lousy timing."

"It looks like your sense of geography isn't so hot either," Maddie noted, wryly gesturing at the wooded landscape that surrounded them. "There's no semblance of a town within twenty miles of here."

The petite blonde threw up her hands. "Of course. My cell phone can't get a signal here, either."

Maddie pointed toward the open cargo bay. "Let me help you out. I assume you're trying to unearth a spare?"

"Thanks. I know I packed one." The blonde smiled at her—all traces of wariness now absent from her green eyes. She appeared to be about Maddie's age, or slightly younger. She was very pretty.

In tandem, they lifted out cartons of house wares, books, and linens, and stacked them along the bank next to the shoulder.

"Moving?" Maddie asked. The woman nodded. "Where are you headed?"

"Jericho."

Maddie raised an eyebrow.

"I'm setting up a new library there."

"Oh." Maddie nodded with recognition. "I'm familiar with that project. It's a wonderful thing for the area—long overdue."

"My name's Syd, by the way."

"Sid?" Maddie asked, confused.

"S-Y-D—like Sydney. It's a family name," she explained. "A nickname. My first name is Margaret, but only my mother calls me that."

"I'm Maddie." She smiled at her. "And the stunning natural blond up there is my dog, Pete."

Syd craned her neck around the car to look more closely at Pete, whose strong head jutted from an open back window. His nose was bobbing up and down as he sniffed at the air outside the Jeep.

"He's gorgeous."

"He knows it," Maddie said with an affectionate glance at Pete. "Don't let him hear you."

Syd laughed. "Are you from this area?"

"Yes and no. I was born about thirty miles from here, but I've only been back here to live for about eighteen months."

Syd nodded and gestured toward Maddie's Jeep. "Hence the PENN sticker on your bumper?"

Maddie regarded her with interest. "That's pretty observant."

"Librarians. We notice things."

"Ah, that accounts for it." Maddie smiled as she lowered the last box to the ground. "Yes. I went to school in Philadelphia and stayed on there to work—although that seems like a lifetime ago."

"So, it's quite a change being back here?"

"You could say that. But, on the whole, it's been a nice one."

Syd pried open the door to the spare tire well. "That's comforting. I'd hate to think that I hauled all of my worldly possessions up here to this lovely roadside only to be miserable."

Maddie looked at the litter of items spread out along the shoulder. There were many boxes of books. "I dunno. At least you won't want for something to read."

Syd smiled as they lifted the grimy tire from its mooring and rolled it toward the front of the car. "I sure wish I hadn't cut driver's ed the day they did this." She wiped her hands on the seat of her jeans.

Maddie walked back to the rear of the Volvo and extracted the t-bar socket tool clipped to the side of the wheel well. She knelt by the front tire and looked up at Syd with a wide smile. "Let's pray that your lug nuts aren't rusted."

Syd wrinkled her nose. "I just know there's a one-liner lurking in there someplace."

Maddie laughed. "Well, with me, that's usually a safe assumption." She forced one of the lugs loose and handed it to Syd.

"I won't let myself take too big a hit for this situation. Car maintenance, or lack thereof, was always my husband's responsibility."

Maddie forced another of the stubborn lugs loose. "Was?"

"Yeah," Syd replied with a shrug. "I'm now an official member of *The First Wives Club*—or I will be shortly."

"Oh." Maddie paused, holding the t-bar against the next lug nut. "Am I sorry about this?"

Syd looked pensive. "No. I'm fine. It's the right thing for both of us." She slowly shook her head like she was clearing it of cobwebs. She met Maddie's eyes. "You seem like you've done this before. I feel worthless just watching you work. Isn't there something I can do to help out? It's *my* mess, after all."

"Sure. Wanna go to the trunk and bring up the jack?"

Syd squinted. "Is that a tool-thingy?"

Maddie rolled her eyes. "Yeah . . . it's a square, flat-looking tool-thingy . . . and it should be the *only* tool-thingy left in the tire well."

"Right." Syd nodded as she headed toward the back of the car. "I'm all over it." She came back with the jack just as Maddie loosened the last of the lug nuts.

Maddie stood up and brushed the dust off the knees of her pants. "Okay, let's give this tool-thingy a whirl."

Twenty minutes later, she finished installing the spare, and they rolled the remains of the flat to the rear of the car. They then repacked all of Syd's boxes of belongings.

Maddie closed the tailgate to the Volvo and turned to Syd. "You're all set."

"I just don't know how to thank you," Syd began.

"Forget about it." Maddie wiped her hands off. "I needed to stop anyway. Old Bowser up there was about due for a swim break, and this is as likely a spot as any." She gestured across the road toward the water glinting through the trees.

Syd seemed interested. "Oh, really? Are you going to let him out?"

"Can I keep him *in* is a better question." She smiled at Syd. "I need to rinse my hands off, anyway." She stood there quietly for a moment as Syd gazed toward the river. She could hear it roaring along below the embankment.

"It flows north, you know."

Syd looked at her. "Pardon me?"

"The New River. It flows north, not south."

"You're kidding, right? That's . . . counterintuitive. Is it some kind of metaphor?"

Maddie smiled. "Well, it may be, but the New is one of the oldest rivers in North America, and, for some strange reason, it flows north."

Syd's eyes narrowed. "Like the Nile?"

"Right. I guess your sense of geography isn't as impaired as I suggested earlier."

"Lucky guess," Syd replied.

"I doubt that somehow." Maddie considered Syd. She was impressed by her obvious intelligence and her dry sense of humor. She would make a welcome and interesting addition to the provincial town of Jericho. She hoped they would run into each other again. She mused that it was very likely they would—she had inherited her father's position on the Tri-County Library Board. She decided not to mention that fact, thinking that it might seem presumptuous, and she was enjoying their easy camaraderie.

"Why don't you stick around for a few more minutes—relax and recover from your roadside trauma before heading on up into the hills?"

Syd wavered.

"I've got a thermos of hot coffee and two cups," Maddie offered, hopefully.

Syd shot her an appraising look. "What *kind* of coffee?"

Maddie gave her a knowing smile. "Oh, very special coffee. I order it online from *A Southern Season* in Chapel Hill and grind it myself." She closed her eyes and hummed. "Oh, yeah . . . it's gooood stuff—practically like coffee-crack."

Syd's eyes glazed over. "All right, already. I'm in. My last cup was from a *Bojangles* in Durham." She shivered. "Trust me. It wasn't special."

"Great. Let me go and unleash the wildebeest." Maddie strode off toward the Jeep, fishing her keys out of a front pocket. As soon as she raised the tailgate, Pete vaulted from the back in a flash of gold and bounded across the road, heading at a high lope for the riverbank.

Maddie tossed Syd a bright green tennis ball.

"Canine pacifier," she pointed out. "Let me just grab the thermos and a blanket."

They slowly made their way down the bank flanking the road and walked through tall grass toward the edge of the river, where Pete was already sloshing about happily.

"Here, Pete!" Maddie took the tennis ball from Syd and heaved it out into the current. The dog plunged in after it and swam back to shore, his trophy proudly clamped between his teeth. "The trick now," Maddie cautioned, washing her hands in the icy water, "is to find a sitting place outside of his shake zone."

"I see what you mean." Syd watched mesmerized as Pete emerged from the water and shook his massive frame. Sparks of sunlight emanated from the shower of spray that flew out from his vibrating coat like shards of glass. Pete then trotted to within ten feet of them, sank to the ground, and chewed contentedly on his tennis ball.

They spread the blanket out on a relatively flat piece of terrain several yards from the water's edge. The air was filled with the pungent scent of pine needles and dry grass. Already, the dogwood trees were turning red—one of the first hints of impending autumn. The repetitive droning of a nearby mockingbird floated on the air above the roar of the river. Over the ridge across the water, the hazy outline of the Blue Ridge Mountains could be seen through the trees.

Syd leaned back on her elbows and looked around at the view. "My god, this is really beautiful."

Maddie nodded as she unscrewed the top to the thermos. The wonderful aroma of coffee wafted up. "I know. I forgot about how much I loved this during my years in Philadelphia. Getting back to this river is one of the best things about being at home again."

Syd looked at her. "You said your father passed away?" Maddie nodded as she poured out two cups of coffee. "I'm sorry about that. Had he been ill?"

Maddie handed one of the steaming cups to Syd and recapped the thermos. "No. It was a massive coronary—completely unexpected. He had been in perfect health—or so we thought." She paused. "It was such a shock. He was so strong and vital. I still can't quite take it in, and it's been over a year and a half."

Syd tentatively touched her on the forearm. "I'm so sorry."

Maddie met her earnest gaze. "Thanks. I miss him a lot." She raised her cup. "How about a toast?" Syd lifted her cup. "Here's to happier days and fewer road hazards." They clinked rims and sipped the hot beverage.

Syd moaned in appreciation. "God . . . you weren't kidding. This is amazing."

Maddie smiled at her. "Glad you think so. I'm kind of a coffee snob." She gave a self-deprecating laugh. "Actually, I'm just kind of a snob. Or, at least, that's what most of the locals seem to think."

"I confess that I worried about that same thing when I came up here to interview for the library position. I wondered if my outlier status might cause problems for me."

Maddie regarded her with a thoughtful expression. "Well, my best advice is to do whatever you can to avoid being isolated. It's easy for that to happen here—especially if you're not from the area." She paused. "I've had my own struggles with that since coming back. It can be lonely."

"I think it might be even harder in my case. I came here from Durham, but I'm not even from the South."

Maddie nodded. She remembered the weekend that the interviews for Syd's position had taken place. She had been out of town at a conference. "I noticed your conspicuous lack of accent. Where are you from originally?"

"Baltimore."

Pete chose that moment to stand up and walk to their blanket. He was still wringing-wet from his sojourn in the river. Maddie sat up defensively. "Uh oh. Take cover. Here comes Lighthorse Harry."

Syd laughed as she drew her legs in closer. Pete flopped to the ground right in front of them and continued to chew contentedly on his tennis ball. Syd ran her hand along his thick, yellow coat. "He really is beautiful. Have you had him long?"

"Just since coming back here. He was my dad's dog." Maddie scrubbed his head affectionately. "He's a good boy. Great company. I love having him—it's like still having a bit of my father with me."

"I can understand that." Syd drained her coffee cup and glanced at her watch. She sighed regretfully. "I suppose I should get on with it. I'm scheduled to meet the county supervisor in an hour to pick up my keys."

Maddie nodded. She recalled that there was a tiny manager's apartment over the old storefront facility the state had leased to house the new library. "I should get rolling, too. I need to be in Charlotte before five."

They stood up together and folded the blanket. Pete raced ahead of them toward the Jeep, sensing where they were headed and not wanting to be left behind. After Maddie stowed the blanket and thermos, she opened the tailgate of the Jeep, and Pete jumped in. He still held the tennis ball in his mouth.

Syd patted his blond head. "So long, handsome. You enjoy the rest of your ride."

Maddie closed the tailgate and turned to her. "Best of luck with the rest of your move." She extended her hand, and Syd shook it warmly. "I hope we see each other again."

Syd smiled. "Oh, just brew a pot of coffee, and I'll come and *find* you." She released her hand and pulled her keys out of her jacket pocket. "I really can't thank you enough for all you've done for me today. You were an absolute lifesaver."

"It was my pleasure. Be safe now."

"You, too." Syd turned back to her car. "So long."

Maddie gave her a casual wave as she climbed into her Jeep. "Bye."

In seconds, they both were underway. Maddie was aware of Syd's Volvo following along behind her for several miles, until she reached the I-74 turnoff in Wilson. Syd blew her horn as she rolled on past the turn and headed on her way toward the tiny hamlet of Jericho.

Chapter 2

Syd had visited the new Jericho Branch Library twice before, but this time was different. Today it was real. As she drove through the Jericho downtown area, she noticed a moderate amount of activity at a corner service station and convenience mart. Several cars and pickups competed for parking spaces out front. Teenage boys, out for the evening in trucks and obvious family sedans, leaned against their cars, smoking cigarettes and loudly calling out to a group of bored-looking young women clustered by the door to the market. A neon sign in the window advertised "Pizza" and "Video Rentals." Innocuously taped below the neon was a hand-lettered placard promoting $24.95 oil changes and stating that this was an Official Virginia Inspection Station.

A Firestone tire dealer was located next door to the mini-mart, and Syd decided that she would venture back on Monday and drop off her damaged tire for repairs.

The rest of the town was fairly quiet. It contained one or two shallow side streets with a litter of small houses, a consolidated school comprised mostly of modular units linked by aluminum-covered walkways, two Baptist churches, a Laundromat annexed to a used appliance dealer, a barbecue restaurant (closed), a hardware store, several auto body shops, and a Volunteer Fire Department.

There was no doctor's office, no bank, no newspaper, and until now, no public library.

"What's it like?" Her mother asked, when Syd called with the news of her successful appointment.

"What? The library?"

"Yes, for a start."

Syd tried for a moment to see the bedraggled structure through her mother's eyes. "I think you'd say that it lacks refinement."

"And the town?"

"Town?"

Her mother feigned exasperation. "The area, then."

"Um . . . somewhat rustic. Not the usual sort of sleepy southern hamlet profiled in Country Living.*"*

There was a pause. The telephone line hissed quietly. "Margaret, how small is this place?"

Syd sighed. No matter how much time or distance intervened, her mother steadfastly refused to call her by her childhood nickname. "Well, to boil the whole of Western civilization down to its least common denominator, the nearest McDonald's is about twenty miles away."

Twenty miles, Syd mused as she pulled into the parking lot beside the low, brick and block storefront, its new tin roof blazing in the late afternoon sun. It might as well be a million. But this back country area of Southwest Virginia, with its virtual anonymity, seemed exactly in keeping with her present state of mind. During her first visit to the area, she was captivated by the landscape. A string of tiny Main Street communities, ringed by ragged-looking farms, spread out along the perimeter of the hazy, brooding Blue Ridge Mountains. The towns, like the people who lived in them, seemed to imitate every dip and sag of the terrain. Faded, weary, worn down by time and the elements, but still hinting at former grandeur and elegance.

In fact, the eighteen-month posting, funded by a grant from the State Library Association, offered just the sort of programmed existence Syd thought she needed. She always preferred to keep the number of options in her life pared down—making decisions was not one of her strong suits. Now, in the wake of a failed marriage, she was willing to hand the immediate superintendence of her life over to the Commonwealth of Virginia. For the next year and a half, while she attempted to sort through the carnage of her personal life, she would lend herself to the citizens of Southwest Virginia.

She had no keys yet to explore the inside, but external improvements were obvious. The brick walls had been freshly painted in bright white, and some enterprising volunteer had built and installed two large window boxes on the front of the building. These planters were choked with bronze-colored chrysanthemums, all craning their springy, fat heads toward the sunny side of the building. A new hand-painted, wooden sign over the door proclaimed that this building was now the Jericho Public Library. In smaller type across the bottom, the sign painter had added, "Highest library in the Commonwealth of Virginia."

A small door wedged between the library façade and the upholstery shop next door led to the tiny furnished, upstairs apartment that would be her home for the next year and a half. Syd glanced up at the big windows of the library that faced out onto the street. The front of the building was in shade, so at least the sun wouldn't be in her eyes in the evenings. There were empty window boxes beneath the upstairs windows as well, and she supposed she could fill those with mums to complement the library plantings at street level.

The window blinds had all been carefully closed, so Syd had no idea how much of her initial inventory had arrived. Behind the building, next to a sagging back porch, an impressive tower of corrugated boxes, broken down for ease of removal, looked promising. She wouldn't really know what awaited her inside until after she met the county supervisor at the courthouse in Jefferson to get her keys and formally assume her position.

Syd had two months before the formal opening of the branch—two months to appoint the interior, unpack, organize, and shelve the meager initial collection, set up her cataloging and circulation systems, recruit and train volunteers and prepare her first acquisitions budget for the state library board.

"Oh, yeah," she pondered. "Grad school *really* prepared me for this."

She walked toward her car and looked across the vacant lot next to the library at the tiny Jericho Post Office. The sun appeared to be on a collision course with the peaked roof of the building. Already, the flat tire and her brief respite on the riverbank had eaten away a good portion of the afternoon. Now, her side trip to visit the library before heading on into Jefferson ensured that when she unloaded the car for the second time that day, it would be in the dark.

Roma Jean Freemantle was a godsend. The redheaded sixteen-year-old volunteered in the branch two afternoons a week after school. In exchange for her practicum with Syd, she earned course credit toward a general business requirement. The vivacious teenager was a hard worker and always very punctual. With Roma Jean as a willing emissary, Syd quickly became enmeshed in the daily lives—and loves—of her new neighbors. Friends of Roma Jean's had a tendency to drop by the library—even on days she wasn't working. Syd got to know them all, and it became clear that the tiny Jericho branch library would quickly evolve into a hub of social activity once its doors formally were opened.

On Monday afternoon, Roma Jean and her BFF Jessie were helping Syd shift stacks of reference materials from her processing area to the front of the building where she had set up study tables and a makeshift computer lab. The two girls carried on an unceasing dialogue while they carried stacks of books and manuals up to Syd, who then carefully arranged them on designated shelves.

"That's like the tenth time they've driven by here in the last hour." Roma Jean sounded exasperated as she plopped six volumes of the Britannica *Macropaedia* onto an oak study table and looked out the big front window toward the street. A vintage black Chevy Nova with shiny silver rims slowly rolled past the building, then gunned its engine at the corner and roared along down the rest of the street.

Jessie's frizzy brown hair bounced around her face as she nodded. "Losers. They're supposed to be at football practice."

"Not today. Jason got hurt on Friday, and they had to take him to Dr. Stevenson's office. He's been benched for a week." Roma Jean huffed. "What a jerk."

Jessie laughed as she pushed up her red-framed glasses. "You're just jealous that he had an excuse to go over there."

Roma Jean shot an anxious look at Syd. "Shut up, Jessie. You're nuts." She turned abruptly and huffed her way to the back of the building to pick up another stack of books.

Jessie rolled her eyes at Syd and turned to follow Roma Jean.

Syd gazed at the two girls with amusement, then stood up and looked out the front window in time to see the black Nova slowly making its way past again. Smiling, she walked forward and waved at the two boys inside the car. They saw her looking at them and quickly jerked their heads away. They gunned the engine so the car lurched forward and squealed as it sped off. It didn't come around again.

The phone rang, and Syd walked to the circulation desk to answer it.

"Jericho Public Library."

"Miss Murphy?" It was Edna Freemantle. "Is Roma Jean still there? She forgot to pick up my shopping list this morning, and I need her to run by Food Bonanza on her way home tonight."

"Hello, Edna." She paused. "Please, call me Syd." She craned her neck toward the back of the building. "Sure, she's still here. She and Jessie are in the back. Let me get her for you."

Syd laid the receiver down and walked to the processing area to fetch Roma Jean. Before she got to the doorway, she overheard the two girls in hushed conversation.

"Don't say crap like that in front of her. I don't want her thinking stuff like that about me. What if she said something to my parents?" Roma Jean sounded desperate.

"Look. I said I was *sorry* . . . what do you want from me?" Jessie held her hands up. "I don't know why you're so upset if it isn't true."

Syd cleared her throat. "Roma Jean. Your mom's on the phone for you." She smiled at the girls and turned around to walk back to the front of the building. *Teenagers. God.*

She snagged a large mailing tube and a box of thumbtacks off the circulation desk as she walked past it and headed to the main entrance. The tube contained several oversized ALA posters that featured colorful photos of pop culture icons happily engaged with their favorite books.

Syd unrolled the posters and placed books on their corners to hold them open while she decided where to hang them. Cesar Milan, Danica Patrick, and Shaquille O'Neal all gazed back at her from the tabletops. Thinking that the posters would look good arranged around the street door, she drug a low step stool over and stood atop it on tiptoes to see how high she could reach without having to commandeer a ladder.

Not high enough. She sighed as she started to climb back down, but jumped at the sound of a car horn, followed by the loud roar of an engine. As she lost her footing and slipped to the floor, she saw a flash of black speed past the front door.

"Damn it." She tried to catch herself, but only succeeded in twisting her left ankle as it tangled up beneath the stool. She landed in an untidy heap on the floor as blinding jolts of pain shot up her left leg.

Roma Jean and Jessie raced to her side.

"What happened? Are you hurt?" Roma Jean asked.

They bent over her in concern.

Syd struggled into a sitting position and tried to straighten out her left leg. "I fell off the stool." She winced as she moved her foot. "I think I might have sprained my ankle." She pulled herself up and sat down heavily on one of the straight chairs arranged around the nearest table. She grimaced in pain. "Damn it. I'm so stupid."

Roma Jean pulled out another chair so Syd could prop her leg up. "Wow. It's already starting to get swollen. We'd better take you to Dr. Stevenson's office right away."

Jessie looked up at her in amazement. "Jeez. You might wait like two seconds before you invent a reason to go flying over there."

"Shut up. Just go and get the car." She gestured at Syd's outstretched leg. "Look at her ankle. It's really swelling."

Syd raised a placating hand. "Girls, please. Give me a minute to catch my breath, okay?" She could feel her pulse pounding—every heartbeat sent answering echoes of pain up her leg. She knew Roma Jean was right, and that she probably needed an x-ray. "Where is this doctor's office, anyway?"

"Oh, I can drive you there," Roma Jean said. "It's no problem at all. It's only about ten minutes from here—right on the road to Jefferson." She waved her hand toward the single road that led out of town.

Syd thought about it. The branch opening was only three weeks away, and she still had tons of inventory to catalog and shelve. She didn't want to waste any of their precious volunteer hours. She looked up into Roma Jean's earnest brown eyes. "I really appreciate the offer, but it would help me more if you and Jessie stayed on here and kept working. I can drive myself with no problem."

"But, Miss Murphy, you can't drive with that ankle," Roma Jean said. "I can take you, and Jessie can stay on here until we get back."

Jessie looked at her in surprise and dismay. "Hey, that's not fair. You're supposed to drop me off at Mrs. Jenkins's house on the way home. My mom'll kill me if I miss another lesson."

Roma Jean looked at Jessie like she wanted to strangle her.

"Girls, really," Syd said in a firm voice. "Stay and finish your work. Roma Jean—your mom needs you to do her shopping on the way home." She struggled to her feet. "Just help me to my car, and I'll be fine." She paused to smile at them as they huddled around her in concern. "Thanks for your help. I really don't know how I'd manage without the two of you."

They smiled shyly as they helped her hobble to the back door. Syd dropped Jessie's arm to grab her purse and keys off the corner of the circulation desk. She stepped outside and grasped the sturdy railing that led down the rear steps. "I think I have it from here, girls. Just be sure you lock the door behind you if you leave before I get back."

Smiling through her pain, she descended the steps and awkwardly climbed into her car. Roma Jean and Jessie continued to stand at the top of the steps and gaze dejectedly at her as she slowly pulled out of the parking lot and began the short drive to the doctor's office.

By the time Syd reached New River Family Medicine, her ankle had swollen to nearly twice its normal size. She feared that it might be fractured, or at least badly sprained, and seriously began to despair over her ability to finish preparations for the library opening.

Roma Jean had been right—the clinic was easy to spot. It was situated on a pretty piece of land on a bend in the road just on the outskirts of Jefferson—the county seat. There was only one other car in the gravel parking lot. As she limped toward the entrance to the small, brick clinic, she wondered if she had been foolish to refuse Roma Jean's offer of support. The slightest bit of weight on her left side sent white-hot bolts of pain surging up her leg. She felt like the cross-trainer on her foot would soon burst its seams. A white painted sign next to the entrance read *M. H. Stevenson, M.D.*, and listed the clinic hours. Grimacing, she pushed open the door and limped inside.

The waiting room was small, but homey and very clean. American primitive antiques lined the walls, and several overstuffed Morris chairs were arranged around a glass-topped coffee table. An older woman, wearing a white shift and a nubby gray cardigan, sat behind a reception desk, organizing a stack of multicolored file folders. She looked up at Syd with unveiled curiosity, noticed her pronounced limp, then quickly stood up and came from behind the desk.

"Are you hurt?" she asked.

"Yes," Syd replied. "I don't think it's too serious, but I fell, and I think I may have twisted my ankle pretty badly."

"Well, you sit right down over here, honey," the woman gushed. She directed Syd into one of the upholstered chairs and dragged an ottoman over. "Prop your leg up on this and let's get that shoe off. Dr. Stevenson will be back in just a few minutes."

"Thank you." Syd gratefully accepted the small, round woman's attentions.

"Now, that's better," the woman pronounced as she dropped Syd's paint-spattered Nike to the floor. "I'm Mrs. Peggy Hawkes," she proudly announced, "and I've worked here ever since old Doc Stevenson opened this clinic twenty-five years ago."

"Oh," Syd looked squarely into a pair of penetrating, steely blue eyes. An implied question hung in the air. "Nice to meet you. My name is Syd Murphy." Syd paused. "I'm the new librarian in Jericho."

Mrs. Hawkes nodded vigorously and rocked back on the heels of her crepe-soled shoes. "Of course," she said. "I read about you in the paper. How you liking it up here in the hills? From up north somewhere, aren't you? I expect you see a lot of Curtis Freemantle out that way. He runs the mini-mart. You just missed his wife, Edna. She was in here this morning to have a neck boil lanced—same one, second time this month. Lord. Would you like some Pepsi, honey? Your color's a little off."

Syd stared in amazement as Mrs. Hawkes droned on, oblivious to her expanding stream of unanswered questions.

Tires crunched on the gravel outside, and a car door opened and closed. Mrs. Hawkes cut her monologue short as something began to rub insistently against the outside of the clinic door.

"I swanny," she said in a huff, as she walked to the door and opened it.

A large, yellow dog bounded into the waiting room. He skidded to a halt on the tile floor when he noticed Syd, then retreated shyly to a corner. He held a bright green tennis ball in his mouth.

Incredulous, Syd extended her hand. "Pete?" Tentatively, the dog approached her and sniffed her outstretched hand.

A striking, dark-haired woman entered the office. The tall woman was wearing a red sweater and a pair of gray corduroys. She carried a large postal bin. She noticed Syd, propped up in a chair with one sock-clad foot extended, and stopped dead in her tracks. Her blue eyes widened, then she laughed.

"S-Y-D, right?"

Syd was equally stunned. "Right. I can't believe this." She rubbed Pete behind the ears. "Do you work here?"

"It's worse than that," Maddie drawled. "I own the joint."

Syd blinked. "You mean *you're* Dr. Stevenson?"

"Dr. Stevenson the *younger,*" cut in a curious-sounding Peggy Hawkes. "This was her daddy's clinic."

"I came back here to practice after my father died," Maddie explained.

Syd continued to stare at Maddie in amazement. "Well, it looks like you're destined to rescue me once again."

Maddie handed the bin of mail to Mrs. Hawkes and crossed her arms. "What happened?"

"I took a nose dive off a step stool at the library and twisted my ankle."

"It looks pretty swollen. How long ago did this happen?" Maddie knelt down next to the ottoman and carefully raised Syd's pant leg as she looked at her ankle.

"About half an hour ago."

"Well, let's get you into an examination room and take a closer look." Maddie stood up and turned to Peggy Hawkes. "Let's get some x-rays of that ankle—AP, Mortisse, and Lateral."

"Can you do that here?" Syd asked, struggling up out of the armchair. Maddie stepped closer and took her arm to steady her as she stood up.

"Sure can," Mrs. Hawkes exclaimed. "Got a better x-ray machine than the county clinic over in Jefferson."

Maddie helped Syd down the hall behind the reception desk and into a small, dimly-lighted room that was dominated by a massive x-ray table.

"Have a seat up here." Maddie tapped the top of the table and helped Syd get settled. "Peggy will be right in to take the x-rays, then we'll fix you up." She smiled, left the room, and closed the door behind her.

For all her flighty presentation, Peggy Hawkes entered and got Syd ready for the x-rays.

"So you two girls met before? Isn't that just the way of things?" Peggy asked. "Where was it—at the library? I remember Maddie talking about needing to order a new PDR for the office. Did you help her with that? Turn this way a little, honey. That's good. I heard from Edna that you're living in that little apartment over the library. Are you going to look for a bigger place? Okay, don't move, now. We'll take this one just like the last time."

Fifteen minutes later, Syd was seated in Maddie's examination room, still reeling from Peggy's inquisition. Idly, she glanced around the office. Several framed diplomas hung on the wall behind the padded examination table. One was an undergraduate degree from Stanford. Syd squinted. *Summa cum laude.* Not too shabby. Another was from the University of Pennsylvania School of Medicine. The third indicated that Madeleine H. Stevenson had served as Chief Resident in Emergency Medicine at Penn Presbyterian Hospital in Philadelphia. Syd shook her head slowly. *God . . . there's nothing like being an underachiever.*

There was a gentle tap at the door, and Maddie entered, now wearing a long white jacket and small, wire-framed glasses. A stethoscope dangled from her pocket. She held a clipboard and a blood-pressure cuff. She smiled at Syd.

"Let's get the routine stuff out of the way." Maddie opened a small drawer, took a foil-wrapped thermometer out, unsheathed it, and placed it under Syd's tongue. "Our digital unit is on the fritz. We're temporarily operating in the dark ages." She took hold of Syd's wrist and counted her pulse.

"A little rapid," Maddie observed. "Probably all the excitement. Let's get your blood pressure."

Syd nodded her assent, and together they rolled up her shirtsleeve. Maddie fitted the cuff into place and fished out her stethoscope. She took readings on both arms.

"No problems there. What's this little gizmo say?" She pulled the thermometer out of Syd's mouth and held it up to the light. "Slightly elevated— also not surprising." She made a few notations on Syd's chart.

"Will I live?" Syd asked playfully.

"I *think* so," Maddie ventured. "But judging by the looks of that ankle, you won't be auditioning for *Dancing With the Stars* any time soon."

"Damn . . . I already had my outfit all picked out."

Maddie was smiling as Mrs. Hawkes entered the room with the x-rays.

"Here you are, Doctor." She turned to Syd. "Now you stop by my desk on the way out, honey, and we'll take care of all your paperwork."

Maddie took the film from her. "Thanks, Peggy."

Peggy bustled out and winked at Syd as she closed the door.

"Wow." Syd exhaled. "She is absolutely exhausting."

Maddie chuckled as she clipped the x-ray films onto a wall-mounted light box. "I know what you mean. My father always said she had more lines than BellSouth. But she's got a big heart, and she's a damn fine nurse."

She studied the x-rays for a minute, and then turned to Syd.

"Those look just fine, but do you mind if I manipulate this thing a little? It may hurt a bit, but I'll try to be quick."

"Twist away, Doctor. At least this time you don't have to contend with rusty lug nuts."

They laughed. Maddie helped Syd to stand so she could sit on the end of the examination table. She took her shoe and sock with her. Maddie lifted Syd's leg in her warm hands and gently rotated her foot—first to the left and then to the right. Syd winced.

"Sorry," Maddie said quickly. "One more, okay?"

She flexed the foot up and down several times, testing the muscle and mobility of the joint.

"How's that feel? Hurt as much as the other way?"

"Not as bad," Syd said through clenched teeth, "but I won't lie and say it's pleasant."

Maddie gently put her leg down and sat back on her rolling stool.

"Well, Madam, there's good news and bad news."

"Okay," Syd prompted.

"The good news is that nothing is broken—or fractured, as near as I can tell. The bad news is that you've got a class-A sprain. And I want you to stay completely off of it for at least three days. No arguments."

"That's impossible," Syd began.

"Look, Syd," Maddie said. "You can stay off it and give it a good chance to heal cleanly, or you can risk re-injuring it and ending up with a more serious and potentially chronic disability. Even though I don't see anything on the films, we can't rule out the possibility of a hairline fracture."

Syd cocked her head. "Don't hold back, Doctor. Tell me what you really think."

The corners of Maddie's blue eyes crinkled as she smiled. "Sorry. Sometimes my bedside manner is more suited to southwest Philly than southwest Virginia."

"It's okay. I know you're right. I've just got so much work to finish before the library opening."

"When is it?"

"November twelfth," Syd answered. "Three weeks from today."

"Do you have any help?"

"Yeah." Syd winced as she pulled on her sock. "Two volunteers. But they only work in the afternoons two days a week."

Maddie sighed. "Well, take my advice. It'll be difficult in the short term, but will do you much more good in the long run."

"Okay, Doc. You're the boss."

"In the meantime," Maddie continued, "just follow the tried-and-true RICE prescription—Rest, Ice, Compress, Elevate. Take it easy. Alternate hot and cold compresses on the ankle for the rest of today, and take aspirin to reduce the inflammation and help ease the pain. You can wrap it with an ACE bandage to make sleeping more comfortable." She reached into a drawer, drew out a cellophane-wrapped bandage, and handed it to Syd. "And keep this leg elevated as much as possible for the next forty-eight hours." She finished jotting notes on the sheet attached to her clipboard. "Give me a call later in the week, and let me know how you're doing."

Syd slowly stood up, still holding her left shoe in her hand.

"And, Syd?" Maddie began.

"Yes?"

"If I don't hear from you, I may just send Peggy by the library to investigate."

"Heaven forefend," Syd declared. "Don't worry. I'll call. I'll write. I'll call *and* write."

"I get the picture." Maddie laughed. She extended her hand. Syd shook it warmly. "Nice to see you again. I'll look forward to hearing from you later in the week."

Chapter 3

Maddie didn't have to wait too long to find out how Syd was faring. Four days later, she ran into her—literally—with her grocery cart.

It was eight o'clock on Friday night, and Maddie had ducked into the local Food Bonanza on her way home from the clinic for eggs and milk. She was famished. It had been a long day, replete with two emergencies, and she hadn't had anything to eat since seven that morning. Deciding that a large chef's salad sounded appealing, she made a quick pass through the deli section for some fresh cold cuts and cheese. She whirled her cart around and slammed right into the cart of another lone shopper, who was several feet away examining boxes of cookies on a lower shelf. Before she could stop it, the second cart lurched into motion and rolled toward a towering display of Vanilla Wafers.

"Holy hell," Maddie cursed and lunged forward to try and grab the handle of the runaway cart. She was too late. It made short work of the display, and a tsunami of cookie boxes fell into its basket, and spread out across the aisle. "Oh, *shit.*" Maddie dropped her arms to her sides as she viewed the carnage.

Syd stood facing her, ankle deep in Vanilla Wafers. "Personally, I was leaning toward the Oreos, but it seems like you feel pretty strongly about these." She picked one of the boxes up out of her cart. A small smile tugged at the corner of her mouth.

Inwardly cursing herself for being so clumsy, Maddie dramatically shrugged. "So much for professional decorum." She looked up to meet Syd's amused green eyes.

"Hello, Dr. Stevenson."

"Hi there. And please, call me Maddie." She paused. "It's a privilege I extend to everyone I rear-end." Syd snorted, and Maddie groaned when she realized what she had just said. "Oh, god. I'm sorry. This just keeps getting worse. Believe me. I'm not normally this accomplished a klutz."

"Really?" Syd crossed her arms. "So you're more of a garden-variety klutz?"

"Touché." Maddie laughed. "How are you? How's the ankle?" She stepped forward and started to pick up the boxes of cookies.

"I'm fine—nearly able to walk in a straight line." Syd pulled boxes of cookies out of her cart.

"You do *not* have to help me clean this up."

"Don't be silly. It's partly my fault. It appears I was blocking the right-of-way—again." She paused, holding boxes in both hands. "Should we try to restack these?"

"Beats me. Maybe we should just ditch 'em and flee the scene."

Syd nodded. "Normally, I'd be way ahead of you with that, but I'm starving, and I really need to find something to eat."

"Long day?"

"Oh, yeah. The branch opening is on top of me, and I still have tons left to do."

"I guess you figured out that all the restaurants around here close at sunset?"

Syd sighed. "Uh huh. I thought about ordering a pizza—again. But I just couldn't face it tonight."

They continued to stack boxes in silence. As they worked, Maddie couldn't keep down her growing curiosity about Syd. On the two previous occasions they had met, she had found herself enjoying Syd's company and wanting to get to know her better. Tonight was no exception. It was rare for her to find someone she felt so immediately at ease with—especially in Jericho. She glanced at her watch. It wasn't *impossibly* late yet, and they both had to eat. She wondered if Syd had any plans for the rest of the evening. She wondered if Syd would find it strange for her to ask.

They were nearly finished, and Syd looked at Maddie. "Why are *you* here this late on a Friday night?"

Maddie shrugged. "Similar story. I had a couple of emergencies today and didn't get a chance to eat anything. I thought I'd pick up some salad stuff on my way home." She paused after placing the last box on top of their makeshift pile. She turned to Syd. "Wanna join me? I can offer you some great wine and a table with a view."

Syd seemed to hesitate as she considered the offer. "Are you sure? It's late, and I know you must be tired."

Maddie smiled at her. "I *am* tired, but to tell the truth, I'm *more* tired of eating alone. If you're up for it, I would really enjoy the company."

"Well, then sure. I'd love to." Syd's smile appeared genuine.

"Great. Let's go cruise the deli aisle and see what looks tempting. You can follow me to my house—it's not far from here."

Before they turned around and headed for the back of the store, Maddie tossed a box of Vanilla Wafers into her cart.

Syd gave her a strange look.

She shrugged. "Might as well."

They approached the checkout lane, and Syd was surprised to see Roma Jean running the cash register. She had never mentioned that she had a part-time job here—or anywhere.

Roma Jean looked up from the copy of *US Weekly* she was reading. She broke into a wide smile.

"Hi, Miss Murphy." She tucked the magazine back into the display rack and hopped off her stool. "I bet you're surprised to see me here." She smiled proudly.

"Hello, Roma Jean." Syd smiled back as she started removing items from her cart. "I sure am. How often do you work here?"

"Mostly just weekends, but sometimes they call me in if somebody gets sick." Roma Jean's fuchsia fingernails were a blur as she quickly scanned Syd's items and pushed them toward the bagging area. "I have to work until closing tonight.

I don't usually mind that, but it's reeaaalllly slow right now. I keep hoping that some of my friends will come in, but I guess the game isn't over yet. I was supposed to go, but they called me in to work because Mrs. Pollard's car broke down again—that's like the third time this week. I'm bored out of my mind 'cause there's nothing to do."

"Well, if you're desperate, there's a display on aisle nine that could use some serious help," Maddie said in low voice.

Roma Jean looked up with a startled expression. She blushed and spilled the bag of oranges she had just picked up. They bounced across the conveyor belt, and Syd caught one before it hit the floor.

Maddie eyed Roma Jean with an amused expression. "Hello, Roma Jean. I saw your mom today. How's she feeling?"

Roma Jean appeared completely undone. "Oh. Um. Hi, Dr. Stevenson. She's fine—I think." She dropped her eyes, then shyly stole another glance at Maddie.

It was clear to Syd that Roma Jean was in awe of the doctor. She watched their interaction with interest.

"Good. Please tell her not to hesitate to call me at home over the weekend if she has any more problems." Maddie began to unload their assortment of deli items from her cart.

"Okay, um, I will." Roma Jean stared down at the moving conveyor belt. She continued to blush furiously. "Thank you, Dr. Stevenson." She belatedly started to scan the rest of Syd's groceries, but was noticeably slower, and had to scan several items repeatedly before she could get their prices to register.

"So, Roma Jean . . . are you going to be at the fire department barbecue tomorrow?" Syd asked, in an attempt to ease Roma Jean's discomfort.

Roma Jean looked up at Syd gratefully. "I think so. I get off at three, so I should be able to make it. My dad is helping out with the cooking."

"That's what I've heard. Everyone says it's the best barbecue around."

"I have to say that I'm not much of a barbecue fan, generally, but I look forward to this event every year." Maddie grinned at Roma Jean. "To tell the truth, it's really your mom's hushpuppies that draw me out. They're amazing."

Roma Jean gaped at Maddie. "Honey," she blurted out.

Maddie gave her a confused smile. "Excuse me?"

"It's honey," a flustered Roma Jean explained. "She puts honey in the batter." Her cheeks continued to blaze as she quickly looked away and handed Syd her change and receipt.

"Ah." Maddie grinned at her. "So that's the secret."

It was hard for Syd not to laugh at Roma Jean's distress. She clearly had a super-sized crush on the good-looking doctor. It was written all over her face. She stole a discreet look at Maddie to see if she was aware of it, but Maddie seemed oblivious as she piled the remainder of her items on the checkout counter. Syd had never witnessed a bona fide swoon before, but when Maddie stepped forward, and Roma Jean looked up into her clear, blue eyes, she thought she might just get her chance.

She decided that expediting their transaction and getting out of the store was the best way to rescue Roma Jean from complete mortification.

"Here, Roma Jean, let me help bag these things." Syd walked around to the other side of the counter and started packing their groceries into paper sacks.

Maddie laughed. "You must really be hungry." She swiped her debit card through the reader and punched in her PIN. "Maybe we should have opted for the pizza after all." Her smile was dazzling, and its full-frontal, close range impact was nearly the undoing of poor Roma Jean. She looked like she was about to pass out.

Syd gave Roma Jean what she hoped was a reassuring nudge. "Dr. Stevenson is taking pity on me. I didn't realize that none of the restaurants around here stay open past seven." Roma Jean's eyes were like saucers. "She's kindly going to feed me some dinner."

Maddie took the receipt that Roma Jean dumbly held out. "Thanks, kiddo. Maybe we'll see you tomorrow at the barbecue?"

Roma Jean just nodded as Syd and Maddie collected their bags and prepared to leave the store.

"Wait a second," Maddie said to Syd. She stopped, dug into one of the bags, and pulled out the box of Vanilla Wafers. Smiling, she turned and handed it to Roma Jean. "Maybe these will help sweeten the rest of your shift tonight." She winked at her and walked out of the store.

Syd sighed and slowly shook her head as she followed Maddie into the parking lot. The poor kid was a *real* goner, now.

Syd was surprised when Maddie stopped next to a small, silver Lexus Coupe. She hit a button on her key ring and the trunk lid popped open. After stashing her bags in the trunk behind a mesh cargo net, she turned to Syd.

"Do you wanna put your cold stuff in here so we can carry it on into the house with us?"

Syd stepped forward. "Sure. Good idea." She handed her the bag with her dairy items. Looking over the sporty, hardtop convertible, she gave a low whistle. "Did the Jeep get a makeover?"

Maddie gave her an innocent look. "Oh, this old thing?" she drawled. "I don't drive it much—the roads around here just beat the crap out of it." She chuckled. "Not that Philly was much better."

"I've always loved cars that look like they're going ninety miles an hour when they're parked." Syd knew her gaze was lustful. She touched the car's retractable top with her free hand.

Maddie affected an ostentatious southern accent. "Why, Miss Murphy. I never would have expected you to be so shallow."

"Oh, no . . . I love my creature comforts, all right. So, please, allow me these few moments of living vicariously. I don't get many opportunities these days."

Maddie laughed good-naturedly. "Look. Why don't you just stash the rest of your stuff in the trunk and ride with me? I can run you right back out here after we eat. It's not far at all."

Syd looked up into her blue eyes, and for just a moment, she identified with Roma Jean's lapse in composure. Maddie's high-voltage smile at close range really *was* unsettling. She found herself wondering why this beautiful woman was unattached. There had to be some kind of story there.

"Okay, if you really don't mind bringing me back out here." She lowered her gaze to the car. "I'd *love* to ride in this thing."

Maddie took Syd's other grocery bag and added it to the stash in the trunk. After snapping the lid shut, she walked to the passenger side door and grandly opened it for Syd. "Well then, Madame. If you would kindly sit down, we can get underway."

Syd climbed into the surprisingly roomy car and sighed as she sank into the soft, leather seat. Her gaze drifted up to Maddie, who was watching her with an amused expression. "Would it be possible to have my dinner served right here?"

Maddie scrunched her brows. "You mean like Sonic Drive-In?" She fluttered the fingers of her left hand. "Little plastic animals on the cup rims . . . tater tots . . . the whole nine yards?"

"Well, I could do without the tater tots, but the animals would be a welcome addition."

"I'll see what I can do." Maddie smiled as she shut the door and walked around to the driver's side.

Maddie sat down next to her, and Syd detected a faint trace of something sweet and slightly peppery. It was fleeting, but the light fragrance seemed to suit Maddie perfectly.

Maddie started the car, and the dashboard was immediately illuminated with soft, blue light. The cabin filled with the deep and resonant strains of Mahler. It seemed to roll and swell out of every surface inside the car. She recognized the piece at once.

"*Das Lied von der Erde?*" she asked.

Maddie looked at her with happy surprise. "Yeah. Janet Baker. It's one of my favorites."

Syd nodded. "I love it, too. This certainly is the definitive recording."

"You like Mahler?"

"I'd call it more of a love-hate relationship. As a fan of classical music, I love it. As a musician, I hate it." She wrinkled her nose. "It's a bitch to play."

Maddie regarded her with interest. "You're a musician? What instrument do you play?"

"Violin."

Maddie looked at her oddly, then shook her head and eased the car into gear. "We have a *lot* to talk about."

The drive to Maddie's house took about ten minutes. They left the main road about three miles from the shopping center and turned onto a curvy, paved secondary road that wound its way through fenced pastures and rolling land dotted with barns and stands of pine trees.

Maddie slowed as she approached the turn onto a private lane that was flanked by split-rail fencing. The weathered boards at the entrance were covered with vines of sweet autumn clematis. The gravel lane climbed up past pastures and alongside a creek that dipped and turned and switched back beneath the road before it emptied into a pond that stood at some distance from a large, white-framed farmhouse that overlooked it from a low rise. The house had a huge porch that wrapped around three sides. A large, yellow dog stood near the steps with his tail wagging, watching them approach. There were several outbuildings, and Maddie drove the Lexus into the one nearest the house and parked next to her Jeep.

She unclipped her seatbelt and turned to Syd. "Home, sweet home. Let's get inside and make something to eat. I'm beyond famished."

Smiling, Syd joined her at the back of the car, and they lifted out their bags. Maddie led them to the doorway past an impressive tool bench loaded with gizmos and shelves full of small appliances that appeared to be in various states of disrepair.

Outside, Maddie stopped to greet Pete, who danced around them as they approached the steps that led up to the wide porch. She set her bags down on a rustic pine table covered with potted plants and pulled open the screen to unlock the big oak door.

Syd stood next to her on the porch, looking at the pond and the rolling land that spread out beyond it. The view took her breath away. She could hear the sonorous rush of water from the creek and, from somewhere near the house, the teakettle night song of a Carolina Wren. She was enchanted.

"My god. This place is incredible." Syd wanted nothing more than to sink down onto one of the painted Adirondack chairs on the porch and never get up.

Maddie turned to her. "You like? This was the old Ward family farm. My parents bought it back in the seventies when they moved here—not long before I was born." Her voice was quiet. "I spent the best ten years of my life here."

Syd turned her head to look at Maddie. "Well, hopefully you now have many more happy years ahead. It would be hard to imagine anything else in this setting."

Maddie smiled. "I'm glad you think so." She touched her on the arm. "C'mon, let's get inside. We can come back out here to eat if you'd like."

"Oh, god. Can we? I was just thinking seriously about claiming squatter's rights on one of these chairs."

"Pick out one you like and call it yours. You're welcome here any time."

Syd laughed as she turned to follow Maddie. "Oh, you say that *now*. Wait until you get tired of stumbling over me every time you leave your house."

Maddie gave her an amused look. "I think I'm equal to the challenge." She held the door open for Syd and followed her inside with their bags. Pete jogged along beside them and quickly disappeared into the back of the house.

If possible, the interior of the farmhouse was even more amazing than the landscape that surrounded it. Comfortable-looking double parlors with French doors flanked a large foyer filled with antiques. Maddie led Syd down a wide center hallway toward a spacious formal dining room. An open staircase ran along one wall, and a set of double doors led into a huge country kitchen. It seemed that every room of the house had direct access to the wraparound porch. Syd followed Maddie into the kitchen and stopped dead in her tracks. The well-lighted space was dominated by a massive Wolf range with double ovens and a glass-doored Subzero refrigerator with a companion wine storage unit that had to hold at least a hundred bottles. She dropped down onto a stool that stood next to a granite-topped center island.

"I'm not leaving. Ever."

Pete walked back into the room and sniffed at Syd's feet. Then he flopped onto the floor beside her. He had the inevitable tennis ball in his mouth.

Maddie smiled at her as she began removing food items from her bags. "I wish I could take credit for this, but my dad was the chef in the family. This was all his." She walked to the Subzero and stashed Syd's bag of dairy items on a lower shelf. "I can barely boil water." She took off her suit jacket and tossed it over a chair. "How about something to drink while we fix our plates?"

Syd nodded her assent. "I could use it."

Maddie went to the wine fridge and opened the door to the top compartment. "Like red?" she asked.

"Oh, yeah. Love it."

Maddie seemed to deliberate a moment, then pulled out a bottle and carried it to the center island. She handed Syd a corkscrew. "Would you do the honors? The glasses are in that cabinet behind you."

"I'd be happy to." Syd stood up and removed two red wine glasses from a large pine sideboard. She returned to the center island and opened the bottle of Pinot Noir while Maddie got plates and utensils out.

Syd looked around the room. It showcased all the charm of a rustic farm kitchen, but had a tasteful overlay of epicurean convenience. The cabinets looked original—tall doors with glass panels that reached the high ceiling. An old-looking, bib-front porcelain sink probably wasn't old at all. A plank-topped table with mismatched wooden chairs stood in front of large, double windows that dominated the back wall. It was flanked by built-in shelves loaded with cookbooks and stacked pottery. The floor was covered with large Italian terra cotta tile. Several antique oak cabinets completed the furnishings in the room. What appeared to be a man's denim jacket hung on a peg near the back door.

An uneasy silence had settled over them once they entered the house, and Syd realized this was the first time they had really been alone in non-neutral territory. She was dimly aware that she had breached some kind of boundary by being here—and even though she had been invited, she guessed that Maddie probably didn't do this kind of thing often. Her thoughts shifted back to their first conversation on the day Maddie changed her tire along the river road. She had hinted at the feelings of isolation and separateness that had characterized her return to live in the area. She hoped Maddie didn't now regret her impulsive invitation.

Maddie seemed aware of the awkwardness, too, as she quietly moved around the kitchen, opening containers and getting condiments out of the refrigerator. She walked back to the center island with a small baguette. She pulled a large bread knife out of its block on the countertop, placed the loaf on a cutting board, and sliced it.

Syd poured two glasses of the wine and held one out to her hostess.

"Thank you again for your hospitality." She hesitated before continuing. "I probably should have had the grace to refuse."

Maddie gave her a perplexed look as she took the wine glass. "What do you mean?"

Syd opted for honesty. "Now that I'm here, I confess to feeling a bit . . . intrusive. I suspect that you don't normally invite total strangers out here to your . . ." She struggled to find the right words. "Sanctuary? Incredibly-tasteful-and-otherworldly retreat?" She smiled shyly. "Your home?"

Maddie regarded her quietly for a moment. "Well, 'normal' is a fairly broad term. I don't think I've been back in Jericho long enough to know yet what normal for me is going to look like." She took a sip of her wine. "And I know it might seem odd, but I don't really think of you as a stranger." She paused and narrowed her eyes. "On the other hand, you aren't brazenly concealing the fact that you're a homicidal maniac or anything, are you? If so, I definitely need to rethink my choice of wine."

"Why?" Syd looked down into her glass. "What's wrong with the wine?"

"Nothing," Maddie drawled. "That's my point. I wouldn't want to waste a bottle this good on a lunatic who's only here to kill me."

Syd sighed. "So many victims, so little time." She tasted the wine. "Mmmm. Too bad I left my slasher gear in my other suit." Maddie snorted, and Syd looked up at her accusingly. "You really weren't kidding when you told me that you were a snob, were you?"

"I plead the fifth."

Syd smiled. "Forgive my lapse into melodrama."

"No problem. C'mon. Let's fix our plates and go sit on the porch."

They relaxed in wide-armed Adirondack chairs on the front porch. They had inhaled their plates of food and were unwinding with second glasses of wine. Syd kicked off her shoes and propped her feet up on an ottoman. Pete was stretched out near her chair, snoring softly. His now empty food bowl rested behind him.

Maddie had stopped to turn on the stereo before they ventured outside with their meals, and the muted sound of the Bach *Suites for Unaccompanied Cello* blended seamlessly with the ambient night noises that surrounded them.

Syd rested her head against the back of her chair and expelled a deep breath. "You know, there isn't much need for us to talk while this conversation is going on."

"What conversation?" Maddie looked at Syd. The semi-light from the house only dimly illuminated her profile as she sat staring out across the pond.

"The one taking place between Bach and this landscape. It's so perfect. I feel like I'm eavesdropping on something profound." She turned to Maddie. "I can't imagine what it must be like to have this experience every night."

"I'm afraid you'll think less of me if I tell you that I can't imagine it, either." Maddie shifted in her chair. "The truth is, I rarely make the time to do this. I'm normally home so late, I barely have time to eat before falling into bed."

"That's just wrong on so many levels."

"I know it is." Maddie sighed. "Truthfully, I think sometimes that I keep myself that busy so I won't have to confront this."

"This?"

Maddie waved her hand. "*This*—all that being back here implies."

Syd turned in her chair to face Maddie. "That was sure loaded. Are you regretting your decision to come back here?" She paused. "Forgive me if that's too personal a question. I don't want to pry."

Maddie shook her head. "Oh, no. You aren't prying. I brought it up." She took a healthy sip of her wine and set the glass back down on a low table next to her chair. "I really thought I left my demons behind when I packed up and moved away from Philadelphia. But presto. Somehow they all got boxed right up with the rest of my stuff." She remained quiet for another moment. "Wherever you go, there you are." She looked at Syd. "Who was it who said that?"

Syd shook her head. "I don't know, but it sounds like T.S. Eliot meets Gertrude Stein."

Maddie laughed. Syd's green eyes weren't visible in the dim light, but Maddie knew they were sparkling with humor and intelligence. She wished their chairs were closer together so she could see her better. She wished that time would slow down so they could continue to sit here and talk for hours. She wished the small librarian wasn't so damn beautiful. She wished she could just go and submerge herself in the frigid water of her pond.

"I love your sense of humor."

Syd smiled. "It's an acquired taste. I have to keep it under pretty tight regulation up here."

"I know what you mean."

"Well, you aren't alone in the wrestling-with-unwanted-demons category. I have my fair share, too." Syd sighed deeply. "And I don't know about *yours*, but mine is a six-foot-tall spoiled brat with a trust fund and a Durham zip code."

Maddie lifted her chin. "Your ex-husband?"

"Soon-to-be-ex-husband," Syd corrected. "Yeah. I really came up here to get away from him, and to figure out what I want to do with what's left of my life."

"So how's that working out for you?"

"Apparently about as well as your retreat is working out for you."

They smiled at each other in awkward camaraderie.

Maddie lifted her wine glass. "Here's to kicking some demon ass."

Syd clinked rims with her. "I'll certainly drink to that." Just as she raised her glass to her lips, Pete sat up and barked as he charged toward the stairs leading to the ground. He vaulted over Syd's ottoman and knocked the wine glass out of her hand with his tail. The red liquid sloshed out across her lap, but she caught the glass by its stem before it hit the floor.

"Oh, shit." Maddie rushed to her. She took the glass and set it down on a nearby table. "I'm so sorry. He probably saw some deer down by the pond. They come in at night to drink."

Syd struggled to her feet. "It's okay. Really." The wine continued to seep into her blouse and slacks. "But I'd better try to rinse this out now, or these clothes will be ruined."

"Of course. C'mon inside. We'll fix you right up. We can just throw them in the wash. I'll give you something to wear."

They walked back into the house. "Don't bother with that. If I can just rinse them out, I can take them to the laundromat tomorrow."

Maddie led the way back through the kitchen to a laundry room at the rear of the house. "No way. You let that stain soak in over night, and that outfit's gonna be toast. She went to a folding table and pulled a clean set of sweats out of a pile. "Take off your clothes."

Syd arched an eyebrow. "That's not the smoothest offer I've ever had, but you sure get points for an authoritative delivery."

Maddie dropped her chin to her chest. "God, I'm such a steamroller sometimes." She looked at Syd apologetically. "Sorry. I'm used to calling the shots. Occupational hazard, I guess."

Syd took the sweats from her. "It's okay, Doctor. I'll take your advice."

Maddie gestured toward the washing machine and all of its accoutrement. "Know how all of this works?"

Syd nodded.

"I'll be in the kitchen getting us some more wine." She left Syd alone in the room to change.

Back in the kitchen, Maddie stood for a moment, gently knocking her head against the door of the wine fridge in consternation. *Get a fucking grip. You're acting like a moron.* She pulled the door open and looked over the tidy array of bottles. Pinots. Cabs. Zins. Syrahs. Blends.

Wondering which wine went best with pathetic, she pulled out a Spencer Roloson Napa Valley Red. She heard the rush of water as the washing machine started filling, and then Syd walked back into the kitchen. Maddie's sweats were comically large on her. The cuffs of the pants were turned up so many times Syd looked like she had fleece muffs around her ankles. Maddie stifled a laugh.

Syd rolled her eyes. "If we're going to make a habit of this, could you at least try to be shorter so I'll feel less ridiculous?"

"Oh, I promise. Shorter. Yes, ma'am. I'll get to work on that straight away." Maddie went to the island and started to open the new bottle of wine. "You look adorable—like you're twelve."

"Oh, thanks. That's just the look I was going for . . . petulant." She pushed the sleeves of the navy blue Penn sweatshirt up her arms, then noticed the time on her wristwatch. "My *god*. Do you realize it's ten-thirty?"

Shocked, Maddie stopped the corkscrew in mid-twist. "No? Really?" She looked at her own wrist. "Oh." She paused. "Well . . . you can have another glass of wine and wait on your clothes, or, if you need to go, I can take you back to your car now, and bring them to you tomorrow. It's your call. The drill sergeant is off-the-clock."

The seconds ticked by while Syd deliberated, and Maddie stood with the corkscrew wound halfway into the bottle of wine.

"I'd really hate for you to make a special trip into town tomorrow. But, on the other hand, I don't want to keep you up any later, either." She hesitated. "How tired are you?"

Maddie decided to reply honestly. "Strangely, I'm not tired at all. I'm enjoying the conversation." She smiled. "It's nice to have some company out here for a change."

"Okay . . . if you'll promise not to let me overstay my welcome, then I'd love another glass of wine."

Maddie gamely raised three fingers on her left hand in a Girl Scout salute. "I promise." She finished opening the bottle of wine. "Grab yourself another glass, and let's go sit in the parlor—it was getting a little too cool out on the porch, anyway."

"Right behind you," Syd said, retrieving another glass from the sideboard.

They walked back toward the front of the house. Maddie stopped at the front door to let a happily penitent Pete inside, then led them into the large parlor on the left side of the hallway. She flipped a wall switch, and Syd caught her breath at the black baby grand piano in the corner facing the front windows. Its keyboard and soundboard covers were closed, but the cabinet looked immaculate.

"My *god*." She walked to it. "This is a Bösendorfer." She looked up at Maddie. "I've never even *seen* one of these outside of a conservatory." She looked it over with a stunned expression. "Was this your father's, too?"

"Nope. *That* belonged to my mother. She was the musician in the family." She smiled. "Dad and I had to content ourselves with playing the stereo. We were both so unmusical it drove my mother nuts." Maddie set her wine glass and the bottle down on the coffee table situated in front of two leather-upholstered club chairs. "I went through six grueling years of lessons before she realized I was better suited to operating on pianos than playing them. I think it all came to a head the day she got home from work and found me dismantling the soundboard."

Syd gasped in horror.

"Yeah. It wasn't pretty." She dropped into one of the armchairs. "Needless to say, I didn't sit down on *that* bench—or any other surface—for over a week." She laughed. "I never took another piano lesson, either."

Syd shook her head as she set her own wine glass down next to Maddie's. She went back to the piano and lifted the keyboard cover. "May I?"

"Be my guest."

Syd bent over the keyboard and played a chord. Then two. Smiling to herself, she played a sequence of arpeggios. The silvery sound rang through the room. She stood up and closed the cover, then turned to Maddie.

"It's in perfect tune. Perfect pitch. Perfect action." She dropped into the chair next to Maddie's. "It's perfect in every way."

Maddie nodded. "That's good to hear. It actually belonged to my grandmother, so it's been in the family for quite a while. I think she bought it in Austria, so it's a bit different from the U.S. models."

"You keep it tuned?"

"Yeah. Dad always did. I've kept up with it since I've been back." She hesitated. "I know that probably seems odd or morbid."

Syd shook her head. "Not at all." She met Maddie's eyes. "Is . . . did . . . has your mother passed away?"

"Oh, no. She's not dead—just gone. My parents divorced when I was ten, and she moved to the west coast. She left it behind." After a moment, she added, "There were quite a few things she left behind."

Syd could sense that they were venturing into awkward terrain. "Well, that's an amazing instrument. I played a Bösendorfer once in college, and remember how different it was from all the Steinways the department had—heavier action— a different kind of resonance altogether."

"Where did you go to school?"

"Rochester."

Maddie raised an eyebrow. "Rochester?"

Syd shrugged. "Eastman."

Maddie tilted her head as she regarded her. "Impressive."

"It really wasn't—*I* really wasn't." She met Maddie's interested gaze. "I got my artist's certificate—barely. But I wisely changed my major to music education. I just didn't have the temperament for a full-fledged career in performance. The ones who did—they were just so different. Their lives were so focused and pared down. It was like they each had only one life decision to make, and they had made it." She took a sip of wine. "That just wasn't me. It still isn't." She set her glass down on a small side table, next to a worn and bookmarked copy of *David Copperfield.*

"Still . . . you're pretty modest for someone with an Eastman certificate."

"Oh, really, Miss Ivy League? Talk about the pot calling the kettle black."

Maddie feigned umbrage. "I'll have you know that I'm not modest at all. Arrogance was the first thing they taught us in med school." She drew her brows together. "I think it had something to do with billing and fee schedules, but I confess all of that weightier stuff was pretty murky to me."

Syd snorted. She looked around the room and its walls lined with bookcases. Opposite their chairs was a beautiful fireplace with a whimsical, Chagall watercolor hanging over it. She inclined her head toward the picture.

"Was that your mother's, too?"

Maddie followed her gaze. "The Chagall? Nope. That's mine. I bought it years ago at a gallery in Washington. It was my reward for finishing my residency."

Syd stared at Maddie. "You mean it's an original?"

Maddie laughed. "It's a lithograph, but it's signed and numbered." She continued to look at it fondly. "I always loved his *Magic Flute* series."

Syd nodded. "I know what you mean. The murals at The Metropolitan Opera are stunning."

They drifted into silence. At a low volume in the background, a cello played its last, heroic note. Syd heard the faint whirring sound of the CD changer from someplace across the room. After a pause, the sensuous strains of Mendelssohn's violin sonata filled the air. She smiled to herself. It was as if someone had faxed Maddie a list of her favorite recordings.

"Tell me more about your soon-to-be-ex-husband. What went wrong?" Maddie's quiet voice cut through her musings.

Syd stared down at the large red and black patterns in the kilim rug at her feet. She exhaled and looked up into Maddie's friendly blue eyes. "It'd be quicker and easier to tell you what went right. Describing what went wrong would keep us both sitting here until dawn."

Maddie gave her a small smile. "That would be okay, too. Remember. I make great coffee."

Syd brightened up at the mention of Maddie's coffee. "That's right. I forgot about that." She smiled in remembrance of their roadside adventure. "Okay, then. Short version of the long story." She sat back in her chair and draped her arms over the sides. "I met Jeff when I moved back to Baltimore after college. He was there interning with my dad." She looked at Maddie. "My father is an agronomist at College Park. He works mostly in the watershed areas of the Chesapeake. Jeff was a grad student at Duke, and he came to Maryland on a summer research grant. That's how we met."

"How long did he work with your father?"

"About four months. During that time, a professor of mine from Eastman connected me with the Baltimore Symphony. I got a job subbing for a music librarian who was out on maternity leave. That ended just about the time Jeff was leaving to return to Durham."

"Now I know how you ended up in North Carolina."

"And why I decided to go to library school. I really loved the work."

"So the two of you got married?"

Syd shook her head. "Not right away. I moved to Durham with him but we didn't marry until nearly a year later. My leaving with him without getting married totally freaked my mother out. Jeff wanted to get married, too, but I wasn't ready to take a step like that—not so soon. I got tired of fighting the two of them. Finally, they wore me down, and I capitulated." She paused to push the sleeves up on the oversized sweatshirt. "It was impulsive. We got married on a Wednesday afternoon by a Justice of the Peace at Durham City Hall." She absently rotated the tiny gold ring on her right pinkie finger. "We didn't even get dressed up." She shook her head and looked up at Maddie. "It's amazing how something that takes less than two minutes to accomplish can completely change your life."

"What happened?"

"Well, for starters, I didn't realize that I was marrying a perpetual student. He bounced around from one program to another—never completing anything. His parents were—*are*—terribly generous with him, financially. He could pretty much do whatever he wanted." She laughed bitterly. "Still can."

"Tell me more about him. If you married him, he had to have *some* redeeming qualities."

Syd smiled at her. "You flatter me. But to his credit—yes, he was charming." She ticked off his attributes on her fingers. "Only child of wealthy, northeastern parents. Nice looking. Great personality. Loved the outdoors. Loved being around other people—got along well with everyone." She rolled her eyes. "He got along *especially* well with starry-eyed, undergraduate coeds."

"Uh oh."

"Yeah. But I didn't make that discovery until a year after we were married. By then, I was already in the middle of my library school program at Carolina." She shook her head. "I hung in there with him for another year and tried to make it work. But by the time I finished my degree, I knew it was over." She turned in her chair to face Maddie. "So you see, this opportunity came along at just the right time for me."

Maddie's gaze was empathetic. "I'm sorry, Syd. That can't have been an easy decision to make."

"You'd be surprised. The chance to hide out up here and sort out my future fell into my lap like manna from heaven. I jumped at it."

Maddie looked thoughtful. "It's ironic."

"What is?"

"You came here to figure out your future. I came here to confront my past."

Syd gave her a small smile. "Maybe it's no accident that we met on the roadside that day."

Maddie raised an eyebrow. "Are you a fatalist?"

"Not generally, but I try not to miss the really big clues the universe tosses in my path." She picked up her wine glass. "Like this, for example. If I drink any more, I'll never be able to drive myself home—not safely, anyway."

Maddie sighed. "You're right. Frankly, I'm not sure I should even think about driving you back to your car." She deliberated. "There's no way your clothes are going to be ready any time soon. Why don't you just stay over?"

"Oh, no," Syd said. "I could never impose on you like that."

"It's no imposition at all. Trust me. This place is like a B&B. I have three guest rooms all ready to go. You can just take your pick. I can easily set you up with toiletries and something to sleep in."

Syd was torn. She was comfortable with Maddie, and she was enjoying the warmth and ease of their interaction. But she worried, again, about pushing the limits of a new friendship too far too fast. She was aware of how isolated she had felt since coming to Jericho, and she didn't want to let her hunger for meaningful, human interaction make her appear clingy or desperate to Maddie.

Maddie's low voice cut through her silent monologue. "I can see you're struggling. I didn't mean to make you feel uncomfortable."

Syd met her concerned blue eyes. "Actually, what I'm sitting here struggling with is entirely the opposite scenario. If anything, I feel *too* comfortable." She waved her hand dismissively. "I don't want you to think I'm some kind of pathetic weirdo who's out looking for someone to glom onto."

Maddie burst into laughter. "God, what a pair we are. I was just saying a version of the same thing to myself in the kitchen while you were in the laundry room changing clothes." She continued to chuckle. "You know what this means, right?"

Syd nodded, with a wry smile. "We're a couple of total losers?"

"That would be correct." Maddie chortled as she picked up the wine bottle. "May I top you off?"

Syd held up her glass. "You certainly may." She sighed contentedly and kicked off her shoes. Sinking lower into her chair, she closed her eyes. "Is this where I ask for turn-down service?"

Maddie snorted. "One thing you'll learn about me if we spend very much more time together is that I rarely turn *anything* down."

They finished the second bottle of wine and hung up Syd's laundry. Maddie walked back through the house, turning off lights. Pete followed along at her heels. After stashing their used plates and glasses in the dishwasher, she picked up her discarded jacket and walked across the kitchen to a back doorway that appeared to lead to the porch.

"C'mon. Let's go up this way. I can grab you something to sleep in."

To the left of the back door, a narrow staircase led up to the second floor. Maddie flipped some wall switches at the top of the stairs, illuminating a spacious master suite with large windows on three sides. It was plainly her bedroom.

It had a small sitting area in front of a fireplace and beautiful heart of pine flooring. Books and papers were tidily stacked on a low table in front of the fireplace. A brass pharmacy lamp stood on the floor beside an upholstered chaise. A pottery jar full of pens and highlighters sat atop a Shaker candle stand. The rest of the room was decorated with primitive American antiques and brightly-colored kilim rugs. A large bed, neatly made-up with a star-pattern Amish quilt, jutted out into the room from a corner near the entrance to a huge, tiled bathroom. A few colorful art prints and several framed black and white photographs ornamented the walls.

Maddie tossed her jacket across the foot of the bed and went to an oak, five-drawer chest. Pete followed her and plopped down in an oversized dog bed near the door to the hallway.

Syd noticed half a dozen tennis balls in various stages of wear in and around his bed.

"Let's find you something to sleep in." Maddie fished around in a bottom drawer and pulled out a set of bright blue scrubs. "These ought to work. They're left over from my residency." She smirked as she tossed them to Syd. "I was shorter in those days."

Syd caught them and looked them over. The tunic top was stenciled *PPMC*. She held the drawstring pants up to her waist. The legs were impossibly long. "Right. *Way* shorter." She clucked her tongue. "Got any duct tape?"

Maddie chuckled as she closed the drawer.

Syd gestured at the room. "This is beautiful. I don't know how you leave it every day."

Maddie shrugged as she looked around. "I don't really think about it all that much." She smiled at Syd. "Having you here is going to be good for me. It's going to make see all of this with different eyes."

"I'm glad. You *should*. I know people who'd chew their own arms off for the chance to escape to a place like this. I'd be one of them."

Maddie crossed the room and stood beside her. "Well, thankfully, you won't have to resort to anything quite so dramatic." Her tone was warm. "You'll always be welcome here." She gestured toward the hallway. "C'mon, let's pick you out a bedroom."

They walked out of the room toward the front of the house. Pete jumped up and followed along behind them, wagging his tail. Three big bedrooms opened off the wide, center hallway, and Maddie steered Syd toward the front one that overlooked the pond.

"If I were you," she said, flipping on the lights, "this would be my pick. It faces north, so you won't wake up with the sun in your eyes. And it has its own bathroom—a real perk. The other two rooms have to share." She paused. "This was my room when I lived here as a child."

Syd looked up at her, but the Maddie's expression was unreadable. "It's settled, then."

The room was spacious and well-appointed—similar in style to the master suite. The walls were covered with framed photos of small airplanes. It had a craftsman-style desk and chair in front of corner windows, and an oak four-poster bed. A large oak chest, an upholstered armchair, and a small washstand completed its furnishings.

Maddie crossed the room and turned on the lights in the adjacent bathroom. It was tiled in black and white, and had a stall shower and a large, porcelain pedestal sink. She opened a linen closet.

"There are clean towels and toiletries in here." She pulled out a slender box and set it on the sink top. "Here's a new toothbrush." She smiled. "You might want to leave it here after you use it." Her blue eyes were twinkling.

Syd pondered. "Well, now that depends."

"On?" Maddie looked intrigued.

"On whether your coffee is truly as ambrosial as I recall. Sometimes, memory can be deceiving."

Maddie pursed her lips. "I see." She glanced at her watch. "Well . . . I guess time will tell. I'll try not to disappoint you."

Syd smiled shyly. "I'm sure you never will."

They stood there awkwardly for a moment.

"I'll say goodnight then. You be sure to let me know if you need anything." Maddie hesitated. "I'm right down the hall."

Syd found Maddie's momentary loss of composure endearing. Impulsively, she hugged her. "Thanks for a wonderful evening. It turns out, I really needed it."

Maddie returned her hug. "Me, too. I'm glad you're here." She stepped back. "C'mon, Pete—bedtime." Pete raced her to the doorway. Smiling at Syd, she left the room and closed the door softly behind her. Syd could hear the clatter of Pete's feet as he trotted down the hallway behind her.

Syd woke to an almost surreal quality, and she had to shake herself to remember where she was and how she came to be there. The place was even more breathtaking in the daylight, and she marveled at Maddie's ability to shrug it all off as if it wasn't anything out of the ordinary.

After rising and washing her face, she made her way downstairs in search of her hostess. She was still wearing the blue scrubs.

Syd ventured outside where Maddie was sitting on the porch with her coffee. "Hi," she said, feeling a little sheepish.

Maggie turned to her. "Hey."

She seemed to be as aware as Syd of the awkwardness that still hovered around the edges of their developing friendship.

Maddie was casually dressed in faded jeans and a long-sleeved, blue polo shirt. Her shoulder-length dark hair was held back with a copper barrette, showing off the classic planes of her face. She looked relaxed and beautiful as she sat back in one of the wide-armed chairs with a hefty Charles Dickens novel open across her lap. The blue of her shirt matched her eyes perfectly.

Syd could see Pete off in the distance sniffing the ground around the perimeter of the pond. It had rained at some point during the night, and she could hear water dripping from a nearby eaves spout. All the plantings around the porch perimeter glistened with moisture. The air was filled with morning bird song. From somewhere in the distance, she could hear the plodding sound of a tractor.

"The sleeper awakens." Maddie gave Syd a blinding smile. "Are you a morning person, or should I go and amuse myself on the back forty until you have your first cup of coffee?"

Syd answered her smile and dropped into a chair beside her. "I am not normally a morning person but in a setting like this, I think I could become one in short order."

"How'd you sleep?"

Syd stretched contentedly. "Like a rock—better than I have in weeks, actually."

Maddie gestured to a thermos and extra cup on the table between their chairs. "The elixir of life awaits you. Do you need cream or sugar?"

Syd eagerly reached for the thermos. "Nuh uh. Just like this." She loosened the cap, and a heavenly aroma wafted out. "Oh god. This better be as good as it smells." She poured herself a hefty cup and sat back. She took a sip and fought an impulse to moan. "My god, woman, why aren't you married?" She looked quickly at Maddie. "I'm sorry. I didn't intend to . . . I just meant . . . This is amazing coffee."

Maddie smiled good-naturedly at her discomfort. "No offense taken." She regarded Syd for a moment. "It's true that I'm a pretty confirmed spinster. But, believe, me, it isn't by choice." She picked up the thermos and refilled her own mug. "I seem to be unfairly challenged in the relationship department."

Syd shook her head. "That's hard to believe. I'd think you'd have a line of suitors a mile long. What man in his right mind wouldn't want a shot at . . . this?" She raised her mug.

Maddie eyed her with interest. "You'd be surprised."

"No contenders on the horizon?"

"Not down here." Maddie's voice was thoughtful. "My wounds are still too fresh from my last relationship. It fell apart just before I came back here to practice." She looked at Syd with her electric blue eyes. "Another entanglement is the furthest thing from my mind right now."

Syd nodded. "Well, we certainly have that in common. I'm sorry for you, though. Were you together long?"

"About two years. All the cards were pretty much stacked against us—two residents working at different hospitals, trying to find time for each other. We didn't have a chance, really."

"So he was a doctor, too?"

Maddie looked at her for a few moments. "A surgeon—ophthalmology."

They drank their coffee in silence for a few minutes and watched as Pete slowly made his way back to them from the pond.

"Are you a breakfast person?" Maddie asked. "I have some decent bagels and fresh fruit inside. How about we make up a tray and come back out here to enjoy what's left of the morning?"

Syd smiled and got to her feet. "I'd love that. Then I can change and impose on you for a ride back into town."

Maddie stood up and grabbed the thermos. "It's not an imposition, it's a pleasure."

Chapter 4

At four-thirty on Saturday afternoon, Syd locked up the library and walked back to her tiny apartment. She had been working since noon, and had made fair progress cataloging her inventory of New Media software. She felt strongly about the need to provide bilingual resources for the area's growing population of Spanish-speaking residents, and had ordered a significant number of tutorials and reference materials designed for this group of underserved patrons.

In recent years, Christmas tree farms had expanded to be become the dominant industry in the tiny mountain region, and many of the workers who moved to the area to work on the farms were of Mexican descent. Some of these workers were seasonal hires—men who followed the sun from locale to locale and sent most of their earnings back home to their families. Lately, more and more of them had been able to bring their families to live with them in Jericho year-round, and their impact on the community as a cultural and economic force was beginning to be felt.

Syd understood that the public schools were overtaxed with the need to provide rudimentary English language instruction to students across all age groups. Likewise, adults needed help obtaining access to basic services like driver licenses and healthcare. She noticed that more than one church in the area advertised services *en Español*, and it was not uncommon now to see notices in store windows in both English and Spanish. Even Maddie's tiny medical clinic had announcements and instruction leaflets available in both languages. It had occurred to her on more than one occasion that she ought to talk with Maddie about her level of service to this population and mine any ideas she might have about ways the library could better support the town's efforts to integrate and serve this burgeoning subset of the community.

After climbing the stairs to her apartment, Syd dropped her keys and her cell phone on the kitchen table and looked around the tiny space. She knew that her decision to store most of her personal belongings for the eighteen months she would live in Jericho made sense. But on days like this, she regretted not having more of her own things to brighten up or at least humanize the Spartan place. Her thoughts naturally swung back to the night before, and her unexpected sojourn at Maddie's home in the country.

The ringing of her telephone brought her out of her reverie. She answered it, surprised to hear Roma Jean's voice on the line.

"Miss Murphy? Hi, it's me."

Syd smiled. "Hello, Roma Jean. What are you up to on this fine Saturday afternoon?"

"Well, I got off work a little while ago and am at the fire department helping out with the barbecue." Syd could hear talking and laughter in the background. "My mama wanted me to be sure and invite you to come out. She says there's plenty of food left and lots of people here you know."

"That's really sweet of her." Syd glanced at her watch. She had forgotten all about the event. "How much later will you all be there?"

"Oh probably a couple more hours. We don't usually pack it up until everything's sold. There's a big church bus from Elk Creek that just pulled in. It's the seniors group, and they'll be here forever." She paused. "Are you coming? Do you need a ride? Daddy'll come and pick you up if you don't wanna bring your car out in this muck."

Syd had forgotten about the rain overnight. The field around the fire hall would most likely be a morass with all the vehicle and pedestrian traffic. "No, that's okay. I can drive myself just fine." She deliberated. "Tell you what. Ask your mom to save me a plate, and I'll be there in about half an hour."

She could hear the smile in Roma Jean's voice. "That's great. I'll tell her." She heard a voice in the background say something to Roma Jean. "Oh, Mama says that you should park down the road near the old Exxon station—it's dry down there."

"Will do. Thanks for calling me. I'll see you in just a bit."

"Bye, Miss Murphy." Roma Jean disconnected.

Syd hung up the phone and shook her head. So much for her plans to spend a quiet Saturday evening reading. She supposed she could go and eat some of the legendary barbecue and enjoy the hospitality of the Freemantle family. They had been especially attentive to Syd since she arrived in Jericho—mostly due to the auspices of their vivacious daughter.

For today, though, she needed to get out and socialize with her neighbors and future patrons. After changing into jeans and a lightweight sweater, she grabbed a rain jacket and headed out for the county fire station. She took about ten minutes to make the drive, and as she approached the old Exxon station, she saw that she wasn't alone in her desire to avoid the muck of the terrain around the fire house. Cars and trucks were parked at rakish angles all over the place. She finally found a space big enough for her Volvo wagon behind a rusted dumpster that was overflowing with Styrofoam containers and drink cups. She hopped out of her car and began the quarter-mile trek up the hill to the barbecue site.

On the way, she ran into Maddie's chatty nurse, Peggy Hawkes. She was walking back toward the gas station with a heavy-set, middle-aged man. He was wearing a yellow rain slicker and a Wal-Mart cap, and carrying two large plastic bags loaded with barbecue dinners.

"Hey there, honey." Peggy beamed at Syd. "How's that ankle? You look like you're moving around just fine. It must be feeling better." She stopped in front of Syd and gestured to the man. "This is my husband, Al. Al, say hello to Syd Murphy—the new librarian in Jericho. We came by to pick up dinners for the nursing home," she continued before the smiling Al could speak. "Some of the people there can't travel this far, so we were going to drop these off on the way home. Al's mother lives there now, and she can't get out at all these days. But she loves barbecue and can still eat us under the table." She looked around behind Syd. "Did you come by yourself, honey? I saw Maddie here earlier. Pity you two girls couldn't come together. It would have been nice for each of you to have the company. I worry about her being alone too much. She never complains about it, but I think she misses her friends in Philadelphia. It's hard for her to be back here without her daddy. He was always such a social butterfly. She doesn't take after him in that way. But then, I think it's harder for a single woman up here in these parts. Don't you agree?"

Syd's head was reeling. "Um, agree about what?"

Peggy laughed. "About how hard it is to be a single woman around here. You don't get invited out much, and there aren't a lot of ways to meet unattached men." She looked at her very attached husband. "Isn't that right, Al?"

Al just smiled and shifted the weight of the bags full of food around in his hands.

"Well, honey, we'd better be off while these things are still hot." She patted Syd on the arm. "You have a good time today, and be sure you ask Edna for the lemon chess pie. I made that." She winked at Syd. "It's worth the price of admission."

Syd grinned. "I will. Thank you for the tip." She turned to Peggy's husband. "It was very nice to meet you, Al." She gave him a wry smile. "I hope we get a chance to chat some time."

He winked at her, and the two of them continued on toward their car.

Once Syd neared the fire station, she could see that things were still hopping. There had to be several dozen people milling around. Makeshift picnic tables were set up all around the perimeter of the brick building, and people laughed and talked as they ate their plates of chopped pork and coleslaw and drank gallons of sweet iced tea.

The big bay doors of the firehouse were open, and the trucks were parked alongside the building for the event. Syd made her way to the end of the line and stood behind a semi-bald man she remembered from the tire store in town. Two local boys she recognized as band member friends of Jessie's were in line just in front of him.

"Did you see her in that black t-shirt?" the taller of the two boys said. He stood with his hands shoved into the front pockets of his jeans and shifted from foot to foot as they waited for the line to inch forward. "Jeez, man, she's totally *hot.*"

Syd smiled to herself and tried hard not to appear like she was eavesdropping.

"You got that right," his companion replied. "Those eyes of hers are freakin' amazing."

"Who cares about her *eyes*? How about those . . ." he muttered the last word. The boys guffawed.

The second teenager punched his friend on the arm. "Like she'd ever look at your sorry ass twice."

"Hey, at least I'm *taller* than she is, you dwarf."

"Since when is that a problem?"

"You're such a freak," the first teen said. "She's way too classy for you. It's lame the way you keep sniffing around her. I can't believe you faked that concussion during practice last week just so you had a reason to go to her office."

"Shut the fuck up, man. You don't know anything. At least I don't cruise the library all the time, hoping to get a look at that hot, little blonde."

An older man in front of the two boys turned around and frowned at them. He noticed Syd and looked past the boys to nod and roll his eyes at her apologetically. The two teens spun around with shocked expressions on their faces and turned five shades of red. Syd smiled sweetly and looked away, trying to save them from further embarrassment.

She was surprised but not shocked when she realized that the boys had to be talking about Maddie. It appeared that poor Roma Jean wasn't the only teenager in Jericho afflicted with unbridled admiration for the doctor's . . . charms. She was also disturbed but slightly gratified to learn that she hadn't totally lost out to the beautiful woman in the admiration department—although maybe she needed to encourage Roma Jean to stop inviting her friends to help out during her volunteer shifts at the library.

Syd finally got to the head of the line.

"Hey, Miss Murphy," Edna Freemantle said, warmly. "I put back a plate for you, but it looks like we still have plenty left. Let's get you one of these fresh ones."

Edna was wearing a turtleneck sweater, but Syd could see a large bandage poking out above its rolled collar when she bent over to count out the change from her twenty-dollar bill. She remembered Maddie mentioning that Edna had been in her office on Friday and wondered if she was still having problems with her "boil." She had Peggy Hawkes to thank for that recollection. *God, one of the lunacies of life in a small town—you have no secrets.*

"Thanks so much, Edna." Syd took the plate from her. "Please call me Syd." She smiled warmly. "I ran into Peggy Hawkes on my way in, and she said I should ask you for a slice of her lemon pie. Do you know if there's any left?" She cast her eyes back behind Edna where a group of volunteers worked a makeshift assembly line fixing plates and to-go boxes.

Edna warily followed her gaze. "Sure, honey. Let me get you a piece."

She walked back to one of the volunteers and gestured toward a row of precut desserts. She returned and handed her a plate that held a shiny piece of yellow pie—and a brownie.

"Here you go." She dropped her voice to a whisper. "Don't tell Peggy, but this really isn't very good." She smiled. "I gave you a brownie, too. You'll want that."

Syd thanked her and went to the outside area in search of a place to sit down.

"Looking for company?" a low, sexy voice said softly from just behind her.

Syd jumped and barely caught her dessert plate as it started to slide off the Styrofoam box that held her dinner.

She turned around. A smug and smiling Maddie stood behind her near the drinks table. Maddie was dressed in the same faded blue jeans from the morning, but had changed her polo shirt for a fitted, black v-neck t-shirt. She had a straw-colored cotton sports jacket slung over her arm, and her thick dark hair was now loose about her face.

"Fancy meeting you here," she said with a grin. Her blue eyes were twinkling.

"Back at ya," Syd replied with a smile. "I ran into Peggy on my way in, and she said you had been here. I assumed you'd already left."

"Nah. I can't let the local undertaker be the *only* professional working this event." Maddie raked her eyes over the crowd, then nodded at a tall, skinny man in a black suit who was slowly making his way from table to table. "I gotta drum up some business."

Syd followed her gaze. "Oh really? Hoping someone will choke on a piece of gristle and need the Heimlich maneuver?"

Maddie snorted. "Gristle my ass." She bent closer and whispered into Syd's ear, "Wait until you taste that lemon pie."

Syd looked down at her dessert with alarm. "You know, you're the second person to caution me. How do I get rid of this without offending anyone?"

Maddie took her by the elbow and led her across the field toward a couple of unoccupied tables. "Stick with me, kid. I'm a pro at the old bait-and-switch technique."

They sat down at a small table beneath a large red maple tree that vibrated with fall color. Maddie tossed her jacket across the back of an extra chair and folded her arms in front of her on the tabletop.

"Did you already eat?'" Syd asked, as she unfolded her paper napkin and opened her container.

"Oh, yeah. But I wouldn't say nay to one of your hush puppies." Her eyes were hopeful.

Syd pushed the container across the table. "Be my guest—I don't really do well with fried food."

"Amateur." Maddie snagged one of the fried cornbread morsels and moaned happily as she bit into it. She looked down at Syd's meal. "Hey. Do you want some tea? Or water?"

"Sure. I forgot to snag a bottle of water while we were up there by the table." She started to get up.

"No, no. Stay put. I'll go. I want something else, too." Maddie stood up. "Be right back."

Syd watched her cross the field and stop to laugh and chat with several groups of people on her way to the beverage station. She couldn't help but notice how much more relaxed and in command Maddie seemed in this setting—less like the shy and somewhat awkward woman she had been last night when they had been alone together. *It must be her professional persona. I guess she has to be like this in public. It wouldn't do for her to appear unsure of herself.*

She took a few bites of her barbecue. It was amazing—incredibly rich and flavorful with just the right amount of spice to the sauce.

There was a large crash, and Syd looked up, startled, to see a commotion by the drinks table. It looked like someone had tripped and fallen into the table and knocked over a huge tureen filled with iced tea. People in line were scrambling to duck out of the way of the icy brown liquid as it raced across the plastic-covered tabletop and poured onto the ground. Syd stifled a laugh when she saw a beet-red Roma Jean sprawled in an ungainly heap on the grass and wearing a dazed expression as Maddie bent over to help her back to her feet.

Syd shook her head and took another bite of the barbecue. *The poor kid won't get any sleep tonight, either.*

Maddie came back to their table in a few minutes, holding two big bottles of cold water. She sat down across from Syd. "I barely dodged that bullet."

"Do you mean Roma Jean?" Syd asked, innocently.

"Roma Jean?" Maddie looked confused. "No, the tea. It went everywhere."

"Right." *You're so clueless.*

Maddie looked down at Syd's plate. "So . . . what's the verdict?"

"Are you kidding? It's fabulous." She pushed the plate toward Maddie. "Best I've ever had."

Maddie snagged another hush puppy. "I think it's that sauce Curtis makes. He should bottle it."

"So, Doctor," Syd said in a low, conspiratorial voice, "what's your strategy for ditching this pie?"

"Ah, yes. Take the brownie off and slide the plate over here to me."

Syd did as she was asked.

Maddie positioned the plate just to the right of her elbow and casually pushed it toward the edge of the table. Then, straightening her arm out as she reached for another hush puppy, she seamlessly knocked the plate off the edge. Syd heard a soft splat as the pie landed facedown on the grass.

"Oh, damn," Maddie drawled. "How clumsy of me."

Syd looked beneath their table at the gooey yellow mass. "Um, Maddie? Is that grass turning brown?"

Maddie guffawed. "I wouldn't doubt it. My dad used to say that you could use the filling from Peggy's chess pies to grout tile."

"Oh, god. Poor thing. And she thinks they're wonderful."

Maddie smiled. "So, how was the rest of your morning? Did you get your work done?"

Syd nodded. "Yep. I made a real dent in processing the New Media materials I was telling you about."

"I think it's great that you're sensitive to this need in the community. You'll do more to help the population here than any of the social service agencies have done to date."

Syd shrugged. "It's why public libraries exist, really—to fill those gaps that traditional agencies don't or can't address. And I'm lucky that the trustees of this particular grant project have given me so much latitude and autonomy. I can pretty much design the collection any way I want."

"Well, then, the residents of Jericho are fortunate to have *you* in this role. Anyone else probably would have opted for a set of encyclopedias and a bunch of Turner Classic Movies on DVD. What *you're* doing is really going to make a difference to many people who wouldn't otherwise have access to services that could materially improve their quality of life."

"You know, you could be talking about yourself."

Maddie blushed. "It's not the same thing at all. They pay me for my services."

Syd held her ground. "Not all of them. Don't think I haven't heard about your weekend clinic hours for people with no insurance."

Maddie shrugged. "It's not that big a deal. We all do what we can." She gave Syd a small smile. "Don't canonize me yet. I still make a pretty decent living off this practice."

"I know," Syd teased. "I've seen your wine fridge."

Maddie chewed the inside of her cheek. "That you have." She sat back in her chair. "Are you nearly finished?" She looked at her watch. "Wanna go watch the sun set over the river? There's a gorgeous pathway a short walk from here that runs right along the east bank—the views are amazing."

Syd brightened up. "I'd love that."

They stood, collected her leftovers, and discarded everything except the plastic-wrapped brownie in a nearby waste can. Maddie led them away from the fire station and toward a path that snaked back along the edge of the field. Several other couples walked along just ahead of them—clearly motivated by the same idea. It wasn't long until Syd could hear the sound of the river rushing along beyond a dense stand of trees.

After a few minutes, the pathway opened up, and the river came into view, flashing brilliantly in the late afternoon sun. The wind picked up when they reached the clearing, and a cool breeze blew toward them across the surface of the water.

"My god, you weren't kidding. This is beautiful."

Maddie smiled. "Told ya. One of the best things about living up here is that you're never more than five minutes away from this old beauty."

They walked along a few more minutes in silence, and then Syd hit an uneven patch of ground. She lost her footing as the sudden shift in weight stressed her weak ankle. Maddie quickly caught her by the arms and held her upright. Syd fell against her and stood for a few moments with her face pressed into Maddie's shoulder.

"Are you all right? Did you twist it again?" Maddie asked with concern.

Syd pulled herself upright. "No—no. It's okay. I just stumbled on something. I guess my ankle is still pretty flimsy."

Maddie kept an arm wrapped around her. "Let's find a spot to sit down so I can take a look at it."

"No, really. It's fine. Doesn't even hurt." She looked up into concerned blue eyes that now searched her face from inches away.

The landscape seemed to melt and reform itself right before her eyes. The sensation was identical to the one she experienced over a month ago, on her first day in Jericho, when she sat next to Maddie by this same river. She had a feeling that some primal force was giving her mental kaleidoscope a great, wrenching twist—tumbling the colored shards of glass inside into a curious and surprising configuration. Time seemed to stop as they stood there, rooted to the spot like trees, slightly swaying toward each other as the breeze swirled around them and the sun dipped further into the west.

They looked around at the sound of pounding feet.

"Come back here with that, you bastard!"

The two teenaged boys from the food line at the fire station burst through the trees and into the clearing. One raced ahead of the other, waving an open can of beer over his head and swinging the rest of a ringed six-pack in his other hand. Beer and foam flew everywhere as he ran past them. The other teen slowed briefly when he saw Syd and Maddie, then he raced on by—clearly more focused on getting back his contraband than in stopping to admire them.

Syd and Maddie stepped away from each other belatedly. Maddie kept a secure hand on Syd's elbow. "Do you want to go back?"

Syd shook her head emphatically. "Not at all. I promise, it's fine. I'd really like to finish the walk." She smiled at Maddie. "Stop worrying, okay? I'm really not that brave. If it hurt, I'd tell you."

Maddie smiled as she dropped her hand. "Okay. C'mon then. It's not much further."

They continued on along the path until they reached a wide bend where the river turned and headed back away from them. They sat down on a large, felled log near the bank to rest before starting back toward the fire station. The sun was just above the treetops, and its late autumn light bathed everything around them in a warm, gold color.

Syd nudged Maddie playfully. "I wish we had another thermos of your coffee."

Maddie looked at her. "You know, I almost brought one along. If I had known for sure you were gonna be here, I would have."

"Well, next time we'll know better."

"That we will."

Syd stared off across the water at the sunset. "It's so beautiful."

"You can say that again." Maddie's voice was enigmatic.

They sat in silence for a few minutes and listened to the sounds of the water and the occasional notes of distant laughter that drifted toward them on the breeze.

Maddie stretched her long legs out in front of her and leaned back on her hands. She turned to Syd. "So. What do you have on tap for the rest of this fine evening?"

Syd shrugged and ran a hand through her short, blonde hair. "Nothing much. I thought earlier that I might try to relax and do some reading but it's likelier that I'll end up going back into the branch to work for a couple more hours."

"That seems like a shame. I was heading back into the clinic after this but I think

I've succeeded in talking myself out of it." She nudged Syd playfully. "See? You've already guilted me into paying more attention to my life away from work."

Syd studied Maddie. "Really? You're quite a pushover. Are you generally this easy to manipulate?"

Maddie raised an eyebrow. "Depends on who's doing the manipulating."

"Oh, *selective* flexibility. Why doesn't that surprise me?"

Maddie crossed her arms. "You know, as your doctor, I could offer you some studied, professional advice."

"Oh, yeah?" Syd lifted her chin as she regarded Maddie. "Let's hear it."

"I know you have the branch opening breathing down your neck but I think you need to take at least *one* night a week off. Do something else—something personal—something that feeds your soul. You can't underestimate the restorative powers of a few hours of enforced relaxation."

Syd held Maddie's blue gaze. "I thought that's what I did last night?"

Maddie held up an index finger. "No. That's what *I* did last night. And in this case, turnabout is fair play."

Syd wrinkled her nose. "I'm not sure this prescription is covered by my insurance plan."

Maddie laughed. "Tell you what. I'll give you a free sample." She chewed her bottom lip for a moment. "What were you going to do if you went back to work?"

"Oh, it's highly technical—something only a licensed professional can do." She leaned forward and lowered her voice. "I was going to paste cards and pockets onto the backs of about two hundred pieces of media." She sat back up. "It sounds boring, I know, but after about an hour of inhaling the fumes from the rubber cement, you don't mind it at all. I've actually wondered if there were twelve-step programs for this. It's kind of addictive."

Maddie chuckled. "How long will it take you to do this?"

Syd shrugged. "I dunno, a couple of hours. Why?"

"I haven't been high since college." Maddie's voice was dreamy. "I'm thinking it might be fun. How about some company?"

Syd stared at her. "Are you nuts? It's mind numbing. There's no way you want to spend a perfectly good Saturday night, sitting in a dank old storefront up to your elbows in rubber cement."

"Oh, c'mon. Let me exercise my philanthropic muscles a bit. I happen to know that I'm the *only* member of the library board who hasn't ponied up yet with some material support. It's long overdue." She paused. "I'll even make us some coffee."

Syd narrowed her eyes. "Now that's just playing dirty, and you know it."

Maddie grinned. "Whattaya say? I can meet you there in half an hour, and we can knock this out in a fraction of the time it would have taken you. You can have your nose safely tucked into a book by eight-thirty."

"You're pretty persuasive," Syd said with amusement. "It must go with all of those abbreviations after your name."

"Hey, don't knock it. Those abbreviations took ten years to acquire, and I'm still paying for most of them."

Syd slowly shook her head. "I can't begin to understand why you'd want to do this, but I'd be crazy to refuse your help."

Maddie gave her a dazzling smile. "Great. Let's go."

They stood up and walked back up the path toward the fire station. When they made the final turn and the field full of picnic tables came into view, Syd nudged Maddie.

"I wonder if there's any lemon pie left?"

Maddie eyed her with suspicion. "Why? Thinking you might want some dessert later?"

Syd shook her head. "Not at all. I was thinking it might work *better* than rubber cement."

The musical sound of Maddie's laughter trailed behind them as they made their way across the field and headed toward their respective cars.

On Monday night, Maddie worked alone in the clinic, updating patient records. She was in the midst of moving all of the files in her practice to an EMR system she had purchased six months ago, but it was proving to be an arduous and protracted process, and she found herself spending many evenings just like this one—checking and cross-checking data entries for accuracy.

Her father's practice hadn't been all that large, but he had been the chief medical provider to scores of families in the area for over twenty-five years, and the backlog of thick patient files was daunting. She thought again about engaging some extra help to make the tedious transition, but she was uncomfortable with the more customary practice of outsourcing the entire project to an agency, and there were sticky confidentiality issues related to engaging local part-time help. For the time being, she and Peggy continued to plug away at it whenever they could, and Maddie now managed all of her active records electronically.

She was making notes on Mrs. Halsey's sciatica when her cell phone rang. She answered it without checking the caller I.D.

"This is Stevenson."

"Hi ya, sweet cheeks. What's shakin'?"

She smiled. It was David. "Nothing much. I'm just here at the clinic—cooking the books, like normal. What are you up to?"

"Oh, I'm gonna be playing host at an ostentatious soirée, and I need your help."

Maddie pushed her laptop away and sat back in her desk chair. "Why am I suddenly suspicious about this call?"

David sighed dramatically. "Now don't start off with *that* attitude—this is a perfectly legitimate request. Besides—you need to get your self-righteous, hermit ass out once in a while. I'm tired of you hibernating out at that damn farm."

Maddie rolled her eyes. "David? David, are you still there?" She tapped the mouthpiece of her phone with her index finger. "All I hear is a bunch of static that sounds vaguely like preaching."

"Nice try, sawbones. Michael and I are throwing a big dinner at the Inn on

Friday night, and I want you to be there. And before you say 'no,' or invent a reason not to show up, I already told the new librarian that you'd pick her up and be her escort for the evening."

Maddie sat up. "You did what? *Jesus*, David."

"Jesus? I've been promoted. I should set you up more often."

"Are you crazy?" Maddie was beyond exasperated. "She isn't *gay*—and even if she were, I'm certainly not looking for that kind of company."

"Whoa there, Bessie. I don't think I said anything about hooking you up. I said I set you up. With a dinner companion—nothing else." There was a pause. "Is there something you need to share with me? It seems like I might have missed a few plot points here."

Maddie sighed. "No. You didn't miss anything." She mentally kicked herself for her knee-jerk response. Now David smelled a rat, and he'd be relentless. "Sorry, I'm just still pretty raw in that department. I didn't mean to take your head off. Gimme the details."

"Okaaaayy," David demurred. "This is kind of a welcome-to-the-area and congratulations-on-the-grand-opening-of-the-new-library kind of event. We're footing the bill for the food, so Michael is going all-out on the menu. I just figured that you'd rather spend the evening making nice with that cute little Syd Murphy than with Gladys Pitzer—who also will be coming solo. But, honestly, if you'd rather pick Gladys up, I'm sure she'd be *thrilled*." He paused for effect. "And I know she'll be happy to reintroduce you to her genetically-challenged son. Beau is fresh out of rehab, so he's living back at home again. You two *would* look awfully cute together."

Maddie sighed. "All right, already. When and where do I pick her up?"

"Gladys?"

"No, nunchuck. Syd."

"Ah. I thought you'd come to your senses. At the branch—six o'clock." He dropped his voice. "And try to look sexy. We couldn't afford an ice sculpture, so we need something tall to class up the entryway." He hung up before she could respond.

Maddie sat there for a moment, dumbly holding the phone against her ear. *God. I'll live to regret this.* She closed her phone and placed it back on the desk.

David Jenkins was her best friend in Jericho, and she had known him ever since they were children together. Reestablishing her friendship with David—and his partner, Michael Robertson—had been one of the real perks of being back in the area to live. But David was determined to drag her out of her shell of self-imposed isolation. She smiled at his persistence, but she wished that he hadn't involved Syd in his rehabilitation scheme. Already, she was finding it hard to keep an appropriate and safe distance from the attractive woman. The last thing she needed was David honing in on her vulnerability where Syd was concerned—and she might already have compromised her feigned indifference to the newcomer's charms.

Oh well. She sighed in resignation. *If I have to torture myself, I might as well get a great meal out of it.*

Syd was dressed and ready when she saw Maddie's silver Lexus turn into the gravel lot next to the library. She hadn't been sure about what to wear to the event, but since it was an evening affair at the area's best inn, she opted for a green silk crepe "boyfriend" jacket with matching crepe trousers, a camisole, and heels.

She met Maddie at the back door to the branch and tried not to gape at her. She was used to seeing Maddie well but casually dressed in business suits or weekend attire, but this was something different. Maddie was wearing a form-fitting, banded silhouette red dress that hugged her curves in all the right places. It had a plunging, halter v-neck top and fell to just above her knees. She wore a vintage black taffeta bolero jacket, and her long, dark hair was brushed back away from her face, showing off black pearl and diamond earrings. She looked stunning.

"My god, you certainly clean up well, " Syd said.

Maddie looked Syd over appraisingly. "You're not so bad, yourself. I was gonna suggest that we just blow this shindig off and go out for ribs but I guess we'd look pretty ridiculous wearing those plastic bibs over these outfits."

Syd laughed. "You just can't take a compliment, can you?"

Maddie shrugged. "I'm just out of practice, I guess. I really haven't had many excuses to get all glammed-out since I moved back down here."

"Well, that borders on the criminal. You look fantastic." Syd pulled the door closed behind her, and they started down the steps to Maddie's car. She glanced at Maddie, who towered over her in heels. "Look, if you suddenly decide that you have your sea legs back and want to, um, enjoy some local color tonight, don't worry about me. I can easily find another way home."

Maddie gave Syd a perplexed look as she opened the passenger door to her car. "What on earth are you talking about?"

Syd raised an eyebrow at her as she daintily sat down inside the car.

Maddie tossed her head back in mock exasperation. "Oh puh-lease. Just who do you think will be attending this event, hmmm?" She looked down at Syd with sympathetic eyes. "I hate to disillusion you, but this isn't exactly going to be like a night with the Chippendales. Not unless you fancy bloated, blue-haired, Type 2 diabetic women. And if *that's* the case, then maybe we should go out for ribs."

Syd snorted, and Maddie grinned as she shut the door and walked around to the driver's side of the car.

Once they were underway, Syd turned to Maddie. "So, tell me about David, and tell me about this inn he runs. I gather it's pretty swanky?"

Maddie nodded as she turned onto the highway that led into Jefferson. "The Riverside Inn is one of the oldest, continuous inns in Virginia. It's been written up numerous times in travel magazines, and it's a very popular weekend destination for people from Charlotte and Richmond. David and Michael have owned it for about five years now, and they do a tremendous seasonal business in weddings and corporate retreats." She looked at Syd. "Michael is the resident chef, and he's a first-rate one, too. He studied at Johnson & Wales in Charleston. David was there at the same time, interning in hotel management at The Planters Inn near the Charleston Market. That's how they met."

Syd was fascinated. "So they came back here together?"

"Yep. A married couple from England had previously owned the inn, but they retired and went back to the U.K. five years ago. That's when David and Michael took it over. They do quite well—although they don't get a whole lot of local traffic. The accommodations and the restaurant fare are a tad too pricey to attract much of a robust local patronage."

"Have you known David long? He seemed to talk about you with such affection, I assumed that you were good friends."

"We are. I've known him since childhood. We were inseparable in the summer months when I'd come back here to stay with my dad." She slowed the car down and turned onto a secondary road that wound down along the river. "It wasn't always easy for him here. There isn't much of a gay community. That's why he went away to school. His family was never very supportive."

"That's so sad. Is it any better for him now that he's back?"

Maddie shrugged. "Yes and no. His mother seems to have mellowed out a bit. You know her—Phoebe Jenkins?"

Syd was surprised. "The school music teacher?"

"The one and the same."

"Huh. What about his father?"

"Dead—for years now. He was a pretty brutal man—not very open and not very kind. David suffered a lot. My dad was always like a surrogate father to him. David actually lived at our place during his last year of high school. It was a difficult time for him. Dad helped him get into the hotel management program at N.C. State. He flourished once he was away from here."

Syd was perplexed. "Why did he want to come back?"

Maddie looked at her. Her blue eyes were luminous in the dimly-lighted interior of the car. "Maybe just to see if he could. It's hard to feel like an outcast—like you have no place to belong." She looked back out at the road ahead of them. "I think he felt like it was time to reclaim his past—to try and live his life on his own terms, in full view of a community that never really accepted him."

"Wow. That's certainly courageous."

"Or suicidal. But that's David. He never held back on anything." She laughed. "He still doesn't. And you know, he's just stubborn enough to persevere. If anyone can make this experiment work, he'll be the one."

They turned onto a gravel lane that led up toward a sprawling, two story Victorian house with wide porches and gabled dormers. All of the downstairs windows glowed with yellow light. People milled about on the lawn in front of the house or stood in clusters under the deep eaves of the porch. A flagstone walkway led from a secluded parking area to the house. It was lined with gaslights that flickered behind bubbled-glass globes. Syd could hear the mellow sound of jazz as they left the car and slowly made their way up the sidewalk toward the main entrance. Tantalizing smells drifted on the night air as they drew closer to the house. Maddie gently took hold of Syd's elbow as they ascended the wide steps.

A loud voice with an affected Southern accent accosted them as they approached the open front door. "Why, Madeleine Stevenson, as I live and breathe. And lookin' like she just escaped from Belle Watling's house of ill repute. Michael. Fetch the smelling salts. I might just have a fit of the vapors."

Maddie stopped and rolled her eyes at the flamboyantly dressed man who stood clutching at his chest in mock distress just inside the door near a wide staircase.

"Hello, David," she drawled. "Nice to see you, too." She went to him and kissed him lightly on both cheeks, then stood back to admire his magenta-colored smoking jacket. "Nice suit. Get that from the Truman Capote Collection?" She batted her eyelashes at him.

He swatted her on the behind and pushed past her to greet Syd. "And who is this blonde beauty?" He took Syd's hand and kissed it dramatically. "Thank you for consenting to join us at this little soirée." He leaned forward and whispered in her ear, "I apologize for consigning you to an evening in such boorish company." He inclined his head toward Maddie, who had taken off her jacket and handed it with her bag to a white-coated member of the wait staff. Her broad shoulders glowed in the soft light of the foyer. She turned back to them, and it was impossible not to notice how the red dress accentuated every tantalizing curve of her long body. David gave Syd's hand a gentle squeeze. "On the other hand, you could do a *lot* worse."

Syd laughed. "I am not at all inclined to disagree. Thank you for inviting me."

"Oh, honey, the pleasure is mine. *Anything* to lure that one out of her cocoon." He winked at her. "We may need to make a habit of this." He tugged her forward and walked back to stand in front of an amused Maddie. "And here you are in the truly glorious flesh."

"So it would seem." Maddie's tone was ironic. "Are you surprised?"

David ran a hand through his thick dark hair and steered them toward a set of double doors. "Of course I am. I have a healthy respect for your inventiveness when it comes to ducking out of social engagements."

Maddie rolled her eyes. "Don't listen to him, Syd. He'll have you believing that I hide from my own shadow."

David regarded her thoughtfully. "Now that you mention it, we did have six extra weeks of winter last year. Think there was any connection?"

Maddie punched him playfully on the arm. "Whatcha got to drink in this dump? I'm parched."

"Oh? Have a long day bilking the insurance companies? That *does* take it out of one."

Syd chortled. "You two should take this on the road."

David brought his twinkling brown eyes to bear on her. "Oh, we *have*—trust me. The good doctor and I go way back." He led them across the bar area toward a small, round table for two. "Now, what may I get you two bodacious beauties to drink?"

Maddie looked thoughtful. "You know, I think I'd like some champagne. Got any open?"

"For you? But of course. Le Veuve Clicquot—chilled and waiting." He turned to Syd. "And for you, my lovely?"

"I think I'll join my erudite companion. Some champagne sounds wonderful."

David gave them a brilliant smile and drifted off toward the bar, stopping to chat with several patrons along his way.

Syd watched him for a moment, and then turned to Maddie. "He's wonderful. So vibrant and charming. I can't imagine anyone more suited to a place like this." She gestured at their beautiful surroundings.

Maddie smiled. "I'm so glad you think so." She looked at David with affection. "He really is like my family here. I don't know what I'd do without him."

"I can understand that. It would be impossible to feel too isolated with David in your life."

Maddie laughed. "I think you're on the verge of finding out first-hand how true that statement is."

"What do you mean?" Syd was confused.

Before she could answer, their waiter arrived with two chilled flutes of straw-colored champagne. A crimson strawberry sat at the bottom of each glass. After he departed, Maddie held her glass up to Syd. "Here's to new friends . . . and an impending end to solitude."

Syd nervously clinked rims with her and drank, wondering what can of worms her presence here had just opened. Hearing David's raucous laughter ring out from across the bar, she supposed it wouldn't be long until she found out.

Chapter 5

In the hour before dinner, Syd and Maddie took their glasses of champagne and milled about the spacious downstairs area of the Inn. Syd recognized many members of the county library board, and was introduced to their spouses, and to a slew of other guests whose names she would never recall.

Maddie had been whisked away by another doctor from the county hospital in Wytheville, and he held her hostage across the room. He had noticed her immediately when they entered the large front parlor, and had made a beeline for her, insisting that she take a few minutes to meet some out-of-town colleagues of his who were in the area to golf and enjoy the fall foliage.

Syd kept stealing glances at Maddie, as she stood in front of a large bay window with the three, white-haired doctors. It didn't take a rocket scientist to realize that fall foliage wasn't the only thing the men were admiring. She noticed that they seemed incapable of keeping their eyes on Maddie's face. More than once, she looked over to find one of them ogling some other red-clad part of Maddie's physique.

"So, Jessie tells me that you were the one who helped her out with her sight reading." Phoebe Jenkins' voice distracted Syd from her spying. She realized, belatedly, that she had not been paying attention to their conversation.

"I'm sorry, what did you say?" She shifted her full attention back to the older woman. Phoebe was a shorter, rounder version of her son. She had the same lively brown eyes, and the same wavy black hair—although hers was shot through with gray streaks. Her face radiated friendliness.

"Jessie Rayburn. She tells me that you're the one who helped her out so much with her sight reading."

Syd smiled. "Oh, that. Yes, she's a sweet girl, and she's been kind enough to help out at the branch. I thought it was the least I could do to try and repay her." She touched Phoebe gently on the forearm. "I hope that was okay. I don't want to interfere with your methods."

Phoebe laughed. "Oh, heavens, it's *more* than okay. I have over two hundred students at that school, and I can only give private lessons to about a dozen of them. Anything you can do to help out is a gift to me—and to them." She took a sip of her pink wine. "David tells me that you're quite the musician in your own right."

Syd raised an eyebrow. There was only one way David could have learned anything about her background in music. She stole another quick look across the room at her statuesque dinner companion, who now looked like she was ready to impale herself on a cocktail knife. Maddie chose that instant to look Syd's way and gazed back at her in mute appeal.

Syd smiled and turned back to Phoebe. "Yes, I studied violin as an under-graduate, but my skills as a musician might be overstated. But if I can be helpful to you in any way by working with some of the students, I'd be happy to pitch in."

Phoebe smiled at her sweetly. She looked over Syd's shoulder and called out to someone passing by behind her. "Gladys! Come over here and meet our guest of honor."

A short, wiry woman with frizzy red hair and thick glasses stopped and turned her beady gaze on Syd. She looked her up and down without disguise, and then nodded quickly. "You're a looker, all right. I wondered what all the fuss was about."

Syd felt her cheeks warm at the odd woman's directness, and Phoebe rushed to intervene. "Syd Murphy, this is Gladys Pitzer. Gladys is a florist. David and Michael got all the fresh flowers you see here from her shop in Jefferson."

Syd extended her hand. "It's a pleasure to meet you, Gladys. I think the arrangements are just beautiful. I noticed them right away." Gladys took Syd's hand in a claw-like grip and continued to hold on to it long after their handshake had ended.

"I didn't do the arrangements. I just brought the flowers." She cast a sidelong glance at Phoebe. "These boys have their own ideas about things." She tugged slightly at Syd's hand. "Are you married?" Her question hung in the air like an accusation.

Syd was nonplussed. "I—um . . . yes, but I'm separated from my husband right now."

Gladys dropped her hand without ceremony. "Unavailable." She turned on her flat heels and headed straight toward Maddie and the trio of lecherous doctors.

They were all saved from further mortification because Michael Robertson chose that moment to enter the room and announce that dinner was ready to be served. Maddie was at Syd's elbow in an instant, and they beat a hasty retreat from the parlor and made their way down the wide center hallway toward the dining room.

"Thank *god*," Maddie whispered close to Syd's ear. "Five more minutes of that, and I would've grabbed a fire axe and chopped my way through a wall to escape."

Syd laughed at Maddie's distress. "Oh, I dunno. There are worse ways to spend an evening." She looked Maddie over. "They certainly were . . . attentive."

"Right. Attending to every nuance of my *derrière*. I never should've worn this damn dress. I'm gonna kill David."

"David picked out your dress?"

Maddie looked down at her with raised eyebrows. "David *lent* me this dress . . . it's his." She paused. "I don't know how he walks in these shoes."

Syd burst into laughter and clutched Maddie's arm. Several other couples turned and looked their way. "Behave," she hissed. "We'll get tossed out of here." She continued to chuckle as they approached the entrance to the large dining room. Michael Robertson met them at the doorway.

The big man pulled Maddie into a bear hug. "How are you, beautiful?" he asked, placing a kiss on her neck.

Maddie returned his hug, and then stepped back. Her blue eyes glowed with affection. "Why, I'm just fine." She turned to Syd. "Have you met Syd Murphy yet?"

Michael turned to regard her. He was a tall man—taller than Maddie. And he looked strong and solid in his white, double-breasted chef's coat. He was semi-bald and wore tiny, black-framed glasses. His gray eyes sparkled as he stepped toward her. "No, I haven't had that pleasure yet." He hugged Syd warmly. "We don't stand on ceremony around here. Any friend of the good doctor's is a friend of mine." He drew back, but still held Syd by her elbows and looked her over. "You're a welcome addition to our little community."

She smiled at the burly man. "I'm so happy to meet you. I've heard wonderful things about your talent in the kitchen."

Michael squeezed her elbows before releasing her. "Too bad I decided to pick *this* night to have Peggy Hawkes cater the whole damn thing . . ."

Maddie's involuntary gasp was audible.

Michael threw back his head and laughed loudly. "Come on you two. David has a special table set aside for you." He winked at Maddie. "I think you'll like it."

He led them past a dozen larger tables, all set for parties of four or six, to a more remote section of the room near the entrance to a large sun porch. Several smaller, more intimate tables were scattered along a back wall that was lined with windows. They overlooked a rolling lawn that sloped down toward the river. Lighted walkways snaked off in several directions, and other patrons could be seen strolling about outside, smoking or carrying their cocktail glasses as they meandered about in the early evening.

"Here you are. Just what the doctor ordered." He indicated a table set for two and gallantly pulled out Syd's chair. "Or *would* have ordered, if she had the sense god gave Adam's house cat."

Maddie looked up at him with a startled expression on her beautiful face, but Michael only chuckled as he strode off to greet other diners.

Syd pretended not to notice Maddie's embarrassment. She picked up her napkin. "They certainly watch out for you."

Maddie shook her head. "Tell me about it." She picked up the wine list that was already open across her plate. Then she sighed and set it back down. "Look, I'm sorry about subjecting you to their full-frontal disapproval of my . . . lack of social life." She hesitated. "I don't want you to get the wrong idea about their motivation."

Syd sat back and regarded her with interest. "And what would that be? All I see are two charming and loving friends who don't want the extraordinary woman they obviously care about to be lonely." She raised her chin. "Is that the wrong idea?"

"No." Maddie smiled at her sheepishly. "That would be just about the *right* idea. But sometimes, they get a bit overzealous in their attentions. I fear they now think of you as a healthy dose of fresh blood in the water."

Syd laughed. "So I'm a shark?"

"Not exactly." Maddie's gaze was thoughtful. "*They're* the sharks. Be prepared to be enlisted in the Jericho Salvation Army. They'll do whatever it takes to co-opt your assistance in their let's-drag-Maddie-back-into-the-limelight scheme."

Syd continued to regard her with amusement. "So what happens if I turn out to be a willing recruit?"

Maddie sighed and picked up the wine list again. "Then I'd say that I'm probably toast."

Michael had outdone himself on the evening fare. They dined on exceptional Low Country cuisine—starting with his signature She-Crab soup. For her dinner entree, Maddie opted for the grilled, pesto-encrusted grouper with creamy grits and fried green tomatoes. Syd had a shrimp and crawfish étouffée with white rice and scallions. Maddie ordered them each a glass of Charles Krug Sauvignon Blanc. For dessert, they shared a peach praline cobbler served with cinnamon ice cream. Their waiter appeared with two steaming cups of coffee and cordials of Frangelico.

"Compliments of the chef," he explained as he set the cups and glasses down in front of them. He tucked the serving tray under his arm and headed back toward the kitchen.

Maddie sniffed the beverages. "And he has the nerve to call *me* a snob."

Syd laughed as she pushed back from the table. "I can't eat another thing. I've never had so much great food at one sitting." The metallic copper color of her sleeveless camisole reflected the flickering light from the oil candle on their table. Maddie noticed how toned and firm her arms were. The square-cut neck of her top showed off her well-defined shoulders and collarbone. She really did look lovely.

Maddie dragged her gaze away from Syd and cursed herself for the umpteenth time for giving in to David's arm-twisting. *Damn him. I should've agreed to bring Gladys Pitzer.* She looked across the dining room at the table where Gladys now sat poking maniacally at the unhappy floral centerpiece in front of her. She growled and shook her head.

"Something wrong?" Syd asked.

Maddie blinked at her. Syd's short blonde hair was feathered back from her face and her green eyes glowed in the soft light. "Yeah. I'm an idiot."

"What do you mean?"

Maddie sighed with resignation. "Just a general observation." She shifted in her chair. "It's hot in here. Do you wanna walk around outside for few minutes?"

Syd perked up. "Sure. That would be great. I'd love to walk off some of this meal." As they stood up, she retrieved her jacket from the back of her chair. "Will you need your coat?"

Maddie nodded, but gestured toward the sun porch behind their table. "Yeah, but let's go through here and grab it on the way out. I want to avoid the melee."

"I'm all for that. I don't have the stamina for any more inquisitions about my marital status."

Maddie led them through a doorway that led to the sun porch area behind their table. She retrieved her short jacket from a coat closet located just off the main hallway of the house. "Oh really? Who's been grilling you?"

"I lost count after the first half dozen."

"Hmmm. Too bad. I could've hooked you up with the Three Billy Goats Gruff . . . they definitely were looking for some scintillating companionship." They walked down the wooden steps that led from the sun porch to the back lawn. "Dr. Greene commented more than once that he'd been meaning to check out the services at our new library. After seeing you here tonight, I'd venture a guess that it won't be long before he drops by to renew his . . . patronage."

Syd eyed her suspiciously. "Uh huh. Well, the only thing related to me that Dr. Greene can look forward to *checking out* will be a book or a DVD." She pointed a finger at herself. "*This* piece of realia is not in circulation at present."

Maddie chuckled as they strolled along one of the gravel paths away from the house.

Syd nudged Maddie's arm playfully. "Besides, Dr. Greene seemed pretty persistent in his admiration of you. I got the distinct impression that this wasn't an unusual occurrence."

Maddie sighed. "You're right, it isn't." She looked at Syd with a resigned expression. "Because most of my background training is in emergency medicine, I fill in a few nights a month at the county hospital. Tom Greene is the ER chief there." She laughed bitterly. "Trust me, there's nothing he'd love more than the chance to practice a bit of triage—on *me*."

"God. What a sleaze. How do you deal with that?"

"About like you'd expect. Thankfully, med school was an excellent preparation for this. You'd be surprised by how literally many of my mentors took the whole hands-on instruction caveat in the course descriptions."

"Well, I think that in this case, the common denominator might be you and not your profession."

Maddie looked at her. "What do you mean?"

Syd laughed at her confused expression. "Come on, Maddie. You must know that you're drop-dead gorgeous. The poor guy's only human." She paused. "Well, human *and* a sleaze. But it's true that the cards are pretty unfairly stacked against him."

Maddie stared at her blankly. Then she shook her head and looked away.

Syd seemed to enjoy her discomfort. "You really *can't* take a compliment, can you?"

Maddie brought her eyes back to bear on Syd. She narrowed them with mischief. "Well, it's a good thing I'm not the jealous type."

Syd's expression was wary. "I know I'm gonna regret asking, but what is that supposed to mean?"

"Well, let's just say that things have been a tad easier for me since a certain green-eyed blonde moved into the area." She gave Syd a conspiratorial wink. "I've really been meaning to thank you for the division of labor."

Syd blushed and swatted Maddie on the arm. "You totally suck."

Maddie raised an eyebrow. "I don't usually, but if I did, it probably would push my profile up a few notches."

Syd threw her head back and considered the night sky. "What did I do to deserve this?"

"Why if I were a spiritual man, I'd say it's your karmic reward for doing good in a past life," David said from behind them.

Maddie and Syd jumped in surprise and then turned around and glared at him.

"What are you two lovelies doing out here alone in the dark?" He looked them over from head to toe as he took a long drag on his cigarette. "On the other hand, who cares? Whatever you're doing, can I watch?" He sat down on a nearby bench and crossed his legs.

Maddie chewed the inside of her cheek as she turned and considered Syd. "Whattsamatter, Davey? Nothing new on Adult Pay-Per-View?"

David took another drag and blew a line of smoke at her. "Now that insinuation is just cruel. You know we don't get decent satellite reception out here." He turned to Syd. The orange tip of his cigarette made laser-like patterns in the darkness as he waved his hand around. "She just loves to torment me."

Syd laughed. "Yes, I can see what a hapless victim you are."

"At last. Someone who understands my suffering." He bowed to Syd. "I knew I liked you."

"The only thing *you're* a victim of is your own hyperbole." Maddie paused and tugged at the sleeve of his magenta jacket. "And maybe your fashion sense."

David feigned umbrage as he yanked his arm away. "Oh, *nice* one, Miss Thing. I now regret defending your honor when I overheard that trio of mulligans speculating on whether or not your boobs were store-bought."

Maddie gasped. "*What?*" She glared back up at the house.

"Calm down, Xena. There's no need to storm the castle. I assured them that even Gladys Pitzer would look as well-endowed in the same dress." He sighed. "Never underestimate the power of the right foundation garment."

Maddie was still seething. "You know, I'm just one Hippocratic oath away from strangling you."

"Ohhhh, baby, I *love* it when you go all butch on me."

Syd stepped in between them. "I hate to be the one to disrupt this love fest, but, David, I think your mother is headed this way."

David turned around and looked up the pathway toward the house. Sighing, he ground out his cigarette and tucked the butt into the pocket of his jacket. "Yep, that's her. And judging by the way she's walking, she ain't got good news."

"Oh, there you are. We've been looking all over for you." Phoebe was breathless as she faced Maddie. "Dr. Stevenson, your service called looking for you. They said it was an emergency."

Maddie nodded, turned to Syd, and touched her lightly on the elbow. "I'm sorry, please excuse me while I go see what this is about."

"Of course. Go ahead. I'll be fine."

Maddie squeezed her elbow and hurried back to the house with an agitated Phoebe in tow.

David shook his head and pulled a fresh cigarette from his breast pocket. "Aaaand she's *off*. Again." He dug out an old-fashioned silver Zippo and lighted up. "I don't think I've ever gotten through an entire evening with that woman without some crisis intervening."

Syd sat down next to him on the bench. "She's just doing her job."

David gave her a long-suffering gaze. "My dear, her job is *all* she does. She does her job to the exclusion of having a life."

Syd hesitated. "You're pretty hard on her."

"On the contrary. I love her enough to speak the truth. When you get to know her a bit better, you'll see what I mean."

"You're right that I can't pretend to be an authority on Maddie, but I do know that she's aware of feeling . . . isolated. I think she struggles with it and wants to change it. It's just going to take some time." David didn't comment. "She's been through a lot in the last two years—losing her father, ending a relationship, moving away from her life in Philadelphia. That's a lot for anyone to deal with— even someone as exceptional as she is."

David sat there, smoking quietly while he regarded her. "I was wrong about you. You don't need any more time to figure her out." He smiled as he wiped some stray ash off his trouser leg. He looked at her, his eyes narrowed. "So how much did the good doctor tell you about her ill-fated relationship?"

Syd felt vaguely like they were venturing into forbidden territory. "Not much, just that it all ended right about the time of her father's death. I know they were both doctors. That's about it."

David nodded slowly. "Interesting." He ground out his cigarette, stood up, and reached a hand down to her. "C'mon, cutie. Let's go and see what caliber of crisis has descended upon our resident Florence Nightingale."

Once inside the house, Maddie retrieved her cell phone from her purse and called her service. She took down the number of her caller and dialed it quickly. A man answered on the second ring.

"Hello?" He had a deep, bass voice. She could hear music and laughter in the background.

"Hello. This is Dr. Stevenson. Someone at this number called me?"

"Well, hey there, little sweetie. We sure did." She could hear the clink of ice cubes against the side of a glass. "Tom said this would be the quickest way to find you. Where'd you get off to? We were hoping you'd join us for a nightcap."

Maddie's jaw dropped, and she swiveled her head around to see the white-haired trio leering at her from their table in the bar. The phone was still pressed to her ear. "Are you kidding me with this?"

She snapped the phone closed and stood there fuming. Then she straightened her shoulders and walked across the bar to stand in front of their table. She knew her eyes were smoldering. The raucous trio fell silent as they sat there, enduring her scrutiny.

"Dr. Greene, I wonder if I might have a word with you—privately." Her voice was icy.

Tom Greene sat staring up at six feet of barely controlled rage. He got to his feet and set his half-empty tumbler down on the table. "Um, excuse me for a minute, fellas."

Maddie turned on her heel and led them out into an unoccupied corner of the hallway. She stood close to the shorter man, using her greater height to its full advantage. She kept her voice low so no one would overhear her.

"Out of respect for your wife, I'm going to forget about this episode of ridiculous and offensive conduct. Muriel has always been kind to me, and I owe this debt of gratitude to *her*." She stepped even closer. Dr. Greene had to tip his head back to avoid having his nose in her cleavage. "But if you *ever* decide to make me the object of your petty and sophomoric behavior again, trust me, I won't be so charitable." She dropped her voice to nearly a whisper. "Do we understand each other, Tom?"

He nodded stupidly. "I'm . . . sorry, Maddie. Really."

She stepped back. "Oh, one more thing." She held out her hand, palm up. "Give me your car keys. You might want to call Muriel and tell her you've decided to spend the night here with your buddies."

He looked like he was going to argue, but Maddie just stood there glaring at him with her palm extended. Sighing with resignation, he fished his keys out of his trouser pocket and slapped them into her hand.

"You can get these from David in the morning. Good night, Dr. Greene."

He shook his head slowly and turned back toward the bar. "Good night, Dr. Stevenson."

Maddie watched him for a moment and then headed back down the hallway toward the rear of the house. Syd and David met her at the door to the sun porch.

"What's up, Sawbones?" David asked. "You look like you've been chewing on ground glass."

"Nothing. It was a crank call," Maddie said in a tone that indicated the subject was closed. She looked at Syd and tried to lighten her mood. "Would you like something else to drink?"

Syd regarded her with a curious expression. "If it's all the same to you, I'm kinda tired. Wanna call it a night?"

Maddie gave her a grateful smile. "Yeah. That call really got on my last nerve." She looked at David. "Do you mind keeping Syd company a minute longer? There's something I need to ask Michael about before we leave."

"It would be my pleasure. We'll wait for you on the front porch."

Maddie nodded and headed across the sun porch toward the entrance to the dining room. She found Michael at the back of the room in an animated conversation with several members of his kitchen staff. Most of the tables had already been cleared and reset for breakfast. He saw her approach, met her halfway, and kissed her on the cheek.

"Hello again, gorgeous. How was your evening? Enjoy yourself?" His gray eyes sparkled with admiration as he regarded her.

"Well, with about three exceptions, the evening was flawless."

"Three?" He looked concerned. "Care to enlighten me?"

"Remember my trio of admirers?" He nodded. "They went a bit too far in their pursuit of happiness, and I'm afraid I had to come down pretty hard on my pal Tom Greene."

"Ouch."

"Yeah." She handed Michael the set of car keys. "He's going to be spending the night here with his pals. Do me a favor and slip these to him discreetly in the morning. And fix them all something special for breakfast—on me." She smiled sheepishly. "He really did act like an ass, but I feel a little sorry for him."

Michael stood there, regarding her for a minute. "You're a class act, you know that?"

She rolled her eyes. "From your mouth to god's ear. Good night, Michael. It was a wonderful meal—as always."

He kissed her lightly. "Good night, gorgeous. You take care of that little blonde. She's a keeper." She glowered at him, and he backed away with his hands in the air. "Okay, okay. You can't blame a guy for trying."

Maddie turned into the gravel lot beside the Jericho library and parked next to Syd's Volvo. The town looked deserted—pretty typical for ten on a Friday night. The football team was playing at home this week, and most of the kids in the county would be out after the game, dragging the main street in Jefferson or hanging out at the local Pizza Hut. She shut the engine off and faced Syd.

"Tired?"

"Not really. I was wondering if you felt like coming up for some decaf?" Syd added quickly, "But if you'd rather head on home, I completely understand."

"No. I'd enjoy the company. And some coffee sounds great. We didn't really get to finish ours at the Inn."

"Well, I can't promise to equal your facility with a coffeemaker but I'll do my best."

Maddie smiled as she unhooked her seatbelt. "I can't wait to get out of these shoes."

"Well, then, let's go on up." Syd climbed out and led the way across the parking lot toward the front of the library. The weather had turned much colder, and a steady wind blew up the narrow street. A white plastic grocery bag had gotten tangled up with the chrysanthemums in the large planter that stood next to the street entrance to Syd's apartment. Maddie knelt and carefully extracted it while Syd unlocked the door. She stood up and displayed the bag with disbelief.

"Panda Inn Chinese Bistro?"

Syd turned to her. "You're kidding? Isn't that in Roanoke?"

"Yeah." Maddie shook her head and dropped the bag into a nearby trash receptacle. "That's some kind of home delivery."

"Or some kind of wind."

"True. Too bad it didn't blow some fortune cookies our way, too."

They started walking up the narrow stairway. "Why? Are you still hungry?"

Maddie chuckled behind her. "No, I'd just like to know the future."

"Worried about what fate has in store for you?"

"You might say that."

Syd turned on a lamp and dropped her bag and keys on the kitchen table. "Make yourself comfortable. I'll get some coffee brewing."

Maddie looked around the small apartment and its threadbare furnishings. She had been here once before, and she regretted that the county hadn't done better to make the place more inhabitable. Syd insisted that she didn't really mind, and that she spent most of her time downstairs in the branch anyway. She explained that her tenure in the area was likely to be so short that a more truncated, hotel-like existence suited her just fine. She wasn't ready to put down roots. Not yet—and not here.

That unhappy realization hit Maddie again as she kicked off her heels and dropped into an armchair, suddenly feeling deflated. Some lingering traces of anger over the whole Tom Greene episode continued to dance around the periphery of her consciousness, and she still felt vaguely like throttling David for his less-than-subtle insinuations about her developing friendship with Syd.

On the whole, it was an evening fraught with frustration, and it reminded her of all of her good and studied reasons for keeping to herself and staying out of social situations that just ended up making her life more complicated. She turned her head and regarded what was rapidly becoming her biggest complication as it moved around the tiny kitchen making coffee.

"Need some help out there?" Maddie asked.

"Nope. Got it all under control. It'll be ready in two shakes." Syd walked into the living room and turned on the radio. A lyrical passage from Schumann's *Scenes From Childhood* filled the air between them. Syd took off her jacket and tossed it across the back of the sofa before sinking down into its sagging cushions. She kicked off her shoes and dragged a fat ottoman over to rest between their seats. They both propped their tired feet up.

Syd turned a questioning gaze toward Maddie. "So tell me. What really happened with the phone call?"

Maddie sighed. "It was Tom and his cronies trying to track me down for a little moonlight madness."

"You have *got* to be kidding. And they called your service?"

"Yeah. I was pretty pissed."

"No doubt. You really did look like you were spitting fire when you met us in the hallway."

"It wasn't pretty. I felt bad about how angry I got with Tom so I asked Michael to hook them all up with something special for breakfast tomorrow."

"Well, you're a better man that I am, Gunga Din. I'd have ripped them all new ones and not thought twice about it."

Maddie gave her a wry smile. "Well, if I *had* ripped them new ones, chances are I'd have been the unhappy one tagged with the task of stitching 'em all back together." She playfully nudged Syd's leg with a stocking-clad foot. "So, see? In the long run, my motivation was purely a selfish one."

Syd laughed quietly. "I don't know how you do it. That kind of poise just has to come from breeding."

Maddie sighed as she slouched deeper into her chair and closed her eyes. "I don't know about that. Sometimes I think that coming back here was a complete mistake."

"Why? They're just sleazebags, Maddie, you'd run into their ilk anyplace."

Maddie shook her head. "Oh, not because of *them*. It's this whole enforced socialization thing. I'm just not ready for it. I'm still too raw. And nursing my wounds just makes me seem arrogant and stand-offish." She expelled a long breath. "Nothing is further from the truth."

Syd leaned slightly toward her and tentatively touched Maddie's arm. "And what is the truth?"

Maddie turned and met Syd's eyes just as a staccato beeping sound rang out from the kitchen.

Syd slowly withdrew her hand and got to her feet. "I'll go and get the coffee, but don't think this means you're off the hook."

Maddie raised an eyebrow as she gazed up at her hostess. "Oh really? Think you can make me talk?"

"Count on it." Syd walked to the kitchen and got their coffee. She returned with two steaming mugs and a small plate of chocolate cookies.

Maddie took hers eagerly, but gave the cookies a quizzical look. "Are you still hungry?"

Syd laughed. "Not at all, but I confess to having a rampant sweet tooth. And what's coffee without something sweet?"

Maddie leaned back in her chair and took a healthy sip of the hot beverage. "I thought that's why *I* was here?"

"Oh, I see that someone has *finally* regained her sunny disposition."

Maddie met Syd's amused green eyes. "I apologize for that. I shouldn't let stunts like the one Tom and his buddies pulled get under my skin that way. It doesn't do much to ameliorate my whole ice-maiden persona."

"You don't need to apologize to me. I would've been likelier to have made a scene."

"Really?" Maddie was intrigued. "You don't seem like the scene-making type."

"I don't?"

"No."

"Well, then, what type *do* I seem like?" Syd's tone was playful.

Maddie set her mug on the side table between them and tented her fingers in front of her face. "The sweet, sensitive, girl-next-door, Sandra Dee type."

"Sandra Dee?"

"Yeah . . . perky blonde actress—married to Bobby Darin—starred in all those *Gidget* movies . . ."

Syd stared at her in horror. "I *know* who Sandra Dee was, egghead. I just fail to see the similarity."

Maddie gave her an exaggerated once-over. "Reaaallllly? No summers on the shore? No pretty, bronzed boyfriends?" She dropped her voice to a near whisper. "No surfboards in your closet?"

Syd colored. "Well . . ."

"Hah! Told ya."

Syd threw part of a cookie at her. "I'll have you know that I'm not in the *least* like Gidget."

"Oh yeah?" Maddie said. "Prove it."

Syd leaned forward and stared into Maddie's eyes from very close range. The faint scent of Syd's perfume was intoxicating. "Let's just say that *my* pretty, bronzed Moondoggies were *very* happy boys," she said in a low and husky voice.

Maddie stared back at her stunned. They sat in frozen silence for several moments with their faces inches apart. Maddie was overwhelmed by a sudden desire to grab Syd and kiss her. Wasn't that what this moment called for? Wasn't that where their conversation was leading them—where the entire evening had been leading them? She felt for a moment like an actor in the middle of a scene, and her tiny internal director was standing just off-camera waving his arms at her and shouting, "Cue the kiss. Do it, do it!" She thought she saw a brief flicker of something in Syd's eyes. Panic? Desire? Confusion? She didn't know. Then Syd slowly sat back against the sofa.

"Looks like you can dish it out, but can't take it." She gave a small, nervous laugh.

Maddie looked at her with a raised eyebrow, not entirely sure what she meant. How far was she willing to take this? How much was she willing to risk to find out?

Not much.

It was too soon. With a sinking heart, she realized that with Syd, it would *always* be too soon.

"Okay," she replied. "So maybe I was slightly off the mark in my assessment of your relative *innocence* quotient but I continue to maintain that you're a total cream puff when it comes to confrontation."

Syd glowered at her. "I still would've decked those obnoxious drunks."

"Don't think for a moment that I didn't consider it. I'd have had a better time being kidnapped by Somali pirates—at least the boat ride would've been fun."

Syd laughed, and the tension between them dissipated. "You're such a nut."

"Well, don't tell anyone. I'd hate to ruin my image."

"Your secret is safe with me, Doctor."

Maddie met Syd's eyes. "You know, I'm beginning to think that all of my secrets might be safe with you."

They smiled at each other shyly, and drank the rest of their coffee in silence.

After Maddie left, Syd stepped back inside her apartment and stood for a moment with her head pressed against the doorframe. *What in the hell was that about?* She was used to Maddie's playfulness and the easy repartee that normally characterized their interactions, but tonight was different.

She closed her eyes. *My god. I almost kissed her.* She was mortified by her behavior, and had no idea how to make sense of it. Had Maddie noticed? What on earth did she think? She shook her head. *Jesus, how pathetic. I need to get laid.*

She walked through the tiny apartment, turning off lights, and thought back over the evening, trying to catalog her impressions. There had been so much to take in. Maddie and David. She smiled. They were adorable together. But Maddie seemed agitated by David's—and Michael's—obvious efforts to throw the two of them together. Why? She knew that David wanted Maddie to get out more—to socialize more. Yet he didn't seem interested in pairing her off with anyone in particular—at least, not with anyone at the Inn tonight.

She laughed bitterly as she thought back over the whole episode with Dr. Greene and his golf buddies. Certainly, *they* weren't serious contenders for the attentions of the tall beauty. She remembered the look of pure chagrin on Maddie's face when Tom Greene descended upon them in the parlor before dinner. She seemed to resent the intrusion, and she certainly escaped from their clutches with dispatch as soon as Michael announced that dinner was ready to be served. Syd felt spoiled by her ability to monopolize Maddie's attention throughout the evening—like she had won the top prize at a church raffle, leaving all the other ticket-holders to stand unhappily on the sidelines while she paraded about with her trophy.

But Maddie seemed to be a willing participant in their virtual isolation from the other dinner guests. She didn't seem to pay particular attention to anyone else, except David, of course.

David. Why was David so interested in finding out how much Syd knew about Maddie's failed relationship? The nature of his query made her uncomfortable—almost as if there was something unsaid lurking behind his question. What was it? She thought back over the few comments Maddie had made about the demise of her relationship. It was true that the details were sparse. She said that they were both residents, and that their schedules were impossible. She said that he was an ophthalmic surgeon.

But wait. That wasn't right.

Maddie never actually said "he." In fact, she seemed skillfully to avoid using *any* pronoun.

For the first time, Syd wondered if maybe Maddie's ex wasn't a man at all. She had a sinking feeling that she was nearing the truth. That would explain a lot—like why she was still single. And why she stayed so isolated and careful about her social interactions. And why David's suggestive teasing about the two of them was so unsettling to her.

Oh my god. And I nearly kissed her. Syd felt a hot flush surge up her neck. *What if she is gay, and I just acted like a horny teenager? Christ.* She held her hands against her hot face. *On the other hand, what if she isn't gay, and I just acted like a horny teenager? God. There's no good outcome to this. I'm so totally screwed. How on earth do I face her?*

She dropped down into a chair and sat staring blankly into the darkness of her apartment, overcome with embarrassment and confusion . . . and wondering vaguely if the university placement office had any job postings in Tierra del Fuego.

Chapter 6

The grand opening of the Jericho Public Library was scheduled for Sunday afternoon from two to six, and most permanent residents of the county found a reason to drop in. Even those who weren't especially curious about this evolution in public service were lured by the prospect of sampling free food from the Riverside Inn. Although he was unable to attend personally, Michael Robertson had graciously consented to cater the event, and the elaborate spread of cold and warmed appetizers he had prepared evaporated quickly before the steady stream of area residents. They swarmed across the food tables like locusts, and by three-thirty, it became clear that the branch was dispensing more canapés than library cards. Syd was certain that she would run out of food well before the event concluded at six.

The throng of attendees was peppered with luminaries. All of the county supervisors were there, along with two representatives from the state library association in Richmond. Five of the six members of the local library board were in attendance—one tall doctor appeared to be the only holdout. Syd was both relieved and disappointed by Maddie's conspicuous absence. They hadn't spoken or seen each other since their ambiguous encounter in her apartment on Friday night, and she worried that Maddie's decision not to attend the event suggested she was equally uncomfortable with their confusing, late-night interaction.

Roma Jean Freemantle and the inevitable Jessie Rayburn were on hand to help staff the event, and several of their fellow band members were clustered around the punch bowl, laughing and talking behind their hands.

Syd was surprised when she saw Tom Greene making his way across the facility. She made a point of intercepting him as he reached the food tables, and couldn't help but notice the improvement in the older man's demeanor. He was polite and deferential as he greeted her and introduced her to his wife, Muriel. Syd greeted them both warmly and expressed particular pleasure at seeing him in Jericho on a Sunday afternoon. He smiled and explained that since the branch opening coincided with his regular weekend off, he was able to attend the event.

"It's Dr. Stevenson you really need to thank," he added, as he reached for another prosciutto and pear roulade. "She's holding down the fort at the ER today."

Syd didn't know whether to feel elated or disappointed. She remembered Maddie mentioning that she filled in for Tom at the Wytheville hospital several times a month. This plainly was one of those times.

Syd smiled at the older man. "Thank you for solving that mystery for me. I actually was wondering why she hadn't made an appearance yet."

"I tried to get someone to sub for her," Tom said, glancing at his watch. "But she was pretty adamant about working a full shift today." He met her eyes. "You know how stubborn she can be when she's already made up her mind about something."

Syd eyed the rapidly dwindling trays of food. *Probably just as well. There wouldn't be anything left for her to eat if she did stop by.* She gave Tom a small smile. "I think I know what you mean."

By five-thirty, the crowd had thinned considerably, and the branch was all but emptied of patrons. Most of the locals were headed home to their TVs and the six o'clock green flag that would herald the start of the NASCAR race in Talladega. Syd was at the back of the library, stacking empty appetizer platters and clearing away punch cups when she heard laughter and caught a flash of blue out of the corner of her eye. She glanced toward the street entrance and was surprised to see Maddie—striking in bright blue scrubs and leaning against a low bookcase as she listened to an animated David Jenkins.

David was plainly in the middle of chastising Maddie about something. Syd could tell by the way he was waving his hands around that it had to do with her wearing her hospital garb. Maddie seemed unfazed as she calmly crossed her arms and tipped her head to the side while his monologue continued. Syd debated with herself for a moment, then decided to approach them.

As she drew close, she became aware of how much taller Maddie seemed in the scrubs. Her dark hair was loosely pulled back away from her face, and the cerulean-colored fabric gave her eyes an almost neon appearance.

David didn't appear to be losing any steam.

" . . . I'd just like to understand just what this whole retro, scullery-maid ensemble thing is supposed to be about." He clucked his tongue. "I gather we all should just be grateful that you aren't up to your shapely elbows in some kind of blood or gore?"

Maddie sighed. "Is your life really so lacking in drama that you have to seize *every* opportunity to create it?"

Syd stepped to just behind Maddie. "Well, I, for one, wouldn't care if you *were* up to your elbows in blood. I'd still be happy to see you." Maddie turned around with a startled expression. Syd smiled at her. "I'm glad you made it."

Maddie answered her smile with a shy one of her own, and Syd realized that had spoken the truth. She *was* glad to see her. They stood there for a few moments without speaking.

Syd became aware that David was watching their silent interaction with unbridled interest. He rolled his eyes and turned to her. "Well, I suppose you could use the help cleaning up. I *was* gonna stick around, but now that Blue Boy is here, I can leave you in capable hands."

"Got a hot date?" Maddie asked, with a raised eyebrow.

He gave her a condescending look. "Still trying to live vicariously, I see." He pulled on his overcoat. "As it happens, this little shindig ain't the only game in town tonight. We've got a full house at the Inn, and Michael will go ballistic if I'm not back by six." He looked at Maddie and then at Syd. "I trust I can leave the two of you alone to fend for yourselves?"

Maddie nodded. "Oh, sure. I can fend. In fact, I'm terribly good at fending. I've been fending for years."

Syd agreed. "It's true. I've seen her fend. She's checked out."

He sighed. "You two deserve each other." He kissed Syd on the cheek. "Nice job today, kiddo." Then he turned and headed for the street door. He threw a backward wave over his shoulder. "Catch you later, Sawbones."

Maddie watched him depart. "Why do I feel like my chaperone just left?"

"Do you think you need a chaperone?"

Maddie met her eyes. "You tell me."

Syd stared back at her for a moment. She knew that her answer was important, but she wasn't exactly certain why. "No. I think you need something to eat."

Maddie laughed. "You got that right." She seemed to relax, and her blue eyes were mirthful again. "Is there anything left?"

"You're joking, right? You should have seen the food flying off those tables. Thirty minutes after I opened the doors, it looked like the Four Horsemen of the Apocalypse had roared through here. I've never seen anything like it."

Maddie chuckled as they slowly walked toward the back of the building. "I should've warned you. People around here save up for these catered events. Sometimes, they show up with relatives they haven't spoken to in decades—like they all decided that a big platter of crudités was enough of a reason to bury the hatchet. I sincerely believe that a couple of well-placed hors d'oeuvre tables could've shortened the Civil War by at least two years."

Syd laughed as they approached the now-vacant buffet. "I didn't expect to see you here. Tom Greene said you were filling in for him at the ER today."

Maddie nodded. "I was. He offered to get Mike Lewis down from Roanoke so I could be free today, but Mike's wife just had another baby, and I didn't want to eat into their time at home together." She looked at Syd. "I do apologize for showing up in these clothes. Normally, I'd have changed at the hospital, but I really didn't think I'd get out of there in time to make it over here before six." She shrugged. "It just ended up being a pretty slow day." She picked up the last remaining roulade.

"A slow day in the ER means a good day for everyone."

"Unless you're the unhappy M.D. consigned to reworking the same Sudoko eighty-five times while trying *not* to stare at the wall clock." She licked her fingertips as she chewed. "Damn, that was wonderful. Are you sure there aren't any more of those hiding anyplace?" She poked around at the stack of trays.

"Sorry, Doctor. The best I can do on such short notice is a slice of indifferent pizza."

Maddie brightened up. "You have a pizza? Where?" She craned her neck and looked past Syd into the processing area behind the food tables.

"Well, unless you're in a real hurry, we could have one here in about thirty minutes. I confess that I didn't get to eat anything either. I was too anxious and too busy playing hostess."

"How'd it go?" Maddie quickly held up her palm. "And before you answer that question, yes, I'd love to share a pizza."

Syd smiled, relieved that they seemed to be back on their easy footing with each other. She now realized that she probably *had* overreacted to their encounter on Friday night. Even if Maddie had noticed anything odd or unsettling about that evening, she seemed as eager as Syd was to move past it and to continue their relaxed camaraderie.

"Why don't you go into my office and order us some food while I finish clearing these things away? Then we can go upstairs, and I'll fill you in on all the details of the opening."

"It's a deal."

"There's a phone book on my desk," Syd called out, as Maddie retreated toward the back of the building.

The library was empty now. Syd finished stacking the platters and punch cups in the large, plastic bins that Michael had provided. He told her that he would stop by on Monday morning to pick the items up. She was piling the bins against the rear wall when she heard the street door open and close. She dropped her shoulders at the prospect that another bevy of famished locals had decided to drop in. She glanced at her watch. Six-fifteen. *I should've locked the damn street door.*

With resignation, she headed toward the front of the building.

A tall, bearded man with wavy brown hair stood gazing up at the poster of Danica Patrick next to the door. He was slender, and dressed in dark slacks and a bright red Columbia jacket. Syd gasped when she saw him, and he turned around to face her.

"What are *you* doing here?" She was incredulous.

He flashed her a broad smile. "Can't a husband stop in to see his wife?"

Maddie hung up the phone and sat back for a moment in Syd's old, oak Bank of England chair, looking around the tiny office. *Thank god that went better than I expected.* She slowly shook her head. *I must have overreacted. Again.* She idly regarded the stacks of new books spread out across the top of the desk. Half of them were in Spanish. She smiled at that as she pushed the big rolling chair back and stood up to go out and rejoin Syd.

"I hope pepperoni is okay with you," she began as she exited the processing area. She stopped cold when she saw Syd standing near the front door, engaged in earnest conversation with a tall, good-looking man. There was something . . . familiar . . . about the way they stood there. She could tell immediately that, whoever he was, he wasn't a stranger to Syd.

They both turned to regard her. The man looked surprised and slightly wary. Syd looked flustered.

"Maddie. This is my husband, Jeff Simon." She glanced up at him. "He was on his way through the area and decided to make an impromptu visit. Jeff, I'd like you to meet my good friend, Maddie Stevenson. She's our local physician."

Jeff continued to stand there next to Syd so Maddie walked toward them and extended her hand in greeting. "Hello, Jeff. It's nice to meet you." As they shook hands, Maddie was aware of feeling irrationally pleased that, even in her flat-soled shoes, she and Jeff were the same height.

Jeff gave Maddie a curious look, but smiled as he released her hand. "Is it usual to have a physician on hand at these events?" He looked at Syd. "I didn't realize that libraries were so dangerous."

Maddie eyed him coolly. "You'd be surprised."

"Maddie is here as a guest, and as an esteemed member of the county library board," Syd quickly interjected. She smiled at Maddie. "But it never hurts to have all of your bases covered."

"Well then, Doctor, it's a pleasure to meet you." Jeff turned to Syd. "I was hoping you'd be able to take a break and join me for dinner. I don't have any fixed time that I have to be in Roanoke tonight." He shifted his gaze to Maddie. "I'm meeting with the fish and game commission there tomorrow to talk about a watershed project on the Roanoke River." He turned back to Syd. "Whattaya say? Wanna go grab something to eat and get caught up?"

Syd seemed to hesitate. Maddie looked from one to the other. Although her internal voice was clamoring for her to remain silent, she spoke up. "Look, Syd. Don't worry about me. I'm famished enough to eat an entire pizza by myself. I'll just run by there on my way home and pick it up." She gave Syd an encouraging smile. "You do what you need to do. I'll catch up with you tomorrow."

Syd shot her a worried look as she continued to deliberate. She turned back to Jeff, squared her shoulders, and shook her head. "I don't think so, Jeff." His disappointment was palpable. "I already have plans for dinner, and I don't want to change them." He appeared ready to argue with her, but she stopped him with a raised palm. "If you really want to talk with me, give me a call later in the week, and we'll work something out. Impromptu visits like this really aren't a good idea right now."

He stood there, quietly chewing on his lower lip, plainly embarrassed by her dismissive response. "Right. I'll call you, then." He gave Maddie a brief nod, and then took a tentative step toward Syd before stopping himself and backing up. "It was good to see you—even for a minute. I've missed you." He hesitated. "You look beautiful."

Syd colored. "Thanks. It's . . . it's good to see you, too." He smiled at that. "Good luck in Roanoke."

He waved as he walked toward the door. "I'll call you mid-week." He pushed open the door and strode out of the library.

Syd stood there for a moment and then she dropped down onto one of the nearby oak study chairs. "Jesus."

Maddie softly laid a hand on Syd's shoulder. "You okay?"

Syd lifted her head and met Maddie's concerned gaze. "How dare he just show up like that?" She shook her head. "It's so typical. Just like him to waltz in here like nothing has changed. God. *Incredible.*"

Maddie knelt next to her. "I'm really sorry I was here. I know that made it more complicated for you."

"Don't be ridiculous." Syd was emphatic. "I'm relieved you were here. It made it easier for me to get rid of him."

Maddie blinked in surprise.

"Does that shock you?" Syd asked, searching her face.

"Maybe. I guess I thought you might feel . . . ambivalent . . . or curious about why he was here." She removed her hand from Syd's shoulder. "That's why I offered to leave—so the two of you could talk."

"Well, I meant what I said to him. If he wants to talk, he can call me first, and we can arrange something. It's *not* okay with me to have him just show up like this." She stood up. "Were you serious about picking up the pizza and taking it back to your place?"

Maddie got belatedly to her feet and tried to conceal her disappointment. "Sure. Of course you want to be by yourself. I completely understand that."

"Be by myself?" Syd looked confused. "No. That's not what I meant. I was wondering if we could eat out at your place?" She looked around them. "I feel like I've been cooped up in here for *eons*. Now that today is behind me, nothing sounds better than a change of scenery."

Maddie knew she wore a stupid grin. "Grab your coat, and let's get out of here."

Syd locked the street door, and they walked to the rear entrance, turning off lights as they went. As they descended the steps, Maddie punched her key fob to unlock the doors of her Jeep. "Why don't you just ride with me? I'll bring you back after we eat."

Syd gave her a sideways glance. "Okay. But *only* if we both promise to remember that tomorrow is a school day. That means no wine-induced sleepovers." She paused. "No matter how appealing the idea is."

Maddie crossed her heart as they walked across the parking lot. "I hear and obey."

Syd looked at her. "Why do I think *that's* a first?"

"Hey. I think you're spending entirely too much time with David."

Syd sighed. "Many hands make light work."

"Oh, good lord. I knew I'd live to regret having the two of you meet."

"Rethinking the idea of telling me all of your secrets?" Syd asked sweetly.

Maddie considered that. "No. Rethinking the idea of moving to another country."

"Funny . . . I was having the same thoughts just the other night."

"Were you?"

"I was."

Maddie opened the passenger door for her and stood back while she climbed inside. "Hmmm. Too bad about tonight's embargo on spirits."

"Why's that?"

"It seems like we're both in the mood to be truthful." She smiled. "*In vino veritas.*"

Syd met her eyes as she pulled on her seatbelt. "All the more reason to stay sober."

Maddie stood there a moment longer before shutting the door and walking around to the driver's side. She closed her eyes as she grabbed the door handle. *This is* so *not helping. I should've just pulled a double shift at the hospital.*

She climbed in and started the Jeep. She took her cell phone out of the center console and handed it to Syd. "I have every pizza joint in the county on speed-dial. Hit #9 and tell them we've decided to pick it up, instead of waiting on home delivery."

Syd took the phone and dutifully punched in the number while Maddie drove them out of the parking lot and onto the road toward town.

Chapter 7

Jericho—Lunch with David

On Tuesday, David walked into the clinic, carrying a clear plastic bag that contained two Subway club sandwiches and two small bags of apple slices. Maddie was standing at the reception desk, going over a patient folder with Peggy Hawkes. The waiting room was empty except for a pregnant young Hispanic woman and her two small children. One of the children dozed with his head on his mother's lap, while the other quietly worked a puzzle on the bare floor at her feet.

Maddie looked up. "Hello, there. I have one patient left to see, and then I can take a short break. Do you mind waiting in my office?"

David smiled at her. "Nope. That's fine." He turned to Peggy. "Hi ya, Nurse Ratched. You keeping this one in line?"

Peggy winked at him. "Barely. It's a tall order."

"Ain't that the truth?" David looked Maddie up and down. "About six feet of one."

The little boy raised his head from his mother's lap as he was seized with a coughing fit. She tried to soothe him as she ran a hand back and forth across his narrow back.

"*Está bien, cariño. La doctora hará que te sientas mejor.*" The child raised his watery eyes to his mother's and tried to stifle his cough.

Maddie stepped around the reception desk and went to the small family. She knelt in front of the little boy.

"*Hola.*" She pointed to herself. "*Soy la doctora.*" He looked up at her with luminous eyes. "*¿Puedo ver tu garganta?*" She smiled at him. "*Prometo vas a sentirte sienta mejor.*"

He looked at his mother, and then he nodded. Maddie held out her hand. "*Vamos a ir a mi oficina.*" She smiled at his mother as the child extended his hand. "We'll be right back."

As the two of them started down the hallway together, David heard Maddie ask, "*¿Cómo te llamas?*"

"Héctor," a tiny voice answered.

David shook his head and looked at Peggy. "Another conquest, and it isn't even noon." He sighed. "Even the sick ones are not immune to that smile."

Peggy clucked her tongue as she rifled through a stack of papers. "Well, she takes after her daddy where that's concerned. Charmers—both of them."

"*Ella es un ángel,*" the Hispanic woman said so quietly that David barely heard her.

Her soft words hung in the air like an anthem. David turned to her. "Yes. Yes, she is."

He sat down next to her and set the bag containing the sandwiches on the seat between them. He leaned over and watched the other little boy work the puzzle. It was slowly taking shape.

"Is that a boat?" David asked. The little boy looked up at him quizzically.

"*Barco*," his mother clarified.

"*Sí*," the child replied.

David picked up a stray puzzle piece and waved it back and forth between them. "Can I help you?" The boy looked up at his mother again.

"*Él quiere ayudarle.*" The mother smiled at the little boy, who looked up at David and nodded shyly. She met David's eyes. "*Gracias* . . . thank you."

David smiled back and then slid onto the floor to sit next to the child. They worked the puzzle together quietly. The only sound in the small waiting room was the tick of the long second hand on the wall clock, and the occasional shuffle of paper as Peggy continued to manipulate her patient folders.

When Maddie returned to the waiting room with Héctor, she explained to his mother that he was in the early stages of developing a strep infection. She had given him an antibiotic shot, and said that he should be feeling better within twenty-four hours. She knelt next to the little boy and pulled a cherry lollipop out of her lab coat pocket.

"*Fuiste muy valiente.*" She smiled at him.

Héctor took the treat and nodded. Then he stepped forward to hug her before retreating quickly to stand next his mother. Maddie pulled a second lollipop out of her pocket and extended it to his brother, who still sat quietly on the floor beside David.

"*¿Quieres uno también?*" she asked as she extended it. The little boy took it eagerly.

She stood and addressed his mother, explaining that she should call her at once if she or any of the other members of her family developed a sore throat or began running a fever. She handed her a white bag containing throat lozenges and analgesics for Héctor.

The woman took the bag and held onto Maddie's hand for a moment. "*Gracias*, Doctor. Bless you." She looked down at her son. "Gabriel, *escoge un juguete.*"

David helped him collect the puzzle pieces and stow them into a battered box. Gabriel placed it into his mother's canvas bag while she helped Héctor into a coat that was sizes too large for him. She made eye contact with David as he discreetly slipped the Subway sandwiches into her large bag. They stared at each other for a moment, and then she smiled shyly and nodded.

David and Maddie stood together as the small family left the clinic. He nudged her playfully.

"*A-hem.*" He cleared his throat.

Maddie looked at him. "What?"

"What am I, chopped liver? Where's *my* lollipop?"

Maddie rolled her eyes. "*After* your lunch, and then *only* if you eat all of your sandwich." She looked him over. "You know the rules."

"Yeah, well . . . about lunch," David demurred. "Fancy a couple of hot dogs from Freemantle's market?"

"What? Why would we . . . ?" She glanced down at the empty bench behind them and looked at him with unbridled affection. "C'mon, I'll drive."

Maddie and David sat with their hot dogs and bottles of water at one of several small tables scattered along the back wall of Freemantle's mini-mart. The business was primarily a service station, but in recent years, Curtis and Edna had started serving hot sandwiches and pizza by the slice. The hot dogs were surprisingly good, and even though she normally shied away from any kind of fast food, Maddie would often make an exception on busy clinic days and drop by the market for a quick bite to eat.

David shoved his open bag of Cheetos across the chipped Formica tabletop. "Eat some of these. I refuse to be the only person at this table with orange fingernails." He licked his fingertips. "C'mon . . . they're the crunchy ones."

Maddie shook her head. "Forget it. Those things are disgusting. I can't believe you eat crap like that." She took a bite of her hot dog.

David nodded at Maddie. "*This* from a woman with a mouth full of meat by-product?"

Maddie swallowed. "You don't really think you can toss out a phrase like 'mouth full of meat by-product' and think I'm going to let it slide, do you?"

"Oh, I tremble before your rapier wit." He gave the bag another shove in her direction. "Come on. I *know* you hoard junk food at home. I've seen the empty Ambien bottles in your trash."

"You're nuts, David."

He held up a crusty, twisted Cheeto. "You know you want it . . ."

She growled at him.

"It's the perfect remedy for sexual frustration."

Maddie rolled her eyes and snatched the blaze-orange treat from between his fingers. "I hate you," she muttered as she popped the fried morsel into her mouth.

He chuckled. "So tell me all about your tête à tête with the lovely Ms. Murphy on Sunday after the opening."

She eyed him suspiciously. "What makes you think we spent time together after the opening?"

"Puh-lease. My mamma didn't raise no imbecile." He regarded her with an amused expression. "You looked like a deer in the headlights when she walked up behind us." He paused. "It was really pretty sweet. I haven't seen an expression like *that* on your face since the third grade, when you had that crush on Mavis Blankenship."

Maddie looked at him with calm indifference. "I refuse to share any details with you."

"Well now, *that's* a pointless exercise. You know I can make you talk."

Maddie sat back and crossed her arms. "Oh, really? What are you gonna do if I refuse? Hold me down and make me listen to your Judy Garland albums?"

"Maybe."

Maddie shook her head. "God. Mavis." She looked at him with wonder. "How do you come up with this stuff?"

David looked over her shoulder toward the front of the market. "Hold that thought. I think the future Mrs. Stevenson is headed our way."

Maddie twisted around on her plastic chair to see a smiling Syd headed toward their table. She was wearing faded blue jeans and a dark burgundy sweater. Her short, blonde hair shimmered under the fluorescent lights.

Maddie let out a slow breath. *Somebody up there hates me.*

David got to his feet as Syd approached, and Maddie belatedly followed suit. Syd was carrying a container of yogurt and a large package of batteries.

David pulled her into a hug. "Yogurt and batteries? I read about this diet in *O Magazine.* They said that David Hasselhoff lost eighty pounds in two days."

Syd laughed and turned to Maddie. They hesitated for only a moment before leaning in and exchanging quick pecks on the cheek.

"I didn't know you ate here," Syd said to Maddie. "I'm surprised I haven't run into you before now. I probably come in here four or five times a week."

So will I, from now on. Maddie gave her a guilty shrug. "I have a hidden passion for junk food."

Syd smiled as she brushed orange Cheeto dust off the lapel of Maddie's lightweight leather jacket. "Apparently."

"That isn't the only passion she keeps hidden," David added in an undertone, winking at Syd.

Maddie glowered at him. "Whoa there, Miss 'Let's put on a prom gown and go eat at Waffle House.' I really don't think you want to go down *this* road." She lifted her chin in challenge. "Do you?"

He threw up his hands. "Okay, okay. Truce." He touched Syd on the elbow. "Sit down with us." He gestured at her yogurt. "Are you going to eat that?"

She looked down at the small container. "I was, but I don't want to intrude on your lunch. I really just ran in to pick up the batteries. I have to stash some boxes in the crawl space and my flashlight's D.O.A."

Maddie pulled another chair over to their small table. "Well, sit with us for few minutes. I have to be back at the clinic soon, anyway. We were just grabbing a quick bite."

Syd put her items down on the table. "Okay, but let me go and get some water."

"No, no. I've got that. You sit down." David jumped to his feet and trotted down an aisle.

Maddie and Syd sat down and faced each other.

"So, how's your day going?" Syd asked.

"Pretty typical. But I just saw my third case of strep throat in as many days. Be sure to wash your hands a lot at work."

"Yes, Doctor." Syd reached for a Cheeto. "May I?"

"Oh, I insist. David was just trying to browbeat me into eating them by explaining that they're a great cure for sexual frustration." *Jesus . . . why did I just say that?*

Syd paused mid-chew. "Really? I wonder if I can get a case discount?"

Maddie looked at her with surprise before bursting into laughter. "Wanna go halves on a skid?"

Syd's green eyes twinkled. "Maybe strep isn't the only malady making the rounds up here."

David returned with Syd's bottle of water. He also gave her a cellophane-wrapped package of Oreos. "Sweets for the sweet." He fixed Maddie with a level gaze. "I thought about picking up something for you, too, but 'doughnuts for the dour' was too lame an alliteration, even for me."

Maddie smiled sweetly. "I appreciate your condescension."

"So, Syd," David began. "You'll never guess who just booked one of our best rooms for three nights over Thanksgiving weekend."

Syd looked amused. "Oh, I just bet I can. George and Janet Murphy of the *Towson* Murphys?"

He nodded. "That would be correct. Thanks for the sterling recommendation. But I think you might have gone a bit overboard with your praise. Your mother seems to think she's going to be staying at a Helmsley Hotel."

Maddie snorted. "Oh, you can pull that off, David. Just wear the taffeta."

David gave her a withering look. "Don't you have some kidney stones to pulverize? We're having a conversation here."

Syd smiled as she opened her container of yogurt. "Well, be forewarned. My mother makes Mr. Clean tremble."

"Interesting." David snagged another Cheeto. "Well, since Michael emerged from the womb waving a bottle of Windex and a Scotch Brite pad, I'd say she's about to meet her match."

Syd laughed. "Still, I think I'll hedge my bet and go ahead and apologize in advance. I confess that I'm surprised they're making the trip. I wonder if my erstwhile ex doesn't have a sticky hand in this." She looked at David. "My soon-to-be ex-husband made an unannounced visit on Sunday night. I think he's angling for a reconciliation."

Maddie gave her a startled look. "You do? What makes you think so?"

Syd sighed. "He called me last night and said as much. It was no accident that my mother called about thirty minutes later to tell me they'd made reservations at the Inn for Thanksgiving."

David leaned forward on his elbows. "Good lord. What are your thoughts about all of this?"

"I don't know." Syd lowered her eyes as she rotated her plastic spoon around. "I told Jeff I'd meet him for dinner tomorrow night—hear what he has to say." She looked up and met Maddie's concerned eyes. "I can't deny that reconciliation would make a lot of things less complicated for me, but I'm still not certain that I trust him."

Maddie didn't fully trust herself to speak. She wanted to be supportive, but right now, she wasn't sure what form that should take. Should she encourage Syd to give Jeff a fair hearing, or should she fall to her knees and plead with her to roar ahead with the divorce? She was in a ridiculous place—a place she had no business inhabiting. The confusing web of her own emotions was beginning to immobilize her and cloud her judgment. She glanced at David, and saw that his eyes were fixed on her with interest.

She turned to Syd. "Maybe it's best that you *do* meet with him—try to get greater clarity," she said with a calm she didn't feel. "You don't want to make a mistake or do something that you might end up regretting."

Syd looked at her with an expression that was hard to read. "You're right. I don't want to make a mistake."

David sighed. "Well, it seems like there's only one thing for you to do, then."

They looked at him expectantly.

He threw his hands up. "Duh! Tell us where you're meeting him so we can accidentally show up and eavesdrop."

Maddie threw a Cheeto at him. "You seriously need to have your meds balanced." She looked at her watch and sighed. "I feel like this is rotten timing but I have to get back to the clinic." She touched Syd on the shoulder as she got to her feet. "Can I call you later?"

Syd smiled up at her. "That'd be great. I'll be at the library until at least six, then you can find me at the apartment."

David collected all of their trash and tossed it into a nearby receptacle. Syd retrieved her batteries and her small packet of cookies and walked with them to the front of the market. Edna Freemantle was behind the register, restocking a cigarette display. David went to greet her.

"Hello again, Edna. Great hot dogs." He fished his wallet out of his back pocket. "Can I get a pack of Camels?"

"Sure thing." Edna snagged a pack from her display and pushed them across the counter toward him. "That'll be three-fifty."

David pulled out three singles, and then looked expectantly at Maddie. "Got any change?"

She crossed her arms. "You're kidding me with this, right? You don't seriously expect me to collude with you in your pursuit of this vile habit?"

"Why not? You collude with me in the pursuit of most of my *other* vile habits."

"Name one."

"Okaaaayy." He leaned against the counter and prepared to tick items off on his fingertips. "Number one: Cheetos—which we've already established. Number two: a fondness for videos starring a certain tall, leggy—"

"All right, already." Maddie dug two quarters out of her jacket pocket and slapped them into his palm. "Don't come crying to me when your lungs turn to charcoal."

He smiled sweetly at her. "Oh, I promise."

Edna shook her head at Syd as she took the money from David. "Just like peas in a pod. They've been this way since they were knee-high to a grasshopper."

"Sans the cigarettes, of course," Maddie drawled.

David pocketed his Camels. "Thanks, Edna, see you around."

Edna smiled at the three of them. "Have a nice afternoon."

They walked out into the parking lot.

David gave Syd a quick hug. "Keep it between the ditches, cutie pie. Michael will give you a call about food options for your folks. He's all jazzed about cooking some kind of exotic goose concoction on Thanksgiving Day."

Syd smiled into the wool of his blazer. "Thanks, I know it'll be wonderful." She stepped back. "See you soon." She turned to Maddie. "Talk to you later on?"

Maddie smiled at her. "Count on it."

Syd climbed into her Volvo, backed out, and waved goodbye as she pulled onto the main road and headed back toward the library.

"Well, I know one thing for sure," David commented as they watched her car disappear around a bend.

"What's that?"

"Hers isn't the *only* goose that's about to be cooked." He turned to Maddie. His brown eyes were uncharacteristically serious. "Be careful, missy. Don't get hurt."

She thought about protesting, but it was pointless. He knew her better than she knew herself. "I don't *want* to get hurt, and you can help me avoid it by giving up on these clumsy attempts to push the two of us together." She laid her hand on his forearm. "Please."

He covered her hand with his own and gave it a warm squeeze. "I always want what's best for you. I'm just not sure yet what that is."

"Well, I know what it's *not*. And I don't want to wade any further into this particular bed of quicksand."

"For what it's worth, I think she's just as confused as you are."

Maddie gave him a hopeless gaze.

David sighed. "So, I guess that means you're *not* calling her later?"

Maddie shot him a withering look. "Let's go. I've got an appointment in ten minutes."

David chuckled as they climbed into her Jeep. "Thought so."

Syd was glad that she hadn't agreed to let Jeff pick her up at the library. He pressed for that, but she insisted that they meet at the restaurant. She chose McGinty's, a locally owned pub in Wytheville. It was close to the highway, and had a decent atmosphere and a good salad bar. When she arrived a few minutes before seven, she saw that Jeff's dark red 4Runner was already in the parking lot. It was covered with mud and packed to the gills with gear—he rarely traveled light. She saw him waiting for her just inside the door.

He stepped forward as she approached and kissed her on the cheek.

"Thanks for doing this. I was afraid you'd back out." He smiled as he took her elbow and guided her toward the hostess station. He was dressed in stylish outerwear, looking as if he had just stepped from the pages of a *Territory Ahead* catalog.

"I won't pretend that I didn't think about it," she said. She had *no* reason to be less than honest with him.

He gave her a sorrowful look. "Well, that's an auspicious beginning."

"We're way past beginnings, Jeff. You know that as well as I do."

The hostess seated them at a booth near the bar area, and they sat for a moment in awkward silence as they contemplated their menus. Jeff ordered a draft Stella Artois, and Syd settled for a bottle of Pellegrino. She wanted to keep her wits about her, and she didn't want to prolong the evening by lingering over drinks. Fleetwood Mac's "The Chain" pounded away in the background, and she was tempted to smile at the irony. Their waitress brought the beverages and hovered by their table for a moment as Jeff made small talk with her. She was a perky, twenty-something named Randi. In short order, Jeff learned that she was a sophomore at nearby Radford University, majoring in Speech Communication.

Right now, she was having no problems communicating with Jeff.

When she left their table to return to the bar, Syd watched Jeff's eyes as they discreetly moved up and down her retreating back.

She sighed. "Isn't she a little young—even for you?"

He looked at her with surprise. "What do you mean?" He slapped his menu down on the table in exasperation. "Give me *some* credit, Syd. I was just being friendly." He picked up his frosted pilsner glass and took a healthy sip of beer. Syd noticed that he wasn't wearing his wedding band.

"Why don't we cut to the chase? What do you really want?"

He sat back and folded his arms. "What do you think I want?"

"Frankly, I have no idea."

"Why are you being like this?"

"Like what?"

He waved his hand. "*This.* So prickly. I don't deserve it."

She considered that. "Okay. Tell me what you do deserve."

He leaned forward. "I think I deserve another chance. Look, I fucked up, and I know that. I'm sorry. Sorrier than I can say. I don't want to lose you over something that didn't even matter to me."

She sat in silence for a moment, letting his words hang in the air between them. "It's that last part that's the problem. I believe you when you say that your various dalliances didn't matter to you—that's what makes them even more impossible for me to forgive or overlook."

He lifted his hands in supplication. "I don't understand."

She sighed. "I know you don't." She poured a splash of Pellegrino over her tumbler of ice. "The fact that you could be unfaithful to me so easily—so many times—with women who didn't even matter to you is what makes your behavior so intolerable. If your heart wasn't engaged with them, it certainly wasn't engaged with me."

He leaned back against the padded seat. "That's not true. You know that our physical relationship was never really what I needed it to be."

She stiffened.

He shook his head in frustration. "It was hard for me. I know I screwed up, but I should think you'd be happy that I never really got involved with any of them. It was all just harmless. Just me being stupid." He looked at her with puppy dog eyes. "I always loved you. I never wanted us to end up like this."

For just a moment, he resembled the man she had met so many years ago at her parents' home in Towson.

"I know you didn't. I didn't either." She sighed. "But here is where we are. And here is where I need to stay." He started to protest, but she stopped him with a raised palm. "I could never trust you again. I know that. And you should respect what I am doing to try and make a new life for myself."

"And this is your idea of a new life?" He waved his hand at the landscape visible outside the windows. "A two-bit town full of rednecks who probably can't even read the books you're shelving? Come on, Syd. I *know* you. This isn't the kind of life you want."

Her patience with him was waning. "I don't think you have the first clue about the kind of life I want. And don't be so quick to judge. You don't know anything about the people who live here. I've already made better friends here than I ever had in Durham."

"I don't doubt that."

"What's that supposed to mean?" It was against her better judgment to ask, but she took the bait anyway.

"Oh, come on. You don't seriously think I missed the chemistry between you and Dr. Tall, Dark, and Deadly?" He flexed his fingers to make air quotes. "Not that I blame you. She's a real beauty. I'd be tempted myself."

Syd placed her napkin on the table and regarded him coldly. "Am I supposed to know what you're talking about?"

He met her level gaze. "I think you know exactly what I'm talking about."

Syd dug a five-dollar bill out of her wallet and laid it on the table next to her glass. "Trying to make me responsible for your behavior is pathetic, but at least, it's consistent." She collected her keys and stood up. "I'm glad I agreed to meet you here, Jeff. It was great confirmation for me." He reached out a hand to stop her, but she drew back. "Don't waste your time—or mine." She glanced toward the bar to see Randi headed toward their table. "Enjoy your beer."

She walked out. He didn't follow her.

Outside in her car, she cursed herself over and over for her stupidity. *What did I think would come of this? He's never going to change.* She started the car and left the parking lot with no idea about where to go.

If she was honest with herself, she knew that her real motivation for agreeing to meet him was somehow tied to a desire to flee. But what was she trying to escape? Jericho? That made no sense. Jericho *was* her escape.

Her future hung in the distance, formless and murky. Once her work at the branch was complete, she had no idea what direction she would take. Going back to Jeff and her life in Durham would have simplified everything. But ten minutes in his company reminded her of all the reasons why she had left him in the first place.

And then there were his vague insinuations about her friendship with Maddie. It wasn't the first time that he had made retaliatory suggestions like that—usually in response to her rejection of his sexual advances. It infuriated her that he continued to lay the blame for their uneven physical relationship solely at her feet.

The on-ramp for the highway and a twenty-minute ride back to the library was just ahead of her. Impulsively changing her mind, she continued on past the interchange, and headed toward a shopping center where a brand new Wal-Mart Superstore rode the horizon like a three-masted ship of state.

Maddie was sprawled in front of the small gas fireplace in her bedroom sitting area, reading. Correction: trying to read. She had reread the same paragraph *five* times. In frustration, she tossed the journal down on the coffee table. *Who cares about functional dyspepsia? Eat some damn Rolaids.* She sighed and stared at the small mantle clock. 8:25. *I wonder if she's home yet?* She cast her eyes around the room, trying to think of some other way to distract herself from her obsessive clock-watching.

Her eyes fell back to the coffee table, where an open brochure advertised the upcoming AMA conference in Richmond. She picked it up and looked for the hundredth time at the glossy photo of the keynote speaker. That was *another* thing that didn't make sense to her. She tossed the brochure back down and sat, tapping her foot in agitation. *What a loser. I'm gonna take Pete out for a stroll then go to bed.* She slid her long legs off the chaise and stood up just as her cell phone vibrated. She snapped it up from the pedestal table next to her chair and flipped it open.

It was a text message—from Syd.

R U still awake?

Smiling to herself, she quickly typed back.

Yep.

She hit the send button, then sat down to wait for Syd's reply. A bit later, her phone vibrated again.

Up 4 a chat?

Now curious and a tad concerned, Maddie quickly answered.

Sure. Where are you?

A few moments later, her doorbell rang.

Pete raced ahead of her down the stairs and danced back and forth in front of the big front door, barking. Shushing him, Maddie flipped on the front porch light and unlocked the door. Through an etched glass panel, she could see Syd, casually perched on the arm of an Adirondack chair. There was a canvas shopping bag at her feet.

Maddie pulled the big door open and addressed her through the screen. "If you're finally here with my pizza, you need to know that you're about three-and-a-half hours late." She pushed the screen door open, and Pete rushed outside with his tail wagging. "This is going to seriously eat into the size of your tip."

Syd sat affectionately, scrubbing the top of Pete's head. She looked up to meet Maddie's eyes. "If a pizza is the price of admission, then I'm screwed." She lifted the canvas bag at her feet and held it out to Maddie. "Will this work as well?"

Maddie took the bag from her and burst into laughter when she looked inside. It contained a bottle of MacMurray Pinot Noir and a large bag of Cheetos—the crunchy ones.

"I apologize for just showing up this way. I needed a shoulder." Syd stood up as Pete vaulted off the porch and headed for the pond. "I promise not to make a habit of this."

Maddie set the bag down and stepped forward to pull Syd into a hug. "This shoulder will always be available to you." She smiled as she felt Syd's arms wrap around her waist. "And you already figured out your co-pay," she muttered into Syd's hair.

Syd drew back and looked at her with a confused expression.

Maddie reached into the bag and held up the Cheetos. "I might be cheap, but I'm not free."

Rolling her eyes, Syd pushed past her and walked into the house.

Smiling, Maddie followed her inside and closed the big front door. They walked down the long center hallway toward the kitchen.

Syd took off her leather jacket and draped it over a straight-backed chair. "Got anything to eat?"

Maddie raised an eyebrow.

"I'm afraid I didn't last long enough to order any food."

Maddie went to the big Subzero and pulled open a door. "Funny you should mention that. I seem to have missed dinner myself. Let's see what we've got in here." She began to rummage around, shifting through a myriad of plastic containers.

Syd stood beside her, and they peered into the massive depths of the fridge together.

"My god," Syd said, incredulous. "Don't you *ever* cook?" She looked up at Maddie. "You're a doctor, yet you have about the least healthy eating habits of anyone I know." She picked up a round container of pimento cheese spread and held it up like Exhibit A. "I'm surprised no one has ever ratted you out to the union."

"You're joking, right?" Maddie crossed her arms. "There isn't a physician on the planet who hasn't subsisted on a diet of doughnuts and Ramen noodles. We invented the whole 'do as I say, not as I do' credo."

Syd shoved her out of the way. "Yeah? Great. Then do as I say and go find a place to perch while I sort through this recycling nightmare." She began to pull random ingredients out and stack them on a nearby counter. "What's your excuse for not eating dinner?"

Maddie pulled a corkscrew out of a drawer and began to open the bottle of Pinot Noir. She shrugged. "I dunno, just preoccupied. I wasn't really hungry when I got home, and by the time it occurred to me to eat, I was already past caring."

She cast a concerned glance at Syd. "How about you? You gonna tell me what happened at your non-dinner?"

"Oh sure." Syd turned around. "That'll take all of two seconds." She walked to the center island and began to wash some spinach leaves and a big tomato in the prep sink. "Got a pair of kitchen shears handy?"

Maddie opened a drawer and waved her hand across its contents. "Take your pick."

Syd gasped as she looked inside at the neatly displayed array of culinary gadgets. She looked up at Maddie in surprise.

"Don't look at me. I told you—Dad was the chef." Maddie scrunched her eyebrows as she peered into the drawer. "I did a standard surgical rotation, but I confess that I have no idea what half of this stuff is. It looks to me like the contents of Jack the Ripper's tool box."

Syd withdrew a large pair of stainless steel kitchen shears. "Well, take these and walk outside to that impressive winter herb garden and get me a few sprigs of basil and oregano." She pulled out a garlic press before closing the drawer.

"Yes, ma'am," Maddie complied and headed for the porch door. She smiled as she walked outside and descended the steps that led to her father's lean-to greenhouse. *This would please him. I'm glad that Miguel has kept this up.* She resolved to give her landscaper a raise.

The tiny greenhouse was dark, but balmy, and there was enough moonlight to make it easy to locate the right plants. After snipping off a few leaves of each, she turned back toward the kitchen.

On impulse, she walked around the big porch to the front door. Pete met her at the top of the steps. Inside, she ducked into the front parlor and turned on the CD player. Once it spooled up, Alfred Brendel began grunting his way through a Mozart sonata. She smiled to herself as she stood in the center of the room and raised the fresh herbs to her face. The music and the aroma of the plants reminded her of her childhood—of an earlier time, when evenings like this one were typical. A time before everything fell apart. The music. Her mother's music. And down the hallway, her mother and her father would be together in the kitchen, cooking and talking about their days at work. She shook her head. *How did all of that change so fast?*

She continued to stand there. The cartoon-like colors of the Chagall print mocked her with their playful optimism. *And now, here I am again. But Dad's gone.* And although her mother was still alive, she was gone, too.

She raised her head when she caught a whiff of garlic. Syd was sautéing garlic.

And here she is.

Jesus. I'm in trouble.

She walked back toward the kitchen with Pete in tow.

Syd was at the island, chopping the tomato. The spinach leaves were washed and drying on paper towels. On the stove, the garlic sizzled in a flat pan, and a large pot of water was heating on a back burner.

Maddie handed her the herbs. "I see you found your way around." She picked up two wine glasses and poured them each a hefty portion of the Pinot.

Syd took the glass Maddie held out and they clinked rims. "I hope that's okay. Everything was pretty easy to find."

Maddie grinned. "It's more than okay. I think my dad is probably up there smiling right now." She hesitated, and then she stepped forward and kissed Syd lightly on the cheek. "He'd like you." She stepped back and took a sip of her wine. "I'm glad you're here."

Syd stood quietly for a moment. The only sounds in the room were the sizzle of the garlic, and a rapid-fire succession of notes from the *Alla Turca* rondo. She smiled shyly at Maddie and took a sip from her own glass. "Me, too."

Syd's concoction turned out to be wonderful. *Aglio e Olio* with garlic, spinach, and tomatoes—all topped with fresh Parmesan. Maddie was in transports as the intoxicating smells wafted about the kitchen. When it was ready, she took two deep pasta bowls off a shelf and handed them to Syd.

"Let's take these into Dad's study to eat. It's got a small gas fireplace that heats up in two shakes." She picked up their wine glasses and utensils and hovered over the stove as Syd divided the pasta between their bowls. "If this tastes even half as good as it smells, I'm going to have to marry you." Syd looked up at her, and Maddie nodded. "That's right. You'll just have to give up your day job."

Syd smiled. "That sure would simplify concerns about my immediate future."

Maddie bumped her playfully. "Yeah, well, we'll get to that, too. But for now, just hurry the hell up. I'm starving."

"You've got the patience of a gnat, you know that?" Syd set the now-empty pot down in the sink and splashed some water into it. She picked up the two pasta bowls and faced the doorway. "Lead on."

"Goodie." Maddie led them into a small sitting room off the main hallway.

It was dominated by a massive oak desk, but also held two comfortable-looking club chairs with matching side tables. The walls of the walnut-paneled room were lined with overflowing floor-to-ceiling bookcases. Books were stacked on every available surface—even the deep windowsill. There were framed diplomas and photos hanging on every exposed bit of wall space.

"Have a seat," Maddie instructed, as she set their wine glasses and utensils down on the tables. She walked to the small fireplace and knelt to turn on its gas jet. She pressed the igniter, a telltale pop sounded, and the opening filled with warm blue flames. As she sat down in one of the chairs, Syd handed her a bowl heaped with the fragrant pasta mixture. Gleefully, she wound a few strands around her fork and took a bite. Her eyes rolled back into her head.

"God. Fuck Cheetos. Who needs sex when there's food like this?"

Syd slowly chewed her own first bite. "I guess that depends on what you're used to."

Maddie took another bite. She regarded her with interest. "Meaning?"

Syd shrugged. "A good meal can only get you so far." She twirled her fork with practiced ease.

"Color me intrigued. Does our demure and girlish librarian have a checkered past?"

Syd glared at her. "You're not going to start with all that Sandra Dee crap again, are you?"

Maddie put her fork down and raised her free hand in surrender. "Nuh uh. Been there, bought the t-shirt. I think you've already established your . . . credentials." She picked up her wine glass.

"Well, you know what they say—it ain't the years, it's the mileage."

Maddie choked on her wine.

"Wimp." Syd picked up her own glass. "Wanna rethink those Cheetos?"

"Do you and David have some kind of job-sharing arrangement that I'm not privy to, or is it just a perverse twist of fate that I ended up with both of you in my orbit?"

Syd laughed. "Poor baby. Are we really that hard on you?"

"He's pathological, so it isn't really his fault. You, on the other hand, have no excuse."

"I don't?"

"Not from where I sit."

"Hmmm." Syd tapped the edge of her bowl with her index finger. "There's really only one response I can make to a statement like that."

Maddie gave her a suspicious look. "What's that?"

"Change your seat."

"Oh *great*. Already the two of you function like some kind of twisted incarnation of the Bobbsey Twins." She took a big sip from her wine glass. "Soon you'll start dressing alike. It's going to get ugly. I just might have to go off the grid."

"*Off the grid?* Who are you? Jason Bourne? And I can think of worse fates to befall me than having to share David's wardrobe."

Maddie snorted. "Yeah. You'd look fetching in that magenta smoking jacket."

"I was thinking more along the lines of that red cocktail dress. How fetching would I look in that little number?"

Maddie was silent for a moment, as images of Syd wearing the low-cut ensemble raced around inside her head. She needed to step off this gerbil wheel before things got any worse. "Well, I wouldn't recommend the shoes—the enhanced altitude might give you a nosebleed."

Syd's jaw dropped. "Smartass. *Your* usefulness to the species went south when they invented the stepladder." She paused. "And while we're on the subject of genetic abnormalities, just exactly how tall *are* you?"

Maddie sat up straighter. "Five feet, twelve inches—barefoot."

"Five feet, twelve inches?"

Maddie nodded.

"You're *six* feet tall?"

Maddie fixed her with a deadpan expression. "I'll bet you were the unbridled star of math camp."

Syd threw her napkin at her. "*Math* camp? I think you have my past confused with yours. Remember, I'm the one who spent my summers by the shore—tanning, surfing, and having carnal knowledge of brawny young men."

Maddie sighed. "That's right. I forgot. Your mantra was 'If it swells, ride it.'"

Syd gave her a withering look. "You're not half as funny as you think you are." She set her empty bowl down on the table between their chairs. "If I didn't know better, I'd think you were jealous."

"You're more right than you realize."

Smiling, Syd stood up and walked to stand before a large, framed object that hung on the wall just above the desk.

"What is this?" she asked, peering at it from close range. "It looks like part of a shirt."

"It is." Maddie got up to stand just behind her. "My dad was a pilot. It's customary to have the back of your shirt cut out the first time you solo. Your instructors mark it up with the date and the aircraft specifics, and tack it to the hangar wall until you get your private license." She reached around Syd and pointed at the writing on the lower left corner of the yellowed square of fabric.

"That's amazing." Syd leaned closer. "What's *N2527K*?"

"That was the tail number of the plane he soloed in. I'm pretty sure it was a Cessna 152—the workhorse of private aviation."

Syd turned to Maddie. "No wonder your old room upstairs is full of airplane photos. I wondered about that."

"Yeah. We're a bunch of total aviation nerds." She gave Syd a wistful smile. "I always loved flying with Dad—he was a natural."

"I know you miss him."

"I really do. It just doesn't get any easier."

"Some things aren't meant to. You'll probably always miss him as much as you do right now."

Maddie nodded. "But let's shift gears here and talk about you." She walked back to her chair and sat down. "I want to hear about your ill-fated encounter with Jeff."

"Oh, god. I guess I do owe you an explanation for showing up and commandeering your evening." She sat back down and picked up her wine glass. "Is there any more of this? It might help me feel a bit less mortified."

Maddie picked up the bottle and refilled her glass. "There's no reason to feel mortified, and if you'd rather not talk about it, that's totally okay."

"No. It's fine. I *want* to talk about it, I'm just embarrassed. I don't know what I was thinking when I agreed to meet him. I mean, he was ogling our waitress within five minutes of sitting down." She shook her head. "And then he had the gall to suggest that I—" She looked up to meet Maddie's concerned gaze. "Never mind. It doesn't even bear repeating." She took a sip from her wine glass. "Suffice it to say that all of our original issues are alive and kicking. He said some things that really pissed me off, and I'm afraid I stormed out on him."

Maddie was puzzled. "Really? You don't strike me as the storming-out type."

Syd met her gaze. "You don't know what he said."

"That's true."

They looked at each other in silence for a few moments. Then Syd let out a slow breath and shrugged. "Oh, what the hell. He tried to suggest that I wasn't interested in reconciling because of my friendship with you."

"Me?" Maddie was stunned . . . and alarmed. Her thoughts spiraled back to the night Jeff showed up at the library unannounced. There had been a fleeting moment when she thought he might be sizing her up as a potential rival but she had quickly dismissed that idea as being ridiculous, and a product of her overactive imagination. Now, she wasn't so sure.

"Yeah. How absurd is that?" Syd asked. "It infuriated me. Jeff has always blamed our . . . issues on what he chooses to define as *my* ambivalence toward intimacy."

Maddie's heartbeat was accelerating at an unhealthy rate. She could barely take in what she was hearing, and she had no idea how to respond. Syd was regarding her with an earnest and open expression, and Maddie knew she had to say something. "Well . . . that hardly seems like a characterization that's consistent with your life prior to marriage."

"It isn't. But you have to know Jeff. In *his* world, any woman who doesn't immediately want to hop into bed with him has to be demented—or gay." She sighed in frustration. "Of course, once our relationship hit the skids, that axiom was expanded to include me."

"He thinks you're gay?" Maddie was tempted to stab herself in the thigh with her fork just to be sure she was awake and not caught up in some torturous nightmare.

"He thinks *any* woman who doesn't want to sleep with him is gay."

"I still don't see how I factor into this equation." Maddie knew it was a mistake to ask, but she had to know what Jeff said about her to Syd.

Syd lowered her gaze. "He seemed to think that . . . well . . . He found you extremely attractive. And in his book, if *he* finds you attractive then it must mean that I do, too."

The tingling between her ears was getting worse. Maddie was certain she was blushing. "He thinks that we're . . . ?"

"In a nutshell. Yeah." She raised her eyes and saw the distressed look on Maddie's face. "God, I'm sorry." She tentatively touched Maddie's knee. "I must have been crazy to tell you all of this. I should've kept my mouth shut. I never meant to offend you."

Maddie recovered enough to pat Syd's hand with her own. "I'm not at all offended. Honest." She forced a shy smile. "If anything, I should be complimented. It's not often that I get cast as the third part of a triangle." She sucked on the inside of her cheek. "Can you imagine David's reaction?"

"Oh god." Syd covered her face with both hands. "Don't even think about telling him. I'd die of embarrassment."

"You would? Now that's a darn shame." She gave a dramatic sigh. "I sort of liked the idea that I might be the object of fantasy for someone."

Syd peeked at her between her fingers, and then lowered her hands. "You're joking, right? At last count, you had a string of lovesick admirers that stretched from here to the state line."

"Oh, pshaw."

"Did you actually just say *pshaw*?" Syd asked, sounding incredulous.

Maddie glowered at her.

"No, really. You *did*. You said pshaw."

"So what if I did? It doesn't make your insinuation any less ridiculous."

"Ridiculous? You're so clueless. You have no idea how many poor, pathetic people are out there pining for you."

"*Pathetic* would be the operative word, too."

Syd crossed her arms. "Oh, so anyone who finds you irresistible is classified as pathetic?"

"Pretty much."

"Well then it's a good thing I'm *not* gay because if I were, I'd surely be at the top of your list of rejects."

Maddie's stomach suddenly felt like it was doing back-flips. She needed to get this conversation back on solid ground, and soon. "I wouldn't say that."

"You wouldn't?"

"No. In your case, I might be inclined to make an exception."

Syd narrowed her eyes. "Why's that?"

Maddie held up her empty pasta bowl. "I'd never reject the hands that fed me." She winked and gave Syd her best smile. "Whatcha do for an encore, blondie?"

"We *are* still talking about food, right?"

"Were you in any doubt?"

"I'm slowly learning that with you, it's always safer to ask."

"Then, yes. We're still talking about food."

Syd stood up and collected their bowls. "Let's go see what else we can cobble together from your vault of shrink-wrapped delights."

Maddie stood up, too. "Now *I'm* confused. Are you talking about my freezer or my bedside table?"

"Pervert," Syd muttered, as she left the study and headed for the kitchen.

Chapter 8

On the Saturday morning before Thanksgiving, Michael Robertson made an impromptu visit to the Jericho Public Library. The main study area was choked with high school students. They were clustered around several oak tables in the reference area, pouring over encyclopedias and competing for access to the library's four computers. He recognized the inevitable Roma Jean Freemantle behind the circulation desk. She was engaged in an animated telephone conversation, but she waved excitedly at him as he approached. He found Syd at the back of the facility enmeshed in trying to un-jam a photocopier. Piles of torn and crumpled up paper surrounded her. The entire front panel was at her feet. Syd was on her knees and had one arm buried shoulder-deep inside the unit. Michael could hear her soft curses as he approached from behind.

"Come on you sorry piece of shit. I so do not need this today."

Michael laughed as he stopped to stand just beside her. "Well, lucky for you, I have the perfect antidote."

Syd jerked at the sound of his voice and banged her head on an open paper drawer as she quickly sat upright. "Damn it." She raised her free hand to rub the top of her head as she turned to him. "Michael. What a pleasant surprise. I hope by antidote, you mean that you know how to fix this thing."

He slowly shook his head. "Not even close. Honey, if it isn't attached to a KitchenAid mixer, I happily abide in ignorance."

"Great." She pulled her arm free and sat back, still rubbing the top of her head. "Where am I going to find someone who can service this thing on a Saturday? I've had over a dozen calls already this morning from people asking if it's fixed yet." She waved her hand toward the throng of teenagers up front. "It's term paper time, and, apparently, the unit in the post office has been broken for about nine years."

"Desperate times call for desperate measures. You might have to break down and throw yourself on the mercy of the county's resident fix-it wizard."

"We have one of those?" Syd extended a hand and let Michael pull her to her feet. "I'm desperate, *and* out of time. Who do I need to call, and how much do I need to pay him?"

"The fee is usually negotiable. But I've always had great success bartering for repairs with food."

"Really?"

"Yep. In fact, I just might be able to help you out. The reason I stopped by is to ask if you want to play guinea pig tonight. I'm doing a dress rehearsal for Thursday's haute cuisine. Since it's your parents I'll be cooking for, I wondered if you'd like to join us to sample the fare?"

Syd grinned. "You don't have to ask me twice. I'd love that."

"Swell."

"But I don't see how this helps me out with my copier—unless you're offering to supply me with leftovers to use as bargaining chips?"

"Not exactly. I was thinking more along the lines of inviting the tool jockey, too."

Syd looked confused. "Just who is this mysterious Mr. Fix-It?"

Michael held up an index finger. "That'd be *Dr.* Fix-It."

Syd's mouth fell open. "You have got to be kidding me?"

"Afraid not. That woman can fix anything. Don't tell me you failed to notice that she has about twenty broken vacuum cleaners stockpiled in her garage?"

Syd stared at him. "You're right. I *did* notice that the first time I went out there but I was so overwhelmed by everything else, I didn't really think much about it."

He nodded. "There you go."

"Good lord. When on earth does she find time to work on them?"

He shrugged. "Beats me. I don't think she ever sleeps."

Syd shook her head. "I wonder why the post office hasn't called her."

"She won't do government work."

Syd rolled her eyes.

He pushed his glasses up his nose with an index finger. "Look at the bright side: she's totally set up with an alternative career if we ever pass socialized medicine."

"True. I don't suppose there are many places you can go to have your Electrolux rebuilt by a Stanford grad."

He nodded. "Possibly our one claim to fame." He glanced at his watch. "I've gotta run if I'm going to make it to the butcher shop in Wytheville before noon. Do you wanna join us at the Inn around six-thirty? We'll have cocktails before dinner."

"I'll be there." She gave him an affectionate smile. "Thanks for thinking of me. I suppose it's pointless for me to ask if I can bring anything?"

"Well, if you catch up with her before we do, you can bring Ms. Goodwrench. Otherwise, just bring your sweet self. And dress casual. It's just going to be the four of us."

"Casual?"

"I think David's wearing a peignoir set."

"God, I love you guys." She stepped forward and kissed the big man on the cheek. "See you tonight."

Michael was loading a large bucket of cut flowers and a couple of canvas shopping bags into the Inn's white Range Rover when he saw Maddie walk out of the Dunkin' Donuts across the parking lot from Gladys Pitzer's shop. She was wearing bright blue scrubs and carrying a large cup of coffee. Smiling, he let fly with a loud wolf whistle and waited for her to notice him.

She did. Shaking her head, she walked toward him.

He pulled her into a full-body hug, being careful not to spill her coffee. "Hi ya, hot stuff. I didn't know you worked this side of town."

She smiled against his shoulder. "Only on Saturdays." She stepped back. "I just finished seeing patients at the hospital. What's your excuse?"

He picked up the white bucket loaded with flowers and foliage. "Well, as it happens, I'm cooking tonight, and you're invited." He stashed the bucket in the back of the Rover and closed its door. *Riverside Inn* was neatly stenciled across the side of the vehicle.

"Great." She took a sip of her coffee. "What's the occasion?"

"We've got a full boat for dinner on Thursday, and I want to do a dry-run on the currant- and cornbread-stuffed goose." He paused. "Bad choice of words. *Dry* is exactly what I want to avoid."

She smiled. "I'm sure it'll be fabulous."

"I dunno. I don't have the best track record with goose, and since I'll be cooking for the redoubtable Mrs. Murphy, I want it to be perfect."

"Why not switch the menu to something you *are* more comfortable with?"

"Because, my dear. Your future mother-in-law was *very* specific about what constituted a traditional Thanksgiving Day meal. She practically clipped recipes for me."

Maddie looked confused. "*My* future . . ." Comprehension spread across her features. "I'm really going to kill the two of you if you don't knock this shit off."

Michael just laughed at her. "Lighten up, will you?" He kissed her on the forehead. "You're so cute when you're miserable."

"Well, as long as my misery can lighten someone else's burden, I guess it serves a purpose."

He stood there, regarding her. "Do you really want to stay away from her?"

She met his eyes. "No."

He nodded. "Hang in there. It might all just work out the way you want it to."

"To tell the truth, I have no idea what I want."

"Don't you?" He held her gaze.

She relented. "Okay. Maybe I know what I *want*, but what I want usually ends up being the opposite of what I need."

"You aren't alone in that one, sweetheart. It's all a crap shoot. Sometimes, we just get lucky."

She sighed. "Are we talking about life, or about Rolling Stones lyrics?"

He laughed. "Both. So, you wanna join us for dinner?"

"Sure. Who are the other lab rats?"

He just looked at her.

She threw her head back. "Oh, *man*. You really are trying to kill me, aren't you?"

"No, just feed you. Look, it's just dinner. We're not going to play spin-the-bottle, or get drunk and swap room keys."

"Right. And do you think you can promise to keep David muzzled?"

"You're on your own with that one, sister," Michael said. "The last time I tried that, we ended up playing some really twisted boudoir games."

"I didn't mean it literally."

"Oh. My bad." He gave her a wistful look. "But he did look cute all tied up. He was stunned when he realized later that I used his Hermès scarf."

"Beyond being appalled by the charming visual image this summons up, I'm stunned to learn that he *has* a Hermès scarf."

"You know our boy."

"Indeed I do. What time do you want me there?"

"How's six-thirty? And if you stop by the library to rescue your damsel in distress, you can bring her along with you."

Maddie looked perplexed. "What do you mean? Why does she need rescuing?"

"Her copier is on the fritz. She was up to her shapely elbows in toner and cursing like a sailor when I stopped by there this morning."

"What's wrong with it?"

He gave her an incredulous look. "You're asking *me* this question? That's your department. You need to pack up your socket wrenches and roar on over there. I told her she needed to call you, so she won't be surprised to see you if you drop by."

"Okay. I suppose I could go take a look at her on my way home." She caught her mistake. "*It.* I mean it." She gave up, and smiled at him sheepishly. "I'll check it out."

He chucked her on the chin before climbing into his car. "I'm *sure* you will." He started the engine. "See you tonight, sweet pea."

Maddie stood there, watching him drive away. *So much for a quiet evening at home. God, when was the last time I even spent a night by myself?*

When the white Rover left the parking lot and pulled out onto the main road, she slowly turned and walked to her Jeep, marveling at the turn her life had taken since Syd's arrival in Jericho. *It's not like we look for opportunities. We just always seem to end up thrown together.*

She unlocked the Jeep, climbed inside, and set her coffee in the console holder between the front seats. *But it's not like I mind, either.* She smiled to herself. An idea she'd had percolating for a few weeks came to mind again. She decided to go ahead and ask Syd about it.

Maybe tonight. *Tonight. Jesus. David. He'll be impossible. I must be crazy.* She started the Jeep. *I am crazy.* She drove out of the parking lot and headed west toward Jericho.

Syd was elated when the front door to the library opened and she saw Maddie, dressed in blue scrubs, stride across the carpet toward her. Maddie was carrying a small, aluminum toolbox. When she reached the circulation desk, she set the box down and calmly regarded her.

"Does something here need a doctor?"

"As a matter of fact, yes. But I didn't realize that you made house calls." She crossed her arms. "How much is this gonna cost me?"

Maddie scratched her chin thoughtfully. "How much you got back there in petty cash?"

Syd backed up, pulled open a drawer, and sifted through its contents. "About four dollars and seventy-five cents. In quarters." She looked up at Maddie hopefully. "Will that be enough?"

"Hmmm. Lucky for you, I'm not really licensed to practice here, so I can be flexible about my fee."

"What if I sweeten the deal and let you be the first person in the county to check out a copy of—" she reached behind her chair to an overloaded book truck and randomly snagged a volume, "*Glenn Beck's Common Sense?*"

Maddie raised an eyebrow.

"You're right." Syd tossed the volume back onto the truck. "I should pay you double-time just for having the gall to suggest that." She smiled at her. "I take it you heard my tale of woe from Michael?"

"Something like that. I ran into him in Wytheville after making patient calls at the hospital. He told me that he saw you over here going fifteen rounds with your photocopier."

"I couldn't quite go the distance—the damn thing had me on the ropes in about a nanosecond."

"Well, don't throw in the towel just yet. Maybe there's some life left in it."

Syd stood there deliberating for a minute. Then she shook her head. "Sorry, I've completely exhausted all the boxing metaphors I know. Will you take a look at it anyway?"

Maddie lifted her toolbox. "I make no promises but lead on."

They walked to the rear of the building.

"I had no idea that you were such an accomplished repairman. I now understand why you have broken vacuum cleaners strewn all over your garage."

Maddie laughed. "It's true. Remember I told you about taking my mother's piano apart? What I *didn't* tell you was that I generally could get things back together pretty well, too. Dad and I usually had something we were breaking down and rebuilding—lawnmowers, tractors, airplane engines—the list went on and on."

Syd stopped her. "Did you just say airplane engines?"

"Yeah. Why?"

"The mental image of an airplane engine lying in pieces around your barn doesn't help ameliorate my morbid fear of flying."

Maddie set her toolbox down next to the still disassembled copier. "You just haven't flown with the right person." She knelt next to the copier. "So tell me what happened here."

Syd sighed. "Beats me. Roma Jean was copying some inventory sheets for me when it jammed. Instead of stopping it, she kept hitting the copy button." She rolled her eyes. "Half a ream of paper later, it shut itself off and hasn't booted-up since. I tried to un-jam it but I think there still must be paper caught someplace that I can't access."

"You're probably right. Has it been disconnected from its primary power supply?"

Syd stood there regarding her with a deadpan expression. "Why do you repair types always lapse into this obfuscated techno-speak when you're around us mere mortals?"

Maddie sighed. "Is it unplugged?"

Syd knelt and held up the three-pronged end of a fat power cable. "Yep."

"Okay." Maddie squatted next to the unit and pulled out the two paper trays. She flipped a series of concealed green levers inside the machine that unlocked the roller assemblies. She stood up and did the same thing beneath the platform at the output door. The side panel dropped down and a wad of crinkled paper was visible, wedged beneath the feed tires. She opened her toolbox and took out a pair of long tweezers. She carefully extracted the accordion-shaped wads of paper.

"Once we get all of this out of here, we need to look at the pick-off fingers. It might be that the separator is pulling in more than one sheet at a time. What weight paper are you running in this?"

"What?" Syd was watching Maddie with fascination. "I'm sorry. I'm just amazed that you knew how to do this. You said something about finger picks?"

Maddie laughed. "Pick-off fingers. They're those little grabbers that snag the individual sheets of paper from the trays. They can get clogged with dust and paper fiber and don't work properly. What kind of paper are you using in this thing?"

Syd picked up a crumpled wad. "White?"

Maddie pulled the last piece of crushed paper away from the rollers. "Well, that's a start. Do you have one of the unopened packages?" She began to lock everything back into place as Syd walked to a shelf and retrieved an unopened ream of the paper.

"Here it is." She read from the edge of the package. "500 sheets. Bright white. Smooth finish. 20#." She looked up. "Does that tell you anything?"

Maddie nodded. "Yep. It's *cheap*. You need to run at least a 24# weight in these things or they get really cranky. This lighter-weight stuff is very prone to curling—especially if you store too much of it in the trays." She slid the two paper trays back into place after removing about half of the paper from each one. "How many reams of this stuff do you have left?"

Syd looked behind them at the storage shelf. "About five."

"Maybe you can call your supplier and exchange it for the heavier weight. If not, just keep the trays about a third full until you run through it all. It also will help if you keep the unopened reams in a cardboard box. Don't ask me why, but they seem to resist curling better if they're stored that way. I think it's some kind of humidor effect." She paused. "You could keep your cigars in there, too."

Syd gave her a blank look.

"Just seeing if you were still paying attention." She stood up. "Okay. Let's plug 'er in and see what happens."

Syd plugged in the unit, and Maddie pushed its power button. After a second, it beeped, and the display panel illuminated. The readout panel flashed its *ready to copy* message.

Syd's jaw dropped. "I so do not believe this."

Maddie stood back and regarded her with a smug expression. "That's nothing. You should see me fix a broken person."

They were quiet for a moment.

Syd gave her a small smile. "Would that cost me more than four dollars and seventy-five cents?"

Maddie's blue eyes searched her face. "You aren't broken."

Syd shrugged. "Opinions on that vary."

They stared at each other.

Maddie opened her mouth to speak. They swung around at a loud crash. The back door to the branch stood wide open, and a red-faced Roma Jean Freemantle was splayed across the floor next to an upturned waste can. She was staring up at Maddie in embarrassment and dismay.

Maddie and Syd looked at each other for a moment before smiling and walking back to help Roma Jean to her feet.

Michael had set a table for the four of them in front of the stone fireplace located at the back of the dining room, close to the kitchen. A smattering of guests dined at other tables spread out across the room, but, typically, business was slow during the days leading up to the holiday weekend, so they were able to relax and enjoy a leisurely meal.

Apart from the stuffed goose, which was anything but dry, Michael served whole green beans tossed with toasted hazelnuts and brown butter, wildflower honey- and whiskey-glazed sweet potatoes, a pineapple and roasted poblano salsa, and zucchini and cranberry mini-muffins. Most of the dinner conversation was confined to talking about the food with Syd in a state of bliss about getting to experience it all again on Thursday evening.

Maddie pushed her plate away with dramatic intensity. "Make it stop. I can't eat another bite."

David plucked half of an uneaten muffin off her plate and popped it into his mouth. "So that would mean that you are *not* interested in sampling a piece of that chocolate, cashew, and *maple* pie I saw cooling back there in the kitchen?"

Maddie frowned as she seemed to consider her options. "I could maybe manage a tiny slice."

"You're such a weakling."

Maddie looked him over. "This from a man wearing pink socks?"

"I refuse to be goaded by someone who blithely conflates fashion sense with femininity." He took a healthy sip of his Chardonnay. "You're a cretinous lout with the aesthetic sensibility of a Weimaraner."

"A Weimaraner?"

David sat back and regarded her. "Tall. Aloof. Blue eyes. Inordinately fond of flannel bedding." He batted his eyes at her. "Any of this sounding familiar?"

Maddie sighed. "I don't know why I agreed to do this. You always get so fractious during the holidays."

"Me?" David feigned umbrage. "You're the one with the whole *Mourning Becomes Electra* complex."

Maddie rolled her eyes. "I'm not even going to ask what you mean by that comment."

Michael chuckled as he stood up and started collecting their plates.

Syd looked back and forth between the two antagonists. "Okay. I'll bite." She turned to David. "Clearly, you're dying to explain."

Maddie groaned as David leaned forward lacing his fingers together. "Well, just let me point out that our dear, reclusive physician here is the one with the deep-seated, mother-daughter, Chlamydia-Electra family drama going on."

Maddie looked at him. "Chlamydia?"

"Duh," David replied. "Electra's mother?"

"That was *Clytemnestra*, you nimrod. Chlamydia is a venereal disease." She paused. "I should think that you, of all people, would remember that."

David stuck his tongue out at her as Syd stifled a cackle.

Michael walked back to their table, carrying the pie. "So, big slices all around?"

Syd expelled a deep breath. "My god, that looks amazing. Are you making another one of these on Thursday?"

"Sorry, sweet pea." Michael cut a generous piece and handed a plate to Syd. "Your mama was specific about wanting *pumpkin* pie. This one is something special for Dr. Strangelove, there. She just *loves* maple."

"That I do," Maddie said, holding out her dessert plate. "Hurry up and dish, Wolfgang."

"I thought you weren't hungry?" David asked.

"Shut up." Maddie dug into her pie with gusto.

David got up, went to the bar, and returned with a chilled bottle and four fluted glasses. "We picked up this really nice Shelton Blanc De Blanc when we were in North Carolina last week. It's gonna go great with dessert." He tore off the foil top and unscrewed the cage covering the cork. "We thought it might be nice for your folks to sample some of our finer Yadkin Valley wines." He popped the cork without ceremony and poured Syd a glass.

"You guys have gone to entirely too much trouble for my parents. I love you both for it but I'm afraid that you've really put yourselves out." She took a sip of the sparkling wine and smiled. "And if I drink much more of *this* wonderful stuff, I'll have to be poured into Maddie's Jeep."

"That goes double for me," Maddie said, covering the top of her champagne flute. "I can't have anything else, or I won't be able to drive us home."

Michael smiled at them. "Lucky for you, we happen to know the innkeepers. Why don't we just put you both up for the night? We've got a couple of empty rooms, so you can relax and enjoy yourselves."

Maddie looked nervously at Syd. "I don't know about that, Michael, we hadn't planned on a slumber party."

David batted her hand away from the top of her glass and poured her a generous serving of the wine. "Tomorrow is Sunday. The library is closed. The clinic is closed. With all due respect, you're both pathetic loners with nothing better to do than stay up late and watch reruns of *Storm Stories* on the Weather Channel."

"Pete—"

"Pete," David interrupted, "is probably already in the barn, sacked-out on the hood of your overpriced Lexus. Relax. Sit a spell." He winked at her, slyly, and dropped his voice. "Don't look a gift horse in the mouth."

She glowered at him. Then she cast a worried look at Syd, who sat watching the two of them with amusement. "What do you think?"

Syd handed her now empty champagne flute to David. "I'd like another glass, please."

David laughed as he refilled her glass. He locked eyes with Maddie as he sat back down. "Our kind of girl."

They spent the rest of the evening laughing and talking, moving from the dining room to the smaller, front parlor where they shared another bottle of the Shelton wine before agreeing that it was time to retire for the night.

Michael walked them up the grand staircase and down the wide center hallway to two smaller rooms at the back of the house. The rooms were tastefully appointed with period antiques and had dormer windows that looked out over the sloping back lawn. Unlike most of the Inn's larger rooms, these two shared a hall bathroom.

David joined them shortly, carrying two, folded sets of pajamas. "These should work for one night." He handed a pair to Syd. They were a soft and tasteful Nick & Nora creation, decorated with fat counting sheep on a pastel background. "And these are for you, Sawbones." He handed Maddie an oversized pair of faded red Dr. Denton's.

Maddie unfolded the pants. "If these have a drop-seat, I'm *so* outta here."

There was no drop-seat, but the pants had built-in booties.

"*Nice.*" She sighed as she draped the pants over her arm. "Why am I not surprised that you have these?"

"Quit complaining. It's more than you usually sleep in." He turned to Syd. "There are toiletries in a basket in each of your rooms. Help yourselves to whatever you need. We'll be out back in our annex. Give us a call on the house phone if you need anything you can't find." He glanced at Maddie, who stood there frowning as she refolded her red pajamas. "However, that's probably not likely to happen. Last time I looked under *her* hood, she was pretty well equipped."

Maddie looked up and stared at him in disbelief. "Are you off your Ritalin again?"

Syd chuckled quietly.

Michael shook his head and kissed Syd on the cheek. "Sleep tight, cutie pie. I'll see you at breakfast." He walked to the still smoldering Maddie, grabbed her, and dipped her back dramatically and planted a kiss full on her mouth. "G'night, hot lips." He stood up and released her, and then jerked his thumb at David. "C'mon, honey. Let's leave the girls alone now." Quietly whistling a refrain from "Meet Me In St. Louis," he strode off down the hallway toward the stairs.

David stood there a moment longer. "I've got a bad feeling about this."

"Why?" Syd asked.

"Whenever he whistles Judy Garland tunes it means there ain't gonna be much sleeping going on—if you get my drift."

Maddie raised a palm. "Okay, that's way too much information."

"You don't know the half of it. He's really horrifying as Mickey Rooney." David thought about that. "Even Mickey Rooney was horrifying as Mickey Rooney. I'm *so* not drunk enough for this tonight."

Maddie laid a reassuring hand on his shoulder. "Buck up, Judy. The show must go on."

He sighed. "You're right. I wonder where I left those shoulder pads?" He walked off toward the stairs, waving a hand over his head. " 'Night, ladies."

At the bottom of the stairs, he hit a switch and the lights went out, leaving Syd and Maddie standing together in near darkness. The only available light came from the blue glow cast by a small nightlight at the opposite end of the hallway. They heard a door open and close at the back of the house. Then it was deathly quiet—the only sound coming from the monotonous tick, tick, tick of the pendulum on the grandfather clock in the foyer below.

"This seems to happen a lot," Syd said.

Maddie considered that. "You mean being subjected to lurid details of David's private life?"

Syd laughed. "No. I mean that I seem to have acquired a remarkable ability to end up wearing someone else's pajamas."

"That's true." Maddie tapped an index finger against her lips. "Is this a chronic thing . . . or a more recent malady?"

"Oh, I'd say it's a *very* recent malady."

"Interesting. When did you first start exhibiting symptoms?"

"I think it started right about the time a tall, distracted person knocked about two dozen boxes of cookies into my grocery cart."

"Hmmm. Tall person. Cookies. Strange pajamas. Not seeing a connection."

"Maybe it's not a medical condition."

"I agree. You could just be a floozy."

Syd threw her pajamas at her. Maddie caught them before they hit the floor. "Has it occurred to you that you're always throwing things at me?"

Syd frowned. "You always catch whatever it is."

"That might be true, but you're not getting these back until you apologize."

"Apologize?"

"Yes."

"For hitting you with fat, flannel sheep?"

"Yes."

"And if I don't?"

"Then you'd better pray there isn't a house fire tonight so you won't have to run screaming from your room in the unforgettable altogether."

"What makes you think it would be unforgettable?"

Maddie paused. "I have an active imagination."

"You do?"

"Oh, yeah."

Syd paused as if she were thinking it through. "Tall person. Cookies. Strange pajamas. I think there might be a connection, after all."

There was more silence.

"We should have more conversations in the dark," Syd said.

"Why's that?"

"Because you're . . . different."

"I am?"

"Yes."

"How am I different?"

"I don't know—*different*. Shorter, maybe?" Maddie chuckled. "More accessible?" Syd paused. "Less guarded?"

"That's probably true. Right now, I feel supremely over-confident. Especially since I'm standing here with *two* pairs of pajamas and you have, lemme see? None?"

Syd sighed. "Okay. I *apologize*." She held out her hands in supplication. "I promise never to throw borrowed pajamas at you again."

"That's more like it." Maddie smiled as she closed the distance between them. "You're forgiven." She held out a set of nightclothes.

As Syd took the pajamas, their hands met. She peered up through the near darkness at Maddie's face. "Thank you." Her voice seemed miles away. "I guess we should get some sleep."

"Probably." Maddie started to back away, but on impulse, leaned down to plant a soft peck on Syd's cheek. Syd turned her head at that moment, and before Maddie knew what was happening, their warm mouths collided in an accidental kiss. They jolted apart and stood in shocked silence for a moment before sharing a nervous laugh.

"Well. Goodnight." Maddie backed toward her door on shaky legs. "You can use the bathroom first."

"Thanks." There was an awkward pause. "Goodnight to you, too. I hope you sleep well."

"Thanks." The way her lips were tingling, Maddie knew she didn't stand a snowball's chance in hell of sleeping well.

Syd turned away, entered her room, and flipped a wall switch to turn on the bedside lamp.

Maddie quickly retreated into her own room and stood quietly for a moment once she was inside.

"Hey!" She heard Syd's complaint through the closed door.

Smiling through her anxiety, she tossed the set of sheep-covered pajamas onto the bed. Humming a few bars from "Strike Up the Band," she started to undress, preparing herself for another long and sleepless night.

Syd stood leaning against the back of her door, still clutching the footie pajamas to her chest.

Oh my god. I can't believe that just happened. She closed her eyes and took deep breaths, trying to calm herself down. She could feel her heart pounding beneath the folded wads of red flannel. *What the hell was I doing? She's going to think I was flirting with her.* She opened her eyes, went to the bed, and sat, then lay down on the soft mattress. She stared blankly up at the tin ceiling, absently running her fingers back and forth across her lips. She wanted to be anywhere but there.

With a start, she bolted back up into a sitting position. *Oh, Jesus. I told her about Jeff. I told her about Jeff and the whole "you must be gay" thing.* She closed her eyes. *She's really going to think I was hitting on her, now.* Waves of mortification washed over her, and she dropped onto her back again. *Oh god.* She held the Dr. Denton's against her hot face. *Maybe I was.*

Chapter 9

It snowed on Thanksgiving Day. Maddie stood in the kitchen of her farmhouse, watching the fat flakes drift down and cling to every surface. She could tell by the size of the snowflakes that the storm was winding down, but it was beautiful while it lasted. She was surprised when she got up that morning to see the ground white, especially since it had been above the freezing mark when she'd finally retired the night before. Squalls of snow had rolled through off and on all day, and, although the roads were mostly clear, there had to be at least four or five inches on the ground.

Pete was still outside. Maddie could see him nosing around the fence posts near the creek bed, his yellow coat thick with snow. He'd be a pupsicle if she didn't coax him back inside soon. She felt envious, watching him, as he slowly made his way along the fence toward the barn. Life was simple for Pete. He had land to roam, critters to chase, a big porch to sleep on, and a full bowl of food twice a day. He never complained. He never wandered off. He never hesitated to ask for the things he needed. And he never worried about the after-effects of the choices he made.

She was about to put on a jacket and go get him when her phone rang. She stood still for a moment, leaning against the countertop with her eyes closed—persuaded that it was probably someone calling in a panic because they'd choked on a dinner roll, or contracted a bad case of reflux from ingesting too much turkey gravy. For a split second, she thought about not answering it—thought about pretending that she was out of town. Out of town, and in her right mind for once. The phone rang again. It would always ring again. Nights. Weekends. Holidays. The rings would always find her because they now formed the parameters of her life—a set of concentric circles that began and ended with a panicked voice on the other end of a phone line.

"This is Stevenson."

"Final-*fucking*-ly! I thought you'd skipped town." It was David.

"Nope. Happy Thanksgiving to you, too."

"Hey, no time for polite conversation. I've got an emergency out here." He sounded desperate enough.

"What's wrong?" She was all business now. A quick glance at her watch told her it was a few minutes before five. She could probably be out there in fifteen minutes—faster than the EMTs could make it from Jefferson.

"Beats the shit outta me. The goddamn thing is on the *fritz*."

"Excuse me?"

"You heard me. It's on the fritz."

She relaxed. "What's on the fritz?"

He sighed. "The frickin' *espresso* machine. Goddamn Italian piece of shit. And

I've got a dining room full of overstuffed flatlanders who aren't getting out of here any time soon if I don't find a way to sober them up with some double-cappuccinos. Get my drift?"

"What's wrong with it?" She leaned back against the countertop and picked up her own coffee mug.

"How the hell should I know what's wrong with it? It's not *espressing*. It's not steaming. It's not doing *shit*. I can't even get it to turn *on*."

"So, what do you want me to do? Bring mine over?" She glanced at her father's prized DeLonghi. The thing had to weigh over a hundred pounds.

"No, Cinderella." He sounded really exasperated now. "I want you to put on a fucking ball gown and fly over here to do a pole dance on the sun porch. What do you *think* I want you to do? Grab your friggin' tool belt and come fix the damn thing."

She sighed. "David, you're pathetic. It's a holiday, for god's sake."

"Oh, gee, thanks for the news flash, Katie Couric. I *know* it's a holiday. Why else do you think I'm calling your obstinate ass?" David paused in his tirade. "Look, I'm sorry. Really. But I need your help. I'm desperate." He paused again. "Please, Maddie."

That did it. He never called her "Maddie" unless he truly was desperate.

"Okay. I'm on my way. Let me in through the kitchen. I don't wanna parade across the dining room with my toolbox."

David released a long sigh. "I owe you for this one, Cochise."

"You got that right, Tonto."

He hung up. She set her cup down on the counter, took a long, last look outside at the white landscape. Pete was no longer visible, and it had stopped snowing. She could see faint ribbons of yellow light snaking across the horizon. If the clouds rolled out, it would be a very cold night. Some cappuccino might be good. She wondered if Michael had any more of that maple pie. She grabbed her car keys and cell phone, and snagged a jacket off one of the pegs by the back door before going outside to whistle for Pete.

Syd's father pushed his plate away with a moan. "I have never eaten so much wonderful food in my entire life." Too late, he seemed to realize his mistake and reached across the table to touch his wife on the arm. "I mean, out in a restaurant, of course."

Janet Murphy rolled her eyes. "I don't even know how you manage to chew when your foot is always so firmly planted in your mouth."

He squeezed her arm before retracting his hand.

Syd smiled at both of them. "Michael went to a lot of trouble for us, but the few times I've eaten here, the food has always been amazing."

Her mother nodded. "I won't argue with you about that. I wasn't sure what to think at first about the cornbread stuffing, but I think it was a perfect compliment to the currants." She took a sip of her white wine and glanced around the dining room. "Is it usually this busy here?"

Syd followed her gaze. It was true that the place was busier than she had ever seen it. There were even several tables set up on the sun porch adjacent to the dining room. David was running around frenetically, seating guests and taking beverage orders. "No, I've never seen it quite like this. I thought the snow might keep more people at home."

"Me, too," her father said. "When I got up this morning, I was sure we were going to get buried in it, but it's all but stopped now. Maybe we can go for a walk outside after dinner?"

Janet gave him an incredulous look. "What do you intend to wear on your feet?"

"I have my waders in the back of the Tahoe." His green eyes looked hopeful.

"Waders?" Syd asked warily. "Dad, I really think Michael and David might be able to outfit you with something more suitable." She smiled to herself. "They're pretty accommodating when it comes to that."

George sat back and crossed his arms. He looked handsome in his brown tweed jacket and khaki slacks. "Why, baby? Are you afraid your old man will embarrass you if he's seen tramping around in his high-water gear?"

She smiled back. "Something like that, yes."

He shook his head. "Last time I checked, there was something we used to call a river located about a quarter of a mile *that* way." He inclined his head toward the sun porch and the white lawn that spread out beyond it. "I'd love to poke around in it."

"Well, why don't you wait until tomorrow to do your exploring?" Janet picked a piece of white lint off the sleeve of his blazer. "Margaret and I are going to run up to Roanoke and do some shopping. That should give you plenty of time to muck around in the mud." She pursed her lips. "Unless, of course, you'd like to join us?"

"Shopping?" His face took on a tortured expression. "I think I'll pass."

Syd knew her face was a mirror image of her father's. The prospect of spending an entire day in the raw glare of her mother's scrutiny was enough to make her want to hide beneath the nearest bed and not emerge until spring. They still hadn't talked about her recent encounter with Jeff—and she was fairly certain that he had probably already called her mother and given her *his* version of their unhappy exchange.

"You know, Dad, I've grown very passionate about slimy rocks. Do you need any help tomorrow?"

"Nice try, Margaret," her mother drawled. "Don't stave off the inevitable. We're going. You need some new clothes. You don't have anything suitable for a winter up here."

"Well, 'suitable' is a pretty expansive term, Mother. I'm only going to be here for eighteen months. It didn't make sense to bring everything."

"I realize that, but shopping for a couple of new sweaters and some better boots won't kill you."

"What doesn't destroy me makes me stronger," Syd quoted. "Somehow, I don't think Nietzsche was talking about an afternoon at Orvis."

Her father perked up. "Orvis? There's an Orvis in Roanoke?"

Syd felt a surge of optimism. "Oh, yeah, a *big* one. In fact, it's one of their pilot stores." She watched his eyes grow wistful. "Rods. Reels. Waders. Fishing maps of the Smith River with little flies attached to the best sites . . ."

Janet watched the two of them with interest. "And it's conveniently located right next to the downtown mall."

George's face fell. Janet gave her daughter a triumphant nod. Her gray eyes glinted with humor.

Syd drooped her shoulders. She held up her thumb and forefinger. "I was *this* close to cheating death."

She noticed that her father's gaze was now directed toward something going on behind her. She half-turned in her chair to see David, engaged in animated conversation with Michael near the beverage station at the back of the dining room. Michael had his arms crossed and stood there slowly shaking his head, while David gestured wildly toward the espresso machine. She thought she saw Michael say something that looked like "you're crazy," before he walked off. He glanced over and saw Syd looking their way, and abruptly changed direction and stopped at their table on his way back to the kitchen.

Syd smiled as he approached. "Something wrong?"

Michael rolled his eyes. "Only the same thing that's been wrong for about thirty-two years." He smiled at her parents. "How are you folks doing? Everything okay with the meal?"

They replied *en masse* with a chorus of praise for his efforts.

Michael gave them a good-natured smile and placed a large hand on Syd's shoulder. "I apologize in advance for what's about to befall you."

Syd narrowed her eyes. "What's that supposed to mean?"

Michael sighed. "Well, according to David, the espresso machine is broken, and he placed a panicked call, begging for emergency repair service . . . if you know what I mean."

Syd colored. "Oh, god. Is it really broken?"

"Who can say?"

"She's going to *kill* him."

"One can only hope."

Her father and mother looked back and forth between them. Then her father's gaze shifted again to the back of the room. His eyes grew wide. "I've never been much of a fan of those boutique coffee drinks, but if *that's* what you people call a repair person, I'm gonna buy *five* of those contraptions and break them all."

Michael and Syd turned in unison to see Maddie, now standing next to David by the espresso machine. She was dressed in a pair of black jeans and a form-fitting blue sweater. Her long hair was loose and shining, and she held a small aluminum toolbox in her right hand. They watched her set the toolbox down on a nearby bussing table before she pulled the unit away from the wall and peered behind it. After a moment, she stood upright and turned to face David with her lips pursed, lazily swinging a disconnected power cord around in small arcs. They had what appeared to be an energetic exchange, before Maddie shifted her handhold on the power cord and held it up in front of David's neck like a garrote. He was still talking and waving his hands—now defensively.

Michael chuckled and softly whispered, "And in four, three, two, one . . ."

As if on cue, David and Maddie turned to face the Murphy's table. Syd met Maddie's gaze and smiled shyly, lifting her hand in a polite wave. Maddie tossed her head back and closed her eyes, before picking up her toolbox and walking to their table. David, who now was grinning like a Cheshire cat, followed behind her.

George noticed the subtle change in his daughter's demeanor as the tall woman approached their table. She sat nervously clenching and unclenching the napkin in her lap, but her face looked open and welcoming as she exchanged glances with their visitor. It was clear that they knew each other.

He got to his feet as David performed the introductions. "Mr. and Mrs. Murphy, I'd like you to meet the county's most eligible and sought-after tool jockey, and *my* very dear friend, Madeleine Stevenson. Maddie, it's my pleasure to present George and Janet Murphy, of the Baltimore Murphys."

Maddie smiled as she faced Syd's mother. "Mrs. Murphy, it's a pleasure to meet you." She turned to George, extending her hand. "And you, sir."

George took her hand and dumbly gazed into a pair of incredible blue eyes that were on a level with his own. He decided to throw caution to the wind. "I'm not quite sure what it is yet, but I'm fairly certain I'll break something later on. Would you and your toolbox like to join us and wait around until it happens?"

Janet swatted him with her napkin. Shaking her head, she looked up at Maddie. "Forgive my husband's lapse into puberty. But do, please, join us."

Maddie laughed as she released his hand. "You're very kind, but I certainly don't want to intrude on your meal." She looked down at Syd. "I just couldn't be here this evening and not come say hello to Syd's parents."

"I'm glad you did." Syd smiled up at her. "I would have called you myself if I'd thought there was any chance you'd venture out on a night like this."

David snickered in the background. Maddie turned and fixed him with a menacing glare. "Don't think you fooled anyone here with your little manufactured crisis. Paybacks are hell, Davey."

David gave the group a baffled look and feigned innocence. "How was I supposed to know the damn thing was unplugged? I'm not the one who majored in small engine repair—remember?"

Maddie was still glaring at him. "Oh, I remember."

"I have to get back to the kitchen," Michael cut in. "May I assume that you'll all be having pie and espresso?" He looked at Maddie. "You too, Doctor. I've got a slice of something special with your name on it."

Maddie hesitated. George saw Syd discreetly touch her hand. "Please stay."

George and his wife exchanged looks. "Let me get you a chair, Maddie." He started to leave the table but David stopped him.

"No need, Mr. Murphy. I've got one right here." Without ceremony, David shoved an unoccupied chair into the back of Maddie's legs, causing her knees to buckle. She plopped down and half fell across Syd's lap as she tried to avoid hitting the table.

George watched as Maddie tried to right herself without spilling the contents of her toolbox. She was blushing furiously as Syd grasped her by both forearms and helped her slide back onto the seat of her chair.

"Great," Michael said, "that's *four* for pie. C'mon, David," he dropped his voice, "I think your work here is through."

David chuckled as he walked off with Michael.

"Did I hear Michael call you doctor?" Janet asked.

Maddie's blush was starting to subside. "Yes, you did." She carefully set her toolbox on the floor and slid it beneath her chair.

"Small engine repair isn't the only thing she excels at, Mother," Syd added, wryly. "Maddie is our local physician."

"Really?" George asked, surprised.

Maddie's expression was apologetic, but her blue eyes twinkled. "I hope you're not too disappointed, Mr. Murphy. I can still wear a set of greasy coveralls with the best of them."

"I'll just *bet* you can," he said, and nodded enthusiastically. "Please, call me George."

Janet clucked her tongue.

George sobered and cleared his throat, adopting his most fatherly persona. "So it's obvious that you two girls are friends?"

The two girls in question exchanged shy glances.

"I remember now that Jeff mentioned something about meeting the local doctor when he visited Syd here last month." He smiled at Maddie. "I confess from his description, I envisioned someone *crustier*—more of a Marcus Welby type. You're a bit of a surprise."

"Dad—" Syd began.

He raised his hand to stave off her impending caution. "It's okay, honey." He met her eyes. "I know better than to listen to much of what Jeff has to say."

Syd gave him a grateful smile and seemed to relax a bit.

Their server arrived with four generous slices of pie and a fresh pot of coffee. Maddie smiled when she noticed that her plate contained something different than the pumpkin pie the rest of them were having.

"So, Maddie," Janet said, smiling as she picked up her dessert fork. "Tell us about yourself." She glanced at Syd. "Let's see what else Jeff got wrong."

There was an awkward silence as Syd looked back at her mother with an unreadable expression on her face. Neither Syd or Maddie seemed to know quite how to respond to Janet's statement.

"Yes, Maddie," George said. "Are you a local like David?" He saw Syd relax just a bit.

Maddie nodded. "I am—although I spent most of my childhood in California with my mother. I came back here to take over my father's practice about eighteen months ago—shortly after his death."

"I'm sorry for your loss," George said quietly.

Maddie smiled at him. "Thank you."

"Where were you before returning to Virginia?" he asked.

"Philadelphia. I went to med school at Penn and did my residency at Presbyterian. After that ended, I stayed on there as assistant ER chief."

"Really? That's pretty impressive. I've actually been to Presbyterian. That's a huge hospital."

Janet gave him a perplexed look. "When was that?"

"Remember when I participated in that sustainability summit at Drexel two years ago?" She nodded. He looked at Maddie. "I was sharing a cab back to my hotel with another speaker, and he had a heart attack—in the car. The driver took us to Presbyterian. Kudos to you for the quality of treatment he got there in the emergency room. I have to say it shattered a lot of my stereotypes about big city hospitals."

Maddie gave him a wry smile. "It must have been my day off."

Syd swatted her on the arm. As Maddie laughed and dodged her assault, George realized that this was a fairly typical interaction between them, and he marveled at Syd's playful and proprietary demeanor toward the seemingly more reserved doctor.

Maddie composed herself and regarded him once again with her amazing blue eyes. "I hope your friend fared all right?"

"He did. He raves to this day about the quality of the care he got there."

"I'm glad to hear that. We don't often get feedback on the success stories."

"Coming back here must have been quite a change from such an urban environment," Janet interjected. "I can't imagine the adjustment it must have been."

"Still is," Maddie added, thoughtfully. "I have to confess that the most frustrating part is figuring out how to extend care to all of our underserved populations. There are people living in remote areas of these counties who have never had access to even the most rudimentary kinds of health care. My father struggled with that, too."

"I can only imagine," Janet said. "Margaret may have told you that I'm a public health nurse, so I can empathize with your frustration level."

Maddie eyed Janet with interest. "I don't suppose you'd be interested in alternative employment in a picturesque part of the Blue Ridge state?"

Janet laughed. "Not so much. Baltimore County is rustic enough for me. Are you looking for a nurse?"

"I might be. Back in Pennsylvania, I was involved with a parish nurse program in the Lehigh Valley. The nurses there networked through area churches, and were able to deliver basic, on-site preventative care to scores of people who otherwise would have had none." She paused in reflection. "It had a tremendous effect on the overall general health of the region. I'd love to be able to imitate those successes here."

Janet leaned forward, caught up in Maddie's enthusiasm for the idea. "Have you been able to generate any interest for the idea?"

Maddie nodded. "Some. I've had a positive response from one of the local Methodist ministers. His circuit includes four congregations in several of the more remote areas. I'm able to have my clinic underwrite part of the expense to hire a trained R.N., but I need to secure more funding to move ahead with the program."

Syd seemed intrigued. "How about the state? Are there other funding sources akin to the one that's paying my rent these days?"

Maddie shook her head. "My petition to the general assembly for funding met with a fair amount of interest, but little promise of money."

"What about private sources?" George asked.

"Funny you should ask," Maddie replied. "I've become desperate enough to prostitute myself to a couple of pharmaceutical company reps at the next AMA conference. It's conveniently being held in Richmond this year, so it'll be easy to hop up there for a day or two." She sighed. "I'll have to see how compelling I can be, but just between us, I'd rather put a sharp stick in my *eye* than have to fawn on these guys. So many of them are little more than glorified snake-oil salesmen."

George chuckled at that. "I wouldn't worry too much. I think you'll fare just *fine*."

"Just let David handle your wardrobe," Syd said. "I'll guarantee that you'll come back flush with funds."

Maddie looked at her with raised eyebrows. "Are you kidding? If I let David manage my attire I'd be flush all right, but it wouldn't be with *funds*." She paused. "At least, not with anything larger than one-dollar bills."

Syd snorted. George saw how Maddie's eyes softened as she looked at his daughter. He glanced at his wife. Janet met his gaze. She noticed it, too.

"When is this conference?" he asked.

"Late March. I'm going to hop up there on a small plane so I can minimize my time away from the clinic."

George looked at Syd. "Don't you have to go to Richmond in March, too, honey?" Janet kicked him under the table. "Owww. Hey. Why'd you do that? She *does* have to go—don't you, baby?" Janet rolled her eyes at him.

Syd glowered at both of her parents. "Yes, I *do*." She gave Maddie an apologetic look. "I have to meet with the trustees of my grant sometime in March, and present my six-month report."

Maddie seemed to consider this information. "You know, I've been meaning to ask if you'd consider going with me."

George sat back smugly, still rubbing his sore shin.

Maddie and Syd shyly smiled at each other.

"I thought it might just be a nice reprieve for you," Maddie said, quietly, "and I'd certainly enjoy the company. Now that I know you have to go, too, I think it's a no-brainer."

Syd nodded. "Going together might be a no-brainer, but I don't know about that small airplane part." She squinted. "Is the pilot experienced?"

Maddie sighed. "Very."

"And you can promise me that you haven't had your sticky mitts or your tools anywhere near the engine?"

"I don't have sticky mitts."

"Your tools, then."

"What about my tools?"

"Can you promise me that your tools haven't been anywhere near the engine?"

"I can't make that promise."

"So you *have* worked on it?"

"I'm not saying that."

"Well, then, what *are* you saying?"

"I'm saying that I always travel with my tools, and my medical bag. Since I do, occasionally fly on small aircraft, it would be false to say that my tools have never been anywhere near the engines."

Syd's exasperation was starting to show. "Why is getting a straight answer out of you like watching a rerun of *Perry Mason*?"

"Beats me. It's not my fault if you can't ask a direct question."

"Okay, wise guy." Syd leaned toward her and raised a menacing finger. "Can you tell me, unequivocally, that the engine on this airplane, in part or in total, has never been on or near your workbench at the farm?"

Maddie thought about that.

"Well?"

"Yes."

"Yes? Yes, *what?*"

"Yes, I can tell you that this engine has never been on or near my workbench at the farm."

Syd sat back and heaved a sigh of relief. "Finally." She looked at her mother. "Your witness."

After dessert, the group decided to give in to George's entreaties for a walk outside. Most of the pathways behind the Inn were clear—or at least passable—and David happily lent George a pair of his foul-weather overshoes. The women were already wearing boots.

Maddie's earlier surmise was correct, and the night was clear and very cold. White moonlight reflected off the snow, and an eerie quiet hung over the landscape as they meandered away from the Inn and its warmer circle of yellow light. Drifting mounds of snow made the pathway narrower than usual so they walked two abreast, with George and Janet taking the lead.

Syd tucked her chin lower into the red scarf that she had loosely wrapped around her neck. She glanced at Maddie and bumped her playfully as they slowly walked along. "Thanks for staying. I know this probably isn't what you had in mind for the evening."

"No. But that doesn't mean I'm not enjoying myself."

"Even though your emergency ended up being a complete red herring?"

"*Especially* because my emergency ended up being a complete red herring." She laughed. "David drives me insane, but sometimes, he actually dupes me into doing things that end up being good for me. I think this is a case in point."

"I'm glad you feel that way. I really wanted you to meet my parents but I didn't want to intrude on your privacy." She laughed nervously. "Well, not any more than I normally do."

Maddie looked at her. "Why would you think that?"

"Why would I think what?"

"Why would you think that you intrude on my privacy?"

"Are you saying that I don't?"

Maddie sighed. "Have we lapsed into another game of *Twenty Questions*? Of course I don't think you intrude on me. Where would you get such an idea?"

Syd rolled her eyes. "Hmmm. Let me think . . ." She tapered off until Maddie groaned. "But really, David's *Weimaraner* analogy isn't so far off the mark." She paused. "Well, with the possible exception of the flannel bedding part. But then, I've never actually *seen* your sheets, so I can't be sure about that."

Maddie raised an eyebrow in challenge. "We could remedy that mystery in short order."

Syd had stopped to brush some snow off the surface of a birdbath that stood next to a stand of holly bushes. She looked up at Maddie with a perplexed expression. "How?"

Maddie just stared at her. "Is this what they call a legally blonde moment?"

Syd looked back at her with a blank expression before realization hit. "Oh, good *god*." Without thinking, she dipped her gloved hand into the icy water and splashed some of it at the smirking Maddie. "You can be such a *jerk* sometimes."

Maddie just laughed as she ducked out of the way. "So I've been told."

"Damn you," Syd said as she peeled off her soggy glove. "Now this thing is soaked. My hand is gonna freeze."

Maddie stepped closer. "Stick your hand in your pocket."

"I don't *have* any pockets."

"Well, I'd offer you one of *my* gloves, but, unfortunately, they're on the console of the Jeep."

Syd noticed for the first time that Maddie had been walking along with her hands shoved deep down into the pockets of her overcoat. She glanced ahead to where her parents were veering off on a path that led down toward the river.

"Do you wanna go back to the house?" Maddie asked.

Syd looked up to meet her eyes. Even in the moonlight, she could see how blue they were. "No. Let's go on. I can wrap it in my scarf."

Maddie took another step to stand just beside her. "I've got a better idea." She took hold of Syd's cold, wet hand and pulled it into the pocket of her coat. Instead of releasing it, she held it there, and covered it with her larger, drier hand. "Better?" she asked, at very close range. Her frosty breath hung in the air between their faces.

Syd felt a tingle spread up her arm from where their hands were clasped together in the warm confines of Maddie's pocket. She nodded slowly. "Yeah." Her voice was husky. She cleared her throat. "Thanks."

She felt Maddie's fingers tighten around hers. "Let's see if we can catch up with your folks before they reach the river. I'm not sure I trust your father to stay away from any thin ice he might encounter in the dark."

Syd nodded as they set off down the path walking very close together. "He isn't the only one you need to worry about."

"What do you mean?"

Syd laughed nervously. "Let's just say that he isn't the only Murphy with a penchant for skating on thin ice."

They walked in silence along the river path, closely huddled together. The only sound came from the crunch of snow and loose gravel beneath their booted feet.

"What on earth were you thinking?" Janet whispered, glancing nervously over her shoulder to be certain that Maddie and Syd were still out of earshot.

"What do you mean?" George asked, innocently.

"Don't give me that, George. You know exactly what I'm talking about. You can't play twisted games like this with people's emotions. Margaret is in a fragile place right now, she doesn't need to have anyone pushing her into something she's not ready for."

"How do you know what she is and isn't ready for?"

"I know my daughter. She's confused—and scared. Her marriage has just ended, and she's feeling lost and vulnerable. It's ludicrous for you—or anyone—to push her toward something that may not be right for her."

He waved his free hand in exasperation. "Well, I'm not sure what you're talking about. I'm certainly not *pushing* her into anything—other than pursuing a healthy friendship with a strong and stable woman." He stopped and looked at her. "How could she not be ready for that? You know how isolated she kept herself when she was with Jeff. Maddie seems . . . good for her."

"Come on. You heard what Jeff told us about Syd's special friendship with the town doctor. Admit it. You were as shocked as I was when she showed up tonight, and we realized who she was. My god, your jaw about hit your dinner plate."

He paused. "Okay. *Yes*, I was surprised to learn that Syd's so-called, special friend wasn't an older man. But beyond that, I don't lend any credibility to anything Jeff has to say about our daughter." He stared at her. "Besides, you'd have to be nuts to think *that* woman was . . . well . . ."

"Gay?" Janet asked.

"Well. Yeah."

Janet sighed and pushed her short, graying hair back from her face. "I'm reluctant to agree with you because I hate to endorse such a ridiculous stereotype."

"What's that supposed to mean?" He looked wounded.

She linked her arm through his and started walking along the narrow path again. "Honey, being gay isn't a one-size-fits-all proposition. Lesbians now come wrapped in lots of fabrics besides flannel." She smiled at him. "And don't forget her toolbox."

He jostled her. "Now who's tossing out the stereotypes?"

She laughed, and they walked along in silence for a moment. In the distance, Janet could hear the rush of the river as they edged closer to its bank.

"Do you really think she might be gay?" His voice was so low she had to bend her head to hear him.

"Who? Maddie?"

"No. Margaret."

She was stunned by his directness. "I thought we were talking about Maddie."

"I think we're talking about both of them."

She sighed and lifted her gloved hand to his face. "I don't know, honey. I don't think she knows, either. That's why we can't push her. I did that once, and look how it turned out."

"You mean her marriage to Jeff?"

"Yes. I blame myself for that. It was clear that she wasn't ready for it. I have to accept that she may never be ready for it."

"So what do we do?"

"Just love her, and give her the space she needs to figure things out on her *own* timetable."

He nodded. "And you'll be okay with *any* outcome?" he asked. "Even if it involves a certain six-foot-tall brunette with blue eyes and a killer smile?"

She sighed. "I guess I'd have to be. I mean, beggars can't be choosers."

He stopped again and faced her. "What's that supposed to mean?"

She gave him a small smile. "I always said I wanted her to marry a doctor."

Further up the path, Maddie and Syd were startled when they heard George's laughter ring out above the roar of the water. They looked at each other with baffled expressions before tightening their clasped hands and continuing on toward the river.

On Friday morning, George set out early with his waders, rod, and tackle to walk the river bank behind the Inn and try his hand at a bit of cold water fishing. This part of the New River was well stocked with smallmouth bass, and Michael told him to be on the lookout for any natural springs along the banks because these tended to raise the water temperature a few degrees, and the sluggish fish were inclined to stack up in those warmer areas.

He left the Inn shortly after eight in the morning, armed with a thermos of hot coffee and a bag lunch that Michael had graciously prepared, determined to enjoy five or six hours of solitude while his wife and daughter made their shopping trek to Roanoke.

The day was beautiful—cold but clear, and the sun was blinding as it angled through the trees and reflected off the snow-covered riverbank. He walked and fished intermittently for about three hours before stopping to eat his lunch at a boat landing area, where there were a couple of battered picnic tables. The view here was breathtaking as the river widened and ran along next to a well-traveled secondary road. He guessed he was about two miles away from the Inn at this point, and resolved that after relaxing with his meal, he would slowly start making his way back.

He hadn't caught any fish yet, but he didn't really mind. Just being outside in the cold but clear air and having the latitude to walk and explore at a leisurely pace was enough to make the outing worthwhile.

These days, he spent far too many hours cooped up in a classroom. The opportunities for fieldwork were becoming few and far between. Budget cutbacks at the state level had seriously eaten into departmental funding for out-of-doors instruction. He thought, ironically, that if the same economic downturn had occurred five or six years earlier, his daughter would never have met Jeff Simon, a former intern of his, and she would never have ended up living in this backcountry region of Virginia. As sorry as he was for the circumstances and the heartbreak that had led her to her to accept a job posting in this remote area, he was finding it hard to regret her presence here. She seemed happier and more at peace with herself than he had seen her in years—at least, since graduating from college.

His thoughts drifted back to the conversation he'd had with Janet last night after meeting Maddie Stevenson. It was impossible to deny that there was some kind of bond between Syd and Maddie. It radiated off both of their faces whenever they looked at each other. "Chemistry," Jeff had called it, in a voice dripping with sarcasm. It irritated George more than a little bit to admit that Jeff might finally have hit on something to be right about.

What would it mean for Syd if Jeff's—and Janet's—suspicions were accurate? Would *she* ever be able to come to terms with it? Would *they*?

He looked out at the river. The water rolled by, making lazy and determined progress toward its ultimate union with the Ohio and Mississippi Rivers. It might slow down, but it never stopped. It might change size or direction, but it always got where it was supposed to be. It might fight its way around an obstacle, or it might simply wear it down but it always kept moving. It had all the time in the world to get where it was going.

He thought about the Irresistible Force Paradox, and how frequently he used it as a teaching tool to illustrate Newton's second law of the conservation of energy. The river was an irresistible force. The rocks that originally lined the banks of this gully were immovable objects. Yet the river prevailed, and the rocks moved.

It would, therefore, be ineffective for him to wade out into the center of this river, raise his hands toward heaven, and command it to stop—to turn around—to go another way. Ineffective. And it would be equally ineffective for him to try and stop the irresistible force he now saw washing over his daughter.

And in some way, he didn't *want* to stop it. Because, sooner or later, everything ended up exactly where it was supposed to be.

And she seemed . . . happy.

When faced with an irresistible force, an immovable object moves. It really was that simple.

After finishing his sliced duck and apple sandwich, he collected his tackle and began his slow journey back along the riverbank toward the Inn. The sun was well above the horizon and was shining down from directly overhead, illuminating eddies that hadn't been visible earlier. About a mile from the Inn, he saw a spot that looked particularly promising and decided to cast a line out and try his luck one more time.

The bank was fairly steep, and the snow pack made it even more challenging, but he dropped his pack and readied his line—attaching a hefty lunker to make sure it dragged along the bottom once he dropped it near the eddy. It took several casts, but finally he got the position he wanted, and he watched the current draw his line toward the center of the whirlpool. In short order, he felt a hit on the line, then a more determined tug. He gingerly descended the bank toward the edge of the water as he slowly took the slack up out of his line. Suddenly, his pole jerked as the fish hit with a vengeance, causing his reel to whine as fishing line flew out across the water.

"So much for lazy bass," he muttered. "This sucker is flying." He stepped into the water and waded out toward the eddy while he pulled back on his pole and wound up his line. The fish fought him, swimming downstream toward a small island that jutted out in the middle of the river.

"Oh, no you don't," he growled. "I'm not falling for that one." He continued to wrestle with the fish, trying to keep his line away from some fallen tree limbs that protruded from the water near the leading edge of the tiny island. It was hopeless. The fish was apparently too big and too fast, and he couldn't get a good enough purchase on the rocks to keep his line clear of the branches. In short order, it snagged, and he couldn't reel it in any further. He had no choice but to take out his Cliff knife and cut the line, losing both the fish and his lunker.

As he drew his knife out of the sheath attached to his belt, the fish apparently changed direction, and his line broke free—the reel singing as the poll jerked out of his hand. He lunged to catch it before the current swept it away, and his boot slipped on the rocks beneath the surface, and he fell forward into the cold water.

He felt the knife blade slicing into his palm. He righted himself, stood up, and took a look at his hand. The cut was clean, but bleeding profusely and would certainly require stitches—probably a lot of them. Sighing, he retrieved his pole and waded back to the shore, trying to keep his palm submerged in the cold water until he reached his pack. He had only an oversized hand-towel to wrap his hand with, so he did the best he could—packing the cut first with snow to try and staunch the bleeding. It was going to be a long walk back to the Inn, and he wondered, as he climbed the bank, whether or not The Irresistible Force would be found in her clinic on the Friday after Thanksgiving.

Maddie met Michael and George at the door. The clinic was, in fact, closed, but she had been in her office most of the day, entering patient records into her EMR database. When Michael called her cell phone to tell her about George's accident, she insisted that they come right over. There was no way she would consign Syd's father to seek medical care at the ER in Wytheville, where he would likely have to wait several hours for attention.

George looked embarrassed and apologetic as she let them into the clinic through the back door. She could see the blood already soaking through the fresh towel Michael had wrapped around his hand, and his pallor was too ashen to suit her. She directed them into an examination room, seated George, and elevated his forearm on a rolling tray table.

"I can't apologize enough to you for imposing like this on a holiday," he began.

Maddie waved him off. "Don't be silly. I was nodding off over patient files. This is actually a nice break for me." She smiled as she helped him out of his jacket. "Let's unwrap this and see what we've got here." She carefully unwound the blood-soaked towel and dabbed at the long cut with a sterile gauze pad. "Yep. It's a beauty. The good news is that it looks like a nice, clean cut. Can you flex your fingers for me?" He did. "Good. It doesn't look deep—just long. What kind of knife was it?"

He winced as she continued to blot the cut. "A Cliff knife—about a five inch blade."

"Jagged edge?"

"No."

"Good." She looked up at Michael, who was still hovering in the doorway with a countenance paler than George's. "Why don't you head back to the Inn? I'll run George back out after I get him stitched up. I was about to knock off for the day, anyway."

Michael met her gaze gratefully. "Really? I don't mind waiting, if it's out of your way—as long as I can wait someplace that's not in here." He looked at George with round eyes. "I'm not very good around blood or needles."

"Go on back to the Inn, Michael," George said as Maddie prepared a basin of warm water and antiseptic solution to soak the cut in before stitching it closed. "You've already gone beyond the call of duty by running me over here." He looked up at Maddie. "I don't think Maddie would offer if it was really an imposition."

Maddie lifted his arm and carefully submerged his right hand in the pan of warm water. "Nope. I wouldn't. You're just lucky it's not my bowling night." She opened a drawer and withdrew an assortment of paper-wrapped needles, gauze pads, and a large syringe.

Michael winced as she started pulling on a pair of latex surgical gloves.

"In that case, I think I'll head on." He took a step toward the back door. "If Janet and Syd get back before you're finished here, I'll tell them what happened. I'll have a big Scotch ready for you, George." He waved as he retreated down the hallway.

Maddie heard the door to the parking lot open and close. She sat down on a rolling stool and prepared her items.

"So. Whattaya think, Doc? Ten stitches?" George asked.

Maddie lifted his hand from the basin and rested it on a bed of dry, sterile towels. "Nah. You're an overachiever. This is going to take at least fifteen or twenty."

His eyes grew wide. "Really?"

She smiled. "Really. But don't worry. When I took Home Ec, I got an A in sewing."

He laughed. "That's comforting. I should've brought my new pants along, they need hemmed."

She smiled as she placed sterile towels around the wound opening. She picked up the syringe and a small vial. "Do you have any allergies to medications that you're aware of?" He shook his head, and she filled the syringe. "Okay. Now for the not-so-fun part. I have to inject this into the cut so we can deaden the area." She met his eyes. "It's going to sting like crazy, so I apologize in advance. Are you ready?"

He nodded.

Maddie injected the lidocaine into several locations inside and along the wound opening, working as quickly as possible. George flinched and gritted his teeth, but he remained perfectly still until she finished.

She withdrew the syringe and patted his arm. "Nice job. That's the worst. It should start feeling numb in about a minute." She opened up several of the paper packets and threaded a small, wedge-shaped needle. "How did this happen?"

He grimaced. "I was fishing about a mile from the Inn, and had just snagged a big one." He laughed. "At least, I *think* it was a big one. It drug me with it right out into the water. My line got tangled on some fallen limbs, and as I was getting my knife out to cut it loose, the fish got free and pulled the rod out of my hand. I slipped and fell into the water, trying to grab onto it—that's how I ended up with the cut." He paused. "I feel like an idiot—a novice." He sighed. "Janet's going to kill me."

Maddie looked at him. "Want me to fix you up with an extra impressive bandage to ratchet-up the sympathy quotient?"

His jaw dropped. "You'd do that for me?"

"Of course I would."

He sat back with a smug expression. "I knew I liked you."

In that moment, Maddie was caught by how much he looked like Syd. He had the same, mischief-filled green eyes, and the same childlike, snub nose. She laughed and gently tapped along the palm of his hand. "Do you feel this? Do you feel any pain or sensation along here at all?"

He shook his head. She set about methodically closing the wound with a series of tiny, perfect stitches and tying knot after knot with her hooked needle and a short pair of tweezers.

He watched her with fascination. "That's amazing. What do you call that knot?"

"This is what we call a mattress stitch. It's generally the most common type used on palms or soles of feet. It's faster and easier because you don't have to bury the knots."

"Do you miss working in an ER?"

"I still keep one toe in that pool by working a weekend a month at the hospital in Wytheville. But the truth is, I don't miss it nearly as much as I thought I would." She tied off another knot and picked up more silk thread. "It's nice to finally experience what it's like to have a life away from the office."

"I gather you didn't have much of a social life in Philadelphia?"

She gave him a small smile. "Not really. No."

"Well, at the risk of offending you, I guess that explains why someone as beautiful and as charming as you is still single."

Maddie slipped as she attempted to snag the loose end of her thread, and nearly dropped the tweezers. She met his eyes. "That doesn't offend me at all. I'm . . . flattered." She nervously began to wonder where this conversation was headed.

"Good. I think that you and my daughter are both pretty extraordinary women." He paused. "I wish sometimes that she had taken *her* time before getting married. Janet and I worry that we pushed her into something that she wasn't quite ready for."

Maddie wasn't certain how to reply, so she kept silent and continued to work.

"She's a wonderful girl—so vibrant and sensitive. We're both grateful that she ended up in a place so nurturing." Maddie looked up to find his eyes fixed on her face. "And that she has found friends like Michael and David—and you." Maddie felt a slow flush creep up her neck as George continued to gaze at her. "Her mother and I will worry less about her now that we know she has you to lean on."

She laid her implements down and sat back on her stool. "I—" she began, then stopped herself and tentatively patted his arm. "That should do it. Let's get this bandaged up now."

She rolled away from him and tried to compose herself as she lifted a tube of ointment and some clean dressings from a drawer. She returned to the little work-table, and he was still regarding her with an earnest expression. She knew she had to say something—her silence was too compromising.

She swabbed the cut with antiseptic ointment. "No one knows better than I how extraordinary your daughter is." She met his eyes. "Her presence here has been like a gift to me. Michael and David feel the same way."

George nodded. "We worry about her because she's been so isolated for the last few years. She lived in a fairly large city and attended a huge university, but she always seemed so alone . . . even though we knew she had friends."

Maddie carefully wrapped his hand with the sterile gauze. "That's hard to imagine. She's wonderful company."

"I think maybe you're just good for her," he said quietly.

She looked at him again. "I hope so."

"She needs friends right now. It's a confusing time for her."

"You mean, with the divorce?"

He nodded. "That—and other things. She has so much uncertainty ahead of her. We want her to be able to make good decisions."

Maddie regarded him soberly. "I want that for her, too."

"I know you do, Maddie."

They stared at each other for a moment.

He shifted on his chair. "Anyway, Janet and I are just grateful that she found someone like you to confide in. We'll worry a lot less about her when we leave for home tomorrow."

Maddie finished wrapping his hand. "There you go. What do you think? Impressive enough?"

He held it up and rotated around. The bandage was large and puffy and looped up around his wrist. "Oh, yeah. This looks like it's concealing something *really* nasty." He smiled at her. "I owe you one. This ought to get me out of the dog house at light speed." He continued to admire her handiwork. "By the way. How many stitches did you make?"

"Sixteen. Not too shabby." She cleared away the rest of her supplies and stood up. "Ready to head back to the Inn and sit down with that big glass of Scotch Michael promised you? I think he's mortified enough to crack open one of the single malts."

He stood up, too, and fished his wallet out of his jacket pocket. "I have my insurance card in here. Can you help me dig it out?"

She stopped him. "Don't bother, please. I hereby gift you with the coveted family discount."

"Which is?"

"On the house."

"I can't do that. It's bad enough that I made you work on your day off. At least let the State of Maryland pay you for your trouble."

"It was no trouble." She held out his jacket for him. She gazed at him determined. "You don't want to make me mad, do you?"

He met her level gaze. "No, ma'am, I sure don't." Sighing, he put his wallet away, and then shrugged into his coat. "Will you at least let me buy you a drink?"

She smiled. "I might consider that."

His smug expression returned. "I *definitely* like you, Dr. Stevenson."

Later that evening, Maddie was sitting in her father's study, reading dog-eared back issues of the *JAMA* and drinking Earl Grey tea when her cell phone rang. She absently picked it up off the table next to her chair and opened it without looking at its display.

"This is Stevenson."

"This is Murphy." There was a pause. "Well, I suppose I should narrow that down for you. This is *Miss* Murphy."

Maddie smiled at the sound of Syd's voice and laid the open journal down across her lap. "Hmmm. I might need you to be even more specific. Would this also be the short Miss Murphy?"

There was an audible sigh. "This would be the short and grateful Miss Murphy, yes."

Maddie smiled into the phone. "How are you? How was the shopping trip?"

"I'm fine, and my day was apparently nowhere near as eventful as my father's. Or yours."

"Yes. It's safe to say that your father got a real feel for the area today."

"Thank you for taking care of him. He won't stop raving about you." She paused again. "I think he might have a little crush on you. He gets all misty-eyed when he talks about how you fixed him up." She chuckled. "Of course, that could also be the four double-Scotches talking."

Maddie laughed.

"I'm not kidding. Michael keeps pouring like a madman. What's that about?"

"It's a long story. Suffice it to say that Michael doesn't do well around blood and gore. He felt guilty about not being able to wait around on your dad while I stitched him up."

"Ahh. Okay. Now about that other thing."

"What other thing?"

"You stitching my father back together. How do I repay you for that?"

Maddie slouched down into her chair and dragged the ottoman closer, prepared now for a longer conversation. "Hmmm. The possibilities are endless. Do I have to make a snap decision? I'd hate to waste this opportunity on something fleeting."

"Against my better judgment, I'll agree that it doesn't have to be a time-value offer. You just let me know when you figure something out."

"Oh, trust me, you'll be the very first to know."

Syd laughed. "In the meantime, my mother has some serious doubts about your competence."

Maddie sat up alarmed. "What do you mean?"

"Calm down, Stretch. Did you forget that she's actually a nurse? That ostentatious bandage didn't fool her for two seconds. My poor father was crestfallen that she didn't collapse weeping into his arms."

"Oops."

"Yeah. Now you two are tagged as co-conspirators. It's not going to be pretty when you see her tomorrow."

"I'm seeing her tomorrow?"

"Oh, yeah. You're coming out to the Inn for breakfast to help me see them off."

"I am?"

"You are."

Maddie sighed.

"Give it up. It's pointless to resist."

"Oh, really?"

"Really. Once you're caught in her crosshairs, there's no escape."

"Spoken like someone resigned to her fate."

"Tell me about it. You haven't noticed that I've been running around all week with an infrared dot tattooed on the center of my forehead?"

Maddie thought about that. "Well, now that you mention it. I thought maybe it was just some kind of high-tech bindi mark."

"You're not half as funny as you think you are."

"In fact, I think I am."

Syd sighed.

Maddie pressed her advantage. "Deep down, you think I am, too."

"Deep down, I think you're a lunatic. Adorable—but a lunatic, nevertheless."

"Excuse me. I think there was some static on the line. Did you just call me adorable?"

"Lunatic. I called you an adorable lunatic. It's not the same thing."

"It isn't?"

"Nuh uh."

It was Maddie's turn to sigh. "Can't blame a girl for trying."

"Well, don't despair. My father will happily drink your Kool-Aid."

"That's nice, but maybe he isn't the only Murphy I want to impress."

Syd was quiet for a moment. "There are others on your list?"

"Maybe."

"Could you be more specific?"

"Well, let's see. There's the short, grateful one who thinks I'm adorable."

"Lunatic. The short, grateful one who thinks you're a lunatic."

"And adorable?"

"And adorable."

"Yeah. That one."

"That one is already impressed."

"In that case, I'd be happy to join you for breakfast."

Syd laughed. "Great. Eight-thirty sharp. See you then."

"It's a date." She hung up and sat staring across the room for a few minutes, smiling stupidly, and wishing it really was.

Chapter 10

T'was the week before Christmas.

2:42 p.m. Text message from Murphy, S.
Now at BWI. Dad sorry u rn't here 2 take stitches out.

2:45 p.m. Text message from Stevenson, M.H.
Tell him scissors won't reach that far.

2:49 p.m. Text message from Murphy, S.
He says u should improvise.

2:52 p.m. Text message from Stevenson, M.H.
Never mastered folding space.

2:57 p.m. Text message from Murphy, S.
He says Southwest does that 4 u.

3:01 p.m. Text message from Stevenson, M.H.
Is that an invitation?

3:06 p.m. Text message from Murphy, S.
Yep. www.southwest.com

3:08 p.m. Text message from Stevenson, MH.
Subtle. I'll think about it. :-)

3:12 p.m. Text message from Murphy, S.
No pressure. But...

3:14 p.m. Text message from Stevenson, MH.
But?

3:17 p.m. Text message from Murphy, S.
I'd like it 2

3:21 p.m. Text message from Stevenson, M.H.
How much?

3:23 p.m. Text message from Murphy, S.
More than I have left in text minutes 2 tell u.

3:26 p.m. Text message from Stevenson, M.H.
It would be one helluva house call.

3:29 p.m. Text message from Murphy, S.
:-)

3:31 p.m. Text message from Stevenson, M.H.
Can't promise. Will see what I can do.

3:34 p.m. Text message from Murphy, S.
Dad happy.

3:37 p.m. Text message from Murphy, S.
Short Murphy happy 2.

3:39 p.m. Text message from Stevenson, M.H.
Miss you.

4:01 p.m. Text message from Murphy, S.
Prove it. Car here. Murphy out.

Two *days before Christmas.*

8:15 a.m. Text message from Stevenson, M.H.
Have emergency. Not able to get away today. So sorry. Will call later.

8:26 a.m. Text message from Murphy, S.
Sorry 2. Will miss u. Call when u can.

1:22 p.m. Text message from Stevenson, M.H.
Still at hospital. No progress. Will you be at home tonight?

1:42 p.m. Text message from Murphy, S.
After 8—r u ok?

1:53 p.m. Text message from Stevenson, M.H.
Been better.

1:58 p.m. Text message from Murphy, S.
:-(Wish I could hug u.

2:03 p.m. Text message from Stevenson, M.H.
Me, too.

On nine-thirty in the evening at the Murphy's house in Towson Syd heard her cell phone ringing.

Her phone was in her purse on the foyer table, where she had left it after coming in from a late dinner with her aunt and uncle. She ran down the stairs from her old bedroom to try and catch it before it rolled to voice mail.

She skidded to a stop and stared wide-eyed as her brother, Tom, flipped opened the phone.

"Syd Murphy's Pleasure Palace. Remember to ask about our special *Yuletide Smack-Down*—two hot babes emasculating you for the price of one. Will you be paying by cash or credit card?" He waved a slice of cold pizza around to dramatize the words.

"Tom, you asshole. I am *so* going to kill you if you don't hand that to me right now," Syd hissed as she danced around her taller brother in frustration. He backed away and held the phone up over her head. As he slowly inched up the steps, he put it to his ear again.

"What's that?" he asked. "You're interested in a volume discount? Oh? A doctor? In that case, would you like me to set you up with a house account?"

"I mean it, Tom. If you don't want to spend the rest of your life singing soprano, you'll hand that to me right now." Syd grabbed the leg of his faded blue jeans and yanked him down to a sitting position on the stairs. She thought she could hear faint laughter through the earpiece. She finally succeeded in grabbing the cell phone and prepared to unleash another torrent of abuse just as Tom shoved the half-eaten slice of pizza into her mouth. "Motthurphumpks . . . jerksufa!"

Chuckling at her distress, Tom daintily stepped over her and headed back to the kitchen.

On the other end of the line, Maddie's voice was calm. "Excuse me? Do you think you could repeat that last part? I was trying to find my credit card."

Syd furiously wiped at her mouth. "I'm going to kill him."

"You know, I've never regretted being an only child—until right now."

Syd sat back against the stair riser. "You must be joking? If you think his phone manners are bad, you should see his bathroom habits. It's like living with Cro-Magnon man, incarnate."

Maddie chuckled. "I doubt it's as bad as all that. He sounds pretty . . . amusing."

"Amusing? Yeah . . . Well, you're just lucky that you can't see the hair on his palms through the phone."

"Then again," Maddie's voice was thoughtful, "maybe I'm *not* sorry that I won't be able to get up there."

Syd's heart fell, but she tried to keep her tone light. "What happened?"

Maddie sighed. "I have a young patient named Héctor Sanchez—he's seven. I saw him about a month ago when he had a strep infection. But now, he's in the hospital with viral meningitis. It was touch and go for a while. We thought it might be bacterial, and I worried that we'd have to quarantine his entire family. I'm afraid that his older brother has it, too. We're waiting on his lab results right now."

"God. I'm so sorry. Will they be okay?"

"Hopefully—if I can figure out how to keep them in the hospital. They don't have any insurance, and their mother is eight months pregnant. I worry about her ability to manage both of them at home in her condition."

"So, you're going to stay around and keep an eye on them?"

"I am. I feel that I have to. They don't have any other family in the area. Mr. Sanchez works for one of the bigger Christmas tree farms over in Ashe County, and he's traveling right now, delivering trees to lots near the coast." She paused. "I'm sorry. I really did want to try to make it up there, just for a night."

"I know," Syd said quietly. "It was just a whim. We knew it was an outside chance at best. Dad will be disappointed." She smiled to herself. "I think he's rounded up every broken appliance in a three-county radius. He seems to think that you'd look pretty fetching in a tool belt."

"Oh yeah? Whoever gave him that idea?"

"I simply cannot imagine."

"You can't?"

"Nope."

"Maybe it's just as well. I actually don't *own* a tool belt. Your father would be disappointed."

"He's not the only one."

There was a pause.

"Oh, really?" Maddie said.

"Well . . ."

"You know, I've observed that the telephone seems to morph you into some kind of altered state."

"What do you mean?"

"Remember once that you said we should have more conversations in the dark?"

"Yeah?" Syd said, warily.

"Well, I think we should have more conversations on the phone."

"Why's that?"

"Because you're . . . different."

"I am?"

"Oh, yeah."

"How am I different?"

"I don't know—*different*." Maddie paused. "Taller maybe?"

Syd let out the breath she had been holding. "You're such a jerk."

Maddie chuckled.

"Why do you love to torment me?"

"If I knew the answer to that, I'd be a very wise woman," Maddie said. Syd couldn't think of a quick, smart-aleck response to that. "Do I really?"

"Do you really what?"

"Do I torment you?"

"Are you seriously asking me that?"

"Let me see . . . I think I am."

"Well then, yes. You torment the shit out of me."

"I do?"

"You do."

"How?"

"How what?"

"How do I torment you?"

Syd sighed. "Well for starters, there's your whole ridiculous height advantage."

"Hold on a minute. I can't be held responsible because *you're* uncommonly short."

"And then there's your—hey! I am *not* uncommonly short."

"Reeealllly?" Maddie drawled. "Then how come you can't see anything above my waist?"

"You can't even *imagine* how wrong you are about that one, wise guy."

"Oh, yeah?" Maddie's tone was challenging. "What color are my eyes?"

"Oh, give me a break."

"I'm serious."

"You're seriously delusional."

"I knew it."

"What?"

"You can't answer me because you don't know."

"That's ridiculous. The entire world knows what color your eyes are. I think they're even listed in Zagat's *Best of Virginia* guide."

"Very funny."

"So. Where was I? Oh yes. The ways you torment me. Let's see . . . there's your complete and unselfish devotion to your patients."

"Well, I'm hardly Florence Nightingale, but how is that a torment for you?" Maddie sounded confused.

"It means I won't get to see you tomorrow."

They were quiet for a moment, and the only sound was the hiss of the miles between them.

"Wrong again. That's *my* torment."

"Mine, too."

"I'm sorry."

"So am I. We'll . . . I'll miss you."

"Same here."

They were quiet again.

"When are you coming home?"

Syd was surprised by her reaction to the question. She had never really thought of Jericho as home. But something about that characterization now felt comfortable. It seemed to fit—just like her growing relationship with Maddie and her small circle of friends seemed to fit.

"Friday," she answered. "I'm coming home on Friday." In truth, she had planned to stay in Maryland until Sunday, but her ticket had an open return, and she decided right then to take advantage of it.

"Really?" Maddie's tone seemed brighter. "Wanna come over for dinner on Saturday night? We can have a belated celebration."

Syd smiled. "I'd love that."

"Great. Will you cook?"

Syd sighed. "If I want something to eat besides pimento cheese spread, I guess I'll have to."

Maddie laughed. "Well, think about what you'd like to have, and text me a list. I'll do the shopping."

"Good luck with Héctor and his brother. I hope they're soon on the mend."

"Thanks. I do, too. Give my best to your folks—apologize for me."

"I will. Bye."

"Hey?"

"Yeah?"

"Merry Christmas, Shortie."

She smiled and held the phone just a little tighter against her ear. "Merry Christmas, Stretch."

She closed her phone and sat quietly for a few moments, staring straight ahead at the big wreath hanging on the inside of her parents' front door. It flickered with about a hundred tiny white lights. Friday. Three more days.

It felt like a lifetime.

Christmas Eve

Syd and Tom sat with their parents in the living room of the family home in Towson. It had been drizzling most of the day, and the colder, nighttime temperature quickly coated everything outside with a glaze of ice. Syd wished it would snow. She had checked the weather forecast earlier in the evening, and it was snowing in the mountains of Virginia. Snowing on Christmas Eve. In her mind's eye, she could picture the way the landscape looked there. She imagined the muffled quiet on the deserted street below her apartment, and the sticky, sweet smell of cedar twigs burning in her corner woodstove. She'd sit with her mug of hot tea, wrapped-up in blankets on her sagging sofa, reading *Jane Eyre* and trying to ignore the cold air that snaked in around the window frames.

Her father got up and added another log to the fire. In the background, Bing Crosby was crooning. Silver bells. Christmastime in the city. She loved her parents. She even loved her obnoxious brother. She was happy to be with them but she didn't want to be in the city. Not at Christmas. She wanted to go home.

Home. When did Jericho become home? For four years, she had lived in Durham with Jeff, and never once did she call it home. It was confusing. And that confusion joined forces with the rest of what was confounding her—filling up her senses with something unnamed. It disrupted her sleep and kept her on edge, but still it remained formless, just beyond her line of sight. Sometimes, she caught fleeting glimpses of it as it crept closer to her in the predawn hours, before it retreated again into the darkness behind the tree line of her subconscious.

"Want this, Sis?" She looked up. Tom stood in front of her. He was holding a tumbler filled to the rim with eggnog. She could see the hefty floater of rum clinging to the inch of froth at the top of the glass. She gave him a grateful smile.

"Thanks. I could use it." He winked at her before reclaiming his seat next to the fireplace.

"If this drizzle keeps up, it's going to be impossible to get out later." Janet was looking out the big front window toward the street. "We should call Marsh and see if he wants to plan on going to Mass tomorrow morning instead of at midnight."

"Go on and call him. I'm not going *anyplace* tonight." George stretched his legs out on the ottoman in front of his chair. "Too bad all we're getting out of this storm is ice. They're getting tons of snow further west." He glanced at Syd. "Good thing you aren't leaving until Sunday. You might have trouble navigating those mountain roads any time sooner."

Syd gazed back at her father. She hadn't told them yet that she'd decided to leave early. And now wasn't the time. Tomorrow. She'd tell them tomorrow.

"It's probably good that Maddie didn't try to get up here tonight," he continued. "Although I sure do wish she'd been able to join us. Not to mention, it would have been nice to have had *her* remove my stitches." He glowered at his wife as he plucked absently at the palm of his right hand, and the loose pieces of dried skin that lined the path of his healing cut. Janet had grabbed his hand without ceremony that morning, and quickly cut and removed his stitches with a pair of kitchen shears.

"Yeah. Just when do *I* get to check out this gorgeous brainiac?" Tom asked.

Syd looked at him. "Never."

He looked crestfallen. "Why not?" He turned to his father for support. "She's single, right? And hot? Why wouldn't she want to meet me?"

"For starters," Syd began, "She has an I.Q. well into the triple digits. That'd make conversation a little tough for you."

He snorted. "Who said anything about talking? There are all *kinds* of ways to communicate. Right, Dad?"

George seemed to think about that. "In this case, son, I think you're way out of your league."

Syd was pleased with that answer and looked smugly at her brother. "Told you."

"Oh come on. Like *you'd* be one to judge. I bet I could have her eating out of my hand in ten minutes. Hell, I nearly had her there on the phone the other day, and we only talked for two seconds." He paused. "She's got a hot voice, by the way. I mean, like phone sex operator quality."

"Uh huh. And you can make this comparison, *how,* exactly?" Syd asked.

"Hey, Mother Theresa. Don't blame me for having a healthy libido. You're just a frustrated prude, and you wouldn't know what to do with it if it fell into your lap."

Syd opened her mouth, but thought better of it. How could she tell her little brother what she didn't understand herself—that finally she was beginning to inch closer to knowing *exactly* what she'd like to do with "it." The problem was that "it" wasn't anywhere near her lap, or any other part of her life experience. It remained indistinct and out of reach, and probably always would.

Tom took her silence as acquiescence and prattled on. "Don't worry, though. There's probably another loser like Jeff Simon out there, just pining for you to notice him."

"That's enough, Tom." Janet's voice was sharp.

Syd raised her head and looked at her mother with surprise. "It's okay, Mom. He's right." She shook her head slowly. "I was an idiot to marry him. Why pretend otherwise?"

Tom set his glass down and leaned forward in his chair. "Hey, Syd, I'm sorry. Really. That was uncalled for. I didn't mean it to come out that way—honest." His eyes were round and soft. "Jeff was a jerk. He never knew what he had in you. I'd like to punch his damn lights out for hurting you."

She gave her brother a small smile. "I allowed myself to be hurt. It's not all his fault. But that's all behind me now. I won't make a mistake like that again." *Not ever,* she thought. *Not even if I spend the rest of my life alone.*

"Well, I'll drink to that." George got to his feet. "Who else would like a refill?" He collected glasses and headed for the kitchen.

Syd sat in silence, along with her mother and brother, trying to push down aggravating thoughts about Jeff. George returned a few minutes later with a small tray with three fresh glasses of eggnog. He had a cordless phone cradled between his shoulder and right ear, and was having an animated conversation with someone. Syd hadn't heard the phone ring, so it was clear that he had placed the call. She assumed it was to her uncle, and concerned plans for their midnight Mass outing.

George set the tray down on his ottoman and distributed the drinks. He was laughing. "I'm not kidding you. She used kitchen shears. Can you believe it? The same ones she uses to cut up chicken breasts. I'll be lucky if I don't get lockjaw or something."

Syd was perplexed. Who was he talking to? Across the room, her mother rolled her eyes and took a healthy sip from her glass.

"That's what I told *her,*" he gushed. "But she said that you would've done it the same way if you'd been here." He walked to the fireplace and picked up the poker to rotate the top log. "How did all of that emergency business work out? Are the little boys doing better?"

Oh, my god. Syd felt her face grow hot. *He's talking to Maddie. He called Maddie. Jesus.* Her pulse began to race. She took a big gulp of her eggnog to try and compose herself. She needed to look indifferent. She needed to *feel* indifferent. She needed to go outside and stand in the rain until she cooled off.

"I'm glad to hear that," George said. "We're so sorry, though, that you couldn't be here to join us." His eyes tracked across the room to light on Syd. He watched her face as he listened to the voice on the phone. "She's fine. She's right here, in fact, looking like she's about to pass out from the heat of this fire I've got going. Hold on a second, and you can say hello to her." He held the phone out to Syd. "Here, honey. Why don't you take this out on the porch and cool off while you two talk?"

Syd didn't know whether she wanted to fling her arms around her father's neck in gratitude or bolt from the room. Instead, she reached for the telephone and stood up to make her way to the front door. Her mother intercepted her and handed her a folded afghan. "It's cold out there. Bundle up if you decide to sit down."

Syd took the throw and smiled at her mother as she opened the big front door and stepped out onto the porch. She pressed the phone to her ear.

"Hello there," she said, finally. "Fancy meeting you here."

She sat down on the swing and wrapped herself in the warmth and familiarity of Maddie's quiet laughter, forgetting entirely about the blanket in her arms.

Syd's plans for returning to Jericho changed again when she told her parents about her decision to leave on Friday instead of Sunday. They protested at first, but it soon became clear to Syd that they realized she actually was anxious to go. She was anxious—and excited. And she knew that excited was an emotion neither of them had seen in her for too long. They quickly made peace with the change in plans, but suggested that she consider driving back with her brother, instead of flying.

Tom had planned to leave on Friday all along. He was a graduate student at Virginia Tech in Blacksburg—only an hour-and-a-half north of Jericho.

Janet had a large bag of clothing, a desk lamp, and a box of assorted kitchen utensils she wanted Syd to take home with her, so the prospect of having Tom drive her back held great appeal. Syd struggled with the decision. Her car was parked at the Raleigh airport, so she would have the later ordeal of prevailing upon someone to drive her there to retrieve it. And, frankly, she wasn't certain that she felt up to spending six hours in the car with her brother.

"Look," Tom said. "Why don't you just go ahead and fly, and I'll run your stuff down to you on Saturday? I'd like to see the library, anyway. So I can drop your things off, and be back at Tech before the Duke game on Saturday night."

Syd was surprised by his generous offer. "Are you sure?"

He shrugged. "Yeah. I feel bad that I wasn't around to help you when you moved. Lemme at least do this."

She smiled at him. "Thanks, then. I'd really appreciate it. I don't want to have to ask anyone to drive me all the way to Raleigh to get my car."

"Yeah, what up with that? Why didn't you leave out of Charlotte? It's a damn sight closer to Jericho than Raleigh. Shit, by the time you to got to Raleigh, you were halfway here."

"Not quite," she said. "And I wanted to get some work-related stuff out of my storage unit there. Besides, I'm flying free on rewards miles, and Southwest doesn't go into Charlotte."

"Whatever. Let's get your shit packed up. I want to be on the road by noon."

It snowed again on Saturday. Hard. Tom finally reached the tiny hamlet of Jericho a little before two and pulled into the lot next to the old storefront building that housed the library and Syd's apartment.

Syd met him at the street door. "God, I was so worried. I tried to call you on your cell phone, but it kept rolling to voice mail."

He smiled apologetically. "Yeah. I left it at my girlfriend's house this morning. Not the best day for that. If I'd gotten stuck in this, I'd have been screwed." He carried a large, taped-up box and a Hefty bag full of clothing. Syd took the box from him and led the way up the stairs to her small apartment.

"I can't believe you still came. You're not going to get back out of here today."

"Sure I can. I don't think it can continue at this rate much longer. I'll just hang out for an hour or so, and then head on back."

They entered the apartment and closed the door against the frigid air sweeping up the stairs from the street.

Syd put the box down on her kitchen table. "I wouldn't count on it. I've been watching the Weather Channel, and what we're seeing now is just the leading edge of a larger system that's moving in. By tonight, we're going to be in full-fledged whiteout mode. They're predicting ten to twelve inches before it tapers off tomorrow morning." She turned to him. "You're stuck here," she smiled demonically, "with your evil big sister."

"Great." He shrugged out of his leather jacket and looked around her tiny, furnished apartment. "Jeez, Syd. This is the best they could do for you?"

"Well, as Faye Dunaway once said, 'These accommodations ain't particularly de-luxe.'"

He looked at her. "*Bonnie and Clyde*, right?"

She smiled at him.

"Some day, you need to see a movie that was actually made in this century."

"Yeah, well, you got the reference." She walked into the kitchen area and took two mugs out of a cupboard. "Want some coffee?"

He nodded. "I only got the reference because it was just on TCM during *Gangster Week*. Dad watched it about ten times. He drove Mom nuts."

"Apparently you did, too."

"What? Drive Mom nuts?"

"Well, that goes without saying. I meant that apparently, you watched the movie, too."

He sat down on a straight chair. "Sure. Faye Dunaway was pretty hot in those days." He picked at a loose piece of tape on the outside of the big box their mother had packed for Syd. "I'd do her."

Syd snorted. "You'd do a hole in a tree."

He sighed and looked at his watch. "This is going well. I've been here all of four minutes, and we're already insulting each other."

She laughed. "See why I didn't want to spend six hours in a car with you?" She handed him a mug of coffee.

"Well, since it looks like you now get to spend the entire night with me, you may live to regret that decision." He sipped his coffee. "What smells so good?"

"Chili. I started a big pot this morning. It seemed like a good day for it."

"Sweet. Chili and basketball."

"Excuse me?"

"Oh, come on. I have a ticket to the Duke game tonight. There's no way I'm not gonna at least watch it in on TV."

"What makes you think it's going to be televised?"

He gave her a withering look.

"Fine. Fine. Watch your precious basketball game. I'm supposed to go out, anyway."

He looked at her with interest. "Oh yeah? What about the impending whiteout conditions?"

"I don't have that far to go." She walked into the living room and sat down on the sofa. He stood up and joined her, sinking into the room's only upholstered chair. "But, you're right. If this keeps up, I'll probably have to stay in, too."

"So what is this?" he asked. "A date?"

"Hardly."

"Why are you acting so squirrelly?"

She looked at him. "I am not acting squirrelly."

"Are too."

"Am not."

"Are tooooooooo."

"Shut up, Tom. It's not a date. I was just going over to a friend's house for dinner."

"Uh huh. And that's why you're cooking chili—because you're going *out* for dinner?"

"In fact, I am taking the chili *with* me. And if you keep acting like a complete ass, I won't leave any here for you."

"Okay, okay. Truce." He took another sip of his coffee. "So. Who's the friend?"

"God, Tom. You're worse than Mom."

He looked at her in mock horror. "That was a low blow."

She relented. "It's Maddie."

"Maddie?"

She nodded.

"Maddie, as in, I'm a six-foot tall, gorgeous hunk of woman with blue eyes and a genius IQ? That Maddie?"

"Where do you get your information?"

He looked back at her without speaking.

She sighed. "Dad. God." She shook her head. "You guys are so much alike, it's scary."

"Wrong on both counts, *Margaret.* I Googled her ass." His eyes grew thoughtful. "And what a *fine* one it is."

"You did *what*?"

"Don't act so offended, Miss Research-Is-My-Life. It's not like you've never done this."

"You're so full of shit. Stalking people online hardly constitutes research."

"Yeah, well, to each his own. It was an hour well spent, lemme tell you. She was the editor of some hoity-toity med school journal at Penn, and there are lots of pictures of her up on that site, and several from some conferences she participated in while she was still working in Philadelphia. Oh, and apparently she was some kind of high school track star—hardly surprising with those legs."

Syd was incredulous. "You're really starting to scare me now."

"I'd send you the links, but there's really no need. You get to experience it all in the flesh . . . so to speak."

"You're such a perv."

"How does having a healthy sexual appetite make me a perv?"

"This has nothing to do with having a healthy sexual appetite. This is just creepy—like going through someone's underwear drawer."

He sat back and regarded her. "Interesting segue, Sis. How'd we make the leap from looking at *public* photos of her online to sniffing her underwear?"

Syd felt herself blush. "I didn't say anything about sniffing her underwear."

"No, but that's what you meant."

"I did not."

"Did too."

"Did *not*."

"Then why are you blushing?"

"You're a perv *and* an asshole."

The phone rang. Shaking her head at her brother one last time, Syd got up to answer it. She recognized the number on the caller I.D.

"Hello?"

"Enjoying our reprise of *White Christmas*?" Maddie asked. "I hope you know we arranged this little curtain call just for you."

Syd laughed. "You're too kind."

"I'm really not, but it works out well for me that you think so. How was the drive back?"

"Not too bad—long. Boring. But I got the things I needed in Raleigh, so it saved me from having to make a trip back over there next month."

"Good. Are you still up for coming by later?"

Syd looked out her front window. The street below was rapidly blending into the rest of the white landscape. "I don't know. What do you think? It's looking pretty ominous out there. If I come over, I might have to stay until spring."

"Hmmm." Maddie paused a moment. "How much chili did you make?"

Syd smiled. "A lot."

"I'll take my chances, then." She paused again. "Why don't I come and pick you up? I've got 4-wheel drive in the Jeep, and I'm more accustomed to driving on these roads in the snow."

"That could work."

"I do think we should do it sooner rather than later. I want to make a good set of tire tracks on my lane while I can still *see* it."

Syd glanced at her brother, who was watching her with undisguised interest. "There is one other thing I need to share with you."

"What's that?"

"My obnoxious little brother picked *today* to drive down here from Blacksburg with a pile of stuff my mother sent back for me. It's pretty clear that he isn't gonna be going back tonight."

"Well, bring him with you. I'd love to meet him. Unless, of course, you think you should stay at home and do family-bonding-types-of-things. I don't want to intrude on that."

"God, no. I've had enough family bonding to last me until Shrove Tuesday."

"Well then, what's the problem?"

"Basketball."

"Basketball?"

"Hokie basketball."

"Oh . . . *that*. He wants to watch the Duke game tonight?"

Syd sighed. "How do you know everything?"

"I know I'll regret admitting to you that I really *don't*. In fact, I've been sitting around here flipping channels for about two hours, waiting to call you. I saw about twenty ads on ESPN for the game."

"Why did you wait two hours to call?"

"I didn't want to appear too anxious. You see, I really *do* like chili." She paused. "A lot. It's hard for me to relax when I know I'm going to be having it—especially when I *haven't* had it for days and days. The anticipation can be maddening. I have to keep my emotions under tight regulation."

"Oh, really?"

"Yes. Chili and I have a complex and storied relationship."

"You're such a nut job."

"Yes, I am."

"So you don't mind if Tom comes over with me to watch the game?"

"Of course not. We can watch it on the big set in the front parlor. I'll make a fire. That's if you think he *wants* to come over. Maybe he'd rather not spend the evening in the company of someone he doesn't really know."

Syd laughed. "Oh, trust me, *that's* not a problem. He thinks he knows you already."

"Great. Then let's say I come and get you in about . . . twenty minutes?"

"We'll be ready."

She hung up and faced her brother. "Well, wise guy, it looks like you're going to get your wish. Maddie is on her way over here to pick us both up. We're going to watch the game at her house."

Tom's blond eyebrow crept up closer to his hairline. "Really?" He rubbed the palm of his hand back and forth across his chin and cheeks. "Do I need to shave first?"

"To watch a basketball game and eat a bowl of chili? I hardly think so."

"No offense, but I was thinking about sampling something a tad hotter than your chili."

Syd sighed. "Believe me when I tell you this. You've got a snowball's chance in hell of Maddie becoming *your* Miss Right."

He gestured toward the snow falling outside. "And a great day for *that* analogy. Besides, I'm not looking for Miss Right. I'm looking for Miss *Right Now*."

She rolled her eyes. "Perv."

"Prude."

"Get your jacket and help me carry this pot downstairs. We'll wait for her in the library."

"Cool. I wanted to see the sights while I was here. Now that the most remarkable landmark is on its way, we can kill time exploring the other one until she gets here."

Syd picked up her keys. "Whatever."

Syd and Tom met Maddie in the parking lot. Maddie left the engine running on her dark green Cherokee, hopped out, and crossed the lot to meet them as they approached. She was wearing jeans and a brown leather aviator jacket. Her long dark hair was loose and dotted with fluffy bits of snow.

Tom stood slack-jawed, holding the big, covered pot of chili, as he got his first real look at her. Even though he'd seen about a dozen photos of her, nothing quite prepared him for the reality of meeting her face-to-face. *Holy shit,* he thought. *She's fucking gorgeous.*

He watched her stride right up to his sister and envelop her in a full-body hug, before she turned to him with a magazine-cover smile. She still had an arm draped loosely around Syd's shoulders.

"You have to be Tom," she said in that sexy, alto voice. "I'm glad to meet you." She studied him with the most incredible blue eyes he'd ever seen. "I think I'd be able to pick you out of a police lineup." She looked back and forth between Tom and Syd. "You two could almost be twins."

He had to force himself to stop gaping at her and say something. Open his mouth. Make intelligible sounds. It really wasn't that hard. *God.*

"Yeah. Nice to meet you, too." *Wow, that was really impressive.* He tried again. "I hope you don't mind having me crash your reunion dinner?"

She released Syd and smiled at him again. "Not at all. I'm actually a closet college basketball fan, so I'm happy to have a good excuse to watch the game." She winked at him, and he felt an unmistakable twinge of arousal as he stared back at her. *Jesus.*

Syd looked at her. "You are?"

She nodded. "Sure. But when you go to a lame-ass basketball school like Stanford, you don't talk about it much."

Syd chuckled. "I think that's the first time I've ever heard the words Stanford and lame-ass used in the same sentence."

Maddie shrugged. "Let's get going and head on out to my place. We can have a much livelier debate about this once we're safely inside and out of this weather. Tom, do you need a hand with that?"

He was still staring at her stupidly. "Uh—no. No, it's fine. Lead on."

He caught Syd's eye as they started trudging across the snow-covered parking lot toward the Jeep. She was looking at him with an odd mixture of amusement and suspicion. *See?* Her glance seemed to say. *I told you she was out of your league.* But there was something else, too. Syd's demeanor toward the tall woman seemed . . . proprietary. Even possessive.

No. That couldn't be right. She just didn't want him to make an ass out of himself with her new BFF. But that hug. What was *that* all about? They sure looked . . . glad . . . to see each other. If he hadn't been watching Maddie with his sister, it would've been almost hot.

He looked Maddie up and down as she pulled open the two side passenger doors of her Jeep. Her jacket was unzipped and he caught a glimpse of the long body it concealed when she bent over to move something off the rear floorboard. *Shit. There's no way. Not her.* He looked at Syd. *Not her, either. Fuck. Who even knows anymore?* As he climbed into the backseat of the Jeep, he met those hypnotic blue eyes again. *And who cares?*

Maddie led them up the porch steps to the kitchen entrance of her house and stood, shaking the snow out of her long hair. She unlocked the door and stepped inside, barking a command at Pete, who had heard them approaching from the barn. "Sit! Stay."

She ushered Tom and Syd inside. "Let me take your coats. Tom, you can set that right over there on the stove." She gestured across the room toward the massive Wolf range.

Syd unwound her scarf and handed it with her coat to Maddie. She knelt and held her hands out to Pete, who was still seated, but squirming with excitement. "Hey, handsome. Come and see me." The big dog waddled over to her and laid his head in her lap, his tail making a staccato beat on the tile floor. Syd kissed the top of his head. "I missed you. Yes, I did," she cooed as she scratched behind his yellow ears.

Maddie watched them both with affection. "I think he missed you, too. I haven't seen him this animated since Thanksgiving."

Tom walked back across the room and handed his jacket to Maddie. "This place is incredible. Have you lived here long?"

"In fact, this was my father's home, but I did sort of grow up here. I've been living here full-time for about two years now." She took his jacket and hung it next to Syd's on a peg near the back door, and was struck again by his strong resemblance to his sister. He was a handsome man—taller than Syd, but with the same sandy blond hair and green eyes. She guessed that he was pretty popular with the ladies back at Tech. She turned to him.

"So, Tom . . . Syd tells me that you're in veterinary school?"

"Yeah. But not to be a vet—I'm more interested in the lab side of things. I'm working on my MS in Biomed/Vet Services."

She nodded. "So you want to do research?"

"Yeah. In truth, I don't think I could cut it as a practicing veterinarian. I don't really have the stamina for that."

She laughed. "I know what you mean. It's a lot harder than med school."

Syd looked up. "Oh, come on."

Maddie nodded. "I'm not kidding. We only had to learn *one* system—veterinarians have to learn dozens." She shook her head. "That was entirely too daunting for me." She looked thoughtful. "Not that there haven't been times when I've treated patients in the ER who seriously pushed the envelope on what constituted a fair definition of human."

Tom laughed. "I know what you mean. I was an undergrad at Drexel."

"Oh, really? I participated in a couple of job fairs there for premed students when I was working in Philadelphia."

"I know," Tom replied.

Syd stood up quickly. "Why don't we get this chili heating up and go make that fire you promised?"

"Sure," Maddie said, somewhat surprised. "Come on, Tom. You can help me carry some wood in from the front porch." She turned and led the way down the wide center hall, with Pete following close behind.

The game was nearing the end of the second period, and the Hokies were clinging to a narrow lead over the Blue Devils. Duke was suffering from an uncharacteristic number of turnovers and missed free throws, and the Virginia Tech team was cashing in on every mistake. Tom was clearly beside himself, but Maddie had seen the Blue Devils rebound too many times in the final minutes of a game to be so confident that the Hokies had put this one away. She picked up her chili bowl and decided to head back to the kitchen for another helping. In her view, this game was plainly headed for overtime.

"Anybody else ready for more?"

Tom was oblivious, but Syd stood up and joined her. "I'll go with you." She looked down at her brother, whose gaze was fixed on the big, flat screen TV. Duke's best free throw shooter was approaching the foul line. She picked up his bowl, too. "He's in la-la land. I'll bring him some more."

They walked back toward the kitchen. It was the first time they had been alone since Syd got back from Maryland. Maddie didn't want to waste the chance to enjoy a few minutes of solitude with her. She set her bowl down on the center island and turned to Syd. She could hear Tom cursing in the background.

"So. Hello."

Syd put down the two bowls and gave her a quiet smile. "Hi."

They faced each other in silence for a moment, before Maddie held out both arms in invitation. "Come here, you."

Syd stepped forward without hesitation, and they hugged warmly.

"I missed you," Maddie murmured against the top of her head.

"Me, too," Syd said, smiling against her shoulder. "Who knew a week could be so long?"

"Was it really that rough?" Maddie backed up and held her at arm's length.

"Not rough. Just long. Too long. I wanted to be here." She met Maddie's eyes.

"Here?" Maddie felt her pulse begin to race.

Syd laughed. "Here. Jericho." She stepped back and tucked a loose strand of hair behind her ear. "But here with you is pretty nice, too. Thanks for having us over. I know this probably isn't quite the reunion you had planned."

You can say that again, she thought. "It's fine. I get to see you, and eat my weight in this truly fabulous chili. What more could a girl ask?"

Syd looked for a moment like she might have a response, but she was distracted again by groans and curses from the front parlor. She rolled her eyes. "How much longer is this torture likely to last?"

"Do you mean the basketball game? Or my scintillating repartee?"

Syd seemed to deliberate. "Do I have to make a snap decision?"

"Smartass. And here I was trying to be all charming for your brother."

"Oh, trust me. You don't have to *try* to impress him. He was sold on your charms about two seconds after meeting you."

Maddie tried to hide her smile. "Really? Hmmmm."

"Yeah, yeah. Go ahead and gloat. Your conquest of the Murphy men is proceeding apace."

Maddie leaned back against the granite countertop and crossed her arms. "And what about the rest of the Murphy clan?"

Syd lifted her chin. "What about them?"

"How likely are they to fall before my full-frontal charm offensive?"

"Well, I don't know." Syd's gaze was hypnotic. "How important is it for you to find out?"

"It could be very important," Maddie said, quietly.

"Oh, yeah?" Syd's voice was a near whisper.

"Uh huh." Maddie dropped her arms and began to take a step toward her just as Tom entered the room.

"Hey, who took off with my chili bowl?" He stood in the doorway with a surprised look on his face. "Um—did I interrupt something?"

Syd turned toward the stove. "Of course not. Are you ready for another bowl?"

Maddie walked to the Subzero and opened its big glass door. "Want another beer, Tom?" she asked, ducking her head inside to hide it. Her heart was about to hammer through her chest wall, and she was trying desperately not to blush.

"Sure," he said. "The game's gone into overtime. Duke hit four consecutive free throws. Bastards."

Maddie laughed as she stood upright and handed him a cold bottle of Stella Artois. "Told you."

"Yeah, well, it ain't over yet." He took the beer and walked to Syd. "Damn," he said, as he looked out the kitchen window. "That's some storm raging out there."

Not just out there, Maddie thought. "Yeah. We need to keep an eye on it, or you two really will be stuck here until the spring thaw." Syd looked up from ladling the chili to meet her eyes. Maddie felt momentarily woozy. What the hell was happening here? What had she almost done? *Jesus.* "What a shame that would be."

Syd smiled at her without speaking and picked up another bowl.

Tom tilted his head toward the front room. "I'm not going anyplace until this game is over." He picked up his bowl. "You two coming?"

Maddie sighed as she picked up her own bowl. "Right behind you."

It was after eight, and the snow was finally tapering off. Syd was agitated beyond measure by her behavior with Maddie in the kitchen. She had been unable to concentrate on anything else since they had rejoined her brother in the parlor.

If Tom hadn't walked in on them when he did, what would have happened? And even worse, what did she *want* to have happen? Her brain was on overload. Why did she continue to behave the way she did around Maddie—like she was some kind of hormone-addled teenager who was incapable of rational thought? God, she even made her brother look mature. She'd never acted this way before—not around other lovers, and certainly never around another woman. None of it made sense to her.

Maddie sat several inches away from her on the small loveseat. They had been consigned to sit next to each other when Tom commandeered the only other chair in the room. Syd hugged the armrest as tightly as possible, trying to avoid any accidental contact with Maddie, who appeared oblivious to this as she quietly watched the end of the game.

Syd discreetly stole a glance at her. Maddie had an arm propped up on the back of the sofa, and her head was resting on a curled hand. Syd allowed her gaze to travel down her shapely, long torso and along the length of her outstretched legs—crossed on the ottoman in front of them. *God. She's so beautiful.* She lifted her gaze and realized that Maddie was now looking at her.

When she met those blue eyes, something surged through her body like an electric shock. What was it? Panic? Fear? Desire? They stared at each other unblinking as the sports commentator droned on in the background. *Jesus.* Syd's heart was about to pound out of her chest. She was certain that Tom would hear it over the din of the TV. She couldn't think. Couldn't breathe. She was consumed with wanting to touch her—wanting to *kiss* her.

For a split second, she thought that Maddie felt the same way. She saw something flicker in her blue eyes. They seemed to get darker, smokier. She lifted her head from her hand and moved her arm to rest along the back of the sofa behind Syd's shoulders. Almost involuntarily, Syd leaned slightly toward her—heedless of her brother sitting several feet away. Maddie slid her hand behind Syd's neck and pulled her forward, both of them gasping when their bodies finally came together. The broadcast of the basketball game thrummed on. Another foul. Another free throw. It didn't matter. None of it mattered. Syd was lost. Her confusion had dissipated. All that remained was a haze of yearning.

She raised her hands to Maddie's face—her beautiful face with its classic features. She stroked the wide planes of her cheeks and ran her thumbs across her full lips. Then she kissed her. They dissolved into one another and sank down into the cushions as the capacity crowd in Cassell Coliseum exploded in cheers. A ninety-percent free throw shooter had missed another shot. Duke had missed again . . . and Maddie was on top of her, kissing her back.

Somewhere in hell, a snowball got a second chance.

Maddie was kissing her. She was suffused with heat. Her brain was spiraling out of control. But something was wrong. A noise was distracting her. Beeping and grating. It grew louder.

Her eyes fluttered open. It was dark. She was disoriented. The beeping continued. Recognition dawned. A snowplow. It was a snowplow on the street below her window. *God.* She was in her apartment. She was in her bed. Alone. She tugged her pillow out from beneath her head and held it tightly against her face. The beeping continued—a maddening, monotonous, unbroken stream. It was like a heartbeat. Beneath the blankets, she started to shake. *Oh, Jesus. I am so fucked.*

Syd walked back to the small oak study table near her office, carrying two mugs of coffee. She'd asked Michael to meet her at the library because she was going to be there all day, getting caught up on processing and shelving returns that had piled up during her week in Maryland. Tom had left shortly after breakfast that morning—once Syd got confirmation from Curtis Freemantle that county road crews had worked through the night plowing the roads between Jericho and Jefferson.

She was exhausted and on edge. It had been impossible for her to go back to sleep the night before. Details from her dream had meshed so seamlessly with actual events from the evening at Maddie's that she was confused about what was real and what was imagined.

The dream. She didn't understand *any* of it, but she understood all of it. It was a terrifying jumble of known and unknown—things she thought she recognized tumbled together with new and unknown ingredients, creating a mixture that was exciting and strange. It was like her first experience of Indian cuisine—meats and vegetables she'd eaten her entire life were redefined. They exploded in new colors and exotic flavors, paired with spices and sauces in unlikely combinations that shocked her palate and put all of her senses on high alert.

Even in her distress, she had to smile as she thought about how Maddie would react to being compared to a dish of curry. But that's exactly what she was—a dense and powerful combination of hot and sweet spices that made Syd shiver and sweat, but left her gamely craving more.

She handed Michael his coffee and sat down across from him. "Thanks for meeting me here. I know it seemed like an odd request."

He shifted on his chair and stretched his long legs out to the side as he regarded her. "No problem. You sounded more than a little distressed. Did something happen with your brother?" He took a sip of his coffee and regarded her. Behind his dark-rimmed glasses, his gray eyes looked concerned.

"Not with Tom. No." She nervously slid her mug back and forth between her open hands. "I—it's not about anyone else. Not really." She met his gaze. "I need a sounding board. I need a friend, and I need to know that I can share this with you, and have it *just* be with you. And I apologize in advance for even asking that. I know it's unfair."

"First—of course you can talk with me. And, second—I don't think asking me to keep this conversation just between us is unfair at all."

She gave him a nervous smile. "You don't know what I need to talk about."

He reached across the table and stopped her still-moving hands. "Then enlighten me, and we'll go on from there."

She looked down at his hand as it rested on top of hers. "This isn't easy for me to talk about. I don't even know *how* to talk about it." She looked up and met his eyes. "I'm not even sure what *it* is, but it's making me crazy, and I have to figure it out."

He continued to regard her quietly.

"Ever since I moved here, I've been . . . unsettled by something—by *someone*. And I thought . . . at first, I thought it was just a reaction to the separation, you know? To leaving Jeff and moving up here? I mean, I know I've been lonely and I haven't really . . . engaged with anyone in quite a while. I had all those years in grad school to fill up my time, and it was easy to avoid how empty the rest of my life was. Does that make any sense?"

He gave her an encouraging smile. "Not yet, but I know you'll get there."

She sighed. "I haven't had friends like you—like you and David . . . and Maddie—in years." She looked down at her coffee mug. "Maybe never." She looked up at him again. "I mean, I've only been here . . . what? Three months? It's crazy. And already I feel happier and more settled than I've ever felt in my entire life."

He looked confused. "And this is a bad thing, because?"

She shook her head. "It's not—it isn't that it's a bad thing. It's more that it's . . . complicated. I wasn't even aware of it at first. Not really. It just sort of grew up around me, and then I started to notice it from time to time. I still didn't quite get it, even when it was jumping up and down and waving its arms in my face." She expelled a long breath. "And trust me, it's been waving its arms in my face for some time now. I can't pretend to ignore it any more."

"And what is it?"

She leaned forward and raised her hands to her face. "Oh, god. I thought this would be easier."

"Syd?" he asked, gently.

She lowered her hands and met his eyes.

"What is it?"

"I think—Michael, I think I might have . . . feelings for . . . another woman." She bit her lower lip as she looked at him with a lost expression. "For Maddie."

He looked at her for a moment with an expression that was unreadable. Then he nodded. "And that makes you feel—how?"

"Oh, god. How do you think it makes me feel? Lost. *Terrified.*" She shook her head. "Ridiculous. Confused." She paused and added quietly, "Excited." She leaned her forehead against the palm of her right hand. "I don't know what to *do*. I have no frame of reference for this. And even if I did. I don't want to risk losing her friendship."

"Honey, what makes you think you would ever lose her friendship?"

"I can barely trust myself to be around her. Every time I'm near her, I start acting like a horny teenager—like some ridiculous caricature of Roma Jean Freemantle.

I'm terrified that she's going to notice—that she's noticed already. I don't know what to do. I don't even know how to make *sense* out of this." She looked at him with desperation. "I mean, is this a fleeting thing—a product of my years of isolation? Is it just a *phase*? Is it just a function of how starved I've been for meaningful adult companionship? What do I do? How do I understand this?" She rubbed her forehead. "And what if I lose her? I don't think I could stand that."

"Okay. Okay. Let's just dial this back a bit. You can't take all of these issues on at once. You really will make yourself crazy." He paused. "And me, along with you." He smiled at her.

She sat back against her chair. "Okay."

"So, you're saying that you've never had feelings or inclinations like this toward another woman before?"

"Like *this*?"

He nodded.

She thought about it. "No. Not like this." She looked past him toward the front of the library where the large poster of Danica Patrick hung next to the street door. The glamorous, dark-haired Formula One driver sat holding a James Patterson novel, staring back at her. Daring her to be honest with herself. She looked back at Michael. "I mean, sure, I've sometimes found other women to be attractive. But I've never—ever—acted on that or even *thought* about acting on it. No. No, it's never been like *this*." She slowly shook her head. "Not ever."

He sighed. "So your feelings are pretty specific to Maddie?"

For just a moment, Syd felt like the floor had dropped away beneath her chair. "Yes."

"Do you think this is just something you're ready to come to terms with? Something bigger about yourself that finally feels comfortable or safe enough to come out?" He paused. "Pardon the pun."

Against her will, she laughed. "Oh, god. I have *no* fucking idea."

He reached across the table and took hold of her hands. "Here's what I think." She stared back at him expectantly. "You need to try and *relax*. Don't keep trying to dissect this. Let it evolve into whatever it's going to be. Give yourself time to figure it out. It's not some kind of relay race, and you don't have to break land records for speed to reach the next mile marker. Try to calm down. Cut yourself some slack."

"But what if it's true?"

"What if it is? It doesn't change anything about who you are—not *anything*." He raised an eyebrow. "Except maybe it shows that you have incredibly great taste in women."

She rolled her eyes in dismay.

"Seriously. One day at a time. What will be, will be."

She sighed. "I don't know if you just gave me good advice, or an index to your Doris Day recordings."

He laughed. "With me, it's always best to ask."

She sat quietly for a minute, digesting all he had said. "Even if I can manage to calm down, how on earth do I conduct myself around her? How do I manage not to mortify myself or embarrass her while I figure it all out?"

"I don't think you *could* embarrass her. Not with this. Not with anything, really. She's one of the best and kindest people I've ever known. You couldn't have a better partner," he shrugged, "or friend in this." He smiled at her. "Don't worry about Maddie. Don't worry about anything. Just take your time. Try to listen to your heart, and not your fear."

"You make it all sound so simple."

"Well, that's the beauty of it. At the end of the day, it *is* pretty simple. Once you know and understand what the realities are, it's just a matter of choosing to accept them. And either you will or you won't—that's about all there is to it. The rest is just . . . noise."

"Sound and fury?" she added.

He nodded. "Signifying *nothing*."

She sat back and nervously crossed her arms. "So where were you when I was going through puberty?"

He laughed. "When *you* were going through puberty? If I had to guess, I'd say that I was probably seated across a table from someone having exactly this same conversation—except I was sitting in *your* chair."

"Should I try to avoid her? At least, until I have some greater clarity about my . . . motivations?"

He shook his head. "I don't see how that would help you, and it certainly wouldn't be fair to her. She wouldn't understand it. Believe me when I tell you that your friendship is important to her. She doesn't open up to people very easily, and being back here to live has been a difficult transition for her. She needs us—all of us."

"I guess I knew that. I don't think I'd be very successful staying away from her anyway. It's the last thing I want." She sighed, miserably. "And that's the problem."

He took her hand again. "It only feels like a problem today. It won't forever. I promise. You'll get to the other side of this, and when you do, you'll know what the right course of action is. For you."

She squeezed his big hand between hers. "I hope you're right. I feel so ridiculous right now. Like I'm twelve again, with a crush on the most popular kid in school. I just don't want to make a fool out of myself."

"You won't."

"You don't know that."

"Yes, I do."

She shook her head. "I'll just have to be more self-vigilant until I figure things out."

"You don't have to be self-vigilant. This isn't a police action. If anything, you need to relax and be *self-aware*—that's what will set you free. The longer you try to constrain and avoid what you're feeling, the harder this process is going to be. Harder—and longer."

"So you're saying I should just go on like normal?"

He nodded. "Like *your* version of normal, yes."

"And if *my* version of normal means I end up totally losing control and throwing myself at her, what then?"

"Well, for starters, try to give me a heads-up before anything like that happens so I can be sure to sedate David. But otherwise, if you morph into some kind of sex-crazed wanton around her, then that's probably good information for you to have, too."

She raised her hands to her face again. "Oh, god." They sat in silence for a minute. "You know, I dreamed about her last night—in a *graphic* way. And I didn't want to wake up. And I tried all morning to blow it off—to tell myself that it didn't mean anything, but I knew deep down that it did. And I knew that I'd go crazy if I didn't talk with someone about it." She met his eyes. "So I called you. You were the first person I thought about."

He smiled at her. "I'm glad. And look at the bright side."

"There's a bright side?"

"Of course there is. If my advice ends up sucking, I can always make it up to you by keeping you well-supplied in baked goods."

"You mean, like cookies?"

"We could discuss cookies."

"Chocolate cookies?"

"That could happen, yes."

She deliberated. "So, do I *have* to be a sex-crazed wanton to get these chocolate cookies?"

"I'll get back to you on that."

"Well, then, I suppose I can contain myself for a *few* more days."

"That's my girl." He looked over her shoulder toward the back door. "In other news, it looks like the sun just came out." He smiled at her. "Maybe that's a good omen for you?"

They smiled at each other.

Chapter 11

The last day of the year was cold, but sunny and clear. Much of the accumulated snow had melted, but stubborn expanses of it continued to dot the pastures and cling to north-facing slopes. The roads, except for the remotest, unpaved county byways, were mostly clear—good news for local law enforcement, who worried about the presence of any hazardous travel conditions on a night that was sacred to revelry.

Maddie spent the day seeing patients in her clinic. It was a slow day with only four afternoon appointments, so she sent Peggy home shortly after three, and sat at the front desk herself, trying to get caught up on correspondence while she waited on her last patient.

She looked up when the door to the clinic opened, expecting to see Gladys Pitzer, who had called earlier about a puncture wound on her left forefinger. She had run some florist wire into it several days ago, and now thought it might be infected. Although she worked near the hospital, she preferred to see her own doctor, and Maddie encouraged her to stop by the clinic on her way home that afternoon—or to give her a call at home the next morning, and they could make arrangements to meet at the clinic later in the day.

But it wasn't Gladys—it was David. And he was carrying two large cups of coffee.

"Howdy, hot stuff," he cooed as he crossed the small waiting room. "I just got these at Freemantle's. Edna made us a fresh pot. I had a feeling you'd still be here."

She reached across the desk and took one of the cups from him. "Yeah. I've only got one more tentative appointment. Thanks for the coffee. What are you doing over here this afternoon?"

He perched on the edge of the desk. "I had to get a leak fixed on one of the front tires—that damn sensor light was driving me insane. It was like a strobe light cutting on and off."

"I know what you mean." She sat back in her chair and regarded him. He looked snappy in his wool slacks and cashmere sweater. "Isn't this ensemble a tad too GQ for the Firestone garage?"

He looked down at his trousered leg as he slowly swung it back and forth. "I hardly think so. Some of us like to demonstrate that we shop at places other than the Salvation Army Thrift Store. Besides, have you seen the new manager over there?" He fanned his free hand in front of his face. "Oh, honey. He ain't at *all* like the local white meat. I think he commutes in from Abingdon."

"Uh huh. And does Michael share your appreciation of this new natural wonder?"

"Oh, puh-lease. Michael has already had the damn Range Rover in there *three* times since last week. I figured it was my turn to enjoy the view." He took a sip of his coffee. "So, what do you have on tap for tonight? Settling down in your quilted robe to watch the Lawrence Welk marathon on PBS?"

She smiled sweetly at him. "How'd you guess? I really can't keep any secrets from you, can I?"

"I wouldn't advise you to try."

"How about you guys? Are you planning anything at the Inn?"

"Nope. Not this year. We have no guests this weekend—by design. We're going to kick back, make some big, greasy pizzas, and drink our weight in cheap North Carolina wine."

"Sounds charming."

"Care to join us? That's really why I stopped by."

"I had a feeling."

"Rescuing you from a life of drudgery is like a vocation for me, Cinderella. It adds another star to my crown."

"I think you might have mixed your metaphors. Isn't Cinderella the one who ends up with the crown?"

"I was referring to my *celestial* crown. If you weren't such a heathen, and occasionally went to Sunday school, you'd know these things."

"Yes, it's clear how well a life of religious perspicacity has served you."

"Oh shit, I hate it when you start trotting out those five-syllable words. It always makes me feel like my co-pay just jumped another ten bucks."

"You're a lunatic."

"So, what about it? Pizzas? Cheap wine? Eight o'clock? Your place?"

"*My* place?"

"Of course. It's hardly a night off for us if we're slinging hash at the Inn."

She sighed. "Okay. Fine."

"What about Goldilocks?"

She eyed him with suspicion. "What about her?"

He rolled his eyes. "Duh? What are her plans for the evening?"

Maddie shrugged. "Why would you expect me to know?"

David raised his eyes toward the heavens. "Oh, gee . . . I dunno. Maybe because, for some *strange* reason that completely eludes me, she seems to think that *your* porridge is just right?"

"You're nuts."

"I'm nuts?"

"Yes."

He set his coffee cup down on the desk and crossed his arms. "And that's why you're blushing—because I'm nuts?"

"Shut up. I'm *not* blushing, and even if I were, it would only be out of embarrassment for *you*, and how you cling to this persistent delusion."

"Uh huh. And which of my many delusions would we be talking about?"

"Syd. Me. Give it up. It's never going to happen. And I don't want you playing any more of these reindeer games."

He sighed. "In the first place, you're the one harboring persistent delusions. Anyone with opposable thumbs can see that the sprightly and curvaceous Miss Murphy has a more than sisterly fascination with your," he waved his hands around to indicate her shape, "stuff."

Maddie groaned.

"And in the second place," he continued, "even if you *were* right—and you're not—it ain't like we all move in such an expansive social set that we can afford to start editing out smart, funny, and *charming* companions. Especially ones who are so easy on the eyes." He paused. "She's a good friend—to all of us. And I'm not going to avoid her just because you can't keep your libido in your boxer shorts."

She regarded him coolly. "I don't wear boxer shorts."

"Yes you do. You just wear them on your brain."

"If I ever figure out what that's supposed to mean, I'll be sure to come back with a crushing response."

"You do that." He stood up. "But in the meantime, *I'm* going to call her and see if she has plans for the evening. *You* can go home and douse your head in a bucket of ice water, right before you shimmy into your sexiest big girl britches and *deal* with it."

She sighed. "*Fine.* At least if I'm at home, I can get drunk."

"*That's* my girl—always looking for the silver lining."

Maddie heard the sound of a car in the parking lot out front, and the opening and closing of doors.

"And that's my cue to exit." David leaned across the desk and kissed her on the top of her head. "Don't worry so much," he said quietly. "I actually *can* behave myself when it really matters."

She laid a hand on his forearm as he stood up. "David?"

He stopped and looked at her.

"It really matters."

He nodded. "I know it does, sweetness." He winked at her. "I'll see you tonight."

She watched him retreat down the back hall as the front door to the clinic opened and a distressed-looking and very pregnant Isobel Sanchez entered with both of her young sons in tow. Maddie got up from her seat behind Peggy's reception desk and hurried into the waiting room to meet her.

"*¿Qué pasa?* Are the boys sick?"

"*No, no, Doctora.* They are well. *Bien.* It is me." She hesitated. "Much . . . blood. *Estoy sangrando.*" She raised a hand to her forehead and looked nervously down at her little boys. They stood half behind her and gazed up at Maddie with luminous eyes.

Maddie took her by the arm to steady her. "How long? *¿Por cuánto tiempo?*"

"*Dos horas.*"

"I'm going to call an ambulance—*llamare a una ambulancia.* Can you walk?" She gestured toward her examination rooms. "*¿Puedes caminar a mi sala de examinación?*"

"*Sí.*"

"Is anyone with you?" Maddie gestured toward the parking lot.

"No. *Ellos no me pueden esperar.* No one."

"*¿Dónde está Carlos?*"

"Working. *En casa esta noche.*" She hesitated. "To-tonight."

Maddie nodded and turned to the children. "Come with us. I want to make your mother feel better." She crooked a finger to indicate that they should follow her. "*Voy a ayudar para que tu mamá se sienta mejor.*"

"Gabriel, Héctor—*vamos.*" Isobel leaned heavily on Maddie as they started down the hallway, but after only a few steps, she half collapsed. There was a pop, followed by a gush of brownish liquid that pooled about their feet.

Maddie recognized the meconium-stained fluid at once, but hastened to reassure Isobel. "The baby is coming. *Se roto la fuente de agua.*" She directed her into the first room on the left and helped her up onto a padded table. Behind them, the boys looked terrified. They huddled next to the door, trying not to look at the murky liquid on the floor. Their brown eyes were like saucers. Maddie grabbed some clean towels from a closet and placed them around Isobel's legs, then turned to the boys.

"Come in and sit." She pointed to two chairs in the room. "*Sientate con tu mamá.* Don't be afraid. *No tengan miedo.*" They shyly entered the room and perched on the ends of the chairs.

Maddie walked back to the hallway and knelt next to the puddle of brownish fluid. She dipped the end of a towel into it and held it to her nose. It smelled vaguely like Comet cleanser. She dropped several towels on top of the wet area and stood up and grabbed the receiver for the wall phone in the hallway. She quickly punched in the emergency number for the Jefferson EMT service. They answered on the second ring.

"This is Dr. Stevenson. I have a twenty-four-year-old woman here in my clinic. She's in the thirty-sixth week of her pregnancy and has just sustained a meconium aspiration. I need immediate transport to the Wytheville ER, and an OB-GYN surgical team standing by for a probable emergency C-Section. I can stabilize her here. Tell the paramedics to use the clinic's rear entrance. We'll be waiting on them. Right. Yes. None. That's right. Thanks." She hung up.

Inside the examination room, Isobel was quietly reassuring her sons. "*No tengan miedo. Tu mamá esta bien. Tu papá estará aquí, pronto. Sean valiente.*"

Maddie stood there, holding the telephone and deliberating for only a moment before she punched in another number and raised the handset to her ear.

"Hello?"

"It's me. How good are you with kids?"

Syd laughed. "Is this some kind of radio quiz?"

Maddie sighed. "I wish. Look, I need your help. Now. Right now. Can you be at my clinic in ten minutes? I've got an emergency on my hands, and I'm here alone."

"I'm on my way." Syd hung up.

Maddie walked back into the examination room and washed her hands before slipping on a pair of latex gloves and approaching the table. "Let's see what kind of entrance your little one is about to make." She gave Isobel what she hoped was an encouraging smile. "Everything will be just fine. *Todo estara bien.* We'll take *good* care of you." She looked down at the two boys. "You, too. *Ustedes, también.*"

Syd arrived at Maddie's clinic just as the EMT truck was backing toward the rear of the brick building. She walked in the main entrance and met Maddie in the hallway that led to the examination rooms. She noticed the wet towels on the floor between them.

"Thank god," Maddie said. "Perfect timing." She wrapped an arm around Syd's shoulders and stood with her a moment in the waiting room. "I owe you *big* time for this one. A very pregnant Isobel Sanchez is here with her two sons, and her water just broke. She's alone and doesn't have anyone to keep the boys until her husband gets back from Tennessee tonight. If she agrees, would you be willing to keep an eye on them until I can get back from the hospital? It shouldn't be more than a couple of hours."

Syd nodded. "Absolutely. I'm happy that you thought to call me."

Maddie smiled and gave her shoulders a squeeze. "Great. C'mon. I'll introduce you to them."

Syd was anxious and intrigued as they approached an illuminated examination room. "Syd, this is Isobel Sanchez, and these are her sons, Héctor and Gabriel. Isobel is on her way to Wytheville to have her baby, and her husband is on his way back into town from Bristol. I'm going to ride with her in the ambulance, and we were wondering if you would be willing to keep Héctor and Gabriel company until their father can get back, or we can find a neighbor to help out?"

Syd smiled at the two boys. They looked wary, but curious. "Of course." She looked at Mrs. Sanchez, who seemed barely more than a child herself. "I'll be happy to stay with them. Don't worry."

Isobel gave Syd a grateful smile. "Thank you. *Usted es muy amable.*"

"I'm happy to help." She hesitated. "*Con gusto le ayudo.*"

Maddie smiled at her proudly, before leaving the room to greet the EMTs at the back door.

Syd knelt next to the chairs where the two children were seated. "*Hola. Me llamo Margaret. Trabajo en una biblioteca. ¿Les gusta leer?*"

They both nodded.

Isobel encouraged them. "Héctor. Gabriel. *Vayan con la señorita. Debo ir al hospital ahorita, pero el Papá de mis hijos llegara a casa pronto.*" The boys looked at Syd nervously. "*Vayan con la señorita—ya.* Go."

Syd smiled at them encouragingly and held out her hands. The boys stood up and shyly took hold of them. She walked them out of the examination room and toward the lobby as the EMTs entered through the back door with a gurney. Maddie approached her and held out her hand. She was holding a set of keys.

"Why not take the boys to my place? They can play with Pete." She smiled at her. "It's well known that golden retrievers are fluent in *every* language. I'll be home just as soon as I can get her settled, and have an ETA on her husband."

Syd let go of Gabriel's hand and took the keys. "No worries. We'll all be just fine." Maddie gave her hand a warm squeeze before releasing it. "Are the guys still coming by?"

"Yeah. I'll call them on the way to Wytheville. They can give me a ride home." She looked back toward the examination room. "I need to go. With that amniotic fluid compromised, Isobel is sure to be facing an emergency C-Section." She hesitated for just a moment. "I can't thank you enough for this."

"Don't even think about it. I'm glad you called me." She took Gabriel's tiny hand again. "Give me a ring when you can and let me know how she's doing."

"Will do." Maddie knelt next to the boys. "Be good for Miss Murphy. *Tu mamá estara bien. No tengan miedo.* Don't worry." She rubbed them both on the tops of their heads and stood up. "See you later on."

She turned around and walked back to join Mrs. Sanchez.

Syd smiled down at the boys. "Do you like dogs—yellow dogs? *¿Quieren jugar con un perro amarillo?*"

They nodded in unison.

"Let's go, then. *Vamonos.*" She led them across the lobby and out to her waiting car.

M ichael was in a quandary about how he should conduct himself, once they all met up later at Maddie's. He needed to be mindful of Syd's confusion about her fledgling attraction to Maddie. He needed to help insulate Maddie from her full-blown attraction to Syd. And at the *same* time, he needed to somehow short-circuit any of David's continuing attempts to push the two women together.

And he needed to do all of this in secret.

Right, he thought. *A complete no-brainer.* He was halfway home with groceries for the evening when his cell phone rang. It was Maddie.

"Well, hello. I was just thinking about you."

"That's good, because we have a slight change in plans. I couldn't reach David."

"No worries. What's up?"

"I have an emergency, and I'm actually on my way to the hospital now. Syd is already out at my place with a couple of additional dinner guests."

"Really?" He was surprised. "Who?"

"I'll let her explain all of that. But I'm hoping you guys can go on out there a bit sooner than we planned and give her a hand. She's actually babysitting some patients of mine. I don't know how long they'll be there. Their mom's in labor and their father is out of town."

"Oh, gotcha. She's keeping them at your place?"

"Yeah, it seemed easier. Do you think you could go on ahead and help her out? Maybe feed the kids some pizza?"

"Sure. No problem."

"I was hoping that maybe David could give me a ride home from the hospital. My car's still at the clinic."

"No sweat. Just give us a shout when you're ready, and one of us will come and pick you up."

"You guys are the *best*. I knew I could count on you."

Michael laughed. "Some raucous New Year's Eve this is turning out to be."

"You got that right. Look, I need to go, we're turning into the hospital." She paused. "Oh, one last thing."

"Yeah?"

"How's your Spanish?"

avid and Syd were losing the card game. Losing badly. Across the kitchen table from them, Héctor and Gabriel had mounting books of cards. David groaned as he was forced to draw yet again from the dwindling deck.

Héctor giggled. "*¡Vaya y pesque!*"

David rolled his eyes. "Yes . . . that's right. I'm *fishing*. Again." He eyed Syd as he tried to stuff the newest card into his burgeoning handful. "I think these two are shysters."

"Don't look at me. I've got more cards than you have."

The phone rang. Michael left the center island where he was rolling out pizza dough to answer it. "Happy New Year," he said, holding the handset to his ear.

"How are things going out there?" It was Maddie.

Michael turned to the card players. "Great. I'm just about to get the pizzas in the oven, and your two favorite partners in crime are getting their tight little butts kicked in a cutthroat game of *Go Fish*. How are things where you are?"

"Isobel's doing just *fine*. She had a C-Section about an hour ago and is in recovery now. The baby is strong and healthy—a little girl."

"Oh, that's great. Hang on—I know Syd wants to talk with you." He turned to the table and held the phone out toward Syd. "It's Maddie, and she's got good news."

Syd jumped up from her seat and went to take the phone from him.

"Hi there. Tell me everything." She perched on a kitchen stool.

"Hello yourself. It's all good. Isobel and the baby are both doing fine. She had a little girl, and she's beautiful. I just saw her."

"Oh, that's wonderful. Did she have the C-Section?"

"Oh, yeah. It was unavoidable. They couldn't wait on a vaginal delivery. There was too much risk of having the baby take that infected fluid into her lungs."

"Has her husband arrived yet?"

"Yes, he just got here about twenty minutes ago. He's with Isobel now. I told him to stay at the hospital as long as he wanted to, and gave him directions to my place. He'll be by later tonight to get the boys." She paused. "How are they?"

"They're fine. We've been playing cards."

Maddie chuckled. "So I heard. Don't bet the farm, okay?"

"Oh, I promise. Are you coming home soon? We're about ready to feed the kids."

"Yeah. That's another reason I'm calling. Do you think David would come and pick me up?"

Syd smiled and turned to nod at David, who was watching her expectantly. "If it gets him out of this card game, I think he'd volunteer to Simoniz your Jeep."

Maddie laughed. "Tell him I'll wait for him at the ER entrance."

"Okay."

"I can't thank you enough for this. I know it was a lot to ask."

"Don't even go there. Besides, Pete deserves most of the credit. You were right about his effect on the boys. They relaxed immediately when they got here and started playing with him."

"Told ya. I'll see you soon, okay?"

She nodded. "Bye."

David was already on his feet, putting on his coat and fishing his car keys out of a zippered front pocket.

Syd turned to the boys. "*¡Usted tiene a una hermana pequeña! Su mamá es fina, y su papá estará aquí pronto.*"

They smiled as they nudged each other. Then they looked at Michael with concern.

"*¿Cuándo comemos nosotros pizza?*" Gabriel asked, seriously.

Syd sighed. "Men. You're all alike." She looked at Gabriel. "Yes. Soon. *Pronto.*"

They nodded and continued playing cards.

"And with that. I am outta here. I should be back with our wayfaring Sawbones in about an hour." David headed toward the back door.

"We'll go ahead and feed the kids," Michael said. "Then we'll eat together and celebrate when you two get back."

David waved as he walked out of the kitchen. "And get ready to pop a few corks—we've got some *serious* catching up to do."

Maddie and David got back shortly after eight-thirty, just as Syd finished settling the boys down upstairs in one of Maddie's guest rooms. At first, they were reluctant to go and lie down, but when she suggested that Pete looked really tired and needed a rest, they quickly volunteered to go along and help keep him company. Pete happily cooperated and hopped up onto the foot of the big double bed in Maddie's old room, and snuggled down between them. Syd knew that the boys would likely be sound asleep in minutes. She tugged the covers up over them and kissed them both on their foreheads.

"Have a nice nap. *Duerma bien.*"

They nodded and closed their eyes. She walked out and left the door ajar, so they could see the light from downstairs if they woke up before their father arrived. As she started down the hallway toward the back stairs, she smiled when she heard Maddie's voice drifting up from the kitchen below. She paused for a moment in Maddie's bedroom as she listened to the quiet sounds of talking and the unmistakable clink of wine glasses.

She was happy. It felt right to be there—comfortable and right. Right in ways that were both exhilarating and terrifying. She knew that Maddie had probably had her choice of several dozen people who could have helped her out with Isobel's children—yet she had called *her*. Why? Was it because she spoke a little Spanish? Was it because she was coming by her house later anyway?

She turned her head at the sound of Maddie's silvery laughter. Or was it because she wanted to share this with me? With David and Michael—*and me?* Her thoughts drifted back to her conversation with Michael that morning. He was right—Maddie *did* need them. And they needed her. They were like a family—a curious, cobbled-together, but warm and comfortable family.

She looked around Maddie's bedroom. It was like an extension of her: tidy but lived-in, spare but tasteful, functional but personal, and punctuated with surprising flashes of color.

Yes. It felt right to be there.

She walked to the stairs and slowly descended into the kitchen.

Maddie looked up with a broad smile as Syd walked in.

"So you made it." Syd smiled back.

"Oh, I'd never miss out on an opportunity to stuff myself on pizza and champagne." Her blue eyes sparkled as she held a glass out to Syd. "Join us in a toast?"

Syd went to stand beside her. "And just who might we be toasting?" she teased, as she took the glass.

David lifted his glass toward the ceiling. "To the newest little Sanchez, who just made her world debut two hours ago, but still managed to look older than Dick Clark."

"Hear, hear," Michael agreed, clinking glasses with him.

"I'll drink to that," Maddie said, locking eyes with Syd.

"Me, too." Syd laughed.

They all drank together. Michael set his glass down and turned to the oven. "Now clear a space, this pizza is beyond ready."

"And *I'm* beyond ready to eat," David said as he took his place at the table. "C'mon you two—siddown." As they took their places, side by side, David topped off their glasses. "So tell me, Cochise, was it hard for you to hand her off when you got to the hospital? I know how much you *luuuuv* to wield those sharp little knives of yours."

"Nope. I was a good little family practice physician and meekly got out of the way." She plucked a Kalamata olive off the relish tray on the end of the table.

"Oh, yeah. I forgot," David said. "Your track record with surgeons is *serious* bad news."

Maddie shot him a dirty look before she removed the pit from her mouth and flicked it across the table at him.

"Hey. Watch the cashmere."

"Hey, watch the *comments*."

"Girls . . . please. Any more of this, and I'll make you eat outside on the porch." Michael set the large pizza down on a hot pad in the middle of the table. It was fragrant and bubbling, covered with garlic, fresh basil, goat cheese, and sun-dried tomatoes.

"My god, Michael, this smells fabulous." Syd leaned over the pizza and tipped her head back as she inhaled.

"Yeah," Maddie said. "And with the amount of garlic on it—it's a good thing we're *all* going to be eating it."

"Oh, reeaaallly?" David drawled. "Just exactly what kind of activity did you have in mind for after dinner? Some kind of kinky, eclectic group thang?"

Maddie rolled her eyes. "Yes. Precisely. I thought we could play an adult version of your earlier amusement, and engage in a few provocative hands of strip *Go Fish*."

David sat back and considered her. "Interesting. Draw a card—lose a garment. I like it. I'm game."

"You're also an exhibitionist and a lousy card player." She picked up a slice of pizza and put it on Syd's plate. "That's a dangerous combination."

"Hey, I wasn't the *only* loser in the room. Miss Murphy over there was every bit as rotten as I was." He took a sip of his champagne. "She'd end up naked a *lot* faster than I would."

Maddie's hands paused in mid-air as she reached for another piece of pizza.

"Uh huh. *That* got you thinking, didn't it?" He sat back smugly and picked up his own slice.

"Honey, that cheese is *really* hot," Michael said. "Be sure you take a nice *big* bite."

David glowered at him.

Maddie shook her head.

Syd chuckled.

Over their heads, the two little boys slept on.

And twenty-two miles away in the maternity ward of the Wytheville Community Hospital, Carlos Sanchez and his wife Isobel named their tiny new daughter Madelena.

Carlos arrived at Maddie's farm a little before midnight. David and Michael helped him carry the still sleeping boys out to his battered station wagon, where they settled them under a couple of borrowed blankets on the back seat. Thankfully, they didn't have far to drive. Maddie and Syd followed them out to the barn where he had parked and stood by while Carlos got his sons tucked in. He stood and turned to Maddie.

"*Gracias, Doctora. Es muy amable y estamos en deuda con usted.*" He looked at his shoes. "*Siempre estaremos en su deuda.*"

Maddie laid her hand gently on his shoulder. "No. You have a wonderful family. *Es un placer, estamos para servir.*"

He met her eyes and smiled. Then he looked at Syd. "*Gracias por cuidar a mis hijos*. Thank you."

She nodded and smiled at him.

He got into his car and drove slowly away from the house.

The four friends stood at the edge of the yard and watched until his tail lights disappeared.

David sighed. "And they're *off*." He held his wrist up into the light and looked at his watch. "So . . . it's nearly time for that big, gaudy bauble to drop over Times Square. Let's go watch." He took Michael by the arm and steered him back toward the house. "You know, I heard that this year, they're using a set from one of Zsa Zsa Gabor's cocktail rings."

Maddie couldn't hear Michael's muffled response as they walked off. She turned to face Syd in the semidarkness. They were standing in one of the long shadows cast by the light on the front porch, and she could barely make out her features.

"Quite a night."

Syd laughed. "One for the record books, that's for sure."

"I'm sorry about that. I know this probably wasn't the kind of evening you had in mind."

"Don't be silly. I had a wonderful time. Those boys are adorable."

Maddie laughed. "Michael and David?"

Syd chortled. "That goes without saying. But I was referring to Héctor and Gabriel."

"They sure are."

"I have to tell you, something like tonight would never have happened in Baltimore." She looked at Maddie. "Or Philadelphia. We'd have had to turn them over to Social Services."

Maddie nodded. "No kidding. I think that's one of the things I like best about being back here to live. It's possible to practice medicine that includes a healthy dose of human kindness."

"I think that would be part of your practice no matter where you lived."

Maddie was glad the darkness hid her blush.

Syd took a deep breath. "Look at that sky. I've never seen so many stars."

"It's going to get a lot colder," Maddie said.

"Uh huh. I'm freezing."

Maddie wrapped an arm around Syd's shoulders. "Come on then, let's go warm up and welcome the New Year."

They slowly walked back to the house. Syd's arms were crossed against the cold, and Maddie tugged her a little closer as they made their way to the porch. "Are you tired?"

"Strangely, no. I guess it's all the excitement." She looked up at Maddie. "I guess you're a little more accustomed to events like this."

Maddie met her gaze. "Me? No, not really. I have to tell you that no matter how many times I witness it, I'm always awestruck when a woman delivers a baby. There's just something so surreal about being present at the outset of that tiny new life. I mean, there they *are*—perfectly formed, and perfectly unformed. They have everything before them. And for a few finite moments, everything is possible. They've never been hurt, they've never been disappointed, they've never been afraid, they've never made mistakes. They're just wonderfully present and ready to begin it *all*." She laughed and shrugged. "Starting with a meal, a bowel movement, and a good cry."

Syd laughed. "You sound downright humbled."

"I *am* humbled." She stopped and turned to Syd. "You're not now going to follow that sage observation up with some sarcastic remark about my ego are you?"

Syd gave her an innocent look. "Me? Would I do that?"

Maddie narrowed her eyes. "In about half a nanosecond."

Syd laid a hand on her forearm. "Not this time. I like it when you get all sappy and philosophical. It's sweet."

"Sappy?"

"Yeah."

"Sweet?"

"Uh huh."

"*I'm* sappy and sweet?"

"Right now you are, yes."

Maddie sighed and shook her head.

"I never knew you had such maternal instincts," Syd said. "It's sweet."

"Me?"

"Yes, you. I saw how you looked at those little boys—like they were pieces of marzipan."

Maddie gazed at her. "I hate marzipan."

"I don't believe you."

"Oh, now *there's* an informed response to a declarative statement."

"Don't try and goad me into a different train of thought. Just admit that you like kids."

"So what if I like them—sometimes? Occasionally. That doesn't make me all maternal."

"You're not maternal?"

Maddie snorted. "No."

"You don't ever want kids of your own?"

"Let's just say that it's not in my long-range plan."

"You *have* a long-range plan?"

Maddie chewed the inside of her cheek. "I'm beginning to formulate one, yes."

They were startled by a burst of gunshots and firecrackers. The remote chorus raged for several minutes as they stood still to listen, standing close on the lawn near the steps to the porch. Silently, they turned to each other, smiling.

"So. Happy New Year," Maddie said.

"Back atcha," Syd replied, quietly.

They continued to stare at each other while the distant sounds of celebration from neighboring farms rolled across the valley and echoed all around them.

Maddie leaned forward and kissed Syd softly on her forehead.

David walked to the front door and opened it, anxious to fetch Syd and Maddie who were still out in the yard. He had a freshly opened bottle of champagne in his hand, and he was ready to toast the New Year. In the parlor behind him, the voice of Ryan Seacrest could be heard shouting above the din in Times Square. He cast his eyes across the lawn toward the barn and saw them before he could call out.

They were standing close together in the shadows near the porch. He strained his eyes to get a better view. No, they weren't just standing close together—they were hugging. He looked down at the beads of sweat on the cold bottle in his hand and smiled as he raised it to his lips. "It's gonna be a *good* year," he said, before taking a big swig and retreating to join Michael in the parlor.

Chapter 12

On January 10, Tom Greene broke his arm in two places. The story *he* later told was that he sustained the injuries when he slipped on a patch of black ice while crossing a parking lot. The story his wife, Muriel, later told was that he fell off a barstool in their basement media room, and that the only ice he'd been near all evening had been floating in a tumbler of Jack Daniels.

But Dr. Greene's arm was well and truly broken, and it was clear that the Wytheville ER Chief was going to be out of commission for a good six weeks while he recovered.

His first choice for a *locum tenens* was the supremely qualified Dr. Stevenson, who already filled in at the ER two weekends a month. But Dr. Stevenson had her own practice twenty-two miles away in Jericho, and he wasn't certain she could be prevailed upon to inconvenience her patients by managing his ER while he was incapacitated. He also had the option of trying to cherry-pick from doctors at neighboring hospitals, but Stevenson was the ideal choice. She had an impeccable professional pedigree, had previously worked as an assistant ER chief at a major metropolitan medical center, and was already familiar with his hospital's protocols. In addition, she spoke fluent Spanish—an increasing asset, since most of the undocumented Hispanic residents of the area received their medical care in the hospital's ER.

He was determined to persuade her, but he knew it wouldn't be easy. He'd run headlong into her iron will before, and he knew that to succeed, he'd have to couch his offer in exactly the right terms. He picked up the phone on his desk with his left hand, and slowly dialed her number.

"Maddie? Hi, it's Tom Greene. I doubt if you've heard this yet but I fell yesterday and managed to break my arm." He chuckled. "Yeah. It's pretty pathetic. Transverse fractures of the radius and ulna." He looked down at the cast that encompassed his hand and covered his entire forearm. "The right one, of course." He laughed again. "Listen. I'm sure you know why I'm calling you, and before you say 'no,' I want you to listen to my proposal." He paused. "Well, I was giving some thought to that Parish Nurse program you talked with me about a couple of months ago, and I think I have an idea . . . "

Maddie had been working for three weeks as Acting ER Chief of the Wytheville Community Hospital. Through some careful juggling, she had managed to maintain clinic hours in Jericho for two mornings and one afternoon a week. Peggy was holding down the fort the rest of the time, and, soon, she would have the additional support of a licensed Nurse Practitioner.

Tom Greene had managed to shake loose some uncommitted United Way funding, and had pledged to have his hospital underwrite the remaining part of the expense of hiring someone to staff a limited Parish Nurse program in the surrounding county. Maddie had conducted phone interviews with several candidates for the post, and was scheduled to meet with the best of the finalists in her makeshift office at the hospital on Friday afternoon.

It had been a busy day in the ER, replete with a rather grisly leg wound injury sustained during late-season bow hunting for deer. Two brothers had been out on a ridge near the New River Shot Tower, and one had fallen from a tree stand, lodging an arrow in his thigh when he hit the ground and landed on his hip quiver. His brother was able to control the bleeding and drive him to the hospital, where Maddie removed the broadhead-style arrowhead, which, fortunately, wasn't very deeply embedded. She then had to set and cast his broken left wrist.

She was required to report hunting injuries like this to the local fish and game commissioner, and even if she hadn't been, she would have contacted the authorities once she smelled the alcohol on the breath of her patient. She was persuaded that his fall from the tree stand was due more to intoxication than excitement over getting off a clear shot at a retreating deer.

Once her patient had been attended to, and the game commissioner had arrived to interview him, she headed off to her office to check her messages and prepare for the interview. She was surprised when she rounded the corner to see that her candidate had arrived already, and was quietly seated on a straight chair outside her office door. The woman looked up in surprise as Maddie approached and smiled as she got to her feet.

"Are you Dr. Stevenson?" she asked, with a soft southern drawl.

Maddie nodded and extended her hand. "Yes. You must be Elizabeth Mayes." They shook hands warmly.

"Please call me Lizzy. Only my mama calls me Elizabeth—and then, only when I'm in trouble for something."

Maddie smiled at her. "Oh? Are you in trouble often?"

The petite redhead raised an eyebrow. "You don't expect me to reveal a thing like that during a job interview, do you?"

Maddie nodded. "Right. Well, come on in, and let's see what else I can trick you into not telling me."

They walked inside and sat down on facing upholstered chairs. "Was the drive up from Nashville long?"

Lizzy settled her bag and briefcase on the floor next to her chair and crossed her legs at the ankles. "Not too bad. I left at about seven this morning."

Maddie glanced at her watch. It was a little after three. "That's still a long drive. But you have family in the area, don't you?"

"That's right. My sister lives in Jefferson—Rachel Wilson. That's how I heard about the position. She works in the county manager's office."

Maddie nodded. "Would you like something to drink? I have access to soft drinks, or I can get you a cup of the world's worst coffee?"

Lizzy smiled. "That does sound awfully tempting but I think I'm just fine for now."

"Well, then, why don't you tell me a little more about yourself, and why you think the prospect of practicing in a remote area like this sounds appealing to you?"

"Okay. And if you're satisfied with my answers, can I be direct and ask you the same questions?" Lizzy's brown eyes looked directly into Maddie's. They were intelligent and curious, and their corners were crisscrossed with smile lines. Her gaze was open and unguarded. Maddie decided that she liked her.

"I don't see why not," she answered.

Lizzy nodded. "So. I got my BSN at UT and worked for five years at a hospital similar in size to this one." She paused. "I hated it. It was mostly housekeeping and paperwork—not the kind of nursing I'd always dreamed about." She smiled as if to herself. "You know, I had all those Cherry Ames-type fantasies—*Dude Ranch Nurse, Department Store Nurse, Cruise Ship Nurse.* Crazy stuff. But I knew that, for me, nursing was a calling." She met Maddie's eyes. "I won't deny that my faith is important to me, and I see a real parallel between the daily exercise of it and my chosen profession. Don't let that scare you," she quickly added. "I'm not some kind of born-again snake-handler." Maddie chuckled. "And I sure hope you're not either, 'cause if you are, then I just blew the hell out of this interview."

Maddie smiled. "I think your secret is safe with me."

Lizzy let out a long breath. "Thank god. Well. I left the hospital and got a job in Nashville, working out of a community center managed by Lutheran Family Services. That's how I became interested in the whole Parish Nurse model. It just seemed to fit me perfectly. So I enrolled in the NP program at Vanderbilt and finally finished up my degree last spring. The rest, as they say, is history."

"How long have you been with Lutheran Family Services?" Maddie asked.

"Three-and-a-half years."

"Do you do any work out of local church congregations, or are all of your services provided through the community center?"

"Most of the work happens in the center but I do remote visits to several small churches twice a month—on Wednesday nights and Sunday nights. I see about forty regular patients that way. Many of them don't have access to transportation into Nashville, or would be terrified to try getting into the city if they could."

"By comparison to here, Nashville is a teeming metropolis."

"That's true. But you'd be surprised how quickly you get into genuine Tennessee back country once you're five miles outside the Nashville city limits."

"I'm sure that's true."

"And I have a more than a passing familiarity with this area. My sister and her husband have lived here for nigh-on fifteen years now. I've spent a fair amount of time with them on holidays and during the summer months. I'm devoted to my nieces and nephew."

"Well, you have excellent credentials, Lizzy. Your transcripts from Vanderbilt are very impressive."

Lizzy met her gaze evenly. "Thank you for saying so. I worked very hard."

"It's clear that you did. Tell me what you find most appealing about the prospect of living and working here—and why a fledgling program like this one is of interest to someone with your accomplishments?"

"I'm thirty years old, Dr. Stevenson. I want to put roots down someplace—someplace simpler and less frenetic than Nashville. I want to do the good work I've been trained to do in a more direct way—a way that helps people, and that feeds my need to embrace the real meaning of the vocation I've chosen. I want to be a nurse—a good nurse. And I want to know and care for the people I meet in ways that will enrich their lives, and mine." She paused. "I really can't state it any better than that."

They were quiet for a moment.

"I really don't think you could," Maddie said.

"As for this particular program," Lizzy continued, "I love the fact that I'd be getting in on the ground floor, and that I'd have a role in helping structure it to do the most good. And that's especially true during the early phases, while we're scouring around for permanent funding. You don't know this, but I'm a pretty determined cheerleader for the things I believe in. I think I could be a real asset to you as you try to embed this program in the minds and hearts of the people controlling the purse strings."

Maddie nodded. "I freely confess that I royally suck at raising money."

Lizzy laughed. "So, if you hired me, it appears that we would already be starting off with a good division of labor?"

"You might say that."

"So?"

"So?" Maddie replied.

"So—how about you? I won't deny that I did a bit of Google research on you to prepare for today. How on earth did someone with your stellar background end up in an area like this?"

"Oh, there's not much mystery to that. I'm a local. I came back here two years ago to take over my father's practice."

"Oh, I see. That makes sense, then. Do you like being back here? You were at Presbyterian in Philadelphia, weren't you? That makes Nashville look like Mayberry."

Maddie laughed. "It's not quite that dramatic. But, yes, I was at Presby. I did my residency there, and then stayed on to work in the ER. This, though . . ." She paused as she considered her words. "This grows on you in ways you wouldn't expect." She looked up to meet Lizzy's brown eyes. "At least, in ways I didn't expect. I've been practicing medicine for over ten years now, but I can honestly say that I only really became a doctor about eighteen months ago."

Lizzy nodded. "I know exactly what you mean."

Maddie continued to give her an intent look. "I think you do."

They sat for another moment in silence, and then Maddie patted her knees and got to her feet. "So, when would you like to go visit the clinic and see your new office?"

Lizzy looked at her with a stunned expression. "I'm hired?"

"Yep."

"Just like that?"

"Yep."

"Holy cow." She looked up at Maddie with amazement. "You're serious?"

"Usually."

Lizzy laughed. "My sister is gonna freak out."

"Fortunately, you'll soon be licensed to prescribe antidotes for that."

"Don't think that hasn't occurred to me." They smiled at each other. Lizzy shook her head in wonder. "Surely you're at least going to call my references?"

"I already have," Maddie replied. "And don't call me Shirley."

Lizzy snorted as she got to her feet. "Oh lord, another *Airplane!* junkie. This is getting way too weird."

"I think you might be right."

They walked toward the hospital lobby and made plans to meet the following morning at Maddie's clinic in Jericho. Maddie smiled to herself as she headed back toward the ER. Tom Greene was an old letch and a royal pain in her ass, but his little arm-twisting scheme to entice her to manage his fiefdom during his convalescence had certainly just paid off for the county. Big time. Things were definitely looking up.

It was Friday evening, and activity in the library had slowed to a crawl. The local high school basketball team had a home game that night, and most of the teens and half the adults in the county were planning on attending. Roma Jean and Jessie were playing in the school's pep band, so Syd was staffing the place by herself. Her last patron of the day sauntered away from the circulation desk, carrying a stack of fat Chilton manuals. She smiled to herself. Somewhere in town, a late-model Dodge pickup was in for a serious overhaul. She watched him leave, and her eyes drifted again to the poster of Danica Patrick that hung on the wall next to the street door. *I need to move that damn thing.*

She hadn't seen or talked to Maddie in nearly ten days, and she had used that time to good advantage. Through careful and honest introspection, she had managed to dissect her . . . *attraction* to the other woman. She now understood it as a somewhat surprising, but reasonable response to her emotional isolation. In the four months she had lived in Jericho, Maddie had all but shattered her self-imposed barriers, pulling her out of herself and into a warm circle of light that was populated with a quirky and amazing ensemble of friends.

And those friends now were *her* friends. It was an incredible turn of events, and it made sense that her gratitude toward Maddie would overflow and morph into something richer and more indefinable. It made sense. Didn't it?

Of course it did.

She reminded herself of what Michael said the day they talked. None of this changed anything about who she was. It wasn't *that* uncommon to confuse gratitude with . . . something else. And god knows, she'd been alone long enough to realize that she was sitting on a stockpile of suppressed sexual energy that could probably light up a small town. She felt sometimes like one of the dams on the river south of town. If she didn't stop holding it all back, she'd risk cracking into a zillion pieces and flooding everything in her path. God. Even the new manager at the tire store was starting to look good to her. It was no wonder she was such a mess. But at least she hadn't had any more of those dreams.

Well. Not many more.

At six-fifteen, Syd locked up the library for the night. She climbed the stairs to her apartment and unlocked her door. Her cell phone rang.

"Hello?" she said, as she closed the door and dropped her keys on the kitchen table.

"Howdy stranger." It was Maddie. "Remember me?"

Syd smiled. "Barely. How are you?" She pulled out a chair and sat down.

"Want the truth?"

"Of course I do."

"Exhausted."

"I'm sure you are. I ran into Peggy today at Freemantle's, and she said you were burning the candle at both ends—running back and forth between the hospital and the clinic."

Maddie sighed heavily. "Normally, I'd deny that, but this time she's telling the truth. I should have my head examined for agreeing to take this on. When I got home last night, Pete actually growled at me. I don't know if he's mad at me for *ignoring* him, or if he simply didn't recognize me when I got out of the car."

"Poor baby."

"Thanks."

"I meant Pete. I think I'd probably growl at you, too."

"Have I been ignoring you, too?" Maddie's voice sounded genuinely penitent.

"I'm nowhere near selfish enough to complain that you've been ignoring me— not when I know the reasons why you've been so out-of-pocket."

"Really? And here I was kind of hoping you'd say you missed me."

"I do miss you."

Syd's candid response hovered in the air between them for a moment.

"I miss you, too," Maddie said quietly. "But, hey? In three more weeks, Tom Greene will be back in the ER, and I can return to *my* life of simple lassitude."

"I'll let the lassitude comment slide, since I know you're probably not firing on all twelve of your normal cylinders right now. But do you really think you can last three more weeks?"

"Oh, yeah. Especially now." She sounded excited.

"Why now?"

"I had something wonderful happen today, and selfishly, it's something that promises to make my life a whole lot easier."

Syd was intrigued. "Care to enlighten me?"

"Sure. But first things first—have you eaten dinner yet?"

"Dinner? No. I just left the library."

"Great. Wanna split a pizza with me?"

Syd smiled. "I think I could be persuaded." She looked at her watch. "When and where do you want to meet?"

"How about at your street door in thirty seconds? I'm turning into your parking lot right now."

Syd jumped up from her chair and walked to the front window in time to see Maddie's silver Lexus pull into the library parking lot. She felt a rush of excitement as the car pulled to a stop and the driver-side door opened.

"So what would you have done if I hadn't been at home?" she asked, trying to keep her voice neutral, although what she was feeling was somewhere on the opposite side of neutral.

There was a flash of blue as Maddie climbed out of the car and then reached back inside to remove a flat, white pizza box. "I'd have used the five pounds of pepperoni on this thing as bait to buy myself back into my dog's good graces." She shut the car door and stood there, tall in her hospital scrubs, looking up at the window where Syd was standing with the cell phone still pressed to her ear. She smiled up at Syd and held both the pizza box and her cell phone over her head like offerings.

Syd shook her head and smiled back at her as she closed her cell phone and waved her toward the stairs.

They met at the door. Maddie smiled sheepishly, and Syd knew she probably had a stupid grin on her own face. They regarded each other in silence for a moment before Maddie scrunched her eyebrows together.

"I know it's been awhile, but have you grown . . . shorter?"

Syd yanked the pizza box out of her hands. "Gimme this and get in here before I change my mind."

Maddie chuckled as she followed her up the stairs and into the tiny apartment. She put her cell phone and her keys down on the kitchen table, took off her leather jacket, and hung it over the back of a straight chair.

Syd set the pizza down on the countertop and walked to the stove to turn the oven on. Then she faced Maddie. Maddie did look exhausted. She had dark circles under her eyes, and there was an uncharacteristic droop to her shoulders. Before she could think better of the idea, she went to Maddie and kissed her on the cheek.

"I really have missed you. And you look like hell." She backed up a step. Maddie was plainly tired, but her blue eyes were sparkling. "Why don't you go collapse in a chair, and I'll bring you something to drink?"

Maddie squeezed Syd's elbows before turning toward the living room. "That's the best offer I've had in days." She walked across the room and sank down onto the sofa. "Whatcha got? Something alcoholic, I hope. This is the first night in two weeks I haven't been on call."

"Can do, Doctor. Beer or wine?"

"Surprise me." Maddie kicked her shoes off and propped her feet up on Syd's fat ottoman.

Syd opened the refrigerator and pulled two bottles of Corona beer and a lime out and set them on the counter next to the pizza. "Do you want to eat right away?"

"No. Why don't we relax and have a drink first—if that's okay with you?"

"It's more than okay. Let me stick this in the oven to keep it warm." She lifted the pizza out of the box and arranged it on a baking sheet before sliding it into the oven and setting the timer. Then she opened the beer and stuck a narrow wedge of lime into the top of each bottle. She went to Maddie and held out one of the bottles.

Maddie took it from her gratefully and then patted the sofa cushion beside her. "Sit down here so you can prop me up. If you don't, I won't remain upright long enough to eat."

Syd dutifully walked around the barriers created by the ottoman and the coffee table, and sat down on the couch beside her. They angled their bodies to face each other and clinked bottles.

"Here's to Friday-fucking night. At last." Maddie took a long pull from her bottle and half-collapsed against the cushion at her back. "God, I needed that."

"So, tell me what this good news is before you end up comatose on my floor."

Maddie laughed. "Well, I just hired the county's very first full-time Nurse Practitioner."

Syd sat up straighter and regarded her in amazement. "No way."

"Way." Maddie met her gaze with a smug expression. "Her name is Elizabeth Mayes, and she's going to start in two weeks. I'm showing her the clinic tomorrow."

"Oh, Maddie. That's *wonderful* news. You must be beside yourself."

"It is wonderful news." She paused. "But I'm not really beside myself."

Syd was confused. "You're not?"

"Nuh uh. I'm actually beside *you*, and given the choice, the view from here is a whole lot better."

Syd knew that Maddie was just teasing her, but that didn't stop her heart rate from accelerating—nor did it short-circuit the blush that she felt creeping up her neck.

"Why do you do that?" she blurted, before she could stop herself.

"Do what?"

"Say things like that to embarrass me."

"Is that what I'm doing?" Maddie's tired blue eyes seemed to bore into hers.

"You mean it's not intentional?"

Maddie raised her arm to rest along the back of the sofa and opened her mouth to answer, but was interrupted by the sound of the oven timer beeping.

Syd looked toward the kitchen and sighed. "One slice or two?"

Maddie closed her eyes and leaned her head back against the sofa cushion. "Make it three. Maybe it'll help us both out if I have something to stuff into my mouth besides my foot."

Syd ended up bringing the entire pizza into the living room, and they made short work of it, sitting side by side on the sofa and resting their plates on the coffee table. While they ate, Maddie filled her in on the details of her candidate search and her decision to hire Lizzy Mayes.

"She's going to be a godsend to the people who live in the higher elevations around here. We'll be able to extend the services of the clinic to populations who now rely entirely on the ER for routine medical care. It's a win-win scenario: they get better preventative health care, and Tom Greene's budget takes less of a hit on Medicaid expenditures."

Syd nodded. "Will she also be available to see other patients of yours?"

"Oh yeah, on a limited basis. It's going to make it much easier for me to do things like the Richmond trip next month, and I might actually get a weekend off now and then."

"In that case, I think it's an even better idea."

Maddie smiled and sat back, rubbing her temples. "Me, too. I could really use a break." She laughed quietly. "Not to mention, the vacuum cleaners are really starting to pile up on my workbench."

Syd watched her in silence for a moment. "Got a headache?"

"Yeah. It's been hanging around all day. I can't seem to shake it."

Syd picked up a throw pillow and placed it across her lap. "Here," she said, tapping the pillow. "Lie down and let me give you a head rub."

Maddie opened one eye and regarded her. "Are you serious?"

"Do I not sound serious?"

"I just want to be sure before I collapse on top of you." She was already shifting her six-foot frame around. "I'm an unabashed hedonist when it comes to head rubs."

With an audible sigh, she leaned back and rested her head on Syd's lap. Her long legs draped over the arm at the opposite end of the sofa. Syd hesitated for only a moment before she slowly raised her hands and moved them into Maddie's dark hair, using her fingertips to make slow circles along the sides of her forehead. Maddie closed her eyes and moaned in pleasure, and Syd began to think that maybe this wasn't the brightest idea she'd ever had. She kept the soothing motions up and tried to ignore her body's visceral response to touching Maddie in this innocent and well-intentioned way that suddenly wasn't feeling all that innocent.

Maddie's thick hair was surprisingly soft, and its sweet fragrance mingled with the unmistakable scent of antiseptic soap that permeated her blue scrubs. She felt Maddie relax under her touch, and after a few minutes, she realized that the sound of her breathing had deepened. Looking down at her with surprise, she realized that Maddie had fallen asleep. Smiling, she continued with the gentle touches and tipped her own head back against the sofa cushion, content just to enjoy their quiet proximity and not think too deeply about it. There would be plenty of time for that later.

Lots of time, she thought as she closed her own eyes. *Lots of time.*

Maddie sighed deeply and shifted her long frame. Her back was beginning to cramp from sleeping too long in one position. She'd obviously fallen asleep on the sofa again, but this time, she really didn't want to get up. Her head was cradled in a soft nest that smelled faintly of lavender, and the sensation created by the hands moving slowly through her hair was luxurious and sensual.

Her eyes flew open. *Holy shit.* She started to sit up, but immediately felt Syd's hand on her shoulder, calming her. "Oh, my god. I fell asleep, didn't I?"

Above her, Syd sounded amused. "Um hmm."

Maddie rubbed her eyes. "How long?"

"About an hour."

"Jesus. I'm sorry, Syd."

Syd smiled down at her. "Don't apologize. But at least tell me that your headache is gone."

Maddie struggled up into a sitting position. "Oh, yeah—it's way gone." She raked her fingers through her long hair, fluffing it out into some semblance of order. "Wow. You've got some kind of magic in those fingers of yours."

"As much as I'd like to take the compliment, I think you just needed a nap."

"A nap and a lap?" Maddie chuckled. "I'll have to remember this prescription."

"Homeopathic remedies *are* often the best."

"You'll get no argument from me there. And your lap is a *lot* more inviting than Pete's. His is much bonier, and he usually has gas."

Syd rolled her eyes. "You say the most romantic things."

"I try." She gazed at Syd, wanting nothing more at that moment than to crawl back onto her lap and sleep the rest of the night. "I really have missed this—missed *you*. It's been a rough couple of weeks."

"For me, too," Syd said quietly. "It's like something has been out of sync. Of course, my social network is a tad more confined than yours, so I rely on you for stimulation."

Maddie raised an eyebrow. "Oh, reeaaalllly? You find me stimulating?"

Syd sighed. "And here we go. Yes. I find your *company* to be stimulating. But before your head swells to nine times its normal size, let me hasten to remind you that stimulating is a broad term that encompasses many forms of meaning."

"Oh, I know what it means, all right."

"Well, wise guy, a cattle prod is stimulating, too. And far less arrogant."

"But not as cute."

Syd thought about that. "True."

"And not half as much fun to eat pizza with," Maddie added hopefully.

"Also true."

Maddie got to her feet. "On that happy and victorious note, I think I should drive myself home while I can still function with some degree of competence."

"Are you sure you're awake enough to go?"

Maddie looked down at her. "Oh, yeah." She had *plenty* to think about on her drive home.

Syd stood up, followed her into the kitchen, and waited while Maddie pulled on her jacket and picked up her cell phone and keys. At the door, Maddie turned and pulled Syd into a warm hug. "Thanks for tonight. I really needed this."

Syd wrapped her arms around Maddie's waist and squeezed her back. "Me, too." They stepped apart, and Syd crossed her arms over her chest. "Good luck tomorrow."

"Thanks. I'll call you?"

Syd nodded. "Please do."

Maddie left the small apartment and walked down the stairs to the street, feeling better than she had in weeks.

Now if she could just get Pete to forgive her.

Lizzy Mayes was a human dynamo.

She'd been working for Maddie for two weeks, and already she had visited all four of the Methodist congregations participating in their pilot healthcare program. Her daily presence in the clinic had borne fruit as well, and Maddie was able to see a greatly expanded patient base, taking even more strain off the emergency services department of the area hospital. The local weekly newspaper had run a series of articles about the fledgling Parish Nurse program, and Maddie's small clinic was quickly flooded with requests for appointments—most from curious residents who just wanted an up-close look at their new neighbor from Nashville.

Lizzy had an easy and unaffected manner, and quickly endeared herself to the loquacious Peggy Hawkes. In no time, it was as if the two of them had worked together for years, and Lizzy was even able to motivate Peggy to make more determined progress at transferring patient files to the clinic's EMR system. Maddie knew that things were going well the day Peggy showed up at work with a lemon chess pie she had made for Lizzy and her sister's family to share.

Maddie was smart enough to have Lizzy actually *sign* her employment contract before she had a chance to sample the pie.

Maddie had one week left to go as acting ER Chief before Tom Greene returned full time. Having Lizzy on staff made it possible for her to keep her clinic open *during* regular business hours and promised to make her transition back into her normal routine easier and less hectic. She was looking forward to that, and to her upcoming trip to Richmond to attend the AMA conference. For once, she would be able to relax and enjoy the sessions without the added burden of courting pharmaceutical reps to try and interest them in funding her startup healthcare initiative. With Lizzy's level of energy and enthusiasm for the project, she was optimistic that local funding streams would remain robust enough to sustain the effort without the need for external support. And if that changed? Well, there was always next year.

Lizzy was temporarily living with her sister's family in Jefferson, but she was actively looking for a small house to buy. Phoebe Jenkins got wind of this through her son, and saw it as a golden opportunity to sell the small bungalow that had belonged to her recently deceased aunt.

Iris Jenkins had always been a favorite of David's. She was a strong and independent woman who stubbornly lived alone until her death at age ninety-two. She never married. She never trusted god or doctors. She never voted. And she never read a newspaper. Right up until the day she died, she chopped all the wood she burned in her small stove—she never trusted anyone to do that for her, either. She was a catbird—that's what the locals called her. A catbird. Growing up, David was never really too sure what that meant. He just knew that his aunt Iris was special. She never judged him—not even when he left home at age sixteen and moved in with Maddie's father. He was never really certain if she had heard any of the rumors that led up to that last, explosive encounter with his father, but he knew somehow that even if she had, it wouldn't have mattered to her. She was a catbird. And catbirds generally went their own way.

So when David told his mother about Maddie's new nurse and her need for suitable housing, Phoebe quickly surmised that maybe Lizzy Mayes would be the ideal candidate to buy Aunt Iris's river bungalow. The two women agreed to meet, and to go together to visit the property on Wednesday.

Phoebe stopped by the library at lunchtime to drop off some sheet music for Syd. There was a community orchestra concert coming up at the high school, and she had enlisted Syd's help to work with her struggling string section. Unknown to Syd, Phoebe had a rather expansive definition of "help." She was determined to persuade Syd to sit in with the string section during the performance—giddy at the prospect of having someone in the orchestra who might inspire the other players to a higher level of accomplishment. If that didn't transpire, at least she would have a principal who could read music and actually *play* the instrument, and play it very well, as it turned out. They hadn't had a musician of Syd's caliber in the county since Maddie's mother left the area over twenty-five years ago. Phoebe was hell-bent on making hay while the sun shone. This was not an opportunity to be missed.

She entered the library and saw Syd bent over a desktop computer, working with Beau Pitzer on something. Beau sat back on the legs of his chair and watched her while she typed—clearly enjoying this chance to get an unobstructed view of the attractive blonde at close range.

Phoebe clucked her tongue as she crossed the room and approached the makeshift computer lab. She was disgusted that Beau didn't even have the grace to remove his hat. A faded red baseball cap with "Skoal" stitched across the front in white letters obscured part of his face.

"Hello, Syd. I hope I'm not too early."

Syd stood up and turned to her with a smile on her pretty face. Beau dropped his chair forward with a thump and looked up at her with a barely disguised scowl.

"Hello, Beau. Nice to see you again. Any luck with the job search?"

He shook his head and stared at her without speaking.

"Well, don't lose hope. I heard yesterday that the glass plant might be adding a third shift."

He mumbled something unintelligible and looked back at his computer screen.

Syd rolled her eyes and waved Phoebe toward the circulation desk. "Why don't we go back there and talk so we don't distract Beau?"

Phoebe nodded. "Good idea."

They walked to the rear of the library. Phoebe saw several other patrons sprawled in upholstered chairs reading newspapers. Zeke Dawkins, the postmaster, was at the copier running off some flyers. He waved when he saw her. Phoebe figured this had to be bad news. Any time Zeke made flyers, it usually meant the rates for *something* were going up.

She set her big leather bag on the circulation desk and pulled out a bulging file folder full of musical scores.

"Here you go," she said, passing the folder to Syd. "This is what I have in mind for our next concert. Let me know what you think."

Syd took the folder and removed the hefty orchestral scores for Offenbach's *Overture to Orpheus in the Underworld*, the finale to Mendelssohn's *Symphony No. 5*, Copeland's *Shaker Variations*, and Grainger's *Irish Tune from County Derry*. She drew her brows together as she leafed through the selections and looked up at Phoebe with a perplexed expression. "Aren't a few of these pretty advanced for our available talent?"

Phoebe shook her head. "I don't think so."

Syd did not look convinced. "Three of these call for a pretty accomplished string *section*. I think that might be a tall order for us right now."

"We don't need a strong section to play these—we just need a strong principal." Phoebe smiled at Syd.

Syd stared at her for a moment as recognition began to dawn. "Oh *no*—not a chance. Forget it, Phoebe. This isn't what I meant when I said I would help out."

"Syd, I've heard you play. Any of these pieces would be a cakewalk for you. And think of the opportunity it would give you to really inspire the rest of the musicians." She laid a hand on Syd's forearm. "It's exactly the kind of motivation we need to really get this group pulled together. Please. Do this. It will mean so much to the community."

Syd hesitated. "I don't even have anything to wear. I didn't bring any formal attire with me."

"You don't *need* formal attire—just black pants and a white blouse."

Syd sighed.

"Come on. I'm making David play, too—if that's any consolation."

"You are?" Syd narrowed her eyes. "He told me that he used his clarinet for kindling."

"Don't you know better than to believe *anything* that comes out of that young man's mouth? It's true that his band uniform was always more appealing to him than his instrument, but he actually plays a very good woodwind." Phoebe smiled to herself. "It's all the hot air, I'm sure."

Syd laughed. "Let me think about it, okay?"

"Okay. But don't take too long. We start rehearsals on Sunday afternoon."

"I promise. And I'll still help with the string section, regardless of whether or not I agree to perform."

"I can't ask for more than that," Phoebe said with a smile.

They looked up when the front door to the library opened. Phoebe glanced at her watch, then smiled and waved at the redheaded woman who had just entered. "Right on time." She turned to Syd. "Have you met Maddie's new nurse, Lizzy Mayes? I asked her to meet me here. She's going to look at my aunt Iris's old river bungalow."

Syd shook her head. "No, I haven't met her yet, but I've heard great things about her." She watched the other woman approach with a curious and interested expression.

Lizzy was anxious to see the small, riverfront property that Mrs. Jenkins had described to her. Its compact size and isolated location appealed to her, and its rustic appointments held greater attraction for her than any of the more contemporary, ranch-style homes she'd considered that were within her modest price range.

Peggy Hawkes had already filled her in on the particulars of Iris's bungalow, so she knew that the house did, in fact, have a conventional heating system. But, Peggy added, old Miss Jenkins had been too stubborn to use it, and preferred to rely on her wood stove for heat during the long winter months. So Lizzy agreed to meet Mrs. Jenkins at the public library during her lunch hour, so they could drive together to view the property.

She was equally curious about meeting the town librarian—a woman she had heard much about since her arrival in Jericho. By all reports, Syd Murphy was an attractive divorcée who was new to the area, and who had quickly become fast friends with Mrs. Jenkins' son, David, and his partner.

Peggy had also hinted at some kind of special friendship that she saw developing between the librarian and the enigmatic Dr. Stevenson. Lizzy wasn't too certain what she meant by that observation but it did seem clear that there was no implied criticism in Peggy's remarks—although it was impossible to deny that her comments were delivered with a non-verbal wink and nudge. It didn't really matter to her one way or another, but the vague suggestion did go a long way to explain why someone like Dr. Stevenson was still single.

When they met for the first time over a month ago, Lizzy had been surprised—even stunned—by Maddie's appearance. For starters, she was much younger than Lizzy had expected, and although she was functionally attired in hospital scrubs, she was remarkably beautiful.

Lizzy remembered her first thought being that Dr. Stevenson looked exactly like one of the picture-perfect models who adorned the covers of glossy medical supply brochures. She found it hard that day to reconcile the accomplished professional of her Google search—the medico with the gold-plated resume—

with the glamorous, self-deprecating, and quick-witted woman who sat before her conducting her interview. She was a paradox. And Lizzy, who loved puzzles, suspected that working with the engaging and mysterious Dr. Stevenson would be many things, but never dull.

As she approached the circulation desk, she saw Mrs. Jenkins engaged in earnest conversation with an attractive blonde woman, whom she assumed was Syd Murphy.

Mrs. Jenkins smiled and waved her over. "Lizzy, I'd like you to meet Syd Murphy, our town librarian. Syd, this is Lizzy Mayes, Maddie's new nurse."

Syd smiled brightly at her and extended her hand. "I'm so happy to meet you. Maddie has been raving about you."

Lizzy shook her hand warmly. "Likewise. I understand that you're new to the area, too?"

Syd's green eyes sparkled. "Oh, I feel like an old-timer by now—the people here are wonderful at making you feel welcome."

"I'm glad to hear that. How long have you been here?"

"Nearly five months now, but it feels like forever." She paused before adding with a wry smile, "I mean that in the *best* sense of the word, too. It's going to be hard for me to leave here when my grant funding ends next year."

"We've already got other ideas about that whole scenario," Phoebe said in a conspiratorial whisper. "We're not sure we're willing to let her go so easily."

Syd rolled her eyes. "Don't tell me you've been listening to your son? I already told him that threatening me with leg irons and an orange jumpsuit wasn't the best way to entice me to stay."

Lizzy laughed. She liked the perky woman. Her humor was infectious. "I'd imagine that with a little bit of creative thinking, you could make a permanent place for yourself here—if," she added, "that's what you wanted."

Syd seemed to be looking back at her with interest. "I'm not sure about my long-term plans yet. But I do confess that the idea of staying on here continues to grow on me."

Phoebe smiled at her. "And with friends who are as determined to keep you here as David and Maddie are, I can promise that you won't get away very easily."

Syd dropped her eyes and made no response to that comment. Lizzy began to sense that there might be some kernel of truth lurking behind Peggy's vague suggestion. She looked forward to having the chance to see the librarian interact directly with Dr. Stevenson, so she could make her own assessment.

She caught a flash of red out of the corner of her eye and quickly turned to find that a medium-sized man in a red ball cap had walked up to stand close beside her. Uncomfortably close. She took an involuntary step backward as he stared at her without speaking.

"Did you need something, Beau?" Syd asked.

The man slowly drew his eyes away from Lizzy and turned to Syd. "The damn thing's locked up again."

"Okay. I'll come take a look at it." She looked at Lizzy, then back to Beau. "Beau, this is Lizzy Mayes, the new nurse at Dr. Stevenson's clinic. Lizzy, meet Beau Pitzer."

Lizzy smiled at him. "Hello, Beau. It's nice to meet you."

Beau nodded at her without speaking. Beneath the brim of his cap, his eyes looked her up and down.

Phoebe clucked her tongue. "Well, Lizzy. We'd better get going or we won't have much time to look over the property." She collected her bag and keys off the circulation desk. "Bye, Syd. I look forward to hearing from you about Sunday."

Lizzy smiled at Syd. "I hope we get a chance to talk again soon. I really enjoyed meeting you."

"Same here," Syd said as she walked around the desk to join Beau. "Call me anytime. Maybe we can grab lunch or dinner soon and get better acquainted?"

"I'd like that." Lizzy smiled and turned toward the street door. As she walked out with Phoebe, she shook off her uneasy sense that the odd man in the red cap was still watching her.

Valentine's Day provided David with more than a license to offer wildly over-priced dinner packages to couples in search of special, romantic venues. It also gave him a plausible excuse for luring Maddie over to the Inn for an innocent tryst with their favorite blonde.

Valentine's Day, he explained to the dour and doubting doctor, was also Syd's birthday, and he had no intention of letting the occasion pass without staging a suitable celebration. They could, he explained, double-up on the special menu Michael had already crafted for the other diners, and commemorate Syd's birthday without exerting the extra effort that he knew she would balk at under normal circumstances. Maddie smelled a rat, but relented anyway, knowing there was no way she could miss this chance to see Syd on her special day.

"Just how did you find out it's her birthday?" she asked in surprise, when David called to share his plans for the event and invite her to join them.

"I have my ways," he said, with smug certitude.

"Do tell? I'm all agog."

"Agog? What the hell does that actually mean, anyway?"

Maddie sighed. "Agog. Adverb. It means a state of eager desire."

"Ahh. Eager desire. Now I get it. Yeah, that about sums up your attitude where she's concerned."

"Don't start, nimrod. Do you want me there or not?"

"Oh, like I could keep you *away* now that you know it's her birthday."

"Whatever." They were both silent. "So . . . how did you know?"

"I ran into Gladys at the post office. She had just delivered a whopping big arrangement of birthday flowers to Syd at the library. Roses. Two dozen. Long stem. And red. Any clue what *that* must have cost?"

Maddie feigned disinterest. "No idea."

"More than you make freezing warts, wise guy."

"Charming image, David."

"I'm just sayin'. *Somebody* clearly wants to hang their shingle on that hot little piece of real estate."

"Why are you telling me this?"

"Why do you think?"

"To annoy the shit out of me?"

"Yes. Precisely. I want to waste my time annoying the shit out of you while some other schmoe breezes in and walks off with the woman of your dreams."

Maddie was losing patience with him. "You're making me insane, David."

"You were already around the bend on this one, Cinderella. Quit pretending that you don't know it. If the glass slipper fits, I say, wear it."

"I think I'm going to hang up now."

"Aren't you forgetting something?"

"What?"

"Eight o'clock. Glad rags. And make it something revealing. It *is* her birthday, after all. Let's spoil her a little bit."

Maddie mumbled an expletive.

"What was that? I didn't quite make it out?"

"I said I'd be there."

"Thought so." He hung up before she could.

Chapter 13

Valentine's Day. Christ. Of course her birthday would be on Valentine's Day. Maddie turned onto the gravel road that led down toward the Inn. Ahead, she could see the parking lot, filled to near capacity with cars. Off to her left, she saw Syd's blue Volvo, and her heart rate accelerated.

God. I'm acting like a teenager at my first prom. She parked her Lexus and sat for a few moments, listening to the final strains of *Beim Schlafengehen*, trying to regain her composure. Renée Fleming's rich voice soared and filled the space inside the car with a rising succession of silvery notes. Maddie shook her head, overwhelmed for a moment by the beauty of the sound and the sentiment of the music. "Time to Sleep."

You got that right, she thought as she shut the car off and looked down at the small, wrapped package on the passenger seat. After some fancy footwork, she succeeded in getting the item in less than twenty-four hours. All it took was some careful deliberation, a phone call to her attorney in Philadelphia, and a small fortune in shipping charges. Was it the right choice? She guessed she'd know soon enough.

She slipped the small package into the pocket of her coat and climbed out of the car. It was a cold night—snow was in the forecast. The Inn was hopping. It was plain that Valentine's Day was good for business. She didn't recognize very many of the cars that filled the gravel parking lot, so she guessed that most of the diners were from areas farther-flung than Jericho or Jefferson. She ascended the wide steps and heard the happy sounds of laughter and music as she crossed the wide porch to the door. David met her just inside. After kissing her cheek, he reached out to take her coat.

"Gimme this and do a quick three-sixty so I can check out your stuff," he said, making rapid circles with his index finger.

Maddie sighed and dutifully turned around so he could inspect her ensemble. Now that she was free from working in the ER, she had actually had time to give some thought to her appearance, and she opted for a long-sleeved black cocktail dress with a deep v-neck and button sleeves. The dress had a wide, fitted waistband that accentuated her tall frame, and its hem fell to just above her knees. She wore tiny, diamond earrings, and no other jewelry. She knew she looked stunning. David was clearly impressed.

"Nice." He smiled at her in approval. "I'd do you."

She looked at him in surprise. "I think that's possibly the nicest thing you've ever said to me."

He winked at her as he took her arm and steered her toward the sun porch at the back of the Inn. "Well, take a deep breath, because your dinner date looks pretty tasty, too."

"Did you just say 'date'—as in singular?" she hissed. "I thought this was a party?"

He chuckled. "Oh, it's going to be a party, all right." He squeezed her arm. "Lighten up, Cinderella. We're going to join you once the dust settles from this first wave." He inclined his head toward the dimly lighted dining room as they walked past. Inside, the tabletops all glittered with candlelight, and a variety of intoxicating smells wafted out toward them. She saw heads turn as they walked past the open doors. "You should only have to be charming for about the next thirty minutes. Think you can manage?"

She scowled at him as they turned the corner and stepped onto the glass-enclosed porch . . . then she saw Syd.

Syd stood with her back to the door. She was holding a wine glass and was in an animated conversation with Michael, who stood near the dining room entrance with his arms folded across his broad chest.

Michael looked up when they entered, and Syd turned around. She was wearing a vintage silk dress in emerald green with a scoop neck and three-quarter length sleeves. The waist was cinched with a matching belt, tied at the front. She looked incredible.

Maddie stopped dead in her tracks and stood, stupefied, as every receptor on every nerve ending in her body decided to stand up and phone home. A giant clue had finally been tied to a biological two-by-four, and it just smacked her right between the eyes.

Oh my god, she thought, as rival sensations of panic and exhilaration chased one another up and down her body. *I'm in love with her.*

David touched her arm. "You okay?" He looked at her closely for a moment. Then he smiled and squeezed her arm. "It's okay, Maddoe," he said softly. "You were bound to figure it out sooner or later." He tugged her forward. "C'mon—she won't bite." He chuckled and muttered under his breath, "Not unless you ask her to."

Maddie gave out a pitiful moan under her breath as they crossed the remaining distance to join Syd and Michael.

Syd stood, talking herself through every mind-control exercise she'd ever tried, and slowed her breathing as Maddie and David made their way across the room toward them. Never before had she experienced this kind of visceral response to another person, and she was terrified that she wouldn't be able to conceal it. Her palms were sweaty, and her face felt hot, and she wasn't sure she could trust her shaky legs to hold her up. The sensations hit her like a tidal wave when she turned around and saw Maddie standing in the doorway. It was impossible for her to deny the nature of her response. There was no way she could continue to dismiss it, falsely classify it, or characterize it as something benign. It was real, and right now, it was bigger than her fear.

Lots bigger.

And she had only an instant to try and recover her poise.

Michael looked back and forth between Maddie and Syd. It was clear to him that something subliminal had just transpired. They both looked shell-shocked, and he couldn't tell which one of them was more unsettled. *Maddie,* he thought. But, no . . . Syd was nervously twisting the stem of her wine glass and seemed shy about meeting Maddie's eyes. *Not that I blame her,* he thought as he took in her ensemble. She looks fantastic in black. *Hell, she'd look fantastic in anything—he* smiled to himself—*or nothing.* He shook his head. *Damn. There must be something in the air tonight.*

Maddie tentatively touched Syd's arm, and said happy birthday. She stepped closer to Syd and kissed her on the forehead. She had a pained expression as her lips hovered near Syd's hairline, then she stepped back and gave him a nervous look that seemed to ask, "What now?"

David, who was the natural enemy of a vacuum, stepped into fill the void. "You two look delicious enough to plop on top of a wedding cake." He thought about it. "A *Red Velvet* wedding cake."

Michael glared at him.

"Hey, don't even start with *that* look," David whined. "It's *my* fantasy. If I wanna put a little *Baywatch* twist on it, it's my prerogative."

"*Baywatch*?" Michael asked, perplexed. "Isn't that the wrong kind of reference for one of *your* fantasies?"

David looked incredulous as he waved his hand between Syd and Maddie's chests. "Hello? Seen what these necklines are barely concealing, big guy?"

That seemed to shock Maddie out of her torpor. She turned to David with a raised eyebrow. "I refuse to *run,* no matter how much sand you haul in here. So don't even ask."

Syd broke into peals of laughter.

Michael shook his head and gestured toward the dining room. "Come on let me seat you. We should be able to join you shortly—most of the other tables are nearing the dessert course. David, why don't you get the girls a bottle of nice wine?"

David adjusted the angle of his red bow tie with both hands. "I can do that." He winked at Syd and Maddie, turned on his heel, and headed back down the hallway toward the bar.

Once they were seated, Maddie felt a bit more in control of her emotions. A bit. Syd looked so beautiful tonight, and the candlelight wasn't helping much, either. Her green dress seemed to glow . . . like her eyes.

She needed something safe to talk about.

"Your dress is lovely. I thought you left all your glad rags in storage?"

Syd smiled at her. "Ever heard of *Mimi's New-to-You Emporium* in West Jefferson?"

Maddie stared at her in surprise. "You're kidding me?"

"Would I do that?"

Maddie pretended to think about it. "In a heartbeat."

Syd lowered her eyes. "Well, maybe I would . . . but in this case, I'm telling you the truth."

Her appreciation for Syd's appearance grew. "So this is a vintage creation?"

"Yep. Circa 1960, I'd say."

Maddie looked her over. "It does exude a certain Jackie Kennedy quality."

"I thought so, too."

"You certainly wear it well. It looks like it was made for you."

"Why thank you, Doctor." Syd took a sip from her water glass. "It's unusual for me to find something that's the right length. Normally, I look like I'm standing in a hole."

Maddie bit the inside of her cheek. "No comment."

"Oh, whatever, Wilma Rudolph. At least I don't get a nosebleed when I stand up in the morning."

Maddie sighed. "Yeah, yeah. Remind me to call you the next time I need to bake brownies."

"We little people *do* have our uses."

"I'll say," Maddie quipped without thinking. She felt the heat rise to her cheeks and thought that maybe Syd was blushing, too, but the candlelight made it hard to tell. "I'm sorry. I must have been channeling David."

Syd met her eyes.

David showed up, wielding a bottle of wine and two champagne flutes. "And to reward you both for your respective birthday hotness, I present you with this fine bottle of Duval-Leroy Rosé de Saignée. And I'd advise you to drink it slowly, 'cause it's the only one of these suckers we've got left." He twisted off the wire cage.

He eyed Maddie as he covered the top of the bottle with a linen towel and held it between his knees, twisting the cork out with exaggerated force. The loud pop echoed through the room, and diners at nearby tables turned and smiled at them.

"That was subtle," Maddie drawled. "Did you skip Boy Scouts the day they explained how to properly open champagne?"

He gave her a look of disdain as he filled their flutes. "Unlike you, I never earned the Fine Wines badge. What troop were *you* in?"

"Me?" She picked up her glass. "I flunked the physical—remember?"

"Hell, my troop would've waived it." He stood back and crossed his arms as he raked his gaze over her. "You sure wouldn't flunk any physicals tonight."

"That's for sure," Syd added with a smile.

Maddie looked at her in surprise.

"What?" Syd asked. "You didn't notice that every head in this dining room turned when you walked in here?"

Maddie raised her eyebrows and looked at her with feigned innocence. "I thought it was because of that piece of toilet paper I had stuck to my shoe."

Syd rolled her eyes. "Yeah. *That,* and the fact that you're drop dead gorgeous and look about nine feet tall in that outfit."

Maddie sat back, trying to ignore the sudden hitch in her breathing. "What makes you think people were only looking at me?"

"Uh huh," David cut it. "Well, I see that you two are doing just *fine* honing your polite conversation skills. Lemme move on and minister to some of our less fortunate guests." He gave Maddie's shoulder an encouraging squeeze as he walked off.

After a momentary silence, Maddie gamely raised her glass of champagne. "There's no place I'd rather be right now, and no one I'd rather be with. Happy birthday, Syd. I'm honored to be a part of your life."

Syd belatedly raised her own glass. Her expression was shy and confused. "Thank you." They clinked glasses and sipped the sparkling wine. "I wish I had the words to tell you how much your friendship has come to mean to me." She dropped her eyes. "I think I'm only starting to understand how alone I was before I came here." She looked at Maddie again with shining eyes. "You—all of you—have become such a part of me now. I can't imagine being without you."

"Why would you need to be without us?" Maddie asked, quietly.

"This grant won't last forever. I only have funding for another year."

"A year is a long time. A lot can happen."

They looked at each other in silence. "I hope you're right."

Maddie gave her a shy smile. "I hope so, too."

Syd shook her head like she was trying to clear it. "But, in the meantime, I have Phoebe Jenkins—who is determined to drag my violin out of retirement and fill my lonely nights with song." She smiled. "Or at least with *some* kind of soundtrack."

Maddie raised her eyebrows. "Oh, yeah? It seems like I heard a rumor about that."

Syd pursed her lips. "I'll just *bet* you did."

"Hey, you can't pin this one on me. You set yourself up as soon as you agreed to start helping the kids out with music lessons."

"Well, I certainly never intended for that gesture to end up resurrecting my ill-fated performance career." Syd picked up the wine cork and rolled it against the tablecloth.

Maddie laughed. "Oh, come on. How bad could it be?"

"Have you ever *heard* the Jericho Community Orchestra?"

"Um. Well. You got me there. I guess it could be pretty bad, after all."

"Exactly."

"But look at the bright side." Maddie fixed her with a hopeful expression. "This is a made-to-order opportunity for a selfless do-gooder like yourself."

"Excuse me? Did you just call *me* a selfless do-gooder?"

Maddie crossed her arms. "I believe I did, yes."

"You must be joking?"

Maddie pretended to consider her comment. "Nope. Don't think I am."

Syd sighed and sat back. "What on earth would lead you to characterize me as a selfless do-gooder?"

"Oh, gee. Lemme think . . . well-educated young professional leaves a thriving metropolitan area to work for pennies in a less-than-glamorous, publicly funded, social service venture in the mountains of Appalachia. Nope. Nothing at all noble about that."

Syd tossed the cork at her.

Maddie chuckled as she caught it and placed it down next to the bottle. "If you're going to start throwing things at me, I'd like to know now so I can go and change. I might need to wear this outfit again in Richmond."

Syd raised an eyebrow. "Oh really? I thought you weren't going to have to seduce any drug reps on this trip?"

"Who said anything about drug reps?"

"Got someone else in mind?"

"You never know." Maddie grinned with amusement. "I might get lucky."

"If you plan on wearing *that* outfit, luck won't have anything to do with it."

"Why Miss Murphy. You'll put me to the blush."

Syd rolled her eyes. "Right."

They fell quiet. Syd looked for a moment like she wanted to say something, but then seemed to think better of it.

"What?" Maddie prompted.

"It's nothing."

"No. Go ahead. What were you going to say?"

Syd shrugged. "It's none of my business, really."

"*What's* none of your business?" Maddie was curious.

"I just . . . I mean, it's obvious that you're not really *seeing* anyone . . . at least, not anyone who lives around here. I was just curious about that. About why that's the case?" She nervously waved her hand. "I know this is really personal, but you've been back here for nearly two years now, and there's no special man in your life. It just doesn't make sense to me. You're about the most eligible person in the county." She lowered her eyes. "I've just never asked you about it."

Maddie bit the inside of her cheek as she puzzled through how to respond. She had already decided to stop lying to herself. Did she also need to stop lying to Syd?

"I'm sorry," Syd said quickly. "I told you it was none of my business."

"Oh, don't be silly." Maddie reached across the table and patted the top of her hand. "I was just trying to figure out how to respond. I mean, I guess I thought you already knew."

"Knew?"

"Well, yeah." Maddie gave her a small smile.

"Knew what?" Syd looked confused.

Maddie opened and closed her mouth. *In for a penny, in for a pound*, she thought. Sighing and leaning forward, she said in a low and conspiratorial voice, "Syd, I'm gay."

Syd's green eyes grew wide, and she sat in stunned silence with her mouth hanging open.

Maddie looked at her with concern. "Are you okay? You look like I just fired a gun next to your head."

Syd raised her fingertips to her forehead. "Oh, god. You must think I'm an idiot."

"Why on earth would I think that?"

Syd looked at her through her spread fingers. "Because I wasn't able to connect the dots, and because I had to ask you in such a *stupid* fashion."

Maddie laughed. "Oh come on. It isn't like I telegraph this information to everyone who moves here. I guess I should be relieved that you didn't figure it out within ten seconds of meeting me."

Syd lowered her hands and shook her head slowly. "Ten seconds? No, I don't think that's something you ever need to worry about."

Maddie was intrigued. "So you honestly had no clue?"

Syd looked uncomfortable. "I won't deny that maybe I thought about it once or twice—briefly, and in a *very* fleeting way. But, no, I didn't have a clue. Not really." She looked at her with an unreadable expression. "Wow."

"Wow? Is that good or bad?"

"It's just . . . wow. You keep amazing me." She added quickly, "And before you ask, that's *not* a bad thing."

Maddie relaxed slightly. "Well, good." She wanted more than anything to take hold of Syd's hand, but knew she couldn't. "I should apologize for not telling you sooner. I hope you know it's not because I didn't think I could trust you."

"Why didn't you tell me?"

Maddie thought about her answer. "It seemed inappropriate at first. I mean, I was your doctor. Then, when we started to become friends, I just didn't want to make a big deal out of it." She shrugged. "I guess I thought you'd simply intuit it from what you knew about my lifestyle, and my best friends." She looked directly at Syd for a moment. "I'm sorry I never told you. I hope you'll forgive me for that."

"God, Maddie. There's nothing to forgive." She slowly shook her head. "So many things make so much more sense now."

Maddie raised an eyebrow. "Oh, yeah? Like what?"

Syd gave her a wry smile. "Well, the whole vacuum cleaner thing, for one."

Maddie laughed out loud. "Oh, *that*. Yeah, it's true. If med school hadn't worked out, I could've have had a stellar career rebuilding transmissions."

"Never say never."

"I rarely do."

"Boy. Things sure don't work out the way you think they will."

"What's that supposed to mean?" Maddie asked.

Syd's gaze drifted over Maddie's shoulder. "I'll tell you later. I think our hosts are finally going to join us."

David pulled up a chair and poured himself a glass of the sparkling wine. "So, did you two lovelies find something to talk about?"

Maddie snorted. "You might say that."

"Okay. What'd I miss?" David raised the glass to his lips.

Maddie sighed. "Nothing much. I just came out to Syd."

David loudly sprayed wine back into his glass.

Michael quickly patted his back.

"You did *what?*" David asked, incredulous

"You heard me."

He looked between Syd and Maddie with shock and dismay. "I *so* do not believe this. How dare you do this without letting me watch? And on *Valentine's* Day, too." He waved his hands in frustration. "That's just sadistic."

Maddie sat back and folded her arms. "Sorry, dude, you snooze, you lose. Film at eleven."

"I hate you." He looked at Syd, then back at Maddie. "How'd she take it?"

Maddie leaned toward him and whispered, "Why don't you ask her?"

Across the table, Michael chortled and laid his arm across the back of Syd's chair. "So it looks like we've got all kinds of things to celebrate tonight." He met Syd's eyes. "I told you not to worry so much."

"What the hell is *that* supposed to mean?" David asked, clearly still agitated.

Michael rolled his eyes. "Will you just calm down, Mary Jane. Maybe if you're a good girl, Spiderman will spin you *another* web."

Maddie topped off her own glass. "Don't count on it. I'm fresh out of secrets."

David demurred. "Well, maybe if we sit here long enough, something else will occur to you."

"Maybe not," Maddie said with determination.

Michael held out a placating hand. "How about you two retreat to your respective corners, and we start this conversation over?"

"Why don't I just make this easier on everyone, and tell you that I more or less forced her to tell me?" Syd said.

David threw his head back. "Oh, and *that's* supposed to make me feel better about missing the revelation of the century?"

Maddie looked at him in amazement. "Why are you so bent out of shape about this? You're acting like I just revealed that I was the one who kidnapped the Lindbergh baby."

He sighed. "You're right. It was hardly a breaking news alert." He fixed Syd with a penetrating gaze. "*Please* tell me that you already suspected. I mean, surely, the tool belt was a dead giveaway?"

"Maddie doesn't have a tool belt." Syd wore a deadpan expression. "And don't call me Shirley."

Maddie chuckled as David gave Syd a withering look. "You two are *so* made for each other."

Michael raised his wine glass. "I was just thinking exactly the same thing. Let's toast to the beginning of new friendships, and an end to old secrets."

They all clinked glasses and drank. Then Michael waved their server over. "Now let's get this birthday feast underway."

"Hear, hear." David turned to Syd and rubbed his hands together gleefully. "And while we eat, I'll regale you with salacious highlights from *Madeleine Stevenson: The Lost Episodes.*"

Maddie kicked him beneath the table with an audible thud. "Or *not,*" she added sweetly.

David moaned as he bent over to rub his shin. "Do you *mind*? I don't happen to be wearing my lead-lined support hose tonight."

"As it happens, I very much mind. How about we agree to confine our conversation to topics related to our guest of honor?"

Syd sighed in disappointment. "That'll certainly be less enthralling."

Maddie met her eyes. "Not from my point of view."

They smiled at each other as the server arrived with their first course.

Syd did her best, during the meal, to appear attentive and engaged, but her head was reeling.

Syd, I'm gay.

She was unprepared for the onslaught of confusing emotions the simple revelation caused. She felt anxious and overwhelmed.

She wasn't ready for this. Not now. Not here. Not tonight. She needed time. Time to sort through it all. Time to understand why Maddie's spare and almost offhand disclosure was so unsettling. Was so *distracting*. Was so absorbing to the point that she was finding it nearly impossible to pay attention to anything else.

Syd, I'm gay.

Jesus.

David was asking her something. Dessert. It was something about dessert. She anxiously looked at Maddie, and found blue eyes fixed on her. Maddie's expression was concerned—perplexed.

Maddie reached across the table and touched the top of Syd's hand. "Are you all right?"

Syd turned her own hand palm up and gave Maddie's fingers a quick squeeze before retracting her hand and pushing her chair back from the table. "I'm fine." She turned to David. "Did you say something about dessert in the parlor?"

He was already on his feet. "Yes indeed. Let's have our coffee in there. We've got a nice fire going, and it'll be a much more private venue for you to open your presents."

That got her attention. "Presents? Please tell me you're joking?"

"Oh, honey, I *never* joke about presents. They're sacred." He looked at Michael. "Aren't they, baby?"

"Ah, yeah. That would be a big 10-4." Michael gave Syd an apologetic glance. "My best advice is just to kick back and try to roll with it. It's fruitless to protest. He'll just enjoy it more."

Syd sighed. "I've got a very bad feeling about this."

"Wise woman," Maddie quipped.

David twirled the ends of his red bow tie. "Enough chatter. Let's go and see what the birthday fairy has in store for you."

"Birthday fairy?" Maddie asked.

"Yes. I got a promotion."

Maddie rolled her eyes. "This promotion didn't, by chance, come with anything like a special costume, did it?"

"Don't worry, Cinderella. The only way you'll ever get to see *my* birthday suit is if you shell out about sixty-thousand bucks, and undergo at least four operations."

"Well, thank god for small mercies."

He slapped her on the shoulder. "Hey. One thing I can promise you is that there's nothing *small* about it."

They left the table and made their way across the dining room to the hallway that would take them to the front parlor. The crowd had noticeably thinned out, and only a few tables of diners were left. Maddie fell into step beside Syd.

"What's wrong?" she asked softly. "It's obvious that you're distracted."

Syd met her concerned blue eyes and quickly looked away. *Distracted? You think?* "I'm okay. I'm just feeling a bit . . . thoughtful."

"About?"

Syd shrugged. "I'm not sure, exactly. Maybe it's just the enormity of all of this."

"This?" Maddie prompted.

Syd absently waved her hand to encompass their surroundings. "*This.* All of this." She met Maddie's eyes again, but didn't look away this time. "All of you. I can't take it in. How much my life has changed in just a year." She shook her head. "In just a few months, really."

"Is that a bad thing?" Maddie's tone was tentative.

Syd quickly laid a hand on Maddie's forearm. "No. No, not at all. It's a *good* thing. I'm just a bit overwhelmed right now by all the changes, and by the uncertainty that's still ahead for me." She gave Maddie a small smile. "I'm sorry to be so somber when you're all being so sweet and kind to me. I really am happy to be here with you." *Too happy.*

Maddie laid a hand over hers and held it there as they walked the rest of the way to the parlor. "Hold that thought—something tells me you're going to need it."

Syd was immediately suspicious. "Do you know something I don't?"

"Not specifically. But it's worth remembering that David has *Babeland* on speed dial."

Syd stopped dead in her tracks. "Oh, god. Please tell me you're kidding?"

"Nuh uh."

Syd closed her eyes in mortification. "If we turn around and run really fast, can we get out of here before he notices?"

Maddie laughed and tugged her forward. "Don't worry. I'll be there to protect you."

Yeah. Having you by my side while I unwrap pleasure aids—that'll help, all right. "I think I'm going to die."

"Trust me. If you begin to die, I'll save you." She leaned closer and whispered near her ear, "See how useful it is to have an accomplished physician as your escort? It simplifies everything."

Not everything, Syd thought as the scent of Maddie's perfume piled up behind her eyes and clouded her vision. "I'll have to take your word for that." Her voice sounded husky. Maddie's proximity was seriously affecting her ability to think straight. *Oh, there's a nice bit of irony.*

They entered the small and richly appointed parlor. A small log fire burned in the corner fireplace, with two chairs and a loveseat in front of it. A coffee table sat in front of the chairs, and it held a silver tray that contained coffee cups, a carafe, cordial glasses, and a full bottle of Bailey's Irish Cream liqueur. David and Michael moved to occupy the two chairs, forcing Syd and Maddie to sit on the small settee.

Maddie's arm brushed against Syd's as she reached forward to take a coffee cup from Michael. Syd felt her heart rate accelerate. *There's no way I'm going to survive this,* she thought, as she bypassed the coffee and went straight for the Bailey's.

From the floor behind his chair, David picked up a small tower of wrapped packages and placed them at Syd's feet. There were four boxes in sizes varying from moderate to very small. Three of them were wrapped in the same, flocked paper and topped with opulent bows. One, the smallest of the group, was more simply appointed.

David pointed at it. "I apologize for the condition of *that* one. At least she didn't use duct tape."

Syd smiled at him and lifted the largest of the boxes onto her lap. It was surprisingly light. With trepidation, she unwrapped it. She lifted the lid off to reveal a dozen, bright orange bags of Cheetos. She sank back against the sofa in relief and laughed, feeling some of the tension drain from her body.

"It's gonna be a long winter," David drawled. "I thought you might need these."

Syd was tempted to rip open a bag right then, but smiled gratefully at him instead. "You're too kind." As an afterthought, she added, "I'll be sure to call you if I run out."

David's brown eyes sparkled as he looked back at her. He shot a look at Maddie. "Thankfully, I know where I can get my hands on an inexhaustible supply."

Maddie rolled her eyes and sipped her coffee.

Syd picked up the next box. It was much smaller, but surprisingly heavy. When she parted the layers of tissue paper inside, the first thing she saw were batteries—*lots* of them. She quickly replaced the paper. "Do I really want to know what else is in here?" She felt Maddie chuckle.

David leaned forward in his chair. "Go on, go on," he urged.

After carefully removing the packs of batteries, she lifted out a tissue-wrapped cylinder. It was very heavy. Holding her breath, she slowly unwrapped it, and was relieved when it turned out to be a high-tech, silver flashlight. She dropped it into her lap. "I'm really going to kill you," she hissed.

"Hey, sometimes you need a little help to find things in the dark." He winked at her.

She began to set the box aside, but David stopped her with a raised hand.

"Nuh uh. That's not everything yet."

She looked at him in confusion.

He sighed. "You *will* notice that the box contained batteries in two sizes?"

"Here it comes," Maddie drawled.

"So to speak," Michael added, in an undertone.

"Oh, god." Syd had a sinking sense of what was about to befall her before she even drew the last item from the box. It was a smaller, wrapped cylinder. Much smaller. Syd was mortified when she realized that she was holding a tiny, finger-shaped vibrator—a bright pink, finger-shaped vibrator with modular tips and a variable speed dial. "Oh, Jesus," she muttered as she immediately dropped it back into the dark recesses of the box.

David burst into merry laughter. "Well, if you use it *properly*, that will always be the response it elicits."

Syd knew she was probably turning pinker than the vibrator. "I don't think I can take any more presents right now," she said, with closed eyes.

Michael handed her the last matching box. "Don't worry, sweet pea. This one's from me."

Syd took it and slowly unwrapped it. It was a book. She turned it over. *Oh my god.* She flipped it open. It was an autographed first edition copy of Arthur Miller's screenplay adaptation of Fania Fénelon's memoir, *Playing for Time*—the incredible story of a group of Jewish musicians who survived the horrors of Auschwitz by playing in the death camp's orchestra. She gave Michael a shocked look.

"Where on earth did you find this?"

He smiled at her. "Vintage clothing isn't the only thing you can find at Mimi's. You just have to know where to look."

She rubbed her fingers over Miller's signature on the bookplate. "I can't believe this. It's incredible."

Michael looked smugly at David, then winked at her. "I thought the content was especially timely, given Phoebe's efforts at conscripting you to play in the community orchestra."

She smiled back as she hugged the book to her chest. "Thank you. This is wonderful."

Maddie leaned closer and gently attempted to pry the book from her hands. "May I?" she asked, from very close range.

Syd turned to look at her, and their faces were only inches apart. It took her a moment to find her voice. "Oh, of course." She released the book and leaned back away from the intoxicating woman. *My god. I need to get a grip on myself.* Ruefully, it occurred to her that David's gift might come in handy after all.

Maddie reverently leafed through the pages of the volume. "You know, this is an extraordinary find, but don't you think it's a little harsh to compare playing in our community orchestra to internment in a death camp?"

Michael snorted. "Have you ever heard David play the clarinet?"

Maddie paused in her inspection of the book. "Good point."

"Oh, the two of you can totally kiss my tight, little *ass*," David hissed, as he poured himself another hefty shot of the Bailey's. "Forget about them, Syd. You've got one more package to open."

Sighing, Syd leaned forward and picked up the last, tiny box. It was simply wrapped in silver paper, and tied with a white silk ribbon. She knew it was from Maddie, and her fingers felt thick and clumsy as she tried unsuccessfully to loosen the bow.

David spoke up. "Jeez, Sawbones. What'd you tie it with? 3.0 silk?"

Ignoring him, Maddie gently stilled Syd's hands and deftly untied the ribbon for her.

Syd's hands were practically shaking as she unwrapped a small, black velvet box. She shot her eyes up to Maddie's. Maddie met her gaze evenly and gave her a quiet smile, silently encouraging her to continue.

With trepidation, Syd opened the box. Inside, on a bed of white satin, was a beautiful gold necklace. She took a closer look at it. The pendant was a small, delicate but ornately carved replica of a violin bridge. It was exquisite. A small printed card tucked in the front corner of the box read *Heifetz Stradivarius.*

She looked at Maddie in disbelief. "This is a replica of the violin bridge from the Stradivarius played by Jascha Heifetz?"

Maddie nodded.

"Oh my god." Syd shook her head in wonder. "I've never seen anything so beautiful." She met Maddie's eyes. "I've heard of these, but I've never actually *seen* one. Where did you get it?"

Maddie smiled shyly. "It was my grandmother's. She was a violinist, too, and I know she'd be happy for you to have it now."

Syd's jaw dropped in amazement. "I can't accept this—it's too much." She offered the box back to Maddie.

Maddie folded her hands around Syd's and returned the box to her lap. "I want you to have it. *Please.*" The expression in her blue eyes matched the intensity of her voice.

Syd could barely speak. She felt tears sting her eyes, and she blinked rapidly to keep them back. She met Maddie's gaze again. "Okay."

They stared at each other for a moment. Then Syd moved closer, and Maddie quickly closed the distance between them, pulling her into a warm hug.

"Thank you," Syd whispered against her ear. Maddie squeezed her tighter in response, before releasing her and sitting back to assume the most respectful distance the small settee would allow.

"Veeeerrrry nice," David said. "I didn't know you had it in you."

Michael simply smiled.

Syd gently lifted the necklace from the box and held it up to the light. She turned to Maddie and shyly asked, "Would you fasten it for me?"

Maddie nodded as she took the necklace from her. Syd sat forward. Maddie leaned closer and reached around her to position the pendant on her chest. She drew the chain around Syd's neck and fumbled briefly with the clasp, but finally succeeded in hooking it. She then briefly rested her warm hands on Syd's bare shoulders and retreated once again to her side of the sofa.

Syd faced her. The small pendant fell to just above the valley between her breasts, and the shiny gold was a perfect complement to the emerald green of her dress.

"Beautiful," Maddie said, quietly. But her eyes were fixed on Syd's face.

"You got that right," David added. "Pretty impressive bit of bling, Cinderella. It's clear that you've been holding out on us."

Maddie turned to him. "Maybe I had a secret or two left in me, after all."

David nodded at her. "I'll drink to that."

Michael held up the bottle of Bailey's and topped everyone off. "Let's *all* drink to that." They picked up their cordial glasses, and he raised his high in the air. "Happy birthday, Syd. May we all continue to make sweet music together."

As they drank, she realized that this was the best birthday she'd ever had. She wished with all her heart that his words would prove prophetic.

Chapter 14

The Tri-County airport was small, even by rural standards. The FBO was a tiny brick building that housed a small pilot lounge, a weather computer, and a telephone used to file and close flight plans. It was outfitted with a couple of shopworn recliners, a sofa, an old console color television, and several vending machines that had seen better days. The air inside was stale from cigarette smoke and smelled like burned coffee. The Spartan accommodations did little to calm Syd's jittery nerves. Outside near the field, she could see a litter of small planes— mostly high-wings. A few of the nicer-looking aircraft were tied down under aluminum t-hangars that ran at a right angle to the runway. While Maddie amused herself playing with the weather computer, Syd watched a fuel truck slowly make its way across the field and wondered when their pilot would show up.

Maddie went to the counter and picked up the telephone receiver just as a squat, middle-aged man entered the room from outside. He was wearing an orange jumpsuit and a cap that read *AeroServ*.

"Hey, Doc!" he called out. "Do you want me to pull her up for you?"

"Sure, that'd be great, Tommy. I have a few minutes 'cause I still need to file my flight plan. Oh, by the way. Top the tips for me while you're at it."

"Can do, Doc." He touched the brim of his cap and headed back outside toward the row of t-hangars.

Syd watched this exchange and the man's departure with a growing sense of dread. "Maddie?"

Maddie turned to her with one eyebrow elevated. "Yeeesss?"

"Is there something about this trip you neglected to tell me?"

"Um . . . like?" A smile pulled at the corner of her mouth.

Syd was losing patience. "Like just *whointhehell* is our pilot?"

"Ahh." Maddie stroked her chin with the fingers of her right hand. "That would be me."

"You? *You?* Are you *kidding* me with this?" Syd was nearly beside herself. "You told me our pilot was *experienced.* You told me our pilot owned his own plane."

Maddie put a hand on Syd's arm to stop her tirade. "She is. I do. You have nothing to be worried about."

"I don't believe this. How could you not *tell* me?" Syd paced back and forth across the stained and faded carpet.

Maddie sighed and leaned her long frame against the counter that held the telephone. She crossed her arms and quietly watched Syd pace. "Once your extremities come to rest," she finally said, calmly, "I'll be happy to share the details of my flight credentials with you."

Outside the plate glass window that faced the field, Syd could see Tommy in a tug, pulling a shiny and sleek-looking low-wing out onto the tarmac. It was brightly painted in blue and yellow, and sported two big engines. She inclined her head toward the scene. "That yours?"

Maddie's eyes followed her gaze. "Yeah. I've had it about five years now. It's a honey."

Syd nodded. "Well, of course it is. It would *have* to be, right? I mean . . . how could it be otherwise?"

Maddie uncrossed her arms and took a deep breath. "Look. I see now that not telling you about this was a mistake, and I apologize for that. I thought it would be a nice surprise for you—honest. Obviously I was wrong. Can you tell me now why this is so upsetting to you? I've been flying since I was sixteen. I'm a careful and experienced pilot. You really will be quite safe with me. I know what I am doing, and I *never* take chances."

Syd turned to her, suddenly a bit ashamed of her overreaction. She put a hand to her forehead and shook her head a couple of times. "I really am sorry. I don't know why that ticked me off so much. I guess it's just . . . I don't know." She waved her hand dismissively. "Shit. Tell me, is there anything you *can't* do?"

Maddie stood there looking pensive. Then she smiled slyly. "I have *many* skills." Syd rolled her eyes. "But . . . yeah. There are a lot of things I positively suck at."

"Like?"

"Well. I can't cook to save my soul. And no matter how hard I try I can never get just *one* of those damn tongue depressors out of the jar." She thought for a minute. "And there's always relationships."

Syd gave her a quizzical look. "What about relationships?"

"I *really* suck at those."

Syd smiled and shrugged. "Well, I certainly can't offer much in the way of advice there, but I might be able to help you out with the cooking thing."

Maddie smiled back. "I'll take you up on that. Now . . . how about letting me file our flight plan, and we'll get on our way?"

Syd sighed, and then nodded. "Go ahead. I'll get our stuff out of the Jeep."

Ten minutes later, Maddie joined her out on the field and unlocked the door to the plane. Syd was shocked by its compact but fairly comfortable-looking interior. "This is really beautiful. What kind of airplane is this?"

Maddie was busy stowing their gear in the cargo hold behind the rear passenger seats. "This is a Cessna 310. It's small, but still nicely sized and fast for a twin-prop plane. My dad and I actually bought this together. We mostly kept it down here, but I often used it to hop back and forth between Jericho and Philly after I finished my residency. It was quicker and more accessible for me than trying to get in and out of Charlotte or Roanoke." She stuffed their last bag into the cargo hold and climbed back out onto the tarmac. "Lemme do my preflight, and we'll get underway."

Syd stood back and watched as Maddie walked around the airplane checking the tires and running her hands along the edges of the wings. Then she checked the props and tested the fuel with a tiny-looking cross between a test tube and a syringe. Then they were ready to head out.

She showed Syd how to step up onto the wing and into the cabin, then climbed in ahead of her and scooted over into the left seat. Once Syd was aboard, Maddie helped her fasten her seatbelt and put on her headset.

Maddie picked up a clipboard from behind her seat and ran through an instrument checklist. She flipped a couple of switches, lowered her window, and called out, "Clear prop!" Then she started the left engine.

Even wearing the headset, Syd was surprised by how loud the noise was. It only increased when the right engine roared into life. She was startled when she heard Maddie's low voice speak over the radio transmitter in her ear. "You okay? I have to take us to the end of the taxiway and do a run-up to test the engines before we take off." Syd nodded. "It'll be loud, and the plane will shake a bit . . . didn't want you to be scared." Syd nodded again. "Syd . . . you can speak. That thing in front of your mouth is a microphone."

Syd smiled sheepishly. "Sorry. I'm not used to any of this. You'll have to bear with me."

"Tri-County traffic, this is Cessna Four Two Nine Whiskey Papa, departing runway two-three, Tri-County," Maddie said into the radio after the run-up. She released the brake, and the plane started rolling down the runway. As it gained in speed, Syd began to feel a sense of exhilaration as the landscape raced by.

"Here we go," Maddie said as she pulled back on the yoke, and the nose of the plane lifted up.

Soon, they were airborne and rotating out over the field. Syd felt a rumble as the gear retracted and stowed away beneath the plane. Below, she could see the brick building of the FBO and the small parking lot where Maddie's Jeep was plainly visible.

Maddie executed a turn and headed them away from the field and toward the eastern horizon. "Tri-County traffic, Cessna Four Two Nine Whiskey Papa is departing the pattern, heading north." After a moment, she said, "Washington Center, this is November Four Two Nine Whiskey Papa. Just departed Tri-County, climbing to 7,500 feet VFR, and would like to pick up my IFR flight plan to Richmond."

"Roger, Four Two Nine Whiskey Papa," a crackled voice answered. "This is Washington Center. You're cleared direct to Richmond. Maintain 9,000 feet. Squawk 3612."

"Two Nine Whiskey Papa, maintaining 9,000 feet direct to Richmond. Squawking 3612. Roger." Maddie adjusted a set of four dials to read 3612. She punched a set of coordinates into the plane's GPS system, and then engaged the autopilot.

She turned to Syd. "So. That's pretty much it. We let the plane do the hard work, now."

Syd looked surprised. "That's *it*? No mystery? No drama? No mile-high heroics?"

Maddie laughed. "You'd better find some wood to knock on. The one thing we *don't* want is any mile-high heroics. What you wish for is a nice, uneventful, and boring flight."

"Oh *now* you tell me," Syd quipped. "Do I at least get a free bag of peanuts for my trouble?"

Maddie smiled and reached behind Syd to rummage around in her flight bag.

"Here." She handed Syd a foil-wrapped breakfast bar. "It's the best I can do on short notice."

Syd smiled. "At least tell me that this trip will count toward my frequent-flier miles."

"Tell you what," Maddie said, unwrapping her own bar. "You may redeem this wrapper for one free round-trip to the destination of your choice."

After landing and taxiing to Million Air, the Richmond general aviation center, they offloaded their gear and carried it inside the slightly more opulent FBO. Syd waited by their bags while Maddie took care of getting her plane safely stowed. They took a cab from the airport and arrived at their downtown hotel shortly after one. Maddie's first session wasn't until four, but Syd's first meeting with the State Library representatives was scheduled for two-thirty.

Maddie unlocked the door of their room, and they both stepped inside. The room was located on the fourth floor of the stately Old Dominion Hotel and overlooked the James River. It was large and comfortably appointed with vintage furnishings. One king-sized bed stood boldly in the center of the room like some kind of fabric-draped behemoth. They both stood stupidly in the doorway for a moment.

Oh shit, Maddie thought, before dropping her bags and looking around the room. "Where's the phone? I'll get this straightened out in no time. I distinctly asked for two beds."

Syd didn't say anything as Maddie crossed to the nightstand next to the massive bed and dialed the hotel's front desk.

A man's voice answered on the fourth ring. "May I help you?"

"Yes. This is Dr. Stevenson in Room 412. I just checked in. I requested a room with two queen-sized beds, but this room has only one king."

"I'm sorry, Dr. Stevenson. Let me check into that for you." There was the sound of clicking on the other end as the clerk typed. "Yes, I can see here that you reserved two queens. Unfortunately, we had a water leak on the second floor yesterday, and several of our rooms are closed for repairs. With the AMA conference in town, we were already overbooked, so we don't have any extra rooms available."

Maddie eyed Syd in agitation as she deliberated. "So there's no potential for you to switch us to another room?"

"I'm sorry, Doctor. To apologize for the inconvenience, I'll code your account so that you and your guest can enjoy complementary breakfasts in the hotel dining room each morning during your stay with us."

Syd walked in behind her and calmly laid her garment bag across the bed with something that seemed like determination.

Maddie sighed. "I understand. Thank you for checking into it."

"It's my pleasure, Dr. Stevenson. I apologize again for the inconvenience. Please let us know if we can do anything to make your stay more enjoyable."

Right. You mean besides make me share a bed with the beautiful straight woman I'm in love with? Yeah. I'll be sure to let you know. "I'll do that," she said instead and hung up the phone.

She turned to Syd and waved her hand in frustration. "Well, it appears we're stuck. They had a water leak, and it took several of their other rooms off-line. They don't have any others available because of the conference."

Syd hesitated for only a fraction of moment. "It's okay. We're both grown-ups. This bed is large enough to declare statehood. I think we can manage."

Maddie was still doubtful. She didn't want Syd to feel uncomfortable, and she noticed that Syd had been unwilling or unable to make eye contact with her since they entered the room. "Are you sure?"

"Absolutely. You're already doing me a *huge* favor by letting me share your room. I have *no* concerns." She finally looked up at her. "Unless, of course, you snore?"

Maddie saw the faint glimmer of humor in Syd's green eyes. She feigned indignation. "I've never had any complaints."

"It's settled, then. Dibs on the bathroom side."

Maddie raised an eyebrow.

"What can I say? I have a pea-sized bladder. It's a curse."

Maddie chuckled as she hefted her suitcase onto the stand at the foot of the bed.

Syd went to the windows and looked out across the city toward the river. "Wow. This is some view. I've never spent much time in Richmond. Do you get here often?"

Maddie joined her at the window. "Hardly ever. But I do know a couple of good restaurants."

"Great. I hope I can remember what to do with a full set of silverware."

"Oh, I think it will come back to you."

Syd continued to stare out the window. "It's odd. You never really think of Richmond as a port city, but that certainly looks like an active waterfront."

"Well, that's why it was the capital of the Confederacy."

Syd turned to her. "I keep forgetting that you're a native Virginian."

"Oh, you're just deluded by the fact that I don't have a stars-n-bars bumper-sticker on my Jeep. It throws a lot of people off."

"I would never have pegged you as a covert secessionist."

Maddie laughed. "Nothing *covert* about me these days—not since I moved back to Jericho. Don't you know by now that intimate details of the local doctor's life are considered public domain?"

Syd nudged her. "Well. Not *all* details."

Maddie smiled sheepishly. "Touché."

"But putting that aside, I have wondered how you cope with it."

Maddie shrugged. "Fortunately, most people are so motivated by self interest that their provincial concerns about the great mystery of my private life are secondary to whatever malady prompts them to seek medical attention. And I have the advantage of being perceived as more-or-less a native. For once, trying to fill my father's shoes is a benefit."

"For once?"

Maddie lowered her gaze from the window to regard Syd. "I knew you wouldn't let *that* comment slide."

Syd glanced at her watch before smiling at Maddie. "Well, you're in luck. Right now I'm faced with the unhappy prospect of trying to fill my *own* shoes. I guess I should go and try to make myself look halfway professional before my meeting."

Maddie laughed and gestured toward the bathroom. "All yours."

Syd leaned her back against the closed bathroom door and stood for a few moments with her eyes shut. *Oh my god, how am I supposed to survive this? I can't let her see how freaked out I am. She'll think it's because she told me she's gay. Jesus.* She opened her eyes, went to the vanity, and looked at herself in the mirror. The face that gazed back at her was completely distracted. *What a mess. How do I act all blasé about this when I'm terrified? What if I have another one of those damn dreams while I'm actually in bed with her? Fuck, fuck, fuck. I so am not up for this.* In desperation, she looked at the tiny window over the commode. *I wonder if I could survive a jump to the street?*

Sighing with resignation, she began to remove cosmetic items from her small travel bag.

Maddie was reclining in a chair with her sneaker-clad feet propped up on the windowsill, reading the entertainment section of the Richmond *Times-Dispatch*. She looked up as Syd entered the room. She felt a twinge of pleasure as she noticed that Syd was wearing the necklace she had given her for her birthday to go with a striking, dark green suit.

"Okay. Who are you and what have you done with the dour librarian I arrived with?"

Syd waved her hand dismissively. "Oh, come on. Hey. *Dour?*"

"You look *great*," Maddie said. "I don't know what dollar amount you've asked for in your budget request, but take my advice and *double* it."

Syd blushed as she transferred items from her handbag into a briefcase. "I hate to disillusion you, but meeting with the state library board won't be anything like your favorite pastime of seducing pharmaceutical reps. The old tried-and-true cheesecake approach won't do me much good."

Maddie was silent for a moment. "Don't underestimate yourself." Syd laughed and turned to her, but Maddie averted her eyes. "You want me to call you a cab?"

Syd nodded. "I'll probably be longer than an hour. Wanna meet back here later on?"

"You betcha. My opening session shouldn't last more than an hour, so I ought to be back here by five-thirty or six. Then we can spend the evening eating and drinking entirely too much." Maddie smiled. "This is one night I don't have to worry about being on call. And I know a great little restaurant in the Fan that we can walk to."

Syd smiled. "I can hardly wait."

After finding the office building and walking up four flights of marble stairs, Syd was shown into a paneled conference room and offered a cup of very stale black coffee. Several minutes later, the door opened, and a middle-aged woman hurried in while apologizing for her tardiness.

"Ms. Murphy? I'm Denise Metcalf—the grant coordinator. Our rural services manger was supposed to join us, but got called away this afternoon."

Syd smiled as they shook hands. "That's okay. I appreciate your willingness to meet with me over a weekend."

"It's a pleasure—really. We don't get many opportunities to talk personally with our field librarians." She was a small woman, with a round, friendly-looking face. "How are you making out?"

"Pretty well—all things considered. The branch opening went very smoothly. I've been the grateful recipient of lots of good volunteer help."

Metcalf smiled and jotted a note on the inside cover of a file folder. "That's what we like to hear. How is the facility shaping up?"

"It's a bit rustic, but the locals have done an amazing job with renovations. We repainted the inside and installed new carpet squares. The interior lighting is still a challenge, so I rely pretty heavily on tabletop fixtures. I have a floor plan for you, in addition to the preliminary operating budget."

"Wonderful. I can't tell you how unusual it is to have this information produced voluntarily and on time. We may want to use you as a poster child for our other branches."

Syd laughed as she passed the documents across the table. "You might want to withhold your praise until you've had a chance to review these. I confess that I am flying blind on this budget."

Metcalf flipped through the neatly typed pages. "Don't worry too much about that. We don't expect you to have an etched-in-stone report until a full year after the branch is up and running. You'll have an opportunity next fall to reassess and modify these figures."

"That's a relief. I never really thought of myself as a science fiction writer until I sat down to draft this."

Metcalf chuckled. "Are there any glaring omissions in your initial inventory? Any critical equipment needs necessary to facilitate operations?"

Syd raised an eyebrow. "Within what dollar amount are we speaking?"

"Oh, roughly in the range of free."

"That's what I thought." Syd drummed her fingers on top of her briefcase. "No. I guess we can manage for now."

Metcalf nodded, then reached into her jacket pocket and pulled out a business card. "Here are all of my numbers. Please give me a call any time I can be of help."

Syd took the card. "Thank you, I will."

"Now, Judy Goldman—who is our state auditor—wants to talk with you tomorrow about some changes in funding that might be coming down the pike next year."

Syd was surprised. "Is this something I should be worried about?"

Metcalf shook her head. "I don't think so—not now, anyway. But it would be disingenuous to pretend that we aren't all concerned about the fate of our less established initiatives in the wake of the hits our state budget has been taking. What we have to hope is that your local economy will be in a position to shoulder the expense of running the branch by the time the grant money runs out next year."

"Well, that sounds vaguely ominous." Syd stood up and buttoned her jacket. "I guess it's a good thing I didn't count on more than an eighteen-month tenure."

Metcalf stood up and extended her hand. "Don't be too worried. We generally find that once they get used to having a library, local governments are reluctant to give them up." They shook hands. "I think your little branch will find a way to survive."

Syd smiled at her. "I hope you're right. I've grown rather fond of the area . . . and the people."

"Oh? So you might be interested in staying on there after the grant ends?"

"I've been giving it some thought lately."

"Well, be sure to tell Judy that tomorrow. It can't hurt for her to know that she's got a potential bird in the hand. It's been a pleasure meeting you, Syd. Your materials look very thorough. I look forward to seeing you again tomorrow. Thanks so much for coming all the way to Richmond."

"Likewise, and I was happy to make the trip up here. I thought a little diversion would do me some good."

"Have you been to our fair city before?"

"Not really. I'm embarrassed to confess that I've never done more than pass through Richmond on the interstate."

"Where are you staying?"

"An older hotel called *The Old Dominion*—in the Fan district."

"Oh, that's very charming. Enjoy your evening, and we'll see you again tomorrow afternoon."

Syd smiled as she grabbed the doorknob. "Thanks. I look forward to it."

Since she had extra time on her hands, Syd told the cab driver to drop her off several blocks from the hotel, thinking that the brisk air would do her good. She browsed in and around several interesting looking storefront shops and wondered how Maddie was faring with the conference. The sky had turned slate gray. She was no expert, but it looked like it could snow. She smiled to herself. *I'll have to ask the resident flying ace and weather maven about that.* She slowly shook her head. *Goofball. I can't believe she sprung that on me.*

She glanced at her watch. Four forty-five. Maddie wouldn't be back for at least another hour, and the weather continued to deteriorate. She decided to head back to the room and change into more comfortable clothes. There was a small café in front of the hotel, and she thought she would order some decent coffee and peruse their complimentary newspaper.

When she got back, she was surprised to see Maddie crossing the lobby. She was striking in a tailored blue dress, walking with long strides across the worn carpet toward the stairs. *Stairs. Of course. Why take an elevator when it's only eight flights?* She crossed to the elevators and decided to do an end-run and surprise her.

Maddie huffed as she bolted up the last flight of stairs. *Damn . . . I really gotta start working out. I wonder if I should pick up one of those Wii Fit thingies while I'm up here?*

At the top, she hauled open the big fire door.

"Hey there, Stretch. Looking for some company?" came a low, sexy voice.

She whipped her head around toward the sound and saw Syd casually leaning against a doorjamb with her arms crossed over her chest and a small smile on her face.

Maddie stood there, slack-jawed, and Syd broke into mirthful laughter. "Oh, poor baby. You look like a deer in the headlights. Did I scare you?"

Maddie took a moment to consider, deciding that a good offense was her best defense. "On the contrary. I was just weighing my options." She stepped closer to Syd so she could tower over her. "I've already sort of made plans with another babe for tonight but I think I can get out of it. She's a librarian, and probably won't last much past seven-thirty." She gave her a rakish wink and bent even closer. "Wanna meet later in the bar?"

Syd dropped her arms in defeat. "Do you have to be better at *everything*?"

Maddie laughed and draped an arm around Syd's shoulders as she steered them toward their room. "Don't be bitter. I already gave you an index to the things I don't do well."

"Oh, yeah. Let's see . . . we can either *cook* something, or fall madly into a relationship." Syd realized what she said and panicked. She looked up at Maddie, quickly trying to conceal her faux pas. "I think those were my options, right?"

Maddie nudged her playfully. "Tongue depressors. You forgot those." She winked at her. "But given the choice, I'd definitely go for the relationship option."

"And why's that?" Syd was intrigued.

Maddie's laugh was self-deprecating. She dropped her arm and retrieved her room key from her bag. "Because even though the ending would be a nightmare, I could promise you a helluva good time getting there."

Syd's pulse raced as she watched her open the door to their room. She wondered what on earth had made Maddie so bitter, and so fatalistic.

Maddie stood aside so Syd could enter the room . . . and looked back at her with an implied question in her clear, blue eyes. Syd knew she needed to make some kind of response to her facetious suggestion.

"Tell you what." Syd smiled. "I'll take it under advisement."

Maddie shrugged into the arms of her leather jacket as they exited the elevator. "Why don't we commemorate having our first appointments behind us and go find some place monstrously overpriced for dinner? I feel like celebrating." She added with a sly grin, "I may even splurge and drink an entire bottle of wine by myself."

Syd raised an eyebrow. "By yourself?"

Maddie playfully nudged her arm as they walked across the lobby toward the street doors. "Okay. I might be persuaded to share a *small* glass with you, if you promise not to question my selection or argue with me about who pays."

"Arguing with you might always be a losing proposition, but I can't promise that I won't try."

They stepped out onto the street. A line of taxis stood at the ready along the curb.

"Do we walk or do we ride?" Syd asked, turning up the collar of her jacket. It was still shy of sunset, but the air was noticeably colder than it had been just an hour ago. She couldn't tell if it was going to rain or snow, but it was pretty clear that something ominous was brewing.

Maddie grasped her elbow and steered her away from the hotel driveway. "We walk." She glanced up at the sky. "But let's hedge our bets and find something closer to the hotel in case the weather turns on us. We can grab some fresh air and look along the river for a nice spot with a view and a good wine list."

"That sounds great to me. I feel like my butt is numb from sitting all day."

"Reeeeaallly?" Maddie asked, stopping to consider Syd's backside. "Want me to take a look at it for you?" She dramatically flexed the fingers of both hands like tentacles.

Syd grabbed her by the arm and yanked her forward. "No, nut job. I think it'll work itself out. Thanks all the same for the offer."

Maddie sighed and shoved her hands into the pockets of her jacket. "Your loss. I'll have you know I was the unbridled star of my session today."

Syd looked at her in disbelief. "And your session on the conference itinerary has exactly what relevance to my backside?"

Maddie shrugged and shook her head. "Medicine is associative. Who can say how seemingly unrelated conditions might intersect in a diagnosis."

"Riiight. Well, I think I'll take my chances and try to walk this particular malady off." Syd smiled at her.

"Well, don't say I didn't offer to help."

After walking a few blocks, they came upon the entrance to a large pedestrian bridge that stretched across the James River. It was located next to an outdoor plaza dotted with bars, quaint looking shops, and neatly landscaped outdoor seating areas. Business people hurried along the sidewalks, talking on cell phones and checking their watches. Lively music, punctuated by raucous laughter, poured out the open doors of one of the bars. Maddie stopped and looked up and down the plaza. She narrowed her eyes as she scanned the row of shops.

"I think there's a—yeah. It's this way. C'mon." She took Syd by the elbow and guided her through the melee of pedestrians.

After walking about a block, they turned down an alley that led away from the plaza toward the riverbank. At the bottom of the tiny street, overlooking the water, stood an old, three-story brick building. A small painted sign that read "River City Chop House" hung on rusty hooks near the large double doors. The legend "1854" was etched into a grimy-looking cornerstone. There were no cars, and no place to park them in any event. A chalkboard on an easel stood on the sidewalk near the entrance.

"It's been a while since I ate here," Maddie explained. "But as I recall, the food is excellent and the atmosphere is even better. You game?"

Syd pulled her eyes away from the tantalizing descriptions of the evening fare and looked at Maddie with a glazed expression. "Are you kidding? *Try* and keep me out of here."

Maddie grinned and walked up the three steps to the door and held it open for Syd. "Well, we're early enough that we should be able to get a seat without reservations."

She opened the door, and an intoxicating blend of odors assailed Syd. She nearly swooned, and had to fight to keep her nose out of the air. The small lobby area was paneled in dark walnut and comfortably, but simply furnished. Wine racks were stashed everyplace—all of them full. The restaurant itself was made up of a series of smaller rooms with spectacular views of the waterfront.

A middle-aged man, wearing a starched white shirt and black bow tie, approached them from inside the restaurant. He wore a knee-length apron and carried several oversized, leather-covered menus. His eyes widened when he saw Maddie.

"Dr. Stevenson. Welcome back. Are you in town for the conference?"

Maddie grinned sheepishly and shook hands with the man. "Hi ya, Willie. Yeah, just here for the weekend. I thought I'd like to treat my friend here to the best food in Richmond. Willie, meet Margaret Sydney Murphy."

Willie shook hands warmly with Syd. "Welcome, Miss Murphy. Let me get you set up some place nice before the crowds arrive." He reached beneath a large stationmaster's desk and picked up a hefty wine list. "If you'll just follow me?"

"Thanks, Willie. You're the best." Maddie gestured for Syd to walk ahead of her.

"Been a while since you ate here, huh?" Syd muttered under her breath as she passed her.

Maddie shrugged. "What can I tell you?" she whispered. "I'm a great tipper."

Willie led them across a faded carpet to a small table in a corner, next to a large set of casement windows that overlooked the river. The view was breathtaking. The late afternoon sun was just starting to set, casting long shadows across everything along the riverbank. Small boats and cargo barges slowly moved along the inner-city waterway. From this vantage point, it was easy to imagine what life had looked like in old, antebellum Richmond. Down here, along the riverfront, there was little to suggest that anything in the city had changed. No cars. No traffic lights. No roads to speak of. Walkways lighted with gas lamps ran along the embankment. There was little pedestrian traffic. Here, the pace of life seemed to move along at the same, unhurried rate of the river itself.

They sat down and began to examine their menus. Maddie ordered them each a glass of cabernet to enjoy while they considered their dining and beverage options. Willie arrived in short order with the two glasses of wine and a loaf of freshly baked sourdough bread. They sipped their wine as he described the chef's specials for the evening, and then left them to their own devices. They eagerly discussed the menu, trying to devise a method to try at least one of everything, while Maddie made happy, groaning noises as she bit into a hunk of the hot bread.

Syd smiled and looked up from her menu. Behind Maddie, she could see a striking, dark-haired woman approaching their table. She wore a tailored navy blue suit and carried a black leather bag. She nodded at Syd as she reached their table, then she touched Maddie lightly on the back of her shoulder.

"Hello, stranger," she said, in a husky voice, tinged with an unmistakable New York accent.

Maddie started and turned to her with a stunned expression on her face. She sat staring at the woman for several seconds. "Gina." It was just one word, but it seemed to speak volumes. "What, uh . . . what are you doing here?" Syd had never seen Maddie lose her composure like this. She was completely rattled.

Gina laughed. She seemed perfectly relaxed. "I'm here for the conference—just like you, I'd imagine." She glanced at Syd, and then shifted her gaze back to Maddie. "Are you going to introduce me to your friend?"

The way she said "friend" bothered Syd. Maddie appeared to notice it, too. Syd saw the muscles in her jaw tighten.

"Of course. Syd Murphy, this is Gina Garcetti. Gina, Syd Murphy."

"Nice to meet you," Gina said as she extended a hand across the table and limply shook hands with Syd. Even while they were shaking hands, her eyes drifted back to Maddie.

"And you," Syd replied, clearly speaking to herself. She studied the small woman. Gina was a looker all right. Glossy black hair, cut stylishly short. Brown eyes with amazing long lashes. A tight-fitting suit. Understated, but expensive jewelry. Prada bag. Manicured nails. Everything about her suggested taste and class. And she was looking at Maddie like she was something that had just rolled out on the dessert cart. Syd had a growing sense that a final piece of a puzzle was tumbling into place right before her eyes.

"Aren't you going to ask me to sit down?" Gina nudged Maddie playfully, adding to her obvious discomfort.

"Um . . . well . . ." Maddie fumbled.

Syd reached across the table to push back the bread basket in an attempt to clear a place for Gina and knocked over her wine glass. The red liquid spread across the tablecloth like a bloodstain and dripped off onto the seat of their only extra chair.

"Damn it," Syd cried, belatedly tossing her napkin on top of the red tide. "I'm so clumsy. God. Please forgive me. Let me get a waiter to help us clean this up."

Gina looked passively at Syd, then down at the lake of cabernet pooling on the chair.

"On the other hand, it looks like this is a bad time." She turned to Maddie again. "Let me catch up with you tomorrow. I'm sure I'll see you at Dr. Heller's keynote." Without waiting for a response, she turned and walked away, tossing an offhand, "Nice to meet you, Syd," over her shoulder.

Syd watched her walk across their tiny dining room as she made her way toward the lobby.

"Bitch," she muttered.

Maddie gave her a startled look.

Syd raised an eyebrow and inclined her head toward their uninvited guest. "Dr. Livingstone, I presume?"

Maddie blinked, then burst into laughter. "Oh my god. You did that on *purpose*, didn't you?"

Syd shrugged and set her glass upright. "It seemed like you needed a diversion, so I made the ultimate sacrifice." She picked up her empty glass and sniffed it. "Too bad. I really liked this stuff."

Willie arrived with the wine steward in tow, and in less than one minute, their table had been cleared and reset. The offending chair was removed. The steward asked Syd if she'd like another glass of the same cabernet.

"Hell no," Maddie roared. "We're celebrating. Bring us a bottle of the *Margaux*."

Syd raised her eyebrows.

Maddie's eyes sparkled as she looked back at Syd. "Thank you for that."

"Why do I think there's a long story lurking here?" Syd asked as she took a fresh piece of bread.

"Probably because there is," Maddie replied with resignation. She sat for a few moments, deliberating as she twisted the stem of her wine glass between her fingers. Then she shook her dark head. "What the hell. You want to hear the ugly truth now or after we eat?"

"Maddie . . . you don't have to talk about it at all if it makes you uncomfortable. I really don't want to pry."

"Oh, trust me. *It* doesn't make me uncomfortable—not like *she* does. I'm just not sure how much of this you really want to know. It might fall into the category of TMI."

Syd smiled. "I'd like to think that we're friends. Unless your story involves pouring over photos of your gall bladder operation, I doubt you could scare me off."

Maddie arched an eyebrow. "You don't wanna see my scars?"

"Only the metaphorical ones."

The steward arrived with the wine and made a ceremony out of opening the bottle. He splashed a bit of it into a fresh wine glass, and Maddie eagerly took a sip.

Her eyes practically rolled back into her head. "Oh, yeah. That'll do."

Maddie cleared her throat. "So . . . where to begin?"

Syd sipped her wine, then met Maddie's gaze. "Let me save you some time," she offered. "I gather that Gina is the infamous ex?"

"That obvious, huh?" Maddie shook her head. "And here I wanted to be all mysterious." She gave Syd a nervous look. "Are you disappointed?"

"Why would I be disappointed? She's certainly beautiful."

Maddie was surprised and slightly embarrassed by Syd's comment. "Well, that isn't exactly what I meant."

"It isn't?"

"No. But, thank you—I *think*."

"You mentioned to me a while back that you had been involved with someone—a surgeon, I think you said—before coming back to Jericho. Was that Gina?"

Maddie nodded.

"And that relationship ended just before you returned to Virginia?"

"Yes."

"That makes sense, now. When we first met, I couldn't figure out why someone like you was unattached."

Maddie raised her eyebrow. "Ditto."

Syd blushed. "Okay . . . I guess I asked for that. What I meant was that you seemed so not of the area—even though I knew you grew up there. It was clear to me that you had some kind of story. That's all."

Maddie considered Syd for a few moments. "Well, as you know, I only did part of my growing up there. After my parents divorced, I spent most of my time living with my mother in southern California. I'd come back to Virginia on holidays, of course, and for a month or so every summer. I saw a lot more of my father during my college years than I ever did during childhood." Syd waited patiently for her to continue. "Dad and I got a lot closer during my years at Penn—his alma mater, too. We shared passions for medicine—and for flying—and spent many weekends together hopping around in our little airplane. He was a frequent visitor to Philadelphia in those days." She smiled at the recollection. "I miss him a lot. My decision to go back there and take over his practice wasn't tough at all. He'd been after me for a couple of years to move back and join him."

"Are you glad you did?"

Maddie nodded. "I am. It just feels right. All except for the secrets I now have to keep. Sometimes I wonder how much longer I can keep it up. It feels so inauthentic—so dishonest."

Syd took a sip of her wine. "If it's not too personal to ask. Who else knows?"

"That I'm gay?"

Syd nodded.

Maddie sighed. "Well, besides David and Michael, my father knew. I don't know if he ever really managed to make peace with the information. I think he may have told Peggy Hawkes. She often lapses into this 'I know something but I'm not telling' posture whenever any aspect of my private life comes up. And, unlike every other woman in the county over the age of sixty, she never quizzes me about my personal life or tries to entangle me with some one or other unattached male."

"Well, that's a cross we both have to bear," Syd pointed out.

Maddie smiled wryly. "I know. But at least you have the singular advantage of having been married. I stand out like some kind of alien species."

Syd quietly considered Maddie. "I don't know," she mused. "We're both anomalies. But in terms of our professions, we're holding true to the stereotypes."

Maddie snorted. "You mean we're both old maids?"

"Exactly."

They sat quietly for a minute or so.

"So?" Syd prompted.

"So?" Maddie repeated.

"So, what happened?"

"You mean in the relationship?" Maddie asked.

Syd nodded.

"Oh, nothing so terribly dramatic. Gina was a third-year surgical resident in ophthalmology at the Wills Eye Hospital in Philly. I was finishing my final year in emergency medicine at Presby. We were introduced by mutual friends, and started seeing each other. It was her first same-sex relationship . . ." She paused. "And my first really serious involvement." She waved a dismissive hand. "We tried living together, but it just never worked out. Our schedules were just too erratic—too dissimilar. In the end, it was all too much for her. Trying to balance a medical career with the stresses of a serious relationship—and her ambivalence about the *nature* of that relationship—just became too complicated. We wanted different things— different lives. It all fell apart pretty quickly. Something had to give." She looked at Syd. "That something ended up being me." She glanced down at her plate and idly picked at her piece of bread. "By the time my father died, I knew it was over. That's when I made my final decision to come back and take over his practice."

They sat in silence again.

"Any regrets?" Syd asked, quietly.

Maddie met her gaze. "Not one."

"Well . . . Gina certainly seemed . . . *composed*. But at the risk of overstepping, you didn't."

"No." Maddie shook her head. "No, I wasn't. I'm *not*. It ended, but it ended badly. And I haven't had any contact with Gina since I left Philadelphia two years ago."

"So seeing her here was a surprise for you?"

Maddie poured herself another half glass of wine. "Yes. No. I mean, I guess I thought there was a pretty good probability that she would be here for this conference—especially for the ophthalmic sessions. I guess I just thought I might be able to avoid running into her." She exhaled audibly and shook her head. "You can see how well that delusion played out."

Syd sighed. "Well, I'm certainly no expert, but it seems like you might have some unfinished business." She paused, and then continued quietly. "Is there a chance you still have feelings for her?"

Maddie's eyes tracked up to Syds. "Oh, I have feelings for her all right. But not the kind you suspect. Believe me, Gina's . . . complicated. Not being around her is altogether in my best interest."

"Okaaaaayyy. But it sounds like your plan to avoid her isn't going to pan out very well if you're in the same session tomorrow. Or is that one you can skip?"

"No . . . no, that's one session I *have* to attend. In fact, it's the real reason I'm here, and that's something else I need to share with you."

"With me?" Syd asked, confused.

"Yeah. Especially since it seems pretty likely that you'll end up being involved in it, too."

Syd sat up straighter in her chair. "It? This is sounding pretty ominous. What is 'it,' and how could I possibly be involved?"

"Weeeellll . . . the conference keynote speaker is one Dr. Celine Heller— associate dean of the UCLA School of Medicine and one of the nation's leading researchers in molecular toxicology."

"Okay, I'm properly humbled. But why is this something *I* need to know about?"

Maddie sighed. "Well, Celine and I have a . . . history. And we haven't exactly been on very good terms for about the last, oh, seven years or so. In fact, I haven't seen her since I graduated from med school. It's fairly certain that she is at least going to want to dine with, um, *us* tomorrow night."

Syd narrowed her eyes. "Okay. We'll get back to that 'us' part. But by history, do you mean . . . ?" She waved her hand.

Maddie gave her a quizzical look, then laughed. "God, no. Celine is my mother."

Syd flopped back against her chair. "Oh my god." She thought about it for a moment. "Heller. Is that the 'H' in Madeleine H. Stevenson?"

"Ding. Would you now like to try for Double Jeopardy, where those dollars can *really* add up?"

Syd tore a hunk off her piece of bread and tossed it across the table at her. "You know, Doctor, you really *might* want to consider parceling out these little revelations of yours. I feel like my brain's about to implode."

Maddie grinned sheepishly and reached across the table to squeeze the top of her hand. "I really *was* going to tell you about Celine tonight—honest. The Gina thing—that just happened. I didn't want to spring the idea of meeting my mother on you any sooner. I didn't want to give you time to back out."

Syd shook her head. "You're a six-foot-tall chickenshit, aren't you?"

"More or less."

"God. Well, I know one thing for sure."

"What's that?"

Syd poured herself another glass of the Margaux. "I'm *not* fighting you for the check."

They lingered at the restaurant until they became uncomfortable, holding the table for so long on such a busy night. Their once quiet dining room was now filled with other patrons, and Maddie was eager to evade any more unwelcome intrusions by over-zealous conference-goers. Already, she had spotted two other physicians she knew from her years working at Presbyterian, and she wanted to avoid any protracted conversations about her mother's scheduled appearance tomorrow. Celine was a luminary in the medical profession, and conference organizers were still crowing about their incredible good fortune at snaring her to deliver the keynote address.

Maddie began to fidget.

"Something wrong?" Syd asked.

"Um . . . if it's all the same to you—how about we get out of here and walk back to the hotel for a nightcap? I think there's a nice little lounge off the lobby that might be a tad less *populated*."

Syd took a quick look around the dining room. "Why? Are there more ex-lovers of yours queuing up?"

Maddie rolled her eyes. "*Very* funny. No. I'd just like to avoid any mind-numbing conference chatter, and that's going to be difficult if we continue to sit here. Already, I see a handful of myopic M.D.'s peering at our table. It's only a matter of time before they muster the courage to pounce."

Syd folded her napkin and placed it on top of the table. "Well, since you've already settled the check and over-tipped to the point that your reputation remains intact—I suppose we can blow this joint with impunity."

Maddie grinned. "I couldn't have said it better."

Syd pushed her chair back. "Let's go, Casanova."

Maddie stood up, too. "Ohhhh, that's *right*. I've got a hot date waiting for me back at the hotel bar . . . don't wanna be late for *that*." She glanced at her watch. "Hmmm. It's eight-fifteen." She looked up at Syd. "Sleepy yet?"

"In your dreams, wise guy."

They collected their coats and left the restaurant. Outside, the night had turned colder, but no precipitation was falling. They walked along the embankment toward the alley that would take them away from the river and back to their hotel.

"You know," Syd said, as she pulled the lapels of her coat closed across her neck, "I'm sure I heard that the first day of spring is just around the corner. What gives with this weather?"

Maddie squinted up at the sky. "I don't think it'll amount to much."

"Oh? Kind of like your chances of getting lucky in the bar later?" Syd bumped into her playfully as they walked along.

"Hey. Doubt me at your peril. I'll have you know that my reputation wasn't built on over-tipping alone."

"Are you telling the truth?"

Maddie gave her a wicked look. "Do you wanna find out?"

Syd sighed. "Here we go again."

Maddie grinned and grasped her elbow. "C'mon. Let's shake a leg. There are a couple of big shots of Bailey's waiting for us back at the hotel."

Thirty minutes later, they were comfortably seated in two plush chairs in a dark corner of their hotel's lounge. A large fire burning in an open fireplace in the center of the room cast giant shadows on the paneled walls. Their waiter arrived and deposited two tumblers of Bailey's Irish Cream and a plate of small chocolate cookies.

Syd immediately snatched one of them up and held it to her nose. "*Oh my god*—these are just like Girl Scout cookies. I might die right here." She happily bit into it.

Maddie laughed, and then shook her head. "Are you telling me that I ordered a Premier Cru Bordeaux at dinner when all I needed to impress you was a lousy box of Thin Mints?"

Syd shrugged and reached for another cookie.

Maddie chuckled and sipped her Bailey's.

Syd picked up her own drink and settled back in her chair. "So. Do you wanna tell me now about tomorrow and what I should expect?"

Maddie met her eyes. "You mean when we meet up with Celine?"

"Yeah."

Maddie sighed. "I hardly know what to expect myself. When I found out that she was attending this conference—or any conference, for that matter—I realized that something was up. Celine hates public speaking, and there's no way she'd make an exception for an event on the opposite side of the country unless she had another motivation. I knew I was right when I got an email from her assistant six weeks ago asking if I was planning to attend."

"From her *assistant*?"

"Oh, yeah. She jobbed that little task out to one of her lab rats. So I took the bait and replied that I'd be here. She emailed me a few days later and suggested that we meet for dinner. I still have no idea why she wants to see me."

Syd gazed at her. "She's your mother, does she really need a better reason than that?"

"Oh, trust me, this has *nothing* to do with maternal instincts. Celine jobbed that out, too. I was pretty much raised by a succession of nannies. But to be fair," she met Syd's eyes, "they all were enormously competent. I even think one or two of them actually cared for me."

Syd leaned forward and touched Maddie's knee. "God. I'm so sorry."

Maddie covered her hand with her own. "Hey, it's okay. I'm not really bothered by any of this."

Syd shook her head. "I know you're not. That's what upsets me."

Maddie sighed and gave Syd's hand a squeeze. "I don't want to pretend that there weren't times when I struggled with this—with Celine's detachment. But eventually, it just became easier to accept my life on her terms." She slowly shook her head. "When it comes to Celine, there is no *there* there. I do okay as long as I don't expect anything."

Syd nodded and sat back. "So what can I do to help?"

"For starters, you can forgive me for taking such shameful advantage of you. For all my bravado, I am a little nervous about seeing her tomorrow." She paused. "Having you there as my friend will help ground me and level the playing field. I'll be less likely to do or say anything I might regret later on."

"Does she know I'll be joining you?"

"No. But if that makes you uncomfortable, I'll call her when we get back to the room and let her know."

Syd tapped her index finger on the side of her glass. "No. I think we should trust your instincts on this. If it becomes clear that my presence is too distracting, I'll invent a reason to leave."

"I really don't know how to thank you for this."

"Oh, don't worry about that." Syd smiled. "I'll think of something."

"Hmmm. I suppose I could just promise to keep you well-supplied with Girl Scout cookies."

"That'd be a hell of a start."

Maddie smiled and drained her glass. "It's a deal. Want another? Or are you ready to head upstairs?"

"Oh, I'm *beyond* ready for bed. But don't let me hold you back. Stay and enjoy yourself."

"If it's all the same to you, I think I'll call it a night, too." She stood up and noticed Syd regarding her with a raised eyebrow. "Hey, even the most accomplished love goddess needs a night off now and then."

Syd rolled her eyes. "Come on. Stairs or elevator?"

"You're kidding, right? After *that* meal? I was thinking about having a porter wheel me up on one of those luggage carts. Of course, you're welcome to ride along . . ."

Upstairs in their room, Maddie changed into a faded, gray Penn t-shirt and baggy, flannel lounge pants, and made a nest in one of the big chairs by the window. She put on a pair of wire-framed reading glasses, pulled a copy of the *JAMA* out of her duffle bag, and opened it to a section marked with a yellow post-it note.

Syd emerged from the bathroom wearing baggy, lightweight pajamas. She looked over Maddie's shoulder and read, "Clinical Outcome and Phenotypic Expression in Cardiomyopathy." She smiled sweetly at her. "A little light reading before bed?"

Maddie looked up from her journal and tried not to show too visible a reaction to seeing Syd in her nightclothes. She looked adorable. "Oh, yeah. This one's a *real* bodice-ripper. I started it yesterday, and I'm simply dying to find out what happens next."

"Well, I'll take pains not to disturb you. I'm going to bed." She squeezed Maddie's shoulder. "Goodnight. Thanks for the wonderful dinner—and the conversation."

Maddie smiled up at her. "Will the light bother you? I don't have to finish this now."

Syd walked to the bed and turned down the covers on her side. "Not at all. I could sleep in the middle of a bus station. Stay up as long as you want." She got into bed and turned off her bedside lamp.

Maddie gazed at her for a few seconds. "G'night, Syd. Sleep tight."

"You, too," Syd replied in a muffled voice.

Maddie settled down for a nice, long read. She wanted to be certain Syd was sound asleep before she got up enough courage to join her in the big bed.

Maddie woke up twice during the night. Once when she felt, more than heard, Syd returning to bed after a bathroom visit. "Everything okay?" she asked, groggily.

"Everything's fine. Just had to pee. Go back to sleep—sorry I woke you."

"S'okay."

The second time she woke up, it was closer to dawn and faint rays of pinkish light were starting to creep in around the edges of the drapes that were pulled tight across their window. She was aware of feeling warm—uncomfortably so— and then realized that the source of the heat wasn't coming from the blankets, it was coming from the softly snoring woman who was draped halfway across her body. Syd's head was tucked between Maddie's neck and right shoulder, and one arm was snugly wrapped around her waist.

For a moment, she panicked. *Oh shit. How did this happen?* Then, as she lay there listening to Syd's quiet snores, she smiled. *God, she fits me like a glove.* She shook her head and silently scoffed at herself. *Who am I kidding?* She closed her eyes. *It's pathetic. I'm shameless. I should wake her up.* She rested her cheek against the top of Syd's head and lay there a few more minutes, quietly warring with herself. Syd smelled like sleep, and soap, and lavender. *On the other hand, I'll never get a chance like this again.* She gave up the struggle with her baser instincts and discreetly moved her own arms up and around Syd. She was out again in minutes.

An hour later, Syd's travel alarm went off, and she woke to find herself comfortably wrapped up in Maddie's arms. "Oh, my *god*." She bolted up into a sitting position, stunned. Her sudden movement shocked Maddie into wakefulness, and she quickly pushed herself up onto her elbows, her dark hair a maze around her face.

"What is it? Is something wrong? Are you okay?" she asked, urgently.

"Maddie . . . I'm . . . I'm so *sorry.*"

Maddie blinked and gave her a quizzical look. "For what?"

Syd waved her hand back and forth between them. "For *this*. For *that.*" She pointed at a big drool spot on Maddie's t-shirt. "God." She shook her head. "I sleep at home with a big, body pillow. I guess I mistook *you* for it. I really apologize. I'm not normally such a . . . space invader."

Maddie laughed and flopped back down on her back. "Is that all? My *god.* I thought the hotel was on fire." She touched Syd on the arm. "No harm, no foul. Body pillow, huh?" She sat up again and tossed her hair back over her shoulder. "Well, I've been called worse." She stood up. "Flip you for the first shower?"

Syd smiled up at her shyly. "You go first. It's the least I can do."

"Well, now you know my motto . . . *always* do the least you can do."

"Then break a sweat. We've got a couple of free breakfasts waiting on us downstairs."

Maddie slowly turned to her with an ironic expression on her face. She raised an eyebrow. "You know, I think you might owe me an apology after all."

Syd stopped smiling. "I really am sorry—"

Maddie cut her off with a raised hand. "Oh, not for *that,*" she teased. "For doubting me last night."

Syd frowned, confused. "Doubting you?"

"Yeah." She dramatically brushed the nails of her right hand across her chest and then blew on them. "Opinions might differ, but it appears that I *may* have managed to score with the town librarian."

Syd sighed deeply, then stood up, and pushed past her. "Uh huh. Do you take comfort in these delusions?"

"Delusions?"

"Delusions." Syd turned to her with a sly smile. "Trust me, Doctor," she dropped her voice, "if you had managed to score with *this* librarian, there'd be no room for divided opinion."

Maddie's jaw dropped, followed soon by her butt, as she plopped back down onto the bed.

Syd smirked at her as she headed for the bathroom. "I'll try to save you some hot water."

She grinned when she heard Maddie mutter, "Don't bother—cold will be just fine."

Chapter 15

The question and answer segment of Dr. Heller's presentation was in full swing. Maddie glanced at her watch for about the twentieth time. Already the session had lasted forty-five minutes longer than scheduled. Judging by the number of hands still waving in the air, it wasn't likely to be over anytime soon. She had intentionally taken a seat in one of the last rows of the auditorium, hoping she could avoid running into Gina and forestalling the inevitable reunion with her mother. She felt vaguely like a stalker. She shook her head in amazement as she watched Celine hold forth at the front of the hall, answering questions with dexterity and precision. *She can still cut the most erudite prick down to size in about ten seconds.*

As if on cue, Celine called on a questioner seated just behind Maddie. When she stepped away from the podium for an angle to see him better, her eyes landed on her daughter for the first time. The two regarded each other while the questioner droned on.

Maddie resisted the urge to sink lower into her seat and met her mother's gaze head-on. Celine pursed her lips, and then nodded slightly in acknowledgement. She then shifted her attention back to her questioner. Without losing a beat, she calmly responded to his query. When she finished, she walked back to the podium.

"I think that's enough for today. I'd like to thank you all for your time and attention. It's been a pleasure to be here with you." The audience responded with a roar of applause as she collected her notes and exited the stage.

Show time, Maddie thought, as she stood up and made her way to the aisle that led to the stage. She made little progress. The throng of attendees in her part of the hall seemed in no particular hurry to exit—many of them standing in place, chatting about Celine's presentation, or making plans for their evening amusements.

After an endless string of polite entreaties and a few well-placed elbows, Maddie was finally able to see Celine leaning against the apron of the stage. Her arms were folded across her chest, and her head was tilted to the side in a manner Maddie recognized as a posture she adopted whenever she was annoyed. *Great. I wonder what put her in a foul mood so fast?* Then she got a clear look at the woman Celine was talking to: it was Gina.

Her first impulse was to turn around and make a beeline for the nearest bar. *Goddamn it to hell. What was I thinking when I agreed to do this?* Her thoughts swung back to Gina's sudden appearance at their table in the restaurant last night. *I should have known by her behavior that she'd pull some kind of stunt like this.* Taking a deep breath, she straightened her jacket and continued on toward the stage.

Celine saw her immediately. She turned away from Gina and watched Maddie approach. "Madeleine. You look well."

"Celine." Maddie turned to Gina. "And, Gina—you're certainly omnipresent." She eyed her short-waisted jacket and shorter red skirt. As usual, Gina was tastefully but provocatively dressed. "I see you've met my mother?"

"Oh, yes. Dr. Garcetti has been *very* entertaining," Celine said, before Gina could reply. "I had no idea that the two of you were so close."

Maddie refused to be goaded. "Really? Well, you can hardly be surprised that you've missed a few plot twists, Celine. Seven years is a long time." She looked directly at Gina. "Dr. Garcetti is so modest that she probably didn't tell you what a brilliant ophthalmic surgeon she is. In fact, she even helped *me* see a few things more clearly."

"Your daughter is too kind, Dr. Heller." Gina's voice was icy. "She didn't need any help from me to find her way. If anything, I was more of a hurdle on her path to self-actualization."

Maddie laughed. "I never was any good at those track-and-field events, was I Celine?" She looked back at Gina. "I caught my foot on every damn one of those hurdles."

Celine held her hand up between them. "*Enough.* I really don't have the time or the inclination to stand here while the two of you engage in this sophomoric repartee." She turned to Maddie. "I came here to have a civilized conversation with *you*, not to get an unsolicited tour of your past indiscretions."

"I can see that I've intruded too long on your reunion." Gina faced Celine and held out her hand. "Thank you, Dr. Heller, for your presentation today and for your many contributions to medicine. It was an honor to finally meet you."

Celine shook Gina's hand. "Dr. Garcetti. I wish I could say the same."

Without a backward look at Maddie, Gina turned abruptly and stormed up the aisle toward the nearest exit.

Mother and daughter stood in silence, watching her leave.

After a minute, Maddie sighed. "Talk about Grant taking Richmond."

Celine exhaled and shook her head. "Madeleine, I don't know what disappoints me more—your decision to waste your talents on an indifferent medical practice, or your penchant for wasting *yourself* on indifferent talent."

Against her will, Maddie laughed out loud. "Dear god, Celine. That's the classiest put-down I've had in ten years."

"Don't prevaricate. You give as good as you get. You always have."

"I had a good teacher."

Celine went to a seat in the first row and collected her coat and briefcase. "As enjoyable as this is, I think we should continue our discussion over dinner. I have an early flight back to L.A. in the morning, and I need to return some calls later tonight."

Maddie regarded her mother calmly. "Let's cut to the chase, shall we? Why did you want to see me?"

Celine straightened the collar of her jacket. "Do I need a reason?"

"Need a reason? No. *Have* a reason? Certainly. What is it?"

"I hate to destroy the dramatic picture you're building up, but I have no motivation other than my desire to take advantage of my presence here and spend an evening with my daughter."

They regarded each other silently.

"So this little reunion is just a glorified homage to geography?"

"If you choose to view it that way—then, yes."

They started walking up the aisle toward the main exit. Maddie looked straight ahead as she addressed her mother. "Great. Then you won't mind if a friend joins us for dinner?"

Celine's back stiffened, but she kept walking forward. "Another friend? Charming." She looked at Maddie. Her expression was unreadable. "I can't wait to meet her."

Maddie didn't bother to correct her. They walked the rest of the way out of the hall in silence.

Syd's morning meeting with the field services librarian was enjoyable and uneventful, but her afternoon session with the state auditor had been sobering. Denise Metcalf was correct in her surmise that government resources were becoming strained to the point that any continuation of funding after the end of the initial grant period was looking increasingly unlikely. Judy Goldman strongly encouraged Syd to use the next twelve months to try and lobby local officials to think creatively about finding a way to fund the library's modest operating budget.

This was a bittersweet development for Syd, who not only had invested tremendous time and energy in setting up her tiny branch, she had actually begun to think seriously about the possibility of remaining on in Jericho after her eighteen-month tenure had elapsed. If, in fact, the state funding dried up and the local economy was unable to shoulder the expense of keeping the branch open, she'd be faced with an unforeseen and confounding scenario.

Six months ago, it would have never occurred to her that she would be so despondent about the prospect of having to leave the tiny mountain community. Six months ago, she worried more about her ability simply to endure the eighteen-month commitment.

Now? Now she was faced with a new and surprising set of issues . . . and emotions.

She didn't want to leave Jericho. Not now. With each passing day, that revelation gained greater clarity. She loved the library. She loved the quirky rural community with its colorful pastiche of residents. She loved her life there with its sense of independence and purpose. She loved the natural opportunity she had been given to dip her toe back into the world of music. And she loved her new friends. She smiled to herself. *A lot.*

She was in no hurry to get back to the hotel, so she decided to take a slow walk along the scenic river embankment. As she lazily made her way toward the hotel, she had time to reflect on all of these things, and on the equally confounding events that were unfolding in her relationship with Maddie. She closed her eyes as she thought for the hundredth time about waking up that morning sprawled on top of her. *My god.* She sat down on an unoccupied bench that faced the water.

Since Maddie's revelation the night of her birthday, she felt that everything between them had changed. Well, that wasn't entirely true. Maddie's behavior was essentially unchanged. Maybe she was bit more relaxed and playful—certainly, she was more direct and self-effacing than usual.

It's me, she thought. *I'm the one who's different. I'm more guarded and suspicious of my motivations. I'm not reacting to her as openly or honestly as I did before I knew the truth.* She gazed out at the inky surface of the water as it slowly made its way toward the Chesapeake Bay. *And what is the truth? That Maddie is gay?* Why was that revelation so unsettling to her? It didn't change anything about their relationship.

She shook her head. No. That was wrong. It changed everything.

It was pointless for her to continue to deny the attraction she felt for the extraordinary woman. It was pointless and dishonest. It didn't help her to pretend it was a fleeting thing that had no deeper meaning. Prior to learning the truth about Maddie's sexual orientation, she had been able to keep the baser threads of her emotions sealed up behind a wall of pragmatism. Maddie was unavailable, so that made any deeper consideration of her as a potential object of desire pointless and futile.

And Syd didn't pursue things that were futile. She might eventually tell herself the truth about her developing attraction to another woman, but she would never act on it. Especially not when the other woman in the equation was so effectively off the table.

But Maddie wasn't off the table. Maddie was gay. Maddie was gay, and she was unattached. Maddie had the word "available" stamped all over her six-foot frame.

And Syd was terrified.

Her biggest fear was that she would do something that would compromise herself and alienate Maddie while she took the time she needed to sort through this tangled-up mess. She needed time—time to calm down and time to understand what, if anything, all of this meant for her. And she needed to stop tiptoeing around her emotions in some ludicrous pantomime of normalcy. She needed to know what, if anything, this revelation about Maddie really meant for her. What would she be willing to do with the information? How would it change the nature of their interactions?

Her emotions were like a house of cards that grew higher and more precarious with each passing day. What did the makeshift structure that was emerging reveal to her? And how long did she have to figure it out before it collapsed beneath the weight of its own simple truth?

She didn't know the answers to any of these things. But she knew that she had to stop hiding from her emotions, and she had to stop withholding herself from Maddie. It wasn't fair. Michael was right. Maddie needed her friendship. And tonight, when they met her estranged mother for dinner, she had a golden opportunity to step up and help her friend in a very material way.

She glanced at her watch. She had an hour before she was scheduled to meet Maddie back at the hotel. An idea began to take shape. She smiled to herself as she thought about it. *Yes, it might just work. If I can't get answers to my own questions, maybe I can at least help her resolve a few of her own.*

She stood up and walked quickly in the direction of the hotel.

Syd watched Maddie drain her Cosmopolitan and signal the bartender for another. They had agreed to meet in the lounge of their hotel for a cocktail before leaving to meet Celine for dinner. One look at Maddie's face told Syd how the meeting with her mother had gone. It only took a few minutes for Maddie to fill in the blanks.

Maddie set her empty glass down on the table.

"Um . . . wanna slow down a little, Stretch?" Syd asked, gently.

Maddie gave her a look that was a perfect blend of irony and despair. "God. A dozen of these might just begin to take the edge off. What the hell was I *thinking*? That woman is just so . . . bloodless."

"Which one?"

"Either. *Both.*" She shrugged. "Flip a coin."

Syd regarded her with concern. "You know, I had all day to persuade myself that going along with you was an okay thing to be doing. Now, I'm not so sure."

Maddie reached across the table and grabbed Syd's hand. "Oh, god . . . *please* don't back out now. I know I'm a shameless coward, but I don't think I can get through this alone. Just ten minutes with her was enough to make the prospect of becoming a Betty Ford alumna sound appealing."

Syd smiled at her. "Buck up. You'll do just fine."

Maddie slowly released her hand. Her beautiful face was a study in desperation. "You'll still come along?"

Syd sighed in resignation. "I will *never* desert you, Mr. Micawber."

Maddie stared at her blankly for a moment, then burst into near hysterical laughter. She leaned across their tiny table and kissed Syd warmly on the cheek. "Oh, man . . . I'm a *sucker* for Dickens." Her blue eyes sparkled. "How'd you come up with that?"

"Please," Syd feigned contempt. "I'm a *librarian*. I notice books. You have at least five editions of *David Copperfield* lying around your house."

Maddie sat back, still chuckling. "Hmmm. So if instead, I had, say, five copies of *The Case of the Velvet Claws*—what would you have said?"

Syd winked at her. "Oh, that's easy. I'd have called you *Chief*, and asked if you'd like another martini."

They stared at each other. Maddie shook her head slowly. "I think I'm in love."

Syd smiled. "Hold that thought, it might actually work to your advantage for the next couple of hours."

"What do you mean?" Maddie looked confused.

Syd leaned forward. "Given what you told me about your mother's reaction to meeting Gina—and to my coming along tonight—why not turn the tables on her and let her think that we *are* a couple?"

Maddie looked at her like she had two heads. "Are you kidding me?"

"No, I'm not."

"Why on earth would we do that?"

"Because I simply don't believe her when she tells you that she has no real reason for suddenly waltzing back into your life. The surest way to get her to come clean is to rattle her cage and see what shakes loose. Let's just *see* how emotionally detached from you she is."

"Now I really need that drink. Are you *nuts*? Celine would see through a ruse like this in a nanosecond."

"You underestimate me, and you underestimate Celine as your mother."

Maddie slumped back against her seat. "It's not that the prospect of toying with Celine doesn't appeal to me, it's that I really just don't get the point."

Their waiter arrived with Maddie's second Cosmopolitan.

"Look," Syd continued, after he had picked up the empty glass and walked away. "You said your mother was pretty pissed-off over the whole Gina exchange today. If she already knew about your sexual orientation and never expressed any interest or concern about it previously, then why would she get so worked up over running into your ex-girlfriend? It doesn't make sense. Something about that whole interaction really yanked her chain. Don't you want to find out what it is that's *really* stuck in her craw?"

Maddie listened to Syd in thoughtful silence. Then she shook her head. "I don't know. I mean, of course I'd like to know what's really going on with her. But I think it's a mistake for the two of us to breeze in there and perform some kind of elaborate pantomime just to try and force her hand. It could totally backfire. I mean, how do we even know we could pull it off? And what about you? Why would you be willing to risk having her—or anyone—think that you're my—my . . ."

"Lover?"

Maddie met her eyes. "Yeah."

Syd smiled at her. "It isn't like I'm going to run into her next weekend at the Junior League rummage sale. Come on. What do we have to lose?"

Maddie thought about it. "You got me there. Not a whole helluva lot." She sat back and looked at Syd with lingering indecision. "Okay." She expelled a breath. "But I have to warn you—when she's cornered, Celine is like Jabba the Hutt in a Chanel suit."

Syd laughed. "Don't worry. I know the type. Some day, I'll tell you about my former mother-in-law. I kept *her* back with wolf's bane and pentagrams."

Maddie shook her head slowly. "God. Why do I think I'm going to live to regret this?"

"Tell you what," Syd said. "You just be your sweet and solicitous self, and leave the driving to me."

"Oh, *that* part," Maddie said, as she raised her glass in a mock toast, "will *not* be a problem."

Celine was staying at The Jefferson, a five-star hotel located near the center of Richmond's financial district. In the interest of time, she and Maddie had agreed to meet for dinner downstairs at her hotel's premier restaurant, *L'Etoile*. She had spent the hours following her conference appearance back in her hotel room, returning phone calls and responding to departmental e-mail. An hour before she was due to meet her daughter, she closed her laptop and made arrangements with the concierge for ground transportation to the airport at five-thirty a.m. Well before the hotel's regular shuttle service commenced. Then she changed into more suitable evening dress.

The cell phone next to her laptop vibrated, and Celine glanced down at its illuminated LCD panel. *Text message from Stevenson, MH.* She flipped the phone open. *On our way. There in 15.* She sat holding the phone for few moments before closing it and placing it into her purse.

She reached into a sleeve on the inside of her briefcase and pulled out a faded, black-and-white photograph of a doe-eyed child sitting with confidence on the shoulders of a tall man. The two wore matching smiles as they posed in front of a small, high-wing plane. Maddie's dark hair was a wind-blown mass under the oversized aviation headset she wore.

Celine turned the photo over to read its inscription: *4.29.79. Maddie's seventh birthday.* Davis had surprised the little girl by taking her for her very first flight in his new airplane. She remembered that Maddie could barely contain her excitement. The child was *so much* like her father—no fear . . . of *anything.* She returned the picture to its resting place.

She thought back to her disturbing encounter with Maddie earlier that afternoon—and with Gina. She shook her head. Toxic. That was the only word for someone like Gina. Her disappointment in Maddie's judgment was palpable. She glanced at her watch, then stood up and collected her room key and purse. Squaring her shoulders, she left the room and headed downstairs to meet Maddie and her newest "friend."

As they exited their cab in front of the Jefferson's impressive façade, Maddie took a deep breath and shook her shoulders like a pugilist trying to loosen up before climbing into the ring.

"Every time I know I'm going to see that woman, I feel like my hands should be taped-up."

Syd gave her a perplexed look. "Why?"

"So I don't break my fingers when I try to punch through her veneer."

Syd sighed and laid a calming hand on her arm. "Why not try a different approach tonight? Instead of gearing up for some predetermined battle royal, why not try to relax and see where *she* wants to go?"

"Oh, I *know* where she wants to go."

"You do?"

"Yeah. And it's the same place I want to go—as far away from *here* as possible."

They crossed the lobby and found the hotel entrance to the upscale French restaurant.

As they entered, Syd tightened her hand on Maddie's forearm. "My *god.*"

Maddie stopped and looked at her in concern. "What is it?"

"I see her," Syd whispered. "It's incredible. You look *exactly* alike."

Maddie looked up and saw Celine, in an elegant and form-fitting black dress, standing next to the *maître d'hotel*. She was listening to her cell phone.

"Yep," she muttered, "that's her—Mommie Dearest."

Celine saw them approach. She closed her phone and stepped forward to greet them. "Thank you for agreeing to meet here," she said to Maddie. "I'm sorry that my flight tomorrow departs at such an ungodly hour." She turned to Syd. "I'm Celine Heller, Madeleine's mother." She held out her hand.

Maddie appeared stunned by her mother's friendly introduction. "Excuse me," she said, belatedly. "Syd, this is Dr. Celine Heller, my mother. Celine, I'd like you to meet my very good friend, Syd Murphy."

As they shook hands, Syd smiled at Celine. "Dr. Heller, I'd like to thank you for allowing me to join you and Maddie this evening. I know the two of you have had only limited time together during this visit, and I am sensible of how intrusive this is."

A flicker of recognition cross Celine's face as her eyes fell on Syd's necklace. She glanced at Maddie before returning an interested gaze to Syd. "Please, call me Celine. May I assume that Syd is short for something?"

"You may, indeed. My full name is Margaret *Sydney* Murphy. Sydney is my mother's family name."

Celine looked thoughtful. "Where are you from?"

"Baltimore."

She paused to consider this. "I taught at Johns Hopkins years ago and had a brilliant young teaching fellow named Marshall Sydney."

Syd stared at her in surprise. "Uncle Marsh?"

Maddie eyed them, looking stunned. "Okay . . . this is getting *waayyy* too weird. If the two of you join hands and start singing 'Kumbaya,' I think my head will explode."

Syd saw the corner of Celine's mouth twitch.

"Let's see if our table is ready, shall we?" Celine nodded to the *maitre'd*, and he led them across the dimly lighted restaurant to their table. When they were seated, Celine picked up the wine list without looking at it and handed it across the table to her daughter.

Maddie took the oversized card from her without comment and began to peruse it. "Red or white?"

"Do you have a preference, Syd?" Celine was regarding her with a raised eyebrow.

Her facial expression was so much like one of Maddie's that it took Syd a moment to stop staring and realize that she had been asked a question. "I'm sorry?"

Celine inclined her head toward the wine list her daughter was examining and gave her a measured look. "Do you have a *preference*?"

"Oh, I *do*." Syd rested her hand on top of Maddie's with slow deliberation. "But in this case, I'm fine with whatever our resident sommelier decides."

Syd and Maddie regarded each other as the deeper meaning of her words hovered in the air between them.

Maddie remained silent. Clearly grateful that she could use the wine list as an excuse not to look at either of them.

Syd gave Maddie's hand a quick squeeze before releasing it to pick up her napkin.

Their waiter approached the table, and Maddie ordered a bottle of the Sang des Cailloux Cuvée. They took a few minutes to review the restaurant's evening fare, and each opted to sample the chef's *Prix Fixe* option, since it promised a fairly representative sampling of the brasserie's Rhône Valley regional cuisine.

When the black-aproned waiter left the table with their orders, Celine took a sip from her water glass and turned her attention back to Syd. "So tell me. How is Marshall? Did he continue his education? We lost track of each other when I left Johns Hopkins for UCLA."

Syd nodded enthusiastically. "Oh, yes. He went on and got his doctorate in neurology. Now he works in product development for GSK in Raleigh."

Celine nodded. "Parkinson's Disease?"

"I think so. I remember that he was very revved-up about the whole embryonic stem cell debate when I saw him at Christmas. He and my mother had a few pretty heated discussions on the topic."

"I take it she's not in favor of the idea?" Maddie asked.

"Oh, no," Syd replied. "My mother is a public health nurse, but she has very traditional—very Catholic—views on social issues. Uncle Marsh was always more of a renegade that way." She paused, and then smiled. "I think that's why he and I always got along so well. I followed his example a *little* too closely to suit her."

Maddie was intrigued. "What do you mean?"

Syd grinned at her. "I got bounced out of Catholic school."

Maddie snorted. "Why doesn't *that* surprise me?"

Syd playfully swatted Maddie on the arm with her napkin. "Back off, Stretch. I'll have you know it was for a *good* reason."

Maddie rolled her eyes. "Oh reeeaaallly? What'd you do? Put bubble bath in the sugar bowls?"

"No, wise guy—and I *saw* that movie. Hayley Mills . . . jeez. Just how old do you think I am?"

Maddie smiled sweetly at her. "Are we talking chronologically or metaphorically?"

Syd turned to Celine. "See what I have to contend with?"

Celine smiled. "I'm afraid that I can't be much help to you in this department. It's really outside my area of expertise. Maddoe has her father's facility for polemics. Arguing with him was always like being on the losing side in a fencing match."

Syd glanced at Maddie, whose wide blue eyes were fixed on her mother in amazement.

"You haven't called me that in years," Maddie said in a quiet voice.

Celine didn't respond. A blanket of silence settled over their table.

Syd watched the interaction between them with a growing sense of anticipation—and dread. Celine seemed embarrassed by her display of candor, and Maddie's face was a study in a hundred conflicting emotions. Syd wasn't sure whether she wanted to say something to try to break their emotional logjam, or push her chair back and flee the restaurant.

She was saved when the wine steward arrived with their bottle of Cuvée. He opened it with a flourish and poured a splash of the fragrant varietal into Maddie's fluted glass. She nodded at him after she sampled it, and he gave each of the women a textbook, four-ounce serving before setting the bottle down and retreating.

Syd decided that trying to pilot the conversation back into safer waters was her best bet.

She turned to Maddie and playfully punched her on the arm. "I feel the need to defend my honor, here." Maddie gave her a grateful look. "If you *must* know, I got bounced from parochial school because I organized a forum on STDs and passed out condoms to all of my classmates. The sisters of Bryn Mawr School tended to frown on that kind of extracurricular activity in the eighth grade."

Maddie chortled. "Margaret Sanger in a plaid jumper. I have *no* problem imagining this."

Syd took a healthy sip of the Cuvée. "Since we're here with your mother, I'll do you a favor and let the combined reference to plaid jumpers and your imagination slide."

Maddie rolled her eyes and picked up her water glass. She glanced across the table at Celine, who was watching Syd with an amused expression.

Syd pressed her advantage. "Besides, Dr. Mensa-baby, not all of us had the great wherewithal to skip half of high school, and then test out of the first two years of college."

Maddie feigned surprise. "Why would you assume I did something like that?"

"I *assume* nothing," Syd replied. "Your Wikipedia bio was very enlightening."

"Stalking me online?" Maddie asked, in a singsong voice.

"In your dreams, egghead."

"Please. You can't seriously lend credibility to a spurious source like *Wikipedia*. What kind of librarian *are* you?"

"Apparently, a very good one," Celine said. She looked directly at Syd. "Don't let her mislead you. In this case, your sources are accurate."

Maddie looked exasperated. "Oh, come on, Celine. It wasn't that big of a deal."

"Madeleine will never tell you that at age sixteen," Celine said to Syd, "she was offered full merit scholarships to four of the nation's best undergraduate institutions. She also had her pick of top medical schools." She paused and looked directly at Maddie. "However, her choice *there* ended up being driven more by sentimentality than ambition."

Maddie sighed in mock resignation and dramatically dropped her chin to her chest. She shot Syd a sideways glance. "*Pow.* Right in the kisser."

Syd looked back and forth between them. She decided to throw propriety out the window. "Okay, you two, don't *make* me stop this car."

In concert, mother and daughter quickly looked at each other, and then back at her. Their expressions formed a perfect tableau of guilt and surprise. They looked so much like misbehaving children that Syd completely lost her composure and laughed.

They were interrupted once again by the arrival of the waiter, who lavishly served their first courses, accompanied by a basket of flower-shaped *Michette* rolls. He refilled their wine glasses and quietly departed.

"So tell me. How long have you two been together?" Celine asked after a long pause.

Maddie, who was in the process of drinking water, choked and noisily sprayed liquid back into the glass. Syd quickly patted her on the back.

"Are you okay, honey?" she asked with exaggerated concern, dabbing at the front of Maddie's jacket with her napkin.

Maddie quickly recovered her composure. Rolling her eyes at Syd, she batted her hand away. "I'm fine, *dear.*" She sat back and regarded her mother coolly. "Whatever do you mean, Celine?"

Celine was unfazed. She picked up one of the rolls and tore off a crusty petal. "We *are* still speaking English, aren't we?"

Maddie's cell phone vibrated. She quickly snapped it up, apologizing for the interruption. She glanced at the readout. "It's my service. I'm so sorry, but I have to take this." She pushed her chair back. "Excuse me. I'll try to be quick." She squeezed Syd's shoulder as she left the table and headed for the solitude of the lobby.

Alone, Syd and Celine faced each other across the table like opponents in a chess match.

Celine's blue eyes were unwavering as they regarded Syd. Her resemblance to Maddie was uncanny. "Madeleine seems happy."

Syd took a deep breath. "I think she is. Mostly."

"Mostly?"

"I think she misses her mother."

Celine lifted her chin. "You speak very frankly."

"Well, based on how limited our time together is, I thought I should make the most of this opportunity to indulge my meddlesome nature. Who knows when I'll get another chance?" Syd paused. "I hope I haven't offended you."

"I'm not at all offended. But I confess that I am unused to this level of forthrightness from any of Madeleine's . . . companions."

Syd laughed. "Now it's my turn to be baffled. You say that like there've been dozens."

Celine smiled. "Not dozens. A few. Most not worth her time."

"You're very hard on her."

"On the contrary. I simply want more for her than she seems to want for herself."

"And that is?" Syd asked, leaning forward on her elbows.

"I want her to be happy." Celine paused and looked down at her uneaten salad. "I want her to find the happiness that eluded me. And I want her to find that with someone who is worthy of her—someone who is a radical departure from her blind succession of *Ginas.*" She looked up at Syd. "Maybe now—finally—she has."

Unprepared for so candid a response, Syd felt her cheeks warm, and she dropped her eyes. The seconds ticked by, and another uneasy silence stretched out between them. Her plan to trick Celine into revealing her true feelings had succeeded, but as a result, Syd was now trapped in a confusing maze that blended fiction and reality so seamlessly, she was unable to tell one from the other.

Celine was eyeing her with curiosity, but looked up when she saw Maddie heading back to their table from the lobby.

Maddie's telephone call concerned Jacob Halsey, an elderly, diabetic patient of hers who had suffered an acute bout of hypoglycemia while visiting his daughter in Charlottesville. Efforts by the family to resolve the problem had failed, and Mr. Halsey began having seizures. EMTs rushed him to the UVA hospital, where he still was not fully responding to treatment. His family insisted that his attending physician at the large university hospital contact Maddie to explain his condition, and to discuss treatment options. After their brief conversation, Maddie assured the family that Mr. Halsey was getting excellent care and promised to stop in Charlottesville tomorrow on her way back to Jericho so she could meet with them all in person.

When she hung up, she tarried in the restaurant lobby a few extra moments to try and puzzle through her mother's uncharacteristic behavior. Celine's casual use of her childhood nickname was surreal—a stunning departure from her customary veil of formality. Maddie had *no* idea what to make of it. It actually seemed that Celine was making an effort at being civil and—even more strangely— that she *liked* Syd.

Maddie continued to stand there, tapping the back of her cell phone in agitation. Celine had taken Syd's bait entirely too easily. Why would her mother, of all people, suddenly have such prurient interest in *this* aspect of her life? Why would she *care* about how long she and Syd had been . . . together? It didn't make sense to her—especially considering their earlier tête-à-tête about Gina.

Maddie shook her head to try and clear it of confusion. She'd had far too much to drink, and she knew she couldn't trust her ability to react safely or smartly to any other revelations tonight. Already, she felt like her emotions were on the brink of a stampede, and she didn't want Syd to get caught in the crossfire if she lost control. On top of it all, the cozy little romantic charade they were putting on for Celine was making it harder for her to submerge the reality of her attraction to Syd and threatening her resolve to keep herself out of danger.

Wistfully, she cut her eyes over to the entrance of the restaurant's bar. Then, with a sigh, she turned away and headed back toward the dining room. As she approached the table, it was clear that Syd and Celine were in earnest conversation about something. They were leaning toward each other from their opposite sides of the table, and neither of their appetizers appeared to have been touched at all. She had a vague sense of panic about what might have transpired during their time alone and regretted, again, that she had been forced to leave Syd sitting there with Celine while she returned the call from her service.

"I apologize again for that interruption," she said as she sat down. "One of my diabetic patients went into insulin shock while visiting with his daughter in Charlottesville. He's now at the UVA hospital, but isn't responding to treatment." She paused. "The family is necessarily distraught. I spoke with his attending. They're doing all they can for him."

Celine nodded. "The diabetes and endocrinology unit at UVA is purported to be very good."

"It is. If this had to happen to Jake, he picked the right place to be."

"I am sure that having his family present is a huge asset, too," Syd added with concern.

"No doubt," she said, turning to Syd, "but if you don't mind, I'd like to make a detour tomorrow and stop in Charlottesville on our way home to check in on him and see the family."

"Of course," Syd said. "I absolutely do not mind. Do you think he'll pull through this?"

Maddie sighed. "I really have no idea. Jake is an old curmudgeon who refuses to follow his dietary regimen. Even if they can reverse the effects of the insulin shock, it's not very likely that he'll emerge with any greater appreciation for his limitations."

"Some patients simply choose to embrace their diseases, instead of fighting them," Celine said. "As difficult as that is for us as doctors, we have to accept that it's a reasonable and legitimate response to illness."

Syd was intrigued. "I guess this is the heart of the whole death-with-dignity debate?"

"Actually, it's more like a prequel to the debate," Maddie said. "End-of-life or advanced-care considerations are separate from the conundrum of someone who *seeks* a course of treatment, but then *refuses* to follow it."

"But the same root, psychological considerations are at play even at the outset of the process. They just have less clarity," Celine added.

Maddie thought about her mother's comment. "*Some* would say a person's desire to seek treatment is a reflexive function of the organism, and its innate need to survive."

"Some would say?" Celine asked, sounding very professorial.

Maddie shrugged. "I cut my class in Medical Ethics the day they covered this, so I can't really speak with any greater authority."

Celine rolled her eyes.

Syd laughed. "Well, I think stopping over in Charlottesville so you can see the family is absolutely the right thing to do. Besides, I'm euphoric about the chance to rack up all those extra Air-Stevenson frequent-flier miles."

Celine gave Maddie an incredulous look. "Did you fly here in your own plane?"

"Yep. In the 310."

Celine sighed. "Old habits die hard. I see the torch has been passed to a new generation."

"Well, you can't complain too much, Celine. You once were involved in this particular passion as much as Dad."

"That was a lifetime ago. I grew up."

Maddie shook her head. "No . . . you ran away."

Her words hung in the air like a pall.

Celine stiffened, but didn't respond. "Before your service interrupted, you were going to fill me in on how the two you two met."

"Was I?" Maddie said in an icy voice.

Syd quickly placed a restraining hand on Maddie's thigh. "I moved to Jericho six months ago to manage a state-funded program to improve public library service. In true, superhero fashion, Maddie swept in to rescue me *twice*—first when I was stranded by a flat tire, and later when I was hobbled by a twisted ankle." She lowered her eyes and smiled at the recollection, then she looked up to meet Celine's interested gaze. "We've been . . . *seeing* each other for about the last two months."

Celine looked surprised. "*Only* two months? That's curious." Her eyes took in Syd's gold necklace again. "You seem so intuitive about one another. It normally takes years to attain that level of symbiosis in a relationship."

Maddie reached under the table and grasped the hand that still rested on her thigh. She looked at Syd, then raised their linked hands and placed them in full view on top of the table.

"Well," she replied, leveling a steely gaze at Celine, "as my online biographer has already established. I *am* a prodigy."

Maddie and Syd stood huddled together in the vestibule of the Jefferson, waiting while the concierge called them a cab to take them back across town to their hotel. Maddie was leaning against Syd, as much for assistance in remaining upright as for the moral support her proximity provided.

"Hang on, Stretch," Syd urged, wrapping an arm around her waist. "The cab should be here soon."

Maddie looked at her through a haze of exhaustion. She tried to smile. "I apologize for this. I don't normally subject women to my Gumby impersonation until the *second* date."

Syd laughed and pulled her closer. "God. You're a charmer even when you're three-sheets-to-the-wind."

Maddie gave her a crooked smile. "Glad you think so. I'm not sure my mother would share your charitable view."

"I think you're wrong about that."

"I'm not sure about anything right now."

The large glass door to the street swung open, letting in a cold blast of air. It had started to rain, and the concierge entered, carrying several dripping umbrellas. Over Maddie's shoulder, Syd could see a clear reflection of the lobby interior behind them. She thought she recognized the lone figure standing by an enormous potted-palm situated just in front of the bellhop station.

She leaned her head closer to Maddie and whispered, "Don't react or turn around. Celine is watching us from the lobby."

Maddie dropped her head. "Oh, god. I don't have the stamina for any more of this."

"I have an idea. Do you trust me?"

Maddie lifted her chin and eyed her with suspicion. "What *kind* of idea?"

"The kind that should seal the deal."

Shyly, Syd slipped her hands up behind Maddie's neck and tugged her closer. Maddie's eyes widened in shock as Syd pulled her head down and kissed her full on the mouth. The seconds ticked by as Syd softly pressed her lips against Maddie's. She felt Maddie belatedly raise her arms and wrap them loosely around her waist. When they separated, their faces remained inches apart.

Alert and seemingly back in control of her faculties, Maddie whispered, "If we're gonna do this, let's *really* sell it." She lowered her head to Syd's, and, this time, there was no hesitation on her part as they kissed.

Syd felt her knees unhinge, and her arms tightened reflexively around Maddie's shoulders. *Jesus. What are we doing?* Maddie's lips felt incredible against hers. She was unprepared for the onslaught of competing emotions she felt as all of her hibernating senses woke up and snapped to attention. *God. She's a great kisser.* Maddie continued the contact with scientific precision. It was passionate enough to look convincing, but restrained enough to protect the shifting boundaries of their friendship.

Before it ended, Maddie bussed her mouth a few more times in quick succession. Syd felt a wave of vertigo roll over her when Maddie's teeth tugged gently on her lower lip before she released her and stepped back. Both of them were breathing unevenly, and they stared at each other, lapsing into stunned and stupefied silence.

After what felt like an eternity, Maddie gave Syd a shy smile. "Think that did the trick?"

Unsure of her ability to speak coherently, Syd didn't reply right away. She looked over Maddie's shoulder at the darkened square of lobby reflected in the glass door behind her. There was no sign of Celine.

"She's gone." She shifted her eyes back to Maddie's face. "It must have worked."

Maddie nudged her playfully. "You can say *that* again."

Syd recovered her composure enough to roll her eyes. "Sleaze."

"Hey, don't blame me, Julie McCoy. *You* were the cruise director on this little installment of *The Love Boat*. I was just following orders."

"Yeah. I noticed. How come you're never this cooperative when it's about something that *doesn't* involve your legendary libido?"

"Try me."

"I thought I just did."

Their escalating banter was interrupted when the concierge timidly approached them to say that their cab had arrived.

"Saved by the bellhop," Maddie quipped.

Syd sighed. "Will you *please* just over-tip this poor man so we can get the hell out of here?"

"Sure." Maddie looked thoughtful. "What's the going rate for Sapphically-induced blindness?"

"Oh, good god." Shaking her head, Syd pushed past her and walked out into the rain.

They were quiet during the fifteen-minute cab ride back to their hotel. The rain had picked up in intensity and drummed loudly on the roof of the car. It was punctuated by the occasional strains of Hindi music that floated back toward them from the driver's radio.

Maddie seemed to be in a state of complete sensory overload from too much alcohol, too much time with her mother, and too much feigned intimacy with Syd, and she looked dazed and physically drained. She sat propped against the passenger door with her eyes closed and her head tipped back against the seat. The passing lights of Richmond's downtown illuminated her features with sporadic flashes of color.

Syd kept stealing glances at her as they rode along in silence. Her mind was racing with confusion about whatever it was that had just transpired between them. She found it hard not to openly stare at Maddie. Throughout the long evening, their already complex relationship had begun to unravel and take on a new and mysterious shape.

Syd looked at her now like she was some kind of exotic museum exhibit—halfway expecting to see a small, printed card pinned to her coat that would explain what she was, and how she came to be sitting beside her in this noisy Richmond taxi.

There was no denying that Maddie was a beautiful woman. Her long, shapely legs were stretched all the way across the floorboard of the back seat—her feet nearly touching Syd's. Hidden beneath the black raincoat was the kind of body that women envied, and men fantasized about. Syd shook her head in wonder as she considered all the non-corporeal aspects of what Maddie was—her engaging personality, her intelligence, her decency, and her lively and irreverent sense of humor. She was quite a package. And right now, the sum total of that package was stirring up a confusing volatility of feelings and desires she'd never experienced before. It was a paradox that was becoming impossible to ignore, and she was too tired and too aware of how frayed and compromised her perceptions were tonight to try and confront it.

She thought, ironically, that the Bollywood music the cab driver was playing was exactly right for this evening. It provided a bizarre and cloyingly upbeat soundtrack to the surreal song-and-dance routine the two of them had performed with such precision for Maddie's mother.

"You okay?"

Syd jumped at the sound of the low voice and guiltily looked up to meet Maddie's gaze, realizing that she had been caught staring at her legs. "Oh. Yeah. Just *tired*, I guess."

"Meeee, too." Maddie stretched her long frame before straightening up on the seat. "I can't wait to get back to the room. If we had been out for very much longer, my body would have started molting out of these clothes on its own."

Syd smiled. "I know what you mean. My feet are positively *killing* me. I'm not used to wearing shoes like this all day."

"Lucky for you, I minored in foot rubs at Stanford."

"*Did* you, now? When did that become part of the pre-med curriculum?"

"Oh, just about the time I landed a departmental assistantship with a gout-ridden, forty-something professor of microbiology." Maddie paused, then winked at Syd. "Talk about some creative extra credit assignments."

Syd groaned. "Have you always been this behaviorally challenged, or do you just crank it up when you're around me?"

Maddie clucked her tongue. "You don't really expect me to give you an honest answer to that, do you?"

"I've given up knowing what to expect from you."

"Right back atcha." They lapsed into silence again.

The cab turned into the entrance of their hotel and pulled forward to stop under its covered portico. Syd won the battle to pay the fare, and they climbed out and walked into the lobby. Maddie paused and touched Syd gently on the elbow. "I need to check in at the front desk and see if I have any messages about tomorrow. It should only take a second. Would you mind grabbing us an elevator and waiting on me?"

"Of course not. See you in a minute." Syd continued across the lobby toward the bank of big silver doors. It was nearly ten-thirty, but the hotel was still pretty active. She could hear the clink of dinnerware and laughter coming from the small café behind her.

True to her word, Maddie was back at her side in just a couple of minutes, and they proceeded on up to their room on the fourth floor.

Once inside, they shed their bags and coats and played a quick game of rock-paper-scissors to see who got the bathroom first. Maddie won, and happily breezed past Syd with her sleepwear draped over her arm. Syd dropped into the nearest chair and kicked her shoes off.

Maddie's reading glasses rested on top of her copy of the *JAMA* and what looked like a couple of patient files. There was a yellow pad filled with notations, and Syd picked it up and looked over the tidy, but indecipherable handwriting. Upon closer inspection, she realized that it was only unreadable because most of it was some kind of Latin shorthand. *Good god. Remind me never to play Scrabble with her.*

Just as Maddie emerged from the bathroom, more comfortably attired in her t-shirt and lounge pants, there was a soft knock at the door of their room, and a voice in the hallway announced, "Room Service."

Syd looked at Maddie with a confused expression, and Maddie inclined her head toward the door.

"I ordered us a little nightcap when we were downstairs. Do you mind grabbing it?" She walked toward the closet to hang up her suit.

"Do you think that's a good idea?" Syd asked, as she got up and headed toward the door. "I don't want you to wake up tomorrow with a hangover."

"I think I'll be safe."

Syd opened the door and a white-coated waiter smiled as he handed her a dome-covered tray. "You're all set," he said. "Dr. Stevenson took care of the tip, too. Have a nice night." He turned around and started back down the hall.

Maddie joined her at the small table in the corner of their room. "Oh, *goodie.* This should help us both sleep better."

Syd was dubious. "I don't mean to be overly proprietary, but less than an hour ago, you needed my help to stand up straight. Are you *sure* this is something you want to be doing?"

"Uh huh. C'mon, blondie. Serve it up."

"Okay, but don't say I didn't try to warn you," Syd said as she lifted the dome off the tray. She was stunned to see two small cartons of milk and a plate full of tiny, Thin Mint cookies. She looked up at Maddie, who stood there grinning like a Cheshire cat. Syd was undone by the sweetness of the gesture and felt for a moment like she might cry.

"Oh, god, it's addictive."

"What is?" Maddie asked, a smile still pulling at the corners of her mouth.

"You are." She dropped the dome and reached out to hug Maddie. "*This* is," she mumbled into her chest.

Maddie hugged her back. "I told you I'd keep you in cookies. A deal's a deal."

Syd stepped back from the warm embrace and picked up the plate. She walked across the room, climbed up onto the bed, and piled pillows up all along the headboard. "Well, come on, Stretch," she said, settling back and biting into a cookie. "Get over here with the milk."

Maddie picked up the milk cartons and climbed up next to her. "You don't have to ask me twice." She set the milk down on the nightstand.

Syd regarded her with fondness. "You know, at some point we need to talk about what happened tonight."

Maddie met her gaze. "You mean our little lobby encore for Celine?"

Syd blushed and dropped her gaze. "Well . . . that, too." She absently fingered a loose thread on the coverlet. Then she looked up at Maddie. "But what I meant is that we need to talk about what happened during dinner. I really think it's possible that Celine was trying to make some kind of overture by coming here."

Maddie sighed. "I know. But if it's all the same to you, I need to let it rest—just until tomorrow. I meant it when I told you that I was on sensory overload. I really don't think I can go there right now."

They were silent for a moment. Syd softly touched Maddie's forearm. "Okay."

Maddie shook her dark head, and then smiled as she drew herself up onto her knees. "I do feel up for *one* thing, however," she said, as she moved toward the bottom of the bed. Her blue eyes were twinkling again as she looked back at Syd. "I think I promised someone a foot rub . . ."

Syd woke up well before dawn. She saw white flashes of light behind the drapes and could hear the distant roll of thunder. She was grateful when she realized that she still had hours left to sleep, and burrowed deeper into the warm cocoon that surrounded her. She shifted even closer to the body pressed tightly against her back and tightened her handhold on the arm that held her close. Then she noticed the soft, steady sound of breathing against her ear.

Her eyes flew open. *Oh my god! Not again.* She felt panic overtake her. *What is it with the two of us?* She slowly started to pull her hands away.

Maddie stirred and said quietly into her ear, "It's okay. You were having a bad dream. I couldn't get you to stop thrashing around. This was the only way I could protect my vital organs."

Syd closed her eyes in mortification. "God, Maddie. I'm *sorry.*"

"No problem." She yawned. "Do you wanna move?"

Syd hesitated. "Are you uncomfortable?"

"Nope."

"Me either." She smiled and opted for the truth. "Chances are we'd just end up back in the same position anyway."

"Probably. This bed has a *lot* of explaining to do."

Syd chuckled and lightly rubbed her fingers against the arm that was still wrapped tightly around her. "Say goodnight, Gracie."

Maddie lifted her head and gave Syd a featherlight kiss on the ear. "G'night, Gracie."

They didn't speak anymore. The only sound in the room was an occasional rumble of thunder as the storm outside blew itself out. They lay close together for the rest of the night, but Syd didn't get any more sleep and she was sure Maddie didn't get much sleep either.

Chapter 16

The Charlottesville-Albemarle Airport was large enough to be served by express carriers for both United and US Airways. Its busy, general aviation center was home to several corporate jet fleets and two charter services. Maddie and Syd made the short flight from Richmond in less than twenty-five minutes, and Maddie was able to park her Cessna at Landmark Aviation's FBO, and arrange for an on-site rental car. They removed their bags from the airplane and stowed them in the trunk of the rental car as a precaution—since Maddie had not arranged for hangar space, due to the short duration of their stopover.

Syd had never been to Charlottesville, and she was enthralled with its beauty. Nestled in the heart of the Shenandoah Valley, Charlottesville was an inspiring mix of old-world refinement and new-world innovation. The lush geography of the region, with its soaring Blue Ridge Mountain views and temperate climate, made it a haven for artists and writers, and the rich, cultural life of the area remained one of its greatest attractions.

The city itself had been named for Princess Sophia Charlotte of Strelitz, wife of King George III, and its roots in history were rich and multifaceted. The sprawling University of Virginia, founded by Thomas Jefferson in 1825, dominated the life and the commerce of the area, and its full-time residents still referred, deferentially, to the former president as Mr. Jefferson. As she and Maddie drove past the imposing red brick, Classical-style pavilions that formed the heart of the university campus, Syd began to regret that their time in the captivating city would be so short. She resolved to return for a longer visit later in the spring.

In short order, they arrived at the massive UVA Medical Center complex, and after parking in a garage the size of a small city, Maddie led them through a maze of tunnels to an information kiosk located near one of the hospital's numerous entrances. Once she deciphered directions to the diabetes and endocrinology unit, she turned to Syd.

"How about we find you a nice lounge or coffee shop to wait while I check in with Dr. Gibson about Jake and see if any family members are here?" She handed Syd the keys to the rental car. "If it looks like I'll be tied-up for more than an hour, you can take the car and see some sights. I'll give you a call when it looks like I can shake loose, and we can head back to the airport."

Syd took the keys, but shook her head at Maddie's unselfish suggestion. "If it's all the same to you, I'd rather just tag along." She looked around them at the towering hospital complex. "Frankly, I'm afraid that if we separate, I'll never *see* you again. I promise not to get in your way. You can deposit me in the waiting room of the unit, and I'll be just fine until you're through."

Maddie looked dubious. "Are you sure?"

"Absolutely. The only other building I've ever been in that was *this* big was the Atlanta IKEA, and it took a pack of bloodhounds to rescue me." She gestured toward the map. "Unless you've got a convenient stash of bread crumbs in your purse, I'm not letting you out of my sight."

Maddie smiled at her. "Okay, then. Let's go and see if we can find this unit." She glanced at the kiosk map again and rolled her eyes. "With any luck, we might just make it by nightfall."

Fifteen minutes and four banks of elevators later, they entered a long hallway that terminated at a large pair of stainless-steel doors. A blue and orange sign announced the entrance to the endocrinology unit. Syd noticed a visitor's waiting room just to the right of the entrance, and she touched Maddie on the elbow and pointed toward it.

"You'll find me right *there*," she said, with determination. "I've got a book with me, but if that fails, I can always amuse myself by pouring over ten-year-old copies of *Guideposts* magazine."

Maddie eyes were twinkling as she nodded at her. Then she pushed through the double doors, and went in search of the nurse's station.

When Syd entered the small waiting room, she noticed three other people in various stages of somnolence, sprawled across chairs with garish upholstery. There was a large, wall-mounted TV set on in the corner but, thankfully, the volume had been turned off. It appeared to be tuned to the FOX News Channel, so Syd was especially grateful for the quietude.

She sat down in the chair that was closest to the hallway and pulled a well-worn paperback copy of *Jane Eyre* out of her bag. Finding her place, she recalled that poor Jane had been in a lot of trouble when she last put the book down. She had fled her post as governess at Thornfield Hall and was wandering the countryside in search of—what? Comfort? Safety? Succor? Certainly not happiness. She had left her chances at finding that behind when she ran from her mounting passion for Mr. Rochester.

Lost in the story, Syd was surprised when she heard Maddie's low voice next to her ear. "I always thought that St. John Rivers was an arrogant prick."

Syd looked up, startled to see Maddie kneeling next to her chair. She glanced at her watch and realized she'd been reading for an hour.

"Well," she said, closing her book, "we can't *all* be as fortunate in our rescuers as I was."

Maddie dramatically stood up to her full height. "Damn straight. I bet I could totally kick his ass in a tire-changing contest."

"You'll get no argument from me there." Syd smiled as she stowed her book back inside her purse. "How did it go?"

Maddie's expression changed as she sat down next to Syd. "Not well," she answered, grimly. "Jake has slipped into a diabetic coma. Dr. Gibson isn't very optimistic. I talked with the family—his wife and daughter were in his room when I went in to see him."

"Oh, Maddie, I'm so sorry. How are they holding up?"

"About like you'd expect. They've called the other family members. Jake's son and granddaughter should be arriving later this afternoon."

"God." She searched Maddie's face. "What do you want to do?"

Maddie shook her head. "There's not much I can do, except wait with them. I think—if you don't mind—I'll run you down to Jericho, then pop back up here for the evening. I haven't known Jake for very long, but he was a patient of my father's for many years. I think they feel a real connection to me because of that, and it might be helpful for them to have a friendly face on hand while they wrestle through this. It shouldn't be long—tonight or tomorrow morning at the latest."

Syd searched her face. "Don't be ridiculous. I can drive back to Jericho tomorrow, if need be. For tonight, why don't we just find a place to stay near the hospital?" She held up her bag. "Jane and I will be fine on our own. You do what you need to do."

Maddie looked like she was going to argue for a moment. Instead, she took Syd's hand and warmly squeezed it. "You're a real pal, know that?"

"Not at all. I'm selfishly completing my self-guided 'Civil War Battlefields of Virginia' tour. After this trip, I only have one hundred and forty-three to go."

Maddie laughed. "Oh *really*?" Her blue eyes twinkled. "And what do you get for all that effort?"

"Well," Syd said, standing up, "at the rate I'm going, it seems I get a ready-made excuse to spend a *lot* more time with you."

Maddie got to her feet as well and steered them toward the nearest elevator. "Silly girl. You don't *need* an excuse for that."

They left the hospital, intending to find a hotel for the night, but on their way to the parking deck, they heard a voice call out, "Dr. Stevenson!"

They turned around to see a tall, slender man with silver hair approaching. He wore a starched white coat with the name *Arthur Leavitt, M.D.* embroidered over the front pocket. He quickly closed the short distance between them and swept a stunned Maddie up into a bear hug.

"Maddoe," he gushed into her hair. "I thought that was you. What on earth are you doing in Charlottesville?" He stepped back, but continued to hold on to her elbows.

Maddie's face was glowing. "Uncle Art. It's wonderful to see you. I'm here checking on a patient." She gestured to Syd. "Let me introduce you to my good friend—and one of Jericho's newest residents—Syd Murphy. Syd, this is Arthur Leavitt. A *very* close friend of my family."

Syd shook his hand. "It's a pleasure to meet you, Dr. Leavitt."

"Please, call me Uncle Art. Any friend of Maddoe's is family to me."

Syd decided that she liked the tall man. "Okay—Uncle Art." He grinned at her.

"Art and my dad went to UVA *and* med school together," Maddie explained, proudly.

Art smiled warmly at Syd. "That was about a thousand years ago, when *this* one," he gestured at Maddie, "was just a gleam in her daddy's eye." He turned back to Maddie. "So how are you? How are you finding life back in the sticks?"

"It's challenging." Maddie glanced at Syd. "But it has its compensations."

Art looked back and forth between them. "So I see."

Syd felt a slow blush creep up her neck as Dr. Leavitt gave her an appraising once-over. He turned to Maddie. "Are you two here for long? I'd love to see more of you and really get caught up."

"Unfortunately, no. We really only intended to be here for an hour or two, but my patient is now in a diabetic coma and is unlikely to last through the night. We thought we'd find a hotel room and head back to Jericho tomorrow."

"A hotel? For tonight?" He looked dubious.

Maddie nodded. "Yeah."

He sighed and shook his head. "You can kiss that idea goodbye, honey. This is alumni weekend at the university, and there are about twelve-thousand drunken Cavaliers besieging the city. You won't find a room within spitting distance of Albemarle County tonight."

Maddie expelled a long breath. "*Wah-hoo-wah*," she muttered.

Art laughed. "Exactly." He paused for a moment. "Well, as it happens, *Uncle Arthur's Youth Hostel* just might be able to accommodate you lovely young ladies for one evening. I have to work the graveyard shift tonight, anyway, so you'll have the place entirely to yourselves." He raised a hand as Maddie opened her mouth to protest. "And don't even bother to say no. Your daddy would never forgive me if I let you stay elsewhere, and I would never forgive myself."

He pulled a key chain out of his pocket and unhooked a silver key. "Here you go, kiddo," he said as he held it out to Maddie. "Do you remember how to find my place?"

Maddie glanced at Syd in resignation and sighed as she took the key. "I sure do. I don't know how to thank you for this—"

"Don't even *go* there. You go drop off your things and give me a jingle in the ER when you get back to the hospital. I'll come and find you." He turned his gaze to Syd, smiled, and held out his hand again. "It's been a real pleasure meeting you, Syd. I hope we'll get a better chance to chat over breakfast."

He pulled Maddie into another quick hug. "The guest room bed is all made up. You should find everything you need." He turned away and headed toward the hospital entrance. "Make yourselves at home," he called over his shoulder.

Syd dumbly watched him depart. "Wow." She raised her eyes to Maddie, who looked equally overwhelmed.

"You can say that again." Maddie slowly shook her head. "See why he's chief of the ER here? He generally gets his way."

Arthur Leavitt lived in an old Norcross Transfer Station warehouse that had been converted to luxury apartments about ten years ago. It was located in the heart of Charlottesville's historic district, and was within walking distance of restaurants, galleries, and the city's downtown mall—which boasted dozens of high-end shops.

Leavitt's condo was on two levels, and had floor to ceiling windows that overlooked the city and its hazy, Blue Ridge Mountain backdrop. The view was dazzling.

Syd laid her garment bag across the back of a settee as she tried to take it all in. "God . . . I could get used to this."

Maddie nodded as she walked toward the gourmet kitchen that was open to the main living area.

"Tell me about it." She picked up the extra house key that hung on a peg by the phone and pocketed it, knowing she would need to return the original to its owner when she went back to the hospital. She leaned against a granite countertop for a moment. "I used to love it when dad and I came up here to visit. Art is a fabulous cook and a *great* storyteller. We'd stay up half the night, laughing and eating amazing meals that went on for hours."

Syd smiled. "When did you see him last?"

"At Dad's funeral." She dropped her gaze. "It was a very difficult time—for all of us."

They were quiet for a moment.

"Then it's good you ran into him today."

Maddie nodded slowly. "Yes, I guess it is."

Syd walked toward a sideboard table that was filled with framed photographs. In one photo, a pretty, dark-haired child laughed from her perch on the shoulders of a tall man. His light-colored hair was wind-blown and his face looked open and happy. He was very handsome. They stood in front of a small airplane, and the little girl was wearing a pair of headphones that were sizes too large for her. Syd picked up the picture and studied it. "My god, Maddie, this is *you*, isn't it?"

Maddie went to stand just behind her. "Yep—in all my faded glory." She squinted at the photo. "Looks like I was having a bad hair day."

"Is this your father?"

"Yeah. That's him," Maddie said in a soft voice. "This was taken on my seventh birthday. Dad took me for my very first airplane ride. Uncle Art was there—and Celine, of course. I think she took this photo, in fact."

"You were adorable."

Maddie playfully bumped her. "Whattaya mean I *was* adorable?"

Syd sighed and set the photo back into its place on the sideboard. "Forgive my oversight. I must have taken momentary leave of my senses."

Maddie nodded with understanding. "I do tend to have that effect on women."

Syd rolled her eyes and faced Maddie. "C'mon, Lothario. How about you show me the guest room so we can get our things out of Art's living room?"

"Of course. Follow me." Maddie led Syd up a flight of open stairs to an expansive loft area that was at least half the size of the downstairs living space. It doubled as Art's home office and library, and its interior walls were lined with enormous, Craftsman-style bookcases. There were several colorful paintings—

most were landscapes of the Shenandoah Valley region. Against the far wall, well away from the windows, stood a queen-sized platform bed.

Maddie looked at Syd shyly and shrugged. "Here we go again." Syd smiled at her. "Look, Syd . . . I'll bunk downstairs on the couch. Who knows what time I'll get back in from the hospital tonight."

Syd shook her head as she crossed the room. "Forget it, Stretch. You aren't going to sit up half the night and then come back here to try and cram that six-foot frame of yours onto a pint-sized love seat." She pulled her book out of her bag and set it on the nightstand next to the bed. "Besides, Jane and I will sleep better if we know where you are."

"How can I refuse an offer like that?"

"I can't imagine that you would even try."

Maddie smiled and checked her watch. "It's just now three-thirty. How about I run back over to the hospital for a bit, then come back by here and collect you around six for an early dinner?"

"That sounds great to me. Maybe we can finally have some time to talk about our evening with your mother."

Maddie rolled her eyes. "On the other hand, maybe I'll just sleep on a couple of chairs in that waiting room . . ."

"Nice try. You can't avoid the topic forever, you know."

"Wanna bet?"

Syd crossed her arms.

"Okay, okay . . . we'll *talk* about it."

"Good."

Maddie gave her a crooked smile. "Do you want me to leave the car for you?"

Syd thought about that. "No. I don't think there's a thing I could need that I'd have to drive to find."

Maddie handed her the extra house key. "Keep this so you can get back inside. I'll call you from the hospital if anything changes." Syd nodded and took the key. Maddie turned, and Syd grasped her forearm and held onto it. Maddie looked down at her with a confused expression.

Syd stepped forward and kissed her softly on the cheek. "I think what you're doing for this family is wonderful. I'm glad I could be here with you." She slowly released Maddie's arm and stepped back.

Maddie stood there for a moment without speaking, and then she gave Syd a small smile. "I'm glad you're here, too. See you in a bit." She turned and walked down the stairs.

At six-fifteen, Syd's cell phone rang. It was Maddie.

"Syd? It's me. I'm sorry to be late. Jake died about thirty minutes ago. I've been here with the family. I just stepped out to call you."

Syd's heart sank. "Oh, god. I'm so sorry."

"I know." There was a pause. "Look, I'll be here about another hour. Can you wait on me to eat?"

"Of course. Take your time. I'm not going anyplace."

"Thanks. I'll see you soon." She hung up.

Syd walked back out onto Art's patio and sat down, facing the distant mountains. The sun was starting its slow descent, and the street below her hummed with energy, as pink and gold light reflected off a thousand windowpanes. Her heart went out to the Halsey family—and to Maddie, who she knew would not take the loss of a patient lightly. All in all, it had been an exhausting few days for the complex woman, and Syd was beginning to appreciate how difficult it was for Maddie to let her guard down. She held her emotions under tight regulation and kept people at bay by wielding her extraordinary wit like a light saber.

She guessed that the last thing Maddie would feel like doing tonight would be going back out in public—especially when going out meant fighting their way through the throngs of raucous university alumni who surely would be crowding every bar and bistro in the city. She watched a group of people on the street below laughing and carousing as they walked toward an outdoor café. Smiling, she picked up her cell phone and headed inside to find Art's telephone directory.

Maddie tapped on the door to Art's condo a few minutes before seven-thirty. As Syd opened the door, Maddie began to apologize for her lateness when she noticed that Syd was wearing faded jeans and a blue, oversized UVA sweatshirt. Her short, blonde hair was tousled. She looked . . . adorable. Maddie drew her brows together as she looked her up and down.

"When in Rome?" she asked, with exaggerated confusion.

Syd smiled. "No . . . I found the sweatshirt hanging in the guest room closet. I guess it's Art's version of the complimentary robe." She pulled Maddie inside and closed the door. "You look like you're about ready to fall over."

"I feel like it."

"How are the Halseys?"

"Exhausted. In shock. They've gone home for the night."

"How are you?"

"Glad to be here with you."

Syd took her arm and led her outside to the patio. "Well, sit down and take a load off. I picked up a nice bottle of wine on my little outing, and have it all ready for you."

Maddie sighed happily as she sank onto a chaise and stretched her long legs out in front of her. "When I grow up, I wanna be a doctor just like you."

Syd smiled as she poured her a big glass of Sculpterra Petite Sirah. "Why like me?"

Maddie took the glass from her. "Because you get to prescribe the *fun* stuff."

Syd filled her own glass and clinked rims with Maddie. "Here's hoping."

Maddie took a sip and slowly rolled her head back against the chaise. "Now *that* doesn't suck."

"I'm glad."

"You know, this might be a mistake. I don't know if you'll be able to get me up out of this thing to go in search of food."

Syd sat down on a chair opposite her. "Hmmm. A conundrum. What's a girl to do?"

"Call the local hose, hook, and ladder company?"

"Nah. Too dramatic. I have a better idea."

"You do?" Maddie asked, intrigued.

"Yep. It's called the hot bar at Whole Foods Market. Even as we speak, our dinner reposes in the warming drawer of Art's overpriced Viking range."

Maddie gave her a slow grin. "Have I told you lately that I love you?"

Syd batted her eyes. "Flatterer." She stood up. "Why don't you go change into some more comfortable clothes? I'll get our dinner ready."

Maddie changed into a long-sleeved t-shirt and jeans and walked downstairs to explore Art's impressive CD collection until she found something she liked. Strains of Puccini filled the air as she walked back toward the kitchen area to join Syd.

Syd was lighting a couple of oil candles that were artfully placed at various locations around the kitchen. She cocked her head. "Is that opera?"

Maddie shrugged. "Yeah. Is that okay?"

"You ask that of a violinist?"

Maddie bowed her head. "A momentary lapse, borne of exhaustion."

Syd returned the lighter to its basket on the countertop. "What is this? Puccini?"

Maddie refilled their wine glasses. "Uh huh. *La Rondine*—one of my favorites."

Syd narrowed her eyes in thought. "*La Rondine.* That means *The Swallow.* Right?"

Maddie was impressed. "You know, you really could make a fortune on *Jeopardy.*"

Syd laughed. "No, I remember this one. It has that gorgeous soprano aria with the piano."

"The 'Canzone di Doretta'?"

"Yes. I once heard Renée Fleming sing that in recital with the Baltimore Symphony. My god, it nearly stopped my heart."

Maddie smiled. "Well, it's supposed to, isn't it? The story of a young woman whose entire life is transformed by a single kiss. What's not swoon-worthy in that?"

They were silent for a moment.

Syd belatedly turned away and walked to the Viking to retrieve their warm dinner plates.

Syd did a better-than-credible job, cobbling a gourmet meal together with her Whole Foods assortments. They dined on rare slices of beef tenderloin with Béarnaise sauce, asparagus and saffron risotto, and an arugula salad with tangy mango dressing. They sat at Art's bistro-sized kitchen table, finding it more appealing than the massive glass-topped dining table that dominated nearly a quarter of the downstairs living space.

Maddie was in transports over the meal. "I still can't believe you did all of this. God, it's wonderful."

Syd smiled at her. "I'm glad you think so. You're eating like it's your last meal."

Maddie nodded. "Well, if you'll recall, I didn't get to enjoy much of my Rhône Valley tour last night."

"I recall." Syd paused. "Celine didn't seem to eat very much, either."

Maddie met her eyes. "Yeah. Next time we decide to do something like that, we should just hit a furniture store and sit around an empty table—it'd be a lot cheaper."

Syd handed Maddie another small slice of herbed foccacia. "Do you think there might actually *be* a next time, or was that suggestion just another opportunity for wit?"

Maddie regarded her with interest. "Trying to figure me out?"

"You might say that. And may I add that your instruction manual reads like a bad translation of Proust."

Maddie considered this. "Are there any good translations of Proust?"

"My point, exactly."

They laughed.

Syd sat back and pushed her plate away. "Okay, Doctor. Your number is officially *up*."

Maddie gave her a quizzical look. "Did I just fold space and end up in line at a bakery?"

"Not even close."

Maddie smiled. "Do you think it's too cold to go sit outside on the patio?"

Syd stood up. "There's one way to find out." She walked through the kitchen and blew out the oil candles.

They picked up their wine glasses and walked across the living room to the large atrium doors that led out to Art's veranda. It was a lovely evening—unusually warm for mid-March. Maddie sighed contentedly as she reclaimed her earlier spot and sprawled across the chaise. Syd sat across from her in another chair and pulled its companion ottoman over so she, too, could prop up her feet. They stared at each other in the semi-darkness. Sounds of laughter drifted up from the street below.

"So," Maddie's low voice seemed to float on the night air, "you wanted to talk about last night?"

"Don't you?"

She sighed. "I guess so. I mean, it was all pretty surreal. For most of the evening, Celine was like someone I didn't even recognize."

"Strange," Syd began, "I had the opposite reaction. To me, she seemed so much like you that I sometimes had a hard time telling you apart."

She could feel Maddie's eyes on her, even though she couldn't see them distinctly.

"What do you mean by that?" Maddie's voice sounded wary.

"I mean, that apart from some pretty astonishing physical similarities, the two of you have more in common than I expected."

"Like?" Maddie sounded uncertain.

"Like the fact that you're both uncommonly intelligent, witty to the point of distraction—and charming when you choose to be. And the fact that *neither* of you is satisfied with the current state of your relationship. That much was perfectly clear to me."

"You got all of that out of one, four-course meal?" Maddie chortled. "Move over, Dr. Phil."

"For once, try to be serious. Think you can manage that . . . for me?"

Maddie expelled a long breath. "I'll try. This isn't easy for me."

"I know, Stretch."

They were silent for a few moments.

"Okay," Maddie said with resignation. "I admit that maybe I'm not as immune to Celine as I postured." She paused. "And I'll also admit that, yes, it *does* still chap my ass that she walked out on us without even a backwards glance . . . *and* that she has never tried to apologize, or explain her actions. *Ever.*"

Syd laid a comforting hand on Maddie's ankle. "Boy . . . when you finally decide to open up, you don't mess around, do you?"

Maddie shook her head slowly. "Nuh uh. Be careful what you wish for. There's no going back once you open Pandora's box."

"That might be true, but as I recall, the best thing in Pandora's box was hope."

Maddie snorted. "Sure, and you got to it right after you fought your way through a litany of evils that stretched from here to Athens," she hesitated, "or Los Angeles."

"Well, maybe the two of you made some progress along that road last night."

"I wouldn't count on it."

"Someday, I'd like to see the list of things you *would* count on."

"It's short," Maddie said after a moment. Syd could hear the smile in her voice. "Only has three items."

"Care to enlighten me?"

"Sure." Maddie held up her fingers and ticked the items off. "Number one: My dog. Science has shown that there is nothing known to man more trustworthy than a golden retriever. Number two: My unwavering belief in the indefatigability and resilience of the human spirit. Number three: You." She paused. "That last one is a recent addition."

Syd was glad the darkness hid her blush.

"And you know, I don't think I'm alone in my assessment. Celine seemed pretty taken with you."

"Oh, I don't know. I think she was more taken with the *idea* of me—as your girlfriend."

"Hard to argue with her about that."

Syd waved her hand in frustration. "Are you just trying to make me blush, or is this some new alternative energy scheme you're using to light up the night sky?"

Maddie laughed. "You asked for it, Goldilocks. It wasn't my idea to parade in there like Ellen and Portia."

"Oh, yeah? Well, you didn't seem to have any problems warming to the idea, did you?"

"Hey, I'm only human. If a great looking woman chooses to lay one on me, I'm certainly not gonna ignore it."

"I noticed."

"Well, thank god you did. I'd hate to think I've lost my touch at the ripe old age of thirty-four."

"Trust me," Syd demurred. "Your reputation remains intact."

They fell silent again, but were kept company by the lively sounds emanating from the street below.

They remained outside until they finished their wine.

Maddie tried, unsuccessfully, to stifle a yawn.

"Tired?" Syd asked, gently.

"Yeah. It's been a tough couple of days."

"I know. Why don't you go get ready for bed? I'll clear away our dishes."

Maddie swung her legs around and sat up. "Normally, I'd argue with you, but I'm really about ready to nod off."

Syd stood up. "Go on ahead. I'll be up shortly."

When Syd climbed the stairs a few minutes later, Maddie had already changed into her sleepwear, and was safely tucked away under the covers on the extreme right edge of the bed. Syd laughed at her ridiculous position. "Think you'll be safe all the way over there?"

Maddie raised a sleepy eyebrow. "I thought I'd give this bed a fighting chance at retaining its virtue. Maybe it will fare better than the one in Richmond."

Syd smiled to herself as she picked up her pajamas and headed for the bathroom. When she emerged, she thought Maddie was already asleep. Quietly, she turned off the light and climbed into the bed, being careful not to disturb Maddie. After a few minutes, she heard Maddie sigh.

"This'll *never* work."

Syd turned her head to look at Maddie's profile, dimly outlined against the darker wall behind them. "What do you mean?" she asked, quietly.

"I'm trying too hard to keep vigilant over here. I'll never get to sleep at this rate." She started to get up. "I think I should just go crash on the sofa."

Syd put out a restraining hand. "No way. You're exhausted." She pushed Maddie back down and, without ceremony, rolled over to stretch out half on top of her. "Desperate times call for desperate measures," she murmured.

"What are you *doing*?" Maddie asked, sounding stunned.

"Saving us each from a sleepless night. Don't worry," she smiled against

Maddie's neck, "we'll have *lots* of time to regret this when we get back to Jericho."

Maddie slowly let out the breath she had been holding and wrapped her arms around Syd. "Speak for yourself, blondie."

They both were sound asleep in minutes.

Chapter 17

Lizzy Mayes had done a more than credible job, holding down the fort at the clinic while Maddie was in Richmond and during her unexpected detour to Charlottesville. For two years now, Maddie had worked in Jericho with little more than an occasional weekend off. Now, with the addition of a licensed nurse practitioner to her staff, she was allowing herself to grow giddy at the prospect of actually being able to take a vacation.

On Monday after their last appointments, Lizzy brought Maddie up to speed about the long weekend while they relaxed over coffee in Maddie's office.

"So Louise Halsey's hip is a lot worse, and I completely agree with your suggestion that she's a candidate for replacement surgery. She could barely walk when she came in here on Friday." She smiled. "I told her that if she'd been a horse on my daddy's farm, he'd have shot her by now."

Maddie laughed. "Now there's a novel approach. How'd she react?"

"It sure got her attention. I thought her husband was gonna drop his teeth into his spit cup."

"Lizzy, if you can succeed in getting that woman to see a surgeon, I'll . . ." She looked around the room in search of some kind of premium to offer up and settled on a small bronze trophy that sat on a shelf behind her desk. "I'll give you this coveted award from last year's Kiwanis 10K Fun-Run." She held it out to her.

Lizzy rolled her eyes. "Gee. *Thanks.*" She took the hideous statuette and turned it over in her hands. "Gosh. First place." She looked up at Maddie with exaggerated wonder. "There's a shocker."

"Oh, shut up. It was hardly a competitive field—most of the other contestants were in wheelchairs."

"I just bet." Lizzy sat the trophy down on the desk. She leaned back in her chair and regarded Maddie quietly for a moment, tapping the side of her coffee mug in agitation.

"What is it?" Maddie asked.

"How . . . What do you know about Beau Pitzer?"

"What do you mean?" Maddie was curious. "In what sense?"

Lizzy shook her red head. "In any sense. He came by on Saturday morning while I was here by myself making notes on the patients we had seen on Friday. I let him in because he said he had hurt his hand working on his truck, but he really seemed fine. Well, *fine* is maybe a relative term." She met Maddie's eyes. "I don't know—something about him just really creeps me out. I felt the same way last week when I met him for the first time at the library."

Maddie narrowed her eyes in concern. "Did he do or say anything inappropriate?"

"Not exactly. It's more just a feeling I have, you know?"

Maddie nodded.

"Phoebe seemed unnerved by the way he was behaving around Syd. I wondered if she had ever mentioned anything about that to you."

Maddie raised her eyebrows. "Syd? No. She's never mentioned anything to me about that. What did Phoebe say?"

Lizzy shrugged. "I dunno. Just that she was concerned about how he was *looking* at her. And she seemed to think that he was spending a lot of time hanging around the library." She paused. "I don't want to be unfair. There was just something unnerving about him."

"I can understand that. He's had some difficulties in the past."

"Drugs?"

Maddie nodded. "Yes. I can't say that I'm very happy about him showing up here on a Saturday like that—not when he knows the clinic is closed." She was thoughtful. "Do you think I should talk with him?"

Lizzy looked surprised. "You'd do that?"

Maddie gazed unwavering at her. "In a heartbeat."

Lizzy shook her head. "No—no, I think it's okay for now. I just wanted to mention it to you—as much for Syd's sake as my own. I thought you should be aware of it."

It occurred to Maddie to wonder why Lizzy assumed that she had such a proprietary interest in Syd's affairs, but she was too concerned about the content of her observations to worry about the style of her delivery. She resolved to check out the substance of Lizzy's—and Phoebe's—observations with Syd later that evening when she left the clinic.

Roma Jean showed up to work in the afternoon and prepared Syd for an onslaught of after-school activity. Spring break was only a week away, and mid-term deadlines were looming at the high school. Starting at two-thirty, the tiny branch quickly filled up with teenagers, all hell-bent on completing their frenzied research for papers on topics that ranged from Shakespeare *to* climate change. One enterprising—and, by Syd's definition, confused—patron, even had a thesis that sought to relate Shakespeare to climate change, and helping him run down credible sources for that project was not an enviable task.

The study tables in the library were filled with students, and Syd was grateful that her nemesis—the photocopier—was cooperating for once. The machine had been running more or less continuously since three o'clock. The mechanical sound of its scanning carriage rolling back and forth filled the air like a monotonous soundtrack, playing at a steady, low-volume behind the chatter and laughter that filled the facility.

By six, activity slowed to a crawl as the teens left to head for home or other evening commitments. Syd headed to the circulation desk to relieve Roma Jean, who needed to leave to meet Jessie and some other band friends for dinner at Pizza Hut. She heard the branch phone ring, and Roma Jean's programmed "Jericho

Public Library" response. Then she heard a thud and the sound of books toppling to the floor.

Syd rounded the corner in concern and saw Roma Jean on her knees, hastily trying to stack a scattered pile of returned books and brandishing the telephone receiver like a hot poker.

She blushed when she saw Syd and meekly held the phone up toward her. "I dropped it. I'm sorry." She lowered her eyes. "It's for you." She stood up and hastily set the stack of books down on top of the desk and ducked past Syd as she handed her the phone. "Bye, Miss Murphy. See you on Wednesday."

Shaking her head, Syd lifted the phone to her ear. "Hello. This is Syd."

"Well, hey there." It was Maddie. "You know, it occurs to me that someone could make a fortune studying the peculiar gravitational characteristics of our public library."

Syd smiled. "Meaning?"

"Meaning that things always seem to be *falling* around there."

"Uh huh. I could point out that this phenomenon only seems to occur when *you're* around. So I think you'd make a better research subject."

Maddie laughed. "Nobody would pay good money to study my sorry ass."

"Is this why you called me?" Syd asked, sweetly. "To engage in a lively debate about the merits of your ass?"

"Hmmm. No. But hearing your thoughts on the subject *would* provide me with a certain amount of vicarious enjoyment."

"I'm sorry. If you want me to talk dirty to you, you'll have to call back after six-thirty. The library is still open right now, and I can't tie up this line."

Maddie sighed. "So close, and yet so far away."

Syd laughed. "You are *such* a nut job. What's going on?"

"Nothing much. I suddenly realized that I had gone almost an entire day without talking to you." She paused. "I didn't like it."

"I know what you mean. It's hard to get back into this daily grind. You'd think we had been away a lot longer than three days."

"You got that right."

Syd could hear wind noise in the background. "Where are you?"

"In my car."

"Oh." She suddenly felt disappointed. "On your way home?"

"Noooooooo . . . on my way to Wytheville to pick up some MRI results at the hospital. I thought I'd grab dinner over there, and wondered if you'd like to join me? And I completely understand if you feel that you need an evening by yourself."

"Think I'm tired of you?"

"Well, let's just say I didn't want to make any assumptions."

"Hmmm." She glanced at her watch. "I *suppose* I could endure your company for another evening. Do you want to pick me up here? I'll be closing up in about ten minutes."

"Works for me. See you in ten minutes." Maddie hung up, and Syd smiled to herself as she began to prepare the library for closing.

An hour later, they were seated in a booth at McGinty's Pub, sipping on Pellegrino and talking about their first days back at work. Syd noted with irony that they were seated in the same booth she had shared with Jeff during their ill-fated conversation several months ago. She was relieved to see that their plucky server, Randi, was nowhere in sight.

Maddie relaxed against the padded backrest and stretched her long legs out beneath the table. "If I kick you, just let me know, and I'll move my legs."

Syd raised her eyebrow. "No way. You kick me, and I'll kick you back."

Maddie pretended to pout. "That's not very sporting."

"Well, neither is kicking me."

"You *do* understand that I wouldn't be doing this on purpose?"

"Uh huh." Syd looked under the table to gaze at Maddie's long legs extended diagonally across the cramped space. She was instantly reminded of Saturday night, and the cab ride after their emotionally-charged dinner with Celine. She quickly sat back up and looked into Maddie's amused blue eyes, trying hard not to blush. Maddie's legs were becoming too much of a leitmotif to suit her. In fact, it wasn't just her legs. Maddie's sheer physicality was becoming too much of a distraction—especially after the events of the weekend. As they continued to stare at each other, she wondered whether Maddie shared any of her consternation about the confusing turns their relationship had taken. She knew that she didn't yet feel confident enough to ask.

"Something on your mind?" Maddie asked in a low voice.

Syd shrugged. "Not really. Why do you ask?"

"I dunno. You seem distracted. Edgy, even."

"Edgy?"

"A little. Yeah."

Syd looked around the restaurant. It was surprisingly busy for a Monday night. She could see that several of the bar TV sets were tuned to the same basketball game. The NCAA Tournament was in full swing, and Virginia Tech had managed to stay alive through the first two rounds. Syd was fairly certain that, wherever he was, her brother was staked out in front of a TV. She looked back at Maddie, who was regarding her with a curious expression.

"Are you really a basketball fan?"

Maddie didn't seem surprised by the irrelevant question. She glanced at the bank of TVs that hung at various angles around the bar area. "Sometimes. I don't get to watch many of the games, though. And Stanford is really better known for the strength of its women's basketball program."

"I forgot about that." She smiled. "I bet you have to keep a low profile whenever they play Carolina or Tennessee."

Maddie laughed. "Oh, honey, you have *no* idea. I usually have to hide my diploma during March Madness."

Maddie's casual use of the endearment caused a thrill to race across Syd's body, and she was annoyed by the involuntary response. Maddie was just being relaxed and friendly, and Syd was overreacting to everything. She knew that the *only* difference between her behavior and Roma Jean's was the fact that she hadn't knocked anything over—yet.

She resolved to make another attempt at safe conversation.

"So, was your first day back at work as busy as mine was?"

Maddie shook her head. "Surprisingly, no. Lizzy managed everything without incident. I don't think they missed me at all."

"Well, I doubt that's the case." She smiled. "But it *is* good news that you can be confident about Lizzy's ability to manage things while you're away. Maybe that means you might actually be able to take some time off now and then."

Maddie lifted her glass of Pellegrino. "A-men to that, sister."

Their server arrived to deposit the two large chicken salad platters they'd ordered. Each was garnished with fresh fruit and a spiced muffin. Syd dug into hers.

"Did you miss lunch?" Maddie asked with amusement.

"Um hmmm." Syd swallowed. "It's term paper time. I pretty much went full-tilt boogie all afternoon."

"Lots of patrons?" Maddie asked, picking up her fork.

"Yeah, the place was crawling with them. I wouldn't have been able to manage without Roma Jean."

"Beau Pitzer around?"

Syd broke off a bite-sized piece of her muffin. "Beau? Yeah, he was there this morning to look over the online job postings. Why do you ask?"

"Lizzy said something about him that concerned me." Maddie sounded a bit guarded. "Something about how much he was hanging around the library. She said that Phoebe had noticed it. And then Beau showed up at the clinic on Saturday morning while it was closed, and Lizzy was there alone. She found his demeanor to be pretty . . . creepy."

Syd set her fork down. "Wait a minute. Lizzy and Phoebe were discussing how much Beau was coming into the library?"

Maddie nodded.

Syd was bothered by the admission, and had difficulty disguising it. "I don't see why they'd have any particular concerns about that. It's a public place. He has a right to be there." She slowly shook her head. "I'm not sure how much I like hearing that I'm a topic of conversation in this way."

Maddie leaned forward. "Hold on. It's not like that at all."

Syd crossed her arms. "It isn't? Okay, then tell me what it *is* like."

Maddie seemed confused by her agitation. "Look, I don't see why you're so bent out of shape about this. Beau is a known-quantity and, like it or not, he's got a less-than-admirable track record around here. It's reasonable for them to be concerned about you."

"I'm not a novice at this. Give me *some* credit. Maybe you all need to remember the meaning of the 'public' part of public library. I don't get to pick and choose who gets to use our services, and I sure won't deny access to someone just because your new Florence Nightingale thinks he's creepy."

Maddie sat back and held out a hand, palm first. "Okay. Let's dial this back a little bit." She waited until Syd assumed a less defensive posture. "I'm tempted to ask you why you're so angry, but I don't think I will. Not right now, anyway." She hesitated a moment before continuing and seemed to choose her words carefully. "I never meant to offend you, and I certainly never meant to suggest that you wouldn't have the sense or the wherewithal to manage Beau if his behavior ever *did* become a problem. Lizzy felt that his behavior toward *her* was vaguely threatening on Saturday. Based on what Phoebe shared with her previously, she was worried about you. That was it."

Syd chewed the inside of her cheek. "So why didn't Lizzy just talk with me herself? Why did she tell you?"

Maddie shrugged. "I don't know the answer to that. I have to admit that I asked myself the same question." She met Syd's eyes. "Is that what you're angry about? The fact that she talked to me about this, instead of you?"

Syd felt her face grow hot. She knew it would be pointless to try to deny the truth—her blush would give her away. She lowered her eyes and stared at the tabletop. "Yeah. I guess so."

"Why does that offend you?" Maddie asked in a soft voice.

Syd shook her head. "Because I'm not a child. Jeff was exactly the same way— always trying to legislate everything for me—never trusting me to make my own determinations about *anything*." She looked up and met Maddie's eyes. "I'm not a piece of property, and I don't need to be protected or taken care of."

Maddie seemed to bite back her initial response and sat quietly for a few moments. Finally, she gave Syd a small smile. "Okay. I'll try to unhitch the steamroller that's tethered to my ass."

Syd was unable to suppress a laugh at that, and she felt some of the tension leave her body. "So, we're back to discussing your ass?"

Maddie made an elaborate show of twisting around to try and examine her derriere. "So it seems." She sighed dramatically and sat back up. "One way or another, things always come back to my butt. It's a curse."

"I don't know about that." Syd gave her an appraising look. "There are worse places to end up."

Maddie rolled her eyes. "Oh, *that* remark deserves a drum roll and cymbals."

Syd picked up her fork and speared a cherry tomato. "So does your butt."

"If I didn't know better, I'd say you were flirting with me."

"Didn't we just establish that you don't always know better?" Syd popped the tomato into her mouth.

Maddie looked a bit shell-shocked. "Did I miss a few lines of dialogue here?"

"Having some trouble keeping up?"

"Apparently." She sat back and stared at Syd in amazement. "You go from zero, to pissed-off to whatever this is in, like, *ten* seconds." She slowly shook her head. "What are we talking about, exactly?"

Syd relented as she met Maddie's confused blue eyes. "I'm sorry. I'm just toying with you—probably trying to get even." She reached across the table and rested her hand on Maddie's. "I didn't really mean anything by it. I'm just being a brat." She squeezed her hand. "Forgive me?"

Maddie sighed. "You were just kidding?"

Syd nodded.

Maddie held her gaze. "Bummer."

They sat in silence for a moment, and then Syd belatedly withdrew her hand.

"So." Maddie cleared her throat. "You're not mad any more?"

"Nuh uh."

"Good. So I can ask you something?"

"What is it?" Syd eyed her with suspicion.

"Florence Nightingale?"

Embarrassed, Syd raised a hand to her forehead.

Maddie chuckled. "Where in the hell did *that* come from?"

"God, I'm sorry." Syd lowered her hand. "I guess I was jealous."

Maddie looked surprised. "Of Lizzy?"

Syd shrugged. "Yeah."

"Why on earth would you be jealous of Lizzy?"

Syd waved her hand in frustration. "Maybe because you seemed to value her perspective more than mine? I don't know . . . it's not rational. I can't explain it in a way that will make sense to either of us."

"But you don't dislike her?"

"Lizzy?" Maddie nodded. "God, no. I like her a *lot*. I'm thrilled that she's working with you—honest." Syd shook her head. "I'm such an idiot."

"Well, I wouldn't say that, but I'm glad you don't dislike Lizzy."

"You really do value her, don't you?"

"Yes, I do, but not as much as I value you."

Syd was embarrassed. "It's not a contest."

"No, it isn't." Maddie held her gaze. "And, Syd?"

"Yes?"

"It won't ever be."

Syd lowered her eyes. Her heart was now hammering so hard she was certain that Maddie could hear it over the din in the bar. "Maybe I was," she said quietly.

"Maybe you were what?"

"Maybe I *was* flirting with you."

Syd found the courage to raise her eyes. Maddie was looking at her with a stunned expression. Before either of them could speak, their server arrived to deposit their check. He noticed their untouched salads with surprise.

"Is your food all right?" he asked with concern.

Maddie looked up at him. "It's fine. We're just taking our time."

"Do you want a couple of to-go boxes?" he asked.

Maddie looked at Syd. She shook her head. "No, we're fine. Turns out we weren't as hungry as we thought we were." She handed him her credit card, and he smiled before walking off.

Syd knew that her emotions were all over the map, and that she was rapidly digging herself deeper into a hole she couldn't climb out of. But part of her didn't care anymore. She was tired of trying to pretend that nothing was happening. It was dishonest, and it wasn't fair to Maddie—who just seemed confused by her erratic behavior.

"I guess I owe you an explanation for that," she said.

"You don't *owe* me anything," Maddie replied. "But I'd like to understand what's got you so rattled."

Syd looked down at her hands and the napkin she had twisted into a knot. She slowly smoothed the fabric out across her lap, then folded it and placed it on top of the table. "Want to get out of here?"

Maddie nodded. "Let me get my credit card back, and we'll leave. Any place in particular you want to go?"

Syd dumbly shook her head. She saw their waiter approaching from the bar area.

"Okay," Maddie said. "We'll figure something out."

Maddie drove them back toward Jericho and impulsively turned off the highway at a public boat landing near the river. Syd had been mostly silent on the drive, but looked at Maddie when they made the turnoff for the river.

"Should I be worried?" she asked. "This looks pretty desolate."

"Well, you once said that we needed to have more conversations in the dark, and at least this will be more private than the restaurant."

"True."

Maddie parked the Jeep near a couple of picnic tables. She reached behind their seats and picked up a long-handled flashlight. "And if you feel threatened, you can always hit me with this." She handed it to Syd.

Syd took it from her. "I don't want to hit you."

"That's comforting to hear. I was beginning to wonder."

"Think it's warm enough to sit outside?"

"C'mon, let's try it. I have a blanket we can sit on."

Syd smiled. "The infamous blanket. Tell me—do you just cruise this river road looking for wayward women to rescue?"

Maddie raised an eyebrow. "*Wayward* is not a term I would apply to you, but then, the night is young."

"You didn't answer my question."

"I know. You don't expect me to give up all my secrets, do you?"

Syd shrugged. "Why not? I seem poised to surrender most of mine."

They were silent for a moment. Maddie unclipped her seatbelt. "In that case, we'll definitely need the blanket."

Syd followed suit and opened her door. "Wiseass."

They got out and walked to a table near the water's edge. Maddie spread the blanket out on the weathered top boards so they could sit facing the river with their feet resting on the bench. The night air was cool but not cold, and there was a gentle breeze blowing toward them from the opposite bank. The moon was nearly full, and its white light made random patterns on the inky surface of the water as it slowly drifted by. Maddie could see a pyramid of fresh-looking cigarette butts on the ground near the base of their table. Clearly, they weren't the first people to sit there that evening.

"So, when did you know?" Syd asked, breaking the silence.

Maddie glanced at her. "When did I know what?"

Syd was looking out across the river. "When did you know you were gay?"

"Oh." Maddie felt her heart rate quicken. "God. I don't know. In high school, maybe? I had a decidedly un-platonic attachment to my track coach. I thought at first that maybe it was just because my relationship with Celine was so crappy, but that's not what it was. By the time I went to college, I was pretty sure that the normal dating scene wasn't really for me."

"But you dated boys?"

"Oh, yeah. I gave 'em the old college try." She laughed. "Quite a few of them, in fact. I didn't actually date another girl until my senior year at Stanford." She looked at Syd again. "I guess you'd call me a late bloomer."

Syd snorted. "You call *that* late? What were you—nineteen?"

"More like twenty. And remember that my primary point of reference for embracing my sexuality was David. So, yeah, twenty seemed late."

"David came out early?"

Maddie looked at her with disbelief. "You're kidding me, right? I'm pretty certain he emerged from the womb belting out Judy Garland tunes."

Syd smiled and playfully bumped Maddie's shoulder. They sat in silence for another minute. Off in the distance, they could hear the whinny of an Eastern Screech Owl. Maddie anxiously wondered where Syd was headed with this train of thought. Given her recent yo-yo-like behavior, she wasn't sure she'd find out any time soon.

"Michael said that it didn't change anything," Syd said.

Maddie was confused. "What didn't change anything?"

"Being gay. He told me that it didn't change anything about who you are. He said that it's all pretty simple, and that once you figure it out, you either decide to accept it or not."

Maddie felt her pulse race again. "Is that what he said?"

"Yeah."

"Care to tell me why he told you this?" she asked, softly.

Syd finally faced her. "Why do you think?"

Maddie stared at her mutely. Syd's expression was unreadable. Her question hung in the air between them. She knew she had to say something, but any response that came to mind seemed too charged with meaning. She felt more petrified than excited. She was tired of hiding, but she was also afraid of revealing too much. She slowly shook her head.

"I really have no idea."

Syd tilted her head as she continued to regard her. "You don't?"

"No."

"Okay." Syd leaned forward, closing the distance between them. "Then maybe this will help explain it."

Maddie was stunned when Syd's lips pressed against hers. She sat there rigidly with her eyes wide open, but as Syd continued the contact, she slowly relaxed into the embrace and raised her hands to rest on the Syd's arms. She was careful not to push her away or pull her closer. As the pressure of Syd's lips against hers became more determined, she felt lightheaded and tightened her handhold simply to hold herself upright. When Syd finally backed away, they both were breathing unevenly.

Syd's eyes looked glassy. She leaned forward again, and this time, Maddie met her halfway. Syd moaned and parted her lips as they surged together. Maddie gasped and tugged her closer when she felt the first tentative touch of Syd's tongue on hers. The contact was electric—the kiss becoming deeper and more consuming as they explored each other. Syd's hands were now on Maddie's face, pulling her even closer as they continued to kiss.

Finally, they broke apart—each taking rapid breaths as they gazed through the darkness at each other.

When she could find her voice, Maddie whispered, "Yeah, that helped."

Syd rested her head on Maddie's shoulder. "I thought it might."

Maddie held her in silence for few moments. "I guess this means we're actually going to have that chat about Richmond?"

She felt Syd smile against her neck. "I tried to tell you that you couldn't avoid it forever."

"Well, you sure found one hell of a persuasive way to get your wish."

Syd sat back and met her eyes. "I just couldn't hide it any more. It was *ridiculous*—to keep pretending that nothing was happening . . . that *this* wasn't happening." She raised her hands and held Maddie's face between her warm palms. "I couldn't keep lying to you—or to myself."

Maddie turned her head and kissed the inside of Syd's hand. "I know. I know." She let out a slow breath. "What now?"

Syd gazed at her in wonder. "You're asking *me* this question? My god, you're the expert. I have *no* idea."

Maddie smiled. "Well, I'd be lying if I didn't say that one or two things occur to me immediately, but I'm really more concerned about you and your comfort level with all of this."

Syd laughed nervously. "I really appreciate that. In all honesty, I'm not sure about *anything* right now." She slowly ran her fingers across Maddie's lips. "Well, that's not entirely true. I'm pretty sure about *one* thing. That's the second best kiss I've ever had."

"The second best?" Maddie raised an eyebrow. "When was the first?"

"Outside Celine's hotel in Richmond."

"Oh." Maddie smiled shyly. "Yeah. Me, too."

Syd looked incredulous. "You, too?"

"Of course. Do you think I'm a block of wood or something?"

Syd leaned back and looked her up and down. "No . . . I can honestly say that *nothing* about you resembles a block of wood."

"Is that a compliment?"

"Oh, yeah."

Maddie smiled smugly. "Cool."

"God." Syd shook her head. "What am I doing?"

"You mean besides freaking both of us out?"

"Yeah."

"I don't know. And I *won't* know until you do. So I think we need to take our time and not rush into anything you may not be ready for."

"What are *you* ready for?"

Maddie hesitated. "I'm ready for whatever you want to give me." She looked down at their tangle of hands. "I guess it's pretty obvious that I'm attracted to you. Even though I've tried, I don't think I've done the best job trying to conceal that."

"What if I don't want you to conceal it?"

Maddie smiled. "Well, that's kind of a moot point now, isn't it? But as much as I want this, I think we need to take it slow so you can be sure about your own feelings."

Syd leaned into her, and Maddie wrapped her in both arms. "God, thank you for that. I'm so confused."

"I know you are. It's okay. This isn't a race. You don't have to hurry. *We* don't have to hurry."

Syd tightened her arms around Maddie. "Michael said the same thing."

"He did?"

"Yeah." She turned her face into Maddie's neck and took a slow, deep breath. "God, you smell so *good*."

Maddie closed her eyes and let the sensation wash over her. "Right back atcha."

Syd lifted her head and met Maddie's eyes. "Can we kiss some more? Before we start all the reality checks?"

Maddie brushed her lips across Syd's and felt the unmistakable hitch in her breathing. "Before, during, and after—if you want." They kissed again, slower this time.

When they separated, Syd whispered breathlessly, "I want."

They spent the better part of an hour sitting by the river, but they didn't do much talking. When the growling of Syd's stomach grew louder than any of the other ambient night noises, it became clear to them that they needed to make progress toward home. It was a weeknight, and they both had early mornings ahead.

When they arrived back at the library, Syd insisted that Maddie accompany her inside long enough to eat a quick sandwich before heading back to her farm. Maddie expressed initial reluctance at this idea, thinking that it probably wasn't the best idea for the two of them to be alone in Syd's apartment, but Syd told her they both were big girls and should be able to handle it.

"Big girls," Maddie said, looking her over. "Therein lies the problem."

Syd swatted her on the arm. "Quit looking at me like I'm some kind of appetizer."

Maddie raised an ironic eyebrow.

Syd blushed. "Oh, good god, let's just get inside."

Once they were upstairs in the tiny apartment, Syd set about raiding her refrigerator to see what kind of makeshift meal she could pull together. Maddie took off her jacket and nervously paced around the living room.

"Maddie, will you please light someplace? You're buzzing around like a gnat." Syd walked back to the fridge. "How about a glass of wine? Will that settle you down?"

Maddie sighed and dropped down onto the sofa. "I don't think a lobotomy would settle me down right now." She sat tapping her fingers against the edge of the sofa cushion.

Syd laughed. "Is that a yes or a no to the wine?" She held up the bottle.

"Oh, that's a yes. A *big* one."

"Coming right up." Syd poured her a generous glass and walked to the sofa to hand it to her. Maddie reached up to take the glass, and their eyes met.

Mistake number one, Syd thought, as she felt an undeniable surge of arousal. Maddie's blue eyes were hypnotic. Syd bypassed her outstretched hand and set the glass down on the end table. Maddie took hold of her free hand and was gently pulled her down. Syd gave in to the pressure and bent forward at the waist to kiss her. *Mistake number two.* An innocent peck quickly became two, then three—each kiss slightly longer in duration. Before she had time to consider what she was doing, she straddled Maddie's lap, and they were kissing deeply. Short-circuiting mistake number three, before it could become mistake number four, Maddie pulled back. She was breathing heavily.

"See why I told you this was a bad idea?" she said in a husky voice.

Syd leaned forward and slowly trailed her lips along Maddie's hairline. "You did?" She continued to kiss her, making steady progress around the side of her face. "Tell me again why this is bad?'" she asked against Maddie's ear.

Maddie moaned, but somehow managed to dislodge her earlobe from Syd's mouth.

"Because it's too fast." She gently maneuvered Syd so that she slid off her lap and sat down on the cushion beside her, but she kept hold of her hands. "As much as I want this—as much as I want you right now—I want us to do this right."

Syd tilted her head as she regarded her. "Were we about to do it *wrong*?"

Maddie laughed nervously. "Well, maybe not *that* part."

Syd smiled at her shyly. Her heart rate was beginning to resume a normal rhythm. "How can you be so strong?"

Maddie sighed. "Trust me, I'm hanging on by a thread here. It's only because I want this so much—want *you* so much—that I want us to take our time and be sure it's right. I've made too many mistakes in the past, and I don't want that to happen with you." She kissed Syd softly on the forehead. "It's too important. This time, it's too important."

Syd nodded. "Okay. I understand." She sat back against the cushion and ran her thumb around in circles across the back of Maddie's hand. "But it has to be a good sign, right?"

"What has to be a good sign?"

Syd met her eyes. "I was just about ready to tear your clothes off. I think that must mean that I've made *some* progress in my journey of self discovery."

Maddie let out a long, slow breath. "You're really trying to kill me, aren't you?"

Syd leaned forward until their faces were centimeters apart. "No, I think I want to keep you alive a little while longer." She gave her as innocent a peck as she could manage and sat back with determination. Then she stood up and reached out a hand. "Come on, let's make something to eat. We can sit on opposite sides of the table if we need to."

Maddie stood up and snagged her wine glass off the end table. "Maybe we should've brought the flashlight inside with us."

"Why?" Syd teased. "Planning on losing something in the dark?"

Maddie rolled her eyes. "No, but *you* certainly seem determined to."

"I've always been a fast learner."

"I'm beginning to realize that."

Syd stopped and leaned slightly toward her, but Maddie took a step back. She sighed. "The table?"

Maddie nodded. "*Opposite* sides."

"I never knew you were so strict."

"You have no idea."

"You know, there are about a hundred quick responses I could make to *that* revelation, but most of them involve items from the Babeland catalog." Syd began ferrying sandwich items from the counter to her small kitchen table.

Maddie looked at her in surprise, and Syd laughed. "Yes, we have David to thank for that. It appears that I've been added to their mailing list. It's the birthday gift that keeps on giving."

"Oh, Jesus."

"You can say that again." She looked thoughtful. "In fact, I'm fairly certain there are a couple of items in their inventory guaranteed to make you say that again—and again."

Maddie shook her head. "You're really starting to scare me. I don't know whether I should ravish you or run like hell."

"Do I get a vote?"

Maddie deliberated for a moment, then nodded.

"Don't run."

They stared at each other. It occurred to Syd that they spent a lot of time staring at each other.

"Okay, I won't," Maddie said. "But you have to help me with this. I can't be strong for both of us." Her blue eyes reflected the intensity of her plea.

Syd sat down opposite her and gripped the sides of the table with both hands. "Okay. I'm sorry. I'll *try*." She sighed deeply and bit her bottom lip. "If I *promise* you that I won't get up or move my hands, will you let me kiss you again?"

Maddie gave her a small smile. "Could I stop you?"

"If you really wanted to," Syd said in a whisper.

"I don't want to."

"Well, thank god." Syd leaned across the table, and Maddie met her halfway. They exchanged a short succession of kisses that started innocently enough, but rapidly progressed to passionate when Maddie parted her lips, and Syd felt the first, fleeting touch of her tongue. Then all bets were off as Syd began devouring her mouth while still tightly gripping the edges of the table. Their lips and tongues were their only points of contact as they touched, teased, and twisted together in an elaborate pantomime of what their bodies wanted. It was all too heady—too intense. She knew they had to stop—that she was losing control. But she had never felt anything like this before—this rush of heat and arousal that overwhelmed her senses and laid waste to her better judgment. Maddie was intoxicating, and Syd licked and probed at her mouth like a crazed addict who was finally getting her first real fix.

In a desperate fit of self-control, she tore her mouth away and tipped her head back, taking urgent breaths. Maddie immediately shifted her attention to her throat and began kissing her way down toward her collarbone.

"Stop," Syd gasped. "Oh, god, we have to *stop*."

Maddie dropped her forehead to Syd's shoulder. She was breathing deeply, too. "I know. I'm sorry."

"It was my fault."

"No. Not this time." She sat up and pushed back onto her chair. "I think I should leave."

Syd looked at her anxiously. "I don't want you to leave."

"Trust me, I don't want to leave, either. But I think I need to." She gave her a crooked smile. "We can talk tomorrow."

Syd dropped her chin to her chest. "Okay, I know you're right." She raised her eyes to Maddie's. "Let me at least make you a sandwich for the road. It won't take a second."

Maddie nodded her assent, and Syd quickly pulled the items together and wrapped them up in a small bag. Maddie stood up shakily and pulled on her leather jacket. Syd walked with her to the door and handed her the paper bag. Maddie took the bag, and then pulled her into a warm hug. They stood there by the door for a full minute, tightly wrapped-up in each other's arms. Neither of them spoke. Then Maddie pulled back, kissed Syd lightly on the forehead, and turned to walk quickly down the stairs.

Syd stood rooted to the spot, feeling dazed and lightheaded as she listened to

Maddie's retreating footsteps. When she heard the street door open and close, she turned back into her small apartment, wondering if she had any more Cheetos.

Maddie wasn't sure how she made the drive back to her farm. Her mind was in a daze, and her body was on overload from too much stimulation. She had already been drifting in a state of angst and confusion from the events of the weekend, and tonight, Syd's revelation had slammed the gears of their blossoming relationship into some kind of hyper-drive. It was exhilarating and stultifying in nearly equal measure. She needed time to take it all in and to make sense of it, and she needed to find a way to calm herself down so she could think clearly.

She entered her house and quickly fixed Pete's dinner, then carried it and her sandwich out to the front porch. She knew she wasn't likely to get much sleep, so she decided to take advantage of the warmer evening and settle down in one of the big Adirondack chairs that overlooked the pond. Pete inhaled his bowl of food and promptly passed out at her feet. Maddie watched him with envy, wishing she could be so lucky. She had poured herself another glass of wine, and sat sipping it as she tried to talk herself into a state of calm she did not feel.

There was no denying that she was happy—even euphoric—over the amazing turn their relationship had taken. She had been beating back her romantic feelings for Syd for so long now that it felt illicit and unnatural to acknowledge them, much less act on them. Even after the events of this evening, there was a part of her that felt guilty to be indulging her thoughts so freely. But Syd had effectively blown all of those best intentions wide open with one simple kiss.

She smiled to herself. *Simple* was hardly an accurate way to describe it. She was still woozy from the after-effects of their intimate contact—woozy, and incredibly turned on. *My god, the woman can kiss. I don't know how I got out of there without taking her to bed. God knows, I wanted to.*

She knew that a big part of her immediate agitation derived from their truncated physical interaction. They both wanted more—that much was clear. The depth of Syd's passion surprised her. It was clear that once she decided to embrace her attraction to another woman, she was going to be relentless in her exploration of it. Maddie closed her eyes as she relived the sensation of Syd's mouth moving against hers. The determined touch of her lips. Her tongue. *Jesus.*

She'd gone too long without this kind of contact—that much was clear. But even allowing for her recent dearth of sexual interaction, she'd never experienced the kind of total sensory explosion she'd had tonight with Syd. Not even with Gina, with whom she'd had her longest and most sexually-charged relationship.

She was in love with Syd. She knew that. She loved her, and she found her desirable beyond imagining. It was only her steadfast belief that there was no possibility of a future with Syd that had prevented her from dwelling too much on how deeply she was attracted to her. Now? Now all of that had flown right out the window, and she was left dazed and adrift in a sea of new possibilities.

She knew that to stand any chance at all of making something lasting out of their fledgling romance, they would have to slow it down. But how? Against her own better judgment, Syd seemed determined to throw caution to the wind and dive right in. And Maddie, who knew too well the hazards of moving so fast, worried about finding the best way rein things in, while still giving Syd the freedom she needed to explore her feelings.

She took a deep breath and stared out across the dark expanse of lawn that sloped down toward the pond. *It is beautiful here. Syd was right about that.* For too long, she had held her own emotions at bay—afraid to let her guard down. Afraid to be hurt again. Afraid to be vulnerable. Afraid to risk embracing what she wanted because her fear of losing it was greater than her need for happiness. Until now.

Seeing Celine in Richmond brought all of that back full circle—that persistent undercurrent of loss and betrayal. There still were too many unanswered questions with no promise of resolution. Why was Celine so cold and so distant? Why, after all these years, did she even care? And the truth was she *did* care. It did matter to her. The pain of her mother's pointed disregard was like a barb in her side, and no amount of distance or passage of time could dislodge it. She'd lived with it for so long that it had warped her developmentally—bent her psyche into a flawed and twisted shape—leading her to hedge every bet in every relationship she'd ever had. Always she withheld herself. Always she kept the deepest parts of who she was boxed-up and stashed conveniently by the nearest exit, ready for flight.

Flight. What a metaphor that was for the passion she shared with her father. They had the same drive to escape and soar above it all. Everything was simpler from ten thousand feet. A landscape that blocked and confounded her on the ground was transformed when viewed from the air. The terrain below fell into geometric patterns that made sense. She understood how to relate to it and how to navigate across it. It wasn't personal, and it couldn't hurt her or trip her up. She could leave it behind, before it left her.

In the distance, she saw some deer slowly making their way toward the pond. At her feet, Pete was snoring softly, and she hoped he wouldn't wake up and chase them away. She wondered sometimes why he bothered—the deer always came back. This drive to push nature back and defend the sacred boundaries of human existence was an ageless contest. But nature always persevered. Nature had time and patience on its side. Nature could wait. Slowly, as the years passed and people grew too old or too tired or too infirm to struggle, the deer would come back— closer, more plentiful, and less timid than before. In the end, human aspirations would wither and die along with the corporeal bodies that once contained them, and nature would have its way.

She shook her head and tried to clear it from fixing too much on these deeper and more distressing channels of thought. She wanted to be less fatalistic. She wanted to find a way to let whatever happened with Syd unfold at its own pace and develop into whatever it would be without the burden of being front loaded with the angst of her previous failures. Above all else, she wanted a shot at a future with Syd, and the best way to let that happen would be to break from the patterns that defined her other relationships. She was determined to do this, even it meant denying herself the joy of indulging in the intimacy she knew Syd was poised to seek. It was too important to her to succeed. This time, she wanted it to be *right*—wanted it to last.

She was jolted from her reverie when Pete sat up with a start. In a flash, he was off the porch, barking and running full out toward the now retreating deer. Maddie could see the flash of their white tails as they leapt over the fence that ran alongside her lane.

Nature, it seemed, would have to wait a bit longer.

On the table next to her chair, her cell phone vibrated. Absently, she picked it up.

"This is Stevenson."

"Doctor, I need your help." It was Syd.

She smiled and shifted lower into her chair. "You do?"

"Oh, I *do*."

"Well, I have been known to make house calls."

"I know . . . and that would be the problem."

"Care to explain what you mean?"

"The kind of house call I have in mind would only make my condition *worse*."

Maddie sighed. "Yeah, I think I know what you mean."

"So," Syd's tone was didactic, "you're the scientist. What do we do about this situation?"

"If I knew the answer to that, I'd be a very rich woman who wouldn't be sitting outside in the cold—*alone*—nursing a facial tic."

Syd laughed. "So much for all those many skills you like to brag about."

"Yeah, well, there are just some things that aren't knowable."

"Really?" Syd asked sweetly. "Then how do you know that?"

Maddie groaned. "Remind me never to have philosophical discussions with you."

"Why?"

"Because you always kick my ass."

"Oh, we're back to your ass already? That happened in record time."

Maddie tapped her index finger against the back of the phone. "Did you call just to make me crazy?"

"No," Syd said softly. "I called to tell you that thinking about you is making *me* crazy."

Maddie didn't trust herself to respond to that. Silence stretched out between them.

"Are you still there?" Syd asked.

"Oh, yeah."

"Was that the wrong thing for me to say?"

Maddie shook her head. "No. No it wasn't wrong at all."

"Why'd you get so quiet, then?"

"Because it's taking every ounce of restraint I have not to jump in my car and roar back over there."

She heard Syd exhale. "I know. I've been walking around here with my car keys in my hand for the last half hour. I'm a *mess*, Maddie. It's pathetic. I've never been like this before."

Maddie felt dizzy. "You haven't?"

"No. Not like this." She paused. "I want you so much—more than I've ever wanted anyone. It's terrifying."

"Syd?"

"Yes?"

"When it *doesn't* feel terrifying, *that's* when we can do something about it."

She heard the deep sigh on the other end of the line. "I know you're right. I'm sorry." Syd paused again. "Is this as hard for you, too." Her voice sounded tentative.

Maddie closed her eyes. "Do you really not know the answer to that?"

"I guess I just needed to hear you say it again."

"Yes." Her voice was barely above a whisper. "Yes, it's hard for me. Yes, I'm crazy with wanting you. Yes, I've kicked myself a thousand times for leaving you tonight. Yes, I want nothing more than to have you in my arms right now. *Yes, Syd—yes to everything.*"

It was Syd's turn to fall silent.

"Are you still there?" Maddie asked after a few moments.

"What's left of me is still here."

"What do you mean?" Maddie was afraid that she'd said too much.

"I think I . . . I just . . ." She sighed. "I think—I think that's the first time I've ever had an orgasm without being touched."

Maddie made a strangled sound that was somewhere between a gasp and a moan.

"God, I'm sorry. I guess that was beyond inappropriate."

Maddie was consumed with the desire to tell Syd that she loved her, but she knew it was too soon. "No. Don't apologize. How could that be inappropriate?"

Syd gave a nervous laugh. "I don't know. Something about you makes me want to tell the truth. I don't want to hide *anything* from you—even if it's embarrassing or too self-revealing. Is that crazy?"

Maddie was incredulous. "No, it's not crazy." She hesitated. "Maybe you can teach me how to do the same thing."

"Do you need help with that?"

"God, yes. I need all the help you can give me. I don't want to muck this up, Syd. I want it to work. I want a future with you."

"Then let's figure it out together. I trust you. I know you would never hurt me."

Maddie's eyes welled with tears. "Not intentionally."

"That's good, then. That's enough for now. I'm not going anyplace. I won't run from you. We have time to see if this is right—to see where it takes us. I realized tonight that this is a trip I'm ready to take . . . with you."

I love you. The three little words that would simplify and complicate everything hung on the end of her tongue. She bit them back. "I'm glad. I want that, too—more than anything." She wiped a hand across her eyes. "I won't run from you, either. I promise."

"Will you do me a favor?" Syd asked, shyly.

"Of course. What is it?"

"Will you call me 'honey' again? I really liked that."

Maddie's heart surged up into her throat. "Goodnight, honey. Sweet dreams."

"*God*, thank you. Goodnight." Syd hung up.

Maddie sat with the phone pressed to her ear for a full minute as she waited for her pulse rate to return to normal. Sweet dreams, indeed. Maybe there were even a few left for her.

Chapter 18

The rest of the week passed uneventfully for Syd, except for the quiet revolution that was systematically transforming the internal landscape of her life. She thought over and over about all those mean-spirited Helen Keller jokes her brother used to tell her when they were kids, consigned to the back seat of the car on long family trips. "How did Helen Keller's parents punish her? Rearrange the furniture." But that's exactly how she felt right now—like she was blindly fumbling across terrain that ought to be familiar, but wasn't anymore. Something had reached down inside her tidy and organized existence and shifted everything around, and it was going to take her some time to get her bearings and feel her way through the surprising new arrangement.

But Michael had been right about one thing—she did still feel like herself. She knew that at some point, she needed to face up to the complex set of realities that loomed ahead of her. She needed to talk with her parents. And she needed to decide what, if any, impact this nascent relationship with Maddie would have on her immediate future, because she couldn't continue to forestall making plans for her life after Jericho.

She had seen Maddie only twice since Monday—the night when everything between them had changed. She had been saddled with back-to-back evening commitments at the library, and on the third night, Maddie had a patient emergency that kept her tied up at the hospital for most of the evening. But they had talked a lot on the phone, and they had made the most of their brief opportunities to be together.

On Tuesday, they met for a quick lunch at Freemantle's market, and they sat in awkward silence at their tiny, plastic-topped table, struggling with their physical proximity in surroundings that made any kind of intimate contact impossible.

Most of their conversation was non-verbal—quiet smiles and casual touches that were anything but casual. Syd laughed when she recalled how Maddie bought a small bag of crunchy Cheetos at the checkout counter, then winked as she handed them to her outside in the parking lot.

"You might need these later on," she said, smiling.

"You promise?" Syd replied, as she snatched the bag and stuffed it into her purse.

On Wednesday night, Syd played host to the regular, monthly meeting of the Tri-County Library Board, and Maddie attended the meeting, in tandem with four other board members. It was abject torture for Syd to have to sit across the large oak table from Maddie while she attempted to give a coherent presentation about her recent trip to Richmond and described likely cutbacks in state funding. She hadn't been one hundred percent certain that Maddie would even attend the meeting, and she felt her heart rate speed up when she saw her enter the library with Phoebe Jenkins—another board member.

Maddie was wearing a tailored gray suit that hugged her long body, and her dark hair fell loose around her shoulders like a thick wave. Syd found it difficult to breathe when she looked at her, so she tried to avoid making eye contact, and she hoped that Maddie would intuit the reasons why.

During a break for refreshments, Syd walked back to her small office to retrieve some funding proposals she had prepared and heard her cell phone beeping from its nest in her purse. She was surprised to see that she had a text message—from Maddie.

8:33 p.m. Text message from Stevenson, M.H.
This is killing me.

She looked around the corner of her office door to see Maddie, standing alone near a shelf of periodicals. She had her cell phone in her hand. She quickly sent a reply.

8:34 p.m. Text message from Murphy, S.
I know. I can't even look at u.

8:35 p.m. Text message from Stevenson, M.H.
Why not?

8:35 p.m. Text message from Murphy, S.
Because I want 2 kiss u.

She looked around the corner again and saw Maddie's eyes fixed on her doorway. Blushing, she ducked back inside and tried to compose herself. Her phone beeped again.

8:36 Text message from Stevenson, M.H.
Meet me in the restroom?

Syd's heart began to pound again. She knew they were flirting with disaster, but she decided to risk it. Taking a deep breath, she walked out of her office and deposited her documents on the meeting table. Maddie was nowhere in sight.

As casually as she could, Syd waked toward the restroom, noting that Phoebe, the only other woman in attendance at the meeting, was standing next to the coffee pot, engaged in earnest conversation with Tom Greene. She pushed open the door to the ladies room and quickly felt a warm hand wrap itself around her wrist.

Maddie pulled her inside and backed her up against the door. She had only a split second to notice how well the dark blue silk blouse Maddie wore brought out the color of her eyes before she was rendered incapable of any rational thought.

Maddie was kissing her hungrily, and Syd felt like her knees were going to give out as she stood there, tightly wedged between the door and Maddie's warm body. She wound her arms around Maddie's back, pulling her even closer as they continued to kiss. When she felt Maddie's tongue graze her own, she knew they were getting out of hand, but she didn't want to stop. There was something wonderfully illicit about this clandestine encounter, and it added to the heady excitement she was now used to feeling whenever she was this close to Maddie.

The sound of laughter from outside finally caused them to break apart. They stood with their foreheads touching, each taking deep breaths. Maddie ran her hands slowly up and down Syd's arms, rubbing and squeezing them.

"God," she whispered. "I can't stand this."

"Me either." Syd leaned back and met her blue eyes. "Can you stay after the meeting is over?"

Maddie sighed. "No. Phoebe rode with me. I have to take her home."

Syd raised a hand and caressed the side of her face. "Can you come back?"

Maddie kissed her palm. "I can, but I don't think I should."

Syd nodded. "Probably not." She raised her other hand so she could stroke the wide planes of Maddie's face. "I suppose we should get back out there?"

Maddie nodded. "Yeah. This would be kind of hard to explain."

"Sooner or later, we'll have to, won't we?"

"That's up to you."

Syd leaned forward and brushed her lips against Maddie's. "No. It's up to *us*."

Maddie pulled Syd away from the door and gave her another incendiary kiss. Then she backed away and straightened her jacket. "I'll call you," she whispered as she pulled the door open and walked back out into the library.

Later that night, when they talked on the phone, they agreed that it was time for them to tell David and Michael about the change in their relationship. Maddie suggested that they invite them to her place for dinner on Friday night and drop the bombshell there. Syd agreed. She was anxious to tell Michael, and to release him from his pledge of confidentiality. She hoped that once their confidence was revealed, David wouldn't hold it against him—or her.

After they discussed possible menu options, Syd shifted gears and decided to tease Maddie. "So . . . Friday night. Should I pack my jammies?"

There was momentary silence on the other end of the line. "You're joking, right?"

"Why would you think I'm joking?"

"Because," Maddie's voice dropped, "the next time you spend the night at my place, you won't *need* any jammies."

Syd's breath caught in her throat. She decided not to tease Maddie anymore. "You don't play fair."

Maddie laughed. "I play to win."

"You've already won."

More silence. "Now who's not playing fair?"

Syd sighed. "We're hopeless, aren't we?"

"Pretty much."

"Well, then, I guess I should drag my hopeless butt off to bed. See you on Friday?"

"If not before. Come early."

"And often?" Syd drawled.

Maddie chuckled. "That goes without saying."

"It sure does now."

Maddie groaned. "You really need to behave."

"But it's so much more fun to be bad."

"One day, I'll find out what you mean by that."

"Yes, you will." Syd sighed. "I guess this is good night, then?"

Maddie exhaled. "Yeah. Good night, honey."

Syd felt a thrill race up and down her body. "Sweet talker. Good night."

She hung up and went to bed, musing about all the possible ways David might react to the news. However it went, it was sure to be one for the record books.

Syd arrived at Maddie's farm half an hour before the men were due. They decided to keep the meal simple—grilled pork tenderloin, salad, and a curried cold rice concoction with nuts and currants that Syd swore was exotic enough to please Michael.

Pete met her in the driveway and happily danced around her legs as she made her way to the porch. Maddie leaned against one of the massive support posts, watching her approach. She was casually dressed in faded blue jeans and an oversized man's black sweater that probably had belonged to her father. Syd thought she looked amazing. But, then, Syd always thought she looked amazing—even when she wore rumpled blue hospital scrubs.

When she reached the porch, Maddie extended her hands to take the large, stoneware bowl from her, then smiled as she leaned forward to kiss her. Syd felt an immediate surge of adrenalin at the contact. *Yep. Zero to turned on in one point two seconds. That's gotta be some kind of record.*

"Do me a favor?" she asked, after Maddie pulled back.

"Okaaaayy." Maddie narrowed her eyes.

"Put that down on the table and come stand right *here*." She pointed to one of the lower steps that led up to the porch.

Maddie complied and dutifully set the bowl down on the large pine table near the door. Then she turned and walked back to stand on the step Syd had indicated. She turned around and held her hands out to the sides as if to suggest, "Now what?"

Syd walked over and draped her arms around Maddie's shoulders. Their eyes were now on the same level.

"Perfect," she muttered as she leaned in and kissed her again—longer this time.

Maddie wrapped her arms around her waist and tugged her closer. When they finally broke apart to breathe, she grinned at her. "Trying to level the playing field?"

"I learned a long time ago that when life doesn't fit, you make adjustments."

"Hmmmm. You should go far with that philosophy."

Syd kissed her on the tip of her nose. "Oh, I plan to."

Maddie pulled her into a full body hug. "God, I missed you."

"Me, too." Syd relaxed into the embrace, kissed her on the ear, and smiled when she heard Maddie moan.

She pulled back, took Maddie's hand, and tugged her toward the door. "We'd better take this inside, or we'll get busted right here in the yard."

"About that," Maddie said as they walked toward the door. "I had some thoughts about how we might share these *developments* with David."

"Oh?" Syd said, picking up the bowl. "Do tell."

Maddie held the door open, and they entered the house and walked down the hallway toward the kitchen. "Yeah. If we're the way we are now when they get here, David will take all of two seconds to figure everything out."

"So?"

"So, I was thinking that this might be a golden opportunity to have some fun at his expense. That's if you're game."

Syd gave her an appraising look. "This is something new. I never realized you had such a devious streak."

"Paybacks, honey. Paybacks."

Syd set the bowl down on the center island and leaned into her. "God, I just melt when you call me that."

Maddie wrapped her long arms around her and kissed her on the head. "Well, then, I'll have to refrain from calling you that until later on."

Syd gave her a squeeze and then stood back. "What's the plan?"

"Just try to behave normally and take your cues from me. If I know David, it shouldn't take too long."

The men arrived shortly after six, and the four of them relaxed around Maddie's large kitchen table with glasses of wine while they got caught up on events of the last week.

David grabbed another handful of Cheetos from the large bowl in the center of the table. "Not that I'm complaining or anything, but what's with the pre-teen treats? Are you still suffering from terminal sexual frustration?"

Maddie smiled sweetly at him. "No. I've just been craving them lately."

Across the table from her, Syd choked on her wine.

David looked back and forth between them. "What gives? You two seem frightfully plucky. Did something happen in Richmond that you need to share with our studio audience?"

"Drop it, David." Michael's voice was cautionary.

"No way." David sat forward in his chair and stared into Maddie's eyes. "She's hiding something. I can tell."

Maddie looked back at him impassively. "It's comforting to see that you're as delusional as ever."

"I'm delusional?"

"In a word—yes."

He sat back. "I simply cannot believe that the two of you spent *three* whole nights together in the same hotel room and *nothing* happened." He shook his head in disbelief. "You really ought to consider donating your libido to science."

Maddie chewed the inside of her cheek, but didn't reply.

"David, I thought we agreed that you were going to drop this ridiculous pipe dream of yours." Michael shot Syd a sympathetic look. "Can't you see that you're just embarrassing Syd?"

"I never agreed to drop *anything* . . . well . . . except for that trial subscription to *Butt* magazine," David said. "I was appalled by all the Photoshop work on those models. It was totally lacking in journalistic integrity."

Michael stared at him in disgust, then turned to Maddie. "I give up. You're on your own with this one."

Maddie sighed deeply and leaned forward, resting both of her hands flat against the top of the table. Her face was less than a foot away from David's. "You're never going to drop this, are you?" Her tone was menacing, and her eyes were fixed on him like twin laser beams.

He was unmoved. "Nuh uh." He casually extended a hand toward the snack bowl, popped another couple of Cheetos into his mouth, and dramatically crunched them in her face.

"Fine." Her voice was hard. "Have it your way." She shoved her chair back roughly and got to her feet. David looked up at her in surprise as she walked around the table and stood next to Syd. She grabbed Syd by the arm, hauled her to her feet, and turned her around so they were facing each other. "Sorry about this, Syd. It's bigger than both of us." Without ceremony, she dipped her dramatically and kissed her—hard and full on the mouth. After a few seconds, Syd raised her arms to grasp Maddie by the shoulders, and energetically kissed her back—both of them moaning into the embrace.

Michael began to chuckle as David coughed and sprayed half-eaten Cheetos across the table. Maddie and Syd started laughing as they playfully continued to nip and peck at each other, before standing upright and facing David with their arms still tightly wrapped around each other.

David dabbed at his mouth and the front of his polo shirt with a napkin. He was incredulous. "You have *got* to be kidding me with this. You two totally *suck*. You know that?"

Maddie raised an eyebrow. "Well, technically, we haven't started any sucking yet, but it probably won't be long."

"You got that right," Syd chimed in and kissed her soundly on the cheek.

David shook his head in stunned disbelief. "I can't *believe* I fell for that. Jesus." He sighed as he stared back at them. "How long has this been going on?"

Syd looked dreamily up at Maddie. "Only since Monday."

"*Monday?*" David climbed to his feet in agitation. "You've been doing—*this,*" he waved his hands to encompass their intertwined bodies, "since *Monday,* and this is the first I hear about it?"

Maddie pretended to consider his question. "Monday? Um, yeah. That's right. Since Monday."

He raised a hand to his forehead. "I need a drink."

"You already have a drink," Michael said, indicating his glass of wine.

"Well, then, I need *another* drink." He looked back at Maddie and Syd, who were now sweetly staring at each other. He smiled and shook his head. "You know, I totally saw this coming."

Syd looked at him. "You did?"

"Hell yes, I did." He shifted his brown eyes to Maddie. "Didn't I, Sawbones?" He looked back at Syd and tipped his head to indicate Maddie. "She's been hopelessly in love with you for months now."

Maddie widened her eyes before she closed them in mortification.

Syd turned to her. "You have?" she asked, in a small voice.

"Jesus, David," Michael hissed.

Before Maddie could speak, her phone rang. Eager for any distraction, she turned to Michael. "Grab that for me, will you?"

"Sure," he said, fixing David with a look of disgust before walking over to the wall phone next to the fridge. "Dr. Stevenson's residence." He stood there for a moment, and then turned to Maddie with a concerned expression. "Hang on, she's right here." He held the phone out to her. "You need to take this, sweetie. It's a Dr. Kramer from UCLA."

Maddie gently disengaged herself from Syd, walked to him, and took the receiver. "This is Dr. Stevenson." They all watched as she listened to the voice on the other end of the line. The color slowly drained from her face. "When did this happen?" Maddie raised her free hand to her forehead. "Where is she now?" she asked, as she sagged against the kitchen counter. "How are her vitals?" She nodded slowly. "Who is her attending?" She looked at her watch. "I'll be on the first flight I can get, but it's probably going to take me at least ten or twelve hours to get there. I'll text you all my contact information." She listened intently for another minute. "Thanks, Dr. Kramer. I'll do that. I'll call you with my flight details."

She hung up and turned toward them. Her face was ashen.

"That was Laszlow Kramer—a colleague of my mother's. There was an explosion in Celine's laboratory about an hour ago—a centrifuge." She looked dazed. "Her lab assistant was killed . . . and she was badly injured." She paused. "She's in surgery now. It . . . it's pretty serious. She lost a lot of blood." She looked at Syd. "I have to go, now. I need . . . I need . . ."

Syd crossed the room and wrapped her arms around her. "Oh, my god. Oh, honey . . ."

Michael already had his cell phone out. "Charlotte to LAX?" he asked. Maddie nodded. "Let's see what we can do. You go get packed."

Maddie dumbly gestured toward the back porch, where her purse hung on a hook by the door. "My credit card . . ."

"Got it," David said. "Go get packed. We'll have the car ready."

She nodded and looked down at Syd, who was still clinging to her. "Help me get ready?"

"Of course." Syd bit her lower lip. "Let's go. I'll help you."

"Okay." Maddie steered her toward the back stairs. "I don't know what to pack." Her voice was vacant.

Syd kept an arm securely wrapped around her waist. "You let me worry about that. Just show me where things are."

They slowly ascended the stairs together. Michael and David eyed each other from opposite sides of the room. Then Michael perked up. "Yes, hello. I need to know what flights you have from Charlotte to LAX that leave *tonight*—it's an emergency."

On the long ride to Charlotte-Douglas Airport, Maddie asked Syd if she would consider staying at the farm while she was away so she could look after Pete. Syd consented immediately. They sat close together on the back seat of Michael's Range Rover, holding hands. David and Michael insisted on driving her to the airport, and Maddie didn't refuse. She knew she was in no position to drive herself, and she didn't want Syd making the trip back to Jericho alone. She had already called Lizzy Mayes and Peggy Hawkes to let them know what had happened, and to relay instructions about how they should manage the clinic and her hospitalized patients during her absence.

Michael succeeded at booking Maddie the last available seat on an American Airlines flight that left Charlotte at 8:55 p.m. They were able to check her straight through to her gate, so she could avoid the obligatory one-hour-before-departure arrival. Her flight was nonstop, but she wouldn't land in L.A. until 1:52 a.m. Pacific time. Dr. Kramer was adamant about meeting her at the airport, insisting that he would be waiting at the hospital all night, anyway. He told Maddie that he would keep her apprised of her mother's condition via text messages as soon as details became available. She knew now that Celine had suffered a penetrating neck injury, a broken arm, and a ruptured spleen. Her condition was listed as critical.

They had little time for goodbyes when they reached the airport—not even stopping to park. Maddie's flight was already at the gate. They dropped her at a curbside entrance with her single bag, so she could rush through security. Syd climbed out and stood back while Maddie hugged David and Michael and thanked them for making the whirlwind trek to Charlotte. She promised to call them as soon as she knew anything definitive about Celine. When she turned to Syd, her eyes were glassy. Wordlessly, they stepped toward each other and embraced. When Maddie pulled back, she took Syd's face between both of her hands and kissed her lightly on the lips.

"I love you," she whispered.

Syd felt her eyes well with tears. "I love you, too."

Maddie gave her a crooked smile and squeezed her hand before turning around and striding toward the large glass door that led to the American Airlines concourses. Syd stood there and watched her retreating back until she lost sight of her as she rounded the bend near the TSA screening area.

It was going to be a long and desolate ride back to Virginia.

On Saturday morning, Syd sat upstairs with Pete in the small sitting area adjacent to Maddie's bedroom. She had wandered around the big farmhouse for most of the morning, feeling unsettled and anxious, trying hard to distract herself from excessive clock-watching as she waited for Maddie's next phone call.

She received a text message from her at five-thirty in the morning, to let her know that she had arrived in L.A. and was en route to the hospital. Celine was out of surgery, and her condition was listed as critical. Maddie called her shortly after eight, to let her know that she'd seen her mother and talked with her surgeon. Celine had sustained a tear in her carotid artery and had been intubated at the scene. She'd also suffered a broken arm and a perforation to her spleen, which had been removed. She now was in ICU, and was still unconscious.

Maddie sounded exhausted, not having slept much on the eight-hour trip. She had managed to book a room at the nearby Beverly Hills Wilshire Plaza Hotel, but was certain to stay at the hospital for as long as Celine remained in critical condition. She promised to call Syd with updates, as her condition warranted. She thanked her again for her willingness to stay on the farm and care for Pete.

"It helps me to know you're there," she said.

"It helps me to be here, too, especially since I'm not there with you."

The line was quiet for a moment. "Thanks for helping me pack. I'm embarrassed that I fell apart like that. I'm usually more in control."

"I know. It's understandable." She wanted to say more, but wasn't sure what words to use. "Did you get anything to eat?"

"I made myself eat a snack on the plane. I found the protein bar you stuck in my bag." Syd could hear the smile in Maddie's voice.

"Good."

"Here comes Dr. Kramer. I'd better go. I'll call you later, okay?"

"Okay." She hesitated. "I . . . you know."

"I know. Me, too. Bye."

"Bye."

They hung up.

That was two hours ago. Syd glanced at the clock over the bedroom fireplace. Not even ten o'clock. She was going to go crazy at this rate. She needed to distract herself.

She pushed the sleeves up on the enormous black sweater that hung off her body and picked up the laptop computer on a small table. Maddie had tossed the sweater on the bed with the rest of her clothes last night, after she had changed for her flight. When Syd had walked up the back stairs later that evening with Pete in tow, she stopped in Maddie's bedroom long enough to fold the discarded garments before making her way down the hall to the guest room. A trace of Maddie's perfume wafted out of the sweater when Syd picked it up, and she held it to her face, trying not to cry. *Oh, what the hell?* She put it on, and had been wearing it ever since.

Maddie's laptop was already plugged in and booted up, so she was able to access its Internet browser easily. She navigated to the *Los Angeles Times* web site and checked to see if there was any local news coverage of Celine's accident. It didn't take her long to find a series of stories and breaking news alerts—the most recent article having been posted only an hour earlier.

DETAILS EMERGE IN UCLA LAB EXPLOSION
Fatality/serious injury reported when CHS centrifuge explodes
By Lynn Hayes

A source at the UCLA David Geffen School of Medicine states that a malfunctioning centrifuge was the cause of yesterday's laboratory explosion. The toxicology research lab was located on the fourth floor of the Center for Health Sciences (CHS) Building adjacent to the Ronald Reagan UCLA Medical Center in Westwood.

Medical Center personnel confirmed that Diego Vaz Peña, a 24 year-old laboratory assistant from Santa Monica, was pronounced dead at the scene. Dr. Celine Heller, Schering Professor of Molecular Toxicology and Associate Dean of the Geffen School of Medicine, was seriously injured, and transported to the Reagan Medical Center complex for treatment. According to sources at the medical center, her condition continues to be listed as critical.

Dr. Laszlow Kramer, a research associate of Dr. Heller's and professor of pathology, reported that the toxicology lab centrifuge was a Beckman L2 that had been slated for replacement over two years ago, but was still in use due to funding limitations. It was housed in an alcove adjacent to Heller's main lab, and was mid-cycle when it experienced massive rotor failure. The unit's safety shielding did not contain the blast, and the explosion hurled metal fragments across the lab, breaking chemical containers and lodging into walls and ceiling tiles. Shock waves from the explosion shattered all of the windows on the southwest side of the fourth floor.

Heller and Vaz Peña were the only occupants of the lab at the time of the explosion.

Vaz Peña was killed instantly. Metal and glass fragments from the blast struck Heller in various locations on her neck and lower back, and the force of the blast hurled her behind an ultra-cold freezer unit, which likely shielded her from sustaining more extensive injuries. EMTs reported that she was unconscious at the scene.

The Ronald Reagan UCLA Medical Center houses a Level I trauma center, acute care hospital, ambulatory care facilities, neuropsychiatric hospital, and schools of medicine, dentistry, nursing and public health. The $3.1 billion

complex opened in 2006, and was the largest building project ever
undertaken by the University of California.

Cal/OSHA has cited the university numerous times for safety violations,
most recently for violations of workplace safety laws in the fatal burning of a
staff research assistant in a Dec. 29 chemistry department lab fire.

Syd sat the laptop back down on the table and tried to compose herself. In a
strange way, reading such a detached and almost clinical account of Celine's
accident made the events seem more real, and yet more surreal at the same time.
The enormity of the circumstances and their implications for Maddie slammed
into her with fresh urgency. She looked around the room at the many indicators
of the quiet life Maddie lived within these walls. She couldn't help but think about
the dinner they'd had with Celine in Richmond just one week ago. It had been her
idea for them to pretend to be a couple—a clumsy attempt on her part to trick
Celine into revealing her real reason for traveling to Virginia.

From the get-go, she had been persuaded that Celine was not as indifferent
to her daughter as Maddie seemed to suggest. Their tête-a-tête when Maddie left
the table to handle a patient emergency proved that she was right. And it proved
something more, too. Celine seemed to see right through her veneer and expose
all of the real emotion that hid behind her pretensions. Never before had she felt
such razor-sharp scrutiny.

Well, her scheme had worked, but not in the way she thought it would. The
clarity she gained that evening was more about her own feelings for Maddie
than Celine's. And it was equally confounding that Celine didn't seem at all
displeased by the reality of what she glimpsed between the two of them. Even
Maddie teased her about that later, when they spent the night at Art's loft in
Charlottesville.

And now? Now they really *were* a couple. Weren't they?

She looked down at a notepad on the table that was covered with Maddie's
illegible handwriting. Beside it was an assortment of pencils and a fat fountain
pen. She sighed.

What were they, exactly? *I love you.* They'd each said it at the airport. Syd had
been surprised by Maddie's admission—and her own. On the long drive back, she
replayed the sound of Maddie's voice saying the words over and over—almost as
if they were being whispered again into her ear. And each time, it felt like a warm
hand had wrapped itself around her heart.

Was that admission too soon? Could it *be* too soon if it were true? Did it even
matter?

David said that Maddie had been in love with her for months. Normally, she
would have dismissed a remark like that from him as just another example of his
serial teasing. But Maddie looked embarrassed—even mortified by his comment.
And then later, Maddie had said the words herself.

And so had she.

Now, Maddie was on the other side of the country, waiting for her mother to regain consciousness, and Syd was here in her bedroom, waiting to regain her equilibrium.

Wanting to keep her cell phone line free in case Maddie called again, she picked up the cordless phone from the table next to her chair and dialed a familiar number. A voice answered on the third ring.

"Hello?"

"Daddy?"

She could hear the surprise in her father's voice. "Hey, baby. This is a treat. What are you up to?"

She gave a nervous laugh. "Well, that's exactly what I called to tell you, but I think you need to sit down first."

He was immediately concerned. "What's wrong, baby?"

"Is Mom there?"

"Not right now. She ran out to the store. But she'll be back in just a few minutes." He paused. "Did you need to talk with her, honey?"

"No. Yes." She sighed. "I need to talk with *both* of you."

"What is it, sweetheart? Did something happen? Are you okay?"

"I'm okay. But, yes, I guess you could say something happened."

He was silent for a moment. "Is this about Maddie?"

Syd was stunned. "Why would you ask me that?"

He laughed. "Because it's nine forty-five on a Saturday morning, and you're calling me from *her* house."

Syd closed her eyes and sank back against the chair. "How do you know that?"

"I'd like to say I'm psychic, but it's really a lot simpler. Ever heard of Caller I.D.?"

"Shit." She was mortified.

"Uh huh. Care to tell your old man what's going on?"

Syd's heart began to pound. "I, uh . . . it's um . . . I need to tell you something." She stopped. The words wouldn't come. She felt ridiculous—like a teenager struggling to confess to a misdeed. But this was bigger than a broken a window or a dent in the bumper of the family car. Lots bigger. She just needed to say it.

"Baby," her father's voice was gentle, "are you calling to tell me that you're in love with Maddie?"

Syd was speechless.

"Are you still there, sweetheart?" her father asked after a moment.

"Yeah." She was incredulous. "I'm here. How, uh . . . how on earth did you come up with that?"

He chuckled. "Are you saying that I'm wrong?"

She deliberated about her answer for only a moment. "No, you're not wrong."

"I didn't think so."

Her amazement continued to increase. "You don't sound surprised—or upset."

"Good. I'm not."

"Why not?"

He sighed. "Honey, it took your mother and I all of about ten minutes to figure it out after we saw the two of you together at Thanksgiving." He laughed. "Well, it only took your mother about ten minutes. I was a bit slower on the uptake. Any lingering doubts I had were taken care of over Christmas."

Syd raised a hand to her forehead. "Oh, my god. I can't *believe* this."

"It's okay, honey. We all knew that Jeff wasn't right for you."

"But, Dad. Maddie is a *woman*."

"Noticed that, too, did you?" His laughter was infectious. "Yeah, she's quite the specimen. I had about resolved that if you didn't soon make a move on her, I was going to have to have a serious sit-down with Tom. I wanted to make sure that *somebody* in this family ended up with her. She's too good a catch to toss back."

Syd sat listening to him in stunned silence. He could have been speaking in an alien tongue.

"So, you're not bothered by the fact that I'm—that I appear to be, um . . ."

"Gay?" her father supplied.

She exhaled. "Yeah." *Gay.* She realized that she had never really said it yet to anyone. "I'm gay."

"Are *you* bothered by it?"

Was she? "No. Not anymore."

"Then I'm not, either. It's all okay, baby. Your mother and I just want you to be happy. And you seem happier with Maddie than we've ever seen you. How can that be bad?"

Syd's eyes welled with tears. "It's not bad. I love you, Dad."

"I love you, too, honey. Is this why you called me? Is Maddie there with you?" He sounded hopeful.

She wiped a hand across her eyes. "Yes, partly. But to answer your other question, no. Maddie isn't here. There was a horrible accident in California yesterday, and her mother was seriously injured. Maddie flew out there last night. Her mother is still in critical condition. We don't know yet if she'll pull through."

"Oh, my god. What happened?"

"Her mother is a member of the research faculty at the UCLA Medical School. A centrifuge in her lab exploded, and she was hit with shrapnel. Her lab assistant was killed."

"Holy shit." His voice conveyed the depth of his concern. "How is Maddie holding up?"

"I think she's in shock. I heard from her early this morning, but not since then. I'm staying here at her farm with Pete, but I'm really about half crazy with worry."

"Pete?"

"Her dog."

"Oh." He was silent a moment. "Are you going to go out there to be with her?"

Syd sank back against her chair. "I don't see how I can. I'd have to close the library, and I really can't afford the last-minute fare. Besides, Maddie may not want the distraction."

"Has she said that?" he asked.

"No, but she wouldn't."

"Do you *want* to go?"

She sighed. "Of course I do."

"Then go."

Her frustration level was growing. "I *can't*."

"Syd." Her father's voice was determined. "From where I sit, there's only one thing you *can't* do, and that's deny your heart."

"But, how—?"

"Your mother and I will take care of your ticket—consider it an early Christmas present."

"Dad. I can't let you do that. It's too much."

"Then Merry Christmas *and* happy birthday."

She shook her head as tears filled her eyes again. "What am I going to do with you?"

He laughed. "Yesterday, I would have said, 'make me a grandfather.' But I can see that we'll have to be a bit more creative about what we wish for."

She smiled at his sweetness. "Don't give up hope. You never know . . . she *is* a doctor."

"Noticed that, too?" He chuckled. "Your mother will be beside herself." In the background, she could hear the sound of a door opening and closing. "And here she is now. Right on cue." He dropped his voice to a near whisper. "Ready to meet your fate?"

Syd closed her eyes in resignation. "I guess."

"Okay, honey, you take care of things on your end, and just let me know the numbers. Call us when you get there and keep us updated. Be sure to tell Maddie how concerned we are, and how happy we are, too."

In the background, she could hear her mother's voice asking him to explain what he was talking about.

"Okay, baby, here's your mother. I love you."

"I love you, too, Daddy. Thank you for everything."

She could hear him handing the phone to her mother.

"Margaret? What's going on?"

She took a deep breath. "Sit down, Mother."

Chapter 19

Maddie arrived at the hospital exactly fourteen hours after her mother was brought up to ICU from the surgical ward. Celine's condition had continued to deteriorate throughout the rest of that night. Her already overtaxed system fought to resist a pernicious blood infection that had taken root after the laryngeal tear caused by metal shrapnel had been repaired. The damage to her carotid artery was confined to an anterior thrombosis that the vascular surgeon had successfully repaired. Her perforated spleen had also been removed.

A day later, she continued to run a high fever, and she had not regained consciousness since being brought in nearly thirty-six hours ago. She was being treated with massive infusions of antibiotics.

Maddie was exhausted. Her emotions were like frayed wires. She sat in a chair next to her mother's bed, quietly holding her hand and listening with her eyes closed to the gentle strains of a Mendelssohn Piano Trio playing from the iPod dock she had placed on a table in the corner of the tiny ICU room.

She felt the slight pressure on her hand as Celine's fingers moved within hers. She opened her eyes.

Keeping hold of her hand, Maddie quickly stood up and leaned over her mother. Celine's blue eyes were open, but they looked dull and hazy. "Hi there. Glad to see you decided to make an appearance."

Celine blinked and moved her lips, but no sound came out. She had been intubated when she first arrived in the ER, but the breathing tube had been removed in the recovery room following her multiple surgeries. Her throat was heavily bandaged.

Maddie squeezed her hand. "No, no. Don't try to talk. You've been extubated, but you sustained some pretty heavy-duty PNIs, and talking won't be an option for a day or so." She smiled at her. "I suppose I should take advantage of this while I can." She felt Celine's fingers weakly squeeze her hand in response.

"I suppose I also should tell you that you weigh a tad less than you did when you arrived here. You suffered a splenic perforation from a piece of rotor shrapnel, and they removed your spleen while you were on the table getting the carotid thrombectomy." She paused and smiled at her mother. "All in all, a typical day for the over-achieving Dr. Heller."

The corners of Celine's mouth twitched.

"Try to rest now. I'll be here when you wake up."

Celine blinked her eyes, before slowly closing them.

Maddie stood over her for another full minute before sinking back down onto the bedside chair. An onslaught of hot tears stung her eyes. Wiping her free hand across her face, she blinked rapidly to clear them away.

As the day wore on, it was clear that Celine had turned a corner. Her fever had abated and she was exhibiting less respiratory distress. She woke up two additional times, and Maddie was at her side on each occasion. By early evening, she was resting comfortably, and the attending vascular surgeon convinced Maddie that she should go on to her hotel and get a good night's sleep. Reluctantly, she consented.

Once she was back in her room at the Beverly Hills Plaza, Maddie phoned room service and ordered a club sandwich and a large cognac from the bar. After showering and changing into a clean pair of scrubs, she sat down on the bed with damp hair and pulled out her cell phone to call Syd. She was disappointed when the call rolled immediately to Syd's voice mail.

"Hi, you've reached Syd Murphy. Sorry I'm unavailable right now. Leave a message, and I'll call you back."

"Howdy, stranger. It's me. I wanted to let you know that Celine has come around. Her fever is down, and she's breathing easier. She woke up a couple of times this afternoon, and was alert and responsive. She's resting now. I'm . . . very relieved, and very tired. I'm back in my hotel room now. Give me a call later, or whenever you can. I miss you." She hesitated. "I love you." She pushed the end button abruptly, closed the phone, and sank back against the headboard of the bed.

The hours that had elapsed since she first got the call about the laboratory explosion had been a whirlwind. She felt vaguely like a bug in amber—lifted out of time and frozen in place. She was unable to do anything but stand by, passively, and observe what had happened to Celine. Her position of helplessness was anathema to her. It left her feeling dull and vapid—drained of all normal and reasonable sensibility. She closed her eyes as, once again, her emotions threatened to overtake her.

She sat up startled when her phone rang. She picked it up and glanced at the readout. It was Syd. She flipped it open. "Hi there."

"Maddie? Oh, god. I'm so glad about Celine."

Maddie smiled at the sound of her voice. "Me, too. It was really touch-and-go there for a while."

"I know. I've been frantic, worrying about both of you. Is she really going to be all right?"

"Yeah. It looks like it. She's a tough old broad. But then, we already knew that, didn't we?"

Syd laughed. "That makes two of you." She paused. "How are you holding up?"

Maddie sighed. "Want the truth?"

"Of course I do."

"Not too well. I nearly lost it in her room today when she finally regained consciousness. I wasn't really prepared for my reaction. It must be some kind of cosmic triple-whammy from stress, sleeplessness, and jet lag."

There was a brief silence on the other end of the line. "It could also be a perfectly human response to finding out that your mother is going to survive this." Syd's voice was gentle. "Why wouldn't you break down?"

Maddie's jaw quivered slightly. "I'm—I . . ." She put her hand to her forehead as she sat there holding the phone to her ear. "Yeah. Maybe." Her voice caught. "God. I almost lost her."

"I know, honey."

Maddie took a deep breath. "I wish you were here," she said, quietly.

"Me, too."

There was a knock at the door. Maddie shook her head to clear it. "Hang on. I think room service is here with my dinner."

"Go ahead. I'll be right here."

Maddie got up, went quickly to the door, and opened it without preamble. Standing in the hallway with her cell phone still pressed to her ear was a shyly smiling Syd. A small roller bag stood on the carpet next to her.

Maddie's jaw dropped, and the hand holding her cell phone fell limply to her side. She stood there with a stunned expression on her face.

Syd lowered her phone and tilted her head as she gazed at her. "If you aren't going to ask me in, then I've *definitely* overplayed this hand."

Snapping out of her stupor, Maddie stepped forward and grabbed Syd. They stood there without speaking, tightly wrapped in each other's arms. Syd could feel Maddie shaking.

"Oh my god," Maddie said into her hair. "I can't believe you did this. I can't believe you're here."

"How could I not be here? It was killing me to be so far away when I knew what you were going through." She lifted her head from Maddie's chest and looked up at her face. The blue hospital scrubs she wore made her eyes look electric. "I had to come."

Maddie pulled her close again and kissed her, heedless of the fact that they were standing in the middle of the hallway. When they separated, her eyes welled with tears. "Thank you."

Maddie released Syd and hastily wiped at her eyes as she stepped forward to retrieve her roller bag. She ushered Syd into the room and closed the door behind them.

An uneasy silence enveloped them. Maddie seemed embarrassed by her tears, and Syd was aware of just how tenuous a hold she plainly had on her over-taxed emotions. She dropped her shoulder bag on a chair and looked around the room.

"So, you mentioned room service. Think it's too late to tag something onto your order for me? I haven't eaten since Charlotte," she glanced at her watch, "eight-and-a-half hours ago."

Maddie brightened up at once. "Absolutely. I called them about fifteen minutes ago. There still should be time to change the order." She picked up a leather-bound hotel directory and handed it to Syd. "See if there's anything that sounds appealing." She gave her a crooked smile. "Frankly, I'm more interested in my bar order than I am in the food."

"I don't doubt that a bit." Syd leafed through the menu offerings. "What did you order?"

"Club sandwich with a side of fruit salad and a ginormous brandy."

Syd snapped the folder closed. "Perfect."

Maddie walked to the bedside table and picked up the phone. "Go get comfy, and I'll change the order."

Maddie had, indeed, changed the order. When it arrived thirty minutes later, the club sandwiches had morphed into two Cobb salads, and the brandy was accompanied by a bottle of MacMurray Pinot Noir. There were also a couple of tiny chocolate cookies sitting on a glass plate that had been dusted with powdered sugar.

They sat down on the bed with the food spread out between them. Syd had changed into sweatpants and a faded UNC t-shirt, and sat propped against the headboard with her knees drawn up in front of her. She held a half-full wineglass between her hands. "God . . . I needed this."

Maddie looked at her with affection and reached across the food scattered between them to rest a warm hand on her knee. "I needed *this*."

Syd covered Maddie's hand with her own. "I did, too."

They leaned toward each other and shared a soft, slow kiss.

Syd sat back, set her wine glass down on the bedside table, and angled her body around to face Maddie. "So tell me more about Celine," she said, picking up one of the salads. "What will her recovery be like? Do you have any idea how long she'll have to remain in the hospital?"

Maddie picked up her own salad. "No idea, really. It could be as long as two weeks, but given the amazing way she seemed to rebound this afternoon, I wouldn't put it past her to be out of there in four or five days."

"That's incredible. It's hard now to believe how tenuous her condition was just yesterday."

Maddie nodded thoughtfully. "You can say that again. I'm still pretty much in shock. I don't think the reality of her turnaround has fully sunk in yet."

"You're exhausted. I'm amazed you're even capable of coherent thought."

"Well, I don't know how coherent I've been. I think I've pretty much spent the last two days communicating in monosyllables." She took a sip of wine. "Celine's surgeon probably thinks I went to med school in Grenada."

Syd snorted.

Maddie looked embarrassed. "Did I actually say that out loud? God."

"I'll forgive you. And I'll even go out on a limb and say it's likely that Celine's little girl has deported herself just fine. I'm sure your mother will be proud of how well you've handled all of this."

Maddie sat back against the headboard. "You know, at this point, I'd settle for her most articulate expression of *dis*pleasure." She closed her eyes. "I can't begin to tell you what it was like to sit there by her bedside, hour after hour, and see her so completely unresponsive. It was frightening . . . surreal."

Syd slowly shook her head. "I can't imagine. Thank god that's behind you now."

Maddie set her salad aside. "I want you to come with me tomorrow to see her."

Syd gave her a surprised look. "Will they let me see her? Isn't she still in ICU?"

"Yes . . . but rank has its privileges." She smiled. "I think Celine would like it, and I'd venture a guess that she'd be pleased to know you're here," she winked at her, "offering me comfort in my hour of need."

Syd rolled her eyes. "Boy, you rebound pretty quickly for someone who was about to crawl under a rock forty-five minutes ago."

Maddie's smile was smug. "Forty-five minutes ago, I was alone and desolate."

"And now?"

"Now, I'm not alone." She raised an eyebrow. "And I'm certainly not desolate."

By nine o'clock, they were fighting to stay awake. In tandem, they turned down the covers on opposite sides of the big bed and climbed in. Aware of the challenge that their physical proximity now presented, they lay side-by-side in forced and rigid silence.

After a few tortuous minutes, Maddie turned to Syd and extended her right arm. "Get over here."

Without argument, Syd scooted over and happily wrapped herself around Maddie.

Maddie sighed with contentment and tightened her arms around her. "Thank you for being here."

Syd lifted her head from Maddie's shoulder and softly kissed her collarbone. "You don't need to thank me. I was miserable at home without you."

They were quiet for awhile.

"I suppose that's something else we need to talk about?" Maddie said.

"Probably." Syd yawned. "Especially the part where I called my father and told him about us." She felt Maddie's sudden intake of breath, and quickly rested her warm hand against the side of her face. "But not tonight. We can talk about everything tomorrow."

"Yeah." Maddie turned her head and gently kissed Syd's palm. "Tomorrow."

When Syd woke up six-and-a-half hours later, they were still wrapped up together in exactly the same position.

Maddie called the hospital first thing in the morning to check on Celine and learned that she'd had a good night, and was still resting comfortably. Dr. Kramer had been there early to check on her, and he gave Maddie a positive assessment of her progress. Her condition had already been upgraded from serious to stable, and they had moved her out of ICU and into a private room. Kramer assured Maddie that she could take her time and get a good meal before heading back to the hospital. Maddie agreed to call him with her own report after she had a chance to see Celine and meet with her attending physician.

By eight, they had showered and dressed and were seated over juice and a basket of croissants in *Le Petit Café*, the hotel's dining room. Maddie quickly downed her second cup of coffee and flagged a passing server, who seamlessly approached their table and refilled her cup.

Syd sat back and watched her with concern. "How much of that have you been drinking?"

Maddie eyed her over the rim of her cup. "You don't want to know."

"Oh, but I do. No secrets—remember?"

Maddie nodded. "I remember."

"I want you to eat something. You barely touched your salad last night."

Maddie shrugged. "I don't have much of an appetite."

"I know. But you won't be any help to Celine if you let yourself get run down."

Maddie let out a long, slow breath. "Okay. You wanna order something for me? I promise to eat whatever it is."

Syd smiled as she picked up the flat menu card. "I think I can handle that. I know your tastes pretty well by now."

"I'll say."

Syd looked up in surprise to see a slight twinkle in Maddie's tired eyes. They gazed at each other in silence for a moment.

"I love you for being here," Maddie said quietly.

Syd felt her cheeks warm. "I can't get used to hearing that."

"Does it bother you?"

"Bother me?" She smiled at her shyly. "It makes me go all soft and squishy inside. No, it doesn't bother me."

"I'm glad."

"It goes both ways, you know."

"What does?"

"*This* does. I wasn't sure about it until I had to say goodbye to you at the airport. But then it hit me like a ton of bricks, and I realized that it had been there all along." She slid her hand across the table until their fingertips were touching. "I don't care if it's too soon. I love you, too."

Maddie looked like she was dangerously close to tears, so Syd changed the subject.

"Are you at all curious about where Pete is?"

Maddie smiled. "I assumed that you sent him to the Inn?" Syd nodded, and Maddie shook her head. "That's fine, but I want you to know that *you're* going to be the one who has to walk the extra five pounds he's going to gain off his blond butt. Michael doesn't understand the concept of moderation."

"No worries. I'll pony up. Now, if memory serves, I promised to tell you about my conversation with my parents."

"You did," Maddie said, as she picked up her water glass. "How did that come about?"

Syd looked past her toward their approaching server. He stopped at their table and regarded them both with a smile. "Have you decided what you'd like to order?"

Syd nodded as she handed him their menus. "Yes. Could you bring us each a slice of the breakfast frittata with fresh fruit on the side?"

He nodded. "My pleasure." He eyed Maddie's empty cup. "Would you like more coffee, ma'am?"

Maddie looked at Syd. "Uh, no. Thank you. Maybe just some more water?"

"Sure thing. I'll have your food out in a jiffy." He turned on his heel and headed back toward the kitchen.

Maddie plucked a croissant out of the basket and dutifully tore off a hunk. "So, you were saying?"

"Yeah. I was wandering around your house all morning yesterday—going crazy—worrying about Celine. Worrying about *you.*" She paused. "Missing you. I knew I had to *do* something. So I decided that it was time to talk with my parents." She smiled. "I got lucky when Dad answered the phone. He made it all so easy for me."

Maddie looked intrigued. "How so?"

"I didn't even have to tell him anything. He just guessed."

"He did?" Maddie looked shocked.

Syd smiled. "It didn't hurt that the caller I.D. tipped him off that I was at your place at an unseemly hour on a Saturday morning. But he told me that he and my mother had already pretty much pieced it all together." She shook her head in wonder as she met Maddie's eyes. "You must know that my father is *still* one of your biggest fans. He actually said that if I didn't somehow manage to end up with you, he was determined to have Tom try and stake a claim."

Maddie laughed, and the silvery sound warmed Syd's insides more than the hot coffee she was drinking.

"I'm glad you find that so amusing," Syd said, once Maddie composed herself.

"Well, can you blame me? I never realized I was such a hot commodity."

Syd gave her an assessing look. "You certainly have the hot part right."

"Flatterer." Maddie sounded surprised and pleased by her directness.

"Get used to it."

They stared at each other in a moment of quiet intimacy.

"So," Maddie continued. "I guess that means your parents are . . . okay with . . . everything?"

"More or less," Syd replied.

"Or less?" Maddie sounded concerned.

"Yeah. Dad still wants grandchildren. He hopes you can find a work-around for that."

Maddie's jaw dropped, and Syd laughed at her shell-shocked expression.

"What's the matter, Stretch? Not one of your many skills?"

"Um. Not the last time I checked." She shook her head. "Is this as surreal for you as it is for me?"

Syd snorted. "Which part?"

"I don't know. A week ago, we were both still fumbling around, trying to avoid or ignore our feelings. And today, we're sitting in a restaurant in Los Angeles, talking about having kids."

"Kinda goes against you're whole not-so-fast mantra, doesn't it?"

"You might say that."

Syd realized suddenly that she probably had gone too far with her teasing. The last thing she wanted to do was add to Maddie's already over-extended stress level.

"I'm sorry," she said, leaning slightly toward her. "Tell me what you need for us to do."

Maddie looked back at her with an even gaze. "I don't know . . . adopt?"

Syd stared at her in stunned silence. Maddie winked at her as their server approached carrying their breakfast plates.

Celine was awake when they arrived at the hospital. She had been moved into a private room early that morning after her condition had been upgraded to stable. Her attending physician confirmed for Maddie that she probably was experiencing more discomfort from the splenectomy and broken arm than from the surgery to repair her PNI. He stated that her color had improved and that the dressing on her throat had been replaced with a more modest bandage. She was still on IV fluids, but her breathing seemed clear and free from obstruction. If she continued to progress at the present rate, he said, she could be looking at discharge in three to four days. It was an amazing turnaround. For now, she just needed rest, and lots of it. They were keeping her fairly well sedated to facilitate her recovery.

Celine was alert, but visibly confused when she saw Syd enter the room behind Maddie. Her eyes widened, and she looked at Maddie with surprise.

Maddie took hold of her mother's hand and bent over to look more closely at her dressing.

"Good morning to you. May I say that you're certainly looking better today?" She stood upright and gestured at Syd. "I'm booked at a great hotel. Look what room service sent up."

Syd stepped forward shyly. "Hello, Dr. Heller. I'm so happy to see that you're doing better."

"Celine." Her voice was barely above a whisper. "Call me Celine."

Syd smiled warmly at her. "Celine. I hope it's all right that I came here with Maddie today."

Celine gave her a faint smile. "Glad you're here." Her eyes tracked up to Maddie. "Did you rest?"

Maddie smiled. "Yes. I had a good night's sleep. Dr. Kramer tells me that you did, too."

She gave a small nod.

"How are you feeling?" Maddie perched on the arm of a bedside chair.

"Okay. Sore throat. Abdominal tenderness. Back ache. Not too bad, considering."

"I'll say. You had us all pretty worried for a while there."

"Sorry for that." Her voice was husky. "Laszlow told me about Diego." Her eyes welled with tears. "Will you call his family for me?"

"Of course." Maddie squeezed her hand as it lay motionless atop the bed. "I'm so sorry."

Celine met her eyes. "I am, too."

For just a moment, it seemed to Syd that they were talking about something else. She felt a lump in her own throat as she watched them struggle with this level of enforced intimacy.

Maddie saw the small iPod dock on the bedside table. "Would you like to hear a little background noise that isn't mechanical?"

Celine smiled at her.

"Let's see what we can do, then." Maddie stood up and bent over the unit. "I'm pretty sure I have something you'll like on this."

While Maddie fussed with the iPod, Celine looked at Syd. "Sit down. Please." Syd complied, and Celine continued to regard her. "How is your library?"

Syd smiled. "Thank you for even asking. It's just fine." A thought occurred to her. "And I need to tell you that my uncle Marsh sends his best regards. He was beside himself when my mother told him that I met you in Richmond. He spoke very highly of you."

Celine smiled. "Tell him it's too late for extra credit."

Syd laughed and heard Maddie snickering, too. Strains of Bach began playing softly in the background.

Celine closed her eyes. "Glenn Gould?"

"Who else?" Maddie replied, sitting back down.

Celine looked up at Maddie. "How long will you stay?"

"That depends on you," Maddie replied. "I, at least, want to see you set up and able to manage when you leave the hospital."

Syd thought that Celine looked relieved. "What about your practice?"

"Oh that's the best part. I didn't get to tell you in Richmond about my new nurse practitioner. I'm in high cotton these days. I'm even thinking about going on one of those golf junkets through Scotland."

Celine rolled her eyes and looked at Syd.

Syd shrugged. "Don't ask me. I keep telling her the wardrobe won't do a thing for her."

Celine looked back at Maddie. "Go to the house. Don't stay in a hotel." Her gaze shifted to Syd. "You, too."

"I don't want to do that. I want to be closer to the hospital." Maddie's voice was gentle.

"I'm fine now. Go to the house. Take my car." She gestured toward the tiny closet in her room. "Laszlow brought my bag from the office. The keys are in it." Her blue eyes met Maddie's. "Please."

"All right," Maddie relented.

Celine seemed pleased. "Remember how to get there?" Even though it was barely above a whisper, her voice still sounded teasing.

"Oh, I *think* so." Maddie tentatively pushed some hair back from her mother's face. She had a nasty-looking contusion on the left side of her head. "Got any headache?"

Celine slowly shook her head. "Not that I'm aware of." Her eyes were starting to droop a little. "Laszlow can help you find the car."

Maddie continued to gently stroke the top of her head. "Okay. You get some sleep now. We'll go check out of the hotel and be back by to see you after lunch."

Celine smiled. "Good. I'm glad you're here." She looked at Syd. "Both of you." Her eyes slowly drifted shut, and the only sounds in the room came from the rhythmic clicking and beeping of the various monitors she was connected to, and the unassuming strains of Bach's *Goldberg Variations*.

Laszlow Kramer was able to direct Maddie and Syd to the area of the staff parking lot that contained Celine's car. From there, it was a short drive back to the hotel where they retrieved their bags and checked out. They stashed their suitcases in the trunk of Celine's black Lexus and made their way back to the medical center to grab lunch, and to spend as much of the afternoon as they could with Celine.

Maddie wanted to have another opportunity to talk with her attending physician, and she needed to visit Celine's office so she could get contact information for the family of Diego Vaz Peña. She had a short, poignant conversation with Mariel Peña, Diego's mother, and conveyed Celine's deepest regrets about her son's untimely death. Mrs. Peña was very gracious, and said they were all very concerned for Celine, and had prayed that she would make a complete recovery. Maddie resolved to represent her mother at the funeral service for Diego in Santa Monica on Thursday.

By five o'clock that afternoon, Celine was adamant that they leave the hospital for the day and head on to her house in Brentwood so they could relax and get a good night's sleep. Rush hour traffic was in full swing, and they crawled along Wilshire Boulevard for nearly twenty minutes before finally heading west on San Vicente.

It was after six when they finally arrived at Celine's house in Crestwood Hills. The Brentwood neighborhood was a community of textbook mid-century Modern homes, ringed by undeveloped greenbelt tracts that functioned as mini-parks. Celine's house was a sprawling, post and beam creation designed by architect Frederick Emmons in 1956. She bought the house shortly after relocating to Los Angeles from Baltimore, and had lived there ever since.

Although Maddie lived in the affluent neighborhood with her mother for over six years, she never truly regarded California as home. She attended local public schools in and around Brentwood before transferring to the prestigious California Academy of Mathematics and Science in the eighth grade. Her tenure there was brief, since she gained early admittance to Stanford University at age sixteen. She never lived with Celine again.

She did, however, return to Brentwood for holidays and summer breaks—dividing her time fairly evenly between her estranged parents and their respective coasts.

Maddie pulled Celine's car into the garage and led Syd through a glass-enclosed breezeway into the house. The interior space was bright, with high ceilings and an open floor plan. Large window panels ran all along the back wall, overlooking a spacious patio and well-landscaped lawn. The décor was clean and artfully spare. Celine's tastes were straightforward, but elegant, and the simplicity and functionality of her home was a perfect complement to her no-nonsense approach to life. The only personal touches were the many books and potted plants that punctuated the interior.

The house was decorated in all neutral tones—the only observable traces of color derived from several pieces of original Bauhaus art—including a Paul Klee that Maddie said she remembered hanging in the New York apartment of her grandparents. The rest of the main living space was dominated by an enormous piano that sat at a right angle to the patio wall and faced into the room. Syd noticed it immediately and hypnotically went to it.

"This is an incredible instrument." She stood next to the six-foot, Steinway Parlor Grand in awe. She ran her hand over its smooth, ebony finish. She bent over the keyboard and played a sequence of chords that resonated throughout the room. "It's in tune. She must be playing this." She stood back and opened the upholstered top of the deep bench seat to reveal an impressive stack of sheet music and several hardbound scores. She lifted out some of the pages.

Maddie went to stand beside her and shook her head in amazement. "I don't know what to say. I didn't even know she *had* this. It wasn't here the last time I visited." She paused. "Of course, that was about seven years ago."

"Well, it's pretty obvious that she's using it, and judging by the caliber of this music, I'd say she's using it well." Syd continued to leaf through the pages of compositions by Debussy, Schumann, and Prokofiev. "My god. She's no amateur, is she?"

Maddie laughed. "Nuh uh. She's a pro, or, at least, she could have been a pro. She started out in piano performance at Columbia before switching to premed. She ended up having to leave home over that decision."

Syd gave her a confused look. "Why?"

"Her parents were both career musicians. My grandmother, Madeleine Heller, was assistant concertmaster at the Metropolitan Opera, and my grandfather, Josef Heller, was on the faculty at Juilliard."

Syd stared in astonishment. "Holy shit. Now I know what Phoebe meant when she told me that your mother was the best musician who'd ever lived in Jericho."

"Yeah."

"What do you think made her change her mind about a career in music?"

Maddie sighed. "I honestly don't know. According to my father, Celine was good enough to gain admission to any top-tier music school. She must have known when she started out in the Columbia/Juilliard joint degree program that music wasn't the path she wanted to follow. I think already being a student at Columbia made her transition to premed less complicated." She smiled. "Even in those days, Celine *always* had a plan."

Syd carefully put the music back into the bench and closed its lid. "The more I learn about your family, the less I seem to understand it."

Maddie chuckled. "What's the matter? Sorry now that you decided to go wading in this part of the gene pool?"

Syd glared at her. "I'll admit that the air is a bit . . . thinner around you. It's harder and harder for me to keep my bearings."

Maddie gave her an appraising look. "Oh, I dunno about that. You're short, but I think you're tall enough for *this* ride."

Syd rolled her eyes. "You know, you're all show and no go."

"Am not."

"Are, too."

"I can prove it."

Maddie crossed her arms over her chest. "Then what are you waiting for? Let's have it."

"Be careful what you wish for." She looked at Maddie with an exaggerated, sultry expression. "Is your mother's living room really the place you want to explore this?"

Maddie raised an intrigued eyebrow. "Oh, please, don't let our location stop you. We have an entire house at our disposal." She waved her hand dramatically. "Carve out any little piece of real estate you'd like."

Syd stood there regarding her, wondering just how far they should take this verbal sparring match. She knew how far she *wanted* to take it. Maddie's eyes were glowing with something more than her usual, harmless challenge. She knew she should probably just back off and change the subject—beat a hasty retreat to safer ground. But, for once, she didn't want to. And judging by the look in Maddie's eyes as their standoff continued, she wasn't ready to wave a white flag either.

Syd felt her pulse drumming in her ears, but she kept her voice steady as she decided to up the ante. "Okay, wise guy. Where's your bedroom."

Maddie suddenly looked like someone had fired a gun next to her head.

"My *what*?" She looked so stunned that Syd burst out laughing.

Maddie threw her head back and sighed loudly as she stared at the beamed ceiling. "You suck. You know that?"

Syd composed herself and touched Maddie's arm. "Why don't we sit down? We probably should talk about a few things."

Maddie eyed her suspiciously. "Am I gonna like this or hate it?"

"Even money on that one."

"Oh, great. You know how much I love sensitive chats." She turned toward the kitchen. "Why don't I find us something to drink, and we can go out and sit on the patio?"

"Works for me. Where should I drop my things?"

Maddie stopped and gestured to a doorway behind Syd. "Down that hallway. First door on the left. It used to be my room. so, please, remove your shoes before you enter."

Syd went to the breezeway and picked up her suitcase. "I'll be sure to genuflect before I approach the shrine."

"Oh, really?" Maddie smiled sweetly at her. "You got that far in your religious education before getting bounced?"

Syd bit the inside of her cheek. "You know, there's really nothing wrong with you that a life-sized condom wouldn't fix."

"You're just saying that because I have an infectious personality."

"Oh, good god." Syd grabbed the handle of her suitcase and headed toward the bedroom. "I hope to hell that Celine has alcohol in this place."

Ten minutes later, they were seated outside on Celine's flagstone patio. Maddie had uncovered a cold bottle of Russian River Pinot Gris in the refrigerator, and she carried it outside with glasses and a corkscrew. They sat on upholstered chairs under a large market umbrella and faced each other as they sipped the spicy, oak-aged wine.

"So. Against my better judgment, you wanted to talk about something?" Maddie set her wine glass down on the table in front of her and regarded Syd, feeling slightly wary.

Syd seemed vaguely uncomfortable, but determined. "Well, I've been doing a little bit of research."

"You have?"

"Yes."

Maddie was intrigued. "On?"

Syd began to color. "On lesbian . . . well . . ." She waved her index finger between them.

Maddie frowned as she looked at her, then recognition dawned. "Sex?" Syd nodded. "You've been researching lesbian sex?" Syd nodded again. She was bright red now. "Well, I sure hope you didn't use one of the library computers—those web cookies are pernicious."

Syd seemed to recover some of her composure as she met her gaze. "Oh, don't worry. I have better sense than *that*. I used yours."

"Mine?"

"Yeah. I had to have something to do while I waited for you to call."

"So." Maddie tapped her fingers on the glass top of the table. "What did you learn?"

"Um. Well, it all seems pretty intuitive."

Maddie nodded. "I wouldn't disagree with that."

"And none of it was particularly scary. Well, maybe *one* thing, but that looked pretty advanced."

Maddie narrowed her eyes. "Just what kind of research were you doing?"

Syd gave her placating look. "What kind do you think?"

Maddie stared in shock. "You were looking at porn?"

Syd exhaled. "You know, it's been an experience discovering how much of a prude you really are."

Maddie was aghast. "I am so *not* a prude."

"Could've fooled me."

"Having a healthy respect for restraint doesn't make me a prude."

Syd took a sip of her wine. "And that's exactly what I wanted to discuss—restraint." She set her glass back down. "Explain the value of this concept to me again, please."

Maddie sighed as she looked at her. "I thought we agreed that we were going to take things slow. Give you time to be sure about what you really wanted before we went too far."

"That's all true," Syd agreed. "But since then, I've made some other discoveries that now demand greater exploration."

"Such as?" Maddie asked.

Syd sighed. "It's more of a *show* than *tell* kind of thing."

Maddie felt her pulse rate begin to pick up. She knew they were playing with fire. "Really?" She tried to keep her tone neutral.

"Oh, yeah." Syd pushed her chair back from the table and stood up. "I can see that I'll have to demonstrate." She extended a hand. Maddie took it, and Syd pulled her to her feet so they stood facing each other. Syd looked left, and then right, before meeting Maddie's eyes. "Great back yard—nice and private." She stepped forward and looped her arms around Maddie's neck. "Put your hands on my hips, please." Maddie slowly complied, and Syd closed her eyes. "Okay. That part appears to be working right."

Maddie was finding it hard to concentrate. "What part?"

Syd pulled her closer until their bodies were touching. "*This* part." Her breath was hot against Maddie's mouth, but she didn't kiss her. She felt Syd's hands moving into her hair, tipping her head back as her mouth traveled an invisible path along her chin and down her neck—gliding, but not quite touching—still managing to singe her with the heat of its exploration. Her nose brushed against the skin at the base of her v-neck t-shirt—the heat of her breath penetrating the thin fabric.

Maddie began to tremble as Syd's hands started to run up and down her arms, gently stroking and squeezing. She felt a tentative lick against the skin at the base of her neck. Syd's warm palms were still in motion, gliding up over her waist and along the base of her ribcage. Her mouth was moving against the underside of her jaw now, leaving a damp trail as it continued on its provocative journey.

White lights danced behind her closed eyes as she pulled her closer and bent down to meet her open mouth. They kissed deeply, their mouths sliding together in a frenzy of emotion. Their tongues touched, probed, and twisted together. She felt Syd's open hands moving against the sides of her breasts in slow, insistent circles. Every touch was electric. Maddie was light-headed. She felt charged and alive in ways she'd never experienced before. She knew they had to slow down or there would be no stopping. She tore her mouth away and pushed herself back.

Syd's lips were wet and open. Her green eyes were shining like pieces of sea glass. She was breathing heavily. They both were. Through the dense haze of her desire, she understood that they would never have another moment like this one, and that what they did now would shape the course of the rest of their relationship. She knew her own heart, but she wanted Syd to be sure.

"Wait. Wait a minute," Maddie said, her voice husky. "We need to slow down."

Syd's chest was still heaving. "We do?"

She raised a shaking hand and ran her finger across Maddie's collarbone, then along her lower lip. Closing her eyes, Maddie moaned and parted her lips. Syd surged forward and kissed her way up Maddie's neck, stopping to suck and nip at her jaw before feasting on her lips again. Their open mouths drifted back and forth—tongues in constant motion.

Maddie slid her hands down to grasp Syd's firm bottom and lifted her up off the flagstones. Syd wrapped her legs around her waist and tightened her arms around her neck—her fingers tangling in her hair as they twined even closer together. They staggered backwards against the patio door, the jolt finally making them break apart.

"Jesus. We have to stop. We have to slow down." Maddie's voice was ragged. She slowly lowered Syd to the ground. She was breathing heavily. "Let's go inside. I feel like I'm gonna pass out."

Trying to get her own breathing under control, Syd nodded and stepped back. She stumbled slightly as she tried to stand on her own, and Maddie grabbed her by the elbow to steady her.

"Come on." Maddie slid open the patio door behind them, and they walked into the house. She went to the sofa and dropped down onto it, pulling Syd down to sit next to her. They sat there in silence while they waited for their breathing to return to normal.

"I can't take this in," Maddie said, filled with wonder. She slowly shook her head. "I've been in love with you for so long. I thought it was hopeless. That I was hopeless."

Syd touched Maddie's arm. "How long? How long have you known?"

"I don't know." Maddie gazed at her. "Since your birthday? Maybe even before that." She smiled at her shyly. "Forever." She angled her body to face her. "You have to believe that as much as I want this, I never *tried* to make it happen. I never wanted to confuse you or complicate your life." She paused. "I still don't."

"I know that." Syd slid her hand down Maddie's arm and linked their fingers together. "I'm not confused—not any more. And the only way you could complicate my life now, would be if you walked away from me." She kissed Maddie softly on the corner of her mouth. "I love you. I'm sure of it. I know this is what I want. You are who I want."

Tears filled Maddie's eyes. Syd gently wiped them away, then kissed her eyelids. "Tell me you love me," she whispered.

"I love you."

Syd crawled over her, straddled her lap, and stroked Maddie's face. "Tell me you want me."

"I want you."

Syd snaked her arms around Maddie's shoulders and brushed a slow line of kisses along the side of her neck and up into her hairline. Twisting her hands into Maddie's hair, she ran her tongue around the outside of an ear and kissed it softly. "Show me how much." Her breath was hot against the side of Maddie's face.

Fresh out of questions, and now in possession of the only answer that really mattered, Maddie stood up, lifting Syd with her. She carried her past the piano and down the hall toward her old bedroom.

She didn't remove her shoes until they got inside.

Maddie was sprawled facedown across the lower half of the double bed, her head resting on Syd's bare abdomen. The steady rise and fall of her back indicated that she had fallen asleep. Her dark hair fanned out across her naked shoulders in random patterns. Syd shifted some the silky strands back and forth between her fingers as she lay awake and looked around the room—Maddie's old bedroom.

For all practical purposes, the woman asleep on top of her had still been a child when she last lived here. Syd found it interesting that Celine had clearly left the room unchanged.

She marveled at the differences between this room and what had been Maddie's room in her father's house back in Virginia. This room seemed less personal—it had fewer clues about the life and character of the person who lived in it. There were a couple of framed photographs on the wall—one of a teenaged Maddie standing in front of a red biplane with her father and a man who, from a distance, looked like a younger Arthur Leavitt. Several other vintage aircraft were visible in the background of the picture. Another photo showed Maddie in a high school track uniform holding up a trophy with three other uniformed classmates.

There was a large bookcase filled with what appeared to be math and science textbooks, but Syd smiled to herself when she noticed one prominently placed copy of *David Copperfield*. There was a small *Dune* poster on a bulletin board over the corner desk, surrounded by numerous award certificates. A Stanford pennant hung from hooks by the large window that looked out into the back yard. Otherwise, the room was unremarkable—decorated much like the rest of the house in a neutral, no-nonsense style.

A Stickley rocking chair with a leather-upholstered seat stood near the bed, and it was there that they had hastily thrown their clothing.

Syd felt a slow blush creep up her neck as she thought back over her actions. She had been like a woman possessed when they entered the bedroom—practically tearing Maddie's clothes from her body. She wanted to consume her—to touch, taste, and discover every part of her. She had never felt this way before, and she had certainly never behaved this way with other partners. The reality of being with Maddie—of finally being able to intimately touch and explore her—was overwhelming. None of her research about the act of making love to another woman prepared her for the reality of being with *this* woman.

In her fast and furious exploration, she needed a dozen hands—not two. She wanted to be every place at once—her mouth, her shoulders, her beautiful breasts, her long shapely legs and thighs. But then Maddie checked her haste—stilled her shaking hands and calmed her frenzy with a single word. "Easy," she'd whispered against her lips. "*Easy.*"

She stood back then and tried to compose herself as Maddie slowly undressed her. Her blouse, her bra, and her pants soon joined the other articles of clothing piled on the oak rocking chair. Maddie's full lips and warm hands softly moved over every newly exposed area, painting her naked body with sensuous touches and whispered words of passion. Syd was drifting on a sea of raw desire, helpless to do anything but respond to Maddie's increasingly intimate attentions with answering gasps of pleasure.

When Maddie gently pushed her down on the bed and moved on top of her, Syd thought she might lose consciousness. The touch and feel of her naked body—the heat and weight of her luxuriously long frame as it slid across hers—was nearly enough to send her over the edge. She clutched at her in desperation, pushing and pulling at her shoulders, her hips, her head—at any part of her she could reach—wanting more, wanting anything, wanting all that Maddie could give her. Maddie's lips seemed to be everywhere at once, continuing on a deliberate and methodical journey down her throat, over her chest—then stopping to linger, endlessly, at her breasts before descending lower to slowly kiss across her abdomen. Syd was impatient for her to continue, and began to writhe and push at her head. "Please," she'd muttered—her voice sounding hoarse and desperate. "*Please*, baby." But Maddie took her time—made her wait while she kissed and licked along the muscles of her legs and up the insides of her thighs. Finally, with interminable precision, she hooked a finger beneath the waistband of her panties and began to tug them down over her hips.

By now, Syd was beside herself, begging Maddie to take her—to possess her in ways no one else ever had. Maddie languorously drew her panties off, and then slid sensuously back up her body so they were face to face—her blue eyes shining with passion. Dark hair fell about both of their faces like a curtain as she lowered her head to lick and tease her mouth. As they kissed, she shifted her weight and ran a hand up the inside of her thigh—gently trailing her long fingers through the wetness she found there. When Syd was certain she'd go mad from the exquisite torture, Maddie shifted her attentions again—gliding back down over the aching terrain of her body, and not stopping until she reached the wellspring of her passion.

Syd thought she might die from the contact—Maddie's touch more intimate than anything she'd ever experienced. Acute waves of pleasure rolled over her again and again, submerging her in pure sensation. This feeling—all encompassing and perfect in its heady mix of love and passion, pushed her beyond endurance to the brink of complete arousal. When, finally, she lifted her dazed head from its position on the rumpled bedspread and saw the naked intensity of Maddie's blue eyes gazing back at her from the heated source of her pleasure, she went over the edge. Willingly. Effortlessly. Endlessly. And soft beneath her, like a musical refrain, she felt more than heard the timbre of Maddie's low voice whispering, "I love you."

Not long after that, as they lay quietly together, her own preconceived fears and inhibitions dissipated as she ventured forth across the sensuous landscape of Maddie's body on her own voyage of discovery. Less patient than her partner, she was on, around, and inside Maddie all at once, in a fast and seamless joining that blinded her to anything but the rush of love and pure physical yearning that had taken her hostage. Appearing overwhelmed by the force and sheer magnitude of her passionate onslaught, Maddie quickly surrendered—throwing back her head and clutching at the bedclothes as she howled out her pleasure.

Then, Syd climbed back up her glorious, long body, and they did it all over again—slower and more deliberate this time—with soft, gentle touches and whispered words of longing.

Looking down at Maddie now, Syd knew that what had happened to her made no sense within the normal context of her life experience. She had always believed that *naming* something she feared robbed it of its power and made it smaller and more manageable than it seemed. But in this case, finally owning up to her feelings had the opposite effect.

Once she dared to make the frightening admission to herself—once she named what she suspected was happening—the emotions just got bigger and more overwhelming. She understood that facing up to her attraction for another woman was one kind of milestone, and that acting on that attraction was another. But nothing could prepare her for the expanse of uncharted terrain that opened up in front of her once she owned up to the glaring truth that she was in love with Maddie.

Maddie raised her tousled head from its resting place on Syd's bare abdomen. She had been dozing, but was startled into wakefulness when a loud gurgling noise rolled and pitched beneath her ear. She pushed herself up on her elbows and met Syd's thoughtful gaze. "My god . . . what's going *on* in there? It sounds like Mount St. Helen's is about to erupt."

Syd stopped stroking Maddie's silky hair. She smiled at her. "I think my body wants you to satisfy one of its *other* appetites." As if on cue, her stomach growled again.

Maddie smiled and bent her head to lightly kiss and lick Syd's tummy. Syd shivered, and Maddie continued her lazy progress up the center of her body, stopping to feast on every piece of real estate she encountered on her maddeningly slow journey. Syd moved her hands into her hair, impatiently urging her forward. Maddie paused when she was fully stretched out on top of her, suspended on her forearms—their faces were centimeters apart.

"I love you," she whispered.

Syd's response was to pull her into a hungry embrace. Maddie sighed happily, relaxed her arms, and sank down onto her as they continued to kiss. Their tongues touched and teased each other in already familiar ways. Syd traced the outside of Maddie's ear with a finger as Maddie gently nipped and sucked on her lower lip.

They drew apart, and Syd sighed deeply. "God, you're good at that."

Maddie gave her a crooked smiled. "You're no slouch yourself."

Syd gazed into Maddie's eyes and stroked her face. "When I was twelve, my parents took us on a family vacation to Steel Pier in Atlantic City. I remember it all so vividly. I had always heard the stories about the legendary diving horses, and even though they had stopped that practice decades earlier, I still couldn't wait to go." She traced Maddie's dark eyebrows with the tips of her fingers. "Tom convinced me to go up with him into one of those Drop Towers—the carnival ride where the floor drops out from under you, and you plunge about a million feet in a free fall." She closed her eyes. "God. I had never experienced anything like that before—that simultaneous rush of fear and exhilaration." She opened her eyes and looked at Maddie, slowly drawing her face closer. "When you kissed me outside Celine's hotel in Richmond—it felt exactly like that." She brushed their lips together softly. "Exactly."

Maddie sighed and touched their foreheads together. "I know." After a moment, she pulled back and kissed Syd's temple. "Are you okay? Is *this* okay? Do we need to talk about . . . anything?"

Syd smiled at her. "Like what?" Her tone was teasing.

Maddie rolled her eyes. "Oh, I dunno . . . effective deforestation methods, long term care plans, the best mutual funds. You know, pillow talk." She lowered her head and fixed Syd with a level gaze. "C'mon. How are you . . . really?"

"How am I *really*?" Syd looked into her eyes. "I'm happy. Overwhelmed. Satiated." Her stomach growled again. She smiled. "Hungry."

Maddie laughed. "I guess we should try and do something about that."

"Do you think Celine has any eggs?"

"There's only one way to find out."

Syd tightened her arms around Maddie. "Does it involve getting up?"

"Afraid so."

Syd frowned and tugged her closer. "On the other hand, we could just stay here a little longer and . . . um . . ."

"Eat each other?" Maddie suggested.

Syd's jaw dropped. "I can't *believe* you just said that."

"I can't believe you just *did* that."

Syd was stupefied. "You really have no shame, have you?"

Maddie lifted the sheet and looked down the length of their naked bodies. "Nope. Must have left it in my other suit."

Syd yanked the sheet back up in feigned outrage. "Oh, my god."

Maddie smirked. "Seems like I've heard *that* before, and quite recently, too."

Syd dropped her head back onto the pillow and rolled her eyes. "What was I thinking?"

"I dunno." Maddie slowly began to kiss her neck. "Maybe I could jog your memory?"

Syd's breathing soon became irregular as Maddie's lips continued to travel across her throat.

"Okay . . . I think it's coming back to me."

Maddie smiled against her skin. "I thought it might."

"I love you so much," Syd whispered.

"I love you, too." They gazed at each other.

"Think we'll always feel this way?"

Maddie kissed her softly. "Oh, yeah. I think this kind of thing rolls around once in a lifetime—if you're lucky enough to recognize it and brave enough to let yourself have it."

Syd smiled. "We have a lot to figure out, don't we?"

"Yeah. But we have lots and lots of time to do it."

"Thank god for that. I may not even have a job next year."

"I've actually been thinking about that." Maddie gazed thoughtfully at her. "How flexible are you?"

Syd smiled wryly. "I thought we just established that."

Maddie groaned. "I suppose I asked for that."

"Actually, you didn't ask for it," Syd reflected. "I think I improvised."

"Hey, let's agree on a division of labor here. *I'm* supposed to be the smartass."

"Sorry, Doctor. I'm in a weakened state due to hunger and exhaustion. I can't be held accountable for my behavior."

Maddie drew back. "Oh, really? Does this disclaimer encompass *all* of your recent activities?"

Syd nodded enthusiastically. "Oh, yes indeed. All of it. You betcha." She sighed. "Who can say what kind of stamina I might have on a full stomach?"

Maddie snorted. "My god. If you had any more stamina than you've already demonstrated, I'd need a B-12 shot just to remain conscious."

Syd gave her a sultry look. "Care to test that hypothesis?" She sat up. "Let's raid Celine's kitchen and see what other discoveries we can make."

Maddie raised an eyebrow. "I told you once that I rarely turned anything down." She sat up. "Here's my chance to prove it."

Syd found it difficult to scramble eggs with any degree of competence while Maddie's arms were wrapped around her waist, and her lips were in constant motion against the side her neck.

"I've never had this much fun in the kitchen," Maddie muttered, licking her ear. "Maybe I should give this cooking thing another try." She moved her hands up under Syd's shirt as she pulled her more snugly against her body.

Syd moaned as she tried to stay focused. The sooner they ate, the sooner they could resume their explorations. In the background, the toaster popped. Against her will, she stopped Maddie's wandering hands. "That's your cue, Stretch. Get over there and start buttering something."

"I thought I was doing that already." Maddie slid her hand dangerously lower.

Ohmygod. Syd's head lolled back against her shoulder for a moment before she forced herself to stand upright and turn around. Maddie's eyes were teasing. She had an unmistakable smirk on her beautiful face.

Syd waved the spatula in front of her. "I'd threaten to spank you if you don't knock it off, but something tells me you'd probably just *enjoy* it."

Maddie snorted. "An interesting suggestion. Wanna try it out later?" Her blue eyes looked hopeful.

Syd raised an imperious eyebrow. "Toast?"

Maddie sighed. "Toast. Okay, I'll make the toast." She kissed Syd on the forehead before releasing her and walking across the kitchen to retrieve the butter from the refrigerator. "Hey, did we leave that wine outside?" She looked toward the living room and the glass doors that led to the patio.

Syd was dividing the eggs between their two plates. "I think so. But I confess that my mind was a little bit fuzzy at the time."

"Oh, yeah? Mine, too. Must be contagious." She set the butter down on Celine's small kitchen table and walked toward the living room. "I'll go out and get it."

"You might want to put on some pants, first," Syd quipped.

Maddie chuckled. "Nah. We're in California, remember? Clothing is optional here."

They finished eating and sat at the table, drinking the rest of the warm white wine.

"You know that I need to go back on Wednesday," Syd said quietly. "I can't keep the library closed any longer."

"I know." Maddie reached across the table to take her hand. "I've been trying not to think about it." They laced their fingers together.

"How long do you think you'll need to stay here with Celine?"

"I don't know. At least a day or two after she's settled in here. Laszlow will be available to help out with meals and any transportation issues that might arise until she can drive herself."

Syd gave her a knowing look. "He certainly seems to be a special friend, doesn't he?"

Maddie smiled. "Yeah. I noticed that, too." She chuckled. "Who knew the old girl had it in her? Maybe she still has a heart lurking in there someplace."

Syd squeezed her hand. "Maddie, she loves you. I'm sure of it. It was all over her face when she looked at you today." She hesitated. "Yours, too."

Maddie shrugged. "Maybe this whole owning-up-to-your-feelings thing is contagious, too."

"Maybe so." Syd stifled a yawn.

"Tired?"

Syd nodded, and then gave her a suggestive look. "But not *that* tired."

Maddie shook her head. "What am I gonna do with you?"

"I have a few ideas."

"I just bet you do. More gleanings from your research?"

"Wanna find out?"

Maddie narrowed her eyes. "I'm not sure. Does any of it require a 220 line?"

Syd shrugged. "Not just yet, but all bets are off once we get back home."

Maddie smiled. "I like the sound of that."

"You do?" Syd was surprised.

"*Home*," Maddie clarified. "I like hearing you talk about home."

"Oh." Syd smiled at her shyly. "Me, too."

"And while we're on the subject," Maddie pushed her chair back and tugged at Syd's hand until she stood up, then pulled her to sit on her lap. "Would you be willing to go back to my place and stay there until *I* get home?"

Syd worked her fingers into Maddie's thick dark hair. "I dunno . . . What's in it for me?"

"Let's see." Maddie leaned forward and nibbled at Syd's throat. "I can offer room service."

Syd tugged her closer. "Tempting, but I can get that at any hotel."

"Not the kind of service I have in mind." Maddie kissed her and ran her hands up under her shirt. Her palms were warm as they moved over her abdomen and covered her breasts.

Syd gasped and arched her back. "God . . . *sold.*"

Maddie lowered her lips to Syd's open neckline and kissed her way down her chest. She kept her hands in motion, and soon, the cotton shirt opened to her waist.

Syd endured the sweet torture for as long as she could before she forced Maddie's head back up and kissed her hungrily. "I'm feeling awfully naked," she muttered against her lips.

"Really?" Maddie ran her hands over Syd's bare breasts again, rubbing and caressing the soft skin. "There's nothing awful about it from where I'm sitting."

Syd pushed herself against Maddie's hands. She was starting to lose focus. She licked and pecked at Maddie's lips. "Maybe you need to make a more thorough examination, Doctor."

Maddie moaned against her mouth. "You think?"

They kissed deeply.

"Oh, I think so." Syd kissed along the side of Maddie's face. She sucked an earlobe into her mouth. "I think I should lie down to make it easier for you," she whispered as she moved her hands over Maddie's body.

Maddie tipped her head back as Syd continued to feast on her neck. "I'll need some kind of co-pay first," she said in a husky voice.

Syd smiled against her neck. "Okay. Will this do?" She quickly found a creative way to demonstrate her good faith. Maddie gasped and moaned against her shoulder, and Syd backed off and slowly withdrew her hand.

Maddie lifted her head and looked up at her with a glazed expression. "Why'd you stop?"

"Stop?" Syd kissed her gently. "I've barely gotten started." She slid off her lap and stood up, pulling Maddie along with her. "Think you can make it to the bedroom?" She tugged at the sides of her open shirt and pulled it off. "Great will be your reward," she said, turning and trailing the garment behind her as she walked out of the room.

Maddie nodded and meekly followed her out of the kitchen.

An hour later, they got up and showered. Syd tidied the kitchen while Maddie called the hospital to check on Celine. Then they remade the bed, climbed back under the covers, and snuggled together in a happy state of exhaustion.

Syd burrowed her nose into Maddie's neck. "I love you."

Maddie chuckled. "I'd say 'prove it,' but you probably would, and it just might kill me."

Syd smiled and tightened her arms around her. "How is Celine?"

Maddie yawned. "She's fine. Actually ate a little bit of solid food. She's asleep now. They're talking about discharging her on Thursday."

"Wow. That's wonderful news."

"It is. I'll still go to the service for Diego in Santa Monica that morning, then head back to the hospital to get her and bring her here."

"Do you want me to stay? I can try to work something out. Maybe Roma Jean—" Maddie laid a finger on her lips.

"Honey, no. Go back on Wednesday like you planned. I'll be just fine. I don't want you to disrupt your work life any more than you have already." She smiled at her. "I'll be back before you know it, and then we can really start complicating things."

"We can?"

"Count on it."

Syd sighed. "How are we going to handle this?"

"Probably no differently than we've handled our friendship up to this point." She chuckled. "Well, with one minor alteration."

Syd slid her hand down from its resting place on Maddie's shoulder and snaked it inside her shirt to stroke a bare breast. "Minor?"

Maddie stifled a gasp. Even in her exhausted state, she felt an unmistakable prick of arousal. "Okay, maybe not minor."

Syd stilled her hand, but did not remove it. Maddie's pulse began to return to normal. "I think our biggest hurdle will be finding ways to manage . . . um, sleepovers."

Syd lifted her head. "Sleepovers?"

Maddie looked at her shyly. "Yeah, you know? Your place . . . my place—the logistics of all of that. Finding ways to be together without compromising your virtue or giving poor Roma Jean a brain hemorrhage."

Syd laughed. "We can save discussions about my virtue for another day, but are you telling me that you finally got a clue about poor Roma Jean?"

"Well, it was kind of hard not to figure out that *something* was going on with her after the first ten or twelve times she fell down right in front of me."

"Oh, so you noticed that?" Syd began running her fingers back and forth across Maddie's breast again.

"I notice *many* things," Maddie replied with a strained voice. "For example, if you keep doing what you're doing with your hand, we're never going to get any sleep tonight."

Syd nuzzled the skin at the base of her neck and slowly moved her hand down to rest on safer territory. "Okay, Doctor. But you're *mine* tomorrow night."

Maddie kissed her on the forehead. "Tomorrow night, and every night after that."

Syd snuggled closer and closed her eyes. "I love you."

"I love you, too, sweetheart. Goodnight."

"G'night."

Maddie could feel Syd's breathing deepen and even out as she quickly drifted off into sleep. In the final moments before she joined her in slumber, she marveled at the sequence of events that led her to be here—in her old bedroom at Celine's house in California—wrapped in the sweet cocoon of a love she never thought she would have.

Chapter 20

The improvement in Celine was incredible. When Maddie and Syd arrived on Tuesday morning, she was sitting up in bed reading the newspaper. Every available surface in her small room was rapidly filling up with get-well cards and brightly-colored arrangements of flowers.

"Wow," Maddie said, taking in the Technicolor display. "It looks like Gladys Pitzer exploded in here."

Celine stifled a laugh. "Funny you should mention her. She actually sent something . . . interesting."

"Really?" Maddie was surprised. News certainly traveled fast.

"Yes. See that basket over there on the windowsill, nearest the corner?"

Maddie walked across the room and picked up the arrangement in question so she could read the small card. "This one?" Celine nodded.

Syd went to stand next to Maddie. "Blue and gold carnations? How on earth?"

"I think she was going for the UCLA school colors," Celine explained. "It's certainly . . . inventive."

Maddie shook her head as she placed the basket back on the sill. "I wonder how she found a florist out here who was willing to torture innocent flowers like that?"

"There's also a slightly more genteel vase of cut flowers from Phoebe and David—with a very sweet note." Celine sounded thoughtful. "It occurs to me that I've had more contact with people from Jericho in the last seventy-two hours than I've had in over twenty years."

Maddie pulled up a chair and sat near the foot of her bed. "Yeah. Nothing like a near-death experience to bring people together." As soon as the words were out of her mouth, she regretted them. "I'm sorry, Celine," she added quickly. "I didn't mean that to sound so flippant."

Celine seemed unfazed by the remark. "I know."

Maddie smiled at her shyly. "Old habits die hard."

Her mother nodded. "Yes, they do." She carefully refolded her newspaper—a task made more difficult by the cast on her left arm. "I have asked the nurses to take the flowers and share them with other patients. They should be coming to get them all shortly."

"That's very generous of you," Syd commented.

Celine smiled at her. "Not really. One or two vases of flowers I can deal with, but this many?" She waved her free hand to encompass them all. "This is just a tad too funereal. I don't really need any more reminders of my mortality just now."

They were quiet for a moment.

"Thank you for allowing me to stay in your home." Syd sat down in the room's only other guest chair. "It's lovely. Stunning artwork."

"Thank you. Although I have to confess that most of it came from my parents—they were the real collectors. I have added one or two pieces over the years."

"I'll say," Maddie cut in. "There's one six-footer that's especially impressive."

Celine seemed embarrassed. "I take it, you noticed the piano?"

"Um hmm," Maddie said. "Kind of hard to miss. When did you get it?"

"About two years ago." She hesitated. "One Saturday, I was listening to a Met Opera broadcast on satellite radio. It was Massenet—*Thaïs*. The music touched me in a way it hadn't for years—almost like I could hear what was *behind* the sounds." She slowly shook her head. "By the time the 'Meditation' played in the middle of Act II, I was sitting on the floor in tears."

Maddie sat forward, stunned by her mother's explanation. She had never known Celine to be so self-revealing. "My god."

Celine met her eyes. "You don't know the half of it. When the broadcast ended, I realized that I had been listening to a vintage recording—your grandmother was the violinist."

Syd's gasp was the only sound in the room.

Maddie quickly ran a hand beneath her eyes and tried to regain her composure. "Why didn't you ask Dad for Oma's piano?" she asked, softly. "You know he would have sent it to you."

Celine nodded. "I know. But I needed to reconnect with this part of myself on my *own* terms, not my mother's. It was only when I finally realized that I could separate the music from the memories, that I was able to let its beauty touch my life again." Her eyes glistened. "Do you understand what I'm saying?"

Maddie bit her lower lip as she nodded slowly, understanding all that her mother was saying, and much of what she was not saying.

"Besides," Celine looked at Syd, "you've got someone in your life now who can make good use of the Bösendorfer."

Syd looked back at her with a startled expression.

Celine smiled. "Phoebe's note contained more than her best wishes for my speedy recovery. She was raving about the newest addition to her community orchestra."

An orderly entered the room, pushing a large metal cart. "Good morning, Dr. Heller. They told me to come in here and get these flowers."

"Yes, thank you. You can take all of those over on that side of the room. I'll just keep the cards."

Maddie belatedly got to her feet and helped the tall man remove the cards and load the flower arrangements onto his cart. When they finished, only two arrangements remained: a vase of cut flowers from Laszlow Kramer, and a small basket of red peonies from the family of Diego Vaz Peña.

"Thank you, Dr. Heller." The orderly slowly backed his cart toward the door. "The folks who are here all alone with no family will really appreciate these flowers."

Maddie looked at Syd and Celine and felt a curious twinge of well-being. For the first time since her father's death, she realized she didn't feel alone.

That evening, Maddie and Syd stopped at a Whole Foods Market on San Vicente in Brentwood and picked out a variety of deli foods and confections for their dinner. They also bought two bottles of Spencer-Roloson Napa Valley Red—one of Maddie's favorite wines. When they arrived back at Celine's house, they quickly changed into more comfortable clothes and took their food items and a bottle of the wine outside to sit on the patio.

It was a pleasant evening and not yet dark. The air was thick with the scent of dark blue Ceanothus, which meandered along the back wall of Celine's garden. The hearty California lilacs were interspersed with desert willow and slender stalks of white sage. Maddie recalled helping her mother plant the white sage not long after they had moved to Brentwood and remembered the stories Celine told her about how the plants were sacred to Native Americans for their curative properties and their efficacy in warding off evil spirits.

For years, Maddie kept several smudge sticks of white sage tied up and hanging from a hook in the back of her closet, hoping the mystical properties of the sweet-smelling incense would push back the darkness that had taken hold of her mother's heart. Tonight, as she sat with Syd and gazed out across the lawn at the row of now mature plants, she wondered if, finally, the magic had worked.

"You're very quiet." Syd's voice was soft and tentative.

Maddie looked at her. She was lovely. Her blonde hair seemed to glow in the fading light.

"You're beautiful. You know that?"

Syd looked at her quizzically. "Thank you, but I think you might be a tad biased."

Maddie shook her head. "No. You are. I noticed it the first time I saw you. There's a wonderful wholesomeness about you. It's captivating."

Syd arched a blonde eyebrow. "Wholesomeness? You're not dredging up that whole Sandra Dee business again, are you?"

Maddie laughed. "Not this time." She thought back to the first time she had made that comparison—the night after their first dinner together at the Inn. She could tell by Syd's expression that she was remembering it, too. "I wanted to kiss you that night. I damn near did."

Syd's eyes widened. "You're kidding me? I spent the rest of that evening kicking myself because I nearly kissed *you*." She sighed. "What a pair we are. To think that we could've saved ourselves all those months of uncertainty."

Maddie reached across the table and took Syd's hand. "I'm not complaining. We're together now, and that's all that matters."

"It's going to kill me to leave you tomorrow." Syd's voice was a near whisper.

"I know." Maddie linked their fingers together. "I'll be home soon."

Syd nodded and sat back, clearly trying to compose herself. "How did your conversation with Lizzy go?"

Maddie released her hand and took another one of the smoked cheese and green salsa taquitos. "Fine. It sounds like everything is under control—no emergencies."

"She really has been a godsend, hasn't she?"

"You can say that again. I don't know how I would've managed this trip without her."

"You know, I owe you an apology."

Maddie looked at her in surprise. "What for?"

"For the way I reacted when you tried to talk with me about Beau. It wasn't fair. I was just bitchy and jealous, and I took it out on Lizzy." She poured herself another splash of the spicy red wine. "He really does give me the creeps. Lizzy wasn't wrong about that."

Maddie regarded her quietly. "Well, I understand what you meant about it being difficult to keep him out of the library. But I don't like him thinking that this means he has carte blanche to pursue you—either of you."

"I know. If it gets any more pronounced, I'll do something about it. I promise."

Maddie sighed. She wasn't persuaded that waiting to see if Beau's behavior got worse was the wisest strategy, but she knew she had to respect Syd's judgment on this. "Okay." She decided to shift the conversation to something less volatile. "I also talked with David this afternoon."

Syd brightened up at once. "You did?"

"Um hmmm. He had a bit of local news. It seems they broke up a meth lab out on the River Road, not too far from the Inn. He was worried that it might hurt their business."

"How? Because it was so close to them?"

Maddie snorted. "No, because they *closed* it. He thought that having a business nearby with such strong local connections would raise their profile among the natives—make the place seem less snooty."

Syd shook her head. "I somehow doubt that this would attract the clientele he's interested in."

"You never know. He also told me that Michael was busy perfecting his recipe for pureed beef liver dog biscuits."

"Oh, my god." Syd stifled a laugh. "That sounds perfectly disgusting."

"Yeah? Well yuck it up while you can. Remember, *you're* the one who gets to work all the extra lard off my dog's ass."

"Oh, I remember. Did he have anything else of interest to impart?"

"To impart? Not really. He did, however, ask me point blank if we'd managed to get horizontal yet."

Syd's jaw dropped. "And what did you say?"

"What do you think I said?"

Syd gazed at her through the declining light with narrowed eyes. "Oh, my god. You *told* him, didn't you?"

Maddie was offended. "I most certainly did *not* tell him."

"You are so full of shit. I can totally tell by your guilty expression that he knows."

"*Ex-cuse* me, blondie, I *told* him nothing. That is not to say that he wasn't able to intuit the details from my stony silence."

"Oh, god." Syd groaned. "Well, I suppose we'll have a few surprises waiting for us when we get back."

"Oh, count on it. At the very least, I'd expect every bed at the farm to be short-sheeted. And if memory serves, he said something about having a U-Haul truck all lined-up and parked at the library for you."

"A U-Haul? Whatever for?"

Maddie rolled her eyes. "I thought you said you did research on lesbian relationships?"

Syd was confused. "I did."

"Well, apparently your sources were a tad too esoteric if you missed the whole 'What does a lesbian take on the second date?' joke."

Syd scrunched her eyebrows together, then she threw her head back and exhaled. "Oh, Jesus."

"Exactly."

"Hmmm. Well, I suppose there are worse things."

Maddie was intrigued. "Than?"

"Than the awful prospect of having to move in with you."

"I would have to agree with—*hey!* Did you just say that moving in with me would be awful?"

Syd smiled sweetly at her. "I guess it would have its compensations."

"That's more like it."

"I mean," she continued, "I *have* always wanted a Wolf range."

Maddie looked at her in disbelief. "Keep it up, Shortie. One more wisecrack like that, and you'll go to bed with no dessert."

Syd snagged one of the chocolate truffles off its plate at the center of the table. "Too late."

Maddie gave her a smoldering look. "That wasn't the dessert I was referring to."

"Oh." Syd met her eyes and slowly lowered the treat. "Did I say awful? What I *meant* to say was awfully tempting."

Maddie folded her arms across her chest. "Awfully tempting?"

Syd nodded enthusiastically. "Awfully."

"How do I know that you aren't just paying lip service to what you think I want to hear?"

"Lip service?" She got up from her chair and sat on Maddie's lap. "What a splendid idea. You read my mind." She kissed her. "I excel at lip service," she whispered against her mouth.

"I'll say." Maddie pulled her closer and allowed Syd to continue with her demonstration. "Okay," she breathed, once they separated. "I'm persuaded. How about we carry all of this stuff inside and explore some of your other gifts?"

Syd pecked at her nose before standing up. "Works for me."

They quickly collected plates and glasses and headed for the house. Syd waited for Maddie to open the sliding door, and as she started to walk past her, Maddie touched her on the arm and shyly asked, "What about the *third* date? Would that be too soon?"

"It just gets better." Syd climbed up Maddie's limp form, then pushed herself up on her forearms and kissed along the solid underside of her jaw. "And I don't see how that's even possible."

Maddie could only moan as she lay there, feeling dazed and weightless. She wanted to lift her arms and wrap them around Syd, but she couldn't remember how to make that happen. Her mind and her body were presently not on speaking terms.

Syd's ability to reduce her to a smoldering heap of gray matter was incredible—and unprecedented. She had never been so responsive before, so willing to surrender control and hand the reins of pleasure over to another person. And *she* was supposed to be the experienced one—the tried-and-tested Sherpa of Syd's novice expedition. Well, some Tenzing Norgay she turned out to be. She could barely move, much less guide or direct the explorations of the inventive woman on top of her.

On the other hand, she thought, as Syd continued to kiss her way across her chest, *I have taken her to the summit.* She smiled. *A lot of times.*

With that realization came a few other welcome discoveries. Her hands appeared to be working now. She slipped them over Syd's smooth back and ran them down to grasp her bottom. Motor control appeared to be a cumulative thing. She was able to lift her head now, and she wasted no time putting her lips to good use against Syd's face and neck. Using her greater strength, she urged Syd forward and leaned up to trail her open mouth over her breasts as she pulled her into a sitting position across her abdomen. Syd wound her hands into her hair and began to moan as Maddie continued her heated attentions to her chest. They were both sitting up now, Syd's legs straddling her lap. Maddie raised her head and kissed her—deep, sensuous kisses that went on and on.

Syd's hips moved and slid against her, and Maddie slowly lowered herself back to the bed. Syd was sprawled out on top of her now—her legs and arms straddling her long body. Maddie continued to kiss her, gliding her lips along her jaw to the side of her face. She moved her hands down to cover her bottom again. Syd's breath was coming in short bursts.

Maddie kissed, licked at her ear, and sucked the lobe into her mouth. "Ever been mountain climbing?" she asked, her words streaming like liquid fire.

She used her hips and her hands to urge Syd forward—up across the plains and peaks of her body toward her waiting mouth.

"*Oh, god, baby.*" Syd's muffled cry was the last thing Maddie heard before they surged together and left the known world behind.

They were mostly quiet on the thirty-minute drive to the Los Angeles airport the next morning. Celine's Lexus glided through the late morning traffic with the grace of a shark, and Syd was impressed by Maddie's ability to navigate the legendary Southern California highways without breaking a sweat.

"You really aren't fazed by much of anything, are you?" she finally asked, as they merged onto the 105.

Maddie glanced at her. "What do you mean?"

Syd gestured out the window at the spaghetti-like maze of traffic lanes. "Well, *this*, for example. It's hardly like your daily commute to work in Jericho."

Maddie laughed. "You forget that I'm not a stranger here, and that this really isn't as bad as driving in Philadelphia."

"It isn't?" Syd was surprised.

"Nuh uh. In Philly, you have a large volume of cars moving at roughly the same rates of speed, but the highways have more potholes than pavement. Driving there was like playing beat-the-clock on an obstacle course that had been carpet bombed."

Syd chuckled and looked out the window at the passing landscape. "This place is such a paradox."

"It is?"

"Yeah. There are so many contradictions."

"Like?"

"Well, think about it." Syd angled in her seat to face Maddie. "I mean, twenty-five million people are crammed into an area that's mostly desert. Bizarre. There are over ten thousand earthquakes a year. And one day, the entire state will probably split apart and fall into the ocean. Pathological. There are well over a hundred colleges and universities in fewer than a dozen counties, making this one of the richest and best-educated regions of the entire country, *and* the lifestyle here is one of the most socially liberal and culturally relaxed on the entire planet. And yet . . ."

"And yet?" Maddie gave her a quizzical look.

"And yet, their chief executive is someone called *The Governator*, and they openly embrace repressive and discriminatory pieces of social legislation that would make someone in Idaho scratch their head."

"You mean Prop 8?" Maddie asked.

"Yeah. It makes no sense."

"Welcome to life on the edge of civilization. See why they call it la la land?"

"I still don't get it."

"It sounds like you've really spent some time thinking about all of this."

"I have."

"Why?" Maddie's tone was teasing. "You suddenly wanna get married to another woman or something?"

"Maaayyybe." Syd placed a hand on her thigh and gave it a playful squeeze. "If it wasn't for the inconvenient fact that I'm *already* married. Let's just say that it's a concept I've been paying more attention to lately." She sighed. "It's *so* ridiculous. I mean, I could fly into Vegas, pick up a random guy in a casino, get married that same night by someone in an Elvis jumpsuit, and my union would be sanctioned and protected by every major religious denomination and civil government in this country. On the other hand," she looked at Maddie's strong profile, etched against the backlight of the driver's-side window, "I could take a year getting to know a wonderful and accomplished woman; fall completely in love with her and want to share my life with her in responsible and mature ways, but be barred from any of that by the *same* laws of god and man that say it's okay to stand up with a stranger in front of Elvis."

Maddie shook her head. "Maybe Virginia isn't the best place for you to settle, then."

"You either, by this definition."

"True. But according to your exhaustive study, the most liberal state in the union isn't very hospitable, either."

Syd smiled at her slyly. "Well, there's always Vermont."

Maddie laughed. "It *is* cold there. Maybe I'd keep better."

"Afraid you're wearing out, Doctor?"

"Not wearing out so much as wearing *down*. I've had a bit more, um, activity than I'm used to, lately."

"Are you complaining?"

Maddie took hold of her hand and placed it back on her thigh. "Does it seem like I'm complaining?"

"Not from my vantage point, no."

"Yours is the only one that counts."

Syd gently ran her hand back and forth over the top of Maddie's leg. The denim of her jeans felt warm and soft. "I'm going to miss you so much."

"Me, too."

Syd yawned. "At least I can catch up on my sleep during the flight."

Maddie smirked at her. "Something been keeping you up at night?"

"You *might* say that. I feel guilty for how much I've been neglecting poor Jane."

"Jane? *Jane Eyre?*"

Syd shook her head. "Austen. I've moved on. I'm afraid I left poor Elizabeth stranded at Rosings with Lady Catherine."

"Oh, dear. Well, I suppose she could always amuse herself by admiring the craftsmanship of Her Ladyship's chimney piece."

Syd swatted her on the arm. "You are *such* a scholar, you know that? Do you trot these tidbits out just to impress me?"

"That depends . . . is it working?"

"Definitely."

"Then, yes, it's intentional."

Syd studied her as she slowed down to make the turn into the airport campus. "You *are* a lot like Mr. Darcy, you know."

"I am?"

"Oh, yeah. Tall, dark, accomplished, gorgeous . . . and vain."

"*Vain?*"

"Oh, lemme guess . . . you're comfortable with *all* of those comparisons but the *last* one?"

Maddie frowned at her.

"I rest my case. Vain."

Maddie turned into the horseshoe-shaped terminal access area. *"Fine.* See if I invite *you* to come fish at Pemberley."

Syd leaned across the console and kissed her cheek, then quickly nuzzled her ear. "I don't need to go fishing any more. I've already bagged my prize." She pecked her cheek again. "And I'm not tossing you back."

Maddie couldn't hide her smile. "Oh, so that's a *hook* in my ass? And all this time, I thought I was sitting on a safety pin."

Syd sighed and sat back against her seat. "You're lucky I love you."

"I sure am." They smiled at each other.

Maddie found a parking spot in one of the pullover lanes near Terminal 1. They got out of the car and unloaded Syd's suitcase from the trunk.

"I wish I could come in and wait with you."

"I know," Syd said. "But you can't go through security with me, and my flight leaves in an hour."

Maddie nodded. "Wanna change your mind and stay here with me?"

Syd smiled at her sadly. "You know I do, but I can't." She took a step forward and laid her hand on Maddie's forearm. "I love you."

Maddie pulled her into a tight hug. "I love you, too." She kissed the top of her head before releasing her. "Call me when you get to Charlotte?"

Syd nodded. They stood there staring at each other for a moment, while other passengers came and went, and diesel fumes from an endless line of hotel shuttles filled the air around them.

Syd squinted as she continued to gaze at Maddie. "We *are* still in California, right?"

"Yeeesss," Maddie answered, with a trace of suspicion.

"Then nobody's going to care if I do this." She pulled Maddie's head down and kissed her soundly.

Maddie smiled. "I sure won't complain."

"Good luck tomorrow. I'll call you." Syd kissed her again quickly, then turned and headed for the entrance to Terminal 1, pulling her small roller bag behind her. She looked back before she entered the security screening area and saw that Maddie was still standing there, leaning against the back of Celine's car. She took a deep breath and turned the corner, heading for a vacant seat on a long row of metal-framed chairs, where she could sit down and remove her shoes.

Maddie spent several hours at the hospital with her mother before leaving in the early afternoon to return to Brentwood and make the house ready for her homecoming the next day. Celine had been up and walking without assistance, so it was clear she would be able to stay in her own bedroom at home, and needed only modest alterations in her bathroom to accommodate her during her convalescence.

With Laszlow's assistance, Maddie had arranged for a nurse to make an in-home visit once a day for the first week, and Celine's housekeeper was available to offer additional assistance with grocery shopping and meal preparation. Maddie had planned to remain with Celine through the weekend, but her mother insisted that by the first of the week, she should be able to manage very well on her own. Celine was grateful for Maddie's assistance, but remained adamant that Maddie should not neglect her medical practice for any longer than was necessary.

Wednesday evening, she sat alone on the patio with her glass of wine, listening to Celine's stereo and thinking back over all that had occurred since she got Laszlow's phone call on Friday night. The changes in her life had been extraordinary. She and Syd had crossed the final relationship threshold and explored the physical side of their attraction—with a vengeance. She smiled to herself. Who would have guessed that, once her passion was unleashed, Syd would be such a dervish in the bedroom?

Guess I just got lucky, she thought. *But, wow, what a turnaround.* And a turn on, as it happened, for Maddie found that she responded to Syd in ways she'd never experienced before. She'd never been so wholly *present* with another lover—so willing to surrender herself to pleasure. It had to be love. That had to be the difference. For the first time in her life, she knew that she was holding nothing back, keeping nothing in reserve. It was exhilarating, and it was terrifying, but it was a risk she was willing to take. Syd was worth it. Together, they were worth it.

Inside the house, the CD changer whirred as it spooled up another disc. Maddie recognized the opening bars of a Schubert lied, "*Sei mir gegrüßt.*" Something about the recording struck her immediately, and she sat up with a start as she realized what it was. The violin and piano parts were seamless—perfectly melded and achingly familiar. Her heart began to race. When had Celine done this? When had she taken those old taped recordings and transferred them to disc?

Then she heard it—like an echo from another time. The voice. Singing in German. German—the language Oma and Opa spoke at home. It was low voice—doleful with a trace of immaturity—but tuneful and full of promise. It was an untrained voice, but it blended beautifully with the simple sentiments of a love lost, and rediscovered. It was her voice—her voice at age nineteen.

They had gone to New York for the Christmas holiday. Opa's seventy-fifth birthday was on the last night of Hanukkah that year, and Oma and Celine planned the family recital as a special gift for him. Maddie had been rehearsing the Schubert song for weeks. The choir director at Stanford had worked privately with her on phrasing and diction.

She remembered that her grandparents' Upper East Side apartment had been full of formally dressed friends and luminaries from the New York music world. Their living room was illuminated by hundreds of candles—the large sterling silver menorah placed prominently on the mantelpiece behind the gleaming Steinway.

She recalled Opa introducing her to the legendary soprano Anna Moffo—

elegant in a dark red gown and diamond earrings. The great singer kissed her warmly on both cheeks and praised her for her moving performance. Maddie could still recall the scent of her perfume. For the rest of the evening, a trace of orange blossom and jasmine stayed with her as she moved through the candlelit rooms trying to avoid notice.

Even her father came to New York for that special night. She remembered how he stood at the back of the room during her performance—tall and handsome in his black tuxedo and gazing at her with a mixture of pride and sadness. It was one of the last times she ever saw her parents together. She recalled seeing tears in Celine's eyes when her father awkwardly embraced her, before leaving to return to his hotel.

Less than a year later, Josef Heller was dead from a brain aneurysm. Six months after that, on the eve of Shabbat, his widow, Madeleine, slipped on a patch of ice and struck her head on the concrete balustrade that surrounded her terrace. She never regained consciousness.

As far as Maddie knew, Celine had not returned to New York since she settled her parent's affairs and sold their Manhattan apartment. The only reminders of those years were a few paintings, the ornate menorah that now adorned a shelf in Celine's study, and the piano that once had belonged to Oma, then to Celine, and now was a permanent fixture in her own life. And, of course, there was the music. Somehow, Celine had reconnected with the music—the silver thread that once had bound them all together in ways the blood they shared never could.

The Schubert lied ended, and there was a prolonged hiss of dead air before the next selection began. Maddie remembered that colleagues of Opa's from Juilliard had been on hand to record the recital, and guests at the gathering politely withheld their applause so the large reel-to-reel recorder could be stopped several seconds after the last note sounded. In her mind's eye, Maddie could see herself, as she stood there, stone-faced in the bend of the big piano. Celine sat behind her at the keyboard, and Oma was seated with her violin on a low chair to her left. After the room had erupted in dignified but enthusiastic applause, Maddie shyly bowed, and then quickly left the front of the room to take her place at an innocuous location in the audience. Celine and her mother continued to play for the better part of an hour, finding in this performance a perfect harmony and balance they had never managed to achieve in the rest of their relationship.

Maddie never sang again after that night. When she returned to Stanford, she withdrew from the concert choir, citing the rigor of her premed curriculum as her excuse.

And Celine stopped playing the piano. Until two years ago, when everything changed for her. Two years ago. Maddie thought about that. *Dad died two years ago.* Was there any connection? It was too coincidental. There *had* to be. She resolved to ask her mother about it tomorrow when they were back at home together.

Home? That was new. She'd never called Celine's house "home" before. She shook her head to clear it. So many things were changing. She couldn't keep up with it all. It was too confusing. On the table next to her wine glass, her cell phone vibrated. She picked it up and opened it.

"This is Stevenson."

"So what was the penalty for contributing to the obesity of a canine? I forget."

She smiled into the phone. "Hey, sweetheart. I take it this means you've picked up the package and are safely back at the clubhouse?"

"Well, you might say that. David and Michael were kind enough to bring Pete back out here to save me the extra trip to the Inn."

"How is he?"

"He's fine—happy and *huge*. You weren't kidding. I think he's put on a good five pounds."

"Told ya. Michael doesn't understand that whole concept of moderation."

"I believe you now. I can see that my blond shadow and I are in for a few robust walks around the property—starting tomorrow." She sighed into the phone.

"What is it?"

"Tomorrow. Tomorrow, I'll go to work, then come back here, and you still won't be at home."

"I know, baby. But it won't be long." She paused. "Are you okay there by yourself? I know it's selfish of me to ask you to stay there."

"Selfish? Are you kidding? I *love* being here. I just miss you."

"I know. I miss you, too."

"Are you okay? How was Celine today?"

"She was fine. Better than fine, really. I think I may be able to come home on Monday."

"Monday?" She could hear the excitement in Syd's voice, and it warmed her heart. "Really? That's wonderful."

"Ummm hmmm. Know anybody who might be willing to pick me up at the airport?"

"Oh, I *think* so." They were quiet for a moment. "Everything okay, Stretch? You seem subdued."

"I'm sorry. I've been sitting here listening to some music I didn't know Celine had—an old recording of her playing with my grandmother in New York." She omitted disclosing her role in the performance, thinking she would save that revelation for later.

"My god. How did you find that?"

"I didn't have to look. She obviously had been listening to it. It was in her CD player."

"Wow." Syd sounded surprised. "She wasn't kidding about reconnecting with her past, was she?"

Maddie shook her head. "Apparently not." She sighed. "Anyway, listening to it brought back lots of memories."

"Maybe you should talk about those with her."

"I was thinking the same thing."

"Do you think you should tell her the truth about us?"

Maddie thought about that. "You mean our little song-and-dance in Richmond?"

"Yes."

"I don't see any reason to correct the record, now, do you? I mean, the end result is the same."

"I agree." Syd was quiet for a moment. "It might make for an amusing anecdote one day."

Maddie smiled. "That's certainly true. Talk about putting feet to your prayers."

"Why, Doctor. Who knew you had such a spiritual side?"

"Oh," Maddie said in a teasing tone. "You'd be amazed. I've been praising god a *whole* lot lately."

"I know," Syd quipped. "I've heard you."

"That you have."

They were quiet again.

"As much as I don't want to," Syd said, "I need to go so I can try and get some sleep. Tomorrow will be tough enough without being bleary-eyed."

"I know. Good luck with that. And prepare to be besieged by people wanting details about Celine."

"No worries, I can handle it. I hope it goes well tomorrow. Call me when you can?"

"Of course. I love you."

"I love you, too. G'night."

"Night, baby. Sleep well."

"In your bed? How could I do otherwise?" She laughed merrily and hung up before Maddie could answer.

The memorial mass for Diego Vaz Peña took place on Thursday morning at the imposing St. Anne Catholic Church on Colorado Avenue in Santa Monica. Diego had been buried on the previous Monday, but his family opted to hold a later, more public service at the home of their largely Spanish-speaking congregation. Maddie sat with other friends and neighbors of the Peña family near the back of the church, which was filled to near capacity with mourners. At the end of the service, she stood, dutifully, in a long line and waited to pay her respects to Diego's family. His mother, Mariel, seemed to recognize her instantly because of her likeness to Celine, and she clamored forward from the receiving line to take Maddie's hands and thank her for being present.

"*Gracias por venir. ¿Cómo esta su mama?*"

Maddie squeezed her hands warmly. "*Esta bien, gracias.* We are so sorry for your loss."

"*Gracias. Rezare para que La Virgen Maria velé por su mama.*" She hesitated, her eyes wet with tears. "She was kind to my son."

Maddie felt tears welling in her own eyes and nodded politely before moving on, allowing the innumerable others behind her access to the Peña family. It was remarkable to her that Celine even knew Diego's family. Clearly, there were whole sides to her mother's character and life in Los Angeles that Maddie knew nothing about. She felt awkward about that—awkward and embarrassed. It was time for her to step up and try to move beyond the pain of their shared past. On the drive back to UCLA, she resolved to do just that.

Celine was dressed and ready when Maddie arrived at her room shortly after one. Her discharge papers had all been signed, and her few personal belongings had been collected and boxed-up. Laszlow Kramer was there, graciously waiting with Celine until Maddie returned from Santa Monica. A nurse arrived with a wheelchair, and the three of them made their way downstairs to the spacious discharge lobby, where Celine waited with Laszlow while Maddie retrieved her car from the parking lot. Laszlow kissed Celine on the cheek and departed to resume his afternoon office hours, saying he would call her at home that evening.

Celine was mostly quiet during the drive, but she did ask Maddie for details about the memorial service for her lab assistant. She was very gratified that Maddie had opted to attend the service and extend her condolences to Diego's family in such a personal way.

"His mother seems very fond of you," Maddie commented, glancing at Celine.

Celine was looking out her window at the passing scenery. "That's more a testament to her character than mine, I'm afraid. I only met her on a couple of occasions when they visited the lab."

"Well, you obviously made a strong impression on her. She said you were always very kind to her son."

Celine shrugged. She seemed uncomfortable with the conversation. "He was an exceptional student. I did what I could to assist him in the program."

"I know. I read the letters you wrote on his behalf to the scholarship committee." Celine looked at her in surprise. "Copies were in the folder your assistant gave me when I asked her for his personal contact information."

Celine nodded, but didn't respond, plainly wanting to drop the conversation. Maddie decided to respect her mother's self-effacing posture—at least where her kindness to Diego was concerned.

In twenty minutes, they were turning into her driveway. Maddie unclipped her seatbelt. "Home again."

Celine looked at her with a small smile on her mostly unlined face. "I can't wait to sit down with a cup of hot tea in my garden."

"I think that can be arranged." Maddie got out and helped her mother into the house. "But let's make it a short one. I don't want you to get overtired."

Celine raised an eyebrow. "Yes, Doctor. I promise to follow orders."

Maddie laughed. "Sorry. Occupational hazard, you know?"

"Oh, I know." Celine walked slowly across her living room and ran a hand along the edge of the piano. "It's going to be a while before I can give this a workout," she said sadly, looking at the cast on her left arm. She sighed and shook her head. Her blue eyes met Maddie's. "So tell me. Is Syd as good a musician as Phoebe says she is?"

Maddie smiled. "Oh, yeah. She's a lot like you."

"What do you mean?" Celine sounded intrigued.

"She got her artist's certificate at Eastman, but switched her major to Music Ed."

Celine seemed surprised. "What instrument?"

"Violin."

"Ah. No wonder you gave her Oma's necklace."

Maddie nodded. "I had other inducements, too."

"I'm sure you did." Celine walked to the large doors that led to her patio. "How about that tea?"

"I'm all over it," Maddie said, walking to the kitchen. "Darjeeling or Earl Grey?"

"Surprise me," Celine said, opening the large door and stepping outside into the sun.

The afternoon light was wonderful. Celine seemed more relaxed than Maddie had seen her in years. She was reclining on an upholstered chaise with her long legs crossed at the ankles. Maddie thought she looked remarkable. If it weren't for the cast on her left arm and the small bandage at her neck, it would be impossible to imagine the ordeal she had just survived.

Maddie sipped from her mug of hot, fragrant tea. This was one of the few rituals she shared with her mother. They often had tea together in the garden, during school breaks or holidays when Maddie was with her in Brentwood. She found the pastime to be quaintly European—a holdover from Celine's childhood in Manhattan and growing up with immigrant parents.

She looked at her mother who was basking in the late afternoon heat. The sun was at treetop level, and the plants along the back wall of the yard were alive with light and color. *It's now or never*, Maddie thought. She set her mug down on the glass top of the table and tried to make her voice sound calmer than she felt.

"I played the CD last night—the recording from Opa's birthday celebration."

Celine looked at her with a startled expression. "You did?"

Maddie nodded.

Celine looked down at her hands, which were folded across her abdomen. Then she looked back up at Maddie. Her expression was undecipherable. "And?"

"And I was surprised. Surprised that you had it, and even more surprised that you were listening to it." She shook her head. "I felt so many things, remembered so many things. Things that I hadn't thought about in years." She met her mother's eyes. "You told us the other day that you bought the piano about two years ago." Celine nodded slowly. "Did that have anything to do with Dad's death?"

Celine closed her eyes and turned her head so Maddie couldn't see her face. "Why would you think that?" she asked, her voice quiet.

"To tell the truth, I don't know *what* to think. I only know that something seems different. You seem different. I *feel* different." She leaned forward. Her heart was pounding. "Celine?" She hesitated. "Mom." Her mother looked at her with surprise. "Talk to me. For once—*please*. Talk to me." She could feel her eyes welling with tears, but she didn't try to staunch them.

"All right." Her voice was softer than Maddie had ever heard it before. "What do you want to know?"

"Tell me what happened with you and Dad. I need to know."

Celine sighed and leaned her head back against the chaise, never breaking eye contact with her. "Why? It won't change anything."

Maddie wasn't going to let this moment pass. "You're wrong. It might change *everything.*"

Silence stretched out between them. Somewhere down the street, a lawnmower roared to life. "I never talked about it—not to anyone," Celine said after what felt like an eternity. She met Maddie's eyes. "Especially not to you. I couldn't."

"Why not?"

"Because he begged me not to tell you. He made me promise." She gave Maddie a smile tinged with sadness. "And I could never refuse him anything."

Maddie looked at her through a haze of confusion. "I don't understand. Why would he make you promise that? What didn't he want me to know?"

Celine sighed. "He loved you so much. We both did. We didn't want to hurt you."

"Hurt me? How could anything hurt me more than losing you? Than losing my home?"

"He made me promise, Maddie." She hesitated. "And I did. I kept my promise, and I lost you. I lost you both."

Maddie was confused. She had to keep Celine talking. "Dad's gone, but *I'm* not lost. Not anymore. Please, Mom. Please. Just tell me what happened."

Celine took a deep breath. "I never loved anyone like I loved your father. He was the entire world to me. When I met him, I felt that finally, *finally* I had found someone who loved all of me. Every part. He was so lively, so strong and so sure of himself. I had never known happiness like that. Not ever. Then you came along." She met Maddie's eyes and smiled at her.

Maddie had the sense that she was looking at her mother through a portal to the past.

"I realized then what true happiness was. You were perfect. We were so happy together, living our fairy tale life in the country." She smiled. "Even Oma began to soften. She actually visited us there, just after you were born. We played Brahms duets while you napped upstairs in your crib."

She sighed and rubbed her eyes.

"Davis was busy getting his practice off the ground. As the years went by, he worked longer and longer hours. He was out of town more and more frequently, attending conferences and serving on state boards. He became a trustee at Penn. Then I got the job with Lilly in Roanoke, and soon we were passing each other in the hallways at home—practically like strangers." She looked at Maddie with sadness. "We kept all of this from you as much as we could. We tried to protect you from how much we had grown apart."

She fell silent again, lost in her memories. "Then one day, I got sick at work. It had been happening a lot, but I hadn't told your father yet. I was pregnant again."

Maddie was stunned, and stared at her mother, unable to say anything.

"I drove home from Roanoke early. You were still at school. When I got to the farm, I was surprised to see that your father was at home, and not at the clinic." She hesitated. "He wasn't alone." She raised her hand to her forehead. "We didn't even make a scene. When I saw who was there, I had some kind of eerie epiphany, and I knew immediately what was happening. And he knew that I knew."

Maddie gasped. "Dad had an affair?"

Celine nodded. "It had been going on for some time. Your father was devastated that I found out, and he was terrified that I would tell you."

Maddie felt like the ground was pitching up beneath her feet. It was incredible. It was impossible. "Who? Who was it?"

Celine looked at her with her heart in her eyes. "It was Arthur Leavitt."

Maddie was dumbfounded. *Uncle Art? Dad? Oh my god.* She saw flashes of white behind her eyes. She was afraid she might hyperventilate. "Jesus. Oh, god."

Celine reached out a hand toward her. "Maddoe . . . oh, honey . . . I'm so sorry. We never should have lied to you. We thought it was for your own good. When it became clear to both of us that you were gay, too, I tried to convince your father that it was time to tell you the truth. But he refused. He couldn't face it. I was bound by my promise to him. A promise I stubbornly kept even as it cost me the love of my only child."

Maddie gazed at her mother with wonder. "What happened to the baby?"

"I lost it. I left Virginia and went back to Manhattan. My parents were characteristically unforgiving. They saw the end of the marriage as *my* failure. I didn't even tell them I was pregnant until I miscarried in the middle of my second trimester. That's why I didn't see you during those first few months after I left your father. I was stupid. I didn't want him to know about the baby." She shook her head. "Then I got the teaching position at Johns Hopkins and sent for you." She paused. "You know the rest."

"Oh, my god." Maddie was beyond stunned. "I feel like my head's gonna explode." She looked at Celine like she was seeing her for the first time. "I don't know what to say, much less what to think." She fell silent. Then she met her mother's eyes. "Where do we go from here?"

Celine gazed back at her with an open expression. "Where do you *want* to go?"

"Honestly?"

Her mother nodded.

"I have no idea. I need some time to absorb all of this."

Celine nodded again, slowly, and lowered her gaze.

Maddie watched her for a moment. "Mom?"

Celine raised her eyes.

"Thank you for telling me. I know it wasn't easy to do."

Celine's eyes filled with tears. "I'm sorry, Maddoe. I'm so very sorry."

Maddie nodded. Her throat felt thick. "I am, too. For everything." She went to sit on the edge of her mother's chaise. She took hold of her hand and kissed her gently on the forehead. "Don't worry. We'll figure it all out. We've got lots of time, now. Lots of time." Celine squeezed her hand and gave her a watery smile. Maddie pulled her into a gentle hug.

Over her mother's shoulder, Maddie could see the white sage plants shining like beacons in the late afternoon sun.

The rest of that evening, Maddie and Celine were understandably shy of each other. Celine seemed to be as emotionally drained as Maddie, and they seemed to agree in nonverbal ways, that enough had been said for now.

But Maddie was aware of a difference in the quality of the silence they shared. If it wasn't exactly companionable, it wasn't hostile either. For once, they were not antagonists. They were more like two exotic fish that had been plucked from separate tanks in a pet store, and then dropped together into the same small bowl. And tonight, they were cautiously swimming around each other in wide circles until their new environment became familiar, and they understood how to relate to it, and to each other.

They ate a light supper from the food that Maddie had picked up the previous evening, and then Celine retired for the night. Maddie helped her get settled in her room, and then sat with her for a few minutes, perched on the side of her bed. She couldn't recall ever having done that before—at least, not in Brentwood. She had rarely entered her mother's bedroom during the years she lived here. It had seemed like an alien place to her—cold and inaccessible, much like her mother's interior life. As she looked around the spacious room now, she realized that her perception had been inaccurate.

This room, unlike the other rooms in the house, was decorated in a richer palette—shades of dark green and gold, with bolder patterns on the upholstered chairs that sat near the large windows overlooking her garden. There were stacks of books and sheet music piled on the table between the chairs, and many framed photographs—some of Oma and Opa, and several of herself, with and without Celine, taken at different signature events in her life. There was even a photo of her with David from her med school graduation ceremony, and that one confused her. Celine had not attended the event, so who had sent her the picture? Dad? David? She remembered that Uncle Art had driven up from Charlottesville to be there. She wondered now if that had been the reason for Celine's absence.

There would be time to ask her mother about that tomorrow. She shifted her gaze away from the photos.

Even the artwork in this room was different—a stark contrast to the Bauhaus paintings that made up the rest of Celine's collection. Maddie saw her mother's treasured Cassatt drypoint etching hanging on the wall opposite the bed. She had forgotten about that picture. The hand-tinted watercolor of a young girl in a bonnet had always hung over the fireplace in the parlor of the Virginia house, and it had been one of the few things Celine had taken with her when she left.

Maddie remembered the day her mother held her at eye-level with the picture and taught her that the Impressionist painter was actually an American from Pennsylvania. Her full name, Celine explained as Maddie traced a stubby finger over the delicate lines beneath the glass, was Mary *Stevenson* Cassatt, and she actually was a distant relative of Maddie's father. The Stevensons and the Cassatts had been among the more prominent families in Allegheny County, and Maddie's great-grandfather had moved to Virginia in 1880 as a manager for the Virginia and Tennessee Railroad, establishing rail service to mines along the Appalachian Coal Basin that stretched from Pittsburgh to Knoxville. Mary Cassatt's father had been one of the investors who helped fund the railroad expansion, and her brother, A.J., went on to achieve great prominence as president of the Pennsylvania Railroad. The lives of the two families intersected again when, more than a century later, Celine acquired the etching at an estate auction in Philadelphia. She had been shocked when she read the provenance of the picture and realized that it once had belonged to relatives of Davis's in Pittsburgh.

"What are you looking at so intently?" Celine asked.

Maddie, startled, looked at her mother, feeling slightly guilty—like she'd been caught eavesdropping. "Oh. I'm sorry. I was thinking about the Cassatt etching. I'd actually forgotten about it until right now." She gave her mother a small smile. "I was remembering when you showed it to me for the first time."

Celine looked at the picture. "I think about that day a lot."

"You do?" Maddie was surprised.

She nodded. "Of course I do. It reminds me of a happier time."

Maddie shook her head. "How did we get so far away from that?"

"That was my fault. I was stubborn and proud, and I made bad decisions that I clung to even after I knew they were wrong." She met Maddie's eyes. "I can never forgive myself for how cold I was—for how much I held you at arm's length. I knew how devoted you were to your father, and how angry you were at me for taking you away from him." She dropped her gaze. "I loved you so much, and I couldn't face the pain in your eyes." She smiled sadly. "So I did what I've *always* done. I just went away. Emotionally withdrew. I submerged myself in work, and I ignored the hurt—mine and yours." She looked at Maddie. "That's what I learned from *my* parents, so those were the reflexive behaviors I resorted to when my own life unraveled."

It was unusual for Celine to be so expansive—especially about anything this personal. Maddie didn't really know what response to make, and she didn't want to do or say anything to disrupt her mother's narrative, so she remained silent.

"I don't want you to think that I'm excusing my behavior, or that I'm blaming my parents for the choices I made," Celine said, after a few moments. "I'm not. I know what I did, and what responsibility I bear for the choices I made. Coming to terms with that has been more painful than you can imagine."

Maddie looked at her with wonder. "What changed?"

Celine sighed. "I did. Your father's death, happening the way it did—so sudden and unexpected—shook me to the core. I was unprepared for the emotion it unleashed. I couldn't contain it—it overwhelmed me. Suddenly, I was confronting everything I'd ever lost—my marriage, my parents," she hesitated, "you." She looked down at the bedspread. "I nearly had a breakdown. I took a three-month sabbatical and went into therapy. Laszlow managed my lab and worked with my grad students. I don't know what I would have done without him."

Maddie tentatively touched her hand. "Why didn't you call me?"

Celine met her eyes. "I couldn't. I knew what you were dealing with, and I had nothing to offer you. I was a *mess*. Finally, about six months ago, I knew I was ready to see you—to try and make amends. That's when the conference opportunity came up. I was fairly certain you would be there since the venue was so close to Jericho, so when the organizers approached me about speaking, I agreed immediately."

Maddie sighed. "But when we met that day after your speech, you seemed so angry and distant."

Celine laughed bitterly. "What was it you said the other day? About old habits dying hard?" She shook her head. "And it was more frustration than anger. I was already terrified about seeing you, and then Gina showed up."

Maddie raised a hand to her forehead. "Oh, god." She gave Celine an apologetic look. "Yeah, I'm certain that little performance didn't help much."

"No, it didn't." She regarded Maddie quietly for a moment. "What on earth were you thinking?"

Maddie shrugged. "I haven't had the best relationship track record, either."

"Until now?" Her mother asked.

Maddie nodded. "Until now."

They sat quietly for a while. The only sound in the room was the monotonous tick of Celine's bedside clock. Celine moved her hand so it rested on top of Maddie's. "About your father. Are you all right?"

Maddie looked back at her for a moment, and then shrugged. "Honestly? I don't really know. I'm shocked, of course. But I'm more distressed than anything. Why on earth would he never tell me he was gay—especially once he knew about *me*?" She shook her head. "I always thought we were so close. But now I find out that I never really knew him at all."

Celine squeezed her hand. "That's not true. You *did* know him. You just didn't know this one thing about him." Her blue eyes were fixed on Maddie's. "You know better than anyone that being gay doesn't define you. Think how many times you've said those words to me, and how frustrated you've been when other people couldn't see past that aspect of your *own* character. Don't do the same thing now to your father. This reaction is what he feared most about telling you, and it's why he kept it a secret."

Maddie shook her head slowly. "I still don't understand it."

"Give yourself time to understand it. This isn't like some new element on the periodic table that you can just review and memorize. You're going to have to live with this for a while before you understand how it fits in with the rest of what you know."

"God." Maddie looked back at her mother with amazement.

"What is it?" Celine asked.

"I forgot what these little instructional chats with you were like." She smiled. "You could've saved me a fortune in shrink bills."

Celine patted her hand. "I don't know about that. Maybe we could've qualified for some kind of family discount."

Maddie chortled. "Yeah. Imagine if we could've bundled Oma in, too?"

Celine gasped. "Oh, good lord. *She* could've put a porch on Freud's house all by herself."

Maddie laughed merrily. The cell phone in her front pocket buzzed, and she quickly placed her hand over it. Celine noticed.

"I'm sorry," Maddie apologized. "It's probably Syd."

"It's fine. Go on ahead and talk with her. I'm fading fast." She smiled. "Tell her I said hello."

Maddie kissed her mother on the forehead. "I will. Call if you need anything?"

Celine nodded. "Count on it. Goodnight, Maddoe."

Maddie smiled. Celine's use of her childhood nickname warmed her heart. "Goodnight, Mom."

Chapter 21

Maddie sat outside on the patio with a glass of wine, smiling as the sound of Syd's voice filled her ear. She had decided to wait until she got home to share Celine's stunning revelation about her father. Just now, Syd was in the middle of a story about how David had managed to twist his ankle during a drunken encounter with a vacuum cleaner hose.

"Do I want to know what he was doing with the hose when this happened?" Maddie asked.

"I *really* don't think you do," Syd replied.

Maddie closed her eyes. "God. I really need to knock some sense into that boy."

Syd laughed. "Well, I told him that was likely to be your reaction when you saw him limping around."

"And?"

"It didn't faze him a bit. He told me there were more old drunks than old doctors."

Maddie sighed. "That sounds about right."

"Then he looked me over and told me how *relaxed* I seemed."

"Oh, Jesus."

"Yeah. He said he was happy that you had apparently not lost your touch."

Maddie chuckled. "It's hard for me know what to say to that."

"*Tell* me about it." Syd exhaled. "I had a few moments of insane jealousy, wondering just who he was using as a basis for comparison."

"Oh, honey, I feel your pain on that one."

"You do?" Syd sounded confused.

"Hell, yes. Remember the night you had dinner with Jeff? I drove myself nuts, thinking about you being out with him."

Syd was quiet for a moment. "You had nothing to worry about."

"I didn't?"

"No. I was already way past gone on you. I know that now."

Maddie smiled into the phone. "So, on a scale of one to ten . . ."

"You'd be about a ten thousand. Relax, Doctor. You've definitely *not* lost your touch."

"God, I miss you."

"I miss you, too. When are you gonna come home and remind me of just how extraordinary you are?"

"I was thinking I'd stay through the weekend and come back on Monday— that's if Mom continues to do as well as she is now."

There was silence on the line. After a few moments, Maddie wondered if their call had dropped. "Are you still there?"

"Yeah." Syd sounded confused. "I'm sorry. I thought I heard . . . Did you just say 'mom'?"

"Oh." Maddie was embarrassed. "I guess I did." She hesitated. "I have some things to share with you when I get back. We've . . . managed to make some peace with each other."

"Apparently. Are you okay?"

Maddie nodded. "I am. Better than okay, actually. We had some difficult conversations. I learned some things I didn't know about her—about both of my parents, actually. It's going to take me some time to work through it all. But, for now, at least, we're in a better place than we've been since I was a child."

"Oh, baby, I'm so happy to hear that."

Maddie smiled, feeling an uncustomary surge of giddiness. "I'm pretty happy about it, too."

"I don't doubt that a bit." Maddie could tell that Syd was smiling. "I like Celine."

"She likes you, too."

"It sounds like we're going to have lots to talk about when you get back."

"Maybe eventually."

"Eventually?"

"Well, lemme put it this way," Maddie deadpanned. "I don't plan on doing much talking for the first few hours."

"Oh, really?" Syd asked, sweetly. "Does that mean you've developed some new ability to remain silent?"

Maddie gasped. "That's between me and my god."

"I know," Syd drawled. "Remember? I've overheard a few of your so-called private exchanges."

"Smartass. You're just begging for it, now."

"In fact, I wasn't, but I'd be happy to start begging if it would help get you home any sooner."

"Be patient. I'll make it worth the wait."

"Smooth talker. Oh." Syd's voice changed timbre. "I forgot to tell you that Lizzy came by the library today."

Maddie was intrigued. "She did?"

"Yeah. She was next in line for the newest Chelsea Cain novel."

"Really?" Maddie was amused. "Should I be concerned that my new nurse is reading books about a serial killer?"

Syd laughed. "Look at the bright side—it might negate the need for a public option in health care reform."

"Hmmm. Murder the infirm? Now *there's* a creative strategy. Would we have to torture them all first, too?"

"Isn't that why we have Medicare Part D?" Syd asked, sweetly.

Maddie laughed. "I think that you and Lizzy could be a dangerous combination."

"Well, hold on to your hat, then, because we're going to be seeing a lot more of each other."

"You are?"

"Uh huh. You apparently didn't realize that your new assistant plays a mean flute. Phoebe's already coerced her into joining the orchestra."

"God," Maddie said, incredulous. "That woman can really sniff them out."

"No kidding. My lazy Sunday afternoons are now a thing of the past."

"Whatever will I do to fill the lonely hours?"

Syd laughed. "You *might* consider making some headway on all those broken toaster ovens in the barn. It looks like the back room at Black & Decker out there."

"Yadda, yadda, yadda." Maddie sighed. "I knew that having you move in was going to be a mistake."

There was silence on the line. "Okay. Let's take these in order, shall we? First: *mistake?* Second: *when* did I move in?"

"Um. Well. 'Mistake' might be an overstatement. I was really going for dramatic effect, there."

"Uh huh. And the moving in part?"

"You can't blame a girl for trying. I mean, you like being there, don't you?"

"Maddie, a gnat with a lobotomy would like being here."

"Was that a yes?"

Syd sighed. "You're making me crazy. You know that?"

"Crazy can be good."

"So can cautious. I don't want us to screw this up. It's too important."

"I don't want us to screw it up, either. And one thing I've learned in the last week is that I'm not going to waste any more time."

"Baby, we've only been . . . *us* . . . for two weeks." Her voice softened. "I don't think we're wasting any time."

"I agree. But I think we've been *us* ever since that day we met on the river road."

There was silence again. "I do, too." Syd's voice was low and earnest. "I'm not going anyplace. You have no worries."

"So, you're saying I've got squatter's rights?"

Syd snorted. "Now there's a phrase that's taken on a whole new meaning for me."

Maddie gasped. "Well, I never."

"Oh, really? Just wait until you get home. I'll make sure you *always*."

Maddie sighed happily. "From your mouth to god's ear."

Any plans Maddie had for catching up on her sleep during the long flight back to Charlotte from Los Angeles were short-circuited by an inquisitive five-year-old UM. The United flight attendant responsible for the little boy asked Maddie if she would mind having the unaccompanied minor seated next to her in business class, since that section was near the front galley of the aircraft, and she would have an easier time keeping an eye on him. Maddie was poised to decline until she made the mistake of glancing at the tiny passenger as he stood there gawking up at her.

"You're really tall," he said. "My daddy is tall, too. He's in the Army. My name is Henry. I'm five."

Maddie smiled at him as he stood there clutching the flight attendant's hand. He was wearing a lightweight denim jacket with a bright blue "I'm Flying Solo" sticker over the breast pocket. She looked up at the harried flight attendant and sighed.

"Sure. I'd be happy to sit next to Henry."

The blonde woman smiled gratefully and winked at Maddie. "Thank you. Once we get underway, I'll be back by to take your beverage order. Ask for anything you want. It's on the house."

She got Henry settled in the seat beside Maddie and stowed his tiny suitcase in the overhead bin. She handed Maddie a plastic bag containing several comics and coloring books.

"I'll be back to check on you shortly, Henry," she said, before she disappeared down the aisle toward the rear of the aircraft.

"What's your name?" Henry asked, turning his small body in the seat to face her.

"I'm Maddie."

"How old are you?"

Maddie chuckled. "I'm thirty-four."

Henry looked confused. "I'm older than you, 'cause I'm a five."

"Well, a five *is* a bigger number than a three, but I'm a three *and* a four. If you add those together, they're bigger than five."

Henry appeared unconvinced.

Maddie decided to change the subject. "Who are you going to see in Charlotte?"

"My gramma. My daddy went to Afostan."

"Afghanistan?" Maddie asked. Henry nodded. "Where's your mommy?"

"I don't have a mommy." His round blue eyes searched her face. "Do you have a mommy?"

"Yes, I do." Maddie wanted to hug him. "I was just visiting her. I'm going home now."

"Where do you live?"

"I live on a farm in Virginia."

"Where's that?"

"It's not too far from where we're going on this airplane. Where does your grandma live?"

"Can Place. She makes socks."

He means Kannapolis, Maddie thought. *She must work in a textile mill.* "Have you visited your grandma before?"

He shook his head.

"Are you going to stay with your grandma while your daddy is away?"

He nodded. "I'm going to a new school."

She smiled at him. "Kannapolis is very pretty. I hope you'll like it there."

"Is it close to your farm?" he asked.

"It's not too far away. Maybe a few hours."

"Are you a farmer? Do you have animals?"

"I have a dog. But, no, I'm not a farmer."

"What do you do?"

"I'm a doctor."

Henry's eyes grew wide. "You are?"

Maddie nodded. "Yep."

Henry tilted his head as he regarded her. His dark hair curled over the tops of his ears. "Why do you have a farm if you don't have animals?"

"It was my daddy's. I live there now."

He seemed to accept that explanation. "Can I come play with your dog?"

Maddie smiled at him. "I don't know. We'd have to ask your grandma about that."

"She won't care. She doesn't like kids."

"Why do you say that?"

"My daddy told me that when he left. He told me to be very good and not to bug her."

"Oh." Maddie felt a surge of sadness as she regarded the earnest little boy. "I'm sure your grandma will like you a lot, Henry."

"She will?"

"I think so. *I* like you."

"I like you, too." He looked down at her purse poking out from beneath her seat. "Do you have a picture of your dog?"

"I don't have one with me. But I'll tell you what. Once they tell us that we're allowed to get the crayons out, I'll describe him to you, and you can draw a picture of him."

He brightened up. "I like to draw."

"It's a deal, then."

Henry continued to look at her. "You're really pretty."

Maddie smiled at his sweetness. "Thank you, Henry. I think you're very handsome, too."

"Are you married?"

She smiled. "No. I'm not married."

"Do you have a girlfriend?" he asked.

Maddie was stunned by his question. "Why do you ask that?"

He shrugged. "My daddy had a girlfriend, but she left."

"Oh. Well." She thought about it. "Yes, I do have a girlfriend."

"What's her name?" he asked.

Maddie smiled. "Syd."

"That's a boy's name." He laughed.

"You're right. It usually is a boy's name. Her real name is Margaret, but Syd is her nickname. Do you have a nickname?"

He nodded. "Daddy calls me Sport." He frowned. "His girlfriend called me Henrietta. I didn't like that very much."

"I can see why. That's not a very good nickname for a little boy."

The plane started to taxi down the runway for takeoff. Henry tensed as they picked up speed. He plucked nervously at his seatbelt.

"Are you afraid?" she asked.

He nodded.

"It's okay, Sometimes I get a little scared, too. But we're really very safe. Would you like to hold my hand?"

He nodded again. Maddie took his tiny hand and held it as the plane rolled faster and faster and the buildings along the runway flew past their window. When the nose lifted up, and they left the ground, she felt Henry squeeze her fingers. He jerked when he heard the loud rumble of the landing gear retracting.

"It's okay, Henry," Maddie said. "That's just the sound of the airplane wheels being put away."

He looked at her with luminous eyes. "Why do they put the wheels away?" His curiosity was plainly overcoming his fear.

"Because they don't need the wheels when we aren't on the ground. In the air, they use the wings to fly—just like birds."

"Oh. Do you like birds?"

"Yes, I do. I like to hear them sing early in the morning."

"Do you have birds on your farm?"

Maddie nodded. "I sure do. Lots of them. My dog likes to chase them."

"I wish I had a dog. The army won't let Daddy have one, and they make Gramma sneeze."

"Well, maybe when your daddy is out of the army you can have one? I never had one, either, until I moved back to Virginia. Pete was my father's dog."

"Pete?" He giggled.

"That's his name. Pete. He's a big, yellow dog."

A bell sounded in the cabin, and the flight attendant announced that the Captain had approved the use of seat-back tray tables and electronic devices. She also stated that they would shortly be beginning their beverage and breakfast service.

"Are you hungry?" Maddie asked Henry.

He nodded.

"Well, let's eat some breakfast, and then we can draw some pictures of Pete."

They each had waffles with hot maple syrup. Henry had apple juice, and Maddie had a large mimosa with her coffee, thanks to her grateful flight attendant. After they finished eating, and their breakfast trays collected, Maddie got out the crayons and paper and helped Henry draw pictures of Pete, and pictures of the birds at her farm.

Henry proudly signed his name in large block letters at the bottom of each drawing, and gave several of them to Maddie to keep. She carefully tucked them inside her briefcase, after promising to show them to Pete, and to her girlfriend with the funny name.

After an hour or so, Henry began to yawn, and Maddie noticed his eyes were drooping.

"Are you sleepy?" she asked.

He nodded. "I had to get up in the dark."

"Do you want to lie down across the seat and take a little nap?"

He nodded. Maddie pushed the call button and asked the flight attendant for a pillow and blanket. She tucked their center armrest up to give him more space, and was surprised when he immediately stretched out across the seat and laid his head on her lap. He was sound asleep in minutes.

She smiled through her amazement. *Reminds me of someone else I know*, she thought, tucking the blanket in around him. Reclining her own seat, she closed her eyes and decided to try and catch a few winks herself, but she guessed that sleep would elude her. Her mind was too active and too full from the events of the last week.

Henry whimpered in his sleep, and Maddie rubbed a calming hand up and down his arm. In moments, he quieted down. She looked down at his small form with an affection that surprised her. *God. I'm so fickle. How do I break the news to Syd that I've lost my heart to a five-year-old stranger I met on the airplane ride home?*

Henry's apparent resiliency and unaffected innocence moved her. Here he was, facing an uncertain future without a mother, and a father on the other side of the globe, and still he was able to fall sleep on the lap of a stranger. She shook her head in wonder as she thought back over her own early childhood years—doted on by both parents in a fairy tale-like environment, surrounded by every possible advantage. And for so many years, after the end of her parents' marriage, she thought of herself as a victim—a loner and an outcast.

Looking down at Henry's sleeping form now, she realized with sadness that nothing had been further from the truth. Her mother had not rejected her. She had withdrawn from her own pain and loss in an ill-fated attempt to insulate Maddie from a truth her father believed she was too young to understand. As the years passed, that mistake became a deception, and even the revelation of her own sexual orientation was not enough to shake her father's resolve. She knew with certainty that she would mourn that loss now—that loss of her father's faith and trust—in the same way she mourned his untimely death.

She ran her fingers through Henry's long, curly hair.

But life ebbed and flowed. The universe took things away and gave things back. She smiled as she thought about her final few minutes with her mother that morning. Laszlow had graciously offered to drive her to the airport for her impossibly early departure. She wanted Celine to stay in bed, but her mother stubbornly insisted on getting up to see her off. She stood in the breezeway next to her while Laszlow stowed her bags in the trunk of his old Peugeot sedan. They were mostly silent—both aware of the awkwardness that still lingered between them. Celine was fully dressed in slacks and a loose-fitting cotton shirt that was large enough to accommodate the cast on her left arm. Finally, she turned to Maddie. She was only a few inches shorter, and their eyes were nearly level.

"Call me when you get to Charlotte?" she asked, almost shyly.

"Of course," Maddie replied, with a small smile.

"I can't thank you enough for being here. It means more to me than you'll ever know."

Maddie searched her mother's blue eyes. "Me, too." She stepped forward and embraced Celine, careful not to jostle the arm that was supported by a bright blue sling. She closed her eyes as she recognized the tangerine and sandalwood scent of her mother's beloved *Farouche* perfume. It was something she remembered from her childhood—from a happier time, when she lived with both of her parents in Virginia.

"I love you, Mom." Her throat felt thick.

Celine's free arm tighten around her back. "I love you, too, Maddoe."

Then she was gone. But they had promised to keep in better contact, and they had talked about seeing each other again in the summer. Celine had even hinted at possibly coming back to the farm for a visit—a suggestion that shocked and pleased Maddie.

Who knew? Maybe she *would* make some headway on those toaster ovens so the barn would be clear of clutter when Celine came back. Syd would be amazed.

Syd. She smiled to herself as she thought about going home to Syd. Right now, life was awfully good. She glanced down at Henry, now drooling on her trouser leg. *I wish I could say the same for you, little man. I wish I could spare you what looks like a rough road ahead.* She tugged the blanket up around his small shoulders, leaned back, and closed her own eyes, drowsiness finally winning out over conscious thought.

Passing by the two passengers sleeping in row seven, the lead flight attendant shook her head and smiled. With their dark hair and blue eyes, they looked like they belonged together. She congratulated herself once again for correctly tagging the right person to watch over her UM.

Half the passengers on board were now dozing, and they had a good tail wind. The rest of this flight was shaping up to be a breeze.

In the busy Charlotte-Douglas Airport terminal, Maddie waited with Henry and the United gate agent until Ada Lawrence, Henry's grandmother, arrived. All around them, other passengers were noisily reunited with friends and family members before bustling off to waiting cars or the lower level baggage claim area. Over the throng of people, Maddie could see the taller form of Michael Robertson making his way to them. She waved him over with a smile.

"Henry, I'd like you to meet a very good friend of mine," she said, as Michael approached them.

Maddie could see the surprise and confusion on his face as he realized that she was standing there with a United Airlines employee and a child. She stepped forward and warmly embraced Michael, before gesturing to her small companion.

"Michael, I'd like you to meet my new friend, Henry Lawrence. Henry kept me company on the long ride from California, and we're waiting here for his grandmother to arrive."

Michael raised an eyebrow before kneeling in front of Henry and extending his hand. "Hello, Henry. It's a pleasure to meet you."

Henry pressed a bit closer against Maddie's leg, but gamely held out his hand. "Hello. Did you know that Maddie is a doctor?"

Michael chuckled. "Yes, I did know that. In fact, Maddie is *my* doctor, and she's given me *lots* of shots."

Henry's eyes grew wide. He looked up at Maddie. "You have?"

Maddie sighed. "Yes, but not nearly as many as he deserved." She gestured to the smiling United gate agent. "Michael, this is Denise. She's waiting with Henry, too."

Michael shook hands with her. "Hi, Denise. These two give you any trouble?"

"Not so far." Denise laughed. She looked past Michael toward the escalators. "I think this might be Mrs. Lawrence."

They all looked at the advancing woman with interest and anticipation. When she saw Henry, she waved and made a beeline for them.

"Is this your grandma, Henry?" Denise asked.

He nodded, but Maddie noted that he didn't seem particularly excited. He remained closely pressed against her leg, clutching his bag of coloring books and crayons.

Ada Lawrence was a medium-sized woman who appeared to be in her early sixties. She had graying, dark hair and watery blue eyes, and she appeared to be more tired than anything. Maddie noticed a slight limp in her gait as she approached them and suspected that she might be suffering from sciatica or fibromyalgia—not uncommon maladies for people who made a living standing in one position for long periods of time. She was nearly breathless by the time she reached them.

"I'm Ada Lawrence, and this is my grandson, Henry," she said. "I'm sorry I'm late. I couldn't find a parking space out front and had to go into the big lot." She bent over and reached out a hand toward Henry. "Hello, honey. Do you remember me?"

Henry nodded and shyly stepped forward to allow the older woman to hug him. Then he quickly retreated to stand next to Maddie. Ada looked up at Maddie with confusion, then at the United agent.

"Mrs. Lawrence, I'm Denise Wilson. Henry has been a model passenger." She gestured toward Maddie. "This is Dr. Stevenson. She kept Henry company on the flight from L.A."

Ada looked back at Maddie. "*Dr.* Stevenson?" She quickly looked down at the little boy. "Are you sick?"

"Oh, no, he's fine," Maddie said. "I just happened to have the good fortune to be seated next to your grandson." She lifted her hand and gently rubbed the top of his head. "We became fast friends." She extended her hand toward Mrs. Lawrence. "It's a pleasure to meet you."

Ada slowly held out her hand. Maddie noticed how warm it felt and how puffy her fingers looked. *Carpal tunnel or diabetes*, she thought. Her heart went out to the woman as she thought about what she was taking on. Mrs. Lawrence looked pallid and fatigued as she stood there. She wondered if there was a Mr. Lawrence. Henry had not mentioned a grandfather.

"Mrs. Lawrence," Maddie said, gesturing to Michael. "This is my good friend, Michael Robertson." Michael nodded and smiled at her.

Denise held out a clipboard. "If you'll just show me some photo I.D. and sign this release form, you can be on your way."

Ada complied, and Denise thanked her and walked off.

Ada turned to Henry. "Come on, honey. We need to get going. Gramma has to work tonight." She looked up and met Maddie's eyes. "Thank you so much for taking care of him on the trip. I really appreciate it."

Maddie smiled. "It was my pleasure." She dug into her jacket pocket to retrieve the card she had placed there earlier while Henry was sleeping on the plane. "This is my contact information. Please don't hesitate to call me if you ever need anything." She paused. "I mean that sincerely." She smiled down at Henry as Ada slowly took the card from her. "I'd love to keep in touch with Henry."

She knelt next to him and placed her hands on his small shoulders. "I really liked meeting you, Henry. Thank you for my drawings. I'll be sure to show them to Pete."

Henry threw his arms around her neck and hugged her. "Can I come and see you on your farm?"

Maddie looked up at Ada as she held him. "We'll see what your grandma thinks about that, and if it's okay with her, I promise to come and get you for a visit." She released him and kissed his forehead. "You be a good boy now. I'll call to check on you, okay?"

"Okay."

"Bye, sweetheart."

When she stood up, she noticed that Mrs. Lawrence was rummaging in her purse for something. Finally, she pulled out a pen and something that looked like a pay stub. She tore off a piece of the paper and wrote down a name and phone number.

"This is my home number," she said, handing the paper to Maddie. "I work second shift, so you can usually catch me in the mornings. My neighbor, Elise Manning will keep Henry at her house until I get home at eleven." She gave Maddie a small smile. "Call whenever you want to. I know he'd like hearing from you."

"Thank you, Mrs. Lawrence. Take care."

She nodded. "Come on, Henry. We need to go now." She took hold of his hand, and they turned to leave the busy terminal.

As they were walking away, Henry looked back at her and waved. "Bye, Maddie."

She waved back at him. "Bye, Henry." She sagged her shoulders as she watched them walk away and leaned into Michael. "Jesus."

"No kidding," he said, wrapping an arm around her. "You're a goner. Who knew you had such maternal instincts?"

"Yeah, yeah. So sue me." She laughed. "Syd's gonna freak."

"Why do you say that?"

Maddie chuckled. "She thinks we need to wait at least a month before we start a family."

Michael laughed heartily as he squeezed her shoulder and turned her toward the street exit. "Come on. Let's get you home so you can confess your sins in person."

Maddie knew that Syd wouldn't be home from orchestra practice until at least four. She intentionally didn't tell her that she was arriving home a day earlier than they had discussed, wanting to surprise her. After Michael dropped her off, she hurried inside, having just enough time to unpack, change clothes, and reunite with Pete before Syd returned.

Upstairs, she noticed that Syd had, in fact, been sleeping in the front guest room down the hall, instead of staying in her larger, master suite. She noted that Pete's dog bed had been moved to that room, too. *I can fix that in short order*, she thought, smiling to herself.

Back downstairs, she put on a pot of coffee and nosed around inside the refrigerator to see if Syd had any intriguing leftovers. She was famished from the long day, and had skipped lunch on the plane, opting instead for a protein bar and some juice. She hoped that she'd be able to prevail upon Syd to cook something for her—even if it was only a couple of scrambled eggs.

Everything in the kitchen was neat and tidy—just like the bedroom upstairs. Except for the few personal items in evidence—a Jane Austen novel on the nightstand, some cosmetics on a shelf in the guest bathroom, a coffee mug in the sink, an extra jacket on a peg near the back door—there was really nothing to suggest that anyone else had even been living in the house. Still, it felt different to Maddie. It felt warmer, more complete. She liked it. She liked coming home to that feeling. It was going to be difficult to have Syd go back to her tiny apartment in town.

Maybe they could talk about that tonight. She smiled to herself as she shut the refrigerator door. Pete started up from his prone position on the floor and darted to the back door with his tail wagging. Then Maddie heard the crunch of car tires on the gravel outside. She walked to the door to the porch and patted the big dog on the head. "I'm right there with ya, big guy. If I had a tail, I'd be wagging it, too." She pulled open the door, let Pete out, leaned against the doorframe, and watched while Syd parked her car.

Syd looked surprised when she saw Pete bounding toward her from the porch, clearly not understanding how he had gotten outside. After a few moments of puzzlement her face lit up and she looked toward the house. She broke into a heartfelt smile, and Maddie's knees weakened. She pushed away from the doorframe and walked down the steps to meet her halfway.

Syd flew into her outstretched arms, muttering, "Oh my god, you're back. I can't believe it."

Maddie hugged her close. "Surprised?"

Syd sank her face into Maddie's neck and took a long, deep breath. "Ecstatic." She planted a string of tiny kisses up her neck and along her jaw line, ending at her mouth. "I missed you so much," she murmured against her lips.

Maddie tugged her even closer and kissed her back. When they drew apart, Syd looked at her with shining eyes and laid the palm of her hand against the side of Maddie's face. "Why didn't you tell me you were coming back today? I'd have met you at the airport."

Maddie turned her head and kissed the palm of Syd's hand. "And miss *this* greeting? Are you kidding me?"

Syd chuckled. "Oh, honey, you'd have received this greeting even if we'd been standing in the middle of Billy Graham Parkway."

Maddie raised an eyebrow. "Somebody is feeling a whole lot of confidence."

"Nuh uh. Somebody is feeling a whole lot in love."

They kissed again.

"I certainly share that sentiment."

Syd smiled up at her. "How about we go inside and continue getting reacquainted? I want to hear about your flight, and I want to hear about Celine."

Maddie released her, but kept hold of her hand. "Good idea. Can I help you carry anything?"

"Nope. Just let me get my violin." They walked to the car, and Syd retrieved her violin case from the front seat.

Inside, Maddie went to the coffeepot and took a cup out of the cupboard. "Want a cup? I made a pot to try and make myself wake up." She smiled at her slyly. "I thought I might need the extra stamina."

Syd arched an eyebrow. "Oh, really? Worried that someone might try and keep you awake later?"

"No. I'm counting on it."

"Hmmm. How about something to eat while we're at it? Are you hungry?"

"Famished. I was hoping you'd offer."

"I guess it's pretty presumptuous of me to offer to feed you in your own kitchen."

"Are you kidding? I fantasized about having you cook for me all the way home from Charlotte."

"Well, I can think of a few other fantasies I'd rather inspire, but I won't complain." Maddie chuckled, and Syd pulled items from the refrigerator. "Who picked you up, anyway?"

"Michael."

"Ahh. That explains it."

Maddie leaned back against the kitchen counter and gave her a quizzical look. "Explains what?"

"Why David was flitting around during rehearsal like the cat that swallowed the canary. I should've known something was up." She turned around to retrieve a couple of utensils from the center island, and Maddie grabbed her by the arm and hauled her to where she was standing.

"I think I need a little appetizer," she said, lowering her head and kissing her.

Syd wound her arms around Maddie's neck and sank into the embrace. "God, I missed you."

"I missed you, too." She kissed the tip of Syd's nose. "I love you."

"I love you, too. As much as I've enjoyed being here, it's been hell without you."

"Yeah, about that . . ." Maddie released her and picked up her coffee mug. "I've been thinking."

Syd walked back to the stove and took a large frying pan down from its hook. "That can't be good news."

"Humor me. At least hear me out."

"I'm all ears."

Maddie ran her eyes up and down Syd's shapely frame. "It truly pleases me to say that you aren't."

Syd shook her head. "Perv."

"Oh, you ain't seen nothin' yet."

Syd laughed. "So. What's your idea?"

"A-hem. Well. Why not just consider staying on here with me? Think of the money you could save the county?" She gave Syd a hopeful look.

"Nice try, Stretch. But, you're nuts. It's way too soon."

"Why do you say that?"

Syd gave her an incredulous look. "Why? Because we've only ever spent *one* night together here, and, even then, we weren't really together. We have no idea how we'd be if we were here full time."

Maddie shrugged. "Why not find out?"

"I agree that we should find out, but I think we need to do that in a more gradual way."

Maddie scowled.

"Baby, I love you. I know that," Syd said in a tender voice. "And I'm not going anyplace. But we need time to learn what being *us* is going to be like before we tempt fate by moving in together." She paused. "You know I'm right."

Maddie exhaled and nodded slowly. "Yeah. I do. I'm just selfish, and I don't want to be away from you now."

"I know. And you won't be—I promise. But I'm not even divorced yet. I, at least, need time to get that behind me. And we need to figure out what the public implications of living together would be for each of us. Are you ready to take on that whole scenario?"

Maddie looked at her intently. "Yeah. I think I am. How about you?"

"Me?" Syd chuckled. "Well, now that I've told my parents, there isn't much more for me to worry about. I mean, my grant money runs out in less than a year, so I don't have to worry too much about what the county supervisors would think about having a big ole lesbian running their library."

Maddie laughed. "In my experience, the less of an issue *we* make it, the easier it is for everyone else to accept it."

"Or ignore it," Syd added.

"That, too. As Celine was quick to remind me—it doesn't define who we are."

"She said that?"

"Uh huh. But it was in quite a different context."

Syd pulled away from Maddie and returned to sautéing chicken breasts in some olive oil and herbs. "Really? What kind of context?"

Maddie sighed. "We had a couple of pretty intense—and revealing— conversations about what caused her to leave my father. It was eye-opening for me, and cathartic, I think, for her."

"What did she tell you?"

"She told me that she came home from work sick one day and found my father here with someone else. It turns out he'd been having a long-term affair."

"Oh, my god."

"Yeah, but that's not the real kicker. It was with another man." She paused. "With Uncle Art, actually."

Syd's jaw dropped. "Oh, sweetheart."

"Yeah. I was pretty stunned, as you can imagine. Still am." She shook her head. "Celine said that Dad made her promise never to tell me. She also never told me that she was pregnant when she left us. She never told Dad, either. She miscarried while she was in New York with her parents. That's why I never saw her during those first few months after they separated."

"Jesus." Syd transferred the chicken to a platter and took the pan off the heat. She turned to Maddie. "Are you okay?"

Maddie nodded. "I am, now. But when she told me, I felt like I had been dropped head first into an alternative universe. Everything looked familiar, but nothing made any sense. Now that I've had a few days to live with this information, it's exactly the opposite. Nothing looks familiar and *everything* makes sense." She sighed. "It's really a paradox."

"I can only imagine."

Maddie touched Syd's arm. "I hope you understand that I wanted to wait until I could tell you this in person?"

"Of course I do." She covered Maddie's hand with her own. "What are you gonna do?"

Maddie shrugged. "I don't know. I need to talk with Art. And I want to ask David if he ever suspected anything during the time he lived here with Dad."

"Would that make any difference to you?"

Maddie thought about that. "I suppose not. But I'd still like to know." She slowly shook her head. "God, Syd. All those years, I thought my mother was shutting me out, and all she was doing was keeping my father's secrets." She sighed. "She admits now that it was a mistake—that she never should have agreed." She looked up and met Syd's eyes. "It was when Dad died that everything started unraveling for her. She nearly had a breakdown—had to take a sabbatical. That's why she came to Richmond. She wanted to see me—wanted to try and make a start at repairing some of the damage." She kissed Syd softly on the cheek. "So it turns out that your instincts on that score were right on the money."

Syd let out a long breath. "How are you now? With Celine?"

Maddie smiled. "Good. Better than good, actually. I mean, we're still like strangers in some ways, but we're both determined to reclaim what we lost so many years ago. I can't tell you what that means to me—to have this chance at getting my mother back. I'm practically giddy whenever I really let myself think about it."

Syd smiled. "I can certainly understand that."

Maddie set her coffee mug down in the sink and rubbed her palms together. "I think I'm ready for a little glass of something cold. How about you? Like some wine? Something white to go with that awesome-smelling chicken?"

Syd nodded. "Sure. I need a little splash of it anyway, to deglaze the pan." She returned the pan to the stove and began to reheat it.

Maddie walked to the wine fridge and pulled out a bottle of Pinot Grigio. "Why does deglazing always sound like you're about to scrape paint off a window?"

Syd chuckled. "Trust me. With cookware other than this, that can be an apt description."

Maddie popped the cork with a flourish. "See? Another reason to move in—ready access to great pots."

"Sweetie, I don't need any more incentives to make me want to move in with you. What I *need* is more strength to resist the temptation."

Maddie handed her the open bottle. "Resistance is futile. I play to win."

"We've had this conversation, Doctor. You've *already* won. You just need to relax and wait a while before claiming your door prize."

Maddie sighed. "Delayed gratification?"

"Yep."

"Damn. I never should have bailed on those twelve steps."

Syd added a hefty splash of wine to the pan and it hissed and sizzled. "You're such a nut job."

"Have I ever told you how much I love your use of scientific terminology?"

"Shut up and pour me a glass of this." She handed the bottle back to Maddie.

"Anything else I can do to help?" Maddie asked, getting two wine glasses out of the sideboard.

"Yeah. You can set the table and feed Pete. There's a big can of green beans in the fridge. I've been giving him a couple of tablespoons of those with his food to make up for the reduction in volume."

"Really? How much are you feeding him?"

"A cup and a half per meal. He doesn't like it, but the beans help bulk it out a bit."

Maddie looked down at her dog, whose brown eyes were gazing up at her forlornly. "Sorry, buddy. Dodge City has a new sheriff. It's bigger than both of us."

Maddie didn't have any trouble convincing Syd to move down the hall and spend the night with her in the master suite. The greatest challenge she encountered was navigating the back flight of stairs after dinner—a task made more complicated by the fact that Syd had climbed halfway up her body and initiated a passionate assault that didn't promise to end any time soon.

The reality was that Maddie's bed was closest to the stairs, and they landed on it in a tangled heap of arms and legs. In retrospect, Maddie doubted whether she would have had the stamina to make it any further. Her head was reeling, and her knees were weak from exhaustion and pent-up passion. With her last few scraps of conscious thought, she realized that finally being here—in her own bedroom, with Syd in her arms—was the fulfillment of her greatest fantasy.

Later, as they lay wrapped up together under the big Amish quilt, Maddie felt a calm and contentment that she hadn't known for decades—not since she was a child and slept beneath all those pictures of airplanes in the room down the hall. Safe, and surrounded by the love of two adoring parents. Her dreams then were whimsical and fantastic. She'd imagine herself performing daredevil feats of aerobatics high above the earth, without danger and without fear. It never occurred to her to think that girls didn't do those things—to consider that society or her parents would disapprove or discourage her. So she believed that she could do it all. Could do anything. She lived in a world of limitless possibilities.

Sighing, she thought about Henry and wondered how he was faring during his first night in Kannapolis. What would his dreams be like tonight?

Syd tightened her arms and tugged her closer. "What are you thinking about?"

"Actually, I was thinking about Henry."

Syd lifted her head from Maddie's shoulder. "Henry? Who on earth is Henry?"

"Henry is a guy I met on the flight back from L.A. He made quite an impression on me. I can't get him off my mind."

"Oh, really? Should I be worried?"

Maddie ran a warm palm down Syd's back and over the naked swell of her hip. "Do you think you *need* to be worried?"

"Not when you put it like that."

"Good. Besides, Henry is five-years-old."

"Five?"

"Uh huh. He was flying across country solo, and the head flight attendant asked if I would keep him company."

Syd smiled into her neck. "You're such a softie."

"Nah. I just have an affinity for short people."

"I'll say." Syd pinched her on the butt. "Perv."

Maddie smiled. "You know, that's a title that seems to get shifted around a lot."

"Don't blame me. It ain't the bait, it's the fishing hole."

Maddie laughed. "You've been living in the South too long."

"Well, I think my tenure here is likely to be even longer, so it's in my best interest to adapt to the local folkways."

Maddie smiled and kissed her on the forehead. "You're off to one helluva start."

"Flatterer. Now quit stalling and tell me more about this little Henry person."

Maddie was silent for a moment. "I don't know. There was just something so sweet and compelling about him. He was traveling from California to North Carolina to live with his grandmother while his father serves out a tour of duty in Afghanistan. No mother in the picture. I don't know the details of that. He was so small, but so serene. Taking everything in stride—like none of what was happening to him was at all difficult or unusual. It was like he didn't expect anything from life, so he wasn't disappointed. It just really got to me."

"I can see why."

"I stayed with him at the airport until his grandmother arrived to pick him up. She was certainly nice enough, but it was pretty clear that taking care of a five-year-old wasn't going to be easy for her. She works in a textile mill in Kannapolis, and, as far as I can tell, she's either single or a widow."

"It sounds like you made a real connection with them."

Maddie nodded. "I think so. It's odd. I gave her my contact information, and I got theirs." She turned her head to Syd. "I'd really like to see him again—see how he's doing. Is that weird?"

"Not at all. And it's not surprising, either. You have great maternal instincts."

Maddie was incredulous. "I do? You're the second person who's said that to me."

"Yes, you do. I noticed it first with the Sanchez children." She chuckled. "You aren't so shabby with teenagers, either."

Maddie groaned. "That hardly counts. There's nothing maternal about my effect on Roma Jean."

"Well, maybe not from *her* vantage point." Syd was quiet for a moment. "Do you want kids?"

"Me? I've never really thought about it. Do you?"

"Oh, yeah. I'd love to have about a dozen."

Maddie felt her stomach lurch. A *dozen*? "Really?"

Syd laughed. "No, nimrod, not really." She thought about it. "A couple, maybe?"

"Wow. I guess if it's too soon for us to consider living together, then it's too soon for us to talk about starting a family?"

"You might say that. Besides, we're not talking about starting a family. We're talking about the idea of having children, in general."

"Is there a difference?"

Syd shifted her head and nuzzled her ear. "There won't be if you knock me up."

Maddie felt a shiver run across her body. "Now there's an interesting idea."

"So tell me more about Henry."

"There isn't much more to tell. He's chatty and charming. He likes animals and drawing pictures. He even sent a few back with me for you and Pete."

"He did?"

"Yeah." She laughed quietly. "He asked me if I had a girlfriend."

"You're kidding?"

"No. It was so sweet and reflexive—like it never occurred to him that it might seem odd to ask a woman that question."

"How did you answer?"

"I said yes." She tugged her closer. "Because I do."

"You got that right."

"He's a real cutie."

"What does he look like?"

"Dark hair. Blue eyes."

"Ahh. Just my type."

"Would you be up for a road trip to Kannapolis sometime to meet him? See how he's doing?"

"Of course." Syd paused. "Should I ask David to extend the rental period on the U-Haul?"

Maddie snorted. "You think you have me all figured out, don't you?"

"Um hmm. Just about."

"Okay, smartass. What am I thinking about right now?"

Syd slid her hand up Maddie's bare abdomen and rested her palm on a warm bit of real estate. "Let me guess." She licked up the side of Maddie's neck. "Is this at all close?"

Maddie sighed and closed her eyes before rolling onto her back and pulling Syd on top of her. "It sucks to be so transparent."

Chapter 22

Maddie's first day back at the clinic was surprisingly low key, thanks to the seamless job Lizzy and Peggy had done managing her patient load during her absence. She was more besieged by well-wishing and curious neighbors inquiring after Celine, than by sick people needing treatment.

By noon, she felt like half of Jericho had checked in. She actually was relieved when Gladys Pitzer showed up complaining about stiffness in the joints of her left hand. Since this had been the hand she had damaged with florist wire on New Years Eve, Gladys was worried that there might be some nerve damage. Maddie had Peggy shoot some x-rays as a precaution, but she was pretty certain what Gladys was suffering from was related more to the strain of repetitive motion after an injury.

She sat down with Gladys in one of her examination rooms and checked her hands and feet for redness, swelling, or inflammation. The discomfort seemed to be confined to her left hand, and more specifically, to her previously afflicted forefinger. She had good range of motion in both hands and feet, and no indications of joint deformity, so Maddie didn't worry too much about a rheumatic condition. As expected, her x-rays were normal.

She finished her examination and sat back on her rolling stool. Gladys seemed jumpier than usual, and that was saying a lot. Maddie often thought of her as the human incarnation of a squirrel—busy and industrious, but furtive and antsy. Today she seemed more agitated and distracted than usual. Her manner was anxious and fretful. She appeared overly concerned with what probably was a simple case of tendonitis. Maddie was determined to try and allay her concerns about her hand, without minimizing the condition.

"Well, Gladys, the good news is that there is nothing seriously wrong with your hand. Your x-rays look fine, and you have excellent range of motion—always a very good sign. I think you have a trace of tendonitis from your injury over the holidays—maybe even a bit of bursitis. I can't be sure about that, but I'd like to give you some antibiotics as a precautionary measure, just in case there was some lingering infection in the wound that might have caused inflammation around the joints."

Gladys nodded rapidly. Her appearance was almost comical. With her beady eyes and frizzy red hair, she resembled a bobble-head clown. "What do I do about work? Easter is coming. It's one of my busiest times. I have to work."

Maddie raised a calming hand. "Easter is still several weeks away. I think we can have you feeling better by the end of the week if you'll do a few simple things to rest your hand. Okay?"

Gladys sighed, plainly still agitated. She nodded again.

Maddie held her gaze. "Okay. I'm going to have Peggy give you some written instructions for how to take care of your hand. Simply stated, I want you to rest it, keep it elevated, and take some over-the-counter anti-inflammatory like Advil or Motrin to reduce any swelling and help you out with the pain. Do this for two to three days, okay? And take the antibiotics as directed until they're all gone. If you don't feel better by the weekend, call me, and we'll go on from there."

Gladys continued to sit on the padded table, holding her afflicted hand in her lap. Her shoulders were hunched together and her compact, wiry form looked like it had been folded up for ease of storage.

Maddie decided to take a chance. "Gladys, is everything okay at home? With Beau?"

Gladys looked up at her with alarm.

"Would he be able to help you out around the house for a few days?" Maddie asked, gentling her voice. "Just so you can rest your hand?"

Gladys shrugged nervously and looked over Maddie's shoulder toward the door that led to the hallway and the other examination rooms. "I don't know where he is right now. He hasn't been at home for over a week."

Maddie felt a twinge of apprehension. "Is he working? Did he get a job some place out of town?"

Gladys shrugged again. "I don't think so. I tried to get him to help me out in the store, but he didn't want anyone to see him working in a flower shop." She looked down at the floor again.

Maddie affected an upbeat tone to try and put Gladys at ease. "Well, maybe you can take advantage of the quiet around the house to really get some rest. I'm sure you'll hear from him soon." When Gladys didn't reply, Maddie leaned forward and met her eyes. "I hope you know that you can always ask for help if you're worried or afraid. No one wants any harm to come to Beau—or to you. Please, don't try to manage anything on your own that feels too big or too frightening."

Gladys nodded curtly and got to her feet. "Where do I get my prescription?"

Maddie sat back and sighed. "I'll write it up and bring it out to you while you're finishing up your paperwork with Peggy. You call me if you need anything. Let me hear from you toward the end of the week, okay?"

"Okay." She refused to make eye contact. "Thanks, Dr. Stevenson."

Maddie watched her narrow back as she exited the room and headed down the hallway toward the reception desk. *Shit*, she thought. *Shit*. She pulled out her prescription pad and started to write.

Maddie had arranged to meet David at the Inn that night after work for a glass of wine. When she had called him to set up the date, he teased her about her seeming formality.

"What's up with the cloak and dagger stuff? I *can't* be in trouble for anything. I haven't even seen you since the night you left for California."

"You're not in trouble. I just need to talk with you."

He was still suspicious. "I know you, Cinderella. You've got something up your poofy sleeve."

Maddie sighed. "We've had this conversation, David. I don't wear poofy sleeves."

"Hey? Allow me *some* artistic license here. If I wanna imagine you in poofy sleeves, then that's my prerogative." He thought about it. "Yeah. *Poofy*. Knowing you, it would be something folksy and tasteless, too—like dotted Swiss."

"Dotted Swiss?"

"You heard me."

"Whatever. I'll be there at five-thirty. Open something expensive."

She arrived at the Inn, and David was actually outside in the parking lot, unloading a couple of boxes from the back of the Range Rover. He stopped when he saw Maddie's Jeep approach and stood back to wait on her to park and join him. They embraced warmly, and he kissed her on the cheek.

"It's good to see you. I'm so glad about Celine. Syd told us how well she rebounded. It must have been harrowing for you."

Maddie held him at arm's length for a moment before releasing him. He looked fit and handsome in the late afternoon light. "It was. You probably understand that better than anyone."

He nodded. "Help me carry these inside?" He gestured at the two boxes sitting on the ground behind his SUV.

"Sure. Whatcha got? New vacuum cleaner hoses?"

He gave her a withering look. "So much for honor among thieves . . . and I thought I could *trust* that blonde vixen of yours."

Maddie laughed as they walked to the Rover. "That was your *second* mistake."

"Hey, don't blame me. Blame that damn Sex Lady on HBO. It was *her* idea."

"I doubt that, somehow."

"Yeah, *whatever*. Besides, this ain't new attachments for the Kirby. It's wine."

"Oh, really?" Maddie noticed the Shelton label stenciled on the outside of the boxes. "Don't I have great timing?" They each picked up a case and headed to the porch.

"Great timing, my ass. I made a special trip to North Carolina in your honor. I know how much you like that Reserve Claret."

"You trying to spoil me?"

"Nope. *Bribe* you. My instincts tell me that I'm in for something, and where you're concerned, I'm never wrong."

He held the door open with his knee, and Maddie entered the Inn ahead of him. They walked to the bar and deposited the two cases of wine on a low table.

"You're not in for anything, David. But I do need to talk with you about something Mom told me the other day when she was home from the hospital."

He stared at her with wide eyes. "Mom?"

Maddie sighed and shrugged. She needed to get used to this reaction. "Yeah. I guess I should tell you about that, too."

"I'll say. What in the hell happened out there?" He took off his jacket and dropped it over the back of a chair. "Sit down. Lemme open one of these."

She complied, dropped into a chair, and pulled another one over to prop up her feet. David returned to the table with two balloon glasses and a corkscrew.

He drew one of the tall bottles out of a box. "You wanna do the honors?" He held the bottle and the corkscrew out toward her.

"Nope." She laced her fingers together and stretched her long arms out, yawning. "I'm dragging. Must still be on west coast time."

David twisted the corkscrew into the top of the bottle. "Oh really? I'd have guessed it was more like sleep deprivation."

She glowered at him. "Nice try. You aren't getting any details from me, so don't even ask."

"I don't have to *ask*—it's all over your face."

"What is?"

"The serene countenance of someone who's getting lots of nookie." He extracted the cork with a loud pop. "This is the first time I've seen you without that annoying facial tic."

"You're nuts. I never had a facial tic."

"Well, then, it *obviously* was some kind of involuntary muscle spasm, discernible only by me." He poured them each a healthy serving of the dark, ruby-colored wine. "I'd say let's let this breathe, but screw it." He clinked glasses with her. "Welcome home, sweetheart."

She smiled. "Thanks." They took a sip, then sat back and regarded each other.

"So," David ran a hand through his dark hair, "what gives?"

Maddie twisted the stem of her wine glass around on the small table. "Mom finally told me the truth about what happened between her and Dad all those years ago." She met his eyes. "Did you know that Dad was gay?"

David's mouth fell open. "*What?*"

She nodded. "Yeah. She found out by accident one day when she came home from work early and found him there—with Uncle Art."

David closed his eyes. "Oh, my god."

"Yeah. He never wanted me to find out, so he made her promise to keep it a secret." She leaned toward him over the small table. "David?"

He opened his eyes and looked at her.

"I have to ask you this. Did you know?"

He hesitated before slowly shaking his head. "Did I *know*? No. I didn't know. Not for sure."

She held his open gaze. "But you suspected?"

He exhaled and took her hand across the table. She did not pull it away. "Yeah. I mean, I thought about it once or twice. But I never knew for sure, and I *never* asked him about it." He shook his head. "Never. I couldn't. My suspicions were too vague, and it just seemed too unlikely to me." He squeezed her hand. "That's why I never said anything to you. I was so sure I was wrong."

She sighed. "Well, it turns out you weren't." She sat back, but allowed David to continue to hold her hand. "What made you suspect it?"

He shook his head. "I dunno. There was never anything . . . *concrete*. It was more like a feeling. And he was so supportive of me, so determined to make sure that I had a positive coming out experience and a better chance at making a life for myself away from here." He lowered his eyes. "I just wondered sometimes, you know? Especially when he never dated anybody else after your mother left. And he spent a lot of weekends in Charlottesville, but Art rarely came to the farm—at least not during the year that I lived there." He looked back up at her. "I guess you never found anything in the house to make you suspect? No books or letters or anything?"

"No. Nothing. And after I moved back down here, I spent a fair amount of time packing up Dad's personal effects. It was all pretty innocuous. No surprises."

"Well. Art was here with him that last weekend. He was the one who called the EMTs when he found your dad in the barn."

Maddie considered that. "Are you suggesting that maybe he took some items out of the house?"

David shrugged. "It would make sense, wouldn't it? I mean, especially if he knew how determined your dad was to hide the truth from you."

"God." Maddie pulled her hand free and rubbed her forehead. "I don't know what to think about *any* of this."

"Maybe you need to talk with Art. I mean, now that you know."

She nodded. "That's exactly what I've been thinking."

They were silent for a while.

"Maddoe, I hope you understand why I never said anything to you," David said, sounding tentative. "I never had more than a vague suspicion, and *that* was only fleeting on one or two occasions. If I had really known something, I would have told you. I never would have let you suffer the way you did all those years after your parents split up. Especially once you figured out that *you* were gay." He shrugged. "That we *both* were gay."

She gave him a small smile. "I know that, Davey. I believe you."

He sat back. "So, when are you gonna go to Charlottesville?"

She took another swallow of the wine. "You know, I'm not sure. I may just live with this a little while before going to see him."

"I can understand that."

"I mean, I remember how devastated he was after Dad's death. Now I understand that in a whole new light." She sighed. "I understand lots of things differently now." She looked at David. "I'm not angry at him—any more than I am at Dad—or Celine. I'm really just sorry. Sorry for all three of them—Dad, Mom, Art." She slowly shook her head. "It's amazing to me that three such highly functioning professionals couldn't find a better way to resolve a painful relationship dilemma."

David expelled a long, slow breath. "Well, at the risk of pissing you off, I think you need to admit that having a string of degrees as long as one of your glorious legs is no guarantee that you'll be able to manage the nitty-gritty of life any better than some poor schmoe on a loading dock. They're just human, and they fucked up. They made bad choices. Just like we have—numerous times. Remember my first *five* relationships? And Gina? Wanna talk about *her* for a while?"

She sighed. "Yeah, yeah. I get your point. But they all had one important thing in common that we didn't have. At least, I'd like to *think* it was important."

"What was that?"

She felt the sting of tears and blinked to hold them back. "Me."

He took hold of her hand again. "Hard to argue with that."

The front door to the Inn opened and closed, and they could hear the voices of several guests as they made their way up the wide stairs to the second floor.

Maddie took advantage of the diversion to regain her composure. "So, I'm thinking I may just write him a letter. Give him the space he may need to respond. Maybe I can go up and see him later on—over Easter, or something. Syd wanted to go back to Charlottesville in the spring, anyway. It might be a chance for us to get away for a night or two."

"I can understand that. How are you two going to manage your relationship now?"

Maddie smiled at him slyly. "You mean, since we didn't take you up on the U-Haul offer?"

He laughed. "That's an open-ended offer. You can redeem it any old time."

"If I had my druthers, we'd have it parked in my driveway tomorrow."

"Now, why doesn't *that* surprise me?" He chuckled and finished his glass of wine. "So who's sandbagging? I know it ain't you."

She stuck her tongue out at him.

"Oh, that's mature. I wish the Penn Board of Governors could see you now. They'd be so proud of their brainiac poster child."

"Bite me."

"Ex-cuse me?" He pointed a finger at his chest. "Do I look like a pygmy blonde?"

"Nuh uh. And *à propos* of *her*," she drained her own glass, "I need to hit the trail. We're having a late supper together."

"And an early breakfast?"

She winked at him. "If I play my cards right."

He laughed. "Lemme walk you out." He stood up and grabbed his jacket, before pulling another bottle of wine out of a case.

They made their way to the front porch. Maddie turned around on the top step to hug him warmly and kiss his cheek. "Thanks, David."

"What for?"

"For always telling me the truth. It would have been easier for you just to lie, and I'd never have known the difference."

He smiled. "You should know by now that I don't do easy."

She looked at him thoughtfully. "No. You never have. That's why I love you so much."

"Really? And here I thought it was for my fashion sense." He handed her the bottle. "Enjoy this with your dinner—on the house."

She took the wine and gave him an affectionate smile. "Thanks. We will." She turned and descended the steps, waving her free hand back over her shoulder as she walked to her Jeep.

Syd smiled broadly when she opened the door to her apartment and saw Maddie leaning casually against the opposite wall. She held out the bottle of Shelton wine like an offering. "From David. I think he wants me to get you drunk."

Syd took the bottle and examined the label. "Really? And why's that?"

"I guess he thinks it might make it easier for me to have my way with you."

"Hmmm. It never occurred to me that holding out might result in such lavish treatment. Maybe I should rethink all of this."

Maddie stepped forward and bent over her so that their lips were close together but not touching. "Really?"

Syd closed her eyes and leaned against her. "No. Not really." Maddie kissed her, and they stood together in the doorway for so long that, finally, the wind sweeping up the stairs made Syd realize how cold it was in the hallway. She drew back from her reluctantly. "Come inside? I have something hot and spicy all ready for you."

Maddie waggled her eyebrows. "I'll just *bet* you do." Laughing, she followed Syd inside and closed the door. She stopped and moaned at the intriguing mixture of smells that wafted from the stove. "What are you cooking? It smells fabulous."

"Chicken and bean stuffed sopaipillas with Spanish rice."

"My god. When do we eat? I'm famished?"

Syd set the bottle of wine down on her small kitchen table and smiled at her. "When are you ever *not* famished?"

Maddie stepped forward and pulled her back into her arms. "I seem to have acquired a hunger for all kinds of things recently."

"I noticed. Lucky me." They kissed again and remained preoccupied until Syd's oven timer went off. Groaning, she pulled herself away. "Wanna open the wine while I fix our plates?"

"Sure. Where do you wanna sit?"

"You pick. Either here or the couch?"

Maddie headed for the small living room. "Couch. That way, I can sit beside you and pick at your goodies."

"Are we still talking about food?"

Maddie laughed. "I'll never tell."

"How did it go with David?"

"Fine. He was nearly as shocked as I was when Celine told me. He said that there were a few times he thought about the possibility, but that he never took the idea seriously." She paused. "I believe him."

Syd went to hand her the wine glasses and some utensils. "Of course you do. Why wouldn't you?"

Maddie shrugged. "Maybe I'm not as trusting as you are?"

"That could be true. But still, I'm glad you believe him. He's your best friend. I don't think he'd ever lie to you—even to protect you."

"I don't either."

"So what happens now?" She returned, carrying two steaming plates of food.

Maddie took one from her and sat next to her on the sagging couch. "I told him that I wanted to live with it all for a bit. Then I might write to Uncle Art—give him some time and distance to decide how he wants to reply. I thought maybe we could head up to Charlottesville later in the spring. See him, and have a nice weekend away. How would you feel about that?"

"Are you kidding? I'd love that." She gave Maddie a sidelong glance. "Would we fly?"

"Do you want to?"

"Absolutely."

Maddie grinned. "It's a date, then." They clinked glasses. "Now let's eat this wonderful meal before it gets cold. Then we can go straight to dessert."

Syd looked at her sadly. "I'm sorry, baby. I didn't plan on anything for dessert."

Maddie leered at her as she lifted a forkful of rice. "I did."

Syd rolled her eyes. "Thank god this is a high-protein recipe."

Later, they dozed in Syd's small bed until it got so late that Maddie knew if she didn't get up and head for home, she'd never make it. Fortunately, she'd already stopped by the farm and fed Pete on her way back to town from the Inn.

She turned her head on the pillow. "I need to go. It's nearly eleven."

Syd sighed dejectedly. "I know. I hate this."

"You'd hate it a lot more if Mrs. Halsey came in to open the upholstery shop at the crack of seven, and my car was still in the parking lot."

"I know." She sighed again. "How are we going to make this work? I don't want to have to sneak around like a horny teenager."

Maddie kissed her on the forehead. "One day at a time, okay? That's what we agreed."

"I know, I know. But this is nuts. I don't want you to leave."

"Trust me. I don't wanna leave, either. But you were right when you said we needed to take more time."

Syd snorted. "Yeah. We're doing great at maintaining some distance, aren't we?"

"Well, I guess we could try and not see each other *every* night."

Syd sat up and looked down at her in disbelief. "You're kidding me, right?"

Maddie chuckled. "Yeah. I'm pretty much full of shit."

"You are if you think there's any way I'll agree to *that*."

Maddie pulled her back down so that her head rested on her shoulder. "Relax. The one thing you can rely on is that I will *always* have less self control than you have."

"Thank god."

"So. Tomorrow night . . . my place?"

"Nuh uh."

"*Nuh uh?*"

"At least not for dinner. I have an extra orchestra practice tomorrow night. Phoebe wants to meet with all the principals. In fact, I'm picking Lizzy up, and we're going to grab some dinner afterward."

Maddie was intrigued. "Really?"

"Yep. Sorry, Stretch. We set this up last week." She lazily ran her fingers back and forth across Maddie's collarbone. "But I *could* stop by on the way back home. I mean, if you're interested."

Maddie sighed. "I don't know. Can I get back to you?"

Syd punched her on the arm.

"Okay, okay. I was joking. Of course I want you to stop by. How late do you think you'll be?"

"I dunno. Maybe eight-thirty?"

"I'll be waiting with bells on."

"Oh, no need to dress up on my behalf."

Maddie thought about that. "Okay, then. I'll be waiting in the nude."

Syd smiled and began to kiss her way across her chest. "Make that seven-thirty."

It was another hour before Maddie finally waved goodbye to her from the parking lot below her apartment.

After rehearsal the next night, Syd and Lizzy stood chatting with David in the parking lot of the high school while they waited on Phoebe to lock up the outside entrance to the auditorium. David was giving his mom a ride home before returning to the Inn, and he took advantage of their few minutes alone together to complain to the other two principals about how much of their spare time his mother's orchestral fantasy was taking up.

He leaned against the back of his Range Rover and took another long drag on his cigarette before blowing out a stream of blue-tinged smoke. "She's really making me insane with all of this. I mean," he waved his hand toward the building, "one or two nights a month are *fine*, but this twice a week shit has simply got to stop. I'm getting seriously behind on my *Project Runway* viewing. I totally missed Nicole Richie's hissy fit last week." He shook his dark head. "You don't get another shot at something like that."

Lizzy laughed as she shifted her flute case from one hand to the other. "It's not *that* bad, David. Besides, ever heard of TiVo?"

"TiVo? Up here in the sticks? Are you kidding me?"

"Well," Syd chimed in. "I suppose you could always break out the old VHS recorder."

"I could, if the damn thing wasn't gathering dust on the esteemed Dr. Stevenson's workbench." David tossed his cigarette to the ground and twisted it beneath the toe of his shoe. "Good thing that tool-jockey has a day job."

Syd and Lizzy laughed as Phoebe joined them. "I want to thank you all again for agreeing to put in this extra time. It's really going to bear fruit for us in the actual performance. See you all again on Sunday at three?"

David groaned. Phoebe smacked him across the abdomen with her handbag, and he made an elaborate pantomime of doubling over.

"Jeez, Mama. What've you got in that thing? Barbells?" His grousing gained momentum. "The damn thing's *big* enough to hold the whole Chuck Norris collection."

She rolled her eyes at him. "Oh, be quiet. You're just bent out of shape because I beat you to it last week at T.J. Maxx." She stroked the sides of her new handbag affectionately.

He rubbed his tummy and glowered at her. "I saw it before you did, and you know it."

She sighed in resignation and turned to Syd and Lizzy. "As I was saying, see you on Sunday?"

They both nodded.

Phoebe smiled and walked around to the passenger side of the Rover.

David sighed, then shrugged and waved goodbye. "Tell that ole sawbones I said hello."

"I will," they said, before looking at one another in surprise.

Syd felt herself blushing, but Lizzy just shrugged and smiled at her. In silence, they climbed into Syd's Volvo and followed David out of the parking lot.

Syd stole a surreptitious look at her watch. It was seven-fifteen. "So, whatcha feel like eating?"

Lizzy looked at her. "You know, I was over at my sister's yesterday, and she sent me home with a big pot of veggie soup. Would you like to just duck into my place and eat a bowl of that with me? She's a great cook—it's pretty tasty."

Syd smiled. "You don't have to ask me twice. I'll take home cooking over fast food any day. Are you sure you're up for that? I promise not to stay very late. I've got a big Baker and Taylor shipment coming in tomorrow, and I need to be at the library earlier than usual."

"No worries. I'll enjoy the company. And you haven't really seen the bungalow since I moved in. I'm anxious to show it off."

"I hear you're doing great things with it."

"I don't know about that. I'm mostly just consolidating piles of kindling. David's aunt had enough wood split to see her through until the millennium."

Syd laughed. "Don't you get lonely being out there all by yourself, with no neighbors in sight?"

Lizzy shook her head. "Nope. I *love* it. After so many years being crammed into a noisy apartment complex in Nashville and listening to kids screaming half the night and smelling everyone else's dinner, it's like heaven. And I love lying in the dark, listening to the sound of the river. It lulls me right to sleep."

"You certainly have seemed to fit right in. I'm amazed at how quickly you've made this transition."

"Why? Nashville was a big enough city, but you forget that I'm really a redneck at heart. Jericho isn't much of a departure for me from the town I grew up in."

"You're far from a redneck. Maddie says that you have about the best nursing credentials she's ever seen."

Lizzy clucked her tongue. "She exaggerates. You should know by now that you can't trust those tall, *smoldering* Ingrid Bergman types."

Syd looked at her. "Smoldering?"

Lizzy smiled. "Okay, maybe not *smoldering*. How about mysterious? That certainly applies."

Syd nodded and gave her a small smile. "I'd have to give you that one."

Lizzy plucked at the bangs of her wavy red hair. "I confess that I don't know her very well yet, but one thing I have learned about her is that she will always exaggerate someone's else's good qualities while downplaying her own."

"That sounds like a pretty apt description."

"I hear she comes by that honestly. Peggy says that her daddy was the same way."

Syd was beginning to feel uncomfortable discussing Maddie in this offhand way. It felt vaguely like gossiping—although she was certain that Lizzy was simply being open and honest in conveying her impressions of her new employer. There didn't seem to be any subterfuge or inappropriate curiosity lurking behind her observations.

She sighed. What was *really* making her feel uncomfortable was the fact that she felt forced to conceal the true nature of her relationship with Maddie. It was hard to act interested and curious about Lizzy's perceptions while maintaining the appearance of an indifference she didn't feel. It was a balancing act she wasn't eager to perfect.

They turned onto the long lane that led down toward the river and Lizzy's small bungalow. Even in the dark, signs of improvement were obvious. Ladders, tarps, and cans of paint were tidily stashed at one end of the big front porch, and a brown construction waste dumpster was positioned just in front of the small detached garage. Lizzy hadn't exaggerated. There were stacked piles of wood in various sizes everyplace. It was already dark, but several lamps were on inside the bungalow, giving it a warm and welcome appearance.

Syd parked her Volvo behind Lizzy's old Subaru wagon, and shut the engine off. Lizzy unclipped her seatbelt and opened her passenger door. "Come on inside. I'll have the soup hotted up for us in no time. You can give me your opinion about some new countertop colors for the kitchen."

Syd smiled and followed her up the steps and into the small house.

"Make yourself at home," Lizzy called out as she dropped her keys and her flute case onto a low table, then walked toward the back of the house.

Syd could hear her opening and closing doors in the kitchen and putting a pot on the stove. She took an appreciative look around the small living room. It was charming—mullioned windows flanked a fireplace with a stone hearth. An antique-looking woodstove jutted out from its opening. Heart pine floors and white, built-in cabinets ran along the back wall, forming her dining area.

"I love this place, Lizzy," Syd called out. "It's really charming."

"Thanks." Lizzy briefly appeared in the doorway to the kitchen. "See why I jumped at the chance to have it?" She held up an unopened bottle of wine. "Want something to drink while we wait on the soup to heat up?"

Syd smiled and nodded. "Thanks. That would be great."

Lizzy disappeared again. "I'll be right out. Have a seat."

Syd took advantage of the few moments of privacy to send Maddie a quick text message. She dug her cell phone out of her purse, sat down on Lizzy's small sofa, and typed quickly.

Still awake? Grabbing a bite 2 eat @ Lizzy's. Won't b long. Ditch clothes. Love u.

She hit send just as she heard Lizzy coming back into the room. She quickly set her phone aside and turned to her.

"Here you go." Lizzy held out a glass of white wine. Syd took it gratefully. It had been a long day.

"Thanks." Syd took a sip. The wine was cold and crisp. "This is *just* what I needed." She inclined her head toward the rest of the small house. "Can I be bold enough to ask for a look around? I really love what you're doing to this place."

Lizzy's smile was genuine. "Of course. I'd love to show it off. Come on. I'll give you the nickel tour." Syd set her wine glass down on the end table next to her cell phone and got up to follow her.

They walked toward the back of the house. Lizzy deposited her wine glass on a sideboard near the entrance to her bedroom and flipped a wall switch. "This is the only bedroom," she began before taking a step into the room, which now was flooded with overhead light.

Syd felt, more than heard, Lizzy's sharp intake of breath. She ran right into Lizzy who had stopped dead in the doorway.

"Oh, my god! What are you *doing* here?" Lizzy pushed back against Syd, stiff with shock and fear.

Over her shoulder, Syd was stunned to see the hunched figure of Beau Pitzer, crouched behind the bed. She had only a moment to notice that all of the dresser drawers had been pulled open, and that clothes and other personal objects were strewn everywhere. Behind him, she could see what was left of a broken window. It took her another moment to realize that he now was standing upright and holding a large hunting knife. He started to advance toward them. He stared blearily at Syd, before fixing a menacing gaze on Lizzy.

"I shoulda known you'd be one of *them*. Fucking dykes." He was breathing heavily, and his eyes looked glazed. He waved the knife at them as he rounded the end of the bed. Syd grasped Lizzy by the upper arms and tugged her back toward the living room.

"What do you want, Beau?" Syd was shaking all over, but somehow managed to make her voice sound authoritative. Lizzy was rigid and trembling with fear.

"What do you *think* I want, bitch?" He took another step toward them.

Syd pulled Lizzy back away from him and stood in front of her, facing Beau.

"Are you looking for money? Do you need money, Beau?" He was high. She was certain of it. He was high, and he was shaking almost as hard as she was. She gestured toward her purse, on the sofa near the front door. "I have some cash, if that's what you need. You can have it."

"Damn straight I can have it." He stumbled against the dining room table, causing a pair of glass candlestick holders to topple over. "I'll take the money . . . and maybe I'll take something else, too." He advanced closer. Syd could tell that he was struggling to remain upright. He waved the knife at her, standing dangerously close. His breath smelled stale and slightly putrid. His pupils were so dilated that his eyes looked black and lifeless.

"You don't want to do this, Beau," Syd said in a near whisper. "You don't want to hurt anyone." She was desperate now. Her heart was pounding so hard she could barely hear herself speak. The sound of her own blood roared in her ears. "Just take the money and leave."

He stared at her through a haze of pain and rage. Then he smacked her across the face with his free hand and knocked her to the floor near the woodstove. "Fuck you, dyke!" He advanced toward Lizzy, who now stood paralyzed with fear. "I know you've been waiting for this." He grabbed her roughly by the arm and started to haul her with him to the door. "You can come with me, and we'll have a nice little party."

Lizzy was crying. Syd struggled to her feet, clutching the side of her face. She felt something wet and sticky beneath her fingers. Her head was reeling. "Beau." She had to try again. "Beau, *stop*. Don't *do* this. You don't have to do this."

He turned to her, nearly losing his balance again. He held the knife out at her, still grasping Lizzy fiercely by the arm. "Back off, bitch. You don't know *anything.*"

Syd's cell phone vibrated on the table. Beau looked at it in alarm. Syd grabbed a piece of firewood from a kindling bucket and slammed it against his arm as hard as she could. The knife went flying, and he doubled over in pain, releasing his stranglehold on Lizzy. Syd pressed her advantage and hit him across the side of the head. The blow reverberated up her arm, and the sharp, fire-like bite of splinters drove into the palm of her hand. He fell to the floor, moaning. Blood poured from a long cut along his hairline.

"Cunt! Fucking *cunt*," he hissed. Dazed, he crawled to his feet and careened toward the door, knocking over a chair and end table on his way out. "You'll *pay* for this." He threw the door open and staggered out, tripping over a pyramid of paint cans and half falling from the porch, before regaining his footing and disappearing into the darkness beyond the house.

Syd dropped the piece of wood and raced to the door behind him. She slammed it shut and threw the deadbolt into place. Then she turned and ran back toward the bedroom, shut that door, and hauled a dining room chair over to wedge beneath the knob. Shaking, she made her way back to the sofa and snapped up her cell phone. Lizzy was sitting in a heap on the floor, shaking.

"*Hang on*, Lizzy. Hang on," she whispered. "We're okay now. We're safe. I'm calling the sheriff." With shaking fingers, she punched 911 and waited only a few seconds before a female voice answered.

"Tri-County 911. How can we help you?"

Quickly, although not very coherently, Syd told the operator what had happened, and that Beau was injured, dangerous, and still at large. She omitted details of her own condition. The operator assured her that help would be dispatched immediately and cautioned her to stay inside with the doors locked. Then Syd collapsed onto the floor next to Lizzy and pulled the shaking woman into her arms. "It's okay. We're okay now. The sheriff is on his way. Lizzy?" She forced Lizzy to look at her. "Do you have any kind of weapon here? A gun? Anything?"

Lizzy dumbly shook her head. She seemed to notice Syd's injury for the first time. "Oh, my god, you're *bleeding*." She raised a shaking hand to the side of Syd's face. "Let me look at that."

Syd's adrenalin rush was subsiding, and she became aware of how much her head hurt, and the pulsing pain in her hand from the splinters. Her insides were cramping, and she felt like she might vomit.

"You need ice on that, and a butterfly bandage to close the cut. I can get those for you," Lizzy said in a monotone—her voice almost robotic.

Syd feared she was slipping into shock.

Lizzy started to climb to her feet, but Syd stopped her. "I'm okay for now. Let's just stay put until the sheriff gets here." Her voice was high and shaky.

She knew she was hanging on by a thread. *What if he comes back?* She glanced around the room. She crawled across the floor on her hands and knees, grabbed hold of the fireplace poker, and hauled it back across the rug with her. *Maddie. I need to call Maddie.* She started shaking again. The minutes dragged by.

In the distance, they heard the wail of a siren cutting through the night like the cry of a screech owl. *Thank god.* The sound got louder and louder, and soon they could see the flash of blue lights through the front windows. Syd got shakily to her feet and went to unlock the front door.

If he hurt her, I'll kill him. If he hurt either of them, I'll kill him. Maddie drove as fast as her car, and her better instincts, would allow. She drummed her fingers on the steering wheel. Syd was all right. They both were all right. *She told me they were fine. Shaken but fine.* The sheriff was there. They were safe. *God, please let her be okay. Let them both be okay.*

She had thought to grab her emergency bag as she ran from the house, and it sat beside her on the front passenger seat of the Jeep. She wondered if she should have called the EMTs, just to be on the safe side. But Syd insisted that they both were fine. She could make her own assessment once she got there.

She turned onto the road that led to Lizzy's bungalow. In the distance, she could see flashing blue lights. There were two sheriff's cars pulled in at angles behind Syd's Volvo and Lizzy's car. Syd told her on the phone that armed officers were combing the area around Lizzy's bungalow, and that the state highway patrol had been alerted to be on the lookout for Beau's pickup truck. As she slowed down and approached the house, an officer near one of the cars held up a hand, signaling for her to stop, and approached the Jeep with a large flashlight.

"Oh, hello, Dr. Stevenson. You can go right on in. I think they're all expecting you."

Maddie nodded. *Frank,* she thought his name was. *Frank Rogers? Frank Smith? Frank something.* Last fall, his daughter had the mumps.

"Thanks, Frank," she said, pulling over and stopping. She grabbed her bag, hopped out, and took the porch steps two at a time. She paused at the open doorway and looked into the house. Her breath caught at the sight that greeted her.

Syd sat next to Lizzy on a small couch. She was holding an ice pack against the side of her face, and her right hand was wrapped in a dishtowel. She looked up anxiously when she heard Maddie's footsteps on the porch. They gazed at each other in silence for a moment, before Syd dropped the ice pack, got belatedly to her feet, and took a halting step forward. Her jaw was quivering. Maddie dropped her bag, strode forward, and pulled Syd's shaking body into her arms.

"It's okay, baby. It's okay. I'm here, now. I've got you," she muttered into her hair and kissed the top of her head over and over. Syd gripped Maddie and pushed her face deep into her chest. After a few moments, Maddie drew back and tried to coax her to lift her head. "Hey? Hey, let me take a look at your face. C'mon, baby. I need to see if you're okay."

"I'm okay. It's nothing." Syd wiped her unwrapped hand across her eyes and drew back to gesture down to where Lizzy sat quietly on the sofa watching them. "I'm worried about Lizzy." Her voice dropped to a whisper. "He tried to take her with him."

Maddie kissed her on the forehead one more time before releasing her and kneeling down in front of Lizzy. She laid a gentle hand on her knee. "Lizzy? Are you all right? Did he hurt you?"

Lizzy met her eyes. Her gaze was steady, but vacant. Her face looked waxy and pale. "I'm okay. No, he didn't hurt me. Syd stopped him." She looked up at Syd in wonder. "You stopped him. You saved me. You saved us both."

"I think she might be a little in shock, Doc," the sheriff said. "We've called her sister. They're on the way to pick her up and take her back to their place in Jefferson."

Maddie nodded. "That's good." She took hold of Lizzy's hands. They felt clammy. She noticed that she was sitting with her shoulders hunched together and her breathing seemed shallow. "Can you lie back for me, Lizzy? I wanna raise your legs a little bit." Lizzy complied, and Maddie used a sofa cushion to prop up her legs. She pulled an afghan off the back of a chair and tucked it in around her. "Lie still now, until your sister gets here. Everything is just fine. There isn't anything to worry about." She stroked her forehead gently.

Maddie stood up, wrapped an arm around Syd, and guided her to a nearby chair.

"Sit down, honey. I wanna look at your face." Maddie pushed back Syd's bangs and looked at the cut and ugly bruise forming near her right eye.

Syd leaned heavily into her. "I'm really okay. I'm just exhausted."

"I know." Maddie knelt in front of her and lifted her hand. "What happened to your hand?" She began to unwrap the towel.

"Splinters." Syd laughed bitterly. "I hit him, Maddie. I hit him with a piece of firewood." She closed her eyes. "God. I thought I killed him, but he got right up again."

Maddie felt a wave of anger wash over her. *That bastard.* She fought to keep her voice calm. "It's okay. I'll take care of it." She grabbed her medical bag and pulled it to where they sat. "Lemme get these out before they get even more swollen." She spread the towel out across Syd's lap and drew a small bottle of antiseptic wash and a long pair of tweezers out of her bag. She looked up and met Syd's green eyes. "I promise to be quick, okay?"

Syd nodded. "Okay." She closed her fingers around Maddie's hand briefly, causing her to look back up. "I love you," she whispered.

The sheriff cleared his throat and walked back toward the fireplace.

"I know," Maddie said softly. "I love you, too." She gave her a small smile and swabbed her palm with the antiseptic.

As she was pulling out the last splinter, the sheriff's radio broke the silence. A crackly voice summoned him. "Sheriff Martin, we've got a 904B in town at the upholstery shop."

He snapped the unit up off a table. "This is Martin. Say again."

"It's Adams, sir. We've got a 904B at Halsey's shop in Jericho. Looks like it started on the loading dock out back."

"Roger that. Anyone inside?"

"Negative, sir. VFD responders say both storefronts were empty, and they checked the apartment upstairs."

He shot a quick look across the room at Syd. "Roger. Seal off the block and evacuate the rest of the buildings on that side of the street. I'm on my way."

"10-4. Adams out."

"What's going on?" Syd looked up at him in alarm.

He walked to them, carrying his radio. "Looks like someone tried to set fire to your library."

"Jesus." Syd try to stand up. Maddie took hold of Syd's hands to restrain her. "How bad is it?"

"Don't know yet."

From outside, they heard the sound of voices, followed by footsteps on the porch. Lizzy's sister and brother-in-law rushed into the house. A sheriff's deputy went to brief them on the situation and to make arrangements for them to take Lizzy back to their house for the night.

Rachel Wilson was like a carbon copy of her sister. She had the same brown eyes and curly red hair, but right now, her face was pale and etched with concern. She perched next to Lizzy on the arm of the sofa and looked up at Maddie with wide eyes.

"Dr. Stevenson. Is she okay? Do we need to take her to the hospital?"

Maddie stood up. "I think she'll be fine, Rachel. She's a little in shock. She just needs some rest and some TLC. Take her home." She smiled down at her nurse. "Give her some hot tea and a warm bed. By tomorrow, she'll be as feisty as ever. Won't you, Lizzy?"

Lizzy gave her a weak smile in return. "I'll sure give it a shot." She looked at Syd. "Will you be all right?"

Syd took hold of Maddie's hand. "I'll be fine. Don't worry about me. Right now, I just want to see if my library's okay."

Maddie turned to the sheriff. "All right if we follow you over there, Byron?"

He sighed. Then gave a curt nod. "I don't suppose it would do me any good to say no." He pulled on his hat. "Come on."

Chapter 23

They could see an unnatural light in the night sky even before they topped the last rise into town. Maddie heard Syd's quick intake of breath as she slowed the Jeep down and stopped behind Byron's car.

"Oh, my god. Oh, my god. What did he do?" Syd was trembling again.

Maddie rested a hand on top of Syd's and squeezed it gently. Ahead of them, the sheriff leaned out his car window and spoke to the uniformed officer who stood in front of a line of orange traffic cones. He gestured toward Maddie's Jeep, and the deputy nodded as he stepped back to wave them through.

The closer they got to the library, the smokier the air became. Maddie pulled over and parked behind Byron's car, about half a block from the fire. Small groups of people were clustered on the perimeter of the scene, standing quietly with stunned expressions.

Several fire trucks, an EMT van, and half a dozen police cars filled the street outside the structure. There was water everywhere. It ran in crooked rivulets along the cracked pavement and pooled in the potholes that were reopened every winter by county snowplows. Maddie stood just behind Syd and kept a protective arm around her shoulders, as much for restraint as comfort. From their vantage point, they could see that the upholstery shop had sustained most of the damage from the fire.

It was clear that the Jericho VFD had most of the fire contained, but some flames were still visible on the second floor of Halsey's shop. All the windows had been broken, and shards of glass covered the pavement in front of the structure. Dark smudges from smoke and water lined the front of the building, tarring the masonry beneath the windows like cheap mascara. The library windows appeared to be intact, and Byron commented that, apparently, the thick firewall between the tandem buildings had done its job. How much of Syd's inventory would be lost to smoke and water damage was another matter. They'd have to wait until daylight to find that out. The fate of Syd's apartment, and all her personal belongings, was equally uncertain.

Maddie felt Syd sink back against her.

"My god. All that work. How could he *do* this?" She looked up at Maddie. Her expression was full of shock and dismay. "He came in nearly *every* day. He used the place more than anybody else in town. *Why* would he do this?"

Maddie tugged her closer. "I don't know, sweetheart. I don't know."

A fireman, walking confidently across a field of broken glass and dirty water, approached the sheriff. He was carrying a white plastic container.

"Hey, Byron? Looks like this might be our culprit. We found it around back, near the dumpster." He held it up.

Byron took it from him. "Acetone." He shook his head. "Same brand as the stuff we found last week at that meth lab on the river. Christ."

Maddie met his eyes. "You think it was Beau?"

He nodded. "Count on it. Don't forget that he was in rehab for meth addiction last year." He sighed as he handed the bottle back to the fireman. "Give this to the fire marshal when he gets here."

From inside her jacket pocket, Maddie's cell phone vibrated. She slapped her free hand to her side, drew the phone out of her pocket, and looked at its display. She didn't recognize the phone number. She opened it and held it up to her ear.

"This is Stevenson."

The voice on the phone was panicked—nearly hysterical. It took her a moment to understand what the woman was saying.

"I shot him! Oh, god. I *shot* him. He isn't moving. You have to help him."

Maddie stood there, dumbly trying to decipher what she was hearing, before realization washed over her like a tidal wave. She clutched the cell phone so tightly she thought she might break it.

"*Gladys?* Where are you?"

"Home. I'm at home. He came here. He was crazy. I couldn't stop him. He wanted money. He . . . he . . ." Her voice wavered. "I had the gun. I told him to stop. I told him to stop . . ."

"Gladys, did you call 911?"

"No! I don't want them. They'll take him away again." She was nearly incoherent. "Come. Come now . . . you have to help him. There's so much blood."

Maddie urgently signaled to Byron. "Gladys, is he still breathing?"

"I don't know. I don't know. He was choking, and now he isn't moving."

"I'm on my way. I'm on my way. I'll call an ambulance. Don't touch him, okay? Don't move him. I want you to wait outside for me? Do you hear me? Go outside and wait for me."

"Hurry. Please hurry." Maddie heard the click as Gladys hung up her phone. She looked up at Byron. "It's Beau. She shot him. He's unconscious and still at the house."

Byron was already in motion. "Ride with me. It'll be faster. We can radio for EMTs on the way."

Maddie and Syd ran after him. Maddie yanked open the back door to her Jeep and grabbed her medical bag while Byron turned his car around. She climbed into the big police cruiser with Syd, and Byron sped off.

The shocked and tired-looking townspeople who had gathered behind the makeshift police barricades that lined the tiny main street watched them go, then turned their gazes back toward the fire, as they continued to keep vigil in a haze of smoke and flashing lights.

Syd was surprised when Maddie climbed into the back seat of Byron's cruiser to sit beside her, instead of claiming the unoccupied front passenger seat. Byron didn't appear to notice, or, if he did, chose not to comment upon it, as they sped away from the scene of the fire. In the darkness of the back seat, Maddie took hold of Syd's hand and gently held it between hers as the car ate up the miles between Jericho and the small community where Gladys lived with her son.

Syd felt like she was fumbling about in a fog—not fully able to take in the evening's rapid sequence of events. Her face hurt like hell and her head was throbbing. She knew she'd have one whale of a shiner by tomorrow morning.

Tomorrow morning. What would tomorrow morning bring? How much of her fledgling library would be destroyed? How many of her personal belongings would survive the smoke and water? And Lizzy. How would Lizzy come to terms with what had nearly happened? Would she ever be able to return to her little house by the river?

The car swerved as Byron careened off the highway onto a side road that would take them to Gladys's house.

And now? Now they were rushing to try and save Beau. Beau—the one who had set all of these horrifying events in motion. Beau—who finally had pushed his own mother beyond all endurance. In a final act of desperation, Gladys had shot her own son.

And the irony of it all was Maddie was now the one who might determine whether Beau lived or died. Syd looked at her. The strong planes of Maddie's face were illuminated by strobe-like flashes of blue from the lights on top of the car. She was staring straight ahead—her expression was unreadable. What was she thinking about all of this? How did she feel about being placed in this position? She could have told Gladys to wait for the EMTs to get there. She could have stayed with Syd in town and not left the scene of the fire. She could have shrugged and let the fates decide what became of Beau. But she didn't.

She didn't.

Maddie must have sensed Syd looking at her, and she turned to meet her eyes. She gave the top of her hand a gentle squeeze and touched their foreheads together. "It's okay. It's all going to be okay. I promise." Her voice was barely audible beneath the constant radio chatter from Byron's police scanner.

Byron ground out the stub of a cigarette he had been smoking and took a long sip from an enormous drink cup. Syd could see a hastily wrapped hamburger perched on the top of the console between the seats. He must have been eating his dinner when he got the call to head to Lizzy's. She sighed. Almost on cue, her stomach growled. Vaguely, she wondered if anyone at Lizzy's had remembered to take the pot of soup off the stove.

Byron slowed down as they made the turn onto the street where Gladys lived.

Gladys lived in a small company house along the north bank of the New River about ten miles east of Jericho. The tiny hamlet had once been a thriving mill town, but the large textile plant that dominated life there had shut down over twenty years ago, and most of the residents had migrated on to other parts of the state in search of work. Now only a handful of families remained behind to care for their tiny scraps of lawn, and to sit in the cool evenings on identical front porches that overlooked the crumbling brickwork of an ancient dam constructed way back in the 1900s. Locals joked that not even the river stopped there any more.

Gladys's house was a standout among the ramshackle structures on her street. It was painted bright yellow and surrounded by container plants in every shape, size, and color. They could see Beau's red pickup truck parked at a rakish angle on the street out front, and, as directed, Gladys was outside, too—her wiry frame plainly visible. She was striding back and forth across her tiny porch in obvious agitation. The EMTs had not arrived yet.

Maddie leapt from the cruiser and ran for the house, carrying her bag. Gladys met her at the top of the steps.

She grasped Gladys by the forearm. "Where is he?"

Gladys gestured toward the open door and led her into the small house without speaking. Syd and Byron followed close behind them. Maddie could see Beau lying at a twisted angle in the doorway to the kitchen. A pool of blood was visible beneath his upper body. He was not moving.

"Gladys, where's the gun?" Maddie asked, as she quickly crossed the room and knelt down next to the unconscious man. She touched her fingers to the side of his neck and bent over to listen to his breathing. It was faint and constricted. His pulse was too rapid to count.

"It's over there." Gladys gestured to a rifle on the floor near the back door of the kitchen. Byron quickly went to secure the firearm.

"It's a 12 gauge—squirrel gun," He called out to Maddie as he broke it open. "One shell has been discharged."

"Right," Maddie responded. "Looks like subcutaneous and deep tissue damage to the face and neck. At least two perforating wounds to the upper chest and thorax." She drew a small flashlight from her bag and opened Beau's mouth to search for any visible airway obstruction. Then she checked his pupils: they were not reactive. She quickly checked the time on her watch.

After carefully rolling Beau onto his back, she saw that he had sustained significant lacerations to the mid and lower face—possibly a mandible fracture. Most of the blood stemmed from a puncture wound on the right side of his neck. She drew the stethoscope from her bag and listened to his heart.

"Sinus arrhythmia. He needs air." She feared that he was lapsing into ventricular tachycardia—a condition unrelated to his largely superficial gunshot wounds. He was clearly in respiratory distress. "Byron, can you find out where the hell the EMTs are?"

"Right." He snapped his radio up off his belt. "Adams, it's Martin. What's the 20 on the ambulance headed to the Pitzer house? I need an ETA, stat."

"Roger, that." There was a brief pause. "They're still about ten minutes out. Dispatch had to send a unit from Jefferson. It was the closest available—the Jericho wagon is at the fire."

He looked at Maddie. She shook her head.

"Too long. I'm going to have to trach him. He isn't getting any air." She looked up at Syd, who stood silently next to Gladys. "I need a straw. A plain old soft drink straw. There's one in the cup Byron had in the car. Can you go and get that for me?" Syd nodded and ran for the door. Maddie shifted her gaze to Gladys. "Gladys, I need a couple of clean bath towels—*fast.*" Gladys continued to stand there and dumbly stare at her. "Now, Gladys! I need towels, *now.*"

Maddie opened her bag and drew out a large container of antiseptic fluid, some gauze pads, and a scalpel. She poured the rinse on Beau's neck and swabbed the front of his throat. Gladys returned with a stack of mismatched blue and yellow towels, and Maddie took two and quickly rolled them up together. Gladys was beyond the ability to speak, and meekly retreated behind a large recliner to stand in stunned silence while Maddie worked on her son.

"Byron, help me lift his upper body a little. I need to get this between his shoulder blades."

Byron knelt beside her, and they carefully raised Beau up so Maddie could slide the towels into position. When they lowered him back to the floor, his head was slightly lower than his torso, and his neck was fully extended.

Syd rushed in from outside, carrying a paper-wrapped straw. "This one was in the Wendy's bag on the floor of the back seat," she said. "It hasn't been used."

Maddie took it from her, smiling gratefully. "Thank god for junk food. Can you get me any kind of bowl or pot from the kitchen? I need to sterilize this."

Syd nodded and ran into the kitchen and returned quickly with a medium-sized ceramic mixing bowl. It had a border of bright red poppies painted around the outside rim. Maddie handed a bottle of alcohol to Syd. "Pour about an inch of this into the bowl." She unwrapped the straw, then quickly drew a small pair of scissors from her bag and cut it in half before dropping it into the bowl. She got a new pair of latex gloves out and rapidly pulled them on. After spreading one of the clean bath towels across his chest, she leaned over Beau and ran her left forefinger back and forth across his Adam's apple, pressing beneath it and then lifting it slightly.

"Syd, put these on." She handed Syd a pair of the surgical gloves. "Then kneel down here and open a couple of these gauze pads. I'm going to need you to swab the blood away from the incision for me after I make the first cut." She looked up and met her eyes. "Are you okay with that?"

Syd nodded and pulled on the tight-fitting gloves before kneeling next to Beau's head. The ugly cut ran along the hairline over his right ear, and the matted blood covered the side of his face. She looked away as she tore open several of the square gauze packets.

Maddie picked up the scalpel and carefully positioned it over Beau's throat just beneath her left finger, and made an incision about two inches wide. Syd held the gauze pad beneath the cut to catch the ensuing small stream of blood. Maddie raised the knife and went back over the incision again, sinking the blade in deeper. She slowly rotated the knife 180 degrees before withdrawing it, then pinched the edges of the incision together, causing it gape open. She picked up one of the sections of plastic straw from the bowl and carefully inserted it into the opening. Beau's chest deflated with a hissing sound. Maddie blew air into the straw, manually inflating his lungs. She drew back and waited for the air to escape, and then repeated the maneuver. When his chest rose and fell without assistance, she sat back, grabbed her stethoscope, and held it to the side of his neck, and then to his chest.

"No good." She checked her watch again, then rummaged in her bag and withdrew a prepared syringe. "Let's try some Heparin." She tugged up Beau's t-shirt and swabbed an area near his belly button. She then unwrapped the syringe and pushed the needle into his abdomen. After administering the shot, she held her stethoscope to his chest.

She shook her head. "He's in V-tach."

She pulled the stethoscope off her neck, snapped up the scissors, and cut the hem of Beau's shirt, and then ripped it open.

"Beginning CPR." She applied rapid chest compressions and looked up at Byron. "Do you have a portable defib unit in your car?"

He nodded as he turned and ran toward the door. "On it."

"Syd." Maddie's voice was gentle. "Help Gladys." She nodded toward the distraught woman who continued to stand rigidly behind the recliner with both hands pressed against her face.

Syd looked up at Gladys, then back at Maddie, who nodded, then leaned over Beau and blew air into the end of the straw that protruded from his neck.

"Okay." She climbed to her feet and went over to Gladys. She wrapped an arm around her shoulders and talked to her in low tones. "It's okay, Gladys. Maddie's doing everything she can to help Beau. It's okay, it's okay."

Byron rushed back into the room with the portable defibrillator and knelt next to Maddie. "Sorry this is one of the older units. The county can't afford the new fangled ones yet."

Maddie was still performing the rapid chest compressions. "No problem. Charge it up and tell me when the LED shows a plus."

He nodded as he unwrapped the two white paddles. "Got a plus," he said, handing the paddles to Maddie.

She took them and positioned them against Beau's chest and side. "Lean back, Byron." She pressed the switch on the paddle and waited. The room was quiet as the unit beeped, and then buzzed. Beau's upper body lifted up as he received a powerful electric shock. Maddie released the paddles and quickly felt his pulse. Shaking her head, she quickly resumed chest compressions and counted to thirty. "Okay—clear," she called out as she took hold of the paddles to administer a second shock. After an interval of about five seconds, Beau's body lifted up again. Maddie released the paddles and quickly felt the side of his neck. Then she grabbed her stethoscope and held it to his chest. She sat back and heaved a sigh. "Okay. We've got a pulse." She dropped the paddles and checked his airway. "He's breathing normally."

Byron placed a hand on her shoulder and gave it a warm squeeze. The distant sound of a siren whined, and within what seemed like moments, EMTs were inside the house and clustered around Beau, carefully lifting him onto a gurney, fixing him with an IV, and taping the short section of straw that protruded from his trachea into place.

Maddie brought them up to speed and related everything that had happened since her arrival on the scene. She asked who was attending in the ER and said she would call ahead and brief him on Beau's condition. She mentioned a probable methamphetamine overdose and cautioned that they should not treat him with any beta-blockers until they ran a full tox screen. She suggested that his cardiac arrest was likely caused by atrial necrosis from prolonged drug abuse, and not related to his gunshot wounds.

She did not offer to accompany them to the hospital, but asked to be kept informed of changes in his condition.

Maddie gave her keys to a sheriff's deputy, and asked if he could have someone drive her Jeep back out to them. She explained that she wanted to spare Syd the ordeal of having to return to the scene of the fire. He consented at once, and was off like a shot, promising to have her car back in less than twenty minutes.

Byron had earlier arranged to have Syd's Volvo retrieved, and Maddie had instructed him just to have it taken to her farm and parked in the barn next to her Lexus. He nodded briefly before walking off with Syd's small ring of keys, seemingly unsurprised by her request.

While they waited for the sheriff's deputy to return with Maddie's Jeep, they walked the short distance from Gladys's lawn to a picnic table across the road on an undeveloped patch of grass overlooking the river. The night now seemed unnaturally quiet—a stark and surreal contrast to the way the evening had commenced. The air was cool and clear—no traces of the smoke that infiltrated everything just a few miles away.

Syd couldn't reconcile the serenity of the scene with the horrors that preceded it. The few neighbors who had been clustered outside Gladys's house during the aftermath of the shooting had dispersed, once the EMTs had departed, to return to their beds or their late-night TV viewing.

Syd tipped her head back and took in a deep lungful of the crisp night air. Maddie sat quietly beside her, perched on top of the table, facing the water.

Syd looked at her. "What you did in there. I still can't believe it."

Maddie met her gaze. Her expression was sad and slightly apologetic. "I can imagine that it wasn't easy for you to see that—to watch me try to save him. Not after what he did to you and Lizzy, and then to the library." She looked down at her hands. "I hope you know that I had to try."

Syd listened to her in confusion, then grasped her arm. "Oh, god, no. That's not what I meant. *Of course* you had to try to help him. I only meant that I had never witnessed anything like that before. I mean, I knew that you worked in a big-city emergency room before coming here, but I guess I never really thought about the kinds of things you did." She shook her head. "It was incredible." She looked deeply into Maddie's blue eyes. "I'm still a little awestruck."

Maddie exhaled and leaned forward, so that her elbows rested on top her knees. "Well, thank god for that. I was afraid you'd be . . . confused. Or angry."

"Angry? God, no." Syd looked down at her feet, perched on the bench seat. Her shoes were stained with black soot. "I'd be lying if I said I could forgive him for all he's done, but he didn't deserve to die because of it."

They were silent for a moment.

Maddie covered Syd's hand with her own and gave it a squeeze. Syd looked up at her, and Maddie smiled. "I love you, you know that?"

Syd nodded. "Yeah. I kinda figured that out."

"Besides," Maddie continued, "you were the real hero tonight."

"What are you talking about?" Syd was incredulous.

"You saved Lizzy. And even after you knew that Beau had started the fire, you still jumped right in to help me try and save him."

Syd shook her head. "Nice try, but all the heroics belong to you. You were *amazing.* I've never seen anything like that before."

"I don't deserve any special credit for that. I was only doing what I've been trained to do. It's automatic." She pulled Syd closer and wrapped an arm around her shoulders. "But *you* . . . What you did shows a depth of character that defies description. At least, it does for me."

Syd buried her head beneath Maddie's chin. "You're nuts."

Maddie snorted. "There you go with the scientific analysis again."

Syd laughed. "I thought you said you liked that? Are you changing your mind?"

"Nuh uh." Maddie kissed her on the top of her head. "When it comes to you, I'll never change my mind."

"I have something else to thank you for," Syd said quietly.

"What's that?" Maddie asked.

"It was your text message coming in that saved us. The sound of the phone buzzing distracted Beau and gave me the chance I needed to hit him."

Maddie tugged her closer, but didn't reply.

Headlights flashed as a car approached, and they turned around in time to see Maddie's Jeep pulling up and parking behind Beau's pickup truck. It was followed by another police car.

"Thank god." Syd sighed. "I just wanna go *home*, crawl into bed, and pretend this day never happened."

"Um, Syd—about that. You know it's probably going to be a while before you can . . ."

Syd placed her fingertips against Maddie's lips. She gave her a small smile. "I want to go home—with you." She lowered her hand, hopped down off the table, and walked toward the Jeep.

They climbed out of the Jeep and walked hand in hand to the big porch, while Pete ran in tight, happy circles around them. Once inside, they dropped their jackets and keys and stood facing each other in the kitchen. Syd looked exhausted.

Maddie ran a hand gently along the injured side of her face. "Why don't you go on up and hop in the shower? I'll turn off these lights and be right behind you."

Syd leaned into her hand. "Promise?"

Maddie nodded.

Syd drew Maddie's face down to hers with both hands and kissed her softly. "Find me something to sleep in?"

"I think I can manage that." Maddie smiled and kissed the tip of her nose.

Syd dropped her hands and turned toward the back stairs that led up to Maddie's bedroom. Maddie watched her disappear around the corner before going through the house, turning off lights.

"C'mon, Pete!" She gave a short whistle, and Pete ran down the long center hallway, carrying a natty-looking tennis ball in his mouth. "Bedtime." The big dog raced her to the back stairs, bounded up ahead of her, and dropped with a huff into his oval-shaped dog bed. He tipped his head back as he chewed contentedly on his prize.

The light was on in her bathroom, and she could hear the shower running. Syd had neatly folded her clothes and stacked them on a low bench that sat just outside the bathroom door. Maddie deliberated only a moment before deciding to join her. She shed her clothing and pulled on an oversized terrycloth robe that hung on the back of the door. She entered the large bathroom, opened her medicine cabinet, and took out a bottle of antiseptic rinse and some butterfly bandages.

"Knock, knock?" She turned and tapped on the shower door. "Would it be all right if I joined you long enough to take a closer look at that cut on your face?"

Syd's naked form was plainly visible through the glass shower door. Against her will, Maddie felt the prick of arousal. As Syd moved toward the door, she realized that maybe this wasn't the best idea—they both were overtired and emotionally drained. Then the door popped open, and a wet arm grabbed her by the lapel of her robe.

"What took you so long? Get in here. It feels *wonderful.*"

Shrugging and sighing happily, Maddie dropped her robe and stepped into the cocoon of heat and steam. The corner shower had jets on both of its walls, and the pulsating, hot water felt marvelous on her tired muscles. *Syd* felt marvelous on her tired muscles. Syd's wet body moving against hers felt so marvelous that soon her muscles weren't feeling tired at all.

Syd moved her hands through Maddie's hair, massaging her scalp, then squeezing the soap out as she tipped her head back under a spray of water. Maddie was basking in the luxurious attention.

"Hey, I'm supposed to be taking care of *you*," she said, as Syd finished washing her hair and ran the washcloth around in slow circles over her breasts.

Syd leaned forward and laid a series of small kisses across her chest. "You *are* taking care of me." She dropped the cloth and moved into Maddie's arms. "I need this. I need you."

Maddie pulled her closer. "You have me." She lowered her head, and they kissed deeply, eventually staggering back against the shower wall. Syd's hands seemed to be every place at once. Maddie threw her head back and gasped. "Good *god.*" She ran her hands down Syd's back and grasped her bottom, desperate for anything to hold on to. Syd's lips were now working their way back up her neck. Her tongue was teasing the outside of an ear. "Baby, *please.* My knees are about to give out. Let's go to bed. I think I'm clean enough."

Syd drew back and looked at her though a haze of steam. Her green eyes were smoldering. "Really? Then let's go and see what we can do to make you good and dirty again."

Maddie threw the lever on the shower valve, shutting the sprays of water off. Every part of her body felt alive. "I thought you were tired?"

Syd backed toward the door and tugged her along. "I seem to have rebounded."

"Apparently." Maddie sighed dramatically as she allowed herself to be led forward.

They quickly toweled themselves off and combed through their wet heads of hair. In the white light of the bathroom, Syd's face didn't look as bad as it had earlier. It was clear that she'd be sporting a class-A shiner, but now that the blood was cleared away, her small cut looked fine. Maddie carefully wrapped Syd up in her discarded robe, picked her up, and carried her into the bedroom.

Syd wound her arms around her neck and nuzzled her ear. "Now this is what I call room service."

Maddie deposited her on the bed and slowly climbed up to straddle her.

"Are you gonna get me some jammies?" Syd asked with an impish smile.

Maddie yanked off the towel she had loosely wrapped around her own body and tossed it to the floor. "I don't think so."

Syd was plainly struggling to remain coherent as Maddie leaned over her and propped up on her forearms. Her dark hair fell around Syd's face like a wet curtain.

"Do you *want* jammies?" Maddie asked, low and husky.

Syd looked up at her, then put her hands and her mouth to good use. Maddie thought she was doing a commendable job and gasped and moaned as she found release.

Then she rolled Syd over and returned the favor.

Wrapped up together under the big, star-patterned quilt, they finally fell asleep—safe and warm, and confident that, together, they had pushed back the darkness that had swirled around them all evening.

As they slept, Maddie's cell phone vibrated in its resting place below them on the kitchen table. Miles away, under the bright lights of an ICU ward equipped with every medical advantage, Beau Pitzer suffered another heart attack. This time, he did not survive.

Maddie left early the next morning. Fortunately, she was scheduled for a lighter day than normal, but knew that with Lizzy out, she'd be seeing all of the patients herself. She kissed Syd goodbye a little before eight and encouraged her to stay in bed a while longer. She promised to head home in the early afternoon so they could go together into town to meet with the fire marshal and review the condition of the library and Syd's upstairs apartment.

When she ventured downstairs, she listened to her messages. She stood for a few moments in the quiet of the kitchen before going back upstairs to tell Syd the difficult news about Beau. They sat in silence, not really knowing what to say or how to feel.

Maddie finally suggested that she intended to talk with Gladys and reassure her that Beau's death was unrelated to his gunshot wounds. In addition to everything else she would have to contend with, she didn't want Gladys wrestling with responsibility for that, too.

After Maddie left, Syd couldn't fall back asleep, so she wandered around the big farmhouse kitchen with a cup of coffee and made mental lists of all the questions she needed to ask related to recovery from the fire. What kind of help would be forthcoming from Richmond? What sort of insurance did the county carry on the facility? How much of her collection would be salvageable? Where did one go locally for disaster relief services? Would she be able to enter her apartment and get her clothes? Her books? Her computer? Who should she contact in Richmond to relate what all had transpired?

This is ridiculous, she thought. *I need a notepad.*

She refilled her cup from the pot of coffee Maddie had left her, went into the downstairs study, and looked around for a pen and a pad of paper. She found an empty legal pad on top of the desk, next to a bronze lamp with a mica shade. Behind the lamp was a framed photo of Maddie with her father—clearly taken at her med school graduation.

Maddie stood tall and beautiful, resplendent in a black gown faced with dark green velvet and a trio of wide green crossbars on the sleeve. She was hanging on to her father's arm affectionately—her head thrown back in laughter and smiling that trademark smile of hers that made Syd go weak at the knees. She was breathtaking, and Syd lost herself for few moments as she stood and stared at the picture and wondered about the amazing chain of events that had led her to be standing exactly where she was at that moment—in Maddie's house, looking at this very photograph.

She was startled when the phone on the desk rang. Uncertain for a moment about the propriety of answering it, she finally opted just to pick it up. *It might be the sheriff,* she thought. *Or Lizzy.*

"Hello?"

"Hello. I'm trying to reach Madeleine Stevenson," a woman responded after a brief pause.

"I'm sorry, she's not at home right now. You can reach her at her clinic, or I can take a message."

There was another pause. "Syd? Is that you?"

Syd felt confused. The voice sounded oddly familiar, but she couldn't quite place it. "Yes . . ."

"It's Celine."

Celine. Oh, my god. "Celine? Hello. How are you?"

"I'm fine. I was hoping to catch Maddie before she left for work this morning. That's why I'm calling her house phone."

Syd glanced at her watch. It was eight-forty—five-forty in California. Celine was an early riser, like her daughter. "She had a hefty patient load this morning, so she went into the clinic an hour earlier than usual. I'm sorry that you missed her. She will be, too."

"That's okay. I can try her cell phone later on. Or if she's that busy today, maybe she can call me back when it's convenient?"

"Um, is everything okay? I mean, are you doing all right?" Syd felt awkward and tongue-tied. She didn't know why she felt so embarrassed to be caught lounging around Maddie's house at such an ungodly hour of the morning. She certainly didn't need for her discomfort to make her sound like an imbecile to Celine.

"I'm *fine*—really. Thank you for asking." There was a pause on the line. "Are *you* all right?"

Syd closed her eyes as she stood there with the phone pressed to her ear. She felt strangely overcome with the need to tell the truth. "No. No, not really. I'm sorry. I'm just . . . I . . ."

"What is it?" Celine's voice contained a trace of alarm. "Has something happened? Is Maddie all right?"

"No. I mean, *yes*." She sighed. "Maddie's fine. But, yes, something *did* happen." She shook her head to clear it and sat down on a leather-covered ottoman. "I'm sorry. I must sound like an idiot."

"Well, not entirely." Celine's drollness was so reminiscent of Maddie that Syd couldn't help but smile. "Look, why not take a deep breath, and then tell me what's going on."

"It's a long story."

"That's okay. I've got a good long distance plan, and I haven't used many of my friends and family minutes up until now. I'd like to change that."

Syd smiled and slid back onto a chair. "We'd like to change that, too."

"Well, then this seems like as good a time as any to start."

Suddenly, Syd wanted very much to talk—not only about the events of last night—but about events of the last six months. After nearly forty-five minutes, she realized with amazement that she had been talking pretty much nonstop. Celine had interrupted her from time to time to react or to ask for clarification, but Syd found that Maddie's mother possessed uncanny reflective listening skills. She expressed concern and amazement about her horrifying encounter with Beau, and was unmistakably proud of Maddie's later, heroic efforts to save him. She was also a good sounding board for Syd to air her mounting anxiety about her immediate future, and her uncertainly about the wisdom of moving in with Maddie so early into their relationship.

"Is there some magic amount of time that you think should elapse before you take this step?" Celine asked, after Syd revealed that one of her greatest concerns was that the fire would force them into something they both thought was happening too soon.

"Well, no. I mean, nothing hard and fast."

"Are you committed to each other?"

"I think so." *No, that wasn't right.* "Yes."

"But you fear that proximity will compromise that?"

"Well, I just don't want us to do anything that might jeopardize our future together."

"And living together in a committed relationship with the person you love, might do that, *how*, exactly?"

Syd laughed. "Now I see where your daughter gets it."

"Gets what?"

"Her annoying proclivity for winning arguments."

"Oh," she could tell that Celine was smiling, "I don't know about that. I think I could learn a thing or two from her."

"Just remind me that I never want to be caught in the crossfire between you two." Celine fell silent, and Syd realized how her innocent gibe might have gone astray. "Oh, god, I didn't mean that the way it sounded."

"I know. It's all right. I'm hopeful that one day we *will* be able to spar with one another again—without the rancor or the baggage."

"I know that Maddie wants that, too."

"You're good for her," Celine said, with authority. "I noticed that immediately when I saw the two of you together in Richmond."

Syd felt embarrassed and wondered again if they should tell Celine the truth about Richmond. "I'm glad you think so."

"You love her." It was a statement, not a question.

"I do. More than I ever thought possible. It's been quite a transition for me—moving here and meeting Maddie." She shook her head. "Going from being married to discovering I'm gay at what seems like light speed. Even though I know it really didn't work that way. I don't know. It's like . . . I feel sometimes like I'm plastered against the cow catcher of a runaway locomotive."

Celine laughed. "Interesting analogy."

Syd shrugged and smiled into the phone. "I love trains. My favorite book growing up was *The Little Engine That Could*."

"Well, lucky for you, this is *one* load you don't have to haul over the mountaintop by yourself. Let Maddie pull her weight. She's up to it. That's what relationships are supposed to be all about—sharing the hard parts along with the easy parts and getting to the same destination together."

Syd smiled. "Thanks for reminding me of that. I tend to over think things."

"That's not always a bad quality. But if every signpost of life seems to be pointing you in the same direction, then the best and wisest course to follow just might be the one laid out in front of you."

"I guess you're right."

"Maybe. But one thing I've learned from my own mistakes is that we're generally better off if we listen to our hearts and not our fears."

Syd was amazed. "You're the second person who's said that to me."

"Well, if a third person says it, then your data will definitely be trending in a certain direction."

Syd laughed. "Thank you, Dr. Heller."

"Syd, may I make another suggestion?"

"Of course."

"If you haven't talked with them yet, call your parents. Tell them what happened last night and let them help you." She hesitated. "I'm sure they'll want to. Maddie spoke very highly of them both."

Syd's eyes brimmed with tears. "Okay. I will."

"Good. You'll be glad you did, and so will they."

Syd sat up straighter in the chair, feeling better—feeling more empowered and less tentative. "Thank you. I mean that." She hesitated. "I hope we can talk again. I've really enjoyed this conversation."

"I have, too. You can call me anytime."

Syd smiled into the phone. "Count on it, then. I'll tell Maddie you called. She'll be so pleased."

"I hope so. Thank you, Syd. Take care."

"You, too, Celine."

They hung up, and Syd sat there holding the phone in her hand, feeling slightly dazed from their conversation. Then she exhaled and dialed a familiar number. When the phone was picked up on the second ring, she took a deep breath. "Hello, Mom?"

Fortunately for Syd, most of the damage the library sustained occurred in the form of smoke, although there was some significant damage to carpet, interior walls—and the books that lined them—from rivulets of soot and water that seeped through cracks in the stairway wall. The upholstery shop was another matter—most of the ground floor of that building was destroyed.

Syd's apartment fared little better. The open stairway that separated the two buildings had acted like a massive chimney—its smooth walls fed a seamless updraft that channeled smoke and soot upstairs, seeking a natural outlet through the open windows on the second floor. Most of the shabby interior furnishings were damaged beyond repair. The walls and the carpet were badly stained with soot.

Most of Syd's clothing and other personal items would be salvageable after extensive odor neutralization and professional cleaning. Some of her books were destroyed—but others would be boxed up and sent to remediation facilities along with affected volumes from the library below. The local dry cleaner in Jefferson had a sizeable ozone chamber, and they graciously offered the use of it to Syd, to expedite the recovery of her non-textile items. In the meantime, a judicious sweep through the Wytheville Wal-Mart would have to tide her over until the rest of her clothing was cleaned and restored.

The library collection was still in its infancy, so the number of volumes affected during the fire was fairly modest. Disaster relief workers from Roanoke were able to quickly box them up and store them on refrigerated trucks. The now frozen books would be transported to a facility where a sublimation process would freeze-dry the volumes to remove all traces of smoke and dampness. The state library of Virginia insured the contents of the facility, but not the physical structure, so these more sophisticated recovery measures were undertaken immediately.

Syd's housing was another matter. It would be days, perhaps a full week, before local insurance adjusters would offer their assessments to the library board, and then the county would be faced with the prospect of determining whether the upstairs apartment could be made habitable again without a significant commitment of funds. In the meantime, Syd was homeless.

Word of the fire, and sketchier accounts of events that preceded it, spread quickly throughout the county, and Syd was besieged with phone calls. With the absence of a local paper, she decided that it made sense to release accurate information selectively using reliable word-of-mouth channels. So, after briefing all members of the Tri-County library board, she stopped by the mini-mart to share details with Curtis and Edna Freemantle. Freemantle's market functioned like a neighborhood wire service, and sooner or later, most residents of the area could be relied upon to stop in and add to or glean from the escalating summaries of what all had transpired the night before. Curtis later reported that they had run completely out of hot dogs and iced tea well before eleven on Tuesday morning—the first time that had happened since the day of the 9/11 attacks.

Across town, Maddie's clinic functioned in much the same way, and Peggy Hawkes happily took up the mantle of official fact-checker and primary information conduit. No, Syd was not at home when the fire started. Yes, the sheriff is sure that Beau Pitzer started it. Yes, Beau did try to rob Lizzy's bungalow. No, he did not rape her. Yes, Lizzy was taking a few days off to recover from her ordeal. Yes, she was staying with her sister in Jefferson. Yes, it's true that Syd was the one who saved Lizzy by chasing Beau off. Yes, Maddie was the doctor who responded when Gladys shot her son. No, he did not die from gunshot wounds. Yes, they think it was a drug overdose. Yes, she had heard that Phoebe Jenkins lost an entire parlor set when Halsey's shop caught fire. Yes, the library was now closed. No, she did not know when or if it would reopen. No, Syd would not be allowed to stay there. No, she did not know where Syd would stay in the meantime, or if she would stay on in Jericho if the county couldn't afford to fix the library. Yes, she was certain that Dr. Stevenson was losing patience with all the phone calls. Yes, she promised to call back later after work.

Maddie and Syd rode home after their meeting with the fire marshal and their preliminary walk through the library and Syd's upstairs apartment. The

Roanoke disaster recovery team was already on-site, thanks to an industrious Elizabeth Metcalf in Richmond—who understood that time was the enemy if there was any hope of salvaging books damaged by water. Other affected items would be disposed of, or aired out and cleaned on site. Once they were allowed upstairs, Syd and Maddie made short work out of stuffing Syd's smoke-infused clothing into large plastic bags and carrying them downstairs to a waiting ServPro truck that was on hand to pick them up and transport them off to Wytheville for cleaning.

After arriving back at the farm, they showered and changed clothes before venturing back downstairs to make dinner. Maddie lent Syd a clean pair of hospital scrubs and her favorite oversized, black v-neck sweater to wear while their clothes were in the wash. In the kitchen, Syd had her first real opportunity to fill Maddie in on the details of her conversation with Celine, and her later phone call to her parents—who now were planning to visit the following weekend.

"I called Michael, and he's going to put them up at the Inn. Secretly, I think Dad was thrilled to have another crack at that infamous bass that nearly drowned him the day after Thanksgiving."

Maddie stopped opening a bottle of wine and looked up at Syd with a disappointed expression. "Why couldn't they just stay here with us? We have plenty of extra room."

Syd smiled at her sweetness, and her apparent lack of introspection. "Honey, it might be true that *you* have lots of extra room. But as far as my parents are concerned, I'm already a guest here, and they wouldn't want to impose on you, too."

"Impose?"

"Uh huh."

"You aren't imposing on me."

"That might be true. But I'm not exactly living here with you, either."

Maddie looked like she was trying very hard not to pout. "You aren't?"

"No, I'm not. Not *yet*, anyway."

"Well, I guess that's something." Maddie resumed twisting the cork out of the bottle.

Syd stood regarding her for a moment, then she walked across the kitchen and kissed her gently on the cheek. "Fire or no fire, you know there's no place I'd rather be than here with you . . . right?"

Maddie met her eyes sheepishly. "I know."

Syd tugged at the sleeve of her shirt. "Then why the long face?" She leaned forward and whispered against her ear, "You know you're going to get your way in the end."

Maddie gave her a small smile. "I am?"

"Of course you are. Don't you always?" She laughed. "Even your mother told me it was pointless to resist." She kissed her again—on the lips this time. "Just be patient for a little while."

"I guess I can do that."

"I know you can. Besides," Syd walked back to the sink and resumed washing a pile of torn lettuce leaves. "I'm not ready to have my mother and father be right down the hall while I'm sleeping with you."

Maddie looked at her. "Not to belabor the point, or anything, but we—I—do have *three* guest rooms."

Syd raised an eyebrow. "Are you suggesting that I could stay here and *not* sleep with you?"

Maddie thought about that. "So, Michael's putting them up again? What a *great* idea. Why don't we have them over here for dinner on Saturday night?"

Syd laughed. "I love you."

Maddie smirked as she poured them each a glass of wine. "I know." She crossed the room and handed a glass to Syd. She turned around and leaned her back against the countertop so she could watch Syd while she worked. "So, tell me more about your conversation with my mother."

"It was amazing, really. I found myself just yammering on and on, like I'd been talking to her that way for years." Syd looked up and met Maddie's blue eyes. "She's so much like you in so many ways. I guess that's part of what made it so easy for me to talk with her. I was impressed by her determination to reach out to you—to us both, really. That part was especially humbling to me."

"Why? She knows how much I love you. She knows that you're a huge part of my life now."

Syd smiled. "I think that's precisely why it was so humbling. It made all of this real for me in a whole new way."

"What do you mean?"

"Hearing your mother talk so matter-of-factly about our relationship—like it was ordinary or unremarkable. And I mean that in the literal sense—not in a judgmental way."

Maddie nodded and crossed her arms. "She likes you. She has right from the outset. Before we even knew where we were headed."

"I know. I came close to telling her the truth about Richmond, but I knew that I couldn't do that without discussing it with you first. I don't like deceiving her—especially now."

"Me either. I guess we do need to come clean about all of that."

"Are you going to call her back?"

"Yeah. I thought I'd do that this evening."

"Why don't you go and call her now, while I'm fixing us some dinner? It's going to be a good forty-five minutes before everything's ready."

"Are you sure you don't need my help with anything?"

Syd smiled at her. "I need your help with *everything*. But in this case, I think I can manage by myself."

Maddie kissed her on the temple. "Okay, then, I'll go and call her." She picked up her wine glass and headed toward the study. "Be back soon."

"Tell her I said hello."

"I will." Maddie disappeared down the hallway, and Syd turned her attention back to the meal preparation.

Maddie reappeared about thirty minutes later, just as Syd was transferring sautéed chicken breasts to a baking sheet. Maddie looked happy and relaxed. Clearly, the conversation with her mother had gone well.

"Mom said to tell you that she was glad the damages to the library were far less serious than they could have been." She paused. "She's happy that you'll be staying on here with me for a while."

Syd shot her a sidelong glance. "Are you two in cahoots now?"

Maddie smiled slyly. "I wouldn't say cahoots, exactly. But we are of the same mind about one or two things."

"Color me *so* surprised."

Maddie affected a high-pitched wail and fluttered the fingers of both hands. "Surrender Dorothy!"

"Very funny."

"Hey, just be glad it's me and not David. He'd have hauled out the costume *and* the makeup."

"Now there's a horrifying thought. What else did you two talk about?"

"Well, she floated the idea of coming for a visit this summer."

"Really? That's wonderful."

Maddie looked smug. "I thought so, too. You, know," she continued, more thoughtfully, "that will be quite an event. She hasn't been back here since the day she left—nearly twenty-five years ago."

"A lot has changed since then."

"It sure has. And speaking of things that have changed . . . You *do* realize that we put on quite a performance for Byron and Lizzy last night, don't you? I think any questions either of them may have had about my sexual orientation have been laid to rest."

Syd turned around to her. "Not just yours."

"No . . ."

Syd shook her head. "The things Beau said to me—about *us*. God. Obviously, he had pieced it all together. I don't know how. He must have been stalking us."

"Probably." Maddie's voice was gentle. "It doesn't matter now."

Syd closed her eyes. "God, Maddie. I'm *so* sorry. It's my fault. I thought I could manage it. I really did. And then when I saw you walk through that door. I just didn't care any more. All I could think about was being close to you. I was so scared. The whole time he was there and waving that knife around at us, I thought I'd never see you again. I really thought he would kill us both—especially after I hit him, and he got back up."

Maddie quickly stepped forward and pulled Syd into her arms. "It's okay, baby. I'm not worried about it—not at all. It doesn't matter. Nothing matters except this. We're together and we're okay, and I don't give a damn who knows about it."

Syd sniffed against her shirt. "I don't care either. Not anymore."

They stood there for another minute, holding each other in silence. Then Syd pushed back and looked up into Maddie's face.

"I guess we need to make a trip to the hardware store tomorrow."

Maddie wiped a tear off her cheek. "What for?"

Syd smiled at her. "Because it looks like I'm gonna need a house key."

George and Janet arrived in Jericho shortly after one on Saturday. Maddie was working a shift at the ER that day, and would be out of pocket until after three, so Syd drove alone to meet her parents at the Inn.

After lunch, they went into town to see the library, and to review the progress being made by the ServPro team from Wytheville. The worst of Syd's black eye had faded by they time they arrived, but traces of the large purple and yellow bruise were still visible enough to make Janet gasp when she saw her for the first time.

"My god. What did he *do* to you?" Janet took Syd's face between her hands and turned her toward the light.

"It's fine now, Mom. Honest. It looks a lot worse than it was."

George ran a soothing hand up and down her back. "I can't believe he hit you. I would've killed him."

"I nearly did—and if I *had*, that would have been even worse." Syd put her arms around both of her parents. "Thank you for coming. I mean that. I didn't realize how much I needed to see you both."

George hugged her warmly. "We would have been here sooner if we hadn't known you were here with Maddie. She told us you were doing just fine."

Syd drew back and met her father's eyes. "You talked with Maddie?"

"Of course I did." He smiled at her. "I called her as soon as you were off the phone with your mother. I wanted to make sure you were as okay as you said you were."

Janet rolled her eyes. "I couldn't stop him. I think he has her on speed dial."

Syd laughed.

"But in all fairness," Janet continued, "If he hadn't, I would have called her myself."

Syd smiled at them. "It's okay. I understand."

"We're happy that you're staying there with her. We didn't want you to be alone right now."

Syd looked at her mother. "Believe me when I tell you that I've never felt *less* alone."

They regarded each other in silence.

"I believe you," her mother said, finally. "And I'm happy about that—for both of you."

Syd couldn't hide her smile. "Thanks." She looked at her father, who stood watching them with a smug expression. "What?"

He sobered and raised his palms. "Don't look at me like that. I told you from the get-go that I didn't care *who* got her as long as she ended up in the family."

Syd poked him in the ribs. "Why are you suddenly talking like Tony Soprano?"

"Hey? Family is important. You only get *one*, you know. And speaking of that—your brother is coming down tomorrow."

Syd was shocked. "He is?"

"Yes, he is. Just for the day. We thought that maybe the five of us could spend some time together. We've already asked Michael if he would cook for us all here." He gave her a small smile. "I think we have a lot to celebrate—don't you?"

She nodded. "I suppose we do."

"It's settled, then. And I'm going to ask Maddie if there's anyone besides David and Michael she wants to invite."

"Dad, is this a family reunion or a block party?"

"Do I have to choose?" His green eyes twinkled. "Besides, I don't think one precludes the other." He looked up at the sky. "Winter is finally over. It's about time we all spent a day in the sun."

Chapter 24

Maddie finished her shift and climbed into her Jeep in the hospital parking lot. Her cell phone rang. She fished it out of her bag and looked at the readout, but did not recognize the phone number.

"This is Stevenson."

"Dr. Stevenson?" It was a woman's voice.

"Speaking."

"My name is Elise Manning. I'm a friend of Ada Lawrence's . . . in Kannapolis." Ada Lawrence. Henry's grandmother. "Of course. Mrs. Manning. Hello."

The woman sounded nervous. "I'm sorry to have to bother you."

"No, please. It's not a bother." She paused. "Is Henry all right?"

"Henry is fine. It's Ada. She's in the hospital."

Maddie was alarmed. "What happened?"

"They aren't really sure. She collapsed at work last night. They think it might have been a stroke."

"Is she conscious?"

"Yes. But she's in intensive care at the hospital in Concord. I've been keeping Henry."

"How is he?"

"Well, that's really why I'm calling." She paused. "He's very upset. Scared. He keeps asking for you. He gave me your card. I think he's been sleeping with it. I asked Ada about it today. She said it was okay to call you."

"Of course it's okay to call me. Is he there? Can I talk with him?"

"Yes. He's right here. Hang on." Maddie could hear the phone being passed to someone.

"Maddie?" Henry's small voice filled her ear. "Gramma's sick. I told them to call you. I told you you could fix her."

"Hey, buddy. It's okay. Calm down, now."

"Will you come and fix her? I know you can."

"Your grandma already has doctors there, buddy. I'm sure they're taking very good care of her."

"But she needs you. I *know* you can fix her." He hesitated. "She told me it was okay to call you."

Maddie closed her eyes and took a deep breath. "Listen, buddy. I'll come down and see you tomorrow, okay? And if your grandma's doctors say it's okay, I'll visit her, too. How does that sound? Can you be a good boy for Mrs. Manning tonight? Be strong and help her?"

She could tell that Henry was nodding. "Yes. I'm scared. I don't wanna be alone."

She felt her throat constrict. "I know you're scared, but you don't have to worry. Mrs. Manning is there to help you, and I'll come see you tomorrow. I'm proud of you. I know you want to help your grandma. The best way for you to do that right now is to be good for Mrs. Manning. I promise I'll be there tomorrow, okay?"

"Okay."

"Can I talk with Mrs. Manning again?"

"Okay. Bye, Maddie."

"Bye, Sport."

She heard him pass the phone over.

"Hello?" Mrs. Manning sounded calmer.

"Mrs. Manning, I told Henry that I would come down tomorrow to see him. Could you get me the name of Ada's attending physician in Concord? Obviously, I can't see her as her doctor, but I can inquire about her condition and stop in to see her while I'm there."

"That would be wonderful, Dr. Stevenson." Mrs. Manning sounded relieved. "I can't thank you enough."

"Don't thank me. I told them both to call me if they ever needed anything. I'm happy to help out, even in this small way."

"I'll call you back this evening with the information, and with directions to my house."

"That would be perfect. Mrs. Manning?"

"Yes?"

"Thank you for taking care of Henry. I know he's in great hands."

"He's a sweet boy. He's been through a lot. I'm glad he met you."

Maddie smiled. "I am, too. Talk to you later on?"

"Sure thing. Thank you, Doctor." She hung up.

Maddie sat quietly in the driver's seat, with one foot inside her Jeep, and one foot resting on the running board. She sighed and held the cell phone against her forehead. Then she sat back and dialed another number. A man picked up on the fourth ring.

"Tri-County Airport."

"Hey, Tommy. It's Maddie Stevenson."

"Howdy, Doc. You wanting to take advantage of this great weather and go out for a spin?"

She smiled. "Something like that. I need to hop down to Concord tomorrow—just for the day. Can you pull her up for me and have her gassed and ready to go by ten?"

"Sure, no problem."

"Thanks, Tommy. I hate to bug you with this on a Sunday."

"No sweat, Doc. I gotta be out here anyway. See you tomorrow."

"Right." Maddie hung up.

She sat for another moment before climbing fully into the Jeep and closing the door. They had dinner with Syd's parents at the farm tonight. She had no idea what they had planned for tomorrow, but she'd do her best to be back in Jericho by dinnertime. She sighed and started the Jeep. *I sure hope she doesn't kill me.*

Syd was incredulous when Maddie told her about the phone call from Elise Manning. She was in the kitchen, washing vegetables for a salad when Maddie got home. Her parents were due in another hour.

"Are you sure you want to do this?" she asked, drying her hands on a cotton towel.

Maddie nodded. "I know it sounds insane, but I *promised* him. I promised him that I would come if he ever needed me."

Syd looked at Maddie with a curious expression. "That's not what I'm talking about. Of course you have to go. What I meant was—are you sure you want to wait until tomorrow?"

Maddie stared at her stupidly for a moment, before stepping forward and pulling her into her arms. "How did I get so damn lucky?"

Syd hugged her back. "Beats me." She lifted her head and kissed Maddie on her collarbone. "You're such an old softie. I love that about you."

Maddie smiled. "I love *everything* about you."

"Oh, really? Do you love me enough to take me with you tomorrow?"

Maddie held her at arm's length. "Are you serious? What about your parents?"

Syd shrugged. "What about them? Dad's dying to hit the river and go angling for his elusive bass, and Mom's going to spend the better part of the day helping Michael cook." She paused. "I think those two have formed some kind of Vulcan mind meld. It's actually pretty creepy."

Maddie laughed. "It's a date then. I'd love to have you with me. You need to meet Henry, in any case, but just remember that I found him first."

"I never thought my biggest rival for your affections would end up being a five-year-old boy."

Maddie smiled sheepishly. Syd tugged her closer and kissed her on the chin. "Good thing you're such a tall drink of water, and that I've got a generous nature."

Maddie ran her hands up and down Syd's back. "Generous? Now there's a hypothesis I'd like to test." She began to kiss along the side of Syd's neck.

Syd stood there for a moment, enjoying the attention, before she reluctantly pushed herself away. "I said generous, not crazy. My mother will be here in less than an hour." Maddie took another step toward her. She quickly laid a palm against her blue-clad chest. "You need to go and get changed. We'll have lots of time later on to explore my generosity."

Maddie sighed. "Promise?"

Syd chewed the inside of her cheek as she slowly looked up and down Maddie's long body. "Oh, yeah."

George and Janet were completely captivated by Maddie's farm. George insisted that Maddie walk him around outside for a tour. He was especially enamored of the pond and the small creek that fed it, and expressed chagrin that he didn't have enough daylight left to explore more of it. Maddie was quick to suggest that he should come back out tomorrow and spend as much time as he wanted tromping around. They walked the perimeter behind the barn and outbuildings until they reached the point where the creek veered off and cut down through a pasture on its inevitable path toward the New River. Pete happily followed along behind them, as they made slow progress back toward the house.

"How many acres do you have here?" George asked, standing up and brushing off his hands. He had been sifting through some crushed rock near a fence post. He looked around in admiration—plainly in his element.

"About eighty, I think. To tell the truth, I'm not really sure. I think Dad bought a few more acres along the county road several years back, when the neighboring farm sold at auction."

"That's just incredible. This is an amazing piece of property. Who maintains all of these pastures?"

She smiled. "Well, that's the best part. I let my neighbors use the land for grazing, and they get the hay in exchange for keeping up the fences. It's a great deal for me. I get all the benefits of living on a functional farm with almost none of the work."

He nodded. "It sounds like a great deal for them, too."

She shrugged. "Dad always managed it this way. It was easy for me just to continue his arrangements. I do have responsibility for upkeep on the ten acres right around the house. But that's about it."

"I love it here."

Maddie smiled at him. "I'm glad. You need to spend more time here with us—with *me*."

He looked at her with a raised eyebrow. "Are you suggesting that my daughter hasn't quite taken up residence with you here yet?"

She sighed. "I guess I'm pretty transparent. Sorry. The truth is, Syd still needs a bit more time before she makes a formal transition like that, and I support her."

He gave her a measured look. "You do?"

"Of course."

He regarded her silently for a moment. "With all due respect, Doctor, you're more full of shit than this pasture."

Maddie looked at him in surprise, before she lowered her head and chuckled. "I guess I am."

George laughed. "Don't despair. She isn't going anyplace. She's enough like her mother that it's just going to have to be *her* idea. And trust me, she'll make you wait for it." He laughed. "But in the end, you'll get what you want."

Maddie looked at him with amusement. "That's pretty much what *she* said."

"See? The apple doesn't fall too far from the tree."

"Lucky for me."

"I dunno about that. Those two can jerk a knot in your tail faster than you can shake a stick. I don't walk with a limp for nothing."

She smiled at him. "I feel your pain, George."

"Not as much as you *will* . . . trust me."

They continued meandering along the split rail fence that bordered the pasture.

"I can't thank you enough for your understanding," Maddie said.

He looked up at her. "About what?"

"Syd. Me." She waved her hand. "Us. It's a lot to take in, I know."

"It's not as hard as you might think. What father doesn't want his daughter to find happiness? And I've never seen her as happy as she is when she's with you. That goes a long way toward overcoming any concerns we might have had. We love her, Maddie. And we know that you do, too. That's all that matters to us."

Maddie was humbled by his comments. "Thank you."

"No need to thank me." They walked on in silence for a moment. He looked at her again. "There is *one* thing that does concern me, however, and I guess this is as good a time as any to bring it up."

Maddie felt a small surge of panic. "What is it?"

He sighed. "My son is simply too unfocused and too unreliable." He met her level gaze. "That means it's going to be up to *you* to provide us with grandchildren." He narrowed his eyes. "At the risk of offending you—neither of you is getting any younger. Syd says you're very creative. So, what ideas do you have about *this* proposition?"

Maddie was stunned. Then she shook her head and laughed. "Funny you should mention kids . . ."

They walked on toward the house in earnest conversation.

In the big farmhouse kitchen, Janet helped her daughter with final preparations for their meal. Syd was roasting an Italian flank steak that was stuffed with prosciutto and roasted red peppers. Her mother was helping her by spooning a big bowl of cheddar-mashed potatoes into a baking dish and sliding them into the second oven on the massive range.

"This is some kind of kitchen," her mother said with obvious admiration. "Did you say that Maddie doesn't cook much?"

Syd laughed. "Maddie doesn't cook at all. She insists that her father was the gourmet in the family—all of this was his."

"It's certainly amazing." She looked at her daughter. "This whole place is amazing. You must love being here." She paused. "You certainly seem to know your way around."

Syd tossed the salad. "I won't deny that being here has its perks, and yes, it *is* amazing." She met her mother's eyes. "But you know that my reasons for wanting to be here have little to do with the accommodations."

Her mother nodded. "I know. She's . . . *unique*, Margaret." She shook her head. "Exceptional. She loves you."

Syd couldn't suppress a smile. "I love her, too."

"I believe you do."

"Are you—are you okay with that? I mean, really okay?"

Janet nodded. "It surprises me just how okay with it I am. But seeing you as happy as you are, especially after all you've been through with Jeff—I couldn't be otherwise."

"Well, in fact, you *could* be, but I'm beyond grateful and relieved that you aren't."

Her mother smiled. "I am, too. And your father is pretty much beside himself, but I think you knew that already."

"Yeah." Syd shook her head in amazement. "At first, it was hard to tell which one of us had the bigger crush on her."

"No kidding. And then your brother met her after Christmas, and it got even *more* complicated."

Syd rolled her eyes. "I know. I thought I was going to have to turn a hose on him because his behavior was so obnoxious. What is it with the men in this family?"

"I wish I knew." Her mother carried a stack of plates and silverware over to the big kitchen table. "Have you talked with Tom?"

"What about?"

"About you . . . and Maddie."

Syd was startled. "No. I mean . . . I just thought that you . . ."

"Margaret, we aren't going to tell Tom—or anyone—about this. Who gets told, and on what timetable, needs to be *your* decision."

"Oh, great. So that means we all get to endure his testosterone-induced, prancing around after Maddie yet again tomorrow?"

"I think you possess a means for short-circuiting that behavior, if you choose to exercise it."

She sighed. "You're right. I'll talk with him."

"Good."

Syd joined her mother at the table and placed the salad bowl on a ceramic trivet. "About tomorrow—are you really okay with me going along to Concord with Maddie?"

"Of course. It sounds important. And I know you're dying to meet the young man who's made such a strong impression on her."

Syd smiled. "I am. She tries to deny that she likes kids, but she has such a sweet way with them. I've seen her with her younger patients, and it's pretty amazing. They just seem to glom onto her." She laughed. "Kind of like everyone else."

"Children are pretty shrewd judges of character."

"They are, aren't they?" She snorted. "And goes a long way toward explaining Tom's fascination with her, too."

"Be nice."

"Okay, okay." The oven timer dinged. "Looks like we're ready to eat. Let's round up the other suspects."

Her mother walked back to the stove. "Good luck convincing your father that he needs to eat his meal inside, and not out on the back forty."

"I think I can manage." Syd went to the back door just as Maddie and her father appeared outside on the porch. She pulled the door open. "Great timing. Dinner's ready. Let's see those hands."

Her father gamely displayed his soiled hands, palms up, before kissing her on the forehead and pushing past her to head for the prep sink. Maddie followed close behind. Syd held up a hand to stop her.

"Okay, you. Get 'em up."

Maddie raised an eyebrow. "You think I got dirty?"

"Were you out there with my father? Of course you got dirty."

Maddie sighed. She held up her hands. The ends of her fingers were gray with dust.

"Uh huh. Thought so." Syd grabbed her by the lapels and tugged her further into the room. "Hose 'em off, Stretch."

"Oh, you're so tough." Maddie kissed her softly. Then she looked quickly over Syd's shoulder with wide eyes.

Syd turned around and followed her gaze. Her parents stared back at them with amused expressions. She turned back to Maddie, who now was a bright shade of red. "Well, that's *one* less thing we have to worry about. Think you can slip up again tomorrow night in front of Tom?"

George's laughter mingled with the sound of running water.

Maddie and Syd landed at the Concord Regional Airport a little after eleven a.m. Maddie had arranged for the use of an airport courtesy car, and they drove the short distance to NorthEast Medical Center, where Ada Lawrence was a patient in the coronary care unit. Elise Manning was meeting them there with Henry at eleven-thirty.

Maddie heard Henry before she saw him, when they stepped off the elevator on the second floor. He was sitting on a sofa near the nurse's station, watching the elevator doors, waiting for their arrival. He jumped up when he saw her.

"Maddie!" He called out as he ran toward her. "You came."

She dropped down on one knee and hugged him as he hurled himself at her. "Hello, buddy. Of course I came. I said I would." She held him for a minute, noticing how small and warm his body was before releasing him. He wore the same denim jacket. She tousled his dark hair as he stepped back and looked up at Syd with a curious expression.

"Is this your girlfriend?" he asked.

Maddie bit the inside of her cheek as she shifted her gaze between Syd, the interested technician watching them from behind the nurse's station, and the advancing, heavy-set woman who obviously was Elise Manning. "Yes, Henry. This is Syd." She stood up. "Syd, this is my friend, Henry Lawrence."

Smiling, Syd bent over and extended her hand. "Hello, Henry. I'm so happy to meet you. Maddie has told me a lot about you."

He stared up at her as he shook her hand. "Hi. You're pretty, too. But you're not as tall as Maddie."

Syd laughed. "No, I'm not. But not many people are." She bent closer to him and whispered, "I kinda like being shorter. It's easier to play with Pete."

His eyes grew round. "Did you bring him?"

"No. We couldn't bring him on this trip. We came on Maddie's airplane."

He looked up at Maddie with wide eyes. "You have an *airplane*? Is it like the one we rode on from California?"

"No, buddy. It's a very small airplane. Maybe I can show it to you later on, if it's okay with Mrs. Manning."

Mrs. Manning had joined them and stood quietly, watching their interaction.

"Mrs. Manning? I'm Maddie Stevenson." Maddie smiled wryly. "And this is my *very* good friend, Syd Murphy."

They shook hands. Mrs. Manning was a short woman with curly brown hair. She appeared to be in her late thirties. She wore round, metal-framed glasses, and carried a large quilted bag that appeared to contain nightgowns, a bathrobe, and magazines. "Hello, Dr. Stevenson. It's so kind of you to come down today." She nodded to Syd. "I'm Elise. It's good to meet you, too."

Syd smiled at her. "I wish it were under better circumstances."

"I do, too." Elise looked back at Maddie. "I haven't seen Ada yet today. I was hoping we'd hear from her doctor while we're here. No one has updated me on her condition yet."

Maddie nodded. "I spoke with the head of the unit last night. He told me that Dr. Patel would be making rounds midday today, so hopefully, we can speak with him. We're in luck. I actually have a slight connection to him. He studied at UVA with a good friend of my father's."

"Really?" Elise sounded amazed. "That's a small world."

Maddie smiled. "Medicine is really like a big game of *Six Degrees of Kevin Bacon*. If you look hard enough, we're all connected in one way or another."

Henry tugged on Maddie's sleeve. "What's kevin bacon?"

Maddie looked at Syd. "Do you wanna take that one, Shortie? I'm gonna go talk with the charge nurse."

Syd rolled her eyes. "Come on, Henry. I brought some photos of Pete to show you. We can sit down over here while Maddie checks on your grandma."

"Okay." He took hold of Syd's hand without hesitation. They walked to the waiting room, while Elise excused herself to call her husband.

Maddie approached the nurse's station.

A harried-looking nurse, carrying an armload of patient folders appeared from behind a large center kiosk. She noticed Maddie standing there and looked up at her over the rim of her glasses. "May I help you?"

Maddie gave her one of her biggest and warmest smiles. "I hope so. I'm Dr. Stevenson, and I spoke last night with Dr. Grainger about your patient, Ada Lawrence. I'm here to visit with her, and, hopefully, to get a few minutes to confer with her attending, Rashid Patel. Can you tell me if Dr. Patel is making his rounds yet?"

The nurse nodded as she dropped her stack of folders on top of a desk and turned to address a tall, white-haired man in bright green scrubs. "Larry, have you seen Dr. Patel yet this morning?" Larry shook his head. "No, but I've been down at the pharmacy all morning, so I might have missed him. I'd ask Lisa. He usually checks in with her."

"I'm sorry, Dr. Stevenson. Let me try to locate Dr. Patel for you. In the meantime, I'll get Lisa Atkins—she's been taking care of Mrs. Lawrence this morning and she can update you on her condition."

Maddie nodded gratefully and glanced down at the nurse's nametag. "Thank you, Wendy. I really appreciate your help."

Wendy smiled. "It's no problem." She pressed an intercom button. "Lisa, can you come by the front desk when you get a second?"

"Sure. Be right there," a crackly voice responded.

"Are you a doctor like Maddie?" Henry asked Syd, once they were seated on a mauve- and teal-colored sofa in the waiting room. It was covered with a vivid and random pattern of indiscernible shapes.

Syd wondered absently why the upholstery on hospital furniture always looked like it was about ready to leap from its frame and suffocate you.

She shifted her full attention to Henry. "No, sweetheart. I work in a library. Have you ever been to a library?"

He nodded and pulled out two, shopworn hardback books from a small Transformers backpack. "Mrs. Manning took me to the library with Jason, and I got these books about Harry." Syd took the copies of the Gene Zion classics from him and smiled when she noticed the Cabarrus County Public Library stamp on the covers.

"I read these books when I was little, too."

"You *did*?" Henry was incredulous. "Harry must be really old."

Syd laughed. "Well, he's a very *special* dog." She held up one of the books. "I especially liked this story about the awful sweater."

"Me, too." He looked at her. "Does Pete have a sweater?"

"No. Pete has very thick, yellow hair, so he doesn't need a sweater."

"Does he get hot in the summertime?"

"Sometimes. But he has a big pond to swim in, and that keeps him cooled off when the days are too hot."

"I like to swim. My daddy taught me how in the big Army swimming pool."

"I know you miss your daddy. I bet he's really proud of how well you're trying to help your grandma."

Henry nodded. "I talked to him last night. He told me to be good and to do whatever Gramma says. I told him about Maddie. He said that Gramma told him she was coming to visit and to see me. He sounded happy about that."

"I'm glad. Maddie likes you a lot."

"I know."

Syd smiled at the simple truth of his acknowledgement. "Do you want to see my pictures of Pete?"

He nodded vigorously and scooted closer to her. Syd reached into her bag and withdrew an envelope full of pictures she had collected that morning. She showed him snapshots of Pete lounging on the front porch of the farmhouse, swimming in the pond, and catching tennis balls. She also had a photo of Maddie posing with Pete, next to her blue and yellow airplane. Henry was fascinated with the photo and looked at it over and over.

"Would you like to keep that picture?" she asked.

His blue eyes grew round. "Can I?"

"I'm sure it would be fine. I think Maddie would like for you to have it."

"Thanks." He tucked the photo inside his backpack. "Do you live on the farm with Maddie?"

Syd was uncertain about how to answer him. "Sort of. I'm staying there with her for a while."

"Do you like it?"

She smiled. "Very much. It's a wonderful place to live."

"Maddie said I could come and visit if it was okay with Gramma."

"I'm sure she'd like that. We both would."

"You're really nice. I'm glad you're Maddie's girlfriend."

Syd wanted to hug him. "I am, too. She's very special."

"Like Harry?"

"Well, sort of. But unlike Harry, Maddie doesn't like to dig in the dirt."

He giggled. "I do."

"That's because you're a little boy, and that's what little boys do."

"I could dig in the dirt with Pete."

"You could. Pete likes to hide his tennis balls."

Henry looked confused. "Why?"

"I'm not sure." She leaned closer. "Maybe you can ask him."

"Okay," he said.

Maddie was still in conversation with Lisa Atkins when the elevator doors opened, and a man wearing blue scrubs and a short white jacket stepped off and approached her. He went to where they stood.

"Are you Dr. Stevenson?" She nodded, and he extended his hand. "I'm Rashid Patel—Mrs. Lawrence's doctor." They shook hands. "I understand you know Arthur Leavitt? He was my adviser at UVA." He smiled. "How is he? I haven't seen him in years."

Maddie smiled back. "He was well enough when I saw him at the end of March. Feisty as ever."

"That sounds like him. Is he still running the ER there?"

"Yep. As tight a ship as ever."

Patel shook his head. "Some things never change. Has Lisa been bringing you up to speed on Mrs. Lawrence?"

"She has." Maddie turned to the duty nurse. "And I thank you for your time, Lisa. You've been very helpful."

"No problem, Doctor. Now that Dr. Patel is here, I'll let him finish briefing you." She handed Ada's chart to Patel, before nodding to them both and turning to head back to the acute care wing.

Patel touched Maddie on the elbow. "Let's get out of this hallway so we can talk more privately." They walked a few feet and entered a small staff break room, where they sat down at a table topped with chipped Formica. "Would you like some coffee?" He gestured at a pot that looked like it had seen better days.

"No, thank you for offering." Maddie sat back and folded her arms. "I appreciate your willingness to discuss Mrs. Lawrence's condition with me. I am certain this probably seems a tad irregular."

"Not at all. I'm actually relieved to know that she has someone knowledgeable interested in her recovery. She told me about your friendship with her grandson. I know she's very worried about how to manage his care during her convalescence."

"Lisa indicated that she might be facing some inpatient rehab. Can you elaborate on that?"

"Of course." He opened her folder. "As near as we can tell, she suffered an ischemic stroke from thrombosis related to atherosclerosis."

Maddie nodded. "Any hemiparesis or aphasia?"

"Mild hemiparesis on the right side with compromised balance and loss of some motor control. Slight aphasia. She tires easily. She'll need a better dietary regimen to keep her diabetes in check and to lower her cholesterol. She won't be returning to work any time soon—if at all. I am recommending inpatient rehab—probably three to six weeks—followed by in-home care."

"Do you know if she has adequate insurance?"

He nodded. "Fortunately, she works for one of the few textile mills in the county that actually provides health care coverage to its full-time employees. And she has some supplemental income from her late husband's social security pension."

"Have you talked with her son?"

"Yes. The Military One Source field officer was very helpful getting us in touch with Corporal Lawrence. He understands the situation and realizes that we may have to look into a foster care arrangement for Henry. There are no other living relatives, and the neighbor, Mrs. Manning, is unable to care for him full time. His tour of duty in Afghanistan is likely to last another twelve to fourteen months. The Army has a Child Development Center office in Salisbury, and they're sending a case worker over to assess the situation and make a recommendation for Henry's care."

Maddie sighed. "Does Henry know any of this?"

"No. Mrs. Lawrence wanted to talk with you before telling him anything."

"Me?" Maddie was surprised. "Why?"

Patel shrugged. "I honestly can't say. Would you like to go and see her now? I was just about to start my rounds."

"Yes, that would be great. I can't thank you enough, Dr. Patel, for your consideration, and for the interest you've obviously taken in the Lawrence family."

"No need to thank me. I was an Army brat myself, and I know what it's like to get shuffled around in the system. I always do whatever I can to help out another service family." He stood up. "Come on. Let's go and talk with her. I know she'll be glad to see you."

Maddie stopped and stole an anxious glance down the hallway toward the waiting room before they made their way back toward the acute care area. She could see Henry huddled close to Syd on the end of a couch. It looked like they were reading a book. Elise Manning was nowhere in sight, but Maddie could see her large quilted bag on the floor at Henry's feet. Syd looked up as Maddie stood watching them, and their eyes met. Maddie raised an eyebrow in question, and Syd smiled at her, before returning her attention to Henry and the book.

Ada Lawrence recognized Maddie at once. She was wan and tired, and her speech was slightly impaired, but there was no mistaking her surge of adrenalin when she saw Maddie enter her room.

"Thank you for coming. I hope it was okay to ask Elise to call you. I didn't know what else to do. She can't keep him. She has four kids of her own." The words tumbled out of her.

Maddie walked to the side of the bed and rested her hand atop Ada's forearm. "I'm glad you thought to have her call me. I want to help out in any way I can."

Dr. Patel checked the stats from the chart at the end of her bed. "How was your night, Ada? Did you rest any better?"

Ada shook her head. "Not really. It's so noisy here. I wanted to get up, but they told me I wasn't ready for that yet."

He made a notation on her chart before hanging it back on the hook at the end of her bed. "Well, they're right. We want to get you a little bit stronger before you go trying to stand up." He picked up her right hand. "Can you squeeze my fingers, Ada?"

Maddie saw the effort it took for Ada to move her fingers ever so slightly.

"That's just fine." He walked back to the end of her bed and lifted up the blanket covering her legs. "How about your foot. Can you push your foot against my hand?"

Her foot barely moved.

"One more time, Ada. Push your foot against my hand."

She made a very slight movement.

Patel replaced the blanket and patted her leg. "Good job. I'm going to go and see a couple of other patients, but I'll be back in to talk with you before I leave today. You have a nice visit with Dr. Stevenson now."

He smiled at them both and left the room. Maddie pulled a chair to the side of the bed and sat down.

"Dr. Patel tells me that you might be looking at some inpatient rehabilitation services. That's a good thing. It will expedite your recovery."

She met Maddie's open gaze with anxious eyes. "I know, but I don't have anyone to take care of Henry. The Army will put him in foster care, and I just can't do that to him. He's already been through so much. I think I just need to try and manage at home—see if they can't get us some in-home childcare help. He's such a good boy. He isn't any trouble."

"Ada, you need to listen to Dr. Patel. He's got your best interests at heart—yours and Henry's. It's going to be better for both of you if you can recover quickly. And your best shot at doing that is getting yourself into a concentrated, inpatient rehab program."

"But what about Henry? Where will he go?"

"What did your son say?"

She waved her hand in frustration. "He said he would go along with whatever I decided. He said I'd just have to figure it out. The Army won't let him come home. He said that's why I'm Henry's legal guardian."

Maddie's heart sank. "I'm sorry. I know this is very difficult for you. And you need to be putting all of your energy into getting stronger. Being anxious about Henry isn't going to help your recovery."

"So what do I do?"

Maddie shook her head. "I wish I knew, Mrs. Lawrence. I guess you need to give the Army a chance to figure something out—see what they recommend."

They were silent for a moment.

"You could take him." Ada's voice was so low that Maddie was sure she had misunderstood her.

"I beg your pardon?"

"I said that *you* could take him. He knows you. He's done nothing but talk nonstop about you ever since he got here from California."

A sense of panic washed over Maddie. "Mrs. Lawrence, you can't be serious."

"Why not? You like him, don't you?"

"Of course I do, but . . ."

"And you have a big house, and someone who could help you?"

"Well, that's *true*, but I'm hardly—I don't—I've *never* . . ." Maddie was completely flustered.

The truth was, she had no good arguments for *not* considering it—not really. But how on earth could she even think about such a step without consulting Syd? She shook her head. *I must be crazy.* She met Ada's desperate gaze. *Syd's gonna think I've completely lost it.* She shook her head again. *I'm crazy.*

"Mrs. Lawrence, you don't even *know* me. Not really. How can you suggest this? What makes you think Henry's father would go along with it? I—*we*—are complete strangers to him."

"I know enough. I know that you love Henry. I could see that when I met you at the airport. I know that you're smart and successful—that you have a great job and a wonderful home. I know that you could afford to take good care of him, and that you'd *want* to, and wanting to matters more to me than any of the rest."

"Mrs. Lawrence, I don't live alone. I have a . . . I'm in a committed relationship with . . . someone."

"I know. It's with another woman. Henry told me. I don't care about that, Doctor. I *do* care about my grandson. Please." She plainly was getting tired. Her speech was getting thicker and harder to decipher. "Please say you'll think about it. The Army said it was up to me to decide what to do. It's only for a month or so. I'd like to have him with someone who cares about him. I'd like to have him with you."

Maddie was stunned. She felt like something was spiraling out of control, and she didn't know how to rein it in. She needed to talk with Syd. She needed to have her head examined.

"All right. I'll think about it. Let me talk with—let me talk with my partner, and I'll let you know something tomorrow. Okay?" She patted her on the arm. "You get some rest now. I'll go and check on Henry."

Ada nodded and closed her eyes. "Thank you."

Maddie stood up and left the room. She stopped to stand for a moment with her head pressed against the wall outside the door. Her pulse was racing. *God. I need a drink. Too bad I gotta fly us home.* Taking a deep breath, she squared her shoulders and headed for the waiting room.

Lunch with Henry was an eye-opening experience for Syd. Maddie and Henry functioned like two halves of a whole, and Syd was amazed at how much alike they were—right down to their quirky eating habits. She quickly found herself playing proctor to both of them, having to take up the unfamiliar mantle of adult supervision.

It amazed her that Henry was actually easier to manage than Maddie. He, at least, seemed to respect her authority. Maddie was hopeless. She laughed and giggled and teased and was every bit as intractable as the worst behaved child in a Vacation Bible School class. Syd was amazed. She always knew that Maddie had a playful and irreverent streak, but she'd never seen her quite as relaxed and spontaneous as she was with Henry. Only with David did she ever come close to this level of playfulness.

Instead of feeling jealous, Syd was charmed by Henry's effect on the normally reserved Maddie. She found their sweetly inspired antics mesmerizing, and it was hard for her to maintain her feigned posture of parental disapproval.

Maddie periodically caught Syd's eye and winked at her lovingly—saying more with a single glance than she could have said if they had been able to converse freely.

After lunch, they took Henry by the Concord airport to see Maddie's plane. He was completely in awe of it. Syd watched the concentration on his tiny features as Maddie explained its operation to him, and she was reminded of the photos she had seen of Maddie at nearly the same age—equally entranced as her father introduced her to his love of flying.

At three, they dropped Henry off at Elise Manning's house in Kannapolis and promised to call him the next day. He hugged them both warmly before he ran off to meet up with Elise's son, Jason, and another boy, who were playing Frisbee in the small front yard of the Manning's mill house. By three forty-five, they were back in the air, en route to Jefferson.

"You want to keep him, don't you?" Syd asked.

Maddie looked at her with a stunned expression. "What makes you say that?"

Syd laughed. "Oh come on, baby. I'd have to be an idiot not to see how you look at him. I've only ever seen that expression on your face when you look at *me*, and that's not something I'm very likely to miss."

"I don't know what to say."

Syd laid a calming hand on her thigh. "Relax, sweetheart. It's not a contest. I'm not jealous."

"Good. You shouldn't be." Maddie covered her hand with hers. "I've never loved anyone as much as I love you."

"I know that. But I also know how much room you have in that big heart of yours. And I think young Mr. Lawrence is on his way to staking out a hefty-sized piece of real estate in there."

"Maybe." Maddie's voice was noncommittal.

"So?"

Maddie met her gaze. "So?"

"So, did Ada ask you to keep him while she's in rehab?"

Maddie looked at her in amazement. "Do you have some secret powers of omniscience or prognostication that you've carefully kept hidden from me?"

Syd smiled back. "What makes you think I wasn't just lurking outside her hospital room door eavesdropping?"

"That was going to be my next guess."

Syd squeezed her thigh. "I'm so sure."

"Come on. How did you know?"

"Well, as much as I'd like to take credit for possessing psychic powers, I guess I have to confess that Elise told me she was going to ask you about it."

Maddie looked incredulous. "She did?"

"Um hmm."

"You mean, you knew about this all afternoon?"

"Yep."

"And still you acted completely calm and seemed to have a good time with him?"

"It would appear so."

"I think I'm having an out-of-body experience right now."

"Well, try and retain the use of your faculties until this thing is safely on the ground, okay? You can take all the time you need to freak out once we're back in Jericho."

"Syd?"

"Yes?"

"I love you."

Syd kissed her warmly on the cheek. "It's a good thing you do, Stretch. You'd be S.O.L. otherwise."

Maddie looked thoughtful for a moment. "Not that I'm disagreeing with you or anything, but why, exactly, would I be shit outta luck if I didn't love you? I mean, I'm asking just for discussion purposes."

Syd sighed. "Because without me on hand to cook for him, Henry would last less than a week on your pathetic diet of Ramen noodles and pimento cheese."

Maddie seemed to think about that. "So, does that mean we're considering Ada's request?"

"Were you in any doubt that we would consider it?"

"I guess not."

"I have only one request."

"What's that?"

"Whatever you do, don't ask my father for *his* opinion."

Maddie laughed. "Understood." After a pause she added, "But you do have to admit that this a damn sight easier than in vitro fertilization."

Syd snorted. "And I thought that getting a spare house key was a big step." She eyed Maddie critically. "Is there *anything* you do with baby steps?"

Maddie looked at her with a raised eyebrow.

"Bad choice of words. Forget I said that."

Maddie squeezed her hand. "I don't think I'll ever forget *this* conversation."

"Me either." They were quiet for a moment. "We must be nuts."

"That's exactly what I was thinking."

They fell quiet again, and then Syd laughed.

"What is it?"

"I was just thinking about poor Tom. Somehow, I think this announcement might trump an accidental kiss."

"Aw, shucks. You mean I don't get to lay one on you in front of him? I was really looking forward to that."

"Honey, I think you've laid enough on me for one day, don't you?"

"I suppose so."

"But you know," Syd moved her hand up and down Maddie's thigh, "maybe later, I can lay something on *you*."

Maddie regarded her with a sober expression. "You do realize that this is an open mike, right?"

Syd felt herself blush up to the roots of her hair. "*Please* tell me that you're kidding?"

Maddie just chuckled and refused to answer. Syd's entreaties ended only with the flight.

Chapter 25

Maddie and Syd arrived at the Inn just after six-thirty. Syd noticed Tom's car in the parking lot, and was surprised to see Lizzy's Subaru. She hadn't seen Lizzy since the horrible events with Beau earlier in the week. She looked at Maddie as they pulled into a space next to Tom's SUV.

"Did you know that Lizzy would be here?"

Maddie shook her head as she unclipped her seatbelt. "No. I suppose it could be a coincidence, but, knowing David, I doubt it."

Syd smiled. "Well, I hope he did invite her. I think she certainly qualifies as extended family, now."

"I do, too." They got out and began the short walk to the wide front porch of the Inn. "She hasn't mentioned anything to me about the dynamics she observed between us that night. I respect her reticence, but I'm sure she's beyond curious about everything."

Syd laughed. "Well, she needs to get in line." She poked Maddie on the arm. "We should charge admission."

"Yeah. Normally, I'd be enjoying this fifteen minutes of fame."

"You mean you aren't now?"

"Not so much."

They started up the steps to the porch. Syd looked up at her in the ambient light. She appeared completely distracted. "Why not?"

Maddie shrugged. "I'm too preoccupied with everything we'll have to do to kid-proof the house."

Syd laughed and tugged her to a dark corner, away from the light that was pouring out of the big front doors. "Honey, he's *five*, not two. He isn't going to be playing with knives or putting his hands on the top of the stove. He already knows how to swim, and I'm fairly certain he knows how to navigate a flight of stairs." She gave her an ironic smile. "And I doubt that he'll have much interest in taking apart your mother's piano." She pulled Maddie closer. "Relax. We can figure all of this out."

Maddie looked dubious. "You sure?"

"Positive."

Maddie sighed, then kissed her on the forehead. "We have to be crazy. Why aren't we starting *smaller*—like with another dog, or something?"

Syd leaned into her for a moment. "I don't want to scare you, but I really do believe that things happen for a reason."

"Syd . . ."

"I know, I know. You're the hardboiled scientist, here. But admit it. Cause precedes effect. We each make the choices we make for a reason." She smiled up at her. "You chose to let Henry be seated next to you on that long flight. You could just as easily have said no."

"But I didn't."

"No. You didn't."

Maddie sighed. "You could have said no to fostering him, too."

"I could have."

"But you didn't."

"I didn't."

"I guess you're right, then."

Syd smiled. "And David says you aren't trainable."

Maddie rolled her eyes. She took Syd by the arm and steered her back toward the entrance to the Inn. "Let's go, Lucy. You got some 'splaining to do."

Inside, they heard voices and laughter emanating from the bar. Tom was the first one to spot them as they entered. He had been standing next to Lizzy near the back of the room, but he excused himself and walked forward as soon as he saw them. He warmly embraced his sister.

"Hey there, shortstop. Clearly, some people will go to *any* lengths to get a few days off." He stood back and looked her over. The bruise on her face had completely faded. He kept an arm around her shoulders as he leaned forward and kissed Maddie on the cheek.

"Hi ya, Doc. Thanks for keeping this one off the streets, and for giving me such a convenient excuse to see more of you."

"It's good to see you again, too, Tom." Maddie smiled. "And don't give me too much credit. I'm getting the better end of this deal."

Tom looked smugly at Syd, clearly pleased with this response.

Syd decided that there was no need to forestall the inevitable. "I hate to be the bearer of bad news, Tom, but I think you've got your wires crossed on this one."

He looked back and forth between them. "Why? Am I missing something here?"

Syd took hold of Maddie's hand. "Don't think of it so much as *missing* something. Think of it more as *gaining* something. In this case, think of it as gaining a sister-in-law."

Tom looked at her in confusion. "What is *that* supposed to mean?"

Syd stepped closer to Maddie and raised their linked hands. She lowered her voice to a whisper. "We're gay, Tom."

Tom stood there slack-jawed. "You're . . . you mean . . ." He waved his hand between them. "You two? No *way*. I don't believe it."

Syd nodded patiently. "Believe it. Mom and Dad know. You can ask them."

Tom stared at her in stunned silence. "You're gay? When the hell did *this* happen?"

"It would take a philosopher to answer *that* question, but we're together now, and I've never been happier."

"Holy shit."

Syd smiled. "My sentiments, exactly."

He looked at Maddie. "*You're* gay?"

Maddie nodded. "It would appear so."

He shook his head. "I need a drink."

Maddie placed a calming hand on his shoulder. "Fortunately, we're in the right place for that. Come on, I'll buy."

He looked at her in amazement. "Thanks . . . Sis."

She laughed and led him back toward the bar.

Syd stood there, watching them depart. Then she made her way to the big front window, where Lizzy stood with a glass of wine.

Syd gave her a hug, stood back, and held her at arm's length. "I'm glad to see you here."

Lizzy inclined her head toward David, who was busy behind the bar. "I didn't have much choice. He can be pretty compelling."

Syd laughed. "Don't I know it? Have you met my parents yet?"

"No." Lizzy gestured toward Maddie and Tom. "But I have met your brother."

Syd laid a hand on her forearm. "I apologize in advance for Tom."

Lizzy looked confused. "Whatever for?"

Syd smiled. "Just consider it a preemptive measure."

Lizzy looked toward the bar. Maddie and Tom stood laughing and talking with David. "I can't imagine why you'd feel the need to apologize. He seems perfectly charming."

Syd looked at her in amazement. "Are you sure you've completely recovered from our recent ordeal? Do you have some lingering fever? Paranoid delusions? Night terrors? Anything that would cloud your normally perfect judgment in this disturbing way?"

Lizzy just laughed. "I can see that you and your brother share the same level of devotion and attachment that my sister and I enjoy."

"Families," Syd quoted. "Can't live with 'em—"

"Can't live without 'em," Lizzy finished.

They smiled at each other.

"How are you, really?" Syd asked.

Lizzy considered her question. "I'm okay. I went back home the next night. I felt I needed to. I didn't want to give Beau that kind of power over me, you know?"

Syd nodded. "I understand perfectly."

"How about you? Will the library reopen? Will you be able to return to your apartment any time soon?"

"The state feels confident that we could reopen the library as soon as the restoration work is completed, but that might take as long as a month. The county, however, is less optimistic. A lot of the decision about whether or not to reopen will be driven by how expensive it is to repair the building itself. The state only insured the contents of the facility, not the physical structure. At best, I think we might be looking at some reductions in the level of service."

"And at worst?"

"It might not reopen at all."

Lizzy's face fell. "Oh, no. That would be a horrible thing for the county." She hesitated. "And for you." Syd noticed her eyes cut quickly to Maddie. "What would you do?"

Syd shrugged. "I don't know. I'd have a lot to figure out."

Lizzy nodded. "You would."

"Well, let's not embrace doomsday scenarios until we have to. For tonight, we have a lot to celebrate." She smiled. "Maddie and I have some interesting news to share, and it's guaranteed to set tongues wagging from one end of this county to the other."

"Really?" Lizzy looked like she was trying hard not to smile.

"Really," Syd replied. "And it's *not* what you think." She paused. "Well . . . it's not *only* what you think." She sighed and shook her head. "Okay, it's *exactly* what you think, but with a surprising twist."

"Okaaaayy. So how long do we have to wait to find out?"

Out of the corner of her eye, Syd saw her mother and father enter the room from the hallway. Michael and Phoebe Jenkins were just behind them. "Not long. It looks like the gang's all here."

David sidled up next to Maddie. Tom had drifted off with a freshly filled mug of beer, plainly headed toward Lizzy. Maddie watched him as he walked away.

"I see that you've dashed the hopes of yet another wannabe suitor," David observed.

Maddie sighed. "Do you ever get tired of spinning all these yarns?"

"Nope. Just call me Clotho. Besides," he nudged her as they watched Tom join Syd and Lizzy, "I think his broken heart might mend, and soon."

Maddie looked at him. "Meaning?"

"Duh. Is there something wrong with your eyesight, Cinderella? Methinks the hot and hunky Mr. Murphy might just want to play a game of tell-me-where-it-hurts with your lovely Miss Clara Barton over there."

Maddie rolled her eyes. "Oh, give me a break."

"Fine. Don't say I didn't call it first."

Against her will, Maddie looked at Tom and Lizzy. They were laughing and standing together in postures that suggested openness, and interest. *Holy shit,* she thought. *Could he be right?* She thought she saw Lizzy pass something that looked like a business card to Tom.

David chuckled.

"Oh, shut up," she said. "Get me a glass of something."

He raised his hands. "I hear and obey."

"That would be a first."

David retreated behind the bar and poured her a generous glass of red wine. "Why do you persist in abusing me?" He shook his head. "I think it *must* be tied to the appalling dearth of male pheromones in your life."

Maddie took a healthy sip of her wine. "Oh, really?"

"Yes. I've spent some time exploring this idea. You lash out at men—me, in particular—because you have next to *no* experience with how to relate to us."

Maddie rolled her eyes. "Don't think the fact that I'm not flinging this drink into your face signifies any kind of agreement with your ridiculous hypothesis. I just happen to be very thirsty."

"On the contrary. I think you know I'm right."

"*You're* right?"

"I am."

"I suffer because I have no experience in how to deal with men?"

"No. I believe what I said is that *I* suffer because you have no experience in how to deal with men."

She set her wine glass down on top of the bar and crossed her arms. "So, illuminate me. Besides knowing that I need to look before I sit down on a toilet seat, what sage and searing insights into the male experience am I missing?"

"I refuse to dignify your lack of sincerity with a thoughtful response."

"Uh huh. Well, hold that thought, because the universe may have provided a means to address what, by your account, are my shortcomings."

David raised an eyebrow. "Does it involve elective surgery?"

Maddie sighed. "No."

"Hormone injections?"

"No."

"Flannel shirts or bowling shoes?"

"Not even close."

"Then color me intrigued. What stunning revelation is about to befall us?"

"What makes you think I'm poised to reveal anything?"

"Why else would we all be gathered together here?"

She waved her hand at the room. "You tell me. *You* invited half the guests."

"That wasn't *me*. Your in-laws were the ones who wanted to host a party. I merely facilitated."

"Right. By setting Lizzy up with Tom?"

"Does it look like she's complaining?"

Maddie looked at the couple in question. They definitely did not seem unhappy to be in each other's company. She sighed. "No. I have to bow to your superior judgment on that one."

"Thank you. I do have my moments."

"That you do."

"And, hey? You aren't the only one with interesting news to impart. My mama has an intriguing announcement of her own to make. That's why I asked her to join us."

Maddie glanced at Phoebe, who was standing with George and Janet. "Really?"

"Really. And keep your fingers crossed, Cinderella. If everything pans out, it could end up being *very* good news for you."

"For me? How?"

"All will be revealed soon enough. For now, let's get this rabble rounded up and into the dining room. That yard bird Janet roasted ain't getting any fresher—if you get my drift."

"Janet cooked?" Maddie was intrigued. Normally, Michael was reticent about letting outsiders anywhere near his kitchen, much less consenting to let someone else cook in it. But then, Janet was more than usually persuasive.

"Oh, yeah. I made the mistake of walking through there earlier, and I thought the two of them were going to come to blows. I heard Michael say something about it not being necessary to kill the damn birds twice. Then I beat a hasty retreat."

Maddie laughed. "At least I now know that Syd comes by it honestly."

"What? Her ability to murder innocent food?"

"No, her ability to get her way."

"Oh, puh-lease. It doesn't take a rocket scientist to figure *that* one out. All she has to do is shake that tight little bootie of hers at you, and she gets whatever she wants." He stroked his chin. "I just wonder who gets tasked with mopping up the drool."

"That is a ridiculous suggestion."

"Oh really?"

"Yes. Really."

"Are you seriously trying to say that Syd *doesn't* get her way with you?"

"Of course not. I'm saying that I don't drool."

"Jesus." He drained his wine glass with a flourish and set it down on the bar. "Grab your talent, and let's go eat."

Michael and Janet had apparently arrived at some acceptable division of labor, because the dinner they prepared was far from dry. The nine of them sat around a makeshift large table near the back of the restaurant and made short work of the roasted orange-herb game hens. Over thick wedges of key lime pie, Phoebe finally prepared to make the announcement David had promised. From her seat next to Syd, Maddie listened to her with open curiosity.

"I want to thank you all for letting me crash this family party," she said, raising a glass. "And I know I'm not the first person to say that I look forward to the day—soon—when our little branch library can reopen and continue the fine work Syd has started here."

Everyone raised their glasses amidst a chorus of well-wishing and drank a toast to Phoebe's best wishes for Syd and the fledgling town library.

"My son, David, will tell you all that I'm a great believer in hedging my bets. And I think it's always wise to have a backup plan." Phoebe turned to Syd. "I turn sixty-five in three weeks, and I think it's time for me to hang up my baton. I've already told the school board that I intend to retire at the end of this semester, and I've *promised* to do my best to help them locate a suitable replacement." She looked at Syd. "Know anyone with the right credentials who might be interested in applying?"

Maddie looked back and forth between Phoebe and Syd with wide eyes. Phoebe had a sly smile on her face, and Syd looked shell-shocked.

By unspoken consent, Maddie and Syd had avoided talking about the direction their lives might take after Syd's eighteen-month tenure in Jericho ended. In the aftermath of the fire, questions about Syd's future grew more immediate, and more emotionally charged. It was like Poe's "Tell-Tale Heart"—banging away beneath their bed like an ominous anthem of uncertainty.

Syd's willingness to help Maddie foster Henry for the six weeks his grandmother would be in rehab offered Maddie some measure of comfort. She knew that Syd would never consent to participate in such an endeavor unless she intended to see it through. Likewise, it seemed to suggest a larger commitment on Syd's part to stay on with Maddie at the farm, even if her apartment in town became habitable once again—an event which appeared increasingly unlikely.

Would Syd consider Phoebe's offer? Maddie's heart raced at the prospect. A nine-month teaching position in the county schools—one that allowed Syd to use her background in music education—would simplify everything.

Well. It would simplify everything for me, she thought, with a tinge of morose. But what would Syd think about it? What about her career track in library science? What about her plans for life after Jericho?

And what would become of me if she doesn't want to consider it? Maddie closed her eyes. She was getting way too far ahead of herself. She took a deep breath and looked at Syd, who was twisting the gold pendant of her Heifetz necklace between her thumb and forefinger. She still hadn't said anything.

George leaned across the table and prodded his daughter. "Well, sweetie? What do you think?"

Maddie held her breath. Syd looked at her, and their eyes met.

Syd smiled and turned to Phoebe. "I think that I need to find out if my North Carolina teaching certificate is valid in Virginia."

Phoebe clapped her hands together. "No worries on that score. I already checked. If you want it, I can guarantee that the job is yours."

Beneath the table, Syd took hold of Maddie's hand. "Do I want it?" she asked in a near whisper.

Maddie felt like her heart was about to pound out of her chest. She laced their fingers together. "Oh, yeah," she said, in a voice loud enough for everyone to hear. "You want it."

At home in bed, Syd shifted closer to Maddie and tightened her arms. It was warm enough that they had left a window open, and she had been lying there listening to the ethereal night song of a Whip-poor-will. The first cry was far away, and she wasn't certain she had heard it at all. But now, the elusive bird had drifted close enough that she could make out the knocking sound that punctuated its haunting calls.

"He's getting nearer," she said.

She felt Maddie nod. "They do that. Then they retreat again before daylight."

"That's kind of sad."

"I think that's why they're so often linked to loss. Legend has it that they can catch a departing soul."

"Then I'd better hold on extra tight."

She could feel Maddie's smile against the top of her head. "I'm not going anyplace."

"Apparently, I'm not either."

"Are you okay with that?"

Syd lifted her head and peered at her through the darkness. "Was there some part of what happened here a little while ago that left you unconvinced? Because I thought we covered all of *those* bases pretty well."

"Oh, those bases were more than covered. In fact, one or two of them are downright sore."

Syd kissed her on the chin. "Then why the worries?"

Maddie shrugged. "It's not rational."

Syd laughed. "When it comes to relationships—any relationships—tell me what *is* rational."

"You've got a point there."

Outside, the Whip-poor-will edged closer. Syd thought he might be perched on the porch railing below their open window.

"Are you afraid I'll change my mind?" she asked.

"About what?" She thought Maddie sounded wary.

"About whether or not I should dye my hair green." She slapped her on the arm. "What do you *think* I mean, goofball? Are you afraid I'll change my mind about you—about *us*? About Henry?"

She could feel Maddie tensing up. "I guess. Maybe."

"Maybe?"

Maddie shrugged again. "Yeah. I'm not proud of it. Don't be pissed," she added, quickly.

Syd sighed and sat up. "Why would I be pissed? Just because it's clear that you *still* don't trust me to know what I want?"

Maddie reached out to touch her arm. "Honey—"

Syd batted her hand away. "Oh, no. We're clearing this up once and for all. I'm not gonna spend the next fifty years with you, having this same conversation every three days." She crossed her arms. "So what's it going to take to get it through your gorgeous head that I'm not viewing you as some kind of human science project?" She shook her head. "I'm not some wide-eyed coed who's getting off on how fun and illicit it might be to fumble around with my college roommate."

"I know that."

"You do? Then what on earth are you worried about?"

Maddie shook her head. "I wish I knew."

Syd sat staring at her. "Oh, my god."

"What?" Maddie sounded alarmed.

"This is it. This is what you *do*, isn't it?"

Maddie stared back at her without speaking.

"In relationships. This is what you do. This is how you insulate yourself."

"What do you mean?" Maddie's voice was barely audible.

"This is how you protect yourself. This is how you push people away so they can't hurt you. You make it about *them*, and not about you." She raised a hand to her forehead. "I get it now. It's not about your fear that I'll leave you. It's about your fear of committing to *me*."

Maddie looked down at the sheets.

Syd laid a hand on Maddie's forearm. "Look at me."

Maddie raised her eyes. Syd wished she could see them more plainly. The darkness in the room continued to hide her expression. "I'm right, aren't I? You're afraid of this. You're afraid you can't make it work—that you can't completely give yourself to it. And that's what scares you."

After a long moment, Maddie slowly shook her head. "No. That's not it—at least, not completely." She slid her hand across the expanse of bed that separated them, and tentatively rested it on Syd's thigh. "I *am* scared. You're right about that. But what scares me is not the prospect of committing myself to you. What scares me is the realization that I've already done it. I'm all in on this Syd—all the way. And I've *never* done that before. Never. And, yes, it scares the shit out of me."

Syd let out the breath she had been holding and covered Maddie's hand with her own. "I can't promise that I'll never hurt you."

"I know that."

"But I *can* promise that I'll never hurt you intentionally."

After a moment, Maddie turned her hand palm up beneath Syd's and squeezed her fingers. "I believe you."

"I hope you do, because if you don't, you're in for a bumpy ride. A *long*, bumpy ride."

"Long?"

"Afraid so."

Maddie inched closer to her on the bed. "What variety of long might you be describing?"

"Let's see." Syd took a moment to consider her response. "Ever read *War and Peace*?"

"Of course." Maddie sounded offended.

"Well . . . longer than that, *and* with more battle scenes."

Maddie laughed. "Oh, great."

"I thought you'd be pleased."

"Yeah. A frozen death march across Russia is *exactly* the metaphor I would have picked to characterize our future together. Thank you for that. I feel *so* much more encouraged, now."

"Another crisis averted." With a sigh, Syd pushed her onto her back and resumed her place, lying half on top of her. "Relax, Stretch. As I recall, the book ended with Natasha and Pierre, happy and safe in their bed, surrounded by their two-dozen adorable children."

"Two dozen?"

"Well. Maybe it wasn't two dozen." Syd nuzzled the base of her neck. "But it was more than a couple."

"True." Maddie wrapped her arms around Syd. "God, I love you."

"I know." Syd could feel Maddie smile. "I love you, too."

"Goodnight, Natasha."

"Goodnight, Pierre."

Below their window, the Whip-poor-will hopped down from his perch on the porch railing and began his slow trek away from the house—ahead of the declining night.

Epilogue

This winter was going to be one for the record books. Another gulf storm had rolled through two days ago, then made its way east to the Atlantic before hooking back around and combining with a massive low pressure system dropping down from the upper Midwest. These double-whammy winter storms were becoming more common, and locals were beginning to chafe under the constant barrage of snow and ice. For the last month, schools in the county had been closed more days than not, and parents were struggling with how to manage their kids and still hang on to their sanity. The Christmas holiday was only a few days away, and more than one family had given up on efforts to try and shop or visit with relatives.

It was clear that Santa was going to be traveling light this year.

Maddie trudged across the narrow walkway she had shoveled from the barn to the porch, carrying a five-gallon container full of gasoline—more than enough to power the big Honda motor through the night. The electricity had gone off two times already, and although county power crews had managed to restore it after just a few hours, the likelihood that it might go off again increased in direct proportion to the amount of snow and ice that continued to pile up on trees and power lines.

After stowing the gasoline near the generator behind the house, she walked back around to the front porch and stood looking out across the eerie expanse of white that stretched down toward the pond. The night sky looked dull, almost opaque. Reflected light cast an orange glow over fields and pastures covered in drifting snow. It was still coming down—larger, wetter flakes now. Not a good sign. Already, trees and shrubs were impossibly bent over under the weight of the heavy stuff. The quiet was deafening.

At least, it *was.*

From inside the house, she heard the arrhythmic sound of six notes being played over and over on the piano. She tilted her head toward the noise. It was familiar—sort of. Then she heard the same notes again. Played this time with authority. She smiled into the scarf tucked around her neck. It was Dvořák. *The New World Symphony.*

Celine was giving Henry a piano lesson. And from the way it sounded, he wasn't faring much better than she had all those years ago when she was the one seated next to her mother on the bench.

Celine had flown in for the holidays. Maddie had managed to fight her way out to the interstate and drive down to Charlotte to pick her up. That had been nearly a week ago, and in that short time, Henry had bonded with Celine in ways that left Maddie dazed. Syd just laughed at her bewilderment over Celine's uncharacteristically maternal behavior.

"She's acting like a grandmother, Maddie," Syd had said earlier in the evening. "It happens."

Maddie shook her head in amazement. "I feel like I fell asleep six months ago, and woke up in some new space/time continuum."

"Maybe you did."

Maddie looked Syd up and down. "How come you're handling all of this so seamlessly?"

Syd shrugged. She was peeling potatoes—lots of them. "We can't both be freaking out."

Maddie watched her for a moment. "What on earth are you making?"

"Mashed potatoes."

"For *what*?"

"For us."

"*Us?* You must have five pounds of potatoes peeled already."

Syd rested her peeler against the side of the sink. "What's your point?"

"Who on earth do you think is going to eat all of that?"

"Well, for starters, you and me. And I suppose Henry and Celine might join us."

Maddie gestured toward the mound of peeled potatoes. "Sweetie, it looks like all the kids in your school orchestra could join us, too."

Syd rolled her eyes and plucked another potato out of the nearly empty bag. "I wanted to be sure we had leftovers. Henry likes them."

Henry.

He had been living with them for nearly six months now. Ada suffered a second stroke during her rehab, and now was consigned to full-time nursing care. They took Henry down to see her twice a month, and were hopeful that she might be able to visit them at the farm in the early spring. Her recovery was slow, but she was making determined progress.

Henry's father still had another eight months of deployment to go, but he wrote letters to his son, and he called whenever he could. Maddie had spoken with James Lawrence on several occasions, and found him to be shy, but beyond grateful to her for her willingness to care for the son of a stranger. He was stationed in the southern province of Kandahar now, and Maddie worried about the increasing number of Taliban attacks in an area that was shaping up to be the center of the Afghan and NATO offensive. For Corporal Lawrence—and for the thousands of other soldiers like him—the prospect of spending another eight months in Afghanistan stretched out like several lifetimes.

Behind her, the big front door opened and closed. She turned her head and saw Syd walking toward her. She was carrying two steaming mugs.

"Here." She held one mug out toward Maddie. "We made hot chocolate." She smiled. "It was the only way Celine could bribe Henry to sit still for another lesson."

Maddie took the mug and smiled at her. "Yeah? Well, he'll figure that one out in a hurry. That's the kind of bribe that only works once." She took a sip. *On the other hand, this was pretty intriguing hot chocolate.* "What's in this?"

"Courvoisier."

Maddie laughed. "Do you want him to sleep until Tuesday?"

Syd glared at her. "I didn't put cognac in *his*."

"Oh. So you just want *me* to sleep until Tuesday?"

Syd thought about that. "I wouldn't mind having you in bed until Tuesday. But trust me, there wouldn't be much sleeping going on."

Maddie wrapped an arm around her and pulled her closer. "Did I really say that this bribe would only work once? I don't know what I was thinking."

Syd pushed her scarf aside so she could nuzzle her neck. "Listen, Santa, we've gotta figure something out. We're running out of time to shop."

Maddie looked out at the falling snow. "I know. Mom and I were talking about that earlier."

"And?"

"I guess a snow blower really wouldn't be at the top of Henry's list?"

"Not so much."

"How about that promo copy we got of Bob Dylan's Christmas CD?"

Syd looked at her like she had suddenly sprouted horns.

"Right. I didn't think so." She sighed. "What do you think he wants?"

"I've only heard him mention two things." She paused. "Well, *three* things. But I hardly think we should take the idea of getting him his own airplane seriously."

Maddie laughed. "What were the other two items?"

"A puppy."

Maddie groaned.

"He's persuaded that Pete is lonely."

"Oh, lord. What's the *other* thing?" she asked, hopefully.

Syd smiled at her. "A doctor's bag."

Maddie was speechless. She looked away, trying to hide her emotion.

Syd used her free hand to force her face back around. "I ought to be jealous, you know."

"Why's that?"

"I don't see him asking for a violin, or a library card."

"He already has a library card."

"True."

"And except for Midori, what five-year-old would voluntarily ask for a violin?"

"Good point."

"He loves you."

Syd smiled. "I know. He loves us both."

"I wish we could give him the one thing he'd like the most."

"Seeing his dad?"

"Yeah."

Syd sighed and snuggled closer. "Me, too."

They stood in silence for a few minutes. The wind started picking up—not a good omen for keeping the power on.

Inside, Henry's lesson continued. Maddie could hear the low timbre of Celine's voice, then the sound of the first few measures of the Dvořák being played again. She assumed her mother had unearthed that old copy of Alfred's *Introduction to Piano* workbook she had groaned her way through so many years ago. It was incredible. Again and again, against all their best efforts to muck things up, the universe found ways to make things right. Heal wounds. Replace darkness with light. And, somehow, these things happened quietly, seamlessly, and without notice.

Off in the pasture, somewhere behind the barn, a loud crack made them both jump. All the lights in the house went out.

"Cool!" Henry's excited voice cut through the darkness.

Maddie and Syd sighed and looked at each other. They turned around and walked hand-in-hand toward the generator behind the house.

Maybe, just once in a while, the universe did need a hand.

ABOUT THE AUTHOR

Ann McMan is a writer by day, and a closet librarian by night.

She was born in the mountains of Pennsylvania, but spent much of her childhood below sea level in northern Delaware. She now lives halfway between the mountains and the sea in central North Carolina, but dreams of one day relocating to Vermont—where the colder climate might help her keep better.

When she isn't working, writing, or rereading *Pride and Prejudice*, she's cruising the circulation desk of her local public library—hoping to be discovered.

Jericho is her first novel.

CPSIA information can be obtained at www.ICGtesting.com
Printed in the USA
BVOW040114081111

275554BV00004B/2/P